SON OF THE POISON ROSE

SON OF THE POISON ROSE

JONATHAN MABERRY

ST. MARTIN'S GRIFFIN
NEW YORK

First published in the United States by St. Martin's Griffin, an imprint of St. Martin's Publishing Group

SON OF THE POISON ROSE. Copyright © 2022 by Jonathan Maberry. Maps copyright © 2022 by Cat Scully. All rights reserved. Printed in the United States of America. For information, address St. Martin's Publishing Group, 120 Broadway, New York, NY 10271.

www.stmartins.com

Library of Congress Cataloging-in-Publication Data

Names: Maberry, Jonathan, author.
Title: Son of the poison rose / Jonathan Maberry.
Description: First Edition. | New York : St. Martin's Griffin, 2022. |
    Series: Kagen the damned ; 2
Identifiers: LCCN 2022043675 | ISBN 9781250783998 (trade paperback) |
    ISBN 9781250784001 (ebook)
Subjects: LCGFT: Novels.
Classification: LCC PS3613.A19 S66 2023 | DDC 813/.6—dc23/
    eng/20220912
LC record available at https://lccn.loc.gov/2022043675

Our books may be purchased in bulk for promotional, educational, or business use. Please contact your local bookseller or the Macmillan Corporate and Premium Sales Department at 1-800-221-7945, extension 5442, or by email at MacmillanSpecialMarkets@macmillan.com.

First Edition: 2022

10 9 8 7 6 5 4 3 2 1

This is for L. Sprague de Camp—friend, mentor, and more. Way the hell back in 1971 you introduced me to *Weird Tales* magazine . . . and now I'm the editor of that book's newest incarnation. You introduced me to the scope and breadth of swords-and-sorcery fiction and encouraged me to try my hand at it . . . and here I've written my second novel in that genre. You believed in me, and I wish you were still with us, because I'd love to sit once more in the comfy chairs in your library/office and talk books and talk shop. Thanks for everything, Sprague!

And, as always, for Sara Jo.

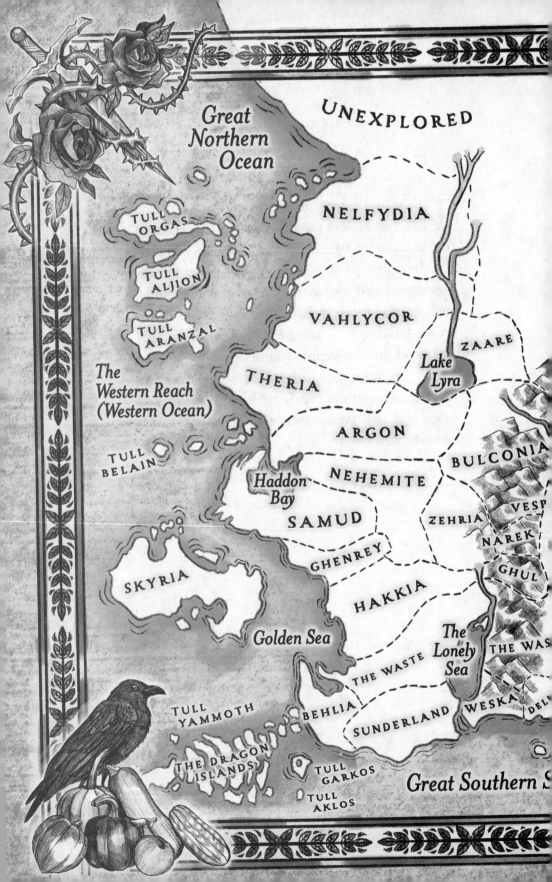

PART ONE
THE UNCLAIMED CROWN

———

Nothing lasts. That is an important thing to keep in mind. The vision of history is long and should always be without bias, especially in times as troubled as these. When looking back, we see that the Silver Empire lasted a thousand years. Before that, the Blue Empire lasted for two hundred, and before that were four thousand years of warring city-states, the rise and fall of kingdoms small and large, and unrelenting tribal warfare. Now the Hakkians are trying to build the Yellow Empire, named for the sacred colors worn by their god, Hastur. Perhaps it will endure for a thousand years, or ten thousand. Or a single day. No one knows because the future is unwritten, and it is always in flux. The past is carved into bedrock; the present is a stormy sea; but the future . . . that floats on a sea of chaos. The potential for radical change is neither good nor evil. It is what it is because change is inevitable. Alas, though, the process of change is as bloody and painful as birth, and we are nearing the birth of something whose shape and size and nature we cannot really predict. We only think we can.

—BRELL UL-TAJEK, ROYAL HISTORIAN TO THE COURT OF KING
HARIQ AL-HUK, THIRTY-SECOND OF HIS NAME, LORD OF SAMUD,
MASTER OF SHIPS, DIVINELY APPOINTED ARCHER OF HEAVEN,
AND DIVINELY ORDAINED PROTECTOR OF THE REALM

CHAPTER ONE

"Repel boarders!"

The cry rang through the ship, tearing Kagen from a dream of his family dining all together, the air filled with conversation and laughter and the smell of the Harvest feast. It ripped him out of the lie of peace and into the reality of horror.

He swung his legs out of his hammock, forgetting in his stupor that he was not on land, not in the palace, but aboard a ship. The deck tilted and he fell heavily and badly, hitting kneecaps and elbows on the oak planking.

It was only then that the words he heard all around him made any sense.

Repel boarders!

"Gods of the burning Pit," he snarled, fumbling for his clothes and weapons. "He's found me already."

The image of his brother's face with the yellow lace veil hanging in tatters as they dueled on the steps of the dais in the throne room of Argentium. In one terrible moment of clarity, the Hakkian Witch-king had become someone and something else. Impossibly, inexplicably, horribly, when that veil was torn it was not the face of some unknown Hakkian. No. It was the face of Herepath, his own brother. His favorite brother—the one he respected and trusted. That was a shock that nearly killed Kagen then, and as the cries rang out through the ship, he felt another pang, as sharp as a knife to the heart.

Herepath knows that I know, thought Kagen as he fumbled for clothes. *He'll stop at nothing to find me. To kill me. To silence me.*

There were screams and yells above, and the *thud-thud-thud* of arrows striking the hull. That, and the heavy clang of steel on steel. Kagen had time only to pull on trousers and run barefoot for the companion ladder, buckling his knife belt as he ran. His pair of matched daggers rattled in their sheaths as if eager to be let out. His body ached still from the battle at the palace a few days before. He had a heavy bandage over a deep chest wound, and more wound around his blistered palms, but he shoved all those concerns away—they belonged to idle moments, and right now he needed to fight.

As he jerked open the cabin door the sounds of battle increased tenfold. Early morning sunlight slanted down through the hatch and as he looked up he could see arrows flitting through the air and steel flashing.

"Shit," he growled as he leapt onto the ladder and began to climb. A piercing scream directly above gave him a half-second warning as a body toppled through the hatch and fell heavily toward him. Kagen leaned sideways off the ladder as the dying sailor dropped past him to smash onto the decking below. It was a Therian, one of the crew of *Dagon's Swan*, and his chest had been slashed open. Blood and pieces of his sternum splattered everywhere.

Kagen swung back and climbed even faster.

He slowed for a heartbeat at the top of the ladder so he could peer out and get a sense of how much trouble he was in.

The ship was totally overrun.

Scores of Hakkian sailors and infantry swarmed the deck, and the crew was being forced back. Many were dressed as poorly as he, proof that the attack had been sudden. There was a bank of dark clouds rolling across the surface of the ocean, and he knew at once that the Hakkians had used it for cover. Nothing less would have fooled the sharp-eyed Therian crew.

He gripped the hatch frame and hauled himself up so he could leap out onto the deck. The ship was dancing drunkenly, and he saw there was no one at the wheel. The craft pitched and rolled and yawed as if it, too, was in panic. Grappling hooks connected it to a half dozen longboats, but the Hakkian ship was still invisible within the clouds. A boat action, then. Swift and silent and damned effective.

"There's another one," roared a Raven, pointing at Kagen with the tip of a cutlass. "Take him, lads."

Five Ravens surged past him, all of them in leather armor and carrying swords or boarding axes.

Kagen drew his daggers and shifted to make sure the hatch was behind him. The soldiers grinned at his daggers, marking him as a fool and an easy kill. Kagen grinned, too.

The first man to reach him had a slender hangar—a curved junior officer's sword—and he twirled it above his head before slashing down. It was a stylish move that Kagen had seen other Ravens do—something that symbolized the flutter of raven wings. But it was a damn-fool thing to do in a fight with someone who knew his trade.

Kagen stepped in and to one side, using his left dagger to check the sword at an angle that sloughed off much of its force, and whipped the tip of the other knife across the man's throat. Blood geysered from the slashed arteries, but Kagen kicked the man's right hip and the dying officer turned and sprayed the men behind him with red. Kagen did not pause but leapt forward, knocking the officer onto the point of another sword while using his own blades to slash and nick.

The movements seemed wrong, and he could tell that from the faces of the men he fought. Even in the heat of battle the Ravens were appraising his style and judging it as too little and too weak.

More fools, they, because Kagen fought with the matched daggers of the greatest artist of bladework of the last century—his mother, the Poison Rose. Her nickname came from those blades and how they were seasoned for combat. The deadly poison *eitr*, known as the god-killer, coated the steel. Within two heartbeats anyone cut by the weapons, no matter how shallowly, felt the sting. The poison exploded the hearts and darkened the minds, and the bodies fell around him. In any fight with one, two, or even three fighters, Kagen liked his odds with unseasoned blades. But this was a riot, and the Therians were badly outnumbered.

The men who rushed forward fell like chaff around him, leaving only their officer, the one with the cutlass, standing close. The whole thing was so fast, the officer was still smiling, but that grin leaked away to be replaced with a mingled expression of confusion and horror. Kagen gave him a wicked grin and then drove one dagger deep into the man's groin. He let the screaming officer fall and turned away.

The invasion had settled down into dozens of personal duels—one to one, one to two, and more. He caught sight of Darch, the captain of *Dagon's Swan*, a man with exceptionally dark skin and arms corded with muscle, wielding a boarding axe as he tried to fight his way to the untended wheel. Heads and limbs flew around him, but then a Hakkian threw a hatchet at his unprotected back. Darch staggered but did not fall and instead whirled with his axe high. The downward swing took off the Hakkian's head and right arm and then the heavy blade buried itself in the deck. Then Darch reeled sideways and coughed dark blood down the front of his chest.

Another Therian caught the captain as he fell, and lowered him to the deck, then rose to stand above him. This man was taller than anyone else on the ship and had tattoos of tentacles reaching up from inside his tunic and wrapping around his throat and face. His eyes blazed with hatred and grief, and he swung a pair of heavy-bladed machetes. As the Hakkians rushed forward to try to capture the wheel, they encountered a storm of steel.

A knot of Ravens circled wide, clearly attempting to both take the wheel and ambush him from his blind side.

"Tuke," cried Kagen. "Ware behind!"

But his friend did not hear him.

Kagen threw himself into the fray, slashing and slicing, but there seemed to be an ocean of Hakkian blades between him and his friend, Tuke, who was fending off a mob. Then a slim figure leapt down from the pilothouse, slashing with a curved Vahlycorian dueling knife. She dropped cat-footed, took the reaching hands of a Hakkian sailor off at the wrists, checked her downward swing, and on the upstroke split another back from chin to bridge of nose. The curved knife was heavy-bladed, ideal for cleaving through bone but short enough to allow her to wade into a crowd and do awful damage. Then she said something over her shoulder to Tuke, and he nodded. Together Tuke Brakson and Filia alden-Bok, Kagen's two best friends, became the eye in a hurricane of bloody slaughter.

Then he saw a gray blur of movement as Filia's great monster of a dog—whom she had named Horse to annoy people—launched himself through the air. Horse slammed his hundred-plus pounds of muscle and fangs at a Hakkian and dragged him down. Blood, hot and red, jetted into the air.

Tuke, who had his own set of bandaged injuries from the fight at the palace, yelled at the top of his voice, and it was a bull's roar of a bellow as he rallied his countrymen. *"Kill the bastards! These sons of whores killed our king!"*

That was almost true. The Therian king had attended the coronation ceremony that was intended to legitimize the status of the Witch-king of Hakkia as the emperor of a new empire. Kagen's play to assassinate the monarch in yellow had resulted in a terrible fight in the great hall of the palace in Argentium, and during that fight the king of Theria was killed. Kagen knew that death was an accident and that he was as much to blame as anyone for having started the fight. But the enemy, regardless of all else, was the Hakkian regime, and in that moment Tuke wanted to set fires in the hearts of his countrymen. The shocked and beleaguered Therians seemed to take heart from him, and they threw themselves into the battle with renewed vigor.

Kagen shouted Tuke's name as he fought his way across the deck, leaving dead and dying in his wake.

However, it was not Hakkian sailors he was killing. Not in his heart. Barely in his conscious mind. One thrust of a dagger was to the heart of the Witch-king. A slash was across the throat of his traitor brother, Herepath. A crisscross slash that severed a head was the death of the usurper who killed his parents. An upward thrust into a groin was for the monster who ordered the deaths of the empress and her precious children.

Kagen saw Herepath in the faces of each enemy, but all around him he saw ghosts. Empress Gessalyn. The Seedlings—all except the twins, Alleyn and Desalyn, because they still lived, though their minds had been twisted into madness by the sorceries of the Witch-king.

He saw his father, his body crisscrossed with mortal wounds, his sword and the hand that clutched it cut off and bloody on the floor.

He saw his older brother, Hugh, headless and lifeless.

He saw his mother, the famed and feared Poison Rose, deadliest fighter of that age of the world. His mentor and tutor, whose knives he now carried.

He saw them all. Friends murdered on the Night of the Ravens. Friends and total strangers raped and desecrated and crucified in the days that followed.

Kagen saw those ghosts everywhere—on the deck, climbing over the rail, standing balanced on the rigging. His mother's ghost stood on the bow, and instead of knives of steel, in each scarred fist she held blades of blazing fire.

These ghosts watched Kagen. Silent. Dead. Murdered.

The fury within his heart grew and grew as the sight of each specter threw fuel on the fire. Kagen fought like ten men. Like a pack of demons. He had barely recovered from the failed assassination attempt in the great hall of the palace of Argentium, but so much had built up inside him and needed—*demanded*—to be let out. There was a black joy in his heart for the opportunity to massacre anyone who marched or sailed under the yellow Hakkian flag.

As he stepped away from one dying man to face the next enemy, the face he saw on each attacker was that of his brother, Herepath Vale, former scholar and Gardener, and now masquerading as Gethon Heklan, rightful heir to the mantle of Witch-king of Hakkia. It made no sense and only proved to Kagen that the world was mad. And he, madder still.

The invading sailors had swarmed toward him, seeing a half-dressed man armed only with a pair of daggers and thinking that he was easy meat. But now, as he attacked *them*, they fell back, stumbling and skidding on the blood of their fellows. He was a madman, a demon, and every Hakkian who rushed him died because they served the man Kagen Vale hated more than anyone who ever lived.

A voice directly behind him whispered, *"Kagen! Ware!"*

He whirled, but there was no one there. The voice echoed in his head. A woman's voice.

"Mother . . . ?" he murmured, confused and frightened.

Then a darkness suddenly covered much of the deck, and he risked a glance upward to see that the sky was filling with black shapes. At first his heart lifted, thinking it was the flock of ragged nightbirds that had been following him since the fall of Argon.

But he was wrong.

They were birds, sure enough, but not crows or starlings, grackles or cormorants.

The sky was filled with thousands upon thousands of ravens. The sacred bird of Hakkia. Servants of the will of the Witch-king, and as one they shot downward like arrows to attack the crew with razor-sharp beaks and talons.

CHAPTER TWO

Kagen spun and began slashing at the birds as they attacked.

Creatures of the Witch-king or not, the god-killer poison slew them with the slightest nick.

But there were so many of them.

Beaks and claws slashed at him, painting his limbs and torso with his own bright blood. He saw sailors fall beneath clouds of them, thrashing and screaming, killing some of the birds that killed them. The Hakkians had paused in their attack, though, every bit as startled as the Therians by the swarm of ravens.

That shock vanished, though, as it became clear the ravens were only attacking the crew of *Dagon's Swan*.

Kagen kept fighting, kept killing, but now his own confidence was waning. With so many enemies, and now these birds . . . hope itself seemed to crumple beneath the weight of reality.

A man with a boarding pike lunged at him, and Kagen had to focus on the moment as he twisted away, feeling the point rip a shallow, burning line along his side. He chopped a blade across the back of the man's hand, but although the man hissed and lost his grip, he did not fall. Kagen's heart sank even more, realizing that the poison was spent and the blades were merely steel.

He kicked the man in the balls, and as the fellow canted forward over the explosion of pain, Kagen slashed him across the eyes.

As that man fell, Kagen battled on, slashing wildly at birds and men. Twice, his blades parted a rope, sending sails flapping out of control. A big hand grabbed his shoulder and turned him for what should have been a mortal stab to the belly, but as he spun, Kagen chopped across his stomach with his elbow, bashing the incoming blade aside. He felt the sword's bite, but he was already bleeding from a score of wounds. He took the pain, though, and let it drive his counterattack as he drove a dagger into the Hakkian's throat in a corkscrew motion that tore a gaping hole. Kagen ripped his knife free and turned, parrying a hatchet swing and cutting another throat.

A pair of Hakkians, both armed with pikes, rushed him, and Kagen crouched, ready to spring to one side or the other, but he was hemmed in. He braced for the incoming weight of men and steel, but something whipped by his face and slammed into the men. It was a large brown bird, a pelican, and it struck both men with its outstretched wings. Kagen heard the fragile bones within those wings break, but even crippled, the bird struck with its long beak, plucking an eye from one Hakkian even as the other stabbed it.

Then another bird hit. A gull this time, white with black on its wings. It impaled the second Hakkian's eye socket, dying of a broken neck as it maimed the man.

Kagen reeled back as the complexion of the day changed again. The ravens wheeled and cried in panic as flight after flight of seabirds dove down and attacked them. And with them were smaller, darker birds.

The nightbirds.

His nightbirds, his strange friends, attacking in vicious squadrons. In flights. In legions.

They slammed into the ravens, three, four, or five striking at once, even unto their own destruction. The ravens fell, and in those first few moments of the counterattack, the invading Hakkians made the most basic, the most crucial and unforgivable mistake. They looked.

At the birds.

Not the Therians.

"At them!" roared Kagen, and instantly Tuke took up the shout. Then Filia uttered a high, ululating screech that would have terrified a banshee, and the tide of carnage on that ship changed. The aerial battle swirled like fury above the deck as the melee below turned into a slaughter. Horse leapt at any raven that flew too low, and soon the deck around the big hound was littered with torn and shattered birds.

A big man with a fierce black beard seemed to materialize out of the chaos directly in front of Kagen. He held a cutlass in one hand and a dagger in the other. The gold braid on his black and yellow uniform marked him as the Hakkian captain, and he attacked with incredible ferocity.

Kagen had to yield ground, parrying the savage blows, barely managing it, because this man could fight. He was every bit as fast as Kagen and at least thirty pounds heavier. His blades were silver blurs and the weight of the cutlass numbed Kagen's arm when twice he had to block rather than parry. The man knew all the tricks, too, for he faked a kick and then, as Kagen reflexively twisted away to protect his groin, the booted foot checked its thrust and stamped down on Kagen's bare toes. White-hot pain exploded and Kagen staggered, hoping and praying that his foot was not broken.

He parried like a madman, knocking aside the sword and dagger and licking out to draw a red line across the captain's thigh. Blood darkened the man's trousers and there were no more kicks, but the cut was on his left leg and the officer was a right-handed fighter. He shifted his weight and changed his fighting style from a brawler's attack to a more sophisticated master duelist's approach, keeping his weight on his good leg, using his left for small sliding and shuffling steps forward and back. The dagger he carried was heavier than Kagen's and had a brass knuckle guard set with spikes, and he used it to try to block as well as trap whichever of Kagen's blades was closest. Then the cutlass would sweep in on short, hard, diagonal slashes. He was a brilliant fighter and Kagen realized that he was in real danger here.

Other fighters drifted away from them, allowing their fight to happen in a clearing around which were corpses of men, women, and birds. Even the roar of the battle seemed momentarily muted as Kagen and the captain dueled.

In moments like this, Kagen's mind seemed to split into two halves—one was fully engaged in the fight, while the other drifted back into memories of when he learned to fight. The Poison Rose was Mother at any time except when there was steel in her hands. Then she transformed from the tender, laughing woman who raised him and his siblings into a warrior so skilled, so feared, that seasoned veterans paled at the thought of crossing blades with her. Her lessons were sometimes arcane for his younger mind, but when he began to get into real battles, the schooling came to crystal clarity.

One lesson—and it seemed ages ago, after everything that had happened since—was on the difference between dueling and fighting.

"The duelist wants to win," she told him, *"but the fighter wants to survive. The duelist relies on the sophistication and dexterity of his attack, and often that is enough. But the fighter, the person who doesn't want to win but needs it, cares nothing for perfection in form. He does not need to see the defeat in his opponent's eyes but rather needs to see him dead on the ground. Remember, my son, there are no judges watching when you fight for your life. The winner is the one who wants it most and can conceive of no reality in which defeat is even a possibility."*

The captain pressed his attack, trying to work Kagen into the cleft between the wheel and the chart table, and it was clear the bastard was going to succeed.

So Kagen let him.

As he backed up, parrying and deflecting with all of his own speed and skill, the captain's eyes grew bright with joy. He knew he was going to win.

Then Kagen felt more than saw the chart table behind him. It was a big and blocky thing, built more like a box, with slab sides made from heavy teak. Kagen waited for a fake-slash combination—something the captain was superb at delivering—and as the cutlass moved, he threw his right-hand dagger at the man's face.

The captain almost laughed as he bobbed sideways and down, letting the weapon pass, but that was the wrong move, because Kagen kicked back against the table and used it to propel himself up and to one side. As the captain evaded to his own right, Kagen leapt like a cat at the man's left, using the fist wrapped around the handle of the second dagger to bash aside the officer's knife and striking with his empty right hand at the captain's forehead. The man reeled, fighting for balance as he sought to bring his sword back into play, but there was no time for it. Kagen's right hand locked closed around the captain's curly black hair and jerked him up and back, snapping his chin toward the sky.

And then Kagen clamped his teeth around the Hakkian's windpipe.

It was so fast and so vicious that the officer collapsed downward as blood erupted from torn arteries and sprayed from a last exhalation of a savaged windpipe.

Kagen dropped down, pivoted, saw his fallen knife, dove for it, rolled, and came up with it, spitting out the shredded meat of the captain's throat.

The Hakkians, seeing their captain slaughtered in such a terrible way, lost heart. With the Therians pressing hard and the nightbirds massacring the ravens, the remaining crew whirled and ran for their ship, some of them even throwing down their weapons as they went. They hurled themselves over the rail.

Those who still had axes or hatchets began chopping at their own grapnel lines.

The Therians were like a horde of madmen now, and they chased down the stragglers, butchering them without mercy even when those Hakkians begged for quarter.

"By the leathery balls of the iguana king, we can't let them escape," yelled Tuke, seeing Kagen a few yards away. "Don't you get it? They'll report our presence, and it will be war with my country."

"Shit," barked Filia. She ran to the companionway and vanished belowdecks with Horse at her heels.

"Where are you going?" yelled Tuke, but she was gone.

Kagen ran toward the fleeing Hakkians, ignoring the pain in his mashed foot. "Maybe we can turn the tide and board them . . ."

But the two ships were already beginning to drift apart. A few Therians had fetched bows and began firing continuously, shooting without aim because the enemy was so densely packed on the near side of their deck.

"Ware, ware," cried a voice, and Filia came swarming up the ladder from below, carrying a cooking pot in which were burning coals from the galley. A bottle of cooking oil was tucked in her belt. Horse barked and danced around her, caught up in Filia's dark excitement.

Tuke and Kagen ran to meet her, then as quickly as they could they began tearing strips of cloth from dead men around them— Hakkians or their own comrades. Tuke yelled for archers, and the bowmen hurried over. Kagen helped them wrap strips of cloth around the barbed heads of the arrows the archers held out. Filia doused the rags with oil and the archers plunged their arrows into the pot of coals. Then they turned and began firing.

Kagen saw a bow lying partly beneath a Therian. He grabbed it and a quiver and began wrapping those arrows. Then he hurried to the rail and fired one flaming arrow after another at the sails of the Hakkian ship.

The morning was hot and the sails dry. They caught at once and the flames devoured them.

Tuke and Filia flanked Kagen, each now with bows. They shot their arrows into the masts and timbers, and even into Hakkians. Within seconds the fleeing ship was fully ablaze. The Hakkians did not even try to douse the blaze, because the sea breeze was whipping it along the rails and lines and sheets. Some of them tried to launch their boats, but now that the ship was ablaze, the Therian archers concentrated on the boat handlers.

The ship died in front of Kagen and his friends. The Therians at the rail cheered when it was clear the massive timbers were involved now. Fire was the thing every sailor feared, though, and as the attacking vessel burned, the cheers of the victors fell away.

The war in the air faded as the last of the ravens flapped away in panic, heading for the coastline, which was a hazy promise in the east. The nightbirds flew after them and, one by one, tore the Witch-king's birds from the sky.

There were Hakkians in the water, swimming away from the conflagration, fighting against the drag of their own armor, screaming and begging for mercy. A few Therian sailors began unlimbering one of their own boats, but Tuke slammed his hand against the hull and snarled at them. They looked at him, perplexed.

"They murdered our king and our captain and our friends," said Tuke in the coldest voice Kagen had ever heard. "Let them drown."

He glanced at Kagen. The deck was painted in blood, and all around, Kagen could see the ghosts of the people he loved who had died beneath Hakkian blades. His mother stood tall and cold and regal, but her body was crisscrossed with red lines from the wounds that had killed her. Kagen blinked his eyes and felt the sting of tears.

"Let them drown," he said, his voice thick and hoarse.

The sailors looked around and saw the only surviving officer, the second mate, a burly man named Jasker, who had coral reef tattoos across his face. The mate looked down at the men in the water, then he turned and nodded toward the captain of their own ship, who lay dead, his body hacked to inhumanity.

"Let them drown," he echoed.

The men stood in grim silence, watching as the Hakkian sailors fought to live.

Fought.

Failed.

And vanished beneath the waters.

CHAPTER THREE

Tuke, Filia, and Kagen knelt with many of the sailors around the body of Captain Drach.

Kagen worked the hatchet loose from the big man's back and tossed the murderous weapon over the rail. Then he and Tuke lowered Drach to the deck, where the captain lay still. His tattooed face looked calm, and his empty eyes stared upward into an infinity none of the living could even imagine.

"He was a good man," said Tuke, grief as potent in his voice as anger. "His wife is my cousin, twice removed. They have seven children. The oldest is seventeen. I spent several Dolphin Festivals with them. Always a lot of laughter and song." He shook his head, and Filia wrapped her arms around his waist and gave him a fierce yet tender hug.

Kagen touched the dead officer's chest. He did not know much of the Therian religion, and much of that was what he'd learned from Tuke over the last few months. But he spoke from the heart, the words just coming to him.

"May Father Dagon and Mother Squid take you into their arms," he said softly. "May you swim the deep waters in peace."

Tuke and some of the sailors gave him strange looks.

"Have you been to a Therian funeral before?" asked Tuke.

"No," said Kagen. "Never. Did I misspeak? If so, I—"

"You did not misspeak, my friend," said Tuke.

"Nor did you," agreed the mate, Jasker. "That was well said."

Tuke continued to study Kagen's face. "That is a very old prayer for the dead," he said. "It's what they say when a sailor is lost at sea. How did you know?"

Kagen shook his head. "I . . . didn't know. It just seemed to be the right thing to say."

Tuke touched the pouch he always wore on his belt, in which was a small carving of the sea god Dagon. "Very curious," was all he said.

Horse sat near the dead captain. He raised his ugly muzzle to the sky and let loose with a long, deep, mournful howl. Tuke looked at the dog, then he too threw back his head and howled. Soon everyone aboard the ship did the same. Even Kagen.

Then Filia touched Horse's shoulder and the howl died away.

"There are wounded to tend to," she said to everyone. "And we have to get under way in case that Hakkian ship had a consort."

The others rose, too; however, Jasker confronted Kagen.

"Those birds," he said, glancing nervously as the scores of dead ravens and other birds littered across the deck. "What was that? How did that even happen? I mean . . ." He let the rest trail off. He looked as frightened of the birds as he was heartsick for his fallen comrades.

Kagen did not answer but instead looked at the coming storm.

"They follow him," said Tuke.

"They . . . *follow* him?" echoed Jasker.

"Ever since the rise of the Witch-king," said Filia.

The mate and other sailors shifted backwards so as not to have any part of Kagen's shadow touch them.

"Knock it off," growled Tuke. "The Hakkians awoke dark powers. Maybe instead of gaping like frightened children you'll take a gods-damned second to realize that Kagen's feathery friends saved your asses."

Jasker's mouth opened, failed to find words, and closed. Several times.

Several of the sailors touched sacred tattoos on their faces, throats, or chests. A few made warding signs or touched the wood rails for luck. Most glanced at the icon of Dagon worked into the mainmast.

"I . . . meant no offense," said Jasker awkwardly.

Kagen stepped close to him and placed a hand on Jasker's shoulder.

"None taken, friend," he said. "And for the record, all of this scares the shit out of me, too."

The moment held, and then the mate nodded and patted Kagen's shoulder in return. He began to turn away, then stopped and said, "Those gulls and crows and such . . . they are the ones who follow you, yes? Not the ravens?"

"Not the ravens."

"Then they saved us because of you. We were losing that fight." A few of the sailors nodded. "There is blood on the ground between us."

It was an old ritual, acknowledging a debt of honor. The custom, though commonplace throughout the Silver Empire, was believed to have started in Theria, a land known for many practices of honor and debt resolution.

Kagen almost told him that no debt was owed, particularly to someone whose own gods had abandoned him, but he did not. Jasker and the sailors, frightened as they were, clung to those traditions. It balanced the world as they saw it.

He glanced around to see if his mother's ghost, or any of the other shades, still lingered, but they were all gone.

"Get us away from here, friend," he said, "and you can consider that debt satisfied."

Jasker studied him, then he nodded. "Yes, sir."

Tuke stood in the mate's way. "Captain Drach is dead. So is the first mate. That means you're the captain now."

Jasker stared at him, and it was clear that in all the shock he had not reckoned on this fact. His mouth hung open for a moment, and then he closed it and straightened. Jasker took a deep breath and exhaled through his nostrils, nodding to Tuke. Then he wheeled and began yelling at the crew to jump to, and soon they were all at work.

Of the original crew of 116 aboard *Dagon's Swan*, forty-six were dead and nineteen wounded. That left fifty-one to see to the wounded, repair lines and reset the sails, and work the ship. It meant that none of them would be getting any sleep for that day, and perhaps for several days. There were storm clouds in the west.

Kagen, who was no kind of sailor, did what he could to help the wounded and to wrap the dead in sailcloth in preparation for a sea burial. Tuke explained that in Therian custom, each sailor would be buried with a knife in his or her hand, ready to cut through their shroud once their sunken bodies reached the realm of the sea gods. Kagen almost made the foolish mistake of asking how that was to be accomplished by sailors who had lost hands or arms, but then decided it was impolitic to ask.

As he set to work, he looked up and was surprised that the rigging was not crowded with the surviving nightbirds and their seabird allies. But the ratlines were clear and only a single crow stood on the rim of the crow's nest. The lookout seemed bemused by its presence and left it alone.

The bird looked down at Kagen. Kagen mouthed, *Thank you, my brother.*

The crow cawed softly. For a fragment of a moment, Kagen thought he heard a woman's laughter woven into that cry. It touched him on a very deep level, and without knowing why, he silently spoke a name.

"Maralina . . ."

The bird looked at him and did not utter another sound.

Within three hours *Dagon's Swan* was under full sail, using the breeze that ran ahead of the storm to make up some distance. They were still technically in Argonian waters, but the Straits of Anthelos were in sight, formed by the two arms of land that enclosed Haddon Bay—one belonging to Samud and the other to Argon. On each side of that narrow passage stood a statue of immense height. On the Samudian side was the image of Grel Uk-Turik, the greatest archer of all time, of whom legends and songs were many, recounting how he took down a mad armored war rhinoceros with a single arrow. Across from him, as if in deliberate counterpoint to theme and message, was the tall and elegant form of Ithilyss, first Silver Empress, a warrior queen of Argon who unified the nations of the west.

To his horror, Kagen saw that, while Grel Uk-Turik's massive statue was intact and unmarred, that of Ithilyss had been defaced. Her beautiful features had been hacked away, leaving a faceless nothing. Hakkian vandals had broken off her hands and painted obscenities all over the eighty-foot-tall statue.

He bowed his head, balled fists resting on the bow rail, jaws clamped shut against the curses he wanted to shout.

The ship sailed between those statues and out into the waters of the Western Reach, then turned north. It stood well out to sea, not wanting to be caught against a lee shore when the coming storm reached them. Theria was directly north of Argon and jutted far out into the ocean. It was not their destination, though. That was all the way up the coast, past Vahlycor and to the very top of Nelfydia before they landed. Far, far from the Hakkian armies. Far from the Witch-king.

For now.

Lightning flashed angrily inside the purple clouds, and their fury mirrored Kagen's own.

"I will find you, my *brother*," he said, conjuring Herepath's face in his mind. "I will find you again and I will kill you, even if it is the last thing I do before I am dragged down to hell with the other damned. This I swear."

No one heard those words except the wind and the coming storm.

CHAPTER FOUR

The bells tolled in Argentium, capital city of Argon and capital of the former Silver Empire.

It was not the capital of the Hakkian Yellow Empire.

No. That entity had died in the womb moments before its birth. The imperial crown lay where it had fallen on the steps of the dais. It was a beautiful yet strange diadem—a band of heavy gold and platinum fashioned to look like the bodies of strange sea creatures writhing and swirling as they reached toward a huge eye whose iris was a yellow diamond of spectacular size and luster. The thing had been meant to replace the Hakkian crown, with its traditional raven iconography, and would rest upon the lord of a new empire. The Yellow Empire that would supplant forever the Silver Empire, as that one had replaced the Blue Empire before it.

It had never been worn, however, and now it lay cracked and twisted in a pool of blood. A set of chains was coiled around it, overlapping it, but slack and cold, as if they were serpents that died in battle with the crown.

It was forbidden to touch either crown or chains. The one person who had tried—a colonel in the palace guard—hung now, flayed and inhuman, on the outside wall of the palace. His hands had been cut off and fed to the hounds.

Inside the great hall, chairs remained overturned, banners in the colors of each of the member nations of the Silver Empire hung in tatters, many spattered with arterial sprays of blood. Broken weapons and pieces of armor littered the marble floor in front of the throne. A wheel cage squatted there, empty and still. To the left of the dais, one entire set of stained-glass windows was in ruins, the colored glass scattered across the floor, the frames bent and twisted, some of the lead and steel melted. Those windows had been destroyed by a bolt of lightning as gods warred in the sky above the palace. Through the gap, the overcast sky brooded. Smoke from sacrificial fires coiled upward like the pillars of a temple to despair.

The vast chamber was a monument to death and spoiled hopes and failed dreams.

The group of generals and advisors were all gone now, having fled the wrath of the Witch-king. Their sole focus now was to find Kagen Vale.

The Witch-king sat upon the throne in robes that were splashed with blood now dried to a muddy brown. The crown that rested heavily on his brow was a replica of the one worn by centuries of Witch-kings. It was elegant, beautifully crafted, set with priceless jewels. But it was the not the crown of an emperor. It was merely the diadem of a usurper, a conqueror. An invader from within the empire. In legal terms, a traitor's crown.

Hunkered down on the steps around and below the throne were his pack of hounds. Mastiffs and half-wolves and other canines bred from hunting dogs to be the protectors of the Witch-king. They sat or lay, but none of them slept. Their baleful eyes scanned the room and ever returned to their master. The bitch who ruled the pack had her massive, shaggy head on the Witch-king's thigh and he stroked her fur slowly. For hours.

On the steps of the dais was a torn piece of yellow lace. The veil he had worn for the coronation. The one that had been torn away during the fight. Only three people had seen the Witch-king's true face during that battle. Two—both soldiers of the elite Hakkian Ravens—had their eyes put out and their bodies torn and devoured by the pack. Their families had been arrested—even to the oldest crone and smallest child—and had been summarily executed. Their property was seized and their homes burned to the ground. Their family names were expunged from all records and histories and were to be officially forgotten. To speak their names would incur the same comprehensive punishment.

The third, though, still lived. Kagen Vale, son of the deadly warrior Lady Marissa Trewellyn-Vale, known as the Poison Rose. That he still lived was a hot poker against the flesh of the Witch-king. It was insult and outrage. And it was so very dangerous.

Days were passing. Four since the bloody fray. The great hall reeked of old blood, rotted meat, dog feces, and fear. And hate. That was the most palpable energy staining the air, polluting the shadows, darkening all skies.

Hate.

The Witch-king stroked the head of the dog to whom he had fed the flesh of the Silver Empress and her children. His fingers were strong, but long and artistic, with spatulate fingertips and a palm callused from decades of training with blades of every kind. His nails were long and sculpted to dagger points, and when he dragged them through the dog's ruff, they left trails that looked like scars.

"Kagen," murmured the Witch-king, and the hounds whined and shifted with deep unease. "I *will* find you."

Beneath his new veil, hidden from all eyes, was a cut that ran from the point of his sharp cheekbone to the corner of his jaw. It was smeared with a mixture of the most potent herbs and stitched by the king's own hand. It was Kagen's dagger that had marked him, and although the poison that had been on the blade—which had helped Kagen fight and kill so many Ravens—had been nearly gone by the time he'd delivered that cut, it still burned. It had made the Witch-king very ill and might have killed him had it not been for the alchemical mixtures of his own devising.

Knowing that he had been that close to mortal death did not fill him with fear. It stoked the fires of his anger. His need to punish Kagen. The burning ache to have that man completely at his mercy . . . and to prove that the well of mercy had long since run dry.

Outside the palace, dominating the sky from one horizon to the next, was a storm. Another in a line of them that seemed intent on battering the whole world. Streams and rivers were flooding. There were mudslides on the sides of the mountains. The last of the autumn crops were drowning in their fields.

The Witch-king did not care.

Lightning burned the sky over and over again, and thunder boomed constantly. The echoes of it found their way, along with icy rain, through the smashed section of wall that had been struck by a thunderbolt during the coronation. The echo of it banged around inside the great hall, and somehow those bass notes were warped and twisted into something else. Like growls of some vast and improbable beast trapped within the walls. It was an awful sound that touched the fears of every listener on an atavistic level. It did not sound like thunder, or even the distorted echo of that, but more like the palace itself was groaning in pain and anger and hate.

The bitch pushed her head against his touch.

"I will find you and kill you," said the Witch-king. "But first I will kill everything and everyone you love. Then, my brother, I will cut your heart out and feast upon it."

Only the dogs heard his promise.

Only the dogs, and the darkness—and all that writhed and coiled within it.

"'is 'ighness is in a mood again," said Zinda, her face beaded with sweat and her arms up to the elbows in a large steaming washtub.

Her particular friend, Jathra, stood nearby, wringing out a sopping towel with her strong hands.

Both women paused as thunder boomed outside with such shocking force that its echoes found them all the way down in the laundry room in the first subbasement of the palace.

"More of that noise," said Zinda, her voice hushed. "Thunder, if thunder it be."

"More like the devils are playing dice with all our souls," countered Jathra.

She set her towel down and made a warding sign in the air—a circle drawn with a finger and then filled with a fist that opened like a blooming chrysanthemum. It was one of the proofs against evil used these many centuries by the followers of the Harvest faith. Technically illegal, now that Hakkia had outlawed that religion, but old habits died hard, especially in such dark times.

Even so, Zinda scowled at her friend. "Don't," was all she said.

They listened as an even greater explosion of thunder seemed to shake the whole world.

"Gods of the . . ." began Jathra, but stopped herself short of saying "Garden" and switched to the more generic and far more acceptable "Pit."

"It's been like that since that coronation business," said Zinda. "Storms and 'alf-storms. Thunder but no rain. Rain out of a clear sky. Lightning when there shouldn't be none." She lowered her voice as if the stone walls themselves were eavesdropping. "It ain't natural. Not by 'alf it ain't."

"T'weren't natural a-tall," agreed her friend. "I been saying it since day one."

The sounds gradually stopped, leaving behind a heavy silence that did not sell the thought that whatever had been making those noises was actually gone. Since the Witch-king had conquered all of the Silver Empire, and most especially since he and his kind had taken up residence in the palace of Argentine, capital of Argon, which was in turn the capital of the empire, there was no real feeling of peace. Instead, shadows seemed to be filled with watching eyes, and things often moved sneakily out of sight, glimpsed only as they disappeared.

"What do you suppose it is?" said Jathra in a hushed whisper. "The weather being all demented like?"

Zinda shook her head. "I don't know, and to tell you the gods' honest truth, I don't want to know," she said quietly. "And you don't want to know either, Jathra Meel."

They looked at each other, having the real conversation they dared not have aloud. Like everyone who worked in the palace, they had awful dreams in which fantastical shapes capered and bit.

After a while they exhaled pent-up breath and returned to their work. For several minutes there was only the splash of sudsy water and the *plop-plop-plop* of what was wrung out.

Jathra looked around as if there could somehow be a listener lurking in the corner, then she leaned closer to Zinda and spoke in an even more hushed voice. "I was talking to Jek last night."

"Which Jek? The blacksmith or the gamekeeper's assistant?"

"Why the blacksmith, of course," said Jathra. "Like you would see me with Old Jek. He hasn't seen the inside of a bathhouse since he was a lad."

"Okay," said Zinda. "I didn't know you were keeping company with *that* Jek. 'e's a brute that one."

"For all his size he has gentle hands," said Jathra, a bit of color blooming in her cheeks. She fished a chain out from under her tunic and showed it to her friend. It was not silver or gold but finely wrought steel from which a tiny metal rose was suspended. "He's sweet on me, he is. Made this for me and gave it to me t'other night."

Zinda admired the piece. "He fancies you for sure," she said. "That's a lot of fine work."

Jathra blushed a deeper shade of red, then her face cleared. "Anyway, Jek told me something I haven't told anyone yet, but I'll tell you." She leaned closer still. "His brother, Fander, is friends with one of the guards."

"Which guards? The 'akkians?"

"Aye."

Zinda turned and pretended to spit on the floor. "There's that for the lot of them."

"No, no, listen to me," said Jathra urgently, "Fander's friend is Hakkian, sure, but his grandmother was from right here in Argentium. He's not like the other Hakkians. He was very upset about what happened on the Night of the Ravens."

"Well, that's nice that one of the soldiers who killed 'alf the people I know is upset about it," said Zinda flatly. "I wonder if he cried while 'e cut the empress to pieces, or did 'e say a prayer afterward then go out drinking with 'is friends?"

"No, no, it's not like that," insisted Jathra. "Fander's friend was in the *second* wave, the ones who marched into town proper like. Not appeared out of nowhere through some bit of magic." She paused and almost made the warding sign again, but restrained herself.

"Well," said Zinda testily, "what did 'e say that 'as you so worked up?"

Once more Jathra glanced around, then she said, "This guard was in the palace during the coronation, and he heard some of what went on. And *he* says that he saw the Witch-king's face."

Zinda stared at her.

"What?" she demanded.

"Hand to the gods. It's what he said. And it weren't no Hakkian face, neither. Nor was it what some people say. It weren't no wolf's face or no demons, either."

"What *was* it, then?" asked Zinda, more curious than she wanted to be.

"It were his brother."

"'oo's brother? The guard's?"

"No, no, it was the brother of the man they brought in chains that night. It was the brother of Captain Kagen."

Zinda snorted. "You're daft if you believe that. The captain's brother was killed at the palace defending the Seedlings. So were his parents. Everyone knows that."

"No, not *that* brother. Not Kagen. Nor Hugh, either, nor the others I heard are scattered hither and yon. No, this was that strange one. The one who went for being a Gardener. The quiet one who went up to the Winterwilds and vanished and everyone thought he was dead."

"You mean Gardener 'erepath?"

"Yes!" cried Jathra, then gasped and put a hand to her mouth. She repeated it in a whisper. "Yes. Herepath it was."

"How would a 'akkian even know who 'erepath was and what 'e looked like?" asked Zinda, her voice sour with skepticism. "What rubbish is this? And 'ow could you believe such a thing, smart as you are?"

"Fander's friend says he's been here to Argentium many times to visit his family. He was at the Games three years in a row, back when all the Vale boys and two of the girls were competing in jousts and such. Herepath was always with his mother, Lady Marissa."

Zinda touched her fingertips to her bosom over her heart at the mention of that name. "May the gods bless the soul of the Poison Rose," she said.

"Bless and keep her," agreed Jathra.

The two women regarded each other.

"Maybe 'e saw the Witch-king's face and maybe 'e didn't," said Zinda, "but in either case it could never 'ave been 'erepath Vale. 'e was a good man, a good son to the Rose, and an ordained Gardener. Not to mention that 'e was Argonian. 'ow could you, a practical woman, believe such tommyrot?"

"It's what he told my friend."

"Then 'e must 'ave been drunk when 'e said it," said Zinda coldly. "Drunk or lying. Think about it. You'd 'ave me believe that 'erepath somehow became the *king* of 'akkia, that 'e learned dark magic, that 'e led his armies against the empire that 'is entire family 'ad fought generation upon generation to defend, and that 'e ordered the murders of 'is parents and brother. Not to mention that 'e 'ad another of his brothers, the poor Captain Kagen, brought to 'im in chains? Tell me, what were *you* drinking when you 'eard this? Or was your blacksmith lover telling you tales to dazzle you so 'e could get into your knickers?"

Mildly offended, Jathra gave a huge sniff and snatched up the towel and gave it a fierce twist. "I only know what I heard from someone who, unlike you, Miss Know-it-All, was actually there."

They lapsed into an angry silence that lasted for nearly a quarter of an hour. Then it softened, and by midafternoon they were chums again.

The memory of what Jathra said, though, never quite left the room.

CHAPTER SIX ▬▬▬▬▬▬▬

"Find Kagen Vale," said the Witch-king of Hakkia. "Find that man and bring him—alive or dead—to me."

The King in Yellow did not yell. But his cold whisper was so much worse because everyone needed to listen that much harder. Every word mattered, every inflection. To misinterpret their master's slightest command was to invite doom—no, to beg for its cold touch. His generals and admirals, chief advisors and spymasters stood in rigid lines before the throne.

"You will send every agent to find him," continued the monarch. "You will put every ship to sea. You will mobilize the militia and order the armies to scour the land. Use no restraint, pause not for screams or pleas, spare no pain or blood. Find him. Kagen Vale is running, but make sure that there is no safe place, no haven, no inch of ground on which he can hide. Hunt him and his allies to the ends of the earth. If any stand between you and that goal, kill them and their relatives to six removes. If a village hides them, burn it to the ground and sow the land with salt. If any offer him succor, skin them and their loved ones alive and crucify everyone in their house, or town, or city."

"Sire," said Lord Nespar, the aged and gaunt chamberlain, "what shall we do if Kagen crosses over into another country? What then? Do we risk open war?"

The Witch-king turned his head very slowly, and although the lace veil hid his eyes, the chamberlain could feel the full weight of that stare.

"Any nation that offers him free passage or sanctuary is our enemy. Send riders ahead to warn them of this. There is no tolerance for rebellion. Hear me, Nespar, there is no mercy for those who would side with an assassin. I may not be the legal emperor, but I still rule all of the west. The other monarchs know this and they rightly fear my wrath. To harbor Kagen is an act of war, and we will lay waste to any kingdom that defies us."

The Witch-king rose to his feet, standing tall and impossibly powerful on the top step of the dais. He looked out across the marble floor, seeing right through his generals and marshals, his aides and advisors, disregarding their reality, and instead seeing the room as it had been seven hours before.

As his eyes swept back and forth, he remembered where the kings and queens of the nations once belonging to the Silver Empire had sat. Where his advisors, Lady Kestral and Lord Nespar, stood, and where his children—Gavran, and his twin sister, Foscor—stood waiting to assist him during the coronation ceremony. Even though the hall was now empty, the Witch-king could remember every placement, every face, every sigil and badge and crest.

The bodies of his soldiers, his Ravens, lay where they had fallen.

The body of the king of Theria, killed during the assassination attempt, was gone now, whisked away by a group of furious and frightened courtiers. Scores of soldiers died in that room, his own as well as the knights of Argonian houses who had come there disguised as the Unbladed. Worse, as the Unseen, the masked members of the Brotherhood of Steel. False, traitorous, murderous. Most of them had died, but not all.

And Kagen was gone.

Gone.

Escaped.

Alive. Unharmed.

And he knew. He *knew*.

During their fight on that very dais, the Witch-king's lace veil was torn away and Kagen, alone of everyone in that crowded room, saw his real face.

Saw it and knew his most hated enemy as his own brother. Not Gethon Heklan, as the official story insisted, but Herepath Vale. Former Gardener and scholar. Brother to murdered siblings. Son to murdered parents.

Kagen knew. And that could not be allowed.

With a force of will more intense than any of the gathered officials could guess, he wrenched his thoughts back to the moment. He sat down very slowly on the throne, not caring that it, too, was spattered with blood.

"Listen to me," he said very quietly. Every officer and tactician in the room snapped to rigid attention, their hands slapping onto the handles of their swords. "The palace has been searched. Kagen Vale has escaped. He attacked me here in my own throne room and then fled, unharmed and unchecked. The security of the coronation was your responsibility. *You* have allowed him to escape. Each of you bear some part of that blame. I will forgive that failure when Kagen is brought to me. Fail me in this and your own lives are forfeit."

The ensuing silence was like iron hands around the throats of everyone there. The only movement was the raising of the heads of each of the Witch-king's pack of hounds. The huge bitch who ruled that pack rose to a seated position beside the throne, and wherever the Witch-king looked, so did she. Her eyes were yellow and filled with hunger, and her lips curled back from enormous fangs that dripped with saliva.

"There is only so far Kagen and his confederates could have gone," said the Witch-king. "You will find him. Do you hear? That is the sole purpose of your lives from this moment on. You will find Kagen Vale and bring him, alive or dead, before me. You will be relentless, obsessed, dedicated to nothing else. You will burn down heaven itself to find him."

The knights and generals remained absolutely rigid. The pack leader growled softly.

"Now go," spat the Witch-king. "Bring me the head and heart of Kagen Vale."

CHAPTER SEVEN

Dagon's Swan made good time for nearly thirty minutes before disaster struck. Lines that had appeared whole after the fight suddenly parted, and immediately sails began flapping wildly and turning on the mast. From one moment to the next the ship went from sailing tight and trim to being a child's toy in raging flood-waters. The line connecting the wheel to the rudder parted and the wheel went slack in the helmsman's hands. The ungoverned ship fought with itself and the wind and the waves. The timbers cried out in distress and the air detonated with breaking spars. Blocks and cordage rained down on the deck, sending everyone scrambling for cover.

Sailors, petty officers, and the captain seemed to be everywhere at once. Kagen and his friends fought their way along the heaving deck to where Jasker was bellowing orders.

"What can we do?"

The newly minted captain wheeled on him. "You can kindly get out of the way."

"But we want to help," insisted Kagen, gesturing to the damage from the battle.

"Are you sailors?"

"I was on a ship for a while," said Tuke.

"In what capacity?"

"Um . . . fighter?"

Jasper sucked a tooth for a moment. "Do you know how to splice a bowline?"

"Well . . . no?"

Jasper glanced at Filia and Tuke. "Can either of you rerig a block, reef a sail, or fit a plug into a hull breach?"

"Not as such . . ." said Filia.

"Do you know how to fish a spar?"

"I know how to fish," said Kagen, but Jasker withered him with a look.

"Fishing a spar is a technique for repairing those poles up there that hold the sails."

"Oh. Then . . . no."

Jasker gave the three of them and the big ugly dog a smile that looked more like a wince. "Understand that I mean this with no disrespect . . . but, please, for the love of Father Dagon . . . get the hell off my deck." He paused, then added, "Now."

They slunk away and settled themselves into the tight booth in the ship's tiny wardroom, which earlier that day Jasker had shared with his fellow officers. Now he would move into the captain's cabin, which, though hardly spacious, was the largest single room on *Dagon's Swan*. The wardroom barely qualified as a *room* at all. Kagen had bigger closets for his clothes back home.

When the Hakkians had grappled their ship alongside *Dagon's Swan*, the hulls had ground together. Neither side had time to drop fenders between the wooden vessels, and the churning waves had played mischief with the seams. Teams of Therian sailors were working inside the ship and on slings lowered over the side to repair cracks and reseal the seams with pitch and tar. One of the sheets of copper used to coat the lowest sections of the hull had come loose and the carpenter and his mate had the precarious job of hammering it back in place, but they could manage only a few swings of their hammer each time the ship rose on the uproll of a wave. Between waves, the poor sailors were swamped with cold seawater.

Inside the craft, the carpenter's mates hammered furiously at a wooden plug over a hole that had been punched through when a fallen spar had been wedged between the ships. Other sailors labored on the hand pumps, which were crude and slow. All of the hammocks and most of the movable cabin walls had been stripped away and stored in the hull to allow freedom of work. Only the captain's cabin and the wardroom were intact, and both were aft, away from the structural damage.

The ship's surgeon—little more than a barber with rudimentary knowledge of anatomy and lots of rum to keep his screaming patients under some measure of control—labored on a table made from hatch covers lashed to barrels. Blood ran in little rivers and drained into the scuppers and out into the ocean, where dozens of sharks followed and fought over discarded hands, arms, and legs.

There was no hot food because the galley fire had been doused during the battle and had not yet been relit. Kagen tried not to take offense at that but privately accepted that he was miffed. In the palace where he'd grown up, there were multiple kitchens and something was always cooking.

Instead, he and his friends found some iron-hard ship's biscuits and a quarter wheel of cheese sharp enough to draw blood and made a meal of it. Kagen was still unnerved by having to tap his biscuits on the tabletop to shake out the weevils. Filia was indifferent to that and tapped away without comment, then wiped the weevils onto the floor for Horse. Tuke ate the weevils and showed his mucked-up teeth to Kagen, enjoying the looks of disgust this inspired. Horse lay down under the table, farted eloquently, and drifted off to sleep.

As the long minutes passed, leaving the intensity of that battle behind, Kagen began feeling the various pains that seemed to be everywhere. His chest was the worst. The Witch-king's sword had cut him through the leather of his jerkin. The muscle and flesh were healing—or had been—but now the bandage was once more soaked with red. The fight had also torn open the blisters on his palms, which he'd gotten when lightning punched through the stained-glass windows of the great hall, sending arrows of electricity through every piece of metal.

CHAPTER EIGHT

Lord Nespar stood over a map table in a room at the heart of the palace. His colleague and friend, Lord Jakob Ravensmere, royal historian, stood beside him. The map covered most of the surface of a large wooden table. Small beads of yellow crystal were used to mark the placement of Hakkian troops, patrols, and ships. Crystals of other colors indicated the known, or likely, positions of military forces belonging to the countries that, like Hakkia, had once belonged to the Silver Empire. There were considerably more of those colors than yellow.

"Well," said the historian, "if there *is* war, songwriters will have a lovely story to tell. A plucky nation outnumbered fifty to one. A nation that dared greatly, shocked the world, held great promise of change, but which was ultimately ground underfoot." He sighed. "I can all but hear the chorus now."

It was meant as a joke, but Nespar was not in the mood for it. "The odds are worse than fifty to one, Jakob," he said darkly. "Closer to five times that, according to the last imperial census."

"So much the better for songwriters and historians."

"Like you?" snorted Nespar.

"Oh, no, not a chance," said Jakob airily. "I'll be among the first to get the chop when the rest of the empire rises against us. They see me as a traitor and collaborator."

"Which you are."

"I prefer, at worst, *opportunist*, and at best, pragmatist."

"Dead either way," said Nespar with a sniff.

"Dead either way," agreed Jakob. He reached for his wine cup and took a delicate sip, then placed a hand on the map as if to halt conversation on the topic of war for a moment. "There's one thing our lord and master has not talked about. Rarely before the coronation and not at all since."

"Which is?"

"His 'children.'"

"Ah," said Nespar.

"Ah," agreed Jakob. "I mean . . . does he expect everyone to believe that they are really his? That would have been a hard sell even before Kagen Vale shouted out who they really are."

"People will believe what he tells them to believe."

"Mm, really? You Hakkians will believe the world is a pimple on the ass of a warthog if he says so, and I get that, I understand and even appreciate that. But that little bit of questionable theater was played out in front of King al-Huk and all the others. Hardly a receptive audience, especially in matters of controversy."

Nespar made a sour face but offered no comment.

"And more to the point," continued Jakob, "it was a very dangerous thing to do. Right there in front of witnesses who are naturally inclined to be hostile, he offers proof that the imperial bloodline still exists. He trotted two legal heirs out in front of the submonarchs and then boldly claimed that they were his own blood kin. I mean . . . adopting those children *after* he was crowned is one thing. By then his position would be locked into place with all of the legal niceties in place. At that point he could have said that those children were rescued from exile and that, out of respect for the empire, he was adopting them as wards. All neat and tidy and with a veneer of compassion."

Nespar scowled, but not at Jakob. Although he would not criticize the Witch-king aloud, he looked into the middle distance for several seconds.

Jakob clapped him lightly on the shoulder. "Never mind, my friend. As the peasants say, that cow has been milked. We can't change what happened, but I think it's crucial that we each spend some time working out the best way to frame what happened with the children in some politically useful way."

"Agreed," muttered Nespar, though it sounded like that word was pulled from his mouth with pliers.

"So, where were we?" mused Jakob. "War?"

They moved to a section of the map that showed Haddon Bay—the massive body of water shared by Argon, Nehemite, and Samud—as well as the Western Reach, the island of Skyria, scores of other islands to the north and south, all the way to the Great Northern Ocean.

Jakob cleared his throat. "Tell me, Nespar," he said, with a touch of nervousness obvious on his voice, "this thing with the birds. The ravens . . ."

"What about it?"

"Will it really work?" asked the historian. "Finding Kagen, I mean."

The chamberlain took a moment with that. He leaned on the table and peered at the waters beyond the Straits of Anthelos, where the bay spilled into the ocean.

"I . . . don't know," he admitted. "It was Kestral's idea, and you saw how His Majesty was after casting that spell."

"Yes. It took much from him," said Jakob, after first glancing at the door. "Too much, I wonder?"

"Hush," warned the chamberlain. But then he nodded. "I hope not too much."

They considered the map, though in truth both men were looking inside their own thoughts. To the rest of the fractured empire, the Witch-king appeared to be capable of anything. The Night of the Ravens was an eloquent statement to that effect. However, to those closest to the monarch in yellow, there were obvious limits and equally obvious costs.

"You'll laugh when I say this," Nespar said after a time. "But I am uncomfortable with magic. As it's used in this kind of thing, I mean. I prefer to rely on spies and assassins, or troop movements when necessary."

"Poisons and daggers in the night," said Jakob. "Or frontal assaults and no quarter asked or given."

"As you say."

Jakob nodded. "I'm not laughing, my friend."

Nespar picked up a small yellow crystal and examined it, then returned it to the map.

"Nespar?" said Jakob.

"Yes?"

"This man, this Kagen Vale . . ."

"What about him?"

"As I've been working on my history of the Night of the Ravens and all that has happened since, his name keeps coming up as someone of great importance. Until the attack on His Majesty, I could not quite understand why. Yes, he was the captain of the guard responsible for protecting the Seedlings, but so what? Your plan worked in that the whore drugged him. By the time he woke up, the killing was mostly done. His parents, his older brother, the empress and her children. There was no one for him left to save. And as for vengeance, so what? A lot of nobles died that night, and all of them would have liked to see the Witch-king's head on a pike. What made Kagen so special from the outset? The Witch-king demanded his head almost from the beginning."

"Because Kagen killed a razor-knight," said Nespar, but the historian snorted.

"That's the story, but do you actually believe it? Yes, the razor-knight was raised by dangerous sorcery, but it was Kestral who invoked that . . . that . . . whatever it actually is. And Kagen used banefire to bring the monster down. That was using magic against magic. Or rather, alchemy against magic. That paints Kagen as either lucky or an opportunist. Why fear him? Why put such a massive bounty on his head?"

"The Witch-king was right to do so," said Nespar, "because it was Kagen who tried to kill him and who ruined the coronation."

"Sure, and placing a king's ransom on Kagen's head *now* makes perfect sense," countered the historian. "But that's now. Why did the Witch-king hate or perhaps fear Kagen before that?"

Lord Nespar straightened and turned away from the map table.

Jakob watched him. "No answer for me, my friend?" he asked. "Is that because you don't know the answer or are afraid to speak it?"

The chamberlain paced over to a buffet table and poured himself a glass of wine. He raised it, sipped, then set his glass down.

"Some things are best left unsaid, Jakob."

The chamberlain turned and regarded his friend. They stood like that for a long while, having a conversation without words, but with deep mutual understanding.

CHAPTER NINE

"You're bleeding all over the damn place," said Tuke.

"So are you," replied Kagen with a weary smile. "Filia, you are, too. We're quite a mess."

Tuke got up, left the cabin, and returned quickly, with fresh bandages and some kind of poultice that smelled truly awful.

"Do you expect me to put that on?" demanded Kagen.

"No. I'm fine with your wounds going septic and you rotting away. You'll find burial at sea quite refreshing."

Kagen told him what he could do with such comments, and into which orifice they would likely fit. But he took the poultice.

"This smells like a donkey's ass."

"I didn't know you were a connoisseur of donkey ass," said Filia, smearing some on fresh cuts on her thigh.

Above and around them were the sounds of bare feet slapping on wood, the creak of blocks as sails were raised or lowered, and the confused splash of water against the hull as the ship rocked in the waves. The bobbing was nauseating, but Filia assured him that the sharp cheese would settle his stomach. It did not.

"Don't fret, city boy," laughed Tuke. "Jasker told me that the rudder line was cut and they're having to splice it."

"And meanwhile we sit here," growled Kagen, "bobbing like apples in a barrel while the entire Hakkian fleet scours the ocean for us. And you know that's what is coming for us. Herepath knows that I know his secret. We can't forget that. He has to find me and shut me up."

"No one can shut you up," sighed Filia, but Kagen ignored her.

"We need to get under sail right damn now, and then we have to make ourselves as scarce as an honest politician. Gods of the Pit, can you even imagine the size of the bounty that's probably now on my head?"

"I can't think of anything else," said Filia, though she winked at Tuke.

Kagen was not in the mood for jokes, though, and he turned on her with a nearly wordless snarl. "That isn't fucking helping."

Filia held her hands up, palms out. "Sorry," she said. "We're safe now. That Hakkian ship found us by—at best—accident. Unless they followed those ravens."

"That'd be my bet," said Tuke. "Those birds had no other business being this far from land." He glanced at Kagen. "Good thing your flock of ugly-ass fowl showed up."

Kagen made no comment.

Filia said, "And at some point I'd like a good gods-damned explanation for *all* of that. Your—what do you call them? Nightbirds? And that swarm of ravens. That's . . . that's . . ." She let the rest hang and shook her head.

"Magic has returned to the world," said Kagen, quoting a line that seemed to be on everyone's lips since the Night of the Ravens—which is what everyone now called the Hakkian invasion a little over three months ago.

"I still don't really understand what that means," said Tuke. "Magic returns . . . how? I mean, I know that the Witch-king did something to make it happen, but none of us know how. Or how *much* magic has returned. Or, to raise another point, how much magic there was already here on earth. No matter how stringently the inquisitors for the Silver Empire labored all those years to stamp it out, clearly they did not. That weird witch in the Tower of Sarsis proves that. She's been around all these years."

"Maralina is not a witch," said Kagen.

"Fine. Half-vampire faerie princess," said Tuke with forced patience. "Quite frankly, I don't know—or care to know—the damn difference. My point is that she was not killed by the Silver Empire, nor was her tower torn down. If what she told you was right, Kagen, she has been very much alive all these centuries. So . . . that brings me back to wondering what magic was actually eradicated, what remained, *how* did it survive, and what's still to . . . I don't know . . . *wake* up?"

Tuke and Filia both looked at Kagen.

"How the fuck should I know?" he said sharply.

"You slept with that sorceress," said Filia. "Pillow talk?"

But Kagen shook his head and then suddenly staggered to his feet and rushed topside to vomit over the rail. He returned in a few minutes, gray-faced, running with sweat, and trembling.

"Gods above and below, I hate ships," he wheezed.

"It's because we're not under sail," said Filia. "Bobbing in the chop like a piece of pork in a pot. Nothing staying still, everything sloshing around and around and—"

Kagen pushed past her and blundered out of the cabin again.

Tuke grinned and shook his head at her. "You are an evil, evil bitch."

"It's a calling," she agreed.

Kagen was longer at the rail, and what returned was a shattered shell of man.

"I hate you," was all he managed to croak out.

"It's okay, lad," said Tuke. "We'll be under way soon and you'll feel worlds better."

He was right. Within a quarter hour the steering cable was

repaired and the helmsman put her before the wind to gain steerage way. The side-to-side rocking stopped, and Kagen's stomach gradually ceased its open rebellion.

"What I don't understand," said Filia, scratching Horse's thick hair, "is why that Raven ship attacked us at all. Even if they thought Kagen was aboard. We're flying the Therian flag. Is Hakkia at war with Theria now?"

Tuke scowled. "I'd like the answer to that myself."

"My guess," said Kagen, his color returning, "is that those birds led them here, and with both ships being out of sight of land, they figured they could take me, kill everyone else, and then do to *Dagon's Swan* what we did to their ship—burn it to the waterline."

"It's such a risk, though," said Tuke. "If word got back home . . . After all, my king died there in the great hall. His body will be on its way to the capital now. It could just as easily have been on this ship. What would the Hakkians do then? Claim ignorance? Or say that this ship went down in a storm?"

"No doubt they have some story concocted," agreed Filia. "They're a bunch of devious bastards, even by Hakkian standards."

Kagen nodded to Tuke. "How will your country react to all of this? The king's death and all, I mean."

The big Therian pondered that for a moment, frowning. "First there will be mourning. We have some sacred rituals that must be performed, and that will take a little time, once the king's body is on home soil. Then his eldest, Princess Theka, will be our new queen. She's no friend to Hakkia, I can tell you. She lost two very close friends on the Night of the Ravens. One was raped and murdered, and the other was crucified for trying to defend a Gardener."

"She's not of the Harvest faith, though," queried Kagen.

Tuke shook his head. "Dagon is our official religion, but we Therians never thought it was a good idea to tell other people how to worship. Plenty of gods to go around, and committing any crime against any kind of church in Theria has always been punished with a heavy hand. You see, we rather like that kind of thing—lots of different points of view. Lots of holidays. No one going out of their way to be an officious ass."

"Right. But how will she react?" asked Kagen. "Watch and wait? Or . . . will Theria go to war with Hakkia?"

"Hell, I couldn't begin to guess. If this was any other country, then it would be war for certain," said Tuke. "But Hakkia is different. The Witch-king conquered the entire empire in a single night. That truth will still stand, and it would have to give any monarch serious pause."

"Sure," said Filia, "but the math is different now. The whole Therian delegation was in that room, as were the delegations of every other nation. They saw Kagen fight the Witch-king. They saw him survive, which pretty much establishes that the Witch-king isn't infallible."

"Right," agreed Kagen. "It also tells everyone that he can't just hurl thunderbolts or whatever wizards do in close combat."

"Point is," said Filia, directing her comment to Tuke, "he lost that fight to our boy here."

"Well, it was more of a draw," said Kagen, but both his friends shook their heads.

"No, it damn well was not," said Tuke. "Filia's correct here. Ever since the Night of the Ravens, everyone in the empire has been shitting their pants thinking about the Witch-king. The great sorcerer who conquered the most powerful empire this world's ever seen and did it in a single night, blah blah blah. People thought he was all-powerful and invincible, but now they know he isn't. If my king knew that before the coronation, he would have absolutely declared war. He'd have had every Raven and their pet mercenaries rounded up and beheaded, and he'd have sent every last head back to Argentium with cocks and balls sewn into their dead mouths."

"Charming," said Kagen. "But I'm all for it."

"Al-Huk of Samud would have joined him," said Filia. "He's a tough son of a bitch, and he loves a good fight. Remember a couple of years back when those corsairs began harrying his trading fleet? Al-Huk loaded every one of his vessels with soldiers, and when the corsairs ambushed them off the coast of Tull Belain, he burned them to the waterline and hung the survivors from the yardarms. No quarter, no hesitation."

Tuke grinned. "I actually thought he was going to join in, back there in the great hall. Wish he had."

"But he didn't," said Kagen. "None of the monarchs did."

"Because, like I said, they thought he was invincible," said Filia. "And they were surrounded by legions of Ravens. Joining our fight would have been nice—we could have used more blades—but it was unwinnable. Al-Huk would have known that. The question now is what *will* happen? Personally, I can't see things going back to the way they were after the conquest. No chance."

Kagen bit into a biscuit without remembering to tap out the worms. He gagged, spit them onto the floor, and tossed the hard roll onto the table.

"So," he said, "you think al-Huk will take Samud to war against the Hakkians just because the Witch-king didn't dazzle everyone with magic spells?"

"Yes," said Tuke.

"Yes," said Filia.

"Damn," said Kagen.

CHAPTER TEN

The Witch-king walked slowly through the formal garden on the east side of the palace. The last of the autumn flowers were fading, but the hardiest ones still shared their vibrant colors with him. Dark purple floss flowers, bloodred garden mums, yellow daisies, spiky blue salvia, and golden strawflowers; canna lilies in bold hues of red, yellow, or orange; bright bronze-orange blanket flowers; and his favorites, the yellow and white calibrachoa. He was fonder of flowers than he was of people, and that had always been the case. And he remembered the color schedule of the flowers here, having walked this garden many hundreds of times growing up.

It was there in that garden, with all the guards banished inside, that he had first kissed the only woman he'd ever loved. Like so many, she was dead now, and her blood was on his hands. He accepted that. His love had been accepted, used, and then discarded when it became both inconvenient and dangerous. It was one of the reasons—one of many reasons—he had gone to the Winterwilds and remained there. The endless ice and bitter cold matched the eternal winter that took hold of his heart when she cast him out.

Now he was back, and the cold had found him here. Winter was descending on the west and these flowers would soon wither and die.

As everything died.

As everyone died.

He stopped in the center of the garden and sat on a stone bench. Unlike those secret assignations of long ago, today the garden was not empty. Guards stood their watches in alcoves. Gardeners—the tenders of flowers, not the scholars or clerics of that hateful religion—worked to take cuttings or prepare the flower beds for their winter nap.

And the children.

They were there. Sweet Gavran and Foscor. Almost six years old now and full of life, humor, intelligence, and mischief. They played at catching butterflies, but the last of the season's insects were too clever to be caught. And that was fine. There would come a time, and not too many years in the future, when those children would be required to kill. He wanted that power for them, but not yet.

Not yet.

They were beautiful, and even though he knew there was darkness growing in each—how could there not be?—he was content to let it blossom in its own time. No need to hurry. Let them be children.

Let them be *his* children.

Behind his yellow veil, he smiled.

Behind his yellow veil, he wept very quietly.

CHAPTER ELEVEN

"They died here," said the little girl.

She and her brother stood together in the doorway. Hands knotted tightly together, eyes wide, hearts hammering.

"Yes," said the boy.

The room was large, with couches and chairs, tables, many shelves for books, and bins for toys. Those shelves and bins were empty. The couches were new. Every item of furniture and all personal possessions were gone. The twins had been forced to burn every single item they once owned. Foscor was still Desalyn when that happened. Gavran was still Alleyn.

That was then.

That was before they had a new father.

It was before *him*.

Now Alleyn and Desalyn were gone. Dead. Like all the others. Their sisters and brothers. Their aunts and uncles. Their mother.

All dead.

The children walked across the room, stopping here and there to touch a piece of furniture that stood where something older and more familiar had been. Some areas pulled one child more than the other, but each time they went together to be in that space or near that thing, they never released the other's hand.

It was different when they held hands.

When that happened, the veil between Foscor and Gavran fluttered away as if in a wind, revealing Desalyn and Alleyn. It was never long, but it was there, and both of them knew, despite their age, that it was a terrible and dangerous secret. To share it with anyone was to lose it, maybe forever. They knew this somehow with absolute certainty.

Most of the time they did not want to disturb that veil. Being the beloved children of the Witch-king—of *Father*—was beautiful and fun and exciting. Like that night in the great hall when they spat on the bad man who tried to force the veil to tear.

Kagen Vale. The man their father hated above all others.

The evil man who tried to stab their father with poisoned knives.

That was the truth they lived with every day.

Except days like this.

Their governess was Lady Kestral, the one who gave them the potions and drew those strange symbols on their skin and placed the special crystals around their beds. But Lady Kestral had not come to them that day, nor had the Witch-king's harpy of a governess, Madame Lucibel; and the veil began to flutter as soon as Foscor took Gavran's hand while they walked down a corridor.

That's when they were not Hakkian children. They became Argonian again. They became Alleyn and Desalyn again.

They became orphans again.

Sneaking into this suite of rooms seemed to make that veil almost vanish. It was here where all the Seedlings lived. *Had* lived. Would never live again.

It was there where every one of their brothers and sisters had been cut to pieces with swords and knives. As one, they turned to a corner where a four-poster bed once stood. Their eyes bulged and filled with tears as they saw ghostly images of their eldest sibling, Hessyla, being held down while very bad men did awful things to her. They had torn her nightdress off. They beat and slapped her and then they forced her to do things that neither of the twins understood but both knew were bad. Like the naughty touching they were told not to do, only much, much worse. And then they killed her. Killed Hessyla and all the others. Leaving only bleeding wounds and desecrated memories in the minds of the twins.

Desalyn squeezed Alleyn's hand hard enough to make their laced fingers hurt.

"I don't want to forget," she said.

"We won't," promised Alleyn.

But then the door banged open and Madame Lucibel filled the doorway, fists on hips, eyes blazing. The Witch-king's governess was a huge woman, with meaty arms and fat thighs and enormous breasts, eyes that could skewer anyone with a glance, and a voice that was sharper than any knife. A flexible "wand of kindness"—a leather-wrapped short whip—was thrust through the sash of her gown. The children well remembered the feel of that rod on their buttocks and stomachs, their thighs and the soles of their feet. Madame Lucibel was quick to use it and was never gentle, even when Lady Kestral ordered only a light "touch of kindness."

"What are you two scamps doing here?" asked Madame Lucibel with her singsong voice that sounded as sweet as summer rain.

"Just looking," said Desalyn at the same moment Alleyn said, "Nothing."

"Which is it?" asked Madame Lucibel. "Nothing or just looking?"

The children were silent.

"Come here," she said. It was still said softly, almost playfully, but for all that she could make her voice sweet, her eyes were hard as fists. As hard as the braided end of the wand of kindness.

They knew the penalty for refusal or hesitation. They went over to her.

Madame Lucibel slid the rod from her sash and offered the handle to the boy.

"Gavran," she said, "take it. Do it now."

His hand trembled, and the other clutched his sister's for dear life. He curled his fingers around the handle.

"Foscor," said the big woman, "turn around and bend over the arm of that couch. No, don't give me that look. Do it now or I'll strip you and make you take it naked. Would you like that? No? Then do what I say."

All in that singsong.

It took so much of the courage Desalyn possessed to let go of Alleyn's hand. She knew what would happen when she did. Alleyn tried to hold on to her, but the weight of Madame Lucibel's glare was too much and the connection broke.

It was Foscor who turned and bent over the arm of the couch.

It was Gavran who beat her with the rod.

But inside, it was Desalyn who screamed. And in his own private darkness, Alleyn screamed every bit as loud. Then, and when Foscor beat him.

But Gavran and Foscor gritted their teeth and took the beatings in silence. Gavran and Foscor smiled with each stinging strike across their upper thighs and buttocks.

Gavran and Foscor laughed.

They laughed and laughed and laughed . . .

CHAPTER TWELVE

Dagon's Swan moved on, heading north by west before a following sea. The clouds above were a mix of puffy white and frowning black, and there was lightning on the seaward horizon.

Below, still exiled to their cabin by Jasker and his busy crew, Filia asked, "How are *you* doing with all this, Kagen?"

"With war?" mused Kagen. "Oh, I'm all in favor of it."

"No," she said, her voice more tender than usual. "I mean with everything. With your brother being a monster. With that level of betrayal. With the fact that it was your favorite brother who murdered your parents and two of your siblings."

Kagen shook his head. "Gods of the Pit, I don't know how to even think about it." He glared down at his hands. "I wish there was a garden I could go to."

In the weeks following the conquest of the Silver Empire, every garden in the west had been ransacked and defiled. The Gardeners, nuns, apprentices, and other staff had all been brutalized. Rape, torture, and mutilation had been specifically mandated by the Witch-king in an attempt to erase that faith from the world. Kagen had heard that mention of the Faith of the Harvest was being systematically expunged from history books, statues, public records, and schools. So, even if his gods had not damned and abandoned him, Kagen had nowhere to go for solace.

Tuke gave his shoulder a squeeze, and Filia patted his forearm. It wasn't much, and it took none of the pain away, but Kagen was nonetheless grateful.

"Tell me something, Kagen," said Tuke. "If—somehow—you manage to get your heart's desire and you carve your brother into pieces . . . what then?"

Kagen shrugged. "Do what I can to help rebuild the Silver Empire. What else?"

"Sure, but with *who* on the throne, exactly?"

"Desalyn is next in line," said Kagen.

"Oookay," said Filia carefully. "We're talking about Desalyn and her brother, Alleyn, who spit in your face and swore they were the children of the Witch-king? How does that make any kind of sense? Politically or otherwise."

Kagen looked away and stared at nothing.

When the empire fell, a team of Ravens had been sent into the imperial quarters to murder the empress and slaughter her children—thereby ending a lineage that had endured for a thousand years. It had been Kagen's oath-sworn job to protect those Seedlings, but he had been off duty, drunk, and asleep in a whore's bed when the invasion began. By the time he'd fought his way into the suite of rooms where the imperial children lived, they were all dead. Chopped to unrecognizable pieces that were later fed to the Witch-king's hounds. The implications of that—and the knowledge that Kagen had sworn by his immortal soul to protect them—led to his damnation.

But the universe was a perverse thing, and during the ceremony that would have made the Witch-king the emperor of a new empire, that madman had brought out two children, a boy, Gavran, and his twin sister, Foscor, and presented them as his own offspring and heirs. Kagen recognized them as Empress Gessalyn's twins—Alleyn and Desalyn—but when he tried to convince the gathered nobles of this, the children rebuked him and spat upon him. They swore that the Witch-king was their father. That, as much as anything that had happened thus far, broke what was left of Kagen's heart. It was a level of failure beyond all that had so far happened.

"I don't know how to talk about that," said Kagen. He dragged a wrist across his eyes and then stared down at the wetness. "Gods damn me to the deepest pit of hell."

"Look, brother," said Tuke, "clearly those children are under some kind of spell. Nothing else makes sense, because it's only been a few months. Whatever that fuckface brother of yours did to make them act like that can be undone."

"Oh yes? And how, exactly?" demanded Filia.

"Hell if I know," said Tuke. "But someone will know. Maybe Mother Frey."

"You're joking," scoffed Kagen. "Didn't she spend her entire life tracking down and persecuting anyone who even breathed the word *magic*?"

"Oh, Frey isn't as simple as that," said Filia. "Tuke's right. I think she's likely to be our strongest ally."

"Right. Sure. An old lady who spent her life in service to the gods who pissed on me. That's terrific. Let's go out of our way to find her," said Kagen.

"No, I'm in earnest," said Filia. "You know that Tuke and I have done work for her. She's not a doctrinist. In fact, I've often thought that her work for the Garden was a convenience to allow her to pursue her own ends."

"Truth," agreed Tuke.

"And what ends are those?" asked Kagen without much interest.

"Trying to prevent bad people from doing bad things," said Filia.

"Ri-i-ight . . ." said Kagen, drawing it out.

"You don't know her," said Tuke. "We do. Trust us that we have a better insight than you do."

"Sure, agreed," said Kagen. "But why should I care? If her life's work was to prevent bad things from happening, it's not unfair to say she's failed."

Filia gave him a hard look. "This is a war, Kagen. We lost the opening battle and then fought the second encounter to a draw. But this isn't over, not by a long stretch. You've said over and over again that you want to kill your brother. You said you want to avenge the empress, the Seedlings, and your family. I know you want to try to rescue Alleyn and Desalyn. We three can't do that. Not without a hell of a lot of help. And not without reliable intelligence. Frey has a thousand times the contacts we have, and her spy network is everywhere."

"Everywhere including in this room," said Tuke.

Kagen snorted but made no other comment.

"Look," said Filia with forced patience, "I think I might have a decent plan for how to make some actual progress in this fight."

"Oh? I can't wait to hear this," said Kagen.

"First, stop being an ass," she snapped. "Second, maybe try to summon a smidgeon of optimism and at least try to show some interest."

Kagen said nothing.

After a long pause during which they listened to the sounds of the ship and the men working her, Tuke ticked his chin at Kagen.

"We're fleeing with some degree of success, but do you have an actual plan for where we're going? Other than what you told Captain Drach—how did you phrase it? Because it was so eloquent: 'Take us north.' Do you have an actual destination, or are you content to sail until we slam into pack ice or sail off the edge of the world?"

"Yes," said Kagen, "I do have a plan."

"A real plan?"

"Yes," said Kagen.

"Any chance you'll actually tell us?"

Kagen almost smiled. "I plan to get to Vahlycor, retrieve our horses from that inn near the Tower of Sarsis, and then head east."

"Why east?" asked Filia.

"I want to find your Mother Frey," said Kagen. "Oh, don't look so surprised. You both told me she's part of a cabal, right? Some disgruntled nobles plotting in basements, as I understand it."

"It's a bit more than that," said Filia, "but close enough."

"And you said she has a network of agents . . ."

"Yes."

"Then she's our best shot of looking for others—in Argon and elsewhere in the empire—to begin putting together a real rebellion."

They sat and looked at him for a while. The lantern suspended from the ceiling swung back and forth, the shadows it cast constantly changing the expression on Kagen's face.

"Once we touch land," said Tuke, "I can send word to her. But the Hakkians will know about her too. She is likely as much a fugitive as we are. So it might be weeks before any message finds her."

Kagen shook his head. "I can't sit idle for that long."

"I started to tell you boys that I had a plan, but you ignored me," said Filia. "I think there's something we should do first while we're waiting for Tuke's message and Frey's reply."

"Such as?" asked Kagen.

"I think we should go further north," said Filia. "I think we should go to northernmost Nelfydia."

Kagen stared at her. "Why on earth would I ever want to go to Nelfydia?"

"Have you ever been there?" asked Tuke.

"No, and there's a good reason for it," said Kagen. "It's nothing but snow and snow and more snow, and I don't like snow."

"City boy."

"The word you're looking for is *civilized*. Which I am. Nelfydia is a frozen nowhere."

"Which makes it a damn good place to hide a training camp of the toughest warriors you'll ever find," said Filia.

Kagen narrowed his eyes. "Such as whom?"

"The Unbladed," she answered.

"Since when did they train at a camp? I thought all of you joined because you're already trained and use it as a kind of union. The *Brotherhood* of Steel," he said, leaning on the word.

"To a degree," said Filia. "But you know as well as anyone that any soldier can improve their skills or learn new ones."

"She's right," said Tuke. "I was an indifferent archer when I was younger, but Ghuraka and her core group of veterans helped me become a hell of a lot better."

"Who in the burning pits is Ghuraka?"

"She is the most respected and feared member of the Unbladed," said Filia. "She's a very tough, very mean, very skilled master teacher. And everyone in the brotherhood respects her."

"She's also ugly as an aardvark's ass," said Tuke, "though I suppose that's beside the point."

"I don't need training," said Kagen. "I need an army."

"If we can get Ghuraka to accept you into the brotherhood," said Filia, "that will give you the best possible opportunity to use the Unbladed *as* your army."

"And how would I pay them?" asked Kagen sourly. "Right now, I couldn't hire a vagrant to move from one side of the street to the other. I have exactly nine copper pennies to my name."

"Frey," said Tuke. "Her friends in the cabal are rich. Very, very rich. I have no doubt they would finance your army even if it beggared them."

Kagen considered that for a moment, then grunted. "Okay, that's promising. But what makes you think this Ghuraka would even agree to see me?"

Filia shrugged. "Anyone can apply for an audition."

"'Audition'?"

"Yes. You can't just up and join the brotherhood," said Tuke. "You have to have what we call a saint—a sponsor—and either of us can take that role. And then you have to do some fighting. Just enough to show that you know your trade."

Kagen grunted. "And then?"

"And then we ask Ghuraka for her help," said Filia.

Kagen got up and walked across the small room. He leaned on the frame around a porthole and stared at the water sluicing past.

"Nelfydia," he said. "Shit."

Dagon's Swan sailed on.

CHAPTER THIRTEEN

Nespar and Jakob sat in big armchairs in the room with the map table. They were alone except for the scuttling of rats in the walls. It was a long evening, pleasant in its way, as they let the conversation flow from topic to topic with the ease of trusted friends.

After a dinner was brought in and devoured and they were settled before the fire, Jakob returned to an earlier topic.

"How exactly did Lady Kestral conjure that razor-knight?" he asked. "There is precious little about that kind of thing in the histories, even those of Hakkian sorcery."

"Oh, it is such a dangerous thing that much of it has been deliberately kept *out* of texts that could too easily fall into the wrong hands," said Nespar. "It is not conjured by any rites of the church of Hastur the Shepherd God but is instead a sorcery associated with Nyarlathotep."

"I've heard of him," said Jakob. "Conflicting stories, really. Some sources list him as a god, or at least godlike. But other histories say he was a man, a wizard of great power."

"Both accounts are correct as far as they go," said Nespar. "The Witch-king explained it to me. He said that the Elder Gods are scattered. Cthulhu dreams in his sunken city. To-Sothoth has returned to the stars, and our own Hastur exists in a space between this world and another, where he, too, dreams. Nyarlathotep, however, has chosen to remain awake and frequently takes human form. Many forms in many places. There are cults who worship him, but all are in hiding. The priests of Skyria worshipped him for thousands of years, and their priests modeled their clothing and dress after one of his aspects. Nyarlathotep occasionally does the will of other gods, taking amusement from such actions, especially when it involves creating trouble for mortal man. His father, after all, is Azathoth, the embodiment of universal chaos."

"Well," said Jakob, "that's genuinely terrifying."

"The expression 'fearing the gods' is hardly symbolic," said Nespar. "Now, as to creating a razor-knight . . . the sorcery involved is very complex. Subtle and variable to some degree."

"You understand it?" asked Jakob, surprised.

Nespar smiled. "I had it explained to me by the lady."

"How does it work? It is essentially necromancy, yes?"

"Necromancy is the core of it, yes," said Nespar, "but there are other factors. In short, the spell depends on having some natural part of a specific person—blood is best, but hair, teeth, skin, even a preserved organ. Lady Kestral says that each part of a person's body holds within it a kind of pattern or code. This is important for a couple of reasons. First, it allows the necromancer to create a physical body for the knight. This allows the razor-knight to essentially search for itself."

"You lost me."

"Consider the Night of the Ravens," explained Nespar. "A spy here in the palace was able to obtain hair from the Poison Rose. When Kestral—at our king's request—created the knight, it was immediately able to sense the presence of Lady Vale and, no matter the distance or obstacles, would follow that scent or trail."

"Why would a creature like that—who is in some way *part* of someone—then go and kill them?"

"The body is linked, and so are some instincts and actions," said Nespar, "but a razor-knight is not simply a golem. Once the body is constructed, the necromancer has to conjure a battle demon to inhabit and drive it."

"Battle demon . . ." mused Jakob. "I'm not familiar with that term, apart from oblique references in old texts."

"There is always war in hell," said the chamberlain. "The spirits of the dead and the demons who populate the realms of the dead are in endless conflict. There is murder and bloodshed, combat and slaughter without end. What makes it truly hell is that there is never a victor, because the combatants are all dead. There is no victory. But when one of these spirits or demons—either will do—is conjured and placed within the body of a razor-knight, and then when it goes out to kill, it can actually win. Such spirits revel in this, and this is why that act of conjuration for such a purpose is often aided by those ghosts and demons."

"That's disturbing."

"But useful. The razor-knight conjured with the Poison Rose's hair was sent to the palace on the Night of the Ravens to guarantee the slaughter of the palace guards, the empress, and her family. And, ultimately, the Poison Rose herself."

"Is that why Kagen was able to kill it, then?" asked the historian. "Because it had accomplished its mission?"

"Oh, no. Once conjured, a razor-knight will continue to serve its master or mistress forever. It is immortal, and it will fight with all of its considerable strength to remain here on earth, where the enemies it fights can actually die." He shook his head. "No, Kagen Vale used one of the very few weapons that have any chance of working against such a creature. Banefire."

"So what happens to the concept of control after the knight has killed its primary target?"

"It remains under the control of whoever has conjured it," said Nespar. "There is a spell of command in which a unique word or phrase—known only to the necromancer, unless he or she entrusts it to someone else—will allow that person to direct the knight toward new targets. But as you can see, that is a dangerous tool."

"What if the necromancer were to die before sharing that command word?" asked Jakob.

Nespar shuddered. "Then it would be free to kill whomever it wanted for as long as it wanted . . . and that would be forever."

"Gods of the Pit . . . has that ever happened?"

"Only once," said Nespar. "Back in the early days of the Blue Empire. A Hakkian priest conjured one in order to exact revenge on a rival who had poisoned him. The razor-knight killed his rival, but the priest died of the poison. It took an army and eight months to bring the razor-knight down, and at the cost of four thousand soldiers and countless civilians."

"I never read about that in any of the histories . . ."

"Nor would you," said Nespar. "Hakkia has a long history of editing its own story."

"That is a blow to any historian," said Jakob. "Even an unrepentant propagandist like me."

They drank.

"There is one other thing about razor-knights," said Nespar. "And this is something Lady Kestral told me before the invasion. She said that the necromantic spell has its own set of variations. For example, a knight can be conjured with blood or hair from more than one victim. If, say, she had used something from the kings of each member nation of the Silver Empire, then the razor-knight would have stalked the entire west, killing kings and queens and the lot."

"I'm glad she did not do that," said Jakob, alarmed. "Think of the total political and cultural chaos. That would have turned the entire west into a bloody brawl."

"Which is why that *wasn't* done," agreed Nespar. "Though there was a plan to try to obtain hair or blood from a few key submonarchs. Al-Huk was at the top of that list."

Jakob nodded. "That might have worked."

"It would have been relatively easy, too, or so she said. Once the razor-knight has found its original victim, then the necromancer would introduce the second target's sample. The knight could be instructed to kill the first victim and immediately head off to kill the next. That has the virtue of singularity of purpose but allows one knight to be a focused assassin for whoever controls it."

The historian looked troubled. "While I understand the value of such a monster, particularly on bold ventures like the Night of the Ravens, I find the concept terrifying and the risks enormous. I can think of a dozen ways that what you've described could go wrong. I mean . . . what if King al-Huk or someone as dangerous were to discover the process and create a razor-knight tasked with slaying the Witch-king? Where would we all be then?"

Nespar's smile was rueful. "And you wonder why I seldom get a good night's sleep? The danger in bringing magic back into the world is that no one—not even our lord and master—can control it all."

CHAPTER FOURTEEN

DREAMS OF THE DAMNED

Kagen crawled into his swaying hammock, dragging his grief and stress and pain with him.

He lay for hours listening to the wild weather and the ten thousand sounds a ship makes when it is in haste and in pain. It made him feel as if *Dagon's Swan* were a living thing, wounded by the Hakkians, abused by the storm, but pressing on, fighting to live.

Those thoughts went with Kagen as he drifted down into sleep, and then changed through the alchemy of dreams into something else . . .

He walked alone through the caverns of ice.

It was rare, strange, to be there without the ghost of the Herepath he had once loved, or the echoes of his younger self. In this dream, Kagen was himself—the adult who was fleeing the wrath of the living Herepath. Living, because Kagen had failed to kill him. The consequences of that failure haunted him like evil ghosts.

He walked for hours, days, weeks—there was no way to tell. Dreams do not follow any rules—he had long since learned that. But as he walked, Kagen realized that he recognized certain corridors, certain places within the world of ice and cold and shadows. He stretched out with his senses, trying to properly orient himself—and stopped.

It was there. The smell of something that did not belong to this world of ice. An animal smell. Strong, but also oddly fragile. And mingled with it was a coppery scent Kagen knew all too well.

He began to run toward it, feeling for the handles of his daggers, assuring himself that even in dreams he was not helpless. The corridor slanted down and then turned, and as Kagen approached the turn, the smell became much stronger. He drew his knives and followed the corridor.

It ended abruptly, opening into a cavern. And there it was. The beast. Massive, bound by chains attached to rings driven deep into the ancient ice. Its head hung low, leathery wings spread wide as if in a cruel mockery of flight, but with iron spikes pinning them to the wall. The creature's body was crisscrossed with countless wounds, some so old they were nothing but gray lines; others were new and bloody and festering.

The dragon in chains. Captive and tortured, its tears and blood harvested by the Witch-king. Kagen's sorceress lover, Maralina, had told him the truth of this creature—that dragons had come to earth countless ages ago. Before their arrival, magic did not exist on the planet. The dragons brought it with them. It was in their flesh and blood, and in their tears. Now this one—Fabeldyr—was the last of them. The last of her kind alive on this world. Abandoned, captured, tortured to give the Witch-king the power to conquer and destroy.

Kagen crept toward Fabeldyr, afraid even in the presence of her utter helplessness. The dragon seemed to be in a daze, or perhaps she slept. He had no way of knowing. But as he approached, that head—three times the size of the largest bullock—moved. Her ancient eyes opened and stared at him with bleak resignation.

"Have you come to bleed me again?" she asked.

Kagen stopped and for a moment looked down at the daggers in his hands. Feeling their weight and heft, seeing the dried gleam of eitr, the god-killer poison on the steel. He wanted to resheathe them, or throw them away.

"No," he said, his voice hollow. "How . . . how can I help you?"

The dragon sniffed the air, and gradually her glazed eyes came into focus.

"You smell like him," she said, "but you are not Herepath."

"No," said Kagen. "He is my brother."

Fabeldyr looked away. "And you are his creature?"

"No," cried Kagen. "He is my enemy. He is everything I hate in this world. But how can I help you?"

The dragon's eyes filled with tears. She opened her mouth to answer.

And Kagen woke.

The ship rose and fell in the night-black water. Kagen tried to sleep, tried to find his way back to that dream, but no matter where he looked, Fabeldyr was not there.

CHAPTER FIFTEEN

They stood at a crossroads in every possible way that metaphor could be interpreted.

The intersection was southeast of Argentium, whence they had all departed in haste that bordered on flight. Eight caravans, eight cadres of mounted cavalry, eight squadrons of foot soldiers with spears, eight clusters of nobility of various ranks.

Eight monarchs of powerful nations that until recently had formed the backbone of the Silver Empire.

Seven of them still lived. One, the king of Theria, lay in a hearse drawn by six horses, one each from the families of greatest wealth and power. The hearse had been an elegant coach, but it was now draped in whatever black fabric the parties could muster. Crow feathers—not those from any raven—had been affixed to the head collars of each horse, and tall soldiers with angry faces stood guard.

Not all of the monarchs were there. Some, including those from the city-states of Tarania, had left the city first. Tarania was not even called that on modern maps anymore, and the region, struck with blight and drought for the last two centuries, was merely known as the Waste. Those small city-states held no real power, and though each had a small militia, there was no national standing army.

A few others were absent as well.

When the Hakkian Ravens launched their rebellion three months before, they struck Argon hardest. That nation, jewel of the empire, had no king or queen but instead was ruled by the Silver Empress, whose governance blanketed the entire empire. Now Empress Gessalyn was dead. And the Hakkian monarch was the Witch-king, who now sat upon the throne in Argentium.

The monarchs gathered together in a loose circle in the middle of an intersection with many roads leading away from it.

King al-Huk of Samud stood with his callused hand on the pommel of the great sword, Kraken, which hung at his hip. Across his broad back hung the storied bow, Saint's Thunder.

To his left was Queen Weska of Behlia, tall and cold-eyed, bearing the family name of a nation other than her own, but a true daughter of a line of revered monarchs. Her country was one of the smaller ones, but highly valued for its strategic importance as the horn at the bottom of the western side of the continent, and with the vast spread of the Dragon Islands extending her control of the sea-lanes. The nation of Behlia itself was not a true part of the Silver Empire and was still a hotbed of political infighting.

Next to her was Ifduril, crown prince of Ghenrey, whose father lay dying back home but whose people had long looked to the strong and steady heir. To al-Huk's right was King Thespo of Sunderland, once known as the Pirate Prince for his activities before accepting the crown upon his father's death.

The others were kings and queens of Nelfydia in the frozen north; vast Vahlycor, the breadbasket of the empire; the grim-faced Nehemitian queen from a long line of warrior-monarchs; and beside her the wily and scholarly king of Zaare, which was the gateway to the east.

King al-Huk looked around at his peers.

"Cousins," he said, "we met in good faith and—let's be frank—optimism that the Hakkian overthrow could be managed into something approximating peace."

Thespo snorted loudly. "Never trust a Hakkian. There's a reason that's been an aphorism for years uncounted."

Queen Weska fingered the filigree on her ancient sword, Espalian. She had some of the same bone structure and coloring as Gessalyn, though her court scholars had never been able to establish a direct blood line. It was well known that her ambition to prosecute a claim for inclusion in the imperial lineage was strong. Her anger and frustration at having her dream torn away was palpable.

She said, "We met in good faith, aye . . . *we* did. But Thespo is not wrong about Hakkia. They have ever been secretive and dangerous, and now we know that they have been planning this for many years. Perhaps since Bellapher massacred their priests and stamped out their religion—or since it was *believed* that the Hakkian religion was dead."

"I'm still confused on that point," admitted Ifduril of Ghenrey. "I know that Hastur was *among* their gods, but since when has he been their principal deity?"

No one had an answer to that.

"And was that truly Hastur we saw in the sky?" asked the old and battle-scarred King Horogillin of Nelfydia. "Or some kind of glamour?"

Al-Huk pursed his lips and glanced at the sky, looking back the way they had come. There was a massive storm brewing, but it looked as if it was moving north, and not all of them were heading that way.

"What else could it have been?" asked the Samudian king uneasily. "Him and that other one. The Dreaming God."

"The Witch-king is a sorcerer," said Queen Lliaorna of Nehemite. She ruled in equal partnership with her brother, who was still at home. At no time did both monarchs leave their country.

"What of it?" asked Ifduril.

"Perhaps he conjured that image," said Lliaorna. "Some kind of trickery."

"To what end?" asked Thespo. "To spoil his own coronation?"

"How can anyone understand the mind of a Hakkian wizard?" sneered the Nehemitian.

"Whether it was their god or not," said al-Huk, "the question is what do we do about it?"

"What *can* we do?" asked Weska. "Even if he could not complete the coronation and remains a conqueror rather than emperor, his troops are still in every one of our nations. They are quartered in our own palaces. They used banefire during the conquest . . . we can assume they have more. And other weapons. They have whatever spell the Witch-king used to transport his troops across the face of the empire on the Night of the Ravens; he still *has* that power. He has all of that, and we have swords and arrows." She paused and shook her head. "Besides, after what happened the other day, he will be expecting some kind of response from us."

"That is true," agreed al-Huk. "He made a point of pleading his case for a legal assumption of power. We each agreed to participate because to do otherwise would incur the wrath of someone who has already conquered us."

He turned aside and spat into the dust, and each of the others did the same. And for the same reasons.

"The Silver Empire cut its own throat by forbidding magic," said Lliaorna bitterly. "I can understand some political control over it, but banning it so forcefully and so unilaterally was a misstep."

"A grave one," agreed Thespo. "It has left us unschooled, unprepared, and vulnerable."

Queen Weska said, "No matter what else we do, cousins, we need to reclaim our understanding of magic. We *know* it exists. Even before the Witch-king rubbed our noses in proof, we knew. The old stories that predate the empire are filled with it."

"Not to mention the travelers' stories from the other side of the Cathedral Mountains. Magic was not banned there."

"In some places it was," said al-Huk. "Kierrod Sund, Gefhelm . . . a few others."

"But not everywhere," she countered. "And as for Kierrod Sund, they outlawed foreign magic but not the kind that is part of their own sacred traditions."

Thespo pointed to the hearse. "Theria was the only nation in the empire that openly practiced the old ways. Granted, it was mostly prayer and catechism, but they believe in it. They never accepted the Harvest Gods as their main deities, no matter what the official records of the Silver Empire insisted."

"Yes," said al-Huk dryly, "and am I the only one who is not convinced that our brother king of Theria did not die by *accident* during the coronation?"

There was a silence, and clearly most of them had already given this some thought.

"What about the scholars over on Skyria?" asked Ifduril. "Don't they continue to practice magic spells and rituals? Can't we get them on our side?"

But Weska shook her head. "It's magic in name only. Old white magic that was used in Harvest cultures before the rise of the Silver Empire. They recite the spells and perform whatever ritual mummery was once used, but it's only to keep alive the memory of white magic. None of those Gardeners are actual magicians. No, cousin, there is no help there."

Thespo said, "And there's the matter of the Witch-king's children. If they are his children at all."

"I've been to court enough in recent years to know a Seedling when I see one," said al-Huk. "Kagen Vale called them by name, and who better than him would know imperial children? He saw them every single day. It is absurd to think he was mistaken."

"Completely absurd," agreed Lliaorna. "Which means what? That those children are under the Witch-king's spell?"

"Given all he has accomplished," said Thespo, "does that stretch credulity all that far?"

"Not as I see it," said Ifduril, and the others nodded their agreement.

Weska said, "They are hostages, whatever else they are."

"All of which calls into serious question the legitimacy of the Witch-king's claim. Conquest is one thing. The gods know there is enough precedent. But treaties have always kept a change of government from becoming all-out war, and sadly, a complete extermination of the previous bloodlines is the only way a new regime can be made legal."

"An absurd law," said Thespo. "But I understand the *why* of it. If it could somehow be proven that those twins were Gessalyn's and not the children of this Gethon Heklan, then . . ." He let the rest trail off.

"So what do we do?" asked Weska. "Do we go back home and have our necks measured for the Hakkian yoke?"

"I, for one," said young Ifduril, "intend to make sure that my court scholars put some real effort into relearning what our forebears knew. Magic is there, and the Office of Miracles could not have completely erased all knowledge of it. The scholars on Skyria prove that much. Perhaps it can be brought back in ways we can use. We need to know, and this I will do as my first act upon returning home."

"And I will be sending my scholars across the Cathedral Mountains," said Thespo, "to see what they can learn from Kortha, Inaki, and Bercless—those eastern nations where magic is still an active part of their traditions."

"Part of traditions, yes," said Lliaorna. "But is it practical magic? Can it be used? I've heard plenty of stories but not one credible report of actual magic being used. My guess is that it is only as real as what the Skyrian scholars are doing. Hand waving and meaningless chants."

"I think we'll all be searching for the secrets of magic," said

Weska. "But I have my doubts about how soon we'll find information of use, and how effective that might be against the sorceries of someone like the Witch-king." She glanced around. "I am surely not the only one of us who will admit to being terrified of that man."

"That *demon*," said Ifduril. He made a warding sign in the air. "That process will not be quick. Relearning magic might take months."

"More like years," said al-Huk. "Possibly many, many years."

"Then what do we do in the meantime?" asked the prince. "Do we go to war in hopes that foreknowledge of the Hakkian tricks will somehow protect us from the Witch-king's wrath?"

"We do not yet know what the Hakkians themselves will do," said al-Huk. "For my part, I will wait."

"Wait and do what?" demanded Weska.

"Wait and very quietly triple the size of my army and my navy, and I recommend that each of you do the same." When no one spoke, the Samudian king nodded and said, "Like it or not, cousins, we now have to live in a world at war. We have been invaded, conquered, but I have never formally surrendered. Have any of you?"

The others shook their heads.

"Then the war is not over," said al-Huk.

"Will you draw your sword now and fight?" asked Thespo.

The Samudian king shook his head and rested his hand once more on Kraken's pommel. "That time may come, but now is not the hour."

"And, cousin," asked Weska coolly, "what do you advise we do in the meantime?"

Al-Huk looked east toward Argentium and then up at the growing storm. "We watch. We smile in the faces of the Hakkian spies. And we prepare for war."

CHAPTER SIXTEEN

Two women sat together in a big window seat, looking out at the trees bending beneath storm winds. They both wore robes of soft wool and had blankets pulled around them, less for physical warmth than as a comfort for their souls.

Their souls needed great comfort.

One of the women was very old, with a face that was lined and seamed. There were bruises on her face that had once been the color of those swelling storm clouds outside, but these were fading now to sickly yellows and greens.

Her friend was much younger and had a broken right arm in a sling. Pain and stress had carved lines into what had been an unmarked face before the madness at the palace.

They sat for a long time in silence, watching the bully winds brutalize the grove of oaks. Branches had already fallen, and one tree—patriarch of the whole line that bordered her estate—was leaning over.

"It will fall," said Helleda Frost. "It will crack and break and fall."

But the older woman shook her head. "It will endure."

Helleda looked at Mother Frey. "You can't know that."

"I can hope for it," said the woman who had once been the chief investigator for the Office of Miracles, a scholarly and secretive branch of the Faith of the Garden. "We've lost so much, but hope endures. Hope is free, and we can take as much of it as we need."

"Hope is a dream," said Helleda, dismissing the comment.

"Everything begins as a dream," said the old woman.

"We need something more substantial than wishful thinking."

"We do, but actions are born of dreams. Any action we take, if not born of hope, is merely reflex. Personally, I have no intention of living what's left of my life merely trying to survive. There is no value in that. No grace. I would rather take inspiration from hope—not vain hope, but based on what *might* be possible—even if at this moment all we can see is rubble in the path of the Hakkian eclipse."

The rest of the room was draped in shadows, and the logs in the fireplace had burned down to a cluster of glowing red coals. The servants did their work elsewhere in the mansion, without sound. The only noises were the rattling of shutters as the fingers of wind tried to pry them open, and the groans of the old house as the storm chilled its bones.

"We should light some incense and say prayers for Hannibus," said Helleda. Her face was pale and drawn from pain, and she had refused any of Frey's offers of draughts for the discomfort because they made her sleepy, and Helleda wanted to be awake and aware.

"Hannibus is resourceful," said Frey. "But, yes, I will light incense and we can pray together later."

The two women had fled the madness and violence of the failed coronation, along with a friend, Hannibus Greel, a wealthy Therian merchant. Hannibus had brought them to Helleda's Argonian country house immediately after their flight from Argentium. Almost immediately afterward, he set off on a mission to Samud, hoping to reach that nation around the same time as the nobles who had attended the coronation. Memories of that debacle and the resulting emotions and political implications would be in sharp relief. It was a very long shot, but Frey thought that the king of that country, the wise and powerful Hariq al-Huk, might be somewhat disposed toward having a useful political discussion. Prior to what happened at the palace, none of the submonarchs whose nations had once formed the Silver Empire had been willing to even entertain a conversation about rebellion, for fear of military and magical retaliation. If that was to change, then now might be the best time.

Helleda shivered, then winced as the involuntary movement sent ripples of pain through her arm. She bit down on a curse and endured it. Mother Frey caressed her face gently.

They had not spoken yet of the fact that they had seen two deities, neither of them belonging to the pantheon of Harvest Gods to which they were devoted. One was Hastur, the Shepherd God, dressed in yellow and standing hundreds of feet tall. The other was the squid-faced monstrosity Cthulhu, the Dreaming God, who was Hastur's half brother, rival, and enemy. Beings that had been worshipped since before recorded history, but in whose existence most people did not believe. Those gods had appeared at the moment of the coronation and battled one another above while Kagen Vale and the Witch-king dueled before the empty throne in the great hall of the palace of Argentium.

Everyone in the great hall—as well as every citizen and visitor in Argentium that day—had seen that appalling and terrifying spectacle. But even on the mad carriage ride away from the palace after the failed assassination and the spoiled coronation, neither of Frey's confidants had spoken of it.

Frey understood why. The very *fact* of those other gods, and the knowledge that they existed in reality rather than in old stories, was dangerous to accept. It hammered cracks into the fundamental beliefs of everyone of every faith. And as belief in those monstrous deities predated the Faith of the Harvest by thousands of years, that was a terrible thing to contemplate. Every Gardener had preached that such old gods were pagan beliefs that had no basis in reality, and that Mother Sah and Father Ar— and their children and fellow gods—were the only true celestial beings. Gods like those who lived beneath the sea—Dagon and his companions—were accepted as real, perhaps as a nod to the Therians, but were mostly relegated to demigod or demon status. Cthulhu and Hastur . . . though the belief in them had been laughable. They were part of something most scholars accepted as the ravings of madmen or, at best, products of poppy-infused dreams.

Now all that had changed but no one seemed yet able to find a way to have that conversation. Not even Mother Frey and Helleda Frost.

Instead, they sat together, sharing warmth, sharing closeness, sharing horror.

"What do we even know about this Witch-king?" asked Helleda. "Gethon Heklan? I've never even heard of him. He was not any kind of political player before the Night of the Ravens."

Mother Frey stared at the storm-lashed tree for a long time before answering. "In the three months since that night," she said, "I've had my agents in Hakkia trying to come up with that answer."

"What did they find?"

"A few details, but it's left me with more questions than answers," said Frey. "What we know is this. Gethon Heklan is a fifth cousin three times removed from the last Witch-king, making him the only person with a potentially legal claim on the throne and title. He was a minor priest of Hastur and a scholar of rising fame within Hakkian circles. Not much known beyond their borders except in certain circles. Nothing at all remarkable about him, and the people from his village are as surprised as anyone that he became their king."

"An imposter, then?" asked Helleda. "Someone else from Hakkia who just *used* Gethon's blood connection in order to rebuild the Witch-king's position, perhaps? Or maybe he was merely groomed to take that role and there are other people—the *real* power behind the Witch-king—in the shadows? Lord Nespar, maybe?"

"Not Nespar," said Frey. "I've met him before while visiting Hakkia on business of the Office of Miracles. No . . . he's smart and cunning as a scorpion, but he isn't brilliant, and everything we've seen speaks to a towering intelligence."

"Then we know nothing about Gethon Heklan?"

"I didn't say that, my dear. I know that he worked briefly with several Gardeners on research projects involved with ancient mysteries, and that is our strongest clue."

"What kind of mysteries?"

"He wrote two notable papers," said Frey. "The first was 'Impermanence, Transition, and Displacement in Ancient Religions.' The other is equally obscure: 'On the Nature of Consciousness, with Additional Notes on Thought Transference and Psychic Theriomorphy.'"

"Theriomorphy?"

"The ability to change one's shape."

"Like a werewolf?"

"Yes. There are many kinds of theriomorphs in folklore—werecats, werefoxes, and so on. Plus monsters like mermaids and elves who use glamours to appear beautiful in order to seduce victims. I don't yet know the actual content of those papers, alas. They were presented to Lord Hroth, Chief Gardener of the Office of Official History, and summarily rejected. If copies were kept on file in his office, they are likely destroyed."

"I remember Hroth," said Helleda. "A distinctly unpleasant man."

"Without doubt. He was pompous, unimaginative, pedantic, and shortsighted. A perfect bureaucrat. That said, I have my agents scouring the empire to collect any documents from a select number of offices. Hroth's, my own Office of Miracles, the Office of War, and others. The fact that the Hakkians were so deliberate in their attempts to utterly destroy the Faith of the Garden, kill the most notable scholars, and collect or burn the libraries is suggestive. The cover story, of course, is that the Garden—in league with the Silver Empire—repressed and oppressed the religion of Hakkia and the practice of magic."

"On that," said Helleda, "since when was Hastur the only

important god of Hakkia?" As I recall, they had an entire pantheon and Hastur was one among many.

"Yes . . . that is curious. My guess—and it's only a guess—is that the cult of magic that has been hiding within Hakkia clung to Hastur because the Shepherd God encouraged magic and miracles. And I think we'll find that he was the patron deity of the Heklan family, though those histories were exceedingly difficult to find *before* the conquest and are now possibly beyond reach."

Lightning flashed and there was a big *boom* as it struck something nearby. Not the oak, though. That still endured.

When the echo of it died away, Helleda asked, "What happened when Lord Hroth rejected Gethon's papers? I know what a crushing defeat that can be for an aspiring scholar."

Frey nodded. "The rejection of his papers resulted in Gethon being dismissed from all official field research. Only one Gardener stood in support of Gethon, and that cleric's letter of appeal was accepted and then sealed by Lord Hroth. I'm working on discovering who that Gardener was. As for Gethon . . . rumor had it that he became despondent and fell into personal decline. Reliable reports say that he became addicted to the Flower of Dreams and as a result became erratic, prone to hallucinations, and also physically ill. He was diagnosed with a wasting disease and seven years ago was predicted to die within a year."

"And . . . ?"

"And nothing. At that point he vanishes from any public records and from all Garden records that I've so far seen. He left his village, and his neighbors thought he died, but then he returned to Hakkia and took up the mantle of the Witch-king."

"Did he find some magic that healed him?" asked Lady Frost. "Something that gave him more agency and personal power?"

"That seems likely, doesn't it?" said Frey.

"That's all you have?"

"It's all that has been verified to some degree. There are bits and pieces of rumors, including one that he undertook a journey to Vespia to find some cure, but we have that from one old man in Gethon's hometown, and that fellow is a bit senile, so the validity is in question."

"And now he is the most powerful and dangerous man in the whole world," said Helleda, and as if in towering agreement, another bolt of lightning struck a birch tree near to the oak and obliterated it.

CHAPTER SEVENTEEN

"This is going to be a mother of a storm," said Filia.

She stood with Tuke and Kagen on the forward deck, each of them clutching lines to steady themselves as the ship rose and plunged in the turbulent sea.

All around them was bustling activity as Captain Jasker and the remaining crew worked to shift ballast and stores to make the vessel better able to withstand what was coming.

In the last hour Kagen had gotten a good lesson in basic ship handling as it related to storms. Because *Dagon's Swan* was a Therian ship, Tuke had managed to secure passage north from Argon, but the challenge was that the vessel had recently off-loaded its cargo of timber and pigs of silver from the northern mines. That left the hull nearly empty, and their newly minted captain had explained that the most dangerous ship in a hurricane is an empty one.

"Why?" asked Kagen.

"Because it's the weight of cargo that helps to stabilize the ship against the waves."

"I thought that was what the ballast was for. I saw a lot of stones down in the hold."

"And in most weather conditions that's enough, sir," said the captain. "But you see, ballast only provides our stabilizing weight.

The weight of cargo—which we don't have—can be shifted to help the ship have better steerage way. If a ship is too light, then it can't push through waves and is more easily tossed about in rough seas." He pointed to the black clouds. "That's more than a squall. That there's a hurricane, and it's going to blow long and hard. When it does that, the seas will get all confused, and if we don't have the weight down below positioned just right, then we're no better than a cork in a flood. So right now we're moving the ballast to give us the right balance, so to speak, so we can lay low enough in the water so as not to get knocked sideways."

"Will it really get that bad?" asked Kagen.

Jasker barked out a harsh laugh. "It'll get bad enough. The *Swan*'s got a wicked roll to her at the best of times, but I've been in blows with her where she rocked thirty degrees to one side and before you can brace your feet, she heeled thirty the other way. Not slow-like. I'm talking in a matter of seconds." He nodded to the storm. "This storm is as big as any I've seen, so if we don't set the ballast just so, then by tonight we'll all be feasting at the sea god's table."

Kagen felt the blood drain from his face. "How can I help?"

Jasker gave him a kindly smile. "Best use you can be, sir, is out of the way."

And so Kagen went forward to stand with Tuke and Filia, each of whom had been given similar orders.

Kagen jabbed Tuke in the chest. "Why aren't you helping? I thought you used to be a pirate."

"I sailed on privateers, not pirate ships, thank you very much," answered Tuke. "And note that I said 'sailed *on*,' not 'sailed.' I'm a fighter and a lover, not a sailor."

"Well," said Filia with a sly grin, "a fighter, anyway."

"Hey!"

A huge wave lifted over the rail and slapped them all with such force that they staggered and would have fallen had it not been for safety ropes. Filia helped Kagen to stand, while Tuke pulled himself upright and stood shivering. They all wore oiled sealskin coats, but the clever water had found every possible opening.

"By the leprous balls of the prince of plagues," sputtered Tuke, wiping saltwater from his eyes. He touched his icon of Dagon in its belt pouch. "I thought I was clear in every one of my prayers, Lord: I want to die in bed, preferably with Filia, if she still has her looks and most of her teeth. I want to be very old at the time, and I want to go with a smile on my face. There was nothing in *any* of my prayers about drowning in a shipwreck."

"If we ever get back on solid ground again," said Filia, "I may slit your throat the next time we're in bed."

"Better that than this," said Tuke.

The winds were howling through the rigging now, and the ship was pitching and rolling with tremendous unpredictability. Life-lines had been rigged fore and aft, allowing sailors to pull themselves along even if the deck was tilted, and to keep them from being washed overboard when a contrary wave sloshed tons of water over the rail.

Time and again a roller would lift the ship so that for a moment all Kagen could see was the night-black sky, and then it would plunge down, slamming into the troughs between one wave and the next.

Kagen heard Jasker yelling orders to two men who were working together to steer the ship. "Steer into the wind, damn your eyes," he roared. "*Into* it . . . that's better. Three points to larboard, lads. Into the low side of the storm. Hold her there and watch those crosswinds."

The sails were reefed high, with very little canvas showing. Tuke explained that even that small amount was enough to take the wind so that *Dagon's Swan* had steerage way, but not so much that it took too much heavy wind, which could tear the masts out. The mathematics involved staggered Kagen, who had never been on anything bigger than a pleasure craft or fishing boat.

Contrary to what Kagen thought was a logical course, the ship turned into the wind, but then he grasped the sense of it. By punching forward into the waves, it allowed the ship to maintain some control, rather than being side-on or stern-on. This way the vessel was not tossed around and battered by each trickster wave. And it prevented the heavier waves from striking side-on, which could easily roll *Dagon's Swan* right over.

The rain, when it came, was biting and cold. There was hail and sleet mixed in, and it felt like flights of arrows.

"Get below," bellowed Jasker.

"I get seasick," Kagen hollered back.

"I don't fucking care. Lubbers below."

But Kagen shook his head. The captain shook his head in disgust. He stabbed a finger at Tuke.

"If he falls overboard, he's for the sharks. We can't fish him out."

"Don't worry, captain," roared Tuke, fighting with the howl of the wind. "I might throw him overboard anyway. Just for fun."

Filia laughed out loud. Kagen hurled obscenities.

The captain turned away, despairing of landsmen of every kind, and went back to try to save his ship.

The rain was a torrent, and the storm was bigger than anything Kagen had ever witnessed. Argon was in a temperate zone, but beyond the Straits of Anthelos, the early winter weather was raw and powerful and angry.

Minutes felt like hours as the ship rose and plunged. Uncountable tons of seawater splashed over the rails, sweeping away anything left loose. The hatches were sealed to prevent that water from sloshing into the hold, though the danger of broaching and foundering was very real.

Despite it all, Kagen was enjoying himself. If this was how he was going to die, then at least there was a grandeur and beauty to it. There was no malice in the storm, only nature's raw power. It made him acutely aware of how inconsequential humans were, like fleas crawling on the skin of a beast so vast it was indifferent to the pests.

Then something rose up out of the water, monstrous and dark, bursting from the upper side of a wave that towered over *Dagon's Swan*. It was so big and so close to the ship that Kagen had no perspective to see what it was. There was a vagueness of a body at least as long as the ship but infinitely more massive.

"Whale," shrieked Filia, but she was wrong.

Or the creature was wrong.

As it reached the apex of its upward lunge and began to fall away, they could see that the body was whale-like, but instead of fins there were clusters of writhing tentacles sprouting from each side. The face was something out of the worst nightmares, with curling barbels like a catfish but each one twisted like a snake, and the mouth—which was big enough to swallow a longboat whole—was filled with row upon row upon row of curved teeth, each as long as a broadsword.

"By the balls of . . ." began Tuke, but words failed him as the monster slammed down onto the next wave and vanished. This sent a shockingly fast wave racing toward the ship, directly off the starboard beam. Kagen could hear Jasker screaming to the helmsmen, and he was aware that the ship was turning. That seemed to happen too slowly, too ponderously, and he found himself praying to the Harvest Gods that had abandoned him.

But *Dagon's Swan* skirted the wave, nimble as a dancer, and the ship moved on.

Kagen stared at the spot where the monster had vanished, his heart hammering in his chest.

The storm grew big and black and impossible, and Kagen felt that it was all he ever needed to know about hell itself.

CHAPTER EIGHTEEN

"Have you found Kagen Vale?"

The King in Yellow sat upon his bloodstained throne with his hounds all around him. Thunder punched the palace walls and rain slanted in through the shattered windows to puddle on the floor. Thunder made threats in the near distance, and the great hall was cold nearly to the point of being unbearable.

Three generals knelt before him, heads bowed low, eyes lowered to the cold marble floor.

"We have several promising leads," said Major General Kiplon. The two officers flanking him said nothing.

"Promising leads," echoed the Witch-king.

"Very promising," insisted Kiplon.

"Stand up," ordered the king.

"Sire?"

"Do I need to repeat myself, General?"

Kiplon got to his feet. He was a thickset man with bandy legs and a black beard going gray.

"Look at me," said the Witch-king.

The effort it took the officer to raise his eyes against the weight of his fear was obvious, but he did it. He stood as straight as possible and looked at the yellow lace veil that covered the features of his king. The hounds, though sprawled, all looked at him, and the muscular bitch who ruled that pack raised her massive head.

"My lord," he said.

"Define *promising*," said the king. "Be precise."

"I . . . well . . . I mean, Majesty, that we believe he took a ship."

"That isn't a lead. It's not even news. We know he and his confederates fled aboard a Therian ship. Surely you have something else? Do you, perhaps, know wither he is bound? Have you determined whether he is an official guest of Theria and if he enjoys diplomatic immunity? Or did he merely *hire* a ship belonging to Theria?"

"Majesty, I . . ."

"The answer to those questions is, I take it, that you don't know."

"We are investigating, Majesty, and—"

"Kiplon," interrupted the Witch-king, "do you consider me a fool?"

"Gods above, my lord . . . *no!*"

"And yet you come here with nothing of use to tell me and yet try to lie and say that you have 'promising leads.'"

"I . . ." The general was sweating badly. The other officers, still kneeling, leaned as far away from him as was possible without losing balance.

"Kiplon . . ."

"Yes, Your Majesty?"

"You disappoint me."

"But, Majesty, it's only been a few days and—"

"Kiplon," interrupted the king. The general snapped to an even more rigid posture of attention.

"Yes, Your Majesty?"

"Run."

"Sire?"

The Witch-king touched the spiked collar cinched around the bitch hound's thick neck.

"Run," he repeated.

The dog's eyes flashed with red hunger. Kiplon staggered backwards as if struck. The other officers scrambled away from him as the hound got to her feet.

General Kiplon whirled and ran. He was fifty-two years old and too heavy to run in full armor. He tried, though. He tried with all his heart and soul. He made it nearly to the big doors before the hound dragged him down and tore the armor from his limbs to get at the quivering flesh. The general's shrieks were dreadful to hear and drowned out the thunder for many minutes.

The other officers made warding signs and tried not to piss in their armor.

The Witch-king did not watch the slaughter. Instead, he looked at each of them in turn, waiting until the force of his scrutiny made them look up.

"Now, gentle sirs," he said softly, "tell me . . . have you found Kagen Vale?"

CHAPTER NINETEEN

A servant brought hot tea for the two women, poured cups, and withdrew without a word.

The storm, already furious, now raged with such ferocity that the tops of all the trees groaned beneath the assault. Branches of all sizes tore away and went flying past the window. It was a bitterly cold rain, too, carrying with it the malicious threat of turning to ice once the sun set.

Helleda shivered and winced. She sipped her tea, which was brewed with echinacea, chamomile, lemon, mint, dandelion root, basil, wolfberry, and chrysanthemum. She closed her eyes for a moment and inhaled the fragrant vapors.

"What will happen now?" she asked.

Frey sighed and gathered her rug more tightly around her thin shoulders. "In the short term? What else . . . things will continue to fall apart."

"Will there be war?"

"That, I'm afraid, is inevitable," said Frey. "It remains to be seen, however, what *kind* of war will break out. The Witch-king has his magicks. We do not have weapons of equal potency yet."

Helleda gave her a sharp look. "*Yet?* A few months ago you told us about three different strategies—three 'pathways' we could follow to try to meet that monster on his own terms. One was the Chest of Algion in the Tower of Sarsis. If Kagen Vale or your agent, Tuke Brakson, found anything there, it was not sufficient to destroy the Witch-king."

"No," said the older woman sadly, "it was not."

"Your other choices were to send an expedition to Vespia—of all places—to find a book of dark magic and to send an even larger force to the Winterwilds in hopes of finding . . . what? You were never specific on that. I mean, originally you seemed to hope that our scouts would find Herepath Vale and enlist his help. Is that still your plan?"

"Yes," said Frey. "But I've changed my view on how to see this done. Despite his failure in killing the Witch-king, Herepath's younger brother accomplished much that should have been impossible. He got all the way to the dais and fought that sorcerer blade to blade. He proved that the Witch-king was not infallible. Nor invulnerable."

"How did that prove the Witch-king's vulnerability?" asked Lady Frost.

"If the Witch-king is unkillable, why would he bother defending himself with a sword?" asked Frey.

Helleda began to comment, then grunted softly. "I hadn't thought of that," she said after a moment.

"Furthermore," said Frey, "the Witch-king did not use magic to defeat Kagen or his friends. That, as I see it, is of at least equal importance. It speaks to limits on his power."

Helleda frowned. "But Kagen lost that fight."

"No, he did not," said Frey firmly. "The fight was interrupted. At best it was inconclusive. Politically it did the Hakkians a great deal of harm, and that, my dear, is something we can use."

"*Instead* of traveling all over creation to find secrets of magic?" asked Helleda.

"Oh no," said the former nun. "But as the Samudian saying goes, 'A smart archer keeps a lot of arrows in his quiver.'"

"So, what then *is* your plan?"

Frey watched the wind and rain for a while. Despite the monstrous wind, a doe walked along the fringes of the forest wall, pausing now and then to take bites of the rain-soaked grass. The sight of the animal—delicate in appearance in ways that completely hid an inner toughness—heartened Frey.

"Tuke was with Kagen, and so was Filia alden-Bok, who, though not an official agent of mine, is nevertheless an ally. A very competent and useful one. I've sent word to both her and Tuke through my network—and before you ask, that is part of what I've asked Hannibus to do. I expect to hear from one or both of them. I'm hoping to meet with this Kagen Vale. I want to know what he knows. About the Tower of Sarsis and the Chest of Algion. About how he got into and out of the palace. And I want to know his mind as regards to that fight with the Witch-king. I am pretty sure I saw that yellow lace veil come loose during the fight. If anyone saw the Witch-king's face, it's Kagen."

"So what? We already know who he is. Gethon Heklan."

"Frankly, I don't know what use any bit of intelligence will be until it is in hand and I've had time to analyze it, and so I will collect every bit of it I can and only then decided what I believe."

"You're a devious old bat," said Helleda, but she said it with a faint smile.

Frey patted her knee. "Nice old ladies don't change the course of history."

A silent half hour later, Helleda asked, "Frey . . . do we have even the slightest chance?"

But Mother Frey did not answer.

Outside, the storm grew and grew until it was a monster.

The oak tree tilted and groaned and tried not to die.

CHAPTER TWENTY

"Your Majesty," said Lord Nespar, bowing very low—much lower than usual, even for him. "She is here."

The Witch-king stood by a high window in the palace, in a small room he used for meditation. His pack of hounds lay sprawled here and there, and though it looked like they were asleep, Nespar saw their ears twitch and turn. The bitch gave a soft huff that was not in any way comforting. The armor of the general that the pack had devoured lay in dented pieces, along with bones that were now covered in flies and maggots. Nespar did not dare to even mention these things. He did not dare to let his eyes linger too long on them.

The monarch in yellow stood with his back to the chamberlain, his hands on the stone window frame as he looked out at the storm. It had raged all day and night, and now there was a hint of dawn's golden light through the fractured clouds. The rain was less intense and the winds half of what they had been.

"Send her in," said the Witch-king.

"At once, Majesty."

"And, Nespar . . ."

"My lord?"

"Only her. Close the door as you leave."

Lord Nespar made the usual obsequious noises as he backed away from the royal presence. At the door he turned and gestured for Lady Kestral to enter. When she saw that he was not joining her she inquired silently with a single lifted eyebrow, to which he responded with a small shake of the head.

He closed the door and fled down the hall.

Lady Kestral walked halfway across the floor, making a wide circle around the bloody armor, and then stopped, bowing to the king even though he could not see it.

"I await your pleasure, Majesty."

"My lady," said the Witch-king, "I want you accompany me to my private study."

Without waiting for an answer, he walked past her, snapping his fingers for the big bitch hound to follow. The dog trotted at his left heel as the Witch-king exited the great hall via a small doorway concealed behind the throne dais. Kestral, surprised, followed dutifully.

She had known her master had a place of private study and experimentation back home in Hakkia, though she had never actually seen it, but she was unaware one had been set up here in Argentium. The Witch-king was intensely, some might say *obsessively*, private, and he withheld many parts of his life even from his most trusted advisors, and so this invitation filled her with excitement and foreboding.

She followed him down the hall and around several corners. The only sound was that of the hound's nails clicking and scratching on the marble floor. The strange procession approached an unadorned ironwood door guarded by Ravens, who snapped immediately to attention. Once through the doorway, Lady Kestral followed her king up a long, winding staircase to a landing with a door that was far more ornate. This one was wide and tall and had a bronze facade in which were warding and protection symbols in a dozen languages, three of which Kestral did not recognize and could not read.

The Witch-king produced a strange-looking key from a concealed pocket in his yellow robes. It was twisted, serpentine, and sprouted spikes of various length, and Kestral could not imagine how a craftsman had devised an internal mechanism to accept such a key. To her mind, there was something unnaturally violative about its design.

However, the door did not immediately open. Instead, the Hakkian king stood in front of it for nearly a minute, his posture straight, eyes closed, lips moving but without sound. Only then was there a *click*, and the door swung inward without being touched.

Stepping into that chamber was like stepping into another world. Or, Kestral mused, like stepping into one room of the Witch-king's mind. The chamber was large but crowded with all manner of objects, both well known to her and completely arcane. There were tall bookcases that reached all the way to the lofty ceiling. The volumes were not filed according to any method she could discern. There were histories mixed in with sacred texts from dozens of religions. There were books of maps sandwiched between codices of ancient healing. There were fat volumes bound in reptile skin and human flesh. There were ancient tomes with titles written in gold leaf and some with no title at all. Some shelves were crammed with scrolls bound in red, purple, or black silk ribbon; others were stacked with clay tablets.

Myriad strange creatures hung from the rafters, each carefully taxidermied. She saw some she recognized—the embryo of a narwhal, a gigantic sloth, a snow leopard, and a titanic boa constrictor. Others were creatures either created to emulate mythical monsters or were—somehow—the real things. Of these, she saw a delicate unicorn and a dwarf; a winged dragon of the kind known as a wyvern; a gnome with an evil twist of fate; and a mermaid whose beautiful torso and elegant fish tail were at odds with a fearsome face with a gaping mouth crammed with razor-sharp fangs. There were goblins and imps, redcaps and sprites, and even the severed head of a gorgon—though its deadly eyes were covered with leather pads.

To one side of the room was a series of tanks that, from their smell, she knew to be filled with spirits of wine. In these floated creatures so obscure that she had no names for them. One was a pop-eyed snaked with a wreath of spikes around its head and a line of many-toothed suckers along its belly. Another was an infant nine-headed hydra.

And in one corner, set in the precise center of a circle of protection, was a block of ice. She felt it radiate cold, and though there was nothing in that room to prevent the ice from melting, it endured. There was a shape within it that looked very human, but the outer surface was frosted and nearly opaque.

Most of the room was filled with tables, and on these sat every manner of alchemical instrument. There were lumps of metal that gleamed with bright gold at one end but were dull lead on the other. A failed experiment, she wondered? Or perhaps a work in progress. There were mortars and pestles made from ceramic or hematite, of jade or rutilated quartz. Most were filled with various compounds, but of their nature she had no clue. Kestral was a necromancer and only skirted the edges of alchemy. She recognized the apparatus, however. There were human organs—heart, liver, spleen, brain, and kidney—in large jars, and these ranged from those belonging to humans of various ages to those of animals.

Many of these tables had all manner of beakers and tubes, flasks and vials, retorts and ampules. There were countless jars and pots of chemicals in liquid, gel, powder, or paste states. Here were stills to condense liquids, and there burners on which tiny cauldrons bubbled and smoked. An antique athanor—a small furnace—occupied the end of one table, quietly burning on a fuel of aromatic ash. On another table was a calcination furnace and a stack of supplies for reducing metals and minerals into fine powder. There was also a cupel, a crucible made of bone ash, and a stout descensory, a different kind of furnace, with a funnel for pouring liquid down to a crystal receptacle. And there were two medium-size dissolving furnaces in which chemical mixtures slowly churned.

Every corner of the room was stacked with raw materials— woods of a hundred kinds; reams of blank vellum or papyrus; bell jars waiting to enclose rare specimens; boxes made of gold, alabaster, lignum vitae, teak, or whalebone; blocks of petrified wood; huge bundles of tallow candles.

The hound went and sat in front of the block of ice and stared at it without moving. Except for the slow movement of her ribs as she breathed, the dog might have been another stuffed curio in this strange place.

"This is all so . . ." began Kestral, but left the rest to hang, because the Witch-king had walked away from her and likewise stood looking at the unmelting block of ice. He touched the dog's muscular neck with one gloved finger and then turned away and went and looked outside. There were two large windows in the tower, and through the clear glass the storm was visibly angry. Furious clouds scowled down, and fierce winds tore banners from flagpoles and leaves from trees and sent them spinning in columns that spiraled up into the darkness. For long minutes the King in Yellow continued to look out at the storm, nodding every now and then as if in agreement with some important thought or insight. Finally, he turned and looked into her eyes. The effect was as palpable and uncomfortable as a physical blow, and Kestral felt her body rock. She took a small backwards step.

"I have a task for you," said the Witch-king, his voice at odds with the storm outside. He sounded calm, even gentle.

"Anything for you, my lord," she said.

"You did me a great service when you worked your spell on the blood of Lord Khendrick Vale. That was how we learned that our enemy is his son Kagen."

"It was my pleasure to do this, Majesty."

He gave the smallest of nods. "Now I have a greater task for you. Of all the sorcerers in my court, you are the only true necromancer. Your skill in this area is extraordinary, and it is why you—of everyone—have earned my trust."

She felt her cheeks grow warm, and she curtsied, as much to

hide that as to show respect for that faith. "Your Majesty is too kind."

"You have done much good work for me over these last few years, and particularly in the weeks leading up to our conquest."

"I am yours to command, Majesty."

"Yes," said the king. "Let's see how far that pledge stretches. I need you to perform that special magic again."

Kestral felt a coldness blossom in her chest, as if her heart had turned to a block of ice.

"Of . . . course, Majesty," she said, tripping only once over the words as the rigors—the *horrors*—of that conjuring came back to her. Necromancy fed in part on the life force of the necromancer, and it took much to recover from so powerful a spell. Even now the echoes of it, the dreadful memories of that conjuring, lit fires in her nerve endings and made her want to scream.

"There is a twist, however," murmured the King in Yellow. "The last time you did this, my lady, I was able to provide you with hair from the Poison Rose. With that you were able to construct a razor-knight who, in turn, was able to defeat her. This was of inestimable value to me, Kestral, because many held the belief that the Poison Rose was invincible, that no one could ever defeat her. I did not want to prolong the fighting here in the palace, nor spend the lives of my best fighters, to bring her down. And down she had to come. That was imperative."

"Yes, my lord."

"This time," he continued, "we do not have any hair nor a definite sample of the blood of the next person whose life and fate stand in the way of our shared destiny. Yet that person must also fall, and I want his death to be a certainty. He has, so far, eluded many attempts and thwarted attacks that should, by all measures, have been his undoing. He still lives and I cannot have that."

Kestral knotted her fingers together over her heart. "Majesty . . . do you speak of the son of the Poison Rose? Of Kagen Vale?"

"I do." The Witch-king gently pushed the hound aside and walked across the room to her, stopped a yard away, towering over her even though she, too, was tall. "Kagen's blood was spilled in the great hall. I saw him bleed."

"Yes, Majesty."

"This is why I have not allowed the hall to be cleaned," he said, "nor will I until we have identified *which* blood is his."

"But . . . my lord . . . the room is awash in blood. Many died there."

"Yes," he said mildly, "and that is the challenge I set before you."

Lady Kestral stood as still as the block of ice, but her mind was a maelstrom of desperate thought. Terror swirled like a whirlwind around her heart.

"You have nothing to say, my lady?" asked the Witch-king softly.

"My . . . my lord . . . what you ask is—"

"Is mine to ask," he cut in. "Or would you refuse your king?"

Kestral felt as if the floor was tilting beneath her. Nausea swept through her like a foul wind.

"Must I ask again, my lady?" asked the Witch-king softly.

"N-no . . . m-my lord . . ." Her teeth chattered as she spoke. Inside her chest, shocks of pain were stabbing into her heart. It took all of her strength to master herself, to at least feign composure, though none was hers in truth. "I will do whatever you require, Majesty. And with a glad heart."

He reached out and with the back of one finger stroked her cheek. It was the same finger, and nearly the same gesture, he had used on his dog.

"The great hall will be reserved for you and guarded night and day," he said. "You may take as many samples of blood as you need from the floor, the furniture, the dais steps, and from the weapons of the soldiers."

"My lord," she said hastily, "I must warn you that what you ask may be too much for me. For anyone. It may kill me before I find Kagen Vale's blood."

The Witch-king studied her for a long time, his eyes only vague shadows behind the lace veil. "My reach extends far beyond the physical world, Kestral. You should take great care to make sure you accomplish this task *before* you die. Whatever it takes, as *much* as it takes." He paused and glanced around his workroom as if to make a specific point. "Do not think that death is a shield against my displeasure."

She opened her mouth to say something more, but he turned away and walked back to the window.

"You may go now, my lady," he said quietly.

CHAPTER TWENTY-ONE

Mother Frey held Helleda Frost's good hand as she bent to kiss the younger woman's cheek.

"I wish I was going with you," said Lady Frost.

"You need to rest and heal, my dear," said Frey. "And in the meantime, be here to receive any news from Hannibus or our friends in the cabal. Some messages may come from my network as well, and I don't trust anyone else to take those messages and have the judgment for what to do. I will send word back to you as I go, and you have my basic itinerary, so you can send word to me."

"Not to be mean, Frey, but you're hardly a young girl and it's a long and dangerous path you'll be taking."

Frey gestured to the carriage standing outside, and the imposing knot of armed guards waiting for her.

"You lent me a squad of brutes, Helleda," said the old woman. "I'll be quite fine."

Helleda did not look mollified, but she nodded, returned the kiss, and then stood watching from the doorway as Mother Frey walked toward the carriage, leaning heavily on a carved walking stick. One of the brutes helped her inside and then climbed in beside her.

Helleda had a last glimpse of Frey's face as the coach turned around in front of the mansion and then moved off. The wheels crunched on the gravel and then the forest seemed to swallow the coach whole.

The big oak stood in the yard. It had survived the storm but was not whole. Branches and even one big limb lay where wind and lightning had thrown them. All of the leaves had been torn away, leaving the tree looking like it was dying. Or dead.

Helleda Frost tried not to take that as a sign.

She went back inside, lit a candle, and prayed all through the night.

CHAPTER TWENTY-TWO

The storm was monstrous, massive, immeasurable.

Dragon's Swan was a tiny thing. Vulnerable. Beaten and battered. Abused by wind and water in ways Kagen had never imagined. Not one of the novels he'd read or songs he'd heard ever painted a picture a thousandth as real as the howling thing that seemed to dominate the entire world.

He sat wedged in between table and wall, feet braced, teeth gritted, hands clamped on the edges of stout furniture as the ship rose and plunged, yawed and pitched, groaned and shrieked.

He closed his eyes and prayed to any god who would listen.

"Let me live long enough to kill him," he whispered in a voice totally drowned out by the storm. "Let me kill Herepath and then you gods can have me for your sport."

Lightning burned the air and thunder punched the hull and every single minute of those five long days seemed to last an eternity.

CHAPTER TWENTY-THREE

The king of Theria lay in state upon a golden bier set atop a dais covered with inlaid tiles showing tentacles swirling around and clutching sharks and whales. Looming above the dais was a representation of the great sea god, Dagon, his eyes downcast as if in sorrow, arms spread to embrace the spirit of the murdered monarch.

The dais stood in the center of a large circular platform fifty yards across. The inlaid mosaic tiles there told stories of fierce gods from the depths of the ocean, strange demigods and heroic men, bizarre demons fighting and taming the greatest of the sea creatures. Torches on tall brass poles ringed the outer and inner circumferences of the great disk. Eight rows of eight soldiers walked slowly around the right, completing eight circuits per hour. Their slow, measured footfalls, landing in perfect unison, echoed like the beats of some titanic heart.

Other soldiers stood in special posts around the outside of the disk, their specific places held by the most important families of Theria. And though the vigil—under the sun in full armor— was grueling, the sons and daughters of those families stood their watch willingly. Their heartbreak and their anger gave them strength and turned their resolve to steel.

The disk was set at the edge of a cliff that reached out over the thrashing waves a thousand feet below. Seabirds wheeled and turned, tearing at the fabric of the air with strange cries. Each night the ocean below was ablaze with fires carefully tended on thousands of military and private ships, and countless smaller fishing vessels.

Princess Theka, the eldest of the royal heirs, tall and strong, walked in front of the soldiers. She carried a fresh bundle of flowers on each circuit, laying them on the lower steps of the dais and receiving new ones from children of the noble born. Theka had her hair tied into long braids that hung nearly to her heels. After the official burial, she would have those braids ceremoniously shorn to shoulder length as part of her ascension to the throne.

Grandstands had been erected in a half circle around the landward side of the disk so that mourners could contemplate the ocean and the mercy of Dagon.

There were no Ravens, or any dignitaries from Hakkia, allowed within eyesight of the dead king. The ambassador from the court of the Witch-king had, with all appropriate flowery apologies, been confined to his quarters in the palace and a heavy drapery hung outside of his window. The princess sent word to him that this was an ancient Therian tradition—no outside spectators were permitted. That tradition, which was indeed hundreds of years old, nullified all official protest from the embassy.

Across Xyria, the capital city, there were no riots, no protests, no mobs shouting for revenge. Theria's customs had never turned that way. They mourned quietly, and if there were any sharp words against the Hakkians or their Witch-king, it was reserved for quiet conversations in family homes or the more secluded back rooms of taverns.

The king was dead.

There were a lot of very quiet conversations, however. The Therians, always known for their restraint and calculating patience, did not share their views with outsiders at the best of times. The most meaningful dialogues were done with glances, with subtle touches of family crests on armor, with a brush of palms on sheathed swords, with stern glances to the southeast. For Therians, each of these gestures was eloquent enough.

All through the day, beneath the weight of the sun, in the teeth of stiff winds off the ocean, Princess Theka walked in front of her retinue of slowly pacing soldiers. Her face showed nothing except to those who knew her best.

They could read her thoughts as if she shouted them aloud.

CHAPTER TWENTY-FOUR

Her name was Ryssa, and although she was not dead, she was nevertheless a ghost.

She spoke rarely, and when she did it was not to any of the people around her. Not to the other women in attendance at the temple. Not to anyone alive.

She spoke to Miri.

Her friend.

Her love.

Dead now. Cold as the stone on which she lay. A small shape dressed in samite and covered with white lace.

Ryssa felt so completely betrayed.

A few months ago she was a girl—barely fifteen—living a quiet life in the keeping of nuns belonging to the Faith of the Garden. And although life was not filled with promise, for she was a poor girl with no real family to provide expectations, she had friends. Miri, one of those nuns, was her best friend. Only a few years older, Miri looked like she could have been Ryssa's sister. Miri, however, was wiser and had traveled all over. She had been an assistant to Mother Frey, senior investigator for the Garden's Office of Miracles.

Then the Ravens came, with their bright swords and their cannisters of banefire that blew down the walls of houses all through Argentium. Those Hakkian soldiers murdered and raped and brutalized the people of the capital city, and had it not been for Miri's quick actions, both of them would have fallen to the dreadful hungers of the invaders. Miri knew many strange secrets, and soon the girls were fleeing down hidden stairs and through strange tunnels that ran beneath the capital. Once free of the city, they fled through the countryside, taking a long and slow path to avoid capture. To Ryssa's surprise Miri arranged passage for them aboard a ship from the strange and distant island of Tull Yammoth.

The journey to the island was fraught with perils, but they arrived safely, welcomed by a beautiful people who practiced a religion entirely unknown to Ryssa. Nothing connected to the Garden at all, but instead dedicated to the worship of a god who slept beneath the tossing waves, where the Western Ocean blends its waters with the Southern Sea. As the Faith of the Garden was torn down by the Hakkians, Miri taught Ryssa the ways of the faith of the Dreaming God.

In those long months, Ryssa leaned the language of R'yleh and was told she was to participate in a ceremony of great importance—to summon Great Cthulhu from his slumber in order to combat that god's half brother, Hastur, and stop the crowning of the Witch-king as the sole emperor in the west.

Had Ryssa known what would happen during that ceremony, she would have run screaming. She would have locked herself in her room and refused to participate. She had been lied to. She had been used, and she knew it.

Miri—beautiful Miri, whom Ryssa had come to love as much more than a sister or friend—warned her when she said, "Remember what I said before, my sweetheart. We all have to make sacrifices. The world we *want* is gone. It is this world here on Yammoth or a grave back in what was the Silver Empire."

But Ryssa did not know how much of a sacrifice was to be asked. The island's high priestess, Lady Sithra, had pressed a ceremonial dagger into Ryssa's hand as Miri lay naked upon an altar. The priestess promised that Ryssa was in no danger and that all she would be required to do was merely prick the skin over Miri's heart. Only that.

And that was true. It was all Ryssa had to do.

No one—not Lady Sithra or Miri—warned Ryssa that there was another action to follow. Once the blade was there, it was Miri herself who gripped her lover's hands and forced the dagger to bite very deep.

Ryssa had fought it. She remembered the vibrations that shivered up through the knife and into her hand and the nerves of her arm as the point punched through skin and muscle, scraping between ribs and plunging into Miri's beautiful heart.

Miri had forced Ryssa to be complicit in her own murder, and as blood flowed, the entire crowd of worshippers howled in ecstasy. The seas churned and the sky broke apart as lightning flashed. Great Cthulhu, roused to the edge of wakefulness, lashed out. Lightning struck Tull Yammoth over and over, shattering stones and burning trees. More of it raced across the sky, across thousands of miles of sea and land, and struck the stained-glass windows of the palace of Argentium. The astral form of Cthulhu appeared in the sky and did battle with his half brother as storms burned the air around them.

Some of this Ryssa knew. Some had been told to her. But she hardly listened. It barely registered on her that the Witch-king's coronation was spoiled.

Ryssa's mind had frozen to ice when Miri's heart stopped beating.

Now she was a ghost haunting the ruined ceremonial area known as the Hall of the Dreaming God. She wore the blood-stained rags of the gown she wore that day. Her hair hung in filthy strings. Her cheeks were hollow, eyes sunken into ashy pits. Time meant nothing to her except as a measure of how soon she could die and go find Miri in whatever afterlife there was.

She slept wherever her body fell each night. She ate whatever the priests forced into her mouth. She knew she was dying, and her only real wish was that she had the courage to throw herself from the tallest cliff, onto the wave-smashed rocks below.

Each night Ryssa came and sat beside the bier on which Miri lay. The part of her mind that was still active—a flame that burned very low indeed—marveled at how Miri looked exactly the same now, many days later, as she had at the moment of her death. Her flesh was full, her lips pink, her breasts not deflated by blood draining to a lower point. Her skin was cold to the touch, though; and when Ryssa kissed her, Miri's lips were like ice.

Torches were lit at the four corners of the altar platform, and they cast weird dancing shadows all around. More than once Ryssa caught sight of one moving oddly across the lace covering and thought Miri had moved. But that was only illusion and wishful thinking.

Only that.

The sun rolled to the edge of the sky and dropped into darkness with no splendor of sunset. More like a candle blowing out in a sudden breeze. Ryssa leaned her back against the platform, put her face in her hands, and wept dusty tears because she had so little moisture left in her body.

She did not see the strange green lights that pulsed slowly and deeply out in the wine-dark sea.

She did not see the albatross that circled overhead. Around and around and around.

She did not see or hear the dolphins that leapt and cried all around the island.

She did not see the lace covering move. And if she had, Ryssa would have blamed it on the wind, trying to deceive her as surely as the capering shadows.

Except at that moment there was no wind at all.

CHAPTER TWENTY-FIVE

Lord Nespar crept into the great hall on legs that trembled so badly it made him stagger as if he were deep in his cups. He was aware of the eyes of the sentries watching him, though every other part of them might as well have been made of cold stone. Nespar did his best not to care about what they thought, but that level of indifference was much easier to affect than genuinely feel. To snap at them, even to order them to keep their eyes front, would be a tacit admission of his own weakness.

Moreover, Nespar had more important matters on his mind, and so he scuttled along the long yellow carpet that stretched from the main doors to the foot of the dais on which the Witch-king sat on his throne. He was particularly careful not to step on any of the brown bloodstains that were spattered here and there—the remnants of the assassination attempt, left there for Lady Kestral. He could see that many showed signs of the knife she used to scrape up flakes of dried blood in her desperate attempt to find the blood of Kagen Vale.

Nespar feared for her. She was a friend and ally. A truer friend than that smiling scorpion Jakob Ravensmere. Nespar truly trusted Kestral, but he trusted the historian only as far as that man's personal interest stretched.

Kestral was doing those dreadful and destructive spells the Witch-king had ordered her to perform, and each day—each hour—she seemed to fade and wither. Her beauty was already gone, leaving a shrewish hag whose skin was like old and brittle parchment, and her vitality—her life force—was spilling away like sand from a cracked hourglass. It was painful to watch, and terrifying to contemplate, because if their lord asked so much of her, what might he one day demand of Nespar himself? That thought kept Nespar awake for much of each night, and often left him a shivering, weeping wreck. His digestion was ruined, and every morning he crouched over his chamber pot as whatever he'd eaten the day before evacuated his trembling bowels like foul-smelling water. He had even taken to wearing extra under-garments in case his digestion betrayed him utterly.

He reached the end of the runner carpet and stopped, bowing low, leaning on his staff of office for fear of his knees giving way. Then he straightened and waited for the monarch in yellow to acknowledge him.

The Witch-king sat with a very old book open on his lap, and one long finger moved at odd angles as he read. Nespar knew this book, one of many ancient texts procured for him by Jakob. It was called *Atlas of Dark Worlds*, but the only time Nespar had seen it open and up close, he saw that the language in which it was written was totally unknown to him. The sentences swirled and turned and writhed like a nest of serpents and followed no order for proper reading that Nespar could detect. Yet the Witch-king seemed able to follow it, his finger moving along with the bizarre narrative structure.

Nespar endured the wait, trying to will his pores not to sweat.

Then the Witch-king nodded to himself and closed the book. He kept it on his lap, though, hands folded quietly on its cover. According to Jakob, the book was bound in the skin of young castrati whose throats were cut as they sang sacred hymns. Nespar had a favorite nephew who was an alto in a choir in southern Hakkia, and the thought of such a lovely child being murdered and skinned was appalling. Even for him.

"Nespar," said the Witch-king, looking down at him. "You look unwell."

The chamberlain waved it away. "A minor indigestion, Majesty. It is of no importance."

Behind the veil of yellow lace, those eyes watched him, and Nespar wondered then, as he so often did, how much the king guessed and how much he knew.

"Each hour I look forward to receiving word that Kagen Vale and his confederates have been apprehended," said the Witch-king. "Or, at very least, located. And yet, another sun has risen and my enemies are not in chains before me. Tell me why this is, my lord chamberlain."

Nespar began to apologize, using a variation of the rote explanations he had used every day since the assassination attempt, but the Witch-king stopped him with a few raised fingers.

"We are not in open court, Nespar," he said mildly. "It is only us here now, and I invite you to speak freely."

"I . . ."

"Speak your mind, my friend," urged the Witch-king. "Nothing you say here will count against you."

Nespar did not know what to make of this. He had enjoyed a more open and frank discourse with his lord earlier in their relationship, but as the Witch-king more fully embraced his power, he had become correspondingly withdrawn and aloof, and eventually quite alien. Where Nespar had once liked him, now he merely feared him. Was the monarch aware of the limitations created by this?

"My lord is generous," said Nespar, happy to say it without a stumble.

"I need truth and frankness, old friend. We are balancing on the edge of a knife and only such freedom between us can be of use, do you agree?"

"Yes, Majesty," said Nespar.

"Good," said the Witch-king. "Now tell me about the search for Kagen Vale and his band of cutthroats."

"Lord," said Nespar, feeling the floor beneath his feet grow solid, "the fighters who disguised themselves as the Unseen were false. They do not belong to the Brotherhood of Steel. In fact, no one at the coronation is known to be one of the Unbladed. They were, without doubt, members of Argonian royal houses. Witness statements have been taken to confirm this."

"Were those statements taken under duress?"

"Some, of course, lord," said Nespar. "But not all. We have friends among the people here. Not many, but enough so that we were able to validate the information obtained by the interrogators."

"How many Argonian houses were involved?"

"Twenty-seven, Majesty. I have a list." He reached into his

robes and selected a sheet of crisp parchment. The Witch-king stretched out a hand and took it from him, then reclined to read through it.

"Many of these families are known to me," he said. "Three are related to the imperial line. Very powerful and influential."

"Yes, Majesty."

"Tell me, Nespar," said the monarch, still looking at the list, "what, in your opinion, would be the likely outcome of our arresting these families on charges of treason and insurrection?" He glanced up. "Be truthful with me."

"War," said Nespar without hesitation, then added, "Your Majesty."

"What kind of war? Are you talking an uprising of the Argonian people?"

"Civil war is almost a certainty, Majesty," said Nespar. "These families are known throughout the land and have been pillars of both Argon and the Silver Empire for centuries. They swore blood oaths to protect the empresses and the empire. They have many friends, and if these families were arrested and executed, then their friends, and the friends of their friends, would consider it a point of honor to rise up."

"They did not do so when the empire fell."

Nespar knew that this was thin ice, but he was taking the monarch at his word and so spoke the truth. "When the empire fell it was because of your power, lord. Your . . ."

"Magic, Nespar," chided the Witch-king. "Never be afraid to call it by its name."

Nespar bowed. "Magic, sire. The Night of the Ravens marked you as the most powerful person in the world. Everyone was terrified of you, and rightly so. That is why there was no real counterattack. It's why in the three months that followed there was no formal declaration of war, no armies put into the field."

"You phrase this in the past tense," said the Witch-king.

"I do, Majesty. I fear we must," said the chamberlain, "because on the night of the coronation, those members of the noble houses who were here in disguise—the ones who survived and escaped—saw what they believed was a limitation of your power. Although Kagen Vale and his friends failed in their attempt to kill you—praise Hastur for his mercy and protection—they also saw Kagen survive. Had he died that night, much would be different."

"You mean, had I killed him that night, then things would be different," said the Witch-king. He did not pose it as a question.

"If Your Majesty pleases . . ."

"You speak truth, my friend," said the King in Yellow. "Though, make no mistake, it was not that I felt overmatched by young Kagen Vale. There were other forces at work that day, as you witnessed."

The memory of Lord Hastur battling in the sky with a monstrous sea creature still gave Nespar nightmares. It shook him to his core and—though he would never admit it, not even to Kestral—had rocked his faith. There were cracks now in his fundamental beliefs in the Hakkian cosmology.

Nespar said, "The unfortunate events of that day continue to send shock waves through the empire, my lord. It has likely emboldened those who were already contemplating revolt, and almost certainly awakened speculation in those who had been previously hesitant. To people here in Argon, and likely elsewhere, Kagen has become the face of that rebellion. He openly defied you, he attacked you, and he yet survives. Where once he was seen as a failure—allowing the Seedlings to die under his care—now he will be a kind of martyr, a symbol for what *we* have taken from the empire."

The yellow king nodded. "I fear you are right, my friend. And I agree that Kagen is the most visible of my enemies. Son of murdered parents, former captain of the guards. He is certainly a symbol, though I wonder if he is bright enough to know it."

"He managed to get all the way to the foot of this dais, lord," said Nespar. "He concocted a way to bypass all of our precautions. He cannot be a fool. And he has friends. Powerful, clever, and resourceful friends. Also, given that he was able to escape the palace from a locked room . . . he or some of those friends may possess some degree of *ability*."

"You mean magic."

"I do, my lord. Nothing else explains how he escaped."

That was true enough. After the fight in the grand hall, Kagen and his two companions—the red-haired woman and the Therian giant—had been chased through the halls. They locked themselves inside a small room, and when the guards broke down the door the found that all three of them had vanished. The room was thoroughly searched for secret passages or trapdoors, but nothing was found. All that remained was a piece of tapestry that crumbled into dust as soon as it was touched. Lady Kestral studied those ashes and determined that the tapestry must have been ensorcelled, though how or by whom was impossible to determine. Its magic was far beyond even her skills, and it belonged to a different school of magic than the necromancy she practiced.

"The tapestry Kagen used was made from ancient and very powerful magic," said the Witch-king. "Such weaving is a highly specialized skill and throughout time there have been only a small handful of sorcerers powerful enough to have created it. Most are still sleeping, for the veils between worlds are slow to open completely. Much must still be done to ensure that magic fully inhabits this world. More so than ever before. As it flourishes so shall my own powers."

Nespar nodded, though he did not entirely understand what that meant. The Witch-king shared only fragments of information on this topic, and even when Nespar and Kestral pooled what they each had observed, all they learned was that they did not know very much. Kestral's own magic, learned in secret over decades, was a single candle lit in the vast darkness that was the unknown. There were many mystery schools in Hakkia, each guarding its own arcane teachings—and even their very existence—from the rest of the magical community. Over the last millennium, and more so these last three hundred years since Lady Bellapher led her army across the face of Hakkia in an attempt to completely and permanently eradicate magical practice from that nation, the mystery schools had been in hiding. Fear of exposure from spies and traitors required that they become obsessed with secrecy. The Witch-king even once admitted that he knew of only a few dozen and believed that more than two hundred others existed in one form or another. It was only after the Night of the Ravens that another dozen came forth from the shadows to offer their services to the new monarch. Others were still silent, unknown, and unseen, and Nespar assumed they were waiting to see if the new Witch-king was as powerful as they all hoped.

The events at the coronation did nothing to allay their fears or inspire confidence.

"Kagen is, as I said, the face of our opposition," mused the Witch-king. "He must be found and brought here to me."

"Yes, Majesty," said Nespar uneasily. "Your . . . ah . . . *remaining* generals are doing their very best."

"Yes," said the Witch-king dryly, "I expect they are. As for the Argonians," he continued, "for now we can let them wonder what we will do. They will expect retaliation and they are likely lining up to be martyrs for a full-on rebellion. Any of the nobles, particularly those with royal or imperial blood, would serve that same purpose beyond the borders of this nation. The kings and queens who attended the coronation will want symbols to rally their own people, to make them believe that it is possible to fight back against an army that has magic on its side. It is likely, even probable, that Kagen's survival will be ascribed to magic. Even more so than his escape. The fact that he fought me and yet lives is the equation that will be sold by every whispered voice, every published tract, even secret conversation. Soon they will be yelling it in their town squares, Nespar, and that will be the flame that ignites true war."

"My lord, I fear that civil war is not our greatest threat," said Nespar carefully. "Although it was an accident, the death of the king of Theria weighs heavily on the peace. I distrust how quietly his retinue withdrew. Nor do I like the silence with which the other submonarchs departed the city. Although there were no threats or hard words, Majesty, there were also no reassurances of loyalty. During that fight, they observed but did not take sides. The fact that they did not side with Kagen is almost immaterial because they more tellingly did not rise to your defense, and every one of them would have laid down his or her life to defend the Silver Empress."

"Yes," said the Witch-king. "Had I *been* crowned before Kagen and his allies attacked, what might they have done?"

"You would have been their liege lord and emperor, Majesty. Even if they disliked you unto hatred from the fall of the Silver Empire, they would have been oath-bound to defend you. The cost of breaking such an oath is at the very core of the Harvest Faith, and they would break that oath at the cost of their own damnation. That they did not defend you, however, means that in their eyes there *is* no empire, and no emperor. To them, without doubt, the west is now a collection of neighboring states. Old alliances are likely being evaluated."

"And old animosities?"

"What is that old saying, Majesty, that the enemy of my enemy is my ally? You conquered them all. And despite our orders to the contrary, the Ravens and, more often, our mercenary troops may have gone to extremes here and there. Rapes and murders, lynchings and crucifixions that exceeded our strategic needs . . ."

"Yes," said the Witch-king, "and I hope your spies are keeping an account of such crimes."

"Of course."

The Witch-king leaned back against the cushioned back of the throne and stared up at the shadowy ceiling. "To a student of history," he said, "this puts a new shine on the old adage that it is easier to conquer a country than to rule it."

"As you say, lord."

"I will tell you something you do not know, Nespar," said the Witch-king, changing the subject.

"My lord?"

"After the fight I sent my ravens . . . my birds . . . to find Kagen Vale."

"You sent *birds* to find him?" asked the chamberlain.

"A simple bit of magic," said the Witch-king, dismissing it. "And find him they did. Kagen took passage aboard a Therian ship, and so I sent one of my fastest raiders to intercept that vessel."

Nespar brightened. "Did you, sire? Have they found him? I can have the admirals send the fleet at once."

The Witch-king was long in responding. "Not one of my birds returned to tell me. Not one."

Nespar touched his throat. "Do you think they were interfered with? Perhaps by those . . . *other* birds?"

During the battle in the great hall, another battle had raged outside as flocks of other birds—crows, ravens, starlings, and more—attacked the ravens that roosted in the palace eaves.

"Yes," said the Witch-king. "The nightbirds."

"Are . . . are those birds servants of the Dreaming God?"

"Cthulhu? No. He cares not for birds of the air."

"Then . . ."

"Because we are speaking so frankly, Nespar, I will admit to you that I do not yet know whence the nightbirds have come. I have read of them and know much of the lore. In ages past, they served the queens of the faerie folk, but they are gone, lost in other realities since the doors of magic were shuddered by the Silver Empire. But . . . perhaps now that those doors are open, however narrowly, it is conceivable that someone connected to the faerie courts. Whatever or whoever it is, some arcane powers have called those nightbirds into service of Kagen Vale."

"Could young Kagen be a sorcerer?" asked the chamberlain.

Again, the Witch-king paused a long time. "Kagen Vale has potential he himself does not grasp. *I* am aware of it and have known about it for some time. It was one of many reasons I wanted him drugged and unconscious when we made our move to conquer the empire."

"We should have had the slut that drugged him cut his throat," said Nespar.

"Runes were cast about that, Nespar, and the voices of the larger world advised against his death then, else things would ill against us on the night of conquest."

"And yet, Majesty, you've since asked for his head and heart brought to you in spirits of wine."

"Yes. What is ill-fated on one day may be propitious at another time."

Nespar waited for more, but there were limits, it seemed, to what the Witch-king wanted to share on that topic. Instead, the Witch-king leaned forward, resting his forearms on the closed book. His whole posture was tense—not like a frightened creature but with the predatory tension of one of the big jungle cats. The air around him seemed to crackle with his energy.

"My lord," said Nespar, "how can I be of best service to you?"

"Find Kagen Vale," said the King in Yellow, laying a hand on the older man's shoulder. "Find his companions as well. Bring them to me, alive or dead. And, Nespar . . ."

"My lord?"

"Spare no effort. Spare no expense. Place a bounty on them that would tempt a saint. A bounty that would corrupt the purest soul and turn all of his friends against him. But do not use threats. Dangle the carrot but hide the stick." He paused. "For now."

"Yes, my lord." Nespar paused. "And what to do about the submonarchs?"

The Witch-king removed his hand. "For now, I will do nothing. At least nothing that will heighten their sense of alarm," said the king. "However, the shepherd god is sending us an ally. Not a friend, exactly, but someone whose interests align nicely with my own. He will advise us on the threat of war."

"Is this person a great general or . . . ?"

"He is not," said the Witch-king. "He is a master of games. The pieces are already on the board and it is time for us to play."

"When should we expect this person, my lord?"

"He will arrive in his own time," said the Witch-king.

"Of course, Majesty."

"Nor will he be my only guest, Nespar. Expect others. When they arrive, you will know them and will not hesitate to bring them here to me."

"Without fail, Majesty."

The Witch-king studied the chamberlain, not yet dismissing him. "Nespar," he said slowly, "understand this . . . while this hunt is on, we will of course prepare for the war that must come. It will not, however, be the war that the empire's rabble-rousers expect. What Kagen and his allies have done is more than an insult to me and to Hakkia. They have insulted our god, and Hastur is not a forgiving god. Nor am I, his priest on earth, forgiving. They have dared to use magic against me. They conjured Cthulhu and fled the palace by no mortal means. If that is the kind of war they want, then by the Elder Gods I will show them a war. I will break the chains of death and raise the dead if needs must. I will tear down the gates of hell to release armies of the damned."

"Majesty . . . but what of our own people? Our armies and navies?"

"Hakkia is beloved of Hastur, Nespar, and if that means we are the only people left alive when the dust settles, then so be it. We will own the west and conquer the world. But I tell you this . . . there will be no peace on this earth until I am crowned Yellow Emperor of all the land." He paused. "Now . . . go and do what I require of you. Do not fail me in this."

"I will not fail you, my lord," said Nespar. He bowed himself backwards and then turned to hurry away and do his master's bidding.

CHAPTER TWENTY-SIX

The storm blew itself out, leaving *Dagon's Swan* bobbing weakly in choppy blue water. Above the vessel the sky transformed from an angry purple-black to a moody gray and then the clouds brightened to a flawless white and sailed away from one another across an ocean of blue sky. The seas settled down and the entire picture nature presented was a sugary confection of calm delight, the kind of sky that drew pleasure boats from the safety of their harbors.

Aboard the ship, the effects of the storm were everywhere. The Hakkians had done their work too well and the hurricane had hit before all of the repairs had been completed. Now it was all worse. There were fallen blocks, parted spars, parted ropes, debris of every kind. The sailors, already tired from the battle with the Hakkian raiders, had been pushed to their limits by the storm, but no rest was in the offing. Several men, sagging with exhaustion, had vanished overboard or fallen from the rigging. A few of the most badly wounded perished from the sheer brutality of the storm-tossed ship.

Through all this, though, Captain Jasker was everywhere, yelling orders, pushing and chopping and working alongside his crew. Kagen offered to help, but the captain fairly snarled at him to go below and let professionals tend to their work. Tuke and Filia were likewise dismissed, though Jesker relented and promised that with calmer seas the cook could relight the galley fire and get something hot into everyone's bellies.

While they waited, Tuke, Filia, and Kagen retreated contritely and squeezed into the tiny cabin they shared. Filia lit a lantern as Tuke and Kagen found unbroken glasses and a big bottle of some dark, sweet liquor.

When their cups were filled, Filia offered a toast to the crew, and they clinked glasses. Tuke followed with a cup raised to his dead king, and that was drunk with solemnity and sadness. There were toasts for the lost members of the crew and the overall safety of the ship. They sipped and brooded. Above them were the sounds of hammering and sawing and the slap of bare feet on planking.

"What I want to know," said Kagen, "is how that Hakkian ship even found us. I mean, did they know we were aboard? If not, why attack a Therian ship?"

Tuke studied him. "Has to be those damned birds," he said.

"My birds?" asked a puzzled Kagen, then he shook his head and corrected his question. "Oh, you mean the ravens."

"Yes," said Tuke. "Nothing else makes sense."

Filia nodded. "Not that *that* makes sense," she said. "Or maybe it does. If your—what do you call them? Nightbirds?—follow you, then maybe the ravens follow their human namesakes. We fled the palace, hid out in Argon for a few days, and then took ship. Plenty of time for the Witch-king's birds to find us and . . ."

"And what? Write a report?" asked Kagen.

"Who the hell knows," groused Filia. "It's all some kind of damned magic."

Kagen sipped his drink, winced, and scowled over the edge of the cup. "Even after all that's happened, I still don't know that I understand what magic really is. I mean, Herepath has clearly become a sorcerer or wizard or whatever word applies, and he conquered the empire in one night. So . . . why didn't he just strike us down in the throne room? If he can create a razor-knight and instantly transport his troops to every capital, how are we even still alive?"

It was not a facetious question, and his friends did not take it as such.

Filia gestured with her cup to Tuke. "I understand some things about magic, and even before the Night of the Ravens I caught some glimpses of it here and there. You tend to do that when you guide caravans through remote places. Especially the Cathedral Mountains, which are filled with stories about vampires and ghouls and all kinds of monsters. But you, Tuke . . . your people believe it more than anyone else in the empire. With the exception of the Hakkians, I mean."

Tuke took a moment to gather his thoughts, glancing now and then at the wall as if he could see beyond it and into the wider and stranger world.

"Sure," he agreed, "we Therians believe in the supernatural, but to us it's part of the natural world."

"Does that make sense?" asked Kagen, but once more considered and answered his own question. "You mean that magic *isn't* unnatural? It's part of what my brother called the 'larger world,' but unlike ordinary things like the weather, animals, and such, we haven't found a way to really *know* it. Is that what you're saying?"

"In part, yes," said the big man. "My aunt Gura was the storyteller of our family. She believed in absolutely everything. On the dark Harvest nights, as we gathered around a big bonfire outside, or the fireplace if it was too cold, she'd tell us all kinds of tales. Legends about wyverns and basilisks and hellhounds; family tales about ghosts and demons . . . and even some songs and ballads handed down one generation to the next. Understand, a lot of it was related to the faith of Father Dagon and Mother Squid, but she seemed to know a lot more."

"How did she know all that?" asked Filia.

"Gods only know," admitted Tuke. "I wish now that I'd asked her. But I was a kid and liked a good spooky story. Especially those with a sexy ghost woman with big tits."

"Idiot," said Filia under her breath. "Are tits all you think about?"

"I was fourteen," protested Tuke. "Of *course* tits were all I thought about."

Filia considered. "Fair enough. Continue."

"She said that magic has been on earth longer than people have," said Tuke. "But that it wasn't *from* earth. She said it came here from beyond the stars. Or maybe from another dimension. I stopped paying attention when she got into that, because I didn't really care. Not then."

Filia began to say something then glanced at Kagen's face. "What's that look on your face? Do you know something?"

"I'm not sure that it's something I *know*," he said slowly. "Listen, there are some things I haven't told you about."

CHAPTER TWENTY-SEVEN

The arrow took the driver in the chest, punching into his heart and ending him as surely as if he were struck down by the gods. The driver did not even make a sound. His body slumped sideways and he fell out of his seat and dropped from the coach. It was so sudden that the horses did not even panic; they continued walking along the road as if everything was normal.

"Hey," said one of the passengers, "what the hell was that?"

There were five of them in the coach—three men and two women. All but one of the passengers was heavily armed. Four were in their mid- or late-twenties and worked as paid guards. The fifth passenger was an old woman in a gray cloak with the hood pulled up. A widow's garb, complete with a mourning veil hiding her face.

"Tell the driver to stop," she cried.

One of the armed guards pounded his fist on the front wall of the carriage.

"Ho! Rolf, stop for a minute."

Rolf did not answer. Rolf was sprawled in the dirt and receding in the distance.

The soldier turned, knelt on the bench seat, and slid open a small window.

"Rolf . . . stop . . . *Oh, shit!*" He turned. "Rolf's not there. Something's wrong."

Without a pause, two others opened the side doors and leaned out. One jumped down and ran to the front set of horses, reaching for their harnesses to try to stop them. The other, the woman guard, grabbed a set of rungs mounted on the outside and wriggled out and began to climb.

They were the next to die.

A half dozen arrows whipped through the air and thudded into them. The running man fell gasping, a shaft in his thigh, but he fell very badly and both wheels on that side of the carriage rolled over him.

The woman was hit in the kidney and the lung and dropped with a wet scream from the side of the wagon.

Suddenly, men poured out of the woods. Eight of them, all dressed in mismatched pieces of light armor, all with bows in their hands and knives hanging from belts. One, a big man with a woodsman's axe, rushed up and buried the blade in the neck of the horse on the right front of the team of four. The animal shrieked in agony and began to bolt, then it canted forward and crashed down, screaming and thrashing, its weight jerking the rest of the team to a nervous halt. The bowmen swarmed the carriage, yanked the doors open, and filled the interior with arrows.

The two remaining soldiers tried to protect the old woman.

They tried.

Their bodies, pincushioned with arrows, collapsed onto her, their slack weight crushing her into the padded seats.

"Get the old witch," snarled one of the attackers. He slung his bow and drew a wicked knife. "Bring her out here."

His men likewise slung their bows, reached inside, and dragged the dying guards out, pausing only to slit their throats. Then they put rough hands on the old woman and hauled her unceremoniously from the conveyance and forced her to her knees in front of their chief.

"Well now, what have we got here, lads?" said the chief in a voice filled with cheery humor. "I think we got us a wanted criminal. And you know what that means?"

They all grinned and nudged one another. Clearly they knew, though their chief answered anyway. He was enjoying the drama and wanted his full moment. He bent and tore away the veil then yanked back the hood, exposing a woman with iron gray hair, a comprehensively lined and seamed face, and eyes that were rimmed with red.

"The Ravens are offering ten gold pieces for every one of you Gardener scum."

The woman looked at him but said nothing. Despite her age and evident fear, her eyes were hard and sharp.

"There is no Garden anymore," she said, each word coming out tight and sharp.

"Yeah, but there *was*, and the Hakkians want all of you holier-than-thou scum rounded up. We've already turned in two Gardeners this month. They made it tough on us, so we had to take a smaller bounty just for their heads. But you, my lady, I think you're going to come along nice and quiet. You ain't gonna struggle and make a fuss, are you? 'Cause I'd hate to have to cut something off to teach you some manners. Like, maybe your tits?

You're long past using them for anything. Do I have to cut them off to get you to behave?"

"Be damned to you," she said. Her voice was hot, but there was ice forming around her heart.

"Or . . . maybe me and the lads can have some fun. You're old as shit but you look like you were something in your day. Maybe we'll blow the dust off your cooze and take you for a ride. Would you like that? My boy Sekk over there is hung like a gods-damn prize bull. I'll let him have your asshole. He likes assholes, young or old."

Sekk, an ugly brute with a filthy beard, grabbed his phallus through his trousers and laughed with genuine delight.

Tears welled suddenly in the old woman's eyes. Her body trembled with equal parts fury and terror. Hope, which had always been her strongest driving force, began to die inside her chest. The last splinter of that hope was the small silver knife she wore, hidden in the gray folds of her robes. If she could get it out quickly enough, maybe she could kill herself before the—

Something slashed the air a handbreadth from her face.

There was a sharp *thwack* and a sudden scream.

She and the chief both turned to see the man Sekk stagger backwards, eyes bulging, mouth uttering a shrill scream, and the hand that had grabbed his crotch was now pinned there with an arrow fletched with red. A darker red welled furiously through his fingers and Sekk sagged to the ground, making a keening noise so loud it scared the birds from the trees.

Then there were arrows everywhere. They came out of the woods and crisscrossed in the air. The highwaymen scattered, but they were in a box.

"Shoot back, for the love of the gods," bellowed the chief as he tore at his own bow. "Kill the fuckers."

That's when the old woman tore her dagger free and buried the blade in the man's chest. She felt it slide between the ribs to the left of his sternum, and when it was buried, she gave it a savage twist. The chief stared at her with a shock so profound that it lit up his face. Then he coughed out a blob of bright blood and fell.

The old woman ran for the woods as fast as her spindly legs could carry her.

The highwaymen were trying to hide in the carriage, but that gave them no room to use bows. They screamed and yelled and prayed and begged for their chief to tell them what to do.

Two figures emerged from the woods on opposite sides of the road. Each had a short, exquisitely made bow—the kind used in close-quarters combat. Quivers hung over their shoulders and they drew and fired, drew and fired with incredible speed and precision. The old woman, crouching behind a tree, saw that they were nearly identical, with the same build and faces, though one was blond and the other had ginger hair.

She waited for more to emerge before it became obvious that all this carnage had been caused by just those two. It was a display of archery so sophisticated that it bordered on the magical.

The last of the bandits boiled from the carriage, raising their own bows, now that they had room to fight. But their foolishness in trying to hide had already stolen away whatever tactical advantage their numbers gave.

One of them managed to close on the blond-haired stranger, drawing a heavy curved sword and weaving a net of glittering steel in the air. The blond tossed his bow aside and drew his own sword, a slender blade of medium length that could not have been even half the weight of the scimitar he faced. He retreated a step and struck a fencing pose that was overly stylized to the point of comedy.

"Have at thee, varlet," he said in a voice filled with mockery and amusement.

The highwayman with the scimitar charged, swinging his heavy blade in a huge overhand arc. The blond sidestepped as nimbly as a dancer, and as the bigger sword cleaved the air an inch from his shoulder, the smaller man pivoted and wove his own steel net. Red lines appeared on the highwayman's arm, chest, shoulder, and face as if by magic. Pieces of him began to slide out of place on a tide of bubbling red.

"Stop fucking around and finish him," yelled the ginger-haired one as he paused to cut the throat of the whimpering Sekk.

"You're no damn fun," yelled the blond, and with a flick of his sword tip he opened the highwayman's throat from ear to ear.

As the last of the brigands tried to flee, he slipped in bloody mud and fell, then tried to crawl backwards on elbows and heels like an overturned crab, begging for mercy.

"Mercy?" echoed the redhead. "Sorry, mate, but I forgot to pack mine."

He killed the man with a pair of crisscrossed slashes that sliced the throat and then lopped off the head.

A silence dropped over everything.

Even the panicked horses stopped whinnying and stamping. The old woman stared in frank amazement. It was all over in seconds. The ginger-haired man checked the coach and the soldiers. The blond cleaned his sword on a dead man's tunic, sheathed the weapon, and retrieved his bow. He fitted an arrow to the string with deft speed, ready for more.

"Damn," he said, "these little pricks got 'em all. Shit on me, we were too late." He walked over and stood at the edge of the woods. "No," he cried. "Here. This one is still alive."

He was looking directly at the lady.

The woman raised her knife in defiance, and in that moment she did not know whether to try another attack or cut her own throat.

The blond bowman smiled. It was a big, warm, genial smile. "After all that, m'lady," he said in a cultured voice that was at odds with his rough woodland clothes, "my guess is that you're not too big on trusting strangers. Fair enough."

He removed the arrow he'd nocked and slid it back into the quiver, then unstrung his bow and laid it on the ground. Then he held his hands up, palms out, but made no attempt to draw closer. The ginger-haired man joined him, and he too set his bow down.

There was something very familiar about these men, and the woman fished in her long, deep memory for what it was.

"We're Argonian soldiers," said ginger-hair.

"*Were* Argonian soldiers," corrected the blond.

"Were. Sure. What we technically are is adventurers." He turned to the blond. "Or is it *are* adventurers?"

"Oh, like I ever paid attention to grammar lessons."

"We're adventurers," said ginger-hair.

"That works," said the blond. "And we are absolutely not going to hurt you."

"Unless you're offended by bad language."

"In which case we apologize in advance," said the blond.

"Fuck yeah we do."

The memory the old woman had been searching for was there. Her mind was crowded with information, but it was all indexed, and she had many mnemonic tricks for finding what she needed.

She lowered the knife. "I know who you are," she said.

The redhead grinned and shook his head. "I doubt that."

"I know your *family*," she said.

They glanced at each other and back at her, but said nothing, letting quizzical expressions be their reply.

"And I know a great deal about your brother," said the old lady. "The one who has been causing such mischief."

There was a long pause.

"Well," said the blond, "from the way you say that, I have a feeling this is a story best told inside."

"And over beers," said ginger-hair.

"Lots of beers," agreed the blond.

CHAPTER TWENTY-EIGHT

The royal twins sat together on a padded bench by a window that commanded a magnificent view of Haddon Bay. Hundreds of boats and ships moved through the sparkling blue water. Flags on poles marked the spots where ships had sunk during the Night of the Ravens, creating a new and somewhat labyrinthine passage from the Argonian ports to the Straits of Anthelos.

A sleek black cat sprawled across Gavran's thighs, and the boy stroked it with an idle hand. Silver rings that were really too big for his small fingers glittered on every finger. His clothes of purple and black were dusted with cat hair, but he did not care. There were people who would clean everything. He even sometimes let the cat piss in the bed just because it was fun to watch grown-ups scramble to change the bedding and clean everything up.

Beside him, his twin, Foscor, played with a tiny but beautifully carved onyx statue of a raven. It was a gift from their father, one of the pawns from their set of Kings and Castles. Neither of them liked the game—it was a bit beyond them still—but the raven pieces were lovely.

The sun peeked at them from behind hedgerows of white clouds.

"Father is angry today," said the boy.

The girl held the raven up to the sun, turning it to see small flecks of hidden colors. Golds and greens and purples. She saw indigo and blue, too, which pleased her because they matched her gown.

"Father is often angry," she said without looking at him.

"Angrier," said Gavran. "I heard yelling earlier."

Foscor looked at him. "Father never yells."

"No," said the boy. "He wasn't the one who was yelling. It was one of the generals."

Foscor frowned. "Yelling, or screaming?"

Gavran thought about that for a moment. "Screaming, I guess."

"Well," said his sister, "he probably deserved it."

"Yes."

They watched the sunlight glitter like polished gold on the knife edges of each little wavelet. Sometimes they caught each other's eyes and then they would both smile. If hungry rats could smile, it would look like that.

Sometimes they stared out the window with eyes grown suddenly vacant, and at such times hours might pass.

Inside their heads, each of them could hear the screams. Not of generals paying for failure to find Kagen Vale, or Argonians reacting to Father's judgments. No. The screams they heard came from within. Stayed within. Trapped there because they were not holding hands.

The screams went on and on. Most of the time Foscor and Gavran ignored them. Sometimes they liked them.

Today was one those days, and as the screams echoed inside the prisons of their souls, the children smiled small and secret smiles.

CHAPTER TWENTY-NINE

"Come, sister," said the woman named Fish as she knelt to take Ryssa's hands. "It's time."

The words seemed to come from very far away, and it took Ryssa a long time to find her way from where she was to a place in her mind where those words made sense. She knew who spoke to her, but even that was almost an abstract thing, like someone half remembered from a fading dream. Everything seemed muted— Fish's voice, the crash of waves far below, the cry of gulls in the clear blue sky above, the lament played by musicians clustered together nearby.

Then, gradually, the sounds became more real, more clear and distinct. To Ryssa it was as if those things moved toward her and settled, with some reluctance, near to where she half sat and half lay at the foot of Miri's bier. She could hear the subtleties of the melodies the musicians played and she heard a soft voice singing a song that felt somehow incredibly ancient. It was not an ordinary song, and the voice that sang it was strange, achieving notes that Ryssa could not comprehend. It sounded more like a human voice trying to sing in the language of whales. When she raised her head and looked, she said that it was Peixe, Fish's friend, who sang. Not once since coming to the city of Ulnagr here on Tull Yammoth had Ryssa heard Peixe speak. Now she heard her sing, and there was magic in it. Sweet and pure and as strange as all the mystery in the sea.

"Let me help you up," said Fish. She pulled gently on Ryssa's hands, and after only a moment of resistance, Ryssa allowed it. But it had been a long time since she stood, and there was so little left of her. In the days since Miri's death, Ryssa had dwindled down to a dry stick. She felt death's soft breath murmur against her cheeks and welcomed its touch. But only Fish's hands were touching her. Fish was alive, and death lingered, hesitating, refusing to accept Ryssa's invitation to dance.

Ryssa swayed, feeling her body pushed this way and that by the slightest puff of breeze. Fish held onto her, steadying her, and guided Ryssa down the marble steps and away from the bier.

"No," cried Ryssa softly, but Fish made soothing noises.

"We have to let Lady Sithra speak the prayers," she said.

Ryssa looked over her shoulder and saw the thin, elegant older woman dressed in a gauzy gown of purest white standing a few yards away. Lady Sithra bowed to her and offered Ryssa a loving smile.

Ryssa hated her and wished it was this woman lying cold and dead on the altar, instead of standing there healthy and whole. She tried to suck enough moisture from the walls of her mouth to spit, but there was not a drop.

Fish took Ryssa to a bench and they sat, near to the highest officials of the island's religion, but not actually with them. Apart, in so many ways. Peixe continued her song, and the deeper into the melody she went, the less human she sounded. It was eerie and uncomfortable to hear, because Ryssa kept trying to understand how the woman even made those sounds. Yet there was something compelling about it. She felt herself trying to understand the meaning, and with each note, that insight seemed to be closer.

But when she opened her own mouth, what she said was merely, "She's gone."

Fish held her close and kissed her dirty face and stroked her filthy hair.

"Gone? Oh, no, Lady Ryssa," she said. "Miri is dreaming with our god."

"She was supposed to be with me," said Ryssa, but her voice broke and all the sound leaked away.

The lament played on, with Peixe's plaintive voice rising to the wind and swirling above the altar. The sea was a thousand feet below, the waves smashing endlessly against the rocks. Ryssa wondered if she had the strength to break free from Fish and make it to the edge and over before anyone could stop her. Gods of the Garden, how she wanted to.

Then a sound caught her attention and she turned to see six strong men walking toward the dais, a casket of gold and hematite balanced on their shoulders. They were naked except for colored cloths wound around their loins, and each of them had incredibly elaborate tattoos covering them from the tops of their feet to the crowns of their shaved heads. Sea creatures of every type and description, from common eels to goblin-faced hagfish, seemed to swim across their limbs and torsos. Tentacles coiled around their thighs and up onto their chests. Sea turtles and jellyfish floated on their broad backs.

Fish and Ryssa watched as the men climbed the steps to the dais and then stood to be blessed by Lady Sithra. They removed the jewel-encrusted lid of the casket and set it to one side.

Lady Sithra spoke in the ancient language of their people. *"N'gha ah mgng nglui."*

Ryssa had learned much of the language and was able to understand the words.

Death is but a doorway.

"I want to go through that doorway with her," she said, but Fish's only answer was to kiss Ryssa's cheek again.

Lady Sithra raised her arms high and wide. *"C' vulgtmoth ehye, Miri, mgep shed h' gn'th'bthnk llll c' uh'eog Cthulhu."*

Our holy one, Miri, has shed her blood for our lord Cthulhu.

The men set the casket down and lined up on either side of the shrouded corpse.

"H' h' goka gn'th'bthnk ng bthnk l' fhtagn r'luhhor," intoned the high priestess.

She gives her blood and body to the Dreaming God.

"No," begged Ryssa.

As one, the six men took hold of the lace shroud, and with great care, even gentleness, they raised Miri's small body up and walked it to the casket.

"Ng c' hai k'yarnak gn'th'bthnk ng orr'e, bthnkor ng orr'e llll c' r'luhhor."

And we now share blood and soul, flesh and spirit with our god.

The men picked up the lid and slowly—so slowly—lowered it onto the coffin.

"C' c' goka ot fhtagn hope l' fhtagn r'luhhor."

As once before, Ryssa noticed that the one word spoken in the common tongue was *hope*. As if that word did not exist in the language of these people.

We offer our dream of hope to the Dreaming God.

The men bent over, each of them setting screws in place and

turning them, fastening the lid down, shutting off forever the dead woman inside from the living woman who loved her.

Then the men lifted the casket and placed it upon the bier. They bowed low, going to one knee and spreading their arms wide as they lowered their heads. Lady Sithra blessed them all and the men rose and left the dais. Then Sithra stood for a long while, her own head bowed as she spoke a prayer whose words did not reach Ryssa's ears. She faced the edge of the cliff, one hand touching the lid of the casket and the other pressed flat against her chest, over her heart.

The cries of the birds and the pitch of Peixe's song rose higher, became much louder. The wind seemed to freshen, too, and Ryssa could hear the sea battering the rocks with more force. It was as if the whole world was crying out in pain for lost Miri.

Lightning snapped jaggedly across the sky despite the lack of clouds, and there was a sound like rocks tumbling down a mountainside. Thunder, perhaps, though if so, it was strangely muted and distorted as if the sound were really a landslide somewhere beneath the waves.

Lady Sithra went to the very edge of the cliff and once more held her arms out high and wide, and in a voice as sharp and piercing as a gull's, cried, *"Ymg' mggoka fhalgof'n wgah'nagl!"*

Take your daughter home.

The gathered people echoed her words. All except Peixe, who continued to sing her whale song. Thousands of voices repeated the prayer.

"Ymg' mggoka fhalgof'n wgah'nagl!"

Over and over.

And Ryssa, despite everything, despite her hatred of everyone here for what had happened, despite her bottomless pain, found herself repeating it, too. In the common tongue and then in the language of R'yleh.

"Ymg' mggoka fhalgof'n wgah'nagl!"

Then there was a sound so big, so deep, so heavy and ponderous that it was felt as much as heard. As if the sea itself cried out in reply, a stentorian bellow tore the air apart. The sea hurled itself at the cliff with incredibly fury, sending boiling white and green clouds of foaming seawater up and up until they spiked above the dais itself and showered everyone and everything. The people of Yammoth never stopped praying, even when uncounted gallons of seawater smashed them to their knees or onto their bellies. Dripping, bleeding, weeping, they climbed back to their feet.

Take your daughter home.

Sithra was screaming now, eyes wide, drops of blood speckling her lips and chin.

Take your daughter home.

Ryssa staggered from the bench onto her knees and pounded the ground with her fists.

Take your daughter home.

The air and the sea and the world itself reverberated with the shout, the plea, the prayer.

And then something rose from the ocean.

It shot out of the waves, punching upward, rising hundreds upon hundreds of feet. Unbearably, impossibly big, covered with rows of suckers, each of which was ringed with teeth like daggers. Ryssa shrieked as it came into view and she fell back into Fish's arms, who caught her and held her. Both women kept praying, though their words disintegrated into screams of terror and ecstasy as a tentacle two thousand feet long and as thick around the hull of a ship rose from the water straight up the cliff and paused there, the delicate tip curled and quivering above the dais.

Then, with a gentleness totally at odds with its immensity and obvious power, it encircled the casket and plucked it up from the marble dais. That tentacle could have crushed the entire cliff wall, it could have torn the city of Ulnagr to pieces and yet it held Miri's casket as gently as if it were the most precious thing.

Ryssa staggered to her feet and reached upward, clawing at the air as if somehow she could reach the casket and tear it away from this monster. But then the tentacle receded, sliding downward, pulling the bejeweled box and its precious contents even further beyond Ryssa's reach. She ran to the edge and would have flung herself over had not Fish caught her and held on with desperate strength. Even then the people still chanted their prayer.

Take your daughter home.

Ryssa clung to the edge, leaning over, reaching down, calling out Miri's name in one long wail as the tentacle and its prize vanished beneath the thrashing sea.

Only when it was gone did the prayers cease.

The seas gradually stopped their thrashing and the winds blew more softly.

Miri was gone.

Her god had taken his daughter home.

CHAPTER THIRTY

"What kinds of things haven't you told us about?" asked Tuke, eyes narrowing.

"About how magic came to earth," he said. "And I think I might know how Herepath got his power."

They gaped at him.

"And you forgot to bring any of this up before now?" growled Filia. "What the fuck?"

"No, listen," said Kagen quickly. "You have to understand that a lot happened to me since the empire fell. The slaughter of the imperial family, the deaths of my parents and two of my brothers. Then . . . what happened with the Harvest Gods. Then . . ."

"Then getting drunk out of your mind for weeks on end," said Tuke.

Kagen took no offense. "I didn't handle things well, I admit. And even now I don't know how steady I am. Mentally and emotionally, I mean."

Tuke, who would normally have plucked a ripe conversational fruit like that, abstained and merely nodded. Filia gestured for Kagen to continue.

"And then there was that whole thing with Maralina," said Kagen.

Maralina was a woman who lived in what was supposed to be an unoccupied tower on the coast of Vahlycor. She had enchanted him, bound him with chains, threatened to kill him, but ultimately freed him. In what Kagen thought was a span of a day or two but was actually closer to a month, they had become lovers. She had told him her story—that she was the daughter of the queen of the faerie folk but was seduced by a handsome wandering nobleman who turned out to be a powerful vampire. He had fed on her but then made her drink of his blood, transforming her into a kind of hybrid—half vampire and half faerie, but no longer truly one or the other. The vampire had tossed her from a high window, not caring if she lived or died. The queen of the faeries found her and resurrected Maralina, but then rejected the thing she had become. Immortal but outcast, Maralina had wandered the world, gaining in knowledge and power, but always alone. Then a curse trapped her in the Tower of Sarsis, and it was there that Maralina fell into legend and ceased to interact with the world outside except remotely. She watched events unfold in her magic mirror and then wove certain images into tapestries of incredible beauty, complexity, and power.

"Yes, Maralina. That's what I want to talk about." Kagen recapped that information in order to frame what he wanted to say next. "When I left her tower, I told you some of what happened to me, but there was no time for the full story because we then set about trying to kill the Witch-king."

"And there *is* more to tell?" prompted Filia.

"There is, and even I had set it to one side in my mind," he said. "Let me tell it now."

Tuke and Filia leaned in, and Kagen bent toward them.

"Ever since I was a child, I have had strange dreams," he said. "I was advised against talking about them. Mostly, I suppose, because of the prohibition against magic, and prophetic dreams are seen as part of that. Unnatural. However, I shared them with my brother. With Herepath. Remember, for much of my life he was the sibling I most admired, the one I confided in and knew I could speak to. I could tell him my truths, my doubts and fears. I could tell him about my dreams. And I told him about a dragon. Fabeldyr is her name. I didn't know it then, but when I spoke of this to Maralina, she told me that was the name of that dragon. She said it was the very last dragon. She told me that the dragon I dreamed of as a lad was real, and that she must be found and protected."

"Protected?" asked Filia. "Why? If dragons are how magic came into this world, then wouldn't killing the last one put an end to magic? Wouldn't that rob the Witch-king of the source of his power?"

Kagen shook his head. "I don't think so. As I understand, the tears—and to some extent, the blood—of dragons are used in spells that open the veils between worlds. In ages past, magic proliferated because there were so many dragons."

"Maralina told you this?" asked Tuke.

"She told me some, and some I . . . well . . . kind of just understood. Partly from dreams, partly from intuition. A few things from cryptic things Herepath said over the years. I don't really understand it all that much, to tell the truth. It's tangled up, because some of it is from old dreams, some is from new dreams I've had since the Night of the Ravens . . . where I am both my younger self and my current self. And, understand this, I somehow know more than I remember her saying in actual words. It's like there was a sharing of information on some level other than speech." He paused. "Yes, I know that sounds crazy."

Tuke pointed to the hull. "A few days ago we saw a giant whale-squid monster thing. You and I have seen flowers growing whose color cannot be described because there is nothing like it on earth. A razor-knight killed your mother. And you have a few thousand birds following you around like a pack of hounds. Crazy? Maybe you are, but the world is no less crazy. Not anymore."

"He makes a point," agreed Filia. "Maybe some of your troubles stem from you trying to deny what is happening all around you. You want things to be the way they were—orderly and measurable and practical. I get that. I'm as pragmatic as the next person. But we have to be realists. This stuff *is* happening. Denial in the face of reality is a short road to losing one's mind."

Kagen nodded and paused to look into the depths of his glass. "I will admit freely that I am not the sanest person in the world. After what I saw that night, and after pickling my brain in strong drink for way too long, I'm not entirely sure I can trust what I believe, let alone my memories. Those dreams now overlap with the visions I had while with Maralina. And with prophecies about me, said by this woman Selvath I met before I met you, Tuke. I seem to be caught up in events I can't even begin to understand, and the person I would have sought out to help me understand all of this is Herepath."

"Shit," said Filia, and reached across to give his forearm a reassuring squeeze.

Tuke shook his head. "Well, *I* have a hard time wrapping my head around the idea that your brother is a wizard, that he conquered the Silver Empire, that he has the ear of a fucking god, and that he wants the three of us dead."

"Yeah," said Kagen, glancing at him, "there's that."

"Magic," prompted Filia. "You've veered off course there, Kagen. What did Herepath say about it—and about dragons—in your dreams?"

"Nothing specific, alas," said Kagen. "Even when we were young, he was always secretive and sly and strange. With all that, though, I would never in a million years have guessed that he would turn evil. I mean the actual, inarguable embodiment of evil."

"When you were young, did you think you'd be a partisan attempting the overthrow of an invading country?" asked Filia. "Did you imagine that you'd be the person you've become?"

"No," said Kagen firmly, "I did not. Not exactly, anyway. I mean, I assumed I'd be some kind of soldier, because that's what most of my family has been, even if they moved on after a term of service. For my part, I assumed I'd do a few years with a patrol, or maybe a fortress battalion, and then move into something else. Music, maybe."

"Music?" said Tuke, surprised. "I didn't know you can play an instrument."

"I can't."

"Then you're a singer?"

"Not a very good one."

"Then . . ."

"Seemed like music was where I would meet girls," said Kagen. "The minstrel life and all that. The travel, the taverns, county fairs . . ."

"But without actual talent . . ." said Filia.

Kagen shrugged. "Hence the reason I became a soldier. Turns out the one thing I'm actually good at is killing people. Even when I was drunk out of my head I was able to kill every Hakkian I met." He sighed. "Hardly something to aspire to, though."

"That's true enough," said Tuke. "I wanted to be an explorer. Sail beyond the horizon, discover new lands. All of that."

Filia glanced at them both. "Am I the only one who actually *did* want to grow up to be a fighter?"

"I guess so," said Kagen.

They lapsed into a shared reverie for a few moments. Drinking, listening to the thumps and curses and other sounds of the crew repairing the storm damage. Hearing the water whispering its way along the hull as *Dagon's Swan* moved through the ocean.

"As for that dragon," said Filia, bringing them back to it, "I wonder what would be best . . . to find it and kill it, ending all chances for the Witch-king to increase his abilities, or—"

"Or to save it and see if we can use its blood to fight Kagen's brother," completed Tuke.

"I don't think we should kill it," said Kagen. "Maralina seemed frightened about what would happen if the last dragon dies."

"Well, she would, wouldn't she," mused Filia. "Maralina's a magical being herself. If the dragons are the source of magic, then killing it might kill Maralina and all her kind."

"Yes," said Kagen darkly. "I've thought about that."

"You know," said Tuke, "I half remember something along those lines from what my aunt said. Let me think for a moment. Ah, yes . . . she said that there were three creatures that embody innocence in its purest and most powerful form. One is a unicorn. Don't suppose your bloodsucking faerie sweetheart mentioned those."

"Don't call her that," said Kagen. "And . . . no."

"What're the others?" asked Filia.

"A nine-tailed fox," said Tuke. "They bring good luck, peace, and prosperity. To kill one invites conflict and famine."

"And dragons are the third?" asked Kagen.

"Yes."

"But what does that mean, exactly?" asked Filia.

Tuke gave them a crooked smile. "To tell the honest truth,

friends, I stopped paying attention when she said they were innocents. I preferred stories about scary monsters and lascivious enchantresses."

"You are still fifteen," said Filia. "Maybe thirteen."

"Well, dear heart, it's not like I knew I was going to ever *need* this information."

Filia sipped her drink. "How would we even go about finding this dragon? This Fabeldyr. I've never once heard about a dragon in an ice cave. Not a live one. Though there's a chap in Zaare who used to take tourists to a granite cave he said was filled with dragon bones, but I think they were really elephants."

"Not helpful," said Tuke.

"I might have an idea where to look," said Kagen. "Or at least begin that search in earnest."

They turned sharply to him.

"Is this another thing you just now remembered from when you were busy getting your brains fucked out by Maralina?" asked Filia.

"No, and kiss my ass," said Kagen. "Look, Herepath was a senior scholar among the Gardeners, and he led an expedition to the Winterwilds. He would send some letters home, and I wrote to him. I may have been the only one doing so, except perhaps for our mother. My point is, I have a good idea where his dig site was." He looked at the others. "Surely you're both thinking what I am."

"That he found something up there that twisted his mind," said Filia, "and also found Fabeldyr. That this is how he was corrupted and made powerful."

"Yes," said Kagen.

"By the prickly balls of the cactus demons," muttered Tuke. "I have a horrible feeling that you two maniacs are going to suggest we trek all the way the hell to the Winterwilds, aren't you?"

Kagen said nothing.

Filia sipped her drink and smiled.

"Well . . . shit," said Tuke.

CHAPTER THIRTY-ONE

Dagon's Swan sailed on, gliding northward out of sight of land. It bypassed Theria and Vahlycor and finally edged its way through a cluster of icy islands, carefully navigating around the first icebergs of the season.

Captain Jasker was a deft hand at both navigation and stealth, and he set his three passengers ashore on a deserted beach at the southern end of Nelfydia. There he bade good-bye to Tuke, Filia, and Kagen, and with no wasted time at all, he turned his ship before the wind and let it drive him south toward home.

The three passengers watched the ship vanish beyond a river of moonlight that painted the ocean from horizon to beach. Then they turned and headed inland.

Early the following morning, they met a Therian agent who had gone on ahead to retrieve the horses and supplies Kagen and his friends had left in the small Vahlycorian town of Arras on the night of the coronation. Tuke paid him well and gave him a message to deliver to Princess Theka. Condolences for her father's death.

"We need to get maps and supplies," said Kagen.

"I have plenty of maps in my saddlebags," said Filia. "Remember, I was a caravan scout. I know every inch of this part of the empire, all the way to the beginning of the snowfields north of Nelfydia."

"We will need supplies, though," said Tuke. "Bedrolls, tents, winter clothes, heavier rugs for the horse. The lot."

"Bedrolls and tents?" echoed Kagen dubiously. "Surely there are inns in every town."

"And Hakkian patrols," Tuke reminded him. "You are the most wanted man in the west." He grinned and clapped Kagen hard on the shoulder. "How's that feel?"

The look of lethal malice Kagen gave him dimmed the Therian's smile.

"Okay, too soon for jests," muttered Tuke. "Touchy subject."

"We can at least bed down in a town near here," said Filia. "I know everyone there, and none of them are friends with the Ravens. It's half a day. Then we can rest, eat, and stock up before we set out." She glanced at Kagen. "Not joking, boy, but this might be the last bed you'll sleep in for a while. Make the best of it."

Kagen said nothing and instead went over and rested his forehead against Jinx's, stroking the big horse's long neck. The animal blew and stamped, happy to see him.

They set out within minutes and rode for five hours, reaching a small village used as a rest and refit stop by traders. Kagen wore a cloak with the hood up and pulled forward. He had not shaved in days. He took some pale roadside dust and rubbed it into his shaggy beard and unkempt hair, and that aged him, making him look at least twenty years older. Sadness and depression hunched his shoulders, aging him even more. In town, he grunted a few words in the island dialect of Tull Garkos, which was so far to the south that it was unlikely even the northern traders could understand him, and so they took him as a foreigner.

In his small room at one of the village inns, he stripped off his clothes, washed vigorously, ate a meal of hot beef and vegetables, crawled under the furs, and was asleep in seconds.

Dreams waited for him in the darkness, and they pulled him down, down, down.

CHAPTER THIRTY-TWO

Major General Culanna yl-Sik, deputy field marshal of Samud, sat upon her horse in the dense shade thrown down by a pair of elm trees that leaned together, their branches intertwined. Those trees were known locally as The Lovers. It was a bittersweet place that threatened to push her into a dark pool of sadness. When she was a girl of seventeen, Culanna had lost her virginity in that very spot with Dul an-Gur, a handsome young lieutenant in the king's guard. Two years later, on the anniversary of that first passionate encounter, she and Dul—by then a captain and her husband—celebrated with another bout of lovemaking. Their first child was conceived that day, exactly on the spot where her horse now stood.

Dul was gone now. He had died as a newly minted general in the army of King al-Huk. Along with his staff and a hastily assembled force of soldiers, Dul had tried to stop the invasion of foreign soldiers on the Night of the Ravens. The son that had been conceived under the trees had fought alongside his father. Beklin, only child of warrior parents, had used his own body to try to shield his father from Hakkian blades.

Now Dul and Beklin were buried in the family cemetery, but Culanna felt them both most strongly there, on that hill, beneath those trees. For her, the trees were no longer The Lovers but had become instead Her Loved Ones.

She leaned her layered palms on the leather saddle horn, a major general's cloak of bright scarlet draped from her shoulder. The cloak had been hemmed in black for the funerals, and though the official time of mourning had passed, she refused to have the mourning color removed. *Her* time of grief would never pass. Not while Hakkians and their mercenary allies still walked abroad in Samud.

Not while the weight of the Witch-king's heel still pressed its crushing weight on the necks of all of Samud. On the whole empire, or what was left of it.

The hill looked down on a shallow valley that was surrounded by dense forests and, on three sides, the upward sweep of a curved mountain range that had once been the cone of a volcano. Massive chunks of jagged obsidian thrust upward from the grassy field that covered the floor of the valley. Every road, trail, and goat path leading to the valley was guarded by Culanna's most trusted scouts. A rabbit could not get in without being seen. Certainly no Hakkian spies could manage it—if any even knew that this was a place worth visiting. The valley was difficult to find and awkward to reach.

That was why Culanna had chosen it.

Below where she sat upon her horse, four thousand Samudian troops—the cream of the archery divisions—were drilling. Skirmish maneuvers. Traps. Sharpshooting at targets pulled by chariots. Tens of thousands of arrows flashed through the moody winter air. The sound of their impact was like steady rainfall.

Although the archers fired at bales of hay, or upright stalks of bamboo wrapped in cloth, all Culanna yl-Sik saw were Hakkians. Every arrow that found its target was another Raven dead.

And Samudian archers seldom missed their marks.

CHAPTER THIRTY-THREE

DREAMS OF THE DAMNED

Dreams are doorways.

That was something Kagen had heard before, though he was not sure when, or who said it. Possibly Herepath. Was it Maralina, during those long and unreal nights in her strange tower? Or had the witch Selvath—the woman he'd saved from a gang of men who were attempting to rape and execute her for her psychic visions—whispered it to him?

Kagen didn't know.

Perhaps each had said it in one way or another. But no matter how, who, or when it was told to him, Kagen knew that it was the truth.

Dreams were doorways.

Not all, to be sure. Most of his dreams were collections of debris picked up by the winds of his conscious or unconscious mind as he moved through any given day. Those kinds of dreams tried to fit disparate elements from one experience with those of another, the way a child might try to fit together pieces of different puzzles. In one dream, the dead sister of an old friend might appear to whisper secrets about where a missing cat was in a castle Kagen had only read about in a book. Or a jackrabbit might chase a hunting dog through the drawing room as the family relaxed by the fire and told tales of things that had happened after their own deaths. Moody and strange, and to the dreamer they seemed like prophecies, but they never were. Rationalization was not insight.

And there were unfiltered memory dreams: a battle, a conversation over beers with friends, a Harvest Day celebration with family, running through the forest with a beloved dog.

Those kinds of dreams did not tear Kagen from slumber with a scream, nor did they trap him in sleep with chains of black ice.

Then there were dreams that seemed to be memories—even memories of past dreams—but which had evolved since their first shadow play in his mind. These were the most disturbing, because they were anchored squarely in both true memory and the certain memory of a specific dream.

That night, Kagen had one of those kinds of dreams. He was fully aware that he was sleeping, aware that he was dreaming, but as the dream unfolded and opened itself to him, he walked through that doorway without hesitation.

Not, though, without fear.

He walked with Herepath through the heart of the great glacier that covered the whole of the Winterwilds, and it was itself part of a cap of ice so vast it covered the very top of the world. What had Herepath said of it? As soon as he reached for that memory the very air seemed to echo with his brother's soft and whispery voice.

"We are not in a castle, little brother. We are in the very heart of a glacier. This is a mountain of ice so high that no one could climb it, and so vast that it would take a journey of a thousand days on the fastest horse to go

from one side to another. It caps the top of the entire world and is bigger than our entire continent. And we, young Kagen, are deeper inside it than anyone else has ever been."

That felt like the truth, especially now that so many dreams had brought Kagen to that place.

"I remember visiting this place with you and the Twins," said Kagen. "You and Faulker had a fight and you beat him pretty savagely."

"We were all younger then," said Herepath, "and passions ruled us more than logic."

The word younger stung Kagen, and he looked down at his body and limbs. Kagen knew that the body he wore in this dream was once again that of his fourteen-year-old self. He was never sure why, though. Perhaps because that was his age when he'd first had those dreams.

Perhaps, as he now wondered, that was before whatever had corrupted Herepath had not fully taken hold. He did not know that this was the truth—there was so much about Herepath that he did not know, and even more that was now called into question—but he believed this was the truth.

No one else had ever been where they were now.

He understood that he was there only as a projection of himself into the dreamlands. How, though, had Herepath himself gotten here? What, indeed, happened to Herepath's official expedition to the Winterwilds? Where were the other Gardeners, monks, nuns, and scholars sent to accompany Herepath here?

In the new dream, Kagen turned to his brother and asked.

"Where is the rest of your team? The other scholars and Gardeners?"

Herepath did not even glance at him, but merely said, "I am not alone, Kagen."

"I don't see anyone. Did they die?"

Then Kagen saw something that jolted him. There were tears in Herepath's lean face. They ran like melted tallow down his cheeks.

"I am not alone, Kagen," he repeated. "Never alone. Never again. Now all the voices speak inside me." Then he stopped and turned sharply, taking Kagen by the shoulders and shaking him. Herepath's fingers were as cold and strong as ice. "You swear so often by the fiery Pits, Kagen, but you should foreswear such careless oaths because you do not know what hell is." Another fierce shake. "I do!" cried Herepath, and his voice broke. "And hell does not burn. It is cold. So . . . very cold."

He flung Kagen from him and turned away, throwing a forearm across his eyes.

Kagen hit the wall so hard that the air was punched from his lungs and stars swam drunkenly around him. It took a few moments for his mind to clear, and when it did, he found that he and Herepath were in a different part of the glacier. There were no tears on his brother's face, and that face itself was subtly different. More careworn, more gaunt. There was a deeper complexity to his eyes and an unpleasant curl to Herepath's lips.

His brother was speaking, and Kagen realized that he was now in a different dream. One he remembered very well. They stood staring at what looked like figures. People. Maybe a hundred of them, only a few short feet inside the ice wall, clustered together or alone . . . scattered by whatever had killed them and then frozen in place. He rubbed at the icy wall to clear it, and through the translucence he could see pale faces. Gray and weathered, as if they were rotting when they were captured by this glacier. What had happened here? Had a tidal surge torn open a graveyard? Or were these dead men and women from some sunken ship who were now eternally entombed in the cold?

Kagen fervently prayed that he would not end up like that—trapped forever in unmelting ice. A prisoner in this kingdom of eternal frost.

A shadow obscured the faces, and Kagen flinched as he turned, expecting one of those frozen dead to be reaching out for him.

But it was only Herepath.

"What are they?" demanded Kagen, and he remembered this moment, and asking the same question. In that older dream, his brother never answered, merely smiled.

Now, though, Herepath touched the ice with his fingertips, and Kagen noticed that those fingers were pale except for the last joints of each, and these were blackened and withered as if with frostbite.

"They are the children of Hastur," he said.

At the mention of that name, all of the figures within the ice opened their eyes, and despite the cold, those eyes burned a bright and terrible yellow.

"Why are they here?" asked Kagen. "How did they become trapped like this?"

Herepath trailed his fingers along the walls as he moved down the corridor. Kagen followed, but he dared not touch that ice.

"Mankind has risen and fallen, risen and fallen," said Herepath. "They rose to great heights and in their hubris believed they were masters not only of the world but of their own fate." He gave a cold snort of laughter. "Such arrogance. Such an infantile lack of understanding. It is like the fleas on a dog thinking that they have conquered the thing on which they live, that they are the reason the sun rises and the stars paint the heavens and the tides ebb and flow."

"The world was made for man," said Kagen, quoting his catechisms. "We were given a garden to tend, and that would feed and clothe us."

Herepath's smile grew colder still. "Lies told by the misinformed to the ignorant. This world is billions of years old, and humanity has been a parasite on its skin for a blink of time's eye. Over and over again the earth—let alone the stars themselves—has scratched those parasites off. With fires and floods, with ice and fire, with disease and with instruments of war."

He turned and looked at Kagen, and now there were yellow highlights in his eyes as well.

"Fifty thousand years ago humanity had reached a pinnacle of culture, of art, of science and medicine. And also of war, of strife, of indifference and hatred. The custodians of that beautiful garden set it ablaze. They poisoned the air with diseases of their own creation and then reeled in shock and horror and surprise when their own foolishness turned to consume them."

Behind the walls, the fire-eyed figures bared their teeth and snapped at the ice as if it were something that could feed them. Or, Kagen thought, that it stood between them and what they wanted to devour. His skin crawled and he took an involuntary step back.

"Everything about that age of the world is gone—lost to time and dust—except what is trapped here in the ice. And"—here, Herepath's eyes took on a secretive, amused aspect—"a few things that the receding ice has already uncovered."

"Are you talking about magic?" asked Kagen.

"Oh yes," said Herepath. "Bright lad. Magic is everything."

"I'm afraid of magic."

"You should be."

"I don't understand what it is."

Herepath looked surprised. "Why . . . magic is chaos unchained, little brother. Magic is energy. It cannot be created or destroyed, only shaped and used."

"But magic was destroyed by the Silver Empress."

"Destroyed! Destroyed? No," said Herepath indignantly. "Magic cannot be destroyed. When the Silver Empire rose in the west, magic was only suppressed. It was forced to sleep, and it did sleep. People were forced to forget it, or to disbelieve in it . . . and that worked. To a degree. But it ultimately failed, because using force to crush out an idea only results in some people holding on to that idea with more passion, to protect it with greater subtlety. Do you think magic is extinct in, say, Hakkia? No. It festers beneath the scab of obedience to the crown. It grows like a cancer in the dark." Herepath shook his head. "The Silver Empresses have never understood this. Our own mother, the so-brilliant Poison Rose, does not understand. She thinks that she and her ancestors, and now her children, are part of an army of the righteous and that it is our sacred duty to continue to suppress even the thought of magic."

"Magic still exists?" asked Kagen, frightened of the thought. That reply was from his younger self, though; inside that shared dream aspect, his older self knew the truth.

"Magic exists," said Herepath distantly. "Here . . . and there. Not everywhere. No . . . not everywhere."

"You mean like Maralina and the Tower of Sarsis?" asked the older aspect of Kagen. "She was always awake, wasn't she?"

Herepath seemed to take the shift in perspective in stride. "Maralina? Yes. That creature has never slept. It is her strength and her punishment. To be the constant eye that watches and never sleeps, but to be unable to act. Never to engage." Then Herepath stiffened. "Except that is not entirely true, is it?"

"What do you mean?"

"Though she cannot interact in this world because she is cursed to remain in her tower, she used you to extend her reach. Yesss . . . I see that now. Be careful, little brother . . . she is not human in any way, and if you are unwise enough to try to understand her by what you know of humanity, you will always come to the wrong conclusions. Maralina is wise and subtle and devious, and you are nothing but a curious toy for her. She is older than the ice on which we stand. She is a monster."

Kagen moved to stand directly in front of Herepath.

"And what about you, brother?" he asked.

Herepath's eyes flickered with yellow light. "Oh . . . I'm a monster, too."

CHAPTER THIRTY-FOUR

"When you say you know our brother," said the young man with curly ginger hair, "which brother do you mean?"

The man who sat next to him looked like an identical twin, though in truth he was a year older. The face and build, the eyes and smile, were the same as his companion, except that his hair was a yellow so bright it looked like spun gold.

"We do have a bunch of them," said the golden-haired man. "I sometimes lose count how many."

"Sisters, too," agreed ginger-hair.

"Two of them," said the blond.

"Pretty sure two of our brothers are dead," said the redhead.

"Hugh's gone now," said the blond. "Never the sharpest cutlery in the pantry, but a good bloke."

"Good-*ish*," said ginger-hair.

"Let's not speak ill of the dead," chided the blond.

"Fair, fair," conceded ginger-hair. "He died a hero."

"And then there's Degas."

"*Lord* Degas," said ginger-hair, pretending to gag. "He always insisted upon being called that, being the eldest. But I guess we can call him that, now he's dead."

"They nailed him to his front door," said the blond, with no humor in his eyes, "and burned him alive. He was an officious ass, but he didn't deserve that."

"I can think of someone who does," said ginger-hair. "A Hakkian bastard whose name begins with *W* and sounds like '*I want to cut his fucking throat out asshole Witch-king.*'"

They both nodded.

The old lady in the traveling cloak pressed her hands to a cup of hot tea and nodded. She was amused by the brothers.

"First," she said, "the death of Degas is not confirmed. The entire house was burned and there were dozens of skeletons in the ashes. But Lord Degas's body was never formally identified."

"Well . . . skeletons . . ." said ginger-hair, as if that explained it all.

"There was no signet ring on any corpse's finger, and his sword, Serpent's Tooth, was missing," she said.

"Missing presumed stolen," said the blond. "Is *he* the one you meant when you said you knew our brother?"

"No," said the old woman. "The brother I am talking about is Kagen."

The room went still.

They were in a small chamber in the basement of an estate owned by Lady Helleda Frost. It was far from where Helleda was recuperating, however, and only a few servants were present. Very loyal, very discreet servants. The place was less than three miles from where the highwaymen had ambushed the coach. The brothers had been content to wait until the staff of the mansion had been notified. They would attend to the honored dead and dispose of the ruffians.

Now the three of them—the old woman and the brothers—sat at a table in a richly appointed room with several bottles of exceptional wine standing open. No beer was available, but they did not seem to mind. Now, though, they sat with wine cups paused halfway to their open mouths.

"What *about* Kagen?" they asked at the same time.

"First," she said, "names." She pointed to the blond. "You are Jheklan Vale."

"Guilty as charged."

"Which makes you," she said to ginger-hair, "Faulker."

"Sure, but who are you? You've waited all this time to give us *your* name."

"My name is Frey."

The brothers exchanged a look, eyebrows raised.

"*Mother* Frey?" queried Faulker slowly.

"As in the chief investigator for the Office of Miracles?" added Jheklan.

"Once upon a time," said Frey.

"Holy shit," they both said.

"Hey, wait," said Faulker. "Mom knew you pretty well, as I recall. Weren't you a midwife or something at one point?"

"Before you became a nun," said Jheklan.

"I delivered your mother," said Frey, nodding. "And may the gods bless her soul."

Both of the brothers nodded, their smiles dimming.

"Still can't believe she's gone," said Faulker.

"I didn't think anyone or anything could beat her in a fight."

"Do you know *how* she died?" asked Mother Frey.

"Killed by Ravens at the palace," said Jheklan.

Frey made a disgusted face. "Ravens? Kill the Poison Rose? Oh please, be your age."

"Then . . . how?" asked Jheklan.

"Magic," said Frey. "The Witch-king had a razor-knight with him, and it was that monster who killed her. Nothing less could have."

They stared at her.

"Get the fuck out of here," said Faulker, laughing.

"A *razor-knight?*" snorted Jheklan. "And was it riding on a hippogriff?"

"With wood elves as footmen?" mocked Faulker.

"Hush," snapped Frey, and they shut their mouths at once. "Your mother died as she lived—a hero. When she passed, a light went out of this world that will never be rekindled. I delivered her and knew her, and you will not make jokes, sons or not, about how she died."

There was a long pause when the brothers looked at the walls, the ceiling, each other, and into their wine cups. Everywhere except at her.

"Sorry," said Faulker.

"Sorry," said Jheklan.

"But . . . a *razor-knight?*" said Faulker. "That's a pretty wild claim."

"Yeah," said Jheklan. "I thought they were storybook monsters."

"You will find," said Frey, "that some of the monsters of stories and legend are quite real. That they have been gone so long from our experience speaks to the power of the Silver Empire. That they are back speaks to the threat we all face. This is the age of the Witch-king, and he has brought dark magic back into our world. The razor-knights are not even the most terrible things we may yet behold."

"I . . ." began Jheklan, but he let it go, unable or unwilling to say more.

"If that's the case," said Faulker weakly, "then we are all screwed. What can *we*—mortal men and women—do against supernatural monsters?"

"Seriously," agreed Jheklan.

Mother Frey smiled thinly. "That razor-knight was killed by a mortal man."

The brothers looked at each other, eyebrows raised.

"Then we need to rally behind him," Jheklan said to Frey.

"Yes," said Frey, "we should rally behind him. And put great faith in him."

Faulker peered at her. "Who is this monster-killing hero of heroes?"

"His name, his name!" demanded Jheklan.

Frey studied them for a cold moment, then said, "That man's name is Kagen Vale."

CHAPTER THIRTY-FIVE

The dairyman grabbed the baker's lad and pulled him off the road as a platoon of Ravens rounded the bend and thundered past.

The soldiers seemed to come out of nowhere, and the road's curve around the gristmill and the thick grove of pecan trees had muffled their approach. The two villagers fell into a drainage ditch, but that was better than being trampled under all those hooves. The lieutenant leading the platoon turned in his saddle and snarled a curse, because it was his horse that had nearly collided with the young baker.

The dairyman lay sprawled in the mud with the lad half smothered beneath him, but he rolled off and let the boy breathe. Then, as the last of the riders passed, he climbed to his feet, gripped the boy's hand, and hauled him upright. They stood shakily by the side of the road and watched the Hakkians vanish around the next bend, disappearing behind the tanner's place.

"Gods of the Harvest," whispered the boy. He was young, but not so young that he was naive enough to say that curse too loudly. Swearing by the Harvest Gods was punishable by—at the very least—a beating across the buttocks, thighs, and kidneys with an inch-thick bamboo rod. The miller's eldest daughter still could not walk upright because of the beating she had received, and the lad heard that the girl was still pissing blood. Her face was waxy and jaundiced, too.

"There's more of them every damned hour of every damned day," complained the dairyman, who was rising thirty but looked older.

The boy nodded. "Pa says they're looking for the Rose's son."

"Aye, lad. There's a bounty on the head of young Captain Kagen."

"Dukis told my sister, who told me, that Captain Kagen nearly killed the Witch-king," said the lad in a conspiratorial voice. "Cut his nose off, he said."

The dairyman spat. "Dukis is the sad half of a half-wit, and t'other half's no genius."

"You saying the captain didn't fight the Witch-king?"

"Well now," said the dairyman, "I didn't say that. He did, and there's plenty of people who saw it firsthand or heard it secondhand from someone worth believing. But as for cutting off noses . . . nay, lad. There was none such mayhem."

"But . . ."

"What I heard was that the Rose's son fought the Witch-king to a standstill, and that's enough of a tale as needs no embellishment. Ordinary man fighting a wizard an' all. Strange times we live in."

They watched the empty road.

"If he didn't actually *hurt* the Witch-king," said the boy, "then why are they tearing up the roads and searching every house and barn to find him? And Dukis also said that there was a reward for turning in the captain. A mountain of gold."

The dairyman grunted. "Well, as for that . . . even Dukis the Dull has to be right once in a while. So, yes, there is a reward that would tempt a saint."

The boy looked troubled. "Do you think anyone we know would turn him in? I mean, with a fortune like that, whoever claimed the reward would be able to live like a king."

The dairyman turned to the boy and gave him a long, hard, flat stare.

"Lad," he said slowly, "you wouldn't be having bad thoughts now, would you?"

The boy blinked. "What? Me? No, I just . . ."

"I know what you were just. That's what the Hakkians are counting on. Someone being so greedy that he starts thinking more about that gold than anything. More than his family and town, more than his country. More, even, than his gods, which the Hakkians have pissed on. Tell me, boy, what kind of person would it take to stop *thinking* about that gold and actually whisper a word to the Hakkians?"

"I—"

"Think it through," said the dairyman, in a way that was not at all friendly. "Captain Kagen is the son of the Poison Rose, and we all know what she did for Argon. For the empire. No better and more honorable fighter ever drew steel. She *died* trying to save the empress and the Seedlings, and they cut her to pieces and fed the empress and her little ones to the hounds. Now, stand there and tell me about that reward and what it would mean to someone who loves his family, his town, his country, and the empire that was. Then you stand here and swear by the Harvest Gods as you start counting the coins the Hakkians want to pay to kill another of our own."

The boy looked at him and then down the road.

"I never would," he said. "I was just thinking out loud."

"And if you weren't my neighbor's boy, I'd take you behind the woodshed and teach you all about history and honor and justice."

"No," protested the lad. "I'd *never* tell anyone."

"Then listen sharp, boy, and chew on what I have to say," growled the dairyman. "If Captain Kagen Vale was in that barn yonder, or this mill right here, and the Hakkians were pulling up ten times ten wagons of gold, I'd cut out my own tongue before I said a word. So would your ma and da. So would all of the decent people in this town and every other town in Argon. Maybe you heard about what's happened to a few loose-tongued louts down in Crossplains and over to Red Valley, or up in Falcon's Pass. If not, ask about *them* before you mouth off about what blood money would buy."

The boy was trembling now and there were tears in his eyes. "I would never," he said. "Never ever."

The dairyman laid his callused hands on the boy's shoulders. They were hard and heavy. "Okay," he said. "I believe you. But loose words, even such as speculating on gold and riches, are nearly as bad as whispering a word in a Hakkian ear. Just saying it aloud might plant a seed in someone else's mind, and you wouldn't want that, would you?"

"No," said the boy in a whisper.

The older man pointed to the road. "Those Hakkians nearly rode us down, and would have done, had I not caught the sound in time to pull us both out of the way. Think about that. The Hakkians want Captain Kagen so bad they'd have trampled us and left us bleeding or dead. And that's the least of what they would do. Think on that. Think about what happened here today and what it means. There's a lesson in it, lad, and I'd like to think you're smart enough—and *loyal* enough—to pick that lesson apart for the best bits. Do that and it'll tell you how to act, what to say, and even what to think. Then use that understanding to plant a better crop of thoughts in your own head. Hear me?"

The boy nodded, slowly at first, then he gave a final and more decisive nod. "I will. And . . . I'm sorry."

"No, boy, I don't want you to be sorry," said the dairyman. "I want you to be *true*. Can you do that?"

The boy slowly straightened his spine and squared his shoulders. "Yes," he said. "I can." Then he corrected himself. "Yes, I will."

The dairyman smiled and gave his shoulders a squeeze. "Good lad," he said. "The Rose would be proud of you."

CHAPTER THIRTY-SIX

Zehria was not the most powerful of nations in the west. It was landlocked and shared its border with several key nations of the Silver Empire—Nehemite, Narek, Ghul, Hakka, and the Waste. But also unaffiliated Bulconia to the north, a land known for the quality of its steel, but feared for how actively its people liked to use steel swords and axes against its neighbor. Granted, Ghul and Narek were much smaller countries, but the former had tin and copper mines and the latter diamonds. Zehria's primary natural resource was sheep and goats.

And espionage.

It was not hard to understand why a nation that shared borders with six other countries would invest so much time and effort in the cultivation of a network of agents. Those spies had kept Zehria safe for two thousand years with but a few stumbles. The invasion by Hakkians on the Night of the Ravens was a hotly debated point among spymasters in Zehria because every other nation had been equally deceived. That left the intelligence networks of each nation in a state of great confusion. After all, spycraft was hardly a match for witchcraft.

Islak Horchleberg was the spymaster general for Vulpion the Gray, king of Zehria. She was a stooped, gaunt woman with very large eyes. That angular posture and those eyes had earned Islak the nickname "Mantis," and it was by that name that the king addressed her.

Mantis never reported to her master in his throne room, nor ever in front of the royal staff. Their meetings were naturally clandestine and were held in a chamber in a tower reserved for the Silent Scribes—a brotherhood who spent their days creating beautiful, illuminated copies of sacred texts. Mantis was publicly believed to be a book merchant specializing in expensive rarities, and so her frequent visits to the tower were taken for granted, and the mundane nature of her false job rendered her virtually invisible. Especially in times like these, when the sale or purchase of dusty old volumes hardly measured against the invasion or the threat of open warfare.

On a fine winter morning—balmy, as it often was in the southern part of the empire—Mantis entered the palace through the tradesmen's door and made her way through the hallways to the tower. The sentries nodded her along without needing to see her papers. She offered each one a bland and meaningless smile and scuttled along with a ribbon-bound bundle of books under one arm.

Halfway up the stairs, at a point where it was not possible for anyone at the foot or the top of the stairs to observe her, she stopped and pressed two tiles in a mosaic of flights of butterflies. There was a faint *click* and a narrow section of wall swung inward. She slipped inside and closed the secret panel behind her.

Mantis groped her way along the inner wall until she reached a more ordinary door made of metal-banded oak. She turned the handle to the left and then to the right and finally straight up, disengaging a complex lock of her own devising. The door opened on silent and well-oiled hinges, and she stepped into a room lit by several oil lamps.

A man sat at the far end of a plain wooden table.

Mantis set her books down and bowed deeply.

"Your Majesty."

The king inclined his head and waved her to a chair. Wine cups stood by a bottle, and the king poured one for each of them, passing hers across. They raised their cups in a shared toast.

"To freedom," said the king.

"And confusion to the Witch-king," replied Mantis.

They drank. It was a rich and complex Bulconian red that was, admittedly, superior to anything made in Zehria.

"How are things progressing?" asked the king. "What have the butterflies told you?"

"Butterflies" was a code name they shared for the field agents of Mantis's spy network. In day-to-day life, a butterfly is often seen but seldom deeply contemplated.

"We are having a bit of fun, Majesty."

"Oh? Tell me."

"My butterflies have started a few minor skirmishes with Bulconian border patrols, tricking them into crossing into our lands and thereby breaking old treaties. Local magistrates have then appealed to the Hakkians to protect us, and that's drawn Raven troops north, and also shifted the focus of their spy network. After all, the Witch-king's occupying forces cannot be seen to fail in their protection of *potential* member states."

That membership was officially pending, because the Hakkian king had not been legally crowned.

The king smiled as he took a sip of wine.

"That's a lovely plan."

Mantis inclined her head. "One of several plans, my lord, each of which draws the eyes of their spies away from any place in which our troops are mustering and training."

The king raised his glass again.

"To deception and obfuscation," he toasted.

"I will always drink to that, Majesty."

CHAPTER THIRTY-SEVEN

"Why are we leaving so gods-damn early?" complained Kagen blearily. He sat on the edge of his bed, knuckling sleep from his eyes. Even with a new stack of logs blazing in the fireplace, the room was frigid. "Sun's not even up."

"That's what 'leave at first light' actually means," said Filia, who was dressed and lounging against the door frame with a tin mug of hot tea cradled between her palms. "By the time you finish packing it'll be dawn."

"Grumble, grumble, grumble," said Kagen, actually speaking the words.

"Soft city boy," said Filia, but her smile was kindly.

Kagen leaned over and fished for his travel bag under the bed. "How long a ride is it to where we're going?"

"Well . . ." she said, drawing it out. "If we went straight along the road, we'd be there in five days."

He looked up at her suspiciously. "And sleep *where* in the meantime?"

"Out of doors."

Kagen pulled out the bag and grunted. "Five days isn't too bad." Then he gave her a suspicious look. "Wait . . . you said *if* we went straight along the road . . ."

"There are Hakkian patrols everywhere," she said. "And since you tried to kill their king, we can assume a certain level of inhospitableness. Not to mention that price on your head. Caution seems smarter than haste, don't you think?"

Kagen stood up and began reaching for his clothes, stuffing them roughly into the leather bag. "And how long will the cautious route take us?"

"A fortnight, give or take."

He stared at her. "And camping outside the whole time? It's almost winter, you know. In the actual frozen north."

Filia sipped her tea and merely smiled.

"I hate you," said Kagen.

"I'll survive."

"Where's Tuke?"

"Seeing to the horses."

"I hate him, too."

"I'll make sure to tell him," she said dryly. "I'm sure he'll want to set aside time later to weep."

Kagen was too fuzzy-headed to conjure a really good insult, so instead he asked, "Can we at least have a hot meal first?"

"We will have something hot to eat on the road," said Filia.

"I really, really hate you."

Filia laughed and went downstairs.

They left at dawn.

CHAPTER THIRTY-EIGHT

"The reports are as we expected," said Nespar.

He stood on one side of a long wooden table that had been brought into the newly minted Hall of Hakkian Heroes. The Witchking sat across from him, and Lord Jakob Ravensmere loitered at head of the table, though he stood, rather than making the error of claiming that seat. Bowls of fruit, plates of bread and cheese, and bottles of wine littered the table. Wine cups acted as weights to hold the edges of large maps in place. The king's hounds chewed lazily on the beef bones tossed to them by their master.

"He's right, Majesty," agreed Jakob. "Everyone is arming for war. Even the unaffiliated city-states in the foothills of the Cathedral Mountains are getting ready."

"The Bulconians as well," said Nespar.

Bulconia was a large and powerful nation crouched on the northeast corner of the old empire, with the mountains forming a sturdy wall to guard its back. It had never joined the Silver Empire and had more than once become a credible and dangerous threat.

"Will Bulconia attack us?" asked the Witch-king. "Or will they begin picking off the small nations around them?"

"The latter is most likely," said Jakob, and the chamberlain nodded agreement.

"Yes, they want the vineyards of Zaare," said Nespar, "and it's a good chance they will attempt to annex the eastern reaches of Nelfydia and Vahlycor to claim governance over caravan routes and, in the latter case, the wheat, barley, and rye fields."

"Agreed," said Jakob. "That way they can claim they are retaking lands once stolen from them. Which is, let's face it, true enough. And it would allow them to do so without overtly offending you, Majesty. Their attack would be a patriotic move rather than an aggressive one. Or at least that's how they'll sell it."

"I think it's likely that Nelfydia may even be working on some kind of under-the-table partnership for that," said Nespar. "They were allies a long time ago, and if you go back two thousand years, they were part of the Northern Alliance."

"Who do we have in Nelfydia?" asked the king.

"Agents in every important town," said Nespar.

"Who is up there looking for Kagen Vale?"

Jakob said, "It's unlikely Kagen would go so far away, lord. The Nelfydians are slow to rally to any cause that doesn't directly serve them, and they rest comfortably knowing that they are strategically unimportant in the present ... ah ... circumstances. We got very little push-back from them during the Night of the Ravens, and even less since."

"All the more reason Kagen might go there," said the Witch-king. "He's clever enough to realize that we would be unlikely to be actively looking for him there, what with Vahlycor, Zaare, and Theria being more usefully placed."

Nespar gave a small bow to acknowledge the point. "I can send a few hundred scouts up there by ship."

"Do that," said the king, "but also put out word through the network of brotherhoods."

Jakob looked confused. "Pardon, Majesty, but the 'network of brotherhoods'? I'm not familiar with that."

Nespar explained. "While we were preparing for the ascension of His Majesty, we seeded the ground—if I may borrow a phrase from the Harvest faith—by providing funding and other kinds of support to various groups of believers. Underground churches, radical cults, and secret temples scattered throughout the Silver Empire. Because Nelfydia is so distant and so inhospitable, it tends to attract some of the more extreme groups of splinter religions. Not necessarily worshippers of Hastur, you understand, but groups seeking the freedom to practice their own beliefs without the Office of Miracles breathing down their necks."

"Ah," said the historian. "I had heard rumors of such cults in the north but did not realize they were under Hakkian protection." He pursed his lips in thought for a moment. "And you say that these groups, despite ideological differences, are allies?"

"They are," said Nespar. "Not necessarily of each other, but of us . . . and our generosity, yes."

"After a thousand years of religious intolerance and repression," said the Witch-king, "you'll learn that we have quite a few very useful allies."

"I am encouraged to hear that, Majesty," said the historian.

The Witch-king nodded and to Nespar said, "Send messengers by land and sea to tell them that Kagen Vale may be coming that way. Offer whatever rewards would best suit each group. Tailor your bribes and encouragements."

"Of course, Majesty," said Nespar.

"What else do you both have for me?" asked the king, changing the subject.

"Theria has begun sending coded messages to Samud and some of the island nations. We intercepted one message and I can verify that the courier did not have the key to that code. And our code breakers have yet to decipher it."

"Will they?"

"In time, Majesty, without doubt," said Jakob. "But it is a clever code. One of the best I've ever seen. I am working with Lord Nespar and his spymaster to try to entice a Samudian noble to our side. Someone who is in a position to know the key to that code."

Nespar smiled. "The noble in question has a taste for little boys," he said. "We are encouraging that but also collecting witness statements. Whereas homosexuality is no crime in Samud, bedding children is."

The Witch-king nodded again.

The meeting went on for another two hours, with one after another report from field agents being presented and discussed, and actions considered. When the entire business was done, Nespar and Jakob waited for their master to comment. The Witch-king brooded over the maps and messages, then sat for long minutes stroking the ugly head of the bitch of his pack. His love for the dog was obvious, and the animal was entirely devoted to him.

Finally, he said, "War is coming."

This was not news, but both of his advisors knew it was a preamble, and so they waited.

"I know our generals and admirals are worried that we will be unprepared, should two or more of the nations form an alliance and make a move. It is, indeed, worrisome. We have more to lose than we have gained."

He let the big hound play-bite his fingers.

"But I want you both to rest assured that we are not unprepared for war," continued the king. "Though the war that is coming is one we will fight on *our* terms and with *our* weapons."

"And, sire, which weapons in particular?" queried Jakob.

"That," said the Witch-king, "will depend on how quickly the other nations complete their preparations, and if they form an alliance that leaves us no other choice."

"Majesty," said Nespar, "is there something we can tell our officers so they have more confidence? That matters, because if they look uncertain, that unease will ripple down through the ranks. There are already reports of some desertions in the more remote provinces."

"Much of what I have planned would frighten our own generals all the more," said the Witch-king, and he gave a rare laugh. "But I take your point, Lord Nespar. Yes, I will prepare something useful to share with our generals. Nespar, arrange a meeting with them. We will have a council of war."

"Excellent, Majesty."

"Between us, though," said the King in Yellow, gesturing to his two advisors, "it is important that you have faith in me. It is important that you have faith in our god, Hastur, for he has not abandoned us. Believe me when I tell you that we have more allies on our side than you know. Powerful allies who will come at my call and who will bring with them all the horrors of hell. Even now these powers rise from a sleep of centuries. Even now veils are being rent asunder and our allies step through from their worlds into ours. The very ground trembles with the footfalls of beings whose nature is so terrible it explains why the Silver Empire labored so long and hard to erase magic from the world. That plan has failed utterly, and Death itself raises the yellow flag of Hakkia." He paused. "Nespar, you may expect some visitors very soon."

"May I know who they are?"

"You will know them when they arrive," said the King in Yellow. "Have no doubts about that."

With that, the Witch-king concluded the meeting and, his pack in tow, left the room.

CHAPTER THIRTY-NINE

Filia knew the region best and led them through the southern forests of Nelfydia, and then took them north. The forests thinned at first but then grew dense as they entered a world that seemed composed of nothing but pine trees. The land was hilly, but Filia steered them away from the taller mountains, each of which was white with new snow.

The going was tough, but safer for all that. They swapped stories as they rode, or sometimes let the miles pass by in silence. The nights were very long and very cold, and more than once the three of them had to huddle together close to a fire. The horses did not like the cold, especially Jinx, who was not at all used to snow. They passed through a small trading outpost far from any city and of no strategic importance to attract the Hakkians. The travelers bought extra furs for themselves and the horses, and thereafter the going was easier.

For all the cold, game was plentiful, and Filia brought down a deer with her bow. Tuke surprised his friends by displaying excellent cooking skills. With a bellyful of roast venison, Kagen felt more enthusiastic about the journey. However, he was delighted to see the lights of a town as dusk caught up to them on that fourteenth day.

"Welcome to Traveler's Rest," said Filia.

"Is that the name of an inn?" asked Kagen.

"Name of the town," she said. "The inn's at the edge of it, near the woods."

His enthusiasm dimmed a bit as they approached it. The place was barely a town. It had a few scattered farms, some houses and businesses clustered together near a frozen river, a stable attached to an inn, and not much else. The residents all looked like they were related, and with more than a little obvious inbreeding. Every building was gray with soot and dirt, and there were damn few smiles to be seen.

"Bear's Mark," announced Filia, nodded at a big old building with pitched roofs, faded shingles, grimy windows, and desultory smoke curling from half a dozen chimneys. "As far from anywhere important as you can get. We'll be safe here."

"Charming place you've brought me to," Kagen groused as they dismounted outside of the dilapidated inn.

A grubby stable lad of about fifteen took charge of their horses and he, at least, seemed to have a flicker of intelligence in his eyes. Kagen thought the kid would leave this town behind him as soon as he could. The inn itself looked about as inviting as a prison, and Kagen said as much as he and the others tramped up the stairs to their rooms.

"Feel free to go camp in the woods," said Filia.

Kagen told her and Tuke what they could go do to themselves. It was obscene, improbable, painful, and humiliating. Filia laughed.

Tuke said, "Hey, what did *I* do?"

"You were born, grew up, fell in love with that witch," said Kagen, jerking his chin toward Filia. "And basically became a pain in my ass."

Tuke considered. "Fair enough."

Kagen had a small room to himself—little more than a closet, really. Tuke and Filia had a bigger suite, and Kagen tried hard not to hate them more than he did.

But the tavern downstairs was warm and there was a massive blaze in the fireplace. The food arrived, plentiful and much better than they expected. They dined on rabbit soup and roast goat, with black bread and salted butter.

Once the meal was demolished, they settled back with a board of cheese and nuts of a kind Kagen had never tried before, which they washed down with beer that was wonderfully bitter and thick.

"So," said Kagen, leaning back in his chair, his tankard resting on a full belly, his mood greatly improved, "when do we meet this Ghuraka?"

"In a few days," said Filia. "I sent word ahead from the port town, so she's expecting us. But she'll decide when—or even *if*—she'll see us."

"If? To the Pit with that," said Kagen. "I didn't come all this way to sit on my hands."

"Relax," soothed Tuke. "She'll see us. Ghuraka enjoys making people wait on her. Worst case is we stay here for a week. Ten days at best."

"It won't be that long," said Filia.

"And what will we be doing all that time?" asked Kagen.

"Relaxing?" suggested Tuke.

"I'm serious."

"So am I."

Filia said, "Look, Kagen . . . there's a garden half a day's ride from here. You could go there."

He looked at her in surprise. "Why on earth would I want to do that?"

She shrugged. "Meditate? Pray? See if the gods have forgiven you?"

He glared at her for a moment before realizing she was in earnest. He left a biting comment unsaid. Instead, he plucked up a piece of sharp cheese and munched it, musing on her suggestion.

"Maybe," he said.

Shortly after, they all went to bed.

Kagen lay awake for a long time. He tried not to hear the gasps and moans and cries coming from the other room. He tried not to remember the feel of Filia—both soft and strong—in his arms. He tried not to think about his murdered parents. He tried not to imagine murdering Herepath. He tried not to feel the weight of his failures and his damnation.

In all of these endeavors, he failed utterly.

Sleep, though, stole up upon him and with the soft fingers of shadows pulled him beneath the surface. He plummeted into his personal darkness, and there, with all other cares now absent from his mind, he dreamed.

CHAPTER FORTY

DREAMS OF THE DAMNED

In the vastness of dreamland, Kagen once more walked through the frozen lands. It was not Nelfydia, though. He was positive that he was once more in the Winterwilds, in the heart of a vast glacier.

He was fourteen again, though only in body. His mind was his adult self, and even though this had happened in other dreams, it nevertheless felt alien and new and unwelcome. The walls were blue-white and seemed as if they were lit from within. And everywhere the air around him seemed to reek, as if meat was stored there but had begun to thaw. And rot.

Far ahead of him there was a sound, and he paused—as he had done in other such dreams—thinking that it was a voice. Either Herepath's or that of some creature speaking in an unknown tongue.

But this was neither. He cocked his head to try to capture what he was hearing and slowly realized that it was a physical sound rather than a voice. A scratching. Very slow, and with the steady regularity of someone or something laboring for a very long time.

He moved forward, following the noise, and could soon make out the distinctive sound of a sharpness to the scraping. Not like that of a tool, but less wholesome.

Fingernails.

Endlessly scratching at the ice.

That realization chilled him more than the ice that surrounded him.

He reached for his daggers, but they were not there. Of course they wouldn't be. At fourteen he owned no fighting knives like that. His mother still lived, and she wore the matched pair. All that hung from his belt was a thin, short ceremonial knife. Hardly a dagger at all, and with a blade better suited to slicing open fruit than fighting. It made him worse than young—he felt naked.

Kagen hurried along, wanting to flee this place and yet drawn to the scratching sounds.

"Gods of the Harvest," he said in a voice that was a child's, filled with the unshakeable faith he once owned. He tried to wrest control of his voice from the child, but that power was beyond him in that moment.

He moved forward, somewhat dazed, as if hypnotized. His feet tripped over irregularities in the ice floor. He caromed off of corners as the corridor twisted and turned. And then the tunnel made a very sharp turn and he jerked to a stop as he was confronted with a dead end.

Kagen began to turn to retrace his steps, but he stopped again as the scratching sound filled the air, much louder and clearer than before.

He looked at the walls of ice, which were as hard as granite, and saw in the dim light that something was inside the nearest wall. A shape, vague and dark. Something trapped in all that ice. Trapped here in the heart of the glacier. What had Herepath once told him?

"The ice here is tens of thousands of years old, little brother. We have found artifacts behind these walls that belong to an age of the world so ancient there are not even rumors about it. No songs or stories tell of these things."

Kagen considered this, fighting to recall everything Herepath had said, knowing there was one thing more. Something very important. It was just there, at the edge of his memory, and he fumbled for it, scrabbling at that memory.

He caught it but it made no sense.

Or it had not when Kagen first had this dream, all those years ago. It startled his adult, sleeping mind to realize that this was, in fact, an echo of a dream. Which was why he had no power over the fourteen-year-old Kagen.

"Such things as these are only hinted at in books," Herepath had said. "Books that no one alive can read. Books no sane mind can decode."

"Then how do you know what those books say?" younger Kagen had asked.

But Herepath's answer was only a smile.

It was an awful smile, stretching too wide, as strange lights ignited in his eyes.

It was then, all those years ago, that his younger self awoke sweating and scared.

But now Kagen did not wake up. He stood there in that young body, watching with his adult eyes as the shadowy thing within the ice pawed at its prison. It scratched and scratched and scratched. Patient as time itself. Indefatigable.

Clawing its way out.

Only then did Kagen Vale come awake, stifling a scream.

But the echo of those scratching fingernails still haunted the air around him.

CHAPTER FORTY-ONE

When they were alone and the hall was quiet as a tomb, Nespar took a bottle of wine over and sat down next to Jakob Ravensmere. He filled their cups and the two men drank.

"How is Lady Kestral?" asked the historian. "I have not seen her in days."

"She is doing the king's work," said Nespar.

"That isn't what I asked."

Nespar sipped and stared at one of the wall hangings for quite a while. "She is dying, I think."

Jakob looked surprised, then his expression softened into concern. "She's more than a colleague, I take it. She is your friend?"

"For years," said Nespar. "Yes. We were the first two people the Witch-king brought into his inner circle. And she was crucial to the events of the Night of the Ravens. Without her . . . well, the credit for removing the Poison Rose as a threat is mainly hers."

"You mean because she conjured a razor-knight?" asked Jakob, and he could not suppress the shiver that rippled through him.

Nespar nodded. "That was a feat of the greatest magic, and it very nearly killed her."

"And now he's asked her to do it again," mused Jakob. "I hope she survives it."

Nespar merely shook his head.

They drank in silence.

"Tell me, Nespar," said Jakob. "Do you have even the *slightest* idea what His Majesty is talking about? These allies? These weapons? What are they?"

Nespar gave another shake of his head.

"Are these actual people? Real armies?" demanded Jakob in frustration.

"Define *real*," said the chamberlain.

The historian looked around and then leaned closer and lowered his voice. "Some might say that such claims speak of wild hope. Or madness."

The older man studied him with shrewd eyes. "Some might say such speculation is treason."

"I did not say *I* said so. But we have generals and nobles and armies. We have an entire people to protect and defend."

"Since when are you a patriot?"

"Since Hakkia has become my country," said Jakob. "I am Hakkian henceforth or I am nothing."

Nespar considered, then nodded. "Fair enough."

"And when I ask these questions, it is because I want my new country not only to succeed but to *endure*. Let's face it, Nespar, the Night of the Ravens could just as easily have gone horribly wrong. Right now we are less of a conquering army and more like an armed camp. If our own people are losing confidence, imagine what that is doing to the zeal of our enemies."

"Oh, I am well aware of that," said Nespar. "It's why my digestion is in total disarray and I haven't had a good night's sleep since I left Hakkia."

"Then tell me what fuels your confidence that everything is well in hand."

Nespar sipped and avoided Jakob's eyes. Finally, he set his cup down, "I know the Witch-king better than you do, my friend. I have been his man for six years now. I've seen him emerge from nothing, a nobody from rural Hakkia that no one ever heard of."

"Gethon Heklan," said Jakob. "I've done the research. He was less than nothing, which makes all of this"—he waved around to indicate the palace and all it represented—"even more incredible."

"Oh yes," agreed Nespar. "Almost overnight he began gathering dissident groups to him, building a base of power. Then he led the purges that removed countless collaborators working with the Silver Empire. He cleansed our schools, our courts, our military, until everyone aligned with him was truly *his*."

"Tell me . . . at what point did he begin wearing that veil?"

Nespar cut him a look. "From the beginning of his political career. From just before I met him."

"And you're certain that the face behind the veil belongs to Gethon Heklan?"

"I am."

"Why are you certain?"

Nespar considered. "Faith," he said. "No, rest easy, Jakob. Our king is the man we think he is."

"Mm," was all Jakob said.

"And I was there, Jakob," continued the chamberlain, "when he first demonstrated the *power* he has."

"You mean magic?"

"Oh yes. Very dark, very powerful, and very *Hakkian*. He revived the religion of Hastur, which had been cruelly suppressed for centuries. He demonstrated powers that could only have come from the gods. He took the mantle of Witch-king without a single voice of dissent from our own people. And in one night he conquered our conquerors."

"And all of this is grand. It's impressive and terrifying and glorious," said Jakob. "But now what? Who are our allies and when can we count on them?"

"The gods only know," said Nespar.

They sat and drank for a long, long time.

CHAPTER FORTY-TWO

The royal twins played in a small courtyard tucked into a corner of the palace. It was surrounded on all sides by high stone walls, open to the sky, though the walls and high towers allowed sunlight to reach the spot for only two hours on either side of high noon. Most of the time the courtyard was shrouded in shadows of varying colors of purple, gray, and black.

Foscor and Gavran liked those darker hours. They hated the sunlight. It made their skin crawl and gave them headaches.

Desalyn and Alleyn hated the shadows and loved the light.

It said everything about the four aspects of those two children. Everything.

CHAPTER FORTY-THREE

"Father," said the little girl, "what *is* that?"

She was seven. A slender child with straw-colored hair, huge eyes, and a slight lisp. Her dress was made from homespun—plain and cheap but cut well and brave in ribbons. A circlet of daisies crowned her head, and a string of smaller flowers hung around her neck. She clung to her father's tunic, peering out carefully around him. He was a big man, a groom with rough hands and kind eyes. He always smelled of horses, but the girl liked that and loved every horse in the vast stables on the estate.

Her father took a long time in answering. He reached back and laid a hand on her back, gently closing her in the protective sandwich of that hand and his thigh. His other hand rested on the handle of a battered old knife he used for everything from cutting weeds from riding paths to dressing rabbits he caught in his traps.

They stood on a slope that was part of the downs used for morning exercise of the racing horses on which his master's fortune had been built. Although the estate was huge, one of the largest in northern Argon, he knew every inch of it, every tree and bird and gully. What he saw now, however, made him frown with unease.

An animal grazed a dozen yards from where father and daughter stood. It rooted in the withered autumn grass for the greenest of the fallen leaves, then stood chewing, looking at the people with large brown eyes.

"Is it a deer?" asked the girl.

"Aye, lass," said her father, though he sounded uncertain.

"Why is it all white?"

Her father chewed the fringe of his thick mustache and studied the beast. It was a deer, though of a kind he had never seen before. It was very frail and moved with a peculiar delicacy. Each tiny hoof was bright, as if polished, and on one shoulder was a spattering of marks that at first appeared to be droplets of mud but on closer observation were more clearly natural coloring. Each mark was a rich brown, nearly the color of beef gravy. What caught the eye was the pattern they made. The marks swirled in a spiral so perfect it looked intentional, as if painted on.

"It's just a deer," said her father. "A bit rare is all."

"It's so pretty."

"Aye, it is that."

"You don't think the gamekeeper will kill it, do you?" she asked, suddenly alarmed. "For the Harvest feast, I mean."

"Not if he knows his trade," said her father. "And old Moegrin is no fool."

Moegrin was a good gamekeeper whose family had done that job for the same family these last three hundred years.

"And we won't hurt 'er either, sweetie. It's bad luck to kill a white deer."

"Bad luck?"

"That's what my gram used to tell me when I was your age. She said that seeing a white deer meant that there was big change coming. Don't ask me what kind, because it was always different. Sometimes good, sometimes bad. But if you *killed* one, then it would be bad indeed. Very bad."

"Who would kill such a thing?" cried the girl. "It's so sweet and gentle."

"Yes, and I think that's the point," said her father, smiling gently. "If someone were to kill something so pure, then it would mean that there was darkness in that person's heart.

"Master Moegrin is a good man, though, isn't he?"

"He is that," her father assured her. "Good, and smart enough to know a good move from a bad one."

The white deer munched an oak leaf and watched the humans. Then it lifted and turned its head as if hearing something they could not. Then it was off with a flick of its fluffy tail, vanishing into the dense undergrowth as surely as if it had truly disappeared.

"Oh," said the little girl sadly. Then she called out, "Run away and be safe, little deer." Then she turned and grasped her father's hand. "Oh no, he's heading toward Prince's Fall."

They looked that way, and neither spoke for a few moments.

Prince's Fall was a section of the woods, by a stream, where shadows seemed to dwell and sunlight always struggled to break through the canopy of leaves. It was an unlucky place, where no one went willingly. The girl's father had expressly forbidden her to ever go that way, and she obeyed without question. She was a sensitive child, and even the thought of Prince's Fall filled her with sickness. Moegrin had once described the big sections of chiseled stone jutting out from a mossy slope. No one seemed certain whether they were the remnants of some fortress that had fallen in ages past or were all that was to be seen of something buried beneath the dirt. Moegrin said that no sane person would ever go there with a shovel to try to find out. A few fools had done so, he said, and were never heard from again.

Now that beautiful little deer was wandering that way.

They stood there, tall father and small daughter, watching the wall of forest. Birds serenaded them from their cloister among the leaves, and the last of the season's dragonflies drifted sleepily in no particular direction. Anywhere except toward Prince's Fall.

After a few quiet minutes the father picked his daughter up and sat her astride his shoulders, holding on to her ankles while she clung happily to his thick black hair. They headed over the hill and back toward the stables.

Deep in the woods, the white deer picked its way carefully through brambles and thorny vines, questing for a safe place to nest, because evening was not too far off. It found a path worn nearly flat by other animals and for a while it meandered that way, drawn by the sound of a chuckling brook.

Then it stopped at a place where a chunk of stone jutted out to the very edge of the game trail. The stone was covered in moss and weeds, but it was more solid and paler than any of the local rocks. The edges, though softened by centuries of wind and rain, were sharply cut, and had there been a more discerning eye to study them, old chisel marks were there to be seen. The rest of the structure to which that errant stone belonged was buried under a mound of dirt that rose high and blended into the rolling hills. Trees had grown tall and old on that hill, and their roots dug deep to clutch at every crack and irregularity in the carved granite.

The deer paused, sniffing at the weeds that grew on the stone. They were darker than others of their species growing elsewhere, their stalks bent and gaunt, their leaves oddly shaped. The deer took a single experimental nibble at one leaf but immediately spat it out, not liking that taste at all.

It began to retreat from the stone—and from the hill—but before it had moved two full steps away, something shot out of the ground and caught it. The thing was shaped like a human hand, but it was far too thin, cadaverous, with dusty tendons mottled with warts and moles and diseased pustules. It smelled not of death but of a life that could never be conquered by death. The skeletal fingers closed around the deer's throat, cutting off its scream of pain and terror. Each finger ended in a wicked black claw, tearing into the flawless white fur, exploding it so that blood sprayed the diseased weeds. The deer fought and kicked, tried to rear, tried to break free . . . but the hand held it fast. Held and squeezed and crushed until the deer's brown eyes rolled high and white. The spindly legs buckled and the deer collapsed, its dying heart pumping blood onto the edge of the stone.

The blood seeped into the ground, soaking the soil but not lingering there. It faded quickly, as if the earth itself sucked it down a dark and hungry gullet. The deer shuddered and then lay still, its eyes glazing and tongue lolling.

A second hand punched through the topsoil and grabbed the deer's shoulder, claws tearing the flaccid flesh. Then, in a flash, the entire animal was pulled down into the dirt.

Silence fell over the forest as every bird and bug held its breath in abject terror. Even the grass trembled there, in Prince's Fall. Far away, on the far side of a cloudless horizon, thunder growled as if the sky itself was in pain.

CHAPTER FORTY-FOUR

Lord Nespar felt the cold creep in at the edges of his awareness.

At first the chamberlain thought it was a vagabond breeze, one of those drafts that seem to thrive in palaces as large and old as the one there in Argentium. He was seated on a couch in a small apartment off the main entrance foyer, a cloak pulled around his narrow shoulders as he read through a stack of reports from his various agents. A stack of big pine logs crackled in the fireplace, and heavy drapes hung in front of the tall windows.

He sipped some mulled wine, sniffed his stuffy nose clear, pulled the cloak more tightly around him, and kept reading. But as he began the process of decoding the message from his man in Zaare, Nespar paused, staring at the air in front of him. His breath plumed out as if he were standing on a country lane in the middle of winter.

"Boy!" he yelled, and on the instant a servant came hustling out of the adjoining scullery. "There you are. Check the windows. One of them must be open. I'm freezing to death in here, damn your eyes."

The servant scurried around the room and reported that all was secure. Nespar cursed him for a fool and ordered him to build the fire bigger, even though the burning logs already threatened to tumble out of the firebox.

Nespar settled back into his chair, cold, disgruntled, and dissatisfied. The news from his spies was not surprising but also not encouraging. Every nation in the former empire was quietly but steadily bulking up its armies. In Behlia they were remanning a line of old forts that had long since been abandoned. In Zaare, merchants working for the crown were buying sturdy horses— ostensibly for farming and hauling timber, but more likely to be used for cavalry. And on and on.

He finished the latest letter, wrote and coded a reply, and then started in on another letter, this one from an agent who was under cover with the Unbladed up in Nelfydia. Less than halfway through the letter he was interrupted by a page, who came in bobbing and bowing and stood looking frightened and uncertain in the doorway.

"What is it?" snapped Nespar waspishly.

"There are . . . um . . . *people* here to see His Majesty," said the page, a girl of thirteen whose uncle was a captain of palace guards.

"Did they present proper credentials?" asked the chamberlain, holding his hand out and snapping his fingers. But the page shook her head.

"No, master," she said, her eyes wide and filled with shadows.

Nespar began to snap at her, but then saw how visibly shaken she was. Frowning, he rose and crossed to her.

"What is it, girl? Why are you trembling like that?"

The girl tried to explain, but she kept shooting nervous glances toward the door. Her explanation became a stammering nothing. Nespar, who liked her uncle, patted her shoulder.

"Very well, child," he said gently. "I'll come and see for myself."

He left her there and went out into the foyer, which was wide and long and grandly appointed with classic statuary on marble platforms, bronzes in niches, and gorgeous paintings from the best artists in the empire. Except for a few statues too heavily connected with the line of empresses, the rest of the artwork was left over from before the invasion. Nespar had thought that fitting, since it showed respect for the culture of all of the member nations of the once and future empire.

As he stepped into the hall, though, he slowed almost to a

standstill. Partly because the air out there was dramatically colder than even his study. The faces on the statuary gleamed dully with a frosty rime. Even the nearby torches in their sconces seemed to withhold any reasonable heat.

The other reason he slowed was because of the visitors who clustered near the main doors. There were six of them, all about the same height and build, and each of them dressed in identical gray robes. The design was plain, even monastic, with rope bents and unusually yellow sigils embroidered on their chests. These monks—for surely that's what they were—had their cowls pulled forward to completely obscure their faces, and they kept their hands hidden in the opposite sleeves, with their arms folded across their middles. As it was, not one inch of their skin was visible.

The monks stood in silence, clearly waiting for someone of sufficient authority to deal with them. Nespar stopped ten feet away, unwilling to draw closer because the bitter cold seemed to hang around them as if they carried the low temperature with them.

"I am Nespar," he said gruffly, "lord chamberlain for His Majesty the Witch-king of Hakkia. Who are you to come here at night and without credentials?"

One of the monks, clearly the leader, took a half-step forward. "We have been summoned and so come here. Tell your master that the Brotherhood of the Yellow Sign have come in service to he who rules the heavens, the Shepherd God Hastur."

Nespar was intrigued but not convinced. "And yet you bring no token?"

The leader bowed slightly and dug into the folds of his robe. Nespar saw that his hand was gloved in gray silk. The item he withdrew was not a card or sealed scroll but was instead a small and ornately carved teak box.

"If a token is required," said the leader, holding the box out, "give your master this." But as Nespar reached for it, the monk added, "Do not dare to open that box, Lord Chamberlain."

Nespar took it gingerly. "Why? What is in it? A scorpion?"

It was a poor joke, and the audience was not receptive to it. The monk said, "It is a gift of great power."

The chamberlain studied the box, attempting to understand words written in some obscure script. But it might as well have been a language from the far side of the world.

"What does it say?"

The monks all made noises that might have been laughter but sounded more like the creaking of rusted chains.

The leader said, "Your master alone can read it."

Nespar gave him a withering glare. "Do you expect me to take an unknown object and hand it to my king? An object you say is so dangerous I should not open it? Forgive me, but that is highly irregular." He offered the box back to the leader. "I cannot accept this presentation on your terms."

The monk did not take back the box and instead stood silent and still.

"I insist that you take this back and leave the palace," said Nespar. "Must I call the guards?"

The leader took another small step forward. "Call your guards," he said quietly. "Call the full armies of Hakkia. We have been summoned by His Majesty and we will not be moved until we have answered that call in its fullest."

There was something in the man's dusty voice that touched Nespar on a deep level. He could feel the cold rolling off the man and felt his own heart grow cold.

"I . . ." he began, and then snapped his mouth shut. He stepped back and snapped his fingers for the guards, who, already alerted by the strangeness of the encounter, moved forward to surround the monks. Their spear points still pointed up, but no longer straight at the ceiling; now they tilted halfway down. Not a direct threat, but an eloquent one.

The monks did not move.

"Wait here," said Nespar sharply. He nodded to the guard sergeant and then whirled and stalked off to the main doors of the Hall of Hakkian Heroes.

Nespar had barely stepped into the chamber when he saw that the Witch-king was already there, surrounded by his hounds.

CHAPTER FORTY-FIVE

"Are we there yet?"

It was not the first—or the fortieth—time Kagen had asked that.

Finally, Filia turned in her saddle, eyes blazing, teeth bared, a savage rebuke on her lips. The vitriolic words nearly exploded from her. Then she saw the sneaky little smile lifting the corners of Kagen's mouth.

"You are a complete bastard," she said instead.

She cut a look at Tuke, whose body was shaking with silent laughter.

"You put him up to it, didn't you?"

He held up his hands. "Me? Innocent me? By the trembling balls of the Prince of Jesters, dare you accuse me of such a heinous crime?"

Filia's eyebrows rose into high, icy arcs.

"Well, guess who's not getting laid anytime soon."

Which made Kagen laugh and Tuke sulk.

They rode on, heading north.

CHAPTER FORTY-SIX

"If Your Majesty pleases," said Nespar, "a rather unusual party has arrived and is waiting in the hall."

The Witch-king stood by one of the ancient tapestries that hung on the wall between tall windows. The guards were forbidden to touch those hangings and were positioned so that not a plume or a flap of their cloaks would transgress. It was the King in Yellow's habit to stand and look at one or another of those tapestries, sometimes for hours, saying nothing. If he moved at all during such times it was not noticeable, as if he was a man transfixed and transformed into a statue.

After Nespar made his announcement, he waited through several long minutes until the Witch-king took a deep breath and exhaled through his nose, causing the yellow veil to flutter. He turned slowly, like a dreamer coming back to the waking world, and for a moment he stared at Nespar as if still not entirely aware.

Then he said, "Guests? Has the Prince of Games arrived so soon?"

"I beg your pardon, my king, but I am unfamiliar with anyone of that name."

"Then it is not he," murmured the Witch-king. "That, I suppose, is to be expected. He is never one to come when called but appears in his own good time."

Nespar had no idea what that meant and did not want to confuse an already challenging moment with another mystery.

"No, my lord," said Nespar. "It is a small group of what look like monks, though they declined to say from which order."

"What colors do they wear?"

"They are all in gray, Majesty," said the chamberlain. "They have no credentials, no papers of any kind. I was going to refuse them and have the guards turn them out, but the leader gave me this and said that it was a token you would recognize."

He held out the small box. After a moment, the Witch-king took it and examined it very closely. Despite Nespar's word of caution, he opened the box to reveal a small glass vial nestled in a bed of cotton. The vial was stoppered with cork and sealed with dark red wax. Nespar could see that it held a small quantity of an ugly red liquid that was thinner than blood but of the same deep shade of scarlet.

"Well, well," murmured the king. "This is indeed a surprise. Tell me, Nespar, are there six of these monks?"

"Just so, lord."

"Excellent. Send them in. But, Nespar . . . be careful not to touch them."

"Sire?"

"It would be inconvenient to have to find a new chamberlain."

Nespar croaked out a reply, then hurried to do this, passing through the tall, ornately carved doors, which the guards closed behind him. The Witch-king mounted the steps of the dais and sat upon his throne. His hounds were all asleep, but as one they snapped awake. Not because of the monarch's presence but because the very air of the great hall changed around them. Although warm sunlight slanted down through one of the huge windows, the temperature in the hall suddenly plunged. Mist seemed to coil out of the darkest corners, and it snaked along the floor, and the air grew moist and clammy. The breath of the dogs and the guards along the wall plumed out and the steam did not evaporate as quickly as it should have.

As the massive doors opened again, the pack shot to their feet, hair standing stiff as brushes along their spines. The great bitch snarled, her lips peeling back from yellow teeth.

The king touched her head very gently and the dog relaxed, but only a little bit.

"Easy, my girl," said the Witch-king. "There is no danger here for you or yours."

The dog turned her scarred and hideous face toward him, a look of vulnerable uncertainty in her brown eyes. He stroked her cheek.

The guards pulled wide the doors to reveal the knot of six figures in gray robes. Lord Nespar entered with them but shifted to stand well to one side. His staff *tap-tap-tap*ped on the marble as he hurried to reach the dais before the guests.

The visitors walked without haste toward the Witch-king, the skirts of their robes billowing with each slow step. They moved with an odd slowness, as if they existed in a dimension on the other side of a veil, one in which time progressed at a slower pace. Even the movement of their robes appeared out of sync with the ordinary pull of gravity. It called to Nespar's mind the way people walked in a pool of water, though the visitors seemed in no way oppressed by any kind of resistance. As they reached where he was standing, Nespar tried to catch some glimpse of their faces within the shadowy folds of their hoods, but he saw nothing. Only darkness and a sense of emptiness that was at odds with the way the robes draped on their shoulders and heads, backs and arms.

The group stopped ten feet from the dais and bowed in perfect unison.

Nespar glanced at the Witch-king for some sign whether to stay or go, but the king did not even glance his way.

"King of golden shadows," said their leader, "our god has called us and we have come."

"All praise to Lord Hastur," said the Witch-king. "I know that you have come a very long way in the service of him who we worship. You are welcome in my court."

"We serve our god and you are his priest on earth," said the leader. "In service of the Shepherd God we would cross oceans of fire."

"This I know," said the Witch-king. "And it is why you are beloved of him who is lord of all."

The monks bowed once again.

The leader spread his hands. "Your enemies are many, my lord. Hakkia, for all the strength it built while in hiding, cannot defend against an entire empire. Even a fractured one. War is coming, and though your enemies will underestimate your powers, when the last blade is bloodied and the last arrow quivering in its target of flesh, Hakkia will fall. Everything you have labored so long to build will be laid waste and the empire that rises from those ashes will do what even the Silver Empresses could not do . . . they will erase Hakkia from the knowledge of men. It will be struck from history. The churches of the Shepherd God will fall more completely than have the gardens your Ravens destroyed. The cities of Hakkia will be torn down and the very ground upon which they now stand will be sown with salt. And you, Majesty, will be burned to ash and those ashes hurled into the sea so that your spirit will have no rest and no substance for all eternity."

Nespar gasped. Had any other visitor—short of a royal person—said such a thing, he would have had the guards drag the offender down to the dungeons for reeducation with thumbscrews and hot pokers. He expected the Witch-king to do as much or worse, but the monarch in yellow merely laid his hands calmly on the arms of the throne.

"You have gone to very great efforts to school me on the realities of troop strength and military probabilities, my friends," the king said without rancor. "Or . . . has our lord Hastur sent you here for some more useful purpose?"

The leader of the monks bowed in acknowledgment of the comment and its implied rebuke. "As Your Majesty says, we are here for a higher purpose. In our dream, the Shepherd God walked among us in the form of a man. He spoke to us in languages spoken only by the dead, and yet we were able to understand everything. With but a thought he transported us to a place of snow and ice. Deep into the heart of a glacier."

The Witch-king sat slowly forward. "Did he now? And to what purpose?"

"He said that there are weapons hidden in the earth, Majesty.

Things of immeasurable antiquity and terrible power. That vial is but the merest artifact of the treasure trove waiting to be found."

"What treasures are these? I have already found the source of power and bled it for my magicks . . ."

The leader shook his cowled head. "We will not speak of dragons," he said.

"Then what? Have you found a cache of swords and shields? Have you found the siege engines of the ancient realms?"

"No, Majesty," said the leader, "our weapons do not cut or stab, nor will they topple stone walls. Look to that vial, Majesty, and you will understand."

"I demand that you tell me," said the Witch-king.

The leader was unmoved. "Majesty," he said calmly, "it would be better that I show you. If you will give me one of your advisors as a witness. Someone whom you trust." He paused and gestured to Nespar. "Not your chamberlain, however."

"I trust him implicitly," said the king.

"He is old and frail and his heart may not endure that which we desire to demonstrate. Besides . . . he is too valuable to you, Majesty. Perhaps your court necromancer? She is known to us and is very strong."

"No," said the Witch-king. "Lady Kestral is engaged in a special task for me and is not available. But I have someone in mind. My court historian."

The leader bowed. "He will do. And a squadron of soldiers. Archers. It is very important that we have archers."

The king studied his guests and then spent a long minute looking at the vial.

"You will have what you require," he said.

"And, beloved of Hastur," said the leader of the Hollow Monks, "so will you."

CHAPTER FORTY-SEVEN

There are places in this world where darkness itself is exulted. Shunned places. Unholy by any definition. Shadows live there, clinging not merely to the underside of rocks or the sides of stones facing away from the sun but even where shadows seem to exist despite the sunlight's assault. Places where darkness seems to hang like vines or creep like moss. Places that seem at all times to be owned by endless night.

The plants that grow there rise from the soil in twisted and painful ways, reaching not for the light but for whatever they can entangle. Their flowers spread great petals with voluptuous slowness, but any bee or butterfly that lands on them is suddenly trapped, enfolded, devoured. Animals—the older and wiser ones—fear such places and will go far out of their way to avoid them, even if those detours put them in the paths and between the teeth of predators. Better a clean and natural death than the alternative.

Those shunned places hide away, sneaky and obscure, subtle and patient. Year after year, century after century, they endure. Most of these fade away entirely, ground to dust by time so that every trace of what they once hid is gone. Others—far fewer—merely wait and endure. These few are infused with a darkness so powerful that it cannot ever really die. Some battlefields are like this, the very soil vibrating with the echoes of the slaughtered, fertilized by the last breaths of the fallen and by vain cries to indifferent gods. Some houses have that pernicious potential, infused with pain and hunger by those who live there and by grotesque acts performed on the innocent behind obfuscatory walls.

In the northernmost corner of Argon, near the shores of Lake Lyra, was such a place.

A slope wandered from the downs where horses exercised to one of the many streams running south from the lake. Most of that region was a paradise of green fields, dense hardwood forests, and plentiful game. Birds sang in the trees everywhere in the forest except in one spot. The only birds that ever flew into that part of the woods sang no songs, then or ever again.

That very morning a young deer, white as snow, died in that awful place. Its blood still glistened on the edges of trembling leaves.

There was a large mound near one of the streams, from which a chunk of chiseled stone jutted. No one alive knew what it had once been, though there were stories. Some claimed it was the cornerstone of a castle that had been destroyed by the first Silver Empress. Others said it was a garden that had been abandoned when the clerics founded the grander one in Kifflein Meadows, many miles to the southeast. A few local songs gave it a romantic bent and told tales of ill-fated lovers meeting there to pledge their troths before meeting tragic ends.

None of these were correct.

The stone was not a remnant of something that had fallen. It was never a sacred space. The stone was the corner of something deliberately buried uncounted ages ago—long before the Silver Empire was even a dream. Wind and rain had begun the process of uncovering the upper corner of a crypt. The door of that fell place had been cemented shut and sealed with another row of dressed stones, cut so precisely that not even a mite could squeeze between them. There were symbols of protection cut into the rock, but erosion had stolen their meaning, blurred their outlines, and made them imprecise. Magic requires precision, and binding spells doubly so.

Thunder battered the sky and gusts of wind whipped the tree-tops, though no rain fell. The sky was littered with torn banners of clouds that seemed unable to decide in which direction they should move. The blue behind them was stained with a greenish gray, looking more like an ocean sky after a volcano has spent its last fury. There was a violent, abused energy to it, and all of the animals in the forest crawled under shrubs or into burrows to hide.

By that chunk of carved stone, a man rose from the ground. He did it slowly, as if time and urgency meant nothing. Clods of dirt fell from his naked limbs. Spiders scuttled from within the threads of his hair. Centipedes fled in panic down his pale legs and leapt away into the brittle grass.

The man unbent, unfolded, and finally stood at his full height. Tendons creaked and bones protested as he moved. His muscles screamed in pain, and through all of this, he smiled.

There was dirt smeared on his naked body, and much of it was so old that it was more dust than soil. Webs of long-dead spiders covered his face like a caul, and when he reached up to pull it away, taloned fingernails rent the flesh of forehead, cheek, and lips. He did not care, did not flinch. Instead, he took the first sensations of pain that he had felt in uncounted years and feasted on it with the same relish with which he had swallowed the blood of the white deer. That blood, along with chewed muscle and ground bone, filled and distended the man's stomach. When he turned and pissed, the discharge was scarlet. That made him laugh.

The woods were black except for a curved fang of moonlight. That glow painted the man's features, picking out the high cheekbones, the high forehead and shelf of brow, the hollow cheeks and pointed chin. And those lips. They were the only part of him that did not look emaciated. The lips were full and sensual, and they curved upward at the corners as if this mouth was meant for smiling.

He smiled now. It was a delighted smile. Cruel and broad and happy and ugly. It was a hungry smile. Very hungry indeed.

Above the smile and the curved beak of a nose, the eyes glittered like jewels. In the uncertain blue-white moonlight they seemed to be a strange mixture of colors. The browns and greens of lesser toads, the green of biting insects, the yellows of sickness. Those colors swirled and swirled as the man looked around. His fingers twitched as if aching to grab and hold and crush.

"Alive," he said. It came out as a long hiss of wicked delight.

He turned in a slow circle, sniffing the air like a dog. When he stopped he was facing southwest. Many, many miles from where he stood was Argentium, capital city of Argon, capital of the old Silver Empire. The man stared as if the miles meant nothing to him. As if time was as irrelevant as distance.

"Yes," he said, drawing that word out so that it scraped the air like a long and rusty sword being drawn from its ancient scabbard.

Then he began walking.

Without haste but with very great purpose.

CHAPTER FORTY-EIGHT

The village was called North Bend, though it was so remote and so underpopulated that the people who lived there simply called it "the village."

There were forty-nine residents spread out in farms laid out with the geometric precision of towns established by the Garden. Each farm was arranged like a slice of pie, with the narrow end touching the small perimeter of the village's few central buildings and the rest of each farm expanding outward from there. The garden—or, what had been a garden before the Ravens came and destroyed it—was in the exact center of the town. It was the seed from which the village grew.

Now the garden was a blackened shell of a building. The fire had, in its mercy, destroyed all traces of the horrors that had oc-curred within. Only a few charred bones remained as relics of the clerics—a Gardener, two monks, and two nuns—who once lived, worked, and taught there. Fresh flowers were placed in bundles at each of the four doors—east, north, west, and south—and the names of those sacred dead were whispered during nightly prayers but never said aloud. Not even among families in the safety of their own homes.

Not that anyone in the village knew that a spy or collaborator lived among them. Most were sure, in fact, that there was no such villain. But the world had changed and the Hakkian heel was felt on every neck, and it was better to withhold trust than to rely on human kindness.

Mylo Elm was thirteen years old when the Ravens came. Like most youths in the region, he cared nothing for politics, had only the vaguest idea where Hakkia even was, could barely write his own name. He had never been talented at math or letters but was good at what he loved: farming. His family owned the fourth-largest farm in town, at least in terms of acreage. When measured by income, they were sixth. His family grew mostly the hardier cold-weather crops—beets, spinach, cabbage, cauliflower, and carrots.

Sowing was its own art form, and Mylo enjoyed the process of tilling the soil, laying compost to help the worms grow fat, and then planting the seeds. Despite his lack of mathematical skills, he nevertheless knew how far apart to place his seeds, which plants should be seeded in clusters and which alone, and which ones liked a lot of sunlight and which preferred a bit of shade.

His sister, Golina, was a dreamer who thought about moving to the city, dressing in fine gowns, and marrying a knight. She was a year older and would probably do just that. Not Mylo, though. There was nothing he wanted to do more than make things grow and see the looks on the faces of people who ate the things that came from his fields.

He was squatting between rows of red cabbage, pulling up some persistent weeds, when something caught his attention. A soft sound combined with a small movement. He pivoted on the balls of his feet and studied the fields, looking for his sister or father, or his youngest brother, Luka, who had only recently started to walk and somehow managed to escape any attempts at keeping him from running free.

The figure in the fields was not one of his kin. He shielded his eyes with a flat hand and tried to see who it was. The sun was behind the figure and that made it hard to pick out details. A man, for sure. About average height and thin. Was it Master Kelton, the landowner who had the adjoining farm? Or Ulri from down the road?

The figure stood perfectly still. Mylo thought that he was looking at the house, which was snugged back beneath the arms of a pair of hickory trees. Smoke curled from the chimney, carrying with it the smell of the rabbit stew Ma was making for lunch.

Mylo began to straighten but paused. There was something odd about the way the man just stood there. Then a small cloud drifted across the face of the sun, and in the resulting moment of shadow, the sun glare vanished and Mylo saw the man more clearly. Definitely not Master Kelton, nor Ulri either. It was a stranger. The fellow was dressed in simple clothes—a tunic over cotton trousers—but the style was wrong. More of a city cut than the rougher country clothes. No embroidery, either, which everyone in farm country had on their tunics, the flowers or plants of which often presented a sense of region if not actual towns. Mylo's own tunic was stitched with cabbages, spinach, carrots, and squash. This man's clothes were bare of such marking, though they were heavily marked by splashes of mud.

Mylo frowned.

The mud was very red, as if rich in clay, and there was nothing like that around here. Not for many miles. The soil in this part of Argon was rich and black. There wasn't much clay closer than the suburbs of Argentium. So, that was odd.

A curious crow flapped lazily from a tree and drifted past to see the stranger, flying low, cawing softly. The man turned to watch it, and even held out a hand like a falconer waiting for his hunter to return. The crow, its sense of play sparked, flew very close and then began to veer away.

The man's raised hand darted out, fast as a striking serpent, and caught the crow by one wing. He snatched it out of the air and shoved the struggling, screaming bird as far into his mouth as he could. Blood and feathers seemed to explode around the stranger's face. He bit and tore with his teeth and wrenched and twisted with his hand. Not merely killing the bird but utterly destroying it. The unfortunate creature died immediately and badly.

The sight of this struck Mylo so hard it tore a cry of horror and disgust from him.

And that was a very bad thing to do.

The stranger turned sharply in his direction. For a moment he seemed unable to see the boy hunkered down between the rows, but then his eyes locked on Mylo's. The ruined bird fell from his mouth, trailing torn feathers and droplets of bright blood. The man—if man it was—raised both hands toward Mylo, fingers curled and clutching. His bloody mouth worked, chewing the meat it had and hungering for the meat it saw.

Then it was running.

It, not he, because Mylo could not reconcile what happened with anything human. Even a starving madman would not do what this man—this *thing*—had just done.

The creature howled like something feral from a nightmare. The sound was only vaguely human but utterly lacking in humanity. There was no trace of language in it. Just need.

Just . . . hunger.

It ran through the rows of vegetables. Tripping over roots and gourds, falling, getting up without acknowledging any injury, speeding up, howling and biting the air.

Mylo turned and ran.

He was young and strong, fit and terrified, and he ran with

every ounce of his strength. He vaulted rows of plants at first, instinctively not wanting to damage good crops, but as the howls rose in volume he merely *ran*.

He ran very fast.

He made it all the way to the center of the little village. He screamed for help, and people thrust their heads from windows and doors. He saw both Master Kelton and Ulri, and his own sister, Golina, who had the baby on her hip. Everyone in the village came to see what was happening.

Mylo screamed as he ran. His screams called them all.

And the madman howled with red delight as he rushed at them, fingers tearing the air, teeth snapping, eyes filled with fire.

Mylo lay in the dirt for a long time.

He could not move. There was not enough of him left for that.

He prayed to the Harvest Gods to take him home. To close his eyes. To shut out the things he saw.

The gods did none of that.

He saw his sister crawling toward an open alley. Half of her face was unmarked. The other half hung in tatters. She dragged with her a bundle that mewled and wept and screamed and bled.

Master Kelton sat with his back to a rain barrel, hands pressed to the ruin of his throat, eyes wide and registering a shock so profound that even if he could talk, there would be no human words to express his horror. Mylo saw the rich farmer's eyes go gradually dull, losing their expression, their clarity. Their life.

He watched Master Kelton slump sideways and fall.

Each time Mylo blinked, the world around him seemed to change. The sunlight shifted as if huge chunks of time jumped forward. He felt himself grow colder.

"Please," he begged to the Harvest Gods. "Please . . ."

The street grew dark as shadows toppled from the row of houses on the western side of the square. He saw his sister, kneeling now, bending to kiss Ulri.

If that's what she was doing.

Mylo tasted something strange in his mouth. Salty. Rich. Blood? He felt weight in his hands. It took a lot for him to look down. To see what he held. To see what it was he ate.

To see who he was devouring.

He screamed. Or tried to. But the sound that came from his throat was a shriek like that the madman had uttered. Wet and phlegmy and wrong.

It was not a scream of pain. It was not a prayer or a plea. That scream spoke to one thought, one need. It was a scream of a vast and bottomless hunger that could never be satisfied.

Never.

Never.

CHAPTER FORTY-NINE

"Archers," said the captain of the squad of Ravens.

A row of a dozen archers nocked arrows and pulled on strings, taking careful aim, adjusting for distance and windage. The strings and yew bows creaked.

Lord Jakob Ravensmere sat on his horse and watched from under the cover of a line of oak trees. He used a scarf to mop cold sweat from his face. His stomach churned but he had already vomited up everything he'd eaten that day. He wished he could vomit out the memory of what he just witnessed.

He glanced at the small man in gray robes who stood apart. The Hollow Monk was as still and silent as a statue. If he felt any human emotions at all about the carnage in the little village, there was no way to tell. Every part of him was covered in gray wool. The yellow sigil on his chest glowed dully as stray bits of sunlight slanted down through the leaves.

"My lord?" queried the captain. "They're coming this way. Shall we . . ."

"Y-yes," stammered Jakob. "Stop them. Kill them. Whatever . . ."

Words failed the scholar as his stomach churned again.

Immediately the archers loosed their shafts. The strings hummed with their strange music and the arrows whipped through the air. Each one struck home, struck clean, but of the mass of people moving toward the group of watchers, only five fell.

"Hearts or heads, damn you for a bunch of poachers," growled the captain, though even his hard voice had a flawed edge. He coughed and barked orders for his men to fire again, and again, and again.

The archers each had twenty-one shafts in their quivers. It took every last arrow to bring the villagers down, and even then there was knife and axe work left to render the whole village down to silence.

Only then did the Hollow Monk turn to the historian.

"And that, Lord Ravensmere," said the ghostly voice, "is how your master will win the war."

PART TWO
THE DAMNED

"Father, why did they call him Kagen the *Damned*? What could any man do to earn such a name?"

"My child, he was damned because he failed at being perfect."

"But Father, I thought perfection was a myth . . . that no man or woman could *ever* be perfect."

"And now, my beloved son, you glimpse the truth behind all stories, behind all legends."

—PHILEAS THE YOUNGER OF THERIA, FROM THE PLAY *A CHILD DREAMS OF GIANTS*, ACT 2, SCENE 1

CHAPTER FIFTY

"Will it be war, then?" asked Grenleth, lieutenant general of the East Ravens.

Every eye at the long table turned to the figure seated at the far end. The Witch-king was elegant in new robes of intense yellow. The ancient crown of the Hakkians sat upon his brow, and from it fell the veil of yellow lace that forever hid his face. There were rings on each of his long fingers, and a necklace of heavy gold hung around his neck, from which a black disk was suspended. It required a certain angle of light to discern the image on the disk—a raven's head facing regardant—body turned dexter with the bird's sharp beak pointed sinister over a stylized eclipse.

This was the first staff meeting since the failed assassination attempt that spoiled the coronation. For most of the officers present, it was also the first time they had heard their king speak since that terrible catastrophe.

The Witch-king leaned against the high back of his chair, hands palm-down and flat on the table. A wine cup sat untouched—and because he had not yet drunk, no one else had. But the generals, lords, and advisors were not eyeing the superb wine; they stared at him in a pregnant silence.

Waiting.

They waited a long time, and no one dared prompt their lord.

His mood following the attack was changeable and seldom pleasant. Dozens of heads leered down from spikes above the main gate; dozens of other officers, soldiers, aides, advisors, and even palace staff had merely vanished, never to be seen or heard from again. Every man and woman at that table had steeled themselves before answering the summons, and each of them dreaded making a wrong move or speaking an ill-received word.

Grenleth's question hung in the air, because he had been the first to dare to speak. His friends among the gathered officers wondered if this was the last time they would hear the general's voice except as screams.

"Yes," said the Witch-king finally, his voice without anger or rancor, "it will be war."

The gathered officials murmured, some gasped, others sighed. One or two looked excited, while others hung their heads. Everyone looked stricken.

"Your Majesty," said General Grenleth, a seasoned veteran with a sword cut running from left eyebrow to his jaw, "will we have the same . . . ah . . . *advantage* as last time?"

The room went quiet again.

The advantage of which Grenleth spoke was central to how Hakkia—a poor and oppressed nation—had managed to conquer the vast and immensely powerful Silver Empire in a single night. On the Night of the Ravens, as it had come to be called, the armies of Hakkia, along with thousands of mercenaries, had suddenly *appeared* in every capital city in the empire. Not at the gates, but inside the palaces themselves. It happened in moments. There was no protracted siege and no warning at all. The entire empire fell in one night, and all of this had been accomplished by powerful magicks employed by the Witch-king. No such assault could have happened any other way.

But the Witch-king shook his head.

"No," he said. "Some miracles cannot be reproduced."

They waited for more, but he did not elaborate. On all the walls the candles burned and dripped and sent shadows capering around the table. A brazier burned in a far corner, filling the air with the scent of herbs and flowers—geranium, peppermint, and sage.

Two figures sat close together at the far end of the table, a gaunt and lugubrious man with a shaved pate and deep-set eyes, and a shrunken shadow of a woman wearing a gray, hooded cloak embroidered with astrological and alchemical symbols. Lord Nespar, the royal chamberlain, and what was left of Lady Kestral. They were the most dedicated advisors to the Witch-king. Of everyone in the room, they knew the most about the Witch-king and shared many of his confidences.

Their involvement with that *miracle* had been extensive and complex and included rounding up dozens of virgin children between eleven and fourteen, making sure that they had no marks, scars, or deformities, paying their families enormous sums, and transporting the children to Xerxith, the capital of Hakkia. None of those children was ever seen again. Rumors of strange sounds—screams, monstrous roars, and prayers spoken in unknown languages and by voices that did not sound even remotely human—were either ignored or shut down by visits from armed royal soldiers.

Anything that needed to be done to save Hakkia, to drag it out of the mud into which the heels of the whole line of Silver Empresses had crushed it, and to ensure a brighter future marked by freedom of action and faith simply *had* to be done. At whatever cost. And yet even they did not know everything about what was, arguably, the greatest feat of sorcery in human history.

Kestral touched Nespar's wrist with a hand that looked like a skeletal claw for all the meat left on it. When Nespar glanced at her, lifting a questioning eyebrow, she gave the tiniest shake of her head. His nod was equally discreet. Kestral's gaunt face retreated into the darkness of her cowl.

"Do you fear the future?" the Witch-king asked into the silence.

"I do not want to displease you, Majesty," began Admiral Orkyan, another old veteran, "but . . ."

The Witch-king took a sip of his wine, lifting the veil to reveal a strong but pointed chin and full, sensual lips. Before he set his cup down, nearly everyone else at the table drank as well.

"Speak your mind, my friend," he said, his voice mild and unthreatening. Much more like it had been before the invasion.

Orkyan nodded his thanks and said, "When we took Argentium, Majesty, we had the element of surprise."

Several old soldiers smiled at that phrasing. *Surprise* indeed.

"We also had banefire and a razor-knight," continued the admiral. "There was no chance for a formal opposition. Right now, we have a standing army of eight hundred thousand spears, thirty thousand light and heavy cavalry, and two hundred fighting vessels of various sizes in our fleet. If Theria and Samud unite against us, we'll be facing an army of vastly more than a million and a fleet seven times the size of ours. If they march on us here, we will be defending from a place that is not ready for a siege. The Silver Empress had Argentium's old defenses torn down as a symbol of the safety of the Silver Empire. We would need two or three years to build proper defenses, and that would mean conscripting half the citizens of Argon. If they send a combined fleet against us, they could burn Argentium to the ground. Our only strategic advantage is that, right now, the other nations don't know that we can't reproduce the magic used during the Night of the Ravens."

The soldiers seated closest to Orkyan leaned slightly away from him as if trying to increase their distance from any flying debris from the Witch-king's wrath.

However, the monarch in yellow merely nodded. "What you say is true, Admiral."

Emboldened, Orkyan said, "I would lay down my life for you,

Majesty, as you know. Every man and woman in this room would do the same."

This won him a round of encouraging shouts. Nespar cut a covert glance at Kestral, who was close to proving the admiral's claim. He wondered how she even had the power to stand, let alone continue to perform the spells required of her by their master.

"But, Majesty," said the admiral with a small smile, "I'd prefer *not* to die in a losing war. I want Hakkia to thrive, and I have prayed all my life to see a Witch-king on the throne of a new empire. Is there nothing we can do to ensure our victory?"

Every eye shifted back to the Witch-king, who took another sip before answering.

"No victory is ever certain," he said. "After all, none of my diviners foresaw the events on the night of the coronation."

Several glances shifted toward Kestral. Nespar, protective of his friend and ally, gave them withering glares, and each officer looked away again very quickly.

"Our enemies are many, and some are quite powerful," said the monarch in yellow. "They are shrewd and subtle. King al-Huk is our most powerful potential enemy, but there are other players we cannot discount. When war comes for us, it will come as a great storm."

The Witch-king looked slowly around the room, and though the veil hid his eyes, each person there felt the sheer power of his gaze when he lingered on them.

"I know that the events of coronation night rattled the whole of the empire," he said mildly. "I daresay we are a laughingstock in many places. My court historian, Lord Jakob Ravensmere, tells me that there are songs about it, and my name is taken in vain, and I have been many times burned in effigy from Sunderland to Nelfydia and from Zaare to Samud. I have become a figure of fun."

He glanced at the royal historian, who responded with a slight bow. Jakob's face was paler and more deeply lined than it had been before. Even since accompanying the Hollow Monks to witness the testing of their weapon, he had looked sick and was less prone to his usual banter with the other officials. The Witch-king's spies within the palace guards said that the historian often screamed in his sleep. And sometimes when he was alone but not sleeping there were screams, sobs, and even prayers heard through the door to his apartment.

The historian's eyes darted away and he looked down at his folded hands.

Privately amused, the Witch-king continued. "What king has not been mocked by the foolish? What invading army has not been thoroughly hated? We Hakkians have borne the brunt of scorn from the earliest days of the Silver Empire. How many songs were written, how many plays produced, how many tales told over beers about how Lady Bellapher and her armies crushed our rebellion three hundred years ago? We have been the pot they piss in. We are the butt of countless bad jokes. But . . . what did that mockery, that abuse and injustice, do? Did it crush us? Did it weaken Hakkian resolve? Did we fade away into a footnote in history? Did we stop believing in our own right to survive, and our own right to stand in the sun rather than skulk in the shadows?"

Admiral Orkyan growled his answer. "Never, Majesty."

Fists pounded the table in fierce agreement.

The Witch-king nodded. "I ask you all now, my brothers and sisters, to have faith that having come this far into the light we will never retreat into darkness again. Never." He looked around. "No, we cannot use the same magicks that won us the victory on that sacred night. But we have many tricks left to play. We have allies that they do not know of. Allies of great power that even *you* do not yet know of, my friends."

He chuckled softly.

"Lord Ravensmere has been in the field, testing a new weapon.

Something vastly different from what we used on the Night of the Ravens."

"Sire," said Grenleth, "may we ask what that weapon is? And how and where it might be deployed?"

The Witch-king took another sip of wine. Jakob Ravensmere shifted uncomfortably.

"In time, General," the Witch-king said in a slow and silky tone. "In time."

CHAPTER FIFTY-ONE

The braided wand of kindness made a soft whooshing sound as it whipped through the air. The impact, though, was hard and loud.

Whack!

Followed by a grunt of pain.

Not a scream. Never a scream. Merely that heavy grunt, torn from young mouths. It was more of sensation than anything. There was no emotion in it.

Whack!

Whack!

Over and over. First on Alleyn's bare buttocks and upper thighs. Then Desalyn's. At first the beatings were fun. Pain was fun. Or so they thought. But with each successive transgression of touch, Madam Lucibel's wand hit harder and harder and the fun disintegrated, leaving discomfort that transformed pain from a delight to a torment.

Whack!

Whack!

And with it, the same words over and over, spoken in Madam Lucibel's singsong voice.

"You will not hold hands."

Whack!

"You will never hold hands."

Whack!
Every morning.
Every night.

CHAPTER FIFTY-TWO

Mother Frey studied their faces. "Have you boys heard about what happened during the coronation?"

"The *failed* coronation," said Jheklan sourly.

"Deferred at best," corrected Frey. "Unless it can be permanently stopped, it will be rescheduled, and with greater security."

"Yeah, fair enough, damn," said Faulker. Then he narrowed his eyes. "Whoa now, wait a minute . . . I think I get where this is going. There's been some wild rumors that the madman who interrupted the coronation was Kagen."

"We thought that was a bit of questionable eyewitness testimony born of wishful thinking or alcohol," said Jheklan.

"Kagen hasn't been heard from since the Night of the Ravens," said Faulker. "We assumed he was dead or in some dungeon."

"He was very much alive the last time I saw him," said Frey. "And yes, it was he who I witnessed dueling with the Witch-king in the great hall of the palace."

They gaped at her.

"Kagen?" they both said.

"Kagen isn't the type," said Faulker.

"Apparently he is," said Frey. "And *I* am the eyewitness."

"You were there? You actually saw Kagen fighting the Witch-king? *Our* Kagen?"

"Kagen's a good fighter," said Jheklan. "Nearly as good as us. But he's a dreamer, not a hero."

Mother Frey studied them. "I think it's fair to say that a lot of people have underestimated Kagen Vale."

Jheklan turned to his brother. "Kagen going at it with a wizard. Are you buying this, Faulker, old son?"

"I'm having a hard time, Jheklan," said Faulker. "I mean, sure, Kagen's a tough monkey, but palace guard was what he aspired to, and even that seemed a stretch for him."

They looked at the lady.

"Maybe tell us what your interest is in all of this, Mother Frey," said Faulker, and a bit of the joviality dropped from his voice. Frey glimpsed the steel those jokes concealed. "Is this just because the Hakkians have pissed on all of the gardens?"

"Burned a lot of them down," said Jheklan to his brother. "Did some pretty awful shit to the nuns and monks." To Mother Frey he said, "Is that it? Is this revenge? Did you put Kagen in the Witch-king's path to try to punch back?"

Mother Frey sipped her tea.

"No," she said. "I witnessed that fight, but I haven't yet spoken with Kagen. The great hall was a shambles and my companions and I barely escaped with our lives."

Faulker twirled a finger. "Maybe give us a little more than that?"

"Just a smidge," encouraged Jheklan. "You brought us all the way here."

"We had plans," said Faulker.

"Big plans."

"Involving black-haired triplets."

Jheklan nodded. "And a lot of very good Therian wine."

Faulker considered his cup. "To be fair, this is pretty good. Better than the average plonk."

"It'll do," agreed Jheklan, and they drank.

Faulker wiped his mouth, stifled a belch, and said, "So, if there's a real point to this, maybe start walking in that direction before we sober up and go find our horses."

Jheklan grinned. "Night's still young."

"Young-*ish*," said Faulker.

"Kagen is somewhere out there," said Mother Frey, jumping in before they burned off a whole hour with their banter, "and he is almost certainly going to try another attack on the Witch-king. He was unusually lucky the first time, and I still don't know how he escaped the palace." She recounted everything she, Helleda, and their friend Hannibus Greel had witnessed. The brothers leaned forward and listened with great interest, not interrupting but occasionally sharing significant looks between them.

"The price on his head is enormous," she said when the main tale was told, "and there is no more wanted a man in all the west. It's only a matter of time before he makes his next move and is killed, or the right group of bounty hunters tracks him down and brings him in chains before the Witch-king."

The brothers, those false twins, stared at her.

"Well," said Faulker.

"Shit," said Jheklan.

Faulker looked dreamy and shook his head. "Kagen, slayer of razor-knights, dueler with magicians, and outright hero. Who'd have thought?"

"The world is mad," said Jheklan.

"The world," said Frey, "is changing."

"Because—how'd you put it?" said Jheklan. "'Magic is back'?"

"Yes."

"Is that how Kagen beat the razor-knight when even *Mom* couldn't?" asked Faulker. "Because so far I haven't had enough wine to make that make sense."

Frey said, "Rumors say that he used some of the Hakkian's own banefire to destroy that foul creature."

"That makes a little more sense," Jheklan grudgingly acknowledged.

"As for magic," said Frey, "it is mostly the darker forms of magic that have returned. Very dark, in some cases. But . . . there are some bright spots. Some natural magic reawakening."

"I have no idea what that even means," said Faulker.

"Yeah," said Jheklan, "because we don't actually believe in that stuff."

"Not even a little," said Faulker.

Frey leaned back and considered them with her intense eyes. "Tell me, boys, how was it you—of all people in the world—happened to be in that forest, on that stretch of road, at exactly the right time to rescue me?"

"Oh that? It wasn't magic," laughed Faulker.

"Nope," agreed Jheklan. "We were hunting. Thought we'd bring some pheasants as courting gifts for the triplets. They have great appetites."

"Curvy girls," said Faulker.

"We like curvy girls," said Jheklan.

"And yet," said Frey, "the exact timing?"

Faulker shrugged. "Luck."

"And what is luck if it is not a nod to the existence of magic?" asked Frey. "Luck, itself, is magic. Do you knock wood? Do you whistle for a wind on a hot day? Do you light candles on the new moon?"

"Well, sure, but . . ." began Jheklan. He stopped. "Okay, I see where you're going with that. Luck. Okay. Small magic. Or a superstition about it."

"More like coincidence," said Faulker.

"You're saying *coincidence* is what brought you two, the brothers of Kagen Vale, to those woods at exactly the right moment to rescue an old woman who delivered your mother and saw your brother fight the Witch-king? Coincidence that you are here with me now, in a room where a cabal meets to discuss a rebellion against the Witch-king of Hakkia. Merely chance and nothing more?"

They sipped and studied her.

"Okay," said Faulker. "When you put it that way."

"It's a little weird," admitted Jheklan.

"What it is, boys," said Frey, "is proof that there *is* magic in the world. It proves that there are forces at work beyond what we can see. Forces that are, for whatever reason, aligned with our desire to overthrow the Witch-king."

"And to stuff magic back into its box if we succeed?" asked Faulker.

"No," said Frey. "I don't think I want to have that happen."

"Then what?" asked Jheklan.

"I think what the Witch-king has done is throw the world out of balance. Dark magic is a hungry thing, and it consumes light."

Faulker jabbed Jheklan in the ribs with an elbow. "That," he said, "is a metaphor."

"I know, dumbass."

Frey said, "It would be wrong to erase all darkness. Wrong and likely impossible. Right now, though, the Witch-king seems bent on bringing his god, Hastur, fully into this world. I do not know what he *thinks* will happen, but from what I have read, it is something so dreadful the ancients and their prophets merely hint at it."

"Not delighted at the sound of that," said Jheklan.

"Wait a sec," said Faulker. "I did pay attention in class *sometimes*. When the Silver Empresses founded the empire, didn't they pretty much do that? In reverse, I mean. They tried to remove all traces of darkness. There are all those stories about how they executed a bunch of wizards and witches and such."

"Yeah," said Jheklan, "and when Bellapher crushed the Hakkian insurrection three hundred years ago, they outlawed even any *mentions* of sorcery in their history books and religious practices and all that, right?"

"Yes," said Frey, "and that was the first swing of the pendulum, going too far into the light. Imbalance is imbalance. Kagen is trying to kill the Witch-king and overthrow his regime. Naturally we want him to succeed. However, swords alone will not get this done."

"Worth a try," said Jheklan.

"Not to mention arrows, pikes, axes, and maces," supplied Faulker.

"A try, yes," said Frey, "but at best it would be a holding action. To *win* we need to reach further and take some incredibly dangerous risks. This is something I need to convey to Kagen, and I have people looking for him. I want to bring him into our cabal before he does something that gets him killed."

"What can *we* do about it?" asked Faulker. "Go searching the whole continent for him?"

"I don't need you to find Kagen," said Frey. "I know where he is."

"You do? So he *is* alive, for sure?"

"He is with two people I trust, and they are in—or will soon be in—Nelfydia."

"Then . . . why are we having this conversation?" asked Jheklan.

"Kagen is one of three possible strategies I hope to employ against the Witch-king," said Frey. "At the present time I'm unsure which strategy is the most likely to work, and so it is my hope to set all three into motion."

"And that involves us . . . *how*?" asked the brothers at the same time and with the same inflection.

Mother Frey smiled thinly. "Rumor has it that you boys once visited one of the cities of the ancients in Vespia."

That wiped the smiles from their faces and seemed to darken an already shadowy chamber. The Vale twins listened, though, and when Mother Frey got to the worst part—the most dangerous and possibly suicidal part—they began to smile once more.

CHAPTER FIFTY-THREE

Kagen had nearly finished a large breakfast of eggs and venison bacon when Tuke and Filia came down to join him. They shared secret smiles and kept making obscure comments that the other laughed at. And they held hands and paused for a lot of hungry kisses. It was all very romantic and charming and Kagen would have loved to knife them both to death.

He hunched over his plate, shoveling eggs into his mouth and sulking.

As if noticing his existence for the first time, Filia said, "Something bothering you today?"

"Bothering me? Oh, no, life's a bowl of freshly picked peaches."

Tuke glanced at him. "Bad night's sleep?"

"I have exactly two things to say about last night," said Kagen, and then counted them on his fingers. "Fuck. You."

"Wow, you're fun," said Filia.

Kagen pushed his plate away and began ticking items off on his fingers. "Herepath is the Witch-king of Hakkia. The Silver Empire has fallen. My soul is damned to the burning pits of hell. And we're no closer to assembling an army to fight back than we are to walking on the surface of the moon. I had to listen to you two screwing each other cross-eyed all night. So . . . sure, let's focus on 'fun,' shall we?"

Tuke sighed and nodded. "Fair enough."

"I want to see this Ghuraka woman," said Kagen. "Sooner rather than later."

"Some things can't be rushed," said Filia.

Kagen actually growled at her.

"Look, brother," said Tuke quickly, "don't despair. I know that it feels like we're just running away, but there's a logic to that. We aren't ready to fight back. Once we get that audience with Ghuraka, then we can go find Mother Frey and listen to what she and her cabal can do for us. They have the money and connections to build your army."

"It's not just his army," said Filia. "We all have dogs in this fight."

Horse, who lay at her feet gnawing a bone, looked up at the word *dog* and then glanced toward the door. It amused Kagen, because Filia's horse was named Dog.

"Yes, we do," agreed Tuke, accepting the correction. "And right now, the kings and queens who were at the coronation are sitting mighty damned uneasily on their thrones. My guess is that they are quietly building their armies while their spy networks are out gathering information."

"Of *course* they are," said Kagen irritably. "Even the ones who might choose to sit back and watch from a safe distance are doing that. What we need is some of those armies to work with us to drive the Hakkians out of the empire and into the sea. Then go the extra mile and wipe Hakkia itself off the map."

"Whoa now," said Filia. "You're talking about massacring all Hakkians?"

"Why the hell not?"

"Because that isn't warfare, Kagen," she said firmly. "Genocide is evil. There's no reason for it or honor in it. Not everyone in Hakkia serves the Witch-king. Think about the farmers and craftspeople. The children. The rural folk who are just trying to get through each season. Gods of the Pit, you'd have us commit greater atrocities as revenge for what the military and political elite have done?"

"She has a point," said Tuke.

"Really?" said Kagen, stabbing the air in Filia's direction with a stiff finger. "And how would you separate the corrupt Hakkians from the innocent?"

"How the hell should I know?" she fired back, face reddening with anger. "But who made you the arbiter of who lives and dies?"

"The Witch-king did, when he slaughtered my parents and the Seedlings," snarled Kagen. A few patrons turned in their direction and Kagen forced himself to speak more quietly, though with the same passion. "Hakkia has been the breeding ground for scum for centuries. Bellapher should have swept that country clean and salted the ashes of what was left."

"In about two seconds I'm going to stand up, take my chair, and beat the living shit out of you," said Filia.

"You can gods-damn well try."

A large, dark, and very powerful hand clamped down on Kagen's wrist as Tuke leaned his considerable bulk over the table. He squeezed Kagen with great force. Not fast, not to damage, but to make a very clear point.

"You need to take a breath, brother," he said. "You have exactly two friends in this world and you are about to lose them both. No, city boy, don't say anything. You don't have the right words now." He turned. "You too, Filia. Both of you hush."

They glared at him.

Kagen tugged against the grip and Tuke let his arm go. The silence that fell around them was massive and ponderous. Kagen got slowly to his feet.

"I'm going to take your suggestion and ride out to the garden," he said slowly. He tossed some coins onto the table, enough for his breakfast as well as theirs. That broke the spell—at least temporarily.

"Kagen," said Filia, "what is really bothering you?"

The temptation to snarl at them like a grouchy old dog was strong, but in a sullen voice he said, "Bad dreams. And no, I don't want to talk about it. You two have a fun day. I'll be back by nightfall."

And with that he turned and stalked off.

CHAPTER FIFTY-FOUR

The door opened and spilled sickly yellow light into the chamber.

The woman who knelt naked on the floor did not look up. She was physically unable to do so. The shadow of the man in the doorway splashed across her, and even though it had no weight in reality, it shoved her down even more. She huddled there, her body curled in on itself as if her stomach was twisted by cramps. Each knob of her spine protruded painfully from jaundiced skin that was too thin. What little moisture remained to her was beaded into cold and greasy sweat along her sallow flesh.

"Kestral," said the man in the doorway. His voice was cultured, soft, almost gentle. "What have you learned?"

All around the kneeling woman was a tableau that looked like a study in madness and slaughter. Bodies were stacked like cordwood against one wall. On the floor, arranged in obscene patterns approximating constellations, alchemical symbols, and secret sigils, were lumps of things that reeked with the sickly sweet aroma of rot. Flies swarmed in the air over the stacked bodies, but any that came close to the woman died and fell to the floor, joining dead roaches and rats. Nothing but the woman lived within a circle drawn with salt and sand and the finely ground bones of crows and starlings and grackles.

A single candle burned in its own small protective circle. And the woman reached her hands out to it to try to draw warmth into her emaciated body.

She tried to speak, but her voice was a cracked and dusty whisper. The woman sucked a few miserly drops of spit into her mouth, swallowed to lubricate her throat, and tried again.

"I have risen the spirits of seventeen of the soldiers who died in the great hall," she said in a ghastly whisper. "And four of those who had survived the battle."

She nodded to the desecrated corpses of three men and a woman—stripped naked and cut apart in ritual fashion.

"And what have the dead told you?" asked the Witch-king.

She turned very slowly, her joints creaking as if ready to crack apart. The King in Yellow was framed against the torchlight of the hall. All she could see was a silhouette edged in fire.

"The blood I harvested from each of them, from shields and blades and armor," she croaked, "belonged to Hakkian Ravens."

"Kagen Vale was cut in that fight," said the Witch-king. "He bled freely. His blood must be there to be found."

She nodded wearily. "I have . . . taken samples from what is still on the floor and the steps of the dais, my lord."

"Which tells me only that you have not found it *yet*."

She flinched as if his words were actual physical blows.

"My lord," she said, tears burning in the corners of her eyes, "this is destroying me. Necromancy of this kind takes so much from me and I don't know how much more I can manage. This is killing me."

The Witch-king was silent for a long moment.

"For the sake of your soul, my lady Kestral," he said softly, "pray that you find what I want before you *do* die. And do not forget that death will not shelter you from my wrath. Do you understand this?"

Lady Kestral bowed her head and her tears fell like rain. She nodded and then buried her face in her bloody hands.

When next she looked up, the Witch-king of Hakkia was gone.

CHAPTER FIFTY-FIVE

The royal twins were only five years old and the knives were too heavy for them.

Foscor dropped hers twice and Gavran cut himself on his.

The fencing master, Sir Giles of Hock, stood like a dancer, one foot angled to the left, the other placed to bisect it and angle to the right. He wore a doublet of yellow over green hose and felt shoes. His hair was blond and swept back in artful waves from a high brow. He had piercing blue eyes, a long nose over a precisely trimmed mustache, and a hero's chin. His lips, though, were thin, and there was a coldness in his smile.

"We will have to do better than that," he said in a crisp voice. His accent was Hakkian laid over urban Berclessian. "Try again."

The children looked at each other with expressions of mingled anger, frustration, and malice.

"Now!" cried Gavran, and he rushed in and tried to stab the fencing master in the groin. At the same instant, Foscor slanted left and slashed at the outside of Sir Giles's knee.

If the swordmaster was surprised or impressed by the fact that five-year-olds were attempting a sophisticated and devious two-pronged attack, it did not show. Instead, he used his rapier to parry the girl and then he kicked the knife from the boy's hand. Foscor was thrown off balance by the parry and stumbled, and Sir Giles kicked her feet out from under her. He was not nice about it.

Before she even fell, Sir Giles snaked out his free hand and slapped Gavron across the face and then reversed and backhanded him. Both children fell hard, tears springing into their eyes.

But there were no cries, no sobs. Instead, they snarled like young wolves as they scrambled to their feet and threw themselves at the man. He backpedaled, using the flat of one hand and the stinging flexible rapier to parry and punish. He let them chase him around the whole of the training room until pain drove them down to their knees.

Then he sheathed his sword, grabbed them by the collars of their padded training vests, hauled them up to their toes, and with no regard for their status or safety, slammed them into each other. He let go on impact and they toppled backwards, blood starting from cracked noses and torn lips. They fell at his feet.

Even then, though, the children did not yield. Gavran wrapped his arms around the swordmaster's ankles and sank his teeth into the man's calf.

Giles hissed in pain and snapped a quick kick out sending Gavran spinning through the air and into a ficus tree. Then he cried out as pain erupted in his left buttock. He whipped around, slapping at Foscor, who had recovered her knife. An inch of the blade's half-sharpened tip glistened with bright red.

The Berclessian slapped the knife away once more, putting much more force into it, and then he grabbed Foscor by the throat and lifted her bodily off the ground. She snarled and writhed like a cat, refusing even in defeat to accept that she was wildly over-matched. Sir Giles looked into the girl's eyes for a long moment and saw no trace of a child's mind in there. No trace of real humanity. What he saw repulsed him. It was like opening the folds of a baby's swaddling clothes to find a scorpion.

With a cry of disgust he flung her into the same shrubbery as her brother. Foscor collapsed there, panting, hissing like a snake.

Sir Giles picked up the two knives and thrust them through his belt. His buttock hurt and warm blood ran down inside his hose. The bite on his calf was nearly as painful. He walked over to the children, making damn sure not to limp, and looked down at them.

"Maggots," he murmured.

Gavran kicked at him, but he moved his leg out of the way.

"Your father wants you trained in weapons," Sir Giles said.

"Father will have you skinned alive for this," snarled Foscor. Nothing in her tone or diction was that of a child.

"Your father told me I could have you beaten every hour of the day or night if you refused," he countered waspishly. "Ask him, if you don't believe me."

"We can fight," snapped Gavran.

"You can sting, I'll grant you, but you cannot fight," said Sir Giles. "You think that viciousness alone is enough? If that was the case, then the barbarians beyond the Cathedral Mountains would have conquered the world. All you can do is annoy and disappoint."

Despite the searing pain it caused, he squatted before them.

"Listen to me," he said softly. "*Hear* me."

They glared at him but said nothing.

"Your father does not want you to be clumsy. You have seen him fight . . . he is an artist with a blade. A master. He knows that there is a time for brutality—time to be a hammer, a fist, a knife in the dark. That's fine. But to win wars and to defend yourself you need to be smarter and more skilled than your opponent. Some will tell you that battles are won by whoever wants it more, but that is seldom true. The winner is the one who can *earn* that victory."

"We'll kill you," said the little girl.

"Maybe you will," he said, "but of what value is that to you? Your father wants you to grow up and *rule* his empire . . . and make no mistake, he will have his empire. Maybe he'll rule the world. But if you don't learn to control your passions, he will have no heirs to pass that empire down to."

There was hatred in their eyes, but he saw that they were now paying attention to him.

"And don't get me wrong," he continued. "You are smarter than your age, and clearly not afraid of anything. That's excellent. That's a secret weapon, like a suit of armor beneath your skin. But it will only serve you well, children, if you learn *all* of the arts of war. Of sophisticated defense and intelligent attack. Today we have drawn blood on one another, but I won. I will always win against savage and unintelligent attacks. If you truly want to kill me, you'll have to learn how to do it, and become more than merely good. I am called swordmaster for a reason. I have killed men in thirty-nine duels, not counting uncountable victories on the fields of battle. If you had succeeded in killing me today, you would have lost a resource you cannot find again. If you attack everyone who wants to teach you, then your father will have no choice but to discard you as worthless. It will break his heart, but he will bury you or lock you away and move on. You will be forgotten, because there will be nothing about you worth remembering."

Gavran glanced at Foscor for a moment, then the eyes shifted back to Sir Giles. They really were listening.

"I will leave you with those thoughts for now," said Sir Giles. "Tomorrow I will be here at the same time. If you show up, then it will be for training. If you choose not to arrive, then I will inform your father than you are untrainable and hopeless. And then, may the gods help you. However . . . if you *are* here, then we can begin in earnest, and I can promise that by the time you are old enough to engage in battle for real, you will bring far more than simple animal ferocity to the field. I will teach you to be masters of every weapon."

With that he rose and turned. When he was halfway to the door he stopped, removed the two training knives from his belt, and tossed them onto the ground. He spat on them and, without glancing again at the children, walked out. He never once limped.

Gavran sat up slowly, wincing in pain. Foscor tried to sit, but her back hurt from the way she'd landed. Without even thinking about it, she reached out her hand to Gavran, who took it and pulled her to her feet.

The connection was made.

The touch of palm to palm tore aside the veil that separated Gavran from Alleyn and Foscor from Desalyn. They looked worriedly around as if expecting Madam Lucibel to suddenly appear with her wand of kindness.

Desalyn touched her brother's face.

He smiled as tears rolled down his cheeks.

"I love you," he said.

"I love you," said Desalyn.

"I . . . I'm always in here," she whispered.

"I know."

"All the time."

"I know."

"But . . . Alleyn?"

"Yes?"

"It's getting darker all the time," said Desalyn. "Every day it's harder to remember."

"I know," he said again.

They dared not hold each other. They dared not burst into tears. But they held on for a very long time. As long as they could.

When Madam Lucibel came into the room, though, it was Foscor and Gavran—the two of them standing a yard apart—who smiled at her.

CHAPTER FIFTY-SIX

Kagen went up to his room, stripped off his shirt, removed the bandage, and studied his chest. The wound, though deep, had knitted quite nicely. Just as Tuke's and Filia's wounds had done. Tuke said it was that gods-awful poultice they found on the ship, and maybe it was, but Kagen was not feeling generous enough at the moment to even think so. He probed the wound, judged it healed enough not to need another bandage, and pulled his shirt back on. The blisters on his palms had long since healed, and the other incidental cuts from the palace fight and the shipboard action were mended enough that he ignored them.

He fetched his weapons and heavy winter clothes from his room and took the back set of stairs out and down to the stables because he did not want to see the happy lovers. He hated that Filia had called him out on what was essentially a stupid knee-jerk reaction.

She was right, but so, to a degree, was he. The Hakkians had to be put down in a way that would prevent them from ever rising again.

He wished he could discuss that with his parents. Father—Lord Khendrick—was a politician and had a broad view of the subtleties of statecraft. For all his coldness and distance, Father had been brilliant. An advisor to two empresses.

As for Mother, her profound understanding of battle on large or small scales was unparalleled in the empire, as far as Kagen knew. Generals often asked her opinion.

Where was that wisdom now? Father's and Mother's. Where?

Dead and lost because of the Hakkians.

"Gods of the Harvest," he swore, and then caught himself, realizing his blunder. But he did not correct the oath.

As he thumped down the stairs, he tried to think about the other thing that was gnawing at him. Tuke and Filia. He wasn't jealous as such, though he did have wonderful memories of making love with Filia. It was more his *lack* than what Tuke *had*. *Envy* was perhaps the better word, he mused, though that wasn't any comfort. The last woman he had slept with was the tragic sorceress, Maralina, and she was both immortal and probably beyond his reach. In that enchanted month in her tower, he had fallen in love with her. At first, in the days after leaving the Tower of Sarsis, Kagen had dismissed those feelings as the effect of her enchantments.

Now, weeks later, the feelings not only persisted but were deepening. Yet to what end? She believed herself doomed to spend eternity in that tower, and Kagen did not want to be either her companion in prison—where she would watch him age, wither, and die—or a temporary guest, with the same realities always hovering over him. Any kind of romance with her would be impossible. And all it would likely do was increase the loneliness for her and feelings of loss and fragility for him.

He paused at the bottom of the stairs and sat for a time, feeling the weight of everything he'd lost. Family, his position as an honored captain, the Seedlings in his charge, the empress. Hell, the entire empire.

And Herepath.

He grieved for Herepath as if his brother had died. And in all the ways that mattered, the older brother he loved and admired might as well be dead. That Herepath was gone, to Kagen and maybe even to himself, for Kagen wondered if perhaps his scholar brother's expeditions to the Winterwilds had exposed him to something that had possessed him. Or maybe some evil force had killed him and adopted his aspect. Now that magic had stepped out of legend and walked abroad in the world, Kagen knew that he had to accept all kinds of possibilities. Things he would have laughed at less than half a year ago were now part of the framework of the world.

"Shit on me," he muttered, and got up and went into the stable to fetch Jinx.

"I'll saddle him, sir," said the stable lad—the one who looked sharper than anyone else he'd met in that town.

"Thanks, boy," he said, tossing the lad a coin.

The youth snatched the coin deftly from the air and made it vanish into a pocket. "I'm not a boy."

That made Kagen pause as he was about to put a foot into the stirrup.

"What?"

"I'm a girl."

Kagen turned and gave the youth a longer, closer look. She had short hair and no trace of a beard, her clothes were oversize and filthy with stable muck, and she wore a scarf around her neck and knotted at the throat.

"You look like a boy."

The girl shrugged. "My pa's idea. So men won't mess with me."

Kagen grasped the saddle horn. "Then why tell me? Aren't you afraid I'll toss you into the hay and try to have my way with you?"

The girl gave him a long, appraising look. "No."

"Why not? Because I'm staying here?"

"No," she said. "Because you don't look like that kind of person."

"What kind of person do I look like? A eunuch?"

"No. You look sad and kind."

Kagen felt those words strike deep in his chest.

"I'm not a good man," he said. "Not at all."

"Yes," said the girl, and there was a strange light in her eyes that reminded Kagen of the witch Selvath. And even a bit of Maralina. "You are."

She turned away and began forking hay into a manger. Kagen studied her, seeing a straight back and hard hands and the side of a face that would never be pretty. He had caught a look at her eyes, though, as she turned. A quick glimpse, but it was enough. Suddenly he felt big and stupid and gruff and grubby, as this girl possessed more integrity and nobility than he could ever hope to have. And maybe some strange quality that either already existed or was awakened by the return of magic.

He tried to come up with something to say, but there was nothing in his personal vocabulary suitable to the moment. So, instead, he climbed into the saddle and walked Jinx out of the barn into the cold, clear morning.

CHAPTER FIFTY-SEVEN

"How are my children?" asked the Witch-king.

Madame Lucibel—muscular, thickset, trollish in aspect and nature—stood before the throne. Lord Nespar, his angular body looking even more sickly and frail in contrast, stood behind her, leaning on his staff.

"They're doing well enough, Majesty," said Lucibel. She had

a peculiar face that wore a perpetually mixed expression—half disapproving frown and half mocking smile.

"Define 'well enough,'" suggested the king mildly.

"They're smart as magpies when it comes to books, math, astronomy, and alchemy," said the governess. "Less so with geography and history. There were some issues with your fencing master, Sir Giles of Hock. Some discipline was required." She touched the braided wand of kindness thrust through her sash. "But we have that sorted now. And Sir Giles tells me that they're becoming quite talented little . . ."

She paused and fished for a word other than the one she intended to use. But the Witch-king waved it away.

"Are they content, madame?" he asked.

"Content?" she echoed, as if that word and its underlying concept were unknown to her. "I . . . I suppose they are, Majesty. All things considered."

The Witch-king leaned forward. "You may teach them and discipline them," he said. "You may scold them and exact any punishment that is appropriate, Madame Lucibel, for I will not tolerate weakness in them. Nor sentimentality. That is the worst of all. But hear me on this: I love my children. I want them to grow up wise and strong. I want them to be fearless and creative and subtle. My son and my daughter will one day sit on matched thrones where I now sit. They will rule the Yellow Empire. Be sure that this is your goal and that in trying to accomplish these things you do not break them."

"I—"

"Do you understand me?"

She straightened, swallowed hard, and then nodded. And in doing that, her own fell light seemed to dim. She did not see Nespar's reptilian smile at her discomfiture.

"I understand, Majesty," said the governess.

"Then be about your work," said the king, dismissing her.

CHAPTER FIFTY-EIGHT ◄━━━━━━━━━━━━

TEN DAYS EARLIER

Lieutenant Vorlon did not like Argon. Not at all.

He had been there twice as a lad, dragged north by his merchant uncle on buying trips. His uncle traded a camel train's–worth of toys fashioned from wood, stone, and scrap metals. Trinkets for the children of middle-class families, decorations for festivals tied to the Harvest faith, and decorations for modest houses through-out that part of the Silver Empire. Even as a boy, Vorlon hated that his uncle, descended from one of the great generals of Hak-kia, scraped by, selling junk. Particularly the festival objects. That faith had been forced upon Hakkia a thousand years ago, first as a heavily endorsed "elective" religion, and then—after the great rebellion three centuries past—as the only legally allowed reli-gion in Hakkia. Their own faith had been crushed under the heels of Lady Bellapher, acting as conquering general and agent of the empress.

Now, years later, it was a different world. Now it was the faith of the Harvest Gods that was crushed and prohibited. Now the Hakkians brought justice and the promise of a new future instead of cheap toys and knickknacks.

Even with that change, the lieutenant still loathed Argon. Con-quered or not, it was the symbol of oppression against his people and their true faith, and that stink would not wash off anytime soon. Certainly not in his lifetime, and likely not in the lifetime of his children back home. He wanted his tour to end so he could put in for a transfer back home.

He knew his men felt the same. After the excitement and tri-umph of the invasion, the challenge of *keeping* what had been taken was less glorious. There were small rebellions—generally no more than a single town or the more aggressive members of a trade union—but mostly his job was chasing minor criminals, posting decrees, and spending endless days on patrol. None of that was the job of a professional soldier. The rebellions should have been left to the regular troops, not to Vorlon and his platoon of Ravens. They were elite and had been promised important work.

There had been some hope—and some chatter among the lads—that with the disaster at the coronation war would erupt. That was something Vorlon wanted, and for weeks he was caught up in the excited anticipation of orders to join a proper battle.

The excitement faded when no armies rose to challenge the Hakkian rule.

His sergeant, Dehla, rode beside him, and as she often did, appeared to read his thoughts.

"Maybe we'll have a good day."

To the Hakkians, a "good day" was when they fought an enemy of equal or greater strength. The kind of battle where every survivor would be celebrated for their valor. Fortunes and promotion were a natural result of such an engagement. Dehla's saying it was not based on any specific or known threat, however. She said that sort of thing at least once a day while on patrol. Ever the optimist.

"That would be nice," said Vorlon sourly. "Before my sword turns to rust in its scabbard."

"I have a good feeling," Dehla assured him. "I dreamed last night that we charged into a storm of arrows and trampled them under our horses hooves."

"That would be *very* nice," sighed Vorlon.

They rode on through dappled sunlight, following a winding road through vast groves of apples and pears. Butterflies and bees flitted from flower to flower along the side of the road, and high above them the sky was a hard blue dome.

"What else happened in your dream?" asked the lieutenant.

"Mine were about frogs. The gods know why. I don't even like frogs. Tell me yours had some fun details."

The sergeant grinned and nodded. "Well," she said, "after the first flight of arrows, we raised shields and—"

She interrupted her own sentence with a heavy grunt.

"What?" asked Vorlon, who was using a small knife to scrape dirt from under his fingernails.

"I . . ." gurgled Dehla as she sagged from her saddle, pawing at Vorlon's leg for balance, and then fell heavily onto the road.

Lieutenant Vorlon gasped and reached for her, and that bend saved his life, as three arrows cut through the air where his head and shoulders had been a moment before. He fished for Dehla, caught a handful of the blue trim on her yellow cloak. Her slack weight pulled him half out of his own saddle, and the second wave of arrows struck his horse.

It was then that he realized what was happening.

The horse screamed and staggered sideways, dumping him onto the ground, on top of Dehla. The impact tore another—and final—grunt of pain from her, but the collision drove the arrows in her side deeper into her, one of them stabbing though lung tissue and into her struggling heart.

Vorlon tried to let go of her, but his hand was snagged by the cloak. He pivoted on his hip and kicked at the cloth while also trying to draw his sword. His ears were deafened by the shrieks of men and horses. He distantly heard the *thunk thunk thunk* of arrows hitting flesh, saddle leather, hard-packed road dirt, and trees on both sides of the road.

He managed to get his hand free and then his sword and was just working his legs clear when a shadow darkened the sky and he looked up to see his horse—a half ton of animal and saddlebags—toppling sideways onto him. The dying creature thrashed and squirmed in panic and agony.

He felt his ribs break, his thighs snap, and his sternum crack.

Suddenly the noise and commotion faded, taking much of the daylight with it. Lieutenant Vorlon flopped back and lay still. His hands and feet hurt but he could feel neither the arms nor legs to which they were attached. There was something warm and salty in his mouth, and taking even a slight breath was like inhaling broken glass.

Everything was quiet, though.

So very quiet.

Then someone came and stood above him, bending a little to peer over the belly of the now dead horse. The man was dressed in simple woodsman's clothes of a hooded green tunic over brown leggings. He wore a cap of soft wool. The man was young, little more than a lad, but there was a hardness in his features and his eyes looked ancient.

"Hakkian," said the young man.

"H-help me . . ." wheezed Vorlon. "By the . . . gods . . ."

The young man turned and gestured to someone Vorlon could not see, and that other person handed something over. The young man accepted it with a nod and showed it to the dying lieutenant. The thing he held was a standard, a flat piece of cloth anchored into a bamboo frame on a pole. There was an image embroidered crudely on the cloth, a disk of silver over which was a circle of thorny rose vines and a pair of crossed daggers. The painting was crude but the details were easy to pick out.

"Wh . . . who are . . . you?" Vorlon asked, forcing the words out with what little breath was left to him.

The young man raised the standard and removed a leather cap on the bottom, revealing a point that was as sharp as a spear point.

"We are the Sons of the Poison Rose," said the man.

And then he stabbed down with all his strength.

CHAPTER FIFTY-NINE

The trail Kagen followed ran straight as an arrow from the main street of town toward the wall of pine trees. Once inside the forest, the road began snaking around and angled upward. Kagen passed a few cabins where smoke drifted lazily from chimneys, but these dwindled behind him and soon vanished entirely.

The forest was dense with red alder, hemlock, black spruce, silver fir, and many other trees he could not put a name to, as well as ground cover of holly, winter rose, and hawthorn. Without the narrow road, the way would be impassible. Even so, the brush leaned out over the path, plucking at Kagen's cloak and snagging in Jinx's blanket.

Halfway to the garden, he passed a huge old mansion that was clearly abandoned. He slowed Jinx and studied the place because it was so strange a sight. There was no defensive perimeter, no fortified towers or moat. Just that mansion, looking as out of place as a palm tree in the middle of a snowfield. The walls were choked with some kind of tough, thorny creeper vines. He paused briefly, trying to work out why anyone would build such a grand place way out here, and why it had been abandoned. Filia had said that these northern forests were wild, with few people and many predatory animals. Bears, wolves, foxes, and even a kind of snow-colored apes, though Kagen thought his friend was bullshitting him about the latter. She had a very dry sense of humor and liked playing on his city-bred credulity.

He rode on, and once the mansion was lost in the distance behind him, Kagen felt his tension begin to ease. He regretted his harsh words at breakfast. Filia was right, damn her eyes, and he was wrong. Her stance was the one he himself would have taken only a few months ago, before the invasion.

And yet he felt a deep, aching frustration over not knowing how to stop the Hakkians, or what to do if the Witch-king was unable to be stopped. The unresolved anger and hurt in his mind festered again as he rode, bringing up new versions of punishment for the Hakkian people. Unfair, immoral, extreme, and yet—at least in thought—deeply satisfying.

He reached for a pendant he no longer had, seeking out of habit to take comfort from the icon of Father Ar. But that pendant was long gone, almost certainly stolen by the whore who got him drunk on the Night of the Ravens. Who possibly drugged him that night.

There were no gods watching over him, and that—as much as anything else—hurt him on a level so deep that it seemed bottomless. His gods had actually turned away from him. Tuke did not believe it had happened and Filia was on the fence, but Kagen knew it had happened.

The hurt turned into an ache in the center of his being that he could not soothe or salve, and that never went away. Before he'd met Tuke, Kagen tried to fill that void with wine, and he did a fair job of it for a while. But hiding from the truth is not the same as accepting or dealing with it.

He threw back his head and yelled a string of obscenities to the open air. Kagen yelled so loud it hurt his throat. The sound startled some birds from the trees, and Kagen saw with some annoyance that they were not the nightbirds. *His* nightbirds. In fact, he had not seen a single one of them since the fight aboard *Dagon's Swan*.

"Even you lot have given me up for lost," he mumbled.

Jinx whinnied nervously.

Kagen rode on, and as he did so he tried to let it all go. The hurt and loss, the fear and heartbreak, the jealousy and longing, the frustration and bloodlust. All of it.

That was a process that took hours and miles, and yet the inner softening did come. Slowly, reluctantly, even grudgingly, but the anger and darkness that had been clinging to him since Argentium began to peel and flake away.

The woods were beautiful. Green trees and white snow. Birds of surprising colors. Plenty of small game darting out of his path. A frozen, sunlit waterfall that looked like a spill of diamonds down the face of rocks rich with quartz and fool's gold. The sun cruised like a great ship between the islands of the clouds, and if it did not greatly warm the day, it at least sold the illusion of warmth, and that was its own kind of gift.

Kagen drifted into thoughts and memories, wondering where his other siblings were. Of all of them, he most missed the two brothers everyone called the Twins, even though they were a year apart in age and one was blond and the other redheaded. Jheklan and Faulker. He hoped they were still alive and outside of the reach of the Hakkian Ravens. How would they react to the news that Herepath was the monster who had killed their parents? How were they processing their own grief at the deaths of their parents and brothers Hugh and Degas? He wished he knew how to contact them. Of all his siblings, they were the ones most likely to sign on with Kagen in an attempt to bring down the Witch-king.

He hoped.

Kagen was chewing on that when the trees seemed to part like curtains, revealing a clearing that had only recently begun to grow wild. There were the remnants of cultivated groves of winter fruits and vegetables laid out in geometric patterns around a dome-like building.

The garden.

It was the northernmost such church in the whole of the Silver Empire, and Kagen knew from Tuke's maps that the line of trees on the other side of the clearing marked the edge of the nation of Nelfydia. Beyond that was a vast wilderness of permanently frozen ground and uncountable miles of snow and ice. Mountains rose from the snowfields like forgotten islands, and between many of those peaks were glaciers of incredible antiquity. The ice there was so compacted, so dense, that it looked more blue than white. No one he had ever spoken with knew what was up there. There were plenty of rumors, tall tales, and legends, but nothing that Kagen felt was reliable. But that was something to consider later. For now, he wanted very much to visit that garden. Jinx seemed to understand that, and he put a little extra effort into reaching it.

When they arrived, Kagen dismounted, adjusted the blankets over his horse and gave him some water and food, then walked to the front door of the old church. Close up, he could see some of the same signs of desecration that marked every garden he'd seen since the Night of the Ravens. Obscenities had been painted on the walls—much of it in what looked like blood or shit. There were yellow stains on the tan stucco from where Hakkian soldiers had pissed on it—something Kagen had learned was required of them by their officers.

The door stood open, and out of habit, he slid one of his daggers from its sheath and held it low by his side. Out of sight but ready.

The inside of the garden broke his heart. It was of the old style, with more exposed wood walls and floor, and a complexity of beams overhead. In this style, no iron nails were used during construction, and instead pegs, holes and slots, and various kinds of rustic methods had been employed. Much more painstaking and difficult, and it stood as tribute to craftsmanship and faith. It implied a devotion to gods-given skills, and also humility. Kagen knew that the Harvest Gods would have been pleased.

Were they watching now? He wondered. Would his pilgrimage count at all in his desire to reclaim his damned soul?

He hoped so. Far more than he let on to Tuke and Filia. With them he pretended an indifference about his separation from the church. Or at least he hoped that's how they saw it. In truth, though, faith had always mattered quite a lot to him. He loved the structures of the Green Faith. The rituals of sowing and planting, the parables and stories that used metaphors of the natural world to explain the challenges of day-to-day life. The forgiveness promised by the Gardeners.

Where was that forgiveness now? Father Ar and Mother Sah had turned their backs on him in the field outside of Argentium. But he had taken their side against the Hakkians. Did that count for nothing? Or was redemption a process? He had learned in Garden school that the gods of the Harvest forgive sinners, and that they were always watching.

Kagen stood in the doorway of the garden and took a deep breath to steady his jittery nerves. Then he pulled the door shut behind him and walked up the aisle toward the altar. There he stopped. The sacred images of the gods had all been hacked away, and the wall hangings that traditionally showed scenes from the history of the gods and their interaction with saints and prophets were gone. Stolen or burned, most likely.

Even so, Kagen knelt and recited a series of prayers he'd first learned as a lad. As he spoke them aloud, he turned clockwise, following the story those tapestries told in every garden through-out the empire. He did not need to have them visible to allow him to see each scene—the creation of the world, the first sunrise, the first rainfall, the planting of the sacred seeds from which all the forests of the world would grow, the child seeds planted in the Grove of Forever, from which the first man and woman bloomed like flowers. On and on, until he had completed a full circle and recited all twenty-four verses of the prayer.

Then he bowed his head, covering his face in his hands, and prayed with his whole heart.

For forgiveness.

For acceptance.

For healing.

For clarity.

He was deep, deep in that prayer when the door burst inward

and a group of killers came rushing in, steel weapons glittering in their hands. They were dressed in crimson robes, like monks or priests. And they raced down the aisle toward Kagen, screaming for his death.

CHAPTER SIXTY

"Damn your soul to everlasting hellfire," snarled the priest.

"Too late," said Kagen as he drew his daggers.

They flooded the room.

Kagen could not even count the number of red-clad maniacs who howled for his blood. He'd come to a spot near the top of the known world, this old building that had once been a garden, here in the northernmost corner of Nelfydia, to escape this kind of thing, looking for safety, for quiet. For a place to rest while he thought through all that had happened, where he could try to get clarity for what to do next.

But they always found him. Not this group—they were unknown to him—but someone aching to end his life and take trophies— proof of death—back to the Hakkians.

Back to the Witch-king.

Kagen backed away, looking for an exit or a clear place to fight. He found neither.

The attackers were of a kind; all of them had shaved heads and tattooed scalps. They wore red robes belted at the waist with rough cord, marking them as monks of some order, or perhaps priests. They carried similar weapons—hatchets or curved daggers etched with swirling patterns of stars, moons, and crawling spiders. They wore sandals that looked homemade and which were laced into intricate patterns.

The one who'd spoken to him—so far, the only one who had said anything—had a thick accent that marked him as a true foreigner. Certainly not from Nelfydia, nor from the nations directly south, Vahlycor or Zaare. Kagen thought he might have been from one of the lands on the eastern side of the Cathedral Mountains. From distant Yehtec or Ashgulan.

His brain recorded all of those details in a flash, in the way a warrior does and must. Details mattered, as his mother had taught him long ago: *"Fight your fight, but learn from it as well. You can never predict which detail will save your life."*

Kagen had his daggers in his fist, using the alligator-tooth guard, the blade in his right held point upward, the one in his left inverted so that he could parry and trap with it.

One of the red priests faked high and then darted in low to try to slash Kagen's leg. It was the kind of move that left the attacker wide open to a downward slash or stab, and only a person dedicated to the result and not to personal safety would ever use it. Even if marginally successful, it would stall Kagen long enough for the others to attack from other angles and slash him to ribbons.

Madmen, thought Kagen, but his body was already in motion.

Instead of dealing with the man diving low, he hop-stepped to his side and let the fool thump down on his chest. Then Kagen swept a dagger up to block the expected follow-up by another attacker and pivoted fast to slash the man across the body, just below the knot of his belt. The twin daggers Kagen used were made from ore taken from a meteor and kept at a razor edge. They parted the cloth, belly flesh, and lower abdominal muscles. The man screamed as his guts spilled out onto the floor in a big, wet pile.

Kagen jagged inward and to the right, ducking a hatchet and slashing another priest's inner thigh. Blood jetted out of the severed artery. Then Kagen stepped on the lower back of the first man, who was still down, and used that to boost him into a leap at a fourth man. He used the inverted dagger to block a knife slash and used the weight of his body dropping down to turn the edge of his other dagger into a chopper. A hand leapt from a wrist.

Kagen kicked another priest in the side of the knee, pivoted off of the impact point, and snapped a second kick into the balls of the man beside him.

All of this happened in seconds. One man with his guts on the ground, another handless; one bleeding from a severed artery, another with a shattered knee; and one curled into a fetal knot with his hands clamped around smashed testicles. Plus the one on whose back he'd stepped, who was flattened like a beached manta on the floor.

But there were more.

They crowded into the small garden.

"Gods of the flaming Pit," he snarled.

Kagen wasted no time gaping, though. His mother had taught him better than that.

He hooked a wooden stool with one foot and lift-kicked it, sending it at the head of the first person in a line of killers rushing down the aisle between rows of pews. The man saw it and bashed it aside with a contemptuous grunt, and as he did that, Kagen slashed him diagonally across the face, taking one eye and slicing neatly through the man's nose. The man screamed and staggered back, right into the knives of the priests behind him. That stalled the line and Kagen left them to sort it out while he stepped onto a pew and from there jumped behind two other men, who were trying to blindside him. As he dropped down, he used the inverted dagger to trap one man's neck between blade and forearm, the weight of his landing body turning that trap into a butcher's cut that opened veins and arteries in the throat. The spray of blood hit the second man full in the face. In that instant of confusion Kagen whipped his other dagger down and the top three inches of the weapon sliced down through the second man's crotch.

That left five more of the killers uninjured. They scrambled over the pews to get at him, but Kagen laughed as he led them on a merry chase. He moved without pattern, knocking over tall candlesticks, upending pews or kicking them so they slid abruptly as the priests tried to step on them. He fought to wound, to maim, rather than kill. Wounded men were a hindrance to their fellows, and badly wounded enemies could be dispatched later.

The priest who'd spoken yelled at him again as he tried to scale the upended pews. His face was smeared with the blood of the others of his order, but he was as yet unhurt.

"You cannot hope to win," screamed the man. "We are legion."

"Then you should have brought the whole legion with you," sneered Kagen. He stabbed the man closest to him and left the blade in the dying man's chest, then used his free hand to pull a short knife from a belt sheath. Kagen reversed it in his hand and whipped his arm up and out. The priest who'd spoken gagged as the blade buried itself in his throat. Kagen tore the dagger free of the first man and with both matched weapons he drove at the remaining priests.

They fought hard.

They tried to surround him, wear him down, cut him to pieces.

They tried.

But Kagen killed them all. He even cut the throats of the wounded.

Almost all . . .

He left one of them alive, though barely. While the man bled, Kagen went outside to see if there were more of the bastards waiting.

━━━━━━━━━━━━━━━━━▶ **CHAPTER SIXTY-ONE**

The fields surrounding the garden were overgrown. Horses were tethered in a pasture of spring grass, indifferent to what had happened to their riders. Kagen's horse, Jinx, munched dandelions nonchalantly, but his eyes were alert and his ears swiveled as he listened to the day.

"Is that the lot?" asked Kagen.

Jinx regarded him for a moment and then took a long and comprehensive shit, ending it with a prodigious fart.

"I guess that about says it," said Kagen, waving the stink away from his nose. He scanned the horizon, saw nothing, turned, and went back inside.

Kagen counted the corpses and was surprised that there were twelve of them. More than he thought. Thirteen soon, he mused, as he went and crouched over the last of them, a black-haired, black-eyed fellow of about thirty. The man lay among the splintered debris that was once a wooden chair. He had his hands clamped over a mortal wound in his chest.

"Who the fuck are you and why the fuck did you try to kill me?" asked Kagen, pitching his tone to be conversational.

"Be damned to you," gasped the priest.

"Thought we already covered that," said Kagen. "I already *am* damned. Don't waste your last breaths on nonsense. Who sent you?"

The man shook his head, but that action sent ripples of agony through him and he cried out. Tears leaked from the corners of his eyes.

"Did my brother send you?" asked Kagen. "Was it Herepath? Was it the Witch-king of Hakkia?"

When he'd spoken his older brother's name, there was no reaction at all in the priest's eyes. However, when Kagen mentioned the Witch-king, those eyes flared for a moment and immediately shifted away.

"You're dying, friend," said Kagen. "We both know it. I can send you on your way quick and clean and you can square things with whatever god you pray to, or I can make this last all day and into tonight. I know how, and trust me when I say that you don't want to know how bad this can get."

Nothing.

"I'm not asking you to betray your god or your vows," continued Kagen. "Just tell me why you and your friends want me dead."

Before Kagen could stop him, the man snatched up a jagged splinter of wood and with an earsplitting cry drove it into his own throat. It was so sudden, so savage, and so unexpected that Kagen recoiled.

"Gods of the burning Pit!" he swore, as blood welled around the wooden spike. The priest's grimace of pain melted into a smile that bordered on the erotic, and then all expression vanished as he faded and died.

CHAPTER SIXTY-TWO

Ryssa walked along a narrow goat path that was one part of a great volcano. There was a bit of heat rising, and a wisp of smoke, but the fiery heart of it still slept. She wondered if the volcano dreamed, as the great god Cthulhu dreamed.

She wondered if Miri was down there beneath the waves, dreaming of her.

Those thoughts brought cold tears to Ryssa's eyes, but they clung to her lower lashes, refusing to fall. Soft winds fluttered the skirts of her gown. The colors of mourning on Tull Yammoth were the same as the colors of celebration—white with the subtlest overlay of sea green. However, Ryssa had searched in market stalls for dark green cloth, which was the mourning color of the Faith of the Harvest. She wore that more somber color as a scarf that wound around her shoulders and over her head, leaving her pale face bare to the sea wind.

Ryssa was aware that people stopped and watched her every time she passed. They smiled at her and bowed, spreading their arms out to the side in a display of openness and emptiness, which was part of their religion. The religion of the Dreaming God.

She knew also that they had a nickname for her, spoken in hushed and reverential whispers. The Widow. No one told her that, but she learned it from overheard whispers.

There goes the Widow.

See? That is the Widow, beloved of the great Dreamer.

Isn't she beautiful in her sacred grief?

And on and on.

The Widow.

At the highest point on the edge of the caldera, Ryssa stopped and stood staring at the waves more than three thousand feet below. Sharp claws of black volcanic rock jutted outward from the base of the cone, and they seemed to scratch at the waves, frothing and churning them. Legions of seabirds, their bellies as white as purity and their eyes as black as sin, clustered on the tips of those rocks or coasted on the slow thermals as if gravity meant nothing to them.

Ryssa leaned out as far as she could and wondered how much and for how long it would hurt if she just kept leaning and let herself fall. Surely it would hurt less than the pain that burned like raging fire in her heart.

Miri was dead. Sacrificed to try to rouse Cthulhu from his slumber of uncounted millennia. Pierced through the heart as she lay on the altar of the Dreaming God. Sacrificed—*murdered*—by a dagger Ryssa held. She had lain as if filled with joy that rose to true ecstasy. The high priestess, Mother Sithra, took a dagger whose blade made from coral and pressed it into Ryssa's hand.

It was all symbolic, they told her. No harm would come of it, they said.

Those words—those lies—still echoed in her head. And her horror for letting herself be fooled into complicity. Ryssa had placed the tip of the knife on the soft, beautiful skin of her friend, her mentor, her true love.

"Oh, Miri," wept Ryssa that day, *"I don't want to hurt you."*

"You won't hurt me, my sweetheart," Miri had promised. *"You can't. You could never hurt me. Now listen to me. Forget everyone else. Forget the thunder and lightning. Just look at me. See me. Do you trust me?"*

Ryssa had nodded, and the action made her tears fall onto Miri's bare skin. *"I trust you."*

"Do you love me?"

"I love you."

Ryssa's hand had trembled, though she fought to hold it steady so as not to cut too soon or too much. The tip of the blade had pressed into Miri's skin, Miri using her fingertips to lightly steady the knife and hold it in its precise placement.

"I love you," said Miri again.

"I love you," said Ryssa, meaning it with her whole heart and soul.

And then Miri's hands had closed like iron around Ryssa's hand, and with a sudden, terrible force, she had plunged the blade deep into her own beating heart.

Every part of that memory was as clear now as when it had happened. Every sight and sound, the smell of the sea, the roaring adoration of the crowd, the feel of the knife in her hand. Miri's touching, guiding her into that terrible, terrible act of commission. It did not matter that it was Miri's own strength that forced the knife to do its ugly work; the knife was still in Ryssa's hand.

If I fall, she wondered, not for the first time, *will I find you, my love?*

The waves seemed to promise that she would. But above and around her the seagulls screamed at her to stay where she was.

The Widow looked down at the water. Wanting to find Miri. Wanting to spend eternity with her. The winds blew past her, and for just a moment—a single, golden, shining, beautiful moment— she thought she heard Miri's voice.

No, my sweet, said the wind. *The world is not done with you. No, not done at all.*

Ryssa staggered back from the edge, turning, as if somehow she could see Miri's ghost in the wind that had just blown past.

But there was nothing at all to see. The echo of those words filled her mind and her heart. On that day, at least, Ryssa did not fall.

The Widow turned slowly and walked away.

CHAPTER SIXTY-THREE

Kagen sat there staring at the man, watching the flow of blood slow and stop. He felt stunned and angry and frustrated. And deeply confused.

"Gods damn it," he yelled, but the chapel was utterly still now, and his words echoed around and came back to him, changing from what he said to "Gods damn you."

He knew it was an illusion, a product of his own despair. For all that, it sounded real and it stabbed him to the heart. The pain ignited his frustration, and Kagen leapt to his feet and spent a useless minute raging around the room, overturning pews, kicking the corpses, yelling at the heavens. His anger was as hot for himself as for these red priests. He knew he could have played it better. Tried mercy and first aid, or tried to reason without threats. He wished he hadn't killed all the wounded, which—though it felt like a smart tactic in the moment—was, on reflection, stupid and ill-considered.

When his rage was spent, he stood breathing harder than he had after the battle. Sweat ran in cold lines down his cheeks and inside his clothes. Kagen grabbed the edge of one toppled pew, jerked it upright, and sat down heavily.

"*Damn you*," he howled, directing his bile to everyone and everything. A few seconds later, in a smaller and more fractured voice he whispered, "Damn you all."

His body trembled with nervous tension from the fight. It was always like that, especially when the battle was a surprise attack. The blood madness was still there, ready to do more, wanting more. The shakes would start soon, he knew. That happened, too, and it was something that used to unnerve him. The first time he'd felt that rush and then those shakes he was afraid that it was fear or, worse, cowardice. But his older brothers assured him that they'd all felt it. Everyone does. Kagen had been a child then. He was a man now, and he accepted every twitch and tremble as natural. He allowed it without hanging any emotional meaning on it. As warriors do.

He looked at the dead men. Now he had no one left to interrogate.

Instead, he tried the old trick of acting calm in order to try to trick his muscles into unclenching and his heart to stop racing. He cleaned his knives unhurriedly on the red robes of the corpse nearest to him, then retrieved his throwing knife and wiped it on the chief priest's chest. After a moment's reflection, Kagen went through their clothes, purses, and saddlebags, finding some food and water, a skin of some strange wine that tasted like a leprous housecat had pissed in it, a pouch of silver and copper, and several small carvings. The man he thought of as the chief priest had such a carving in the leather purse tied to his waist, as did each of the others. He stood the objects all in a row.

Each of the carvings was a variation on the same creature—a demon or god of a kind Kagen had never seen before. It looked like a short, fat creature with a face that was a bizarre blend of toad and bat. He had half-closed eyes that could be interpreted as either sleepy or sly, and the tip of a pointed tongue protruded obscenely from between rows of sharp teeth.

"Who in the burning courts of hell are you?" asked Kagen. His word echoed oddly and uncomfortably in the empty garden.

That sobered him. It reminded him quite sharply that this place used to be a church. And even though his own gods, Father

Ar and Mother Sah, had literally turned their backs on him—something he saw during the horrible night when the Silver Empire fell—he still feared them. He feared all gods nearly as much as he hated them.

Kagen had always been devout in his faith, and if not the most pious of all his brothers and sisters, and with a roster of earthy sins that would never qualify him for sainthood, he never felt unwelcome in any garden. He did now, and very much so. That feeling extended to the trinkets of other faiths. Where once he would have mocked what his family's Gardener would have called "pagan junk," recent events had somewhat broadened his perspective. Any thoughts about smashing the carvings flitted into his mind and were chased out by common sense and natural caution. Being abandoned by gods was bad enough; he did not want to actively encourage their wrath.

Kagen stood, gathered up the idols, and placed them on the floor near the chief priest. He stood them in a half circle around the man's head. He wasn't sure why that position, but it felt right in the moment. A necessary ceremony.

But he kept one of them as he walked outside. There, in the bright sunlight, he held it up, speaking to it as it were a person.

"I killed your priests in self-defense," he said. "You're a god; you saw it. You know that I did what I had to do. That was between them and me. Whoever you are, I give my respects." He paused, and after a moment's awkward hesitation, bowed his head for a few silent seconds. When he was done, he gave the last idol a frank stare. "I'll say this, though . . . If you have influence over your followers, don't let any more of them come after me."

Then he knelt and placed the last idol on the flagstone walkway that wound up to the garden door.

Nothing about the last few minutes made any real sense to him. The priests—if such they truly were—belonged to a church unknown to him. The tattoos on their faces reminded him vaguely of some he'd seen in coastal towns in Theria, but most of them were white men and the greater population of that nation was black. Apart from that, the main god of Theria was Dagon, and Kagen's friend Tuke carried a statue of the fish god. Dagon was nothing at all like the boar-headed idol he'd taken from the red priests.

So who were they? He doubted they were priests of any Nelfydian gods. These northern gods were moody, bitter, and combative giants of ice or rock, and they looked human enough. The local priesthood were shamans in furs and leather hung with many beads and trinkets. No, the boar-headed god's people were not from this part of the world. He stood and looked north. The deserted garden was the northernmost point for both the Silver Empire and the Faith of the Garden. Both were extinct now; they died the night Hakkia invaded the capital cities of every nation in the empire.

Beyond a narrow strip of a pine forest was an area that on most maps was merely marked as "unknown" or "unexplored." Kagen knew people who believed that the actual edge of the world was a couple of thousand miles across the snowy wastes. Kagen's father had always scoffed at such tales and was one of the class of educated nobles who believed the world was not flat but somehow round. That, of course, seemed absurd to Kagen, and he'd spent fruitless hours as a lad trying to make his toy soldiers stand on the bottom of a globe. But they always fell off.

Herepath believed the world was round, too. Kagen felt a sharp pang at that. Although he hated the Witch-king with his whole heart, the younger Kagen—the lad and the young man—had loved Herepath. That part of him mourned as if Herepath were dead. On some level he even hoped that the revelation of seeing his older brother's face that night in the great hall in the palace of Argentium was the product of some sorcery. A glamour, perhaps. After all, how could so fine and noble a man as Herepath ever become so corrupted, so twisted, that he would betray his nation, his empress, and his family?

"Don't walk that path," he told himself aloud.

Kagen took a long breath to steady his emotions, then tried to focus on the issues at hand. The red priests and their monster god. Who were they? That was one question. The other was, Why were they hunting him?

He chewed on that and other, related questions that formed in his mind. How had they found him here? If this was in one of the great cities or a seaport, Kagen could build a case for how these men had located him. But way up here? Right on the edge of a wasteland where only polar bears, gods, and ghosts lived? That made no sense.

He chewed on this as he stripped the saddles from each horse and examined the animals for brands. There were none. Nor any tattoos.

"Maybe the day isn't entire shit after all," he said. One of the horses bobbed her head as if agreeing with him. He gave the mare's nose a friendly stroke and she flicked her tail and blew softly.

Kagen tied the animals into a string and attached the lead to Jinx's saddle. Thirteen healthy and unbranded horses were worth a lot of money.

Kagen was about to mount when an idea struck him. He went back inside and spent a few minutes writing a message on the wall. He stood for a while considering it.

"Be damned to you, too," he said.

Then he mounted Jinx and turned his head to the northeast.

CHAPTER SIXTY-FOUR

EIGHT DAYS EARLIER

The courier brought the artifact to his master, Lord Jakob Ravensmere, Royal Historian in the service of the Witch-king. His title had been that of Imperial Historian, but that had been conditional. Now he used the politically appropriate one. He rather hated that, because Imperial Historian sounded—and moreover *felt*—like what he deserved to be called.

He was poolside at his estate, watching leaves sail across the breeze-touched water. Three of his apprentices were huddled together on the far side, hotly debating translations of a book bought at great expense from a traveler who claimed it was from a crypt in a Vespian city. Jakob's master had an extremely keen interest in such objects—and really, in any items brought from Vespia, the island of Skyria, or the ghost cities scattered throughout the Cathedral Mountains.

The courier, in livery of the road scouts division of the Hakkian intelligence service, stood to attention, eyes staring at nothing as he waited to be acknowledged.

"You may approach," said Jakob, pitching his voice and even inflection to match that of the Witch-king. There were rumors floating around the western lands that Jakob was a distant relative of the Witch-king, which made even higher-placed nobles and officers treat him with cautious deference. Only his most trusted inner circle of apprentices knew that Jakob had started those rumors in order to achieve exactly that effect.

The courier, sweating badly despite the mild day, stepped forward and offered a very low bow. He carried with him a standard that had a sharply pointed bottom and a top crested with a bamboo frame on which a piece of yellow cloth was stretched. The cloth was roughly cut and spattered with dried blood.

"My lord," said the courier, "I was instructed to bring this and to give it directly into your hands." He named the intelligence officer who had sent him, and it was a person of high rank. A person Jakob knew well enough to have trust in this agent.

"Show it to me," said Jakob.

The courier bobbed his head again, stood the pole on its pointed end, and turned the crest toward the historian. The symbol displayed was a circle of thorny rose vine overlaying a silver disk.

"Where was this found?" asked Jakob.

"Northeast of here, my lord," said the courier, naming a small town in central Argon. "It was set atop a mound of heads." He paused. "The heads of a platoon of Ravens."

Jakob rose to his feet. "What is this you say? Tell me every detail."

The courier produced a map of the part of Argon that included his standard route. He placed a finger on the spot where the patrol had been ambushed.

"Who else has seen this?" demanded the historian.

"It was reported by a local farmer," explained the courier. "Several people from the nearby town came to see it, and the town's beadle reported it to my lieutenant. He is trying to match the heads to the register of soldiers who were part of that patrol. Quite a few of the people from that whole area have seen it. There was quite a crowd."

"So now everyone in that part of the country knows about this," said Jakob.

"I'm afraid so, my lord."

Jakob nodded, dashed off a brief note to the lieutenant, and sent the courier away.

Then the historian ordered his servants to pack a bag and prepare his carriage. Within an hour he was on the road back to the palace in Argentium.

CHAPTER SIXTY-FIVE

King Hariq al-Huk, thirty-second of his name, lord of Samud, master of ships, divinely appointed Archer of Heaven, and divinely ordained protector of the realm, sat on his throne.

He was squat, broad, and muscular. His skin was a smooth olive color marked here and there by old scars, and his eyes were so dark that they looked black instead of brown. He wore his beard trimmed into three points like the tines of a trident. Around his neck he wore a small but exquisitely fashioned arrow on a slender gold chain.

A big middle-aged man stood before the throne, but the room was otherwise empty, except for the soldiers stationed beside the door at the far end of the hall. Those soldiers stood with strung bows, though no arrows were nocked. Not that it mattered. If one of the guests attempted to harm the king, he would be dead with two arrows between his shoulder blades before steel could clear sheath. These archers were masters even in a nation known for its archery.

"You've come a long way," said the king. His face was stern, mouth hard and unsmiling. "Coming to my court is risky."

The visitor gave a small bow of acknowledgment. He was a tall, thickset man with the dark skin of a Therian and eyes the color of milky jade. He wore robes of sea green, belted with a gold sash. A thick silver chain around his neck supported an elaborate pendant fashioned to look like a gigantic squid with a sperm whale caught in its tentacles. The ring on his right index finger matched the pale color of his eyes precisely.

"Your Majesty," he said in a rich baritone, "my name is Hannibus Greel and—"

"I know who you are," interrupted al-Huk. There was no hint of warmth in his tone or in his eyes. "And I can guess why you're here. I wonder, though, if you are acting as official envoy for the Therian government, or are you representing *other* interests? No . . . don't look so surprised. I know your family well enough to know that you have political and financial concerns resulting from the Night of the Ravens. You lost eighty-four ships that night, all of them burned to the waterline during the invasion."

Greel nodded. "I am not here as a representative of my country," he said. "Not officially or unofficially. I am here as a citizen of the Silver Empire."

"The empire is dead."

"If I may, Majesty, the empire has fallen," said Greel. "It only dies if a new emperor is named or if the submonarchs vote to dissolve it."

Al-Huk took a wine cup from a table beside his throne and sipped it. "You are still a Therian. Which camp, though? Do you side with those blaming Kagen Vale and the Argonian nobles who attempted to assassinate the usurper or with those who blame the Hakkians themselves? Be careful how you answer, my friend. I am not easily fooled, and there is a high price for attempting to deceive me."

"Majesty, you put me in a dangerous position, because you have not yet made a public statement of where Samud itself lies."

"I went to Argentium to participate in the coronation," said al-Huk, "and I would have seen that crown on the Witch-king's head."

Greel nodded again. "I was there, Majesty. I was in the back of the hall."

The king of Samud said nothing. He sipped his wine and studied the man with reptilian patience.

"I say that I am in a dangerous position," said Greel, "but I do not feel that I am speaking to an enemy. I feel that I may stand in the presence of an ally. A very great ally."

"Allied against . . . ?" asked al-Huk.

"Against the Hakkians."

"You say that, despite my participation in the coronation ceremony?" asked the king.

"Yes, Your Majesty."

"Why?"

"Because you described the Witch-king as a usurper," said Greel.

"That is a flimsy platform on which to stand," said al-Huk. "Perhaps you are naive and hopeful."

"If so, then I am at your mercy, Majesty."

"You're at my mercy regardless, Hannibus Greel," said the king. "You represent no nation, not even your own, which means you have no diplomatic protections. I could order you whipped or hung and be within my rights."

"Yes, Majesty," said Greel, "you could do that. My life is yours to take."

Al-Huk smiled thinly. "I'm glad we are clear on that. Now tell me, who *do* you represent?"

Greel took a breath and said, "I represent a group of nobles, merchants, and important citizens from many of the Silver Empire's nations."

"Ah," said al-Huk. "A partisan."

"A patriot, Majesty."

"Gods of the Pit, save me from zealots."

"May the Gods of the Harvest save us from the coming darkness, Majesty," countered Greel.

"And an idealist," said al-Huk. He sighed and set his cup aside. "You are not the first or the twentieth person to come here begging for troops, ships, or money. Each of those was turned away empty-handed. I do not make it my habit to become involved in pointless intrigues."

"Pointless, Majesty?" said Greel, his tone infused with obvious disapproval. A risky move in such an encounter, and both he and the king knew it. "I believe that there is very valid point."

"The Hakkians conquered the Silver Empire," said al-Huk sharply. "The empress is dead."

"She is dead, yes," said Greel, "but there are heirs."

"Those children? The twins, Gavran and her brother Foscor?" asked al-Huk. "That's who you mean? If you were there in the great hall of Argentium, then you know that Captain Vale called them out as Seedlings of Gessalyn, but the children themselves refuted that claim. They are the same ages, perhaps, as the empress's twins, but no official claims have been made to assert the legitimacy of Vale's claims."

"I *know* those children, Majesty," said Greel. "I have dined with Empress Gessalyn at the palace many times. I have dangled those children on my knees. They were, without doubt, Alleyn and Desalyn, Seedlings of the empress and heirs to the throne of the Silver Empire."

Al-Huk studied him for several long moments. "This is a very dangerous claim, Lord Greel."

"It would hardly be the first time, Majesty, that the truth has been a danger to someone willing to speak it."

"You realize that if I come out officially in support of their claim to the throne, it would be a de facto declaration of rebellion?"

"Yes, Majesty."

"And I would be rebelling against those very children, as they have very definitely and publicly claimed to be the heirs of the usurper?"

"Yes, Majesty."

Al-Huk laughed. "You must think me the biggest fool in the world."

"A fool, Majesty? No. Never that," said Greel. "I have always regarded you as a great king who has never been afraid of the truth."

"Ah, and now we get to the flattery portion of the discussion." His eyes narrowed in shrewd appraisal. "I will give you ten minutes, Hannibus Greel. You have that long to sell your argument. Be careful, though, because if I do not like what I hear, if I think you are lying to me or trying to manipulate me, then you will spend the rest of the day screaming for your mother."

Greel's eyes were equally cold. "After my father's death, my widowed mother took holy orders and became a nun at a garden in Theria. When the Ravens invaded, she was raped and crucified to the wall of that garden and was still alive when they set it on fire. I did all of my screaming then, Majesty. I have nothing left for you but the truth."

CHAPTER SIXTY-SIX

The royal twins crept up the tower stairs without making a sound.

They had learned stealth. Part of it was what their fencing master, Sir Giles of Hock, had taught them about how to move. Now that they accepted the necessity and practicality of his tuition, they threw themselves into the training. The other part was a shared natural talent for slyness. Their feet made no sound, and each had changed into clothes that did not rustle and soft-soled shoes.

Getting past the guards was easier than they thought, and once free of watchful eyes, they slunk up the stone steps, going round and around the tower. They liked the clammy stone and ran their fingers through patches of moss where no light ever fell.

A rat, startled by their sudden appearance, scuttled toward a crack between flat stair and riser, but Foscor—quick as a snake—darted out her hands and caught it. She and Gavran crouched over it, listening to its terrified squeaks and shrieks. They grinned at each other as fleas jumped from the bristling black hair and landed on Foscor's skin.

"Want to see something wonderful?" asked Foscor in a whisper.

"Always," hissed her brother.

"Look!" she said, and with a quick twist she snapped the rat's back. It uttered a piercing shriek but did not die. She handed it carefully to her brother, who kissed it and laid it down on the step. The crippled animal tried to move, but its lower half was as still as death, and that gave its feeble upper half no strength to flee.

The children watched it struggle and almost—*almost*—grabbed each other's hands in delight. But by reflex they each snatched their hands back. The *whoosh-whack* of Madam Lucibel's wand of kindness was too sharp in their minds. And while neither of them minded pain—pain was delightful—sometimes the beatings left them unable to run, climb, play, or fence. And so they eschewed that contact.

They left the rat to gasp and wheeze and die and continued climbing the stairs.

CHAPTER SIXTY-SEVEN

Kagen rode through the frosty afternoon. The map he'd studied gave him a landmark: a huge chunk of rock that Filia said was what was left of a falling star that struck the region five hundred years before. It was the size of a small hut and squatted in a crater that had since been reclaimed by the forest, with all manner of thorny bushes growing so close that the meteor looked like a giant egg in a nest.

The directions said to turn more directly north, which put him on a disused sheep path. The bones of several hundred sheep lined the road, but whatever had killed them—and the why of it—belonged to someone else's story. Twice he got off his horse and squatted along the verge to examine those bones, looking for tool marks of any kind—axe, cleaver, skinning knife—but he found none. Instead, he saw sharp but rounded marks that suggested teeth and claws, but even then, the marks did not match anything he recognized.

He was a moderately competent hunter, but no more so than any other city-bred person. Most of his hunting experience had been from the occasional day out with his older brothers and a group of huntsmen from the palace. It was the latter who did the tracking and skinning, and it was they who knew the difference between a tiger's bite and that of a wolf. Now that Kagen was on the run, his woodcraft and hunting skills were improving, but he was very aware that he still had much to learn. He knew a few dozen footprints, but only just. He could tell horse droppings from bear scat, but rarely many animals in between. It was a dangerous hole in his knowledge, and he felt its lack quite strongly while crouching there among the bones.

He had no real idea what had killed so many sheep. There was a confusion of spoor, but mostly old and small and frozen into the earth from animals passing while the ground was still wet enough to take their prints. Now that the ground was frozen, it would have taken a much savvier eye than his to read the scene. He wished his brother Faulker was there. Of all the family, he had spent the most time with Wurgin, the palace huntsman. Granted, that had been a long game, to try to get Wurgin's daughter, Peony, out of her bloomers—an act that eventually earned him a savage hiding by Wurgin—but the woodland knowledge stuck with Faulker long after his ass and back healed from the huntsman's leather belt.

What, Kagen wondered, would Faulker have read here?

He turned and looked as deeply into the woods as the shadows allowed. The pine trees stood in their millions, huddled together as if trading secrets. He could hear them whispering as the wind stirred the branches. Off to his left an owl hooted, and the strangeness of the moment turned the sound into something threatening. Kagen rested one hand on the handle of one of his daggers.

He looked down again at the bones. There was not a shred of meat left on them. Even the last vestiges of cartilage had been stripped away. When he picked up a heavy leg bone, he saw that it had been cracked open and the marrow sucked out.

By what, though? And why here? Why were so many sheep slaughtered in this spot? Was it, perhaps, some primitive tribe that used weapons fashioned with the teeth and claws of predators? Could that account for the lack of blade marks?

He did not know.

Had it happened all at once? Or was this a special place—a hunter's open-air slaughterhouse? A sacred spot for sacrifices? If so, where was the altar? Or was the ground itself the altar and the pine woods the church?

The Green Faith existed up here—he had, after all, come from what had been a garden—but animal sacrifices of this kind were not part of that religion. Surely a land this far north, bordering on the vast and mostly unexplored icy wastes, had older faiths. Pagan ones, perhaps, with more savage and less formal practices for offering animals to the gods.

If that was what it was.

A familiar sound drew his attention and Kagen stood and walked to the other side of the road and looked up. There, lining the branches of huge pine, were a score or more of nightbirds. Their presence always gave him dual feelings of comfort—for he was certain they were on his side—and unease because they were most often present when something bad was about to happen. Tuke once wondered if they were psychopomps, spirits who guide the dead to the underworld, but that did not seem to explain their presence or actions. If anything, they were like guardian spirits of some kind, but that was one of the many aspects of magic about which he knew next to nothing. He wished he could ask Maralina about them.

He also wished he could speak—or at least understand—their language. Their presence in this place of bones and mysteries was no comfort at all. Despite being forcibly separated from the faith of the Harvest Gods, Kagen made a warding sign in the air and climbed warily back into the saddle. He loosened his daggers in their sheaths and tapped his bow to make sure it was within easy reach. Just because the bones were old did not mean the danger was gone.

"Hunt for me and I'll strip *your* bones," he said aloud, challenging and warning whatever was out there. The wind whipped his words away, shredding them, tearing the meaning and the warning to pieces and scattering them through the woods.

Kagen shivered and blamed the cold for it, but he knew that was a lie. That shiver had started deep inside of him and rippled outward, not the other way.

He rode on and left one section of forest to cross, a wide break through which ribbons of shallow streams lay in frozen silence. He crossed these carefully, but the ice was thick and easily supported the weight of horse and rider. The sky was a hard blue ocean across which fleets of cloud sailed. There were crosswinds up high, so it seemed as if those fleets were about to collide in some heavenly battle. Darker clouds fringed the horizon above the trees, and there was the smell of a storm in the air.

He left the clearing and entered a bigger part of the forest, following the road back to the inn. He supposed he would have to make some kind of apology to Filia and Tuke. He felt ashamed for his moodiness, but he also wished they would light a fire under their asses and help him get things moving. He wanted them to take him to the Unbladed camp to meet the mysterious Ghuraka, and then off to find the even more singular Mother Frey and her cabal. Kagen could feel the lethal passage of time and could not help believing that each spent moment was benefiting the Hakkians more than him.

So, as he rode, his mood darkened just as the sky ahead grew darker. He had always been prone to moodiness, which had not been a big problem for him back in the big city of Argentium. There, he'd had a large family, many friends, a job he loved, and the contentment of belonging to a religion that afforded him comfort.

All of that was gone now.

Gone.

Thanks to Herepath. His brother. Traitor, conqueror, sorcerer, monster. But how? Why? Those questions punched Kagen in the chest as he rode.

"Why?" he muttered aloud. Jinx looked back at him, ears twitching nervously. The animal was sensitive to Kagen's moods, and there was fear in his big brown eyes.

Kagen could not see it, though. Not through the tears that blinded him.

"Why, Herepath?" he snarled. "Why? Why, why, why?"

And then he was falling, sliding, and toppling from the saddle. Landing hard on the ground amid the bones. He knelt there, slamming his fists against the hard-packed dirt.

"Why, why, why, why?" he demanded.

The fleets of warring clouds ignored him. The gods were silent and indifferent.

Jinx stopped and stood looking at him as the tough, fierce, battle-tested soldier covered his head with his hands and descended into tears.

CHAPTER SIXTY-EIGHT

Her name was Pellia and she was seven years old.

She had been seven years old for so many years now.

She would be seven years old forever.

That was how old Pellia was when she died of the winter sickness. It was how old she was when they buried her in the family crypt. It was how old she was when a local artist, Jedthro, painted her picture. Pellia had not sat for Jedthro, but she stood by, silent and unseen, while her mother and grandmother, her father and two older brothers, her aunt and the governess each sat with the artist and described her in loving detail.

If Pellia had been able to weep, she would have, but a ghost can only cry ghost tears and can only sob in a ghost's voice. Unseen, unheard, unknown.

And eventually forgotten.

Every day she stood in the drawing room and watched the

painter work. He was an older man with kind eyes and a face that always looked a little sad. Pellia could understand that, because he was hired for things like this. To paint portraits of the dead. He was known for that, and although Pellia could feel in him the desire to paint landscapes or birds on tree branches, he had become famous for painting the dead.

At times Pellia thought the artist could feel her there, standing nearby. He would turn now and then, head cocked as if listening to the songs she sang in her empty voice. Pellia had always loved to sing, and even sang some of her favorite songs as she lay dying. As the fever burned her from the inside out, she sang of chasing butterflies, of trees with golden leaves standing on a hill, of faerie ladies living in lonely towers, of dragons flying on majestic wings across the face of the heavens. She died with a song unfinished on her pale lips.

She woke to hear that song sung by her aunt. It was sung in a voice as cracked as old porcelain. Slow and sad and full of tears. Pellia knew that it was her own funeral. She ran to her aunt and tried to make her smile, tried to tell her that it was all going to be all right. Death was not painful. There was no fever, no vomiting. Death was soft. It did not hurt at all. It felt like nothing.

Pellia tried so many times to comfort her mother and father. To speak to her brothers and tell them not to grieve so.

Her voice was as silent as a breeze, as silent as a shadow.

When the painting was complete, she watched Jedthro carve and assemble a frame and then hang the painting on the wall.

When it was done, when the family had finished crying and hugging and praying, when they—exhausted from all of that— eventually went off to bed, Pellia felt herself becoming drowsy. She closed her eyes, and in her own way she slept. She knew that she was somehow falling asleep inside the painting, but that was fine. She closed her eyes and did not dream at all.

When she woke, the house was different.

It was gray and filled with dust. There were only a few sticks of furniture there. No laughter filled the rooms. No sobs, either. Pellia stepped out of the painting and turned to look at it. The canvas was pale with dust and a dead spider hung from its own ancient web in one corner.

She heard sounds and turned to look, but it was just rats scuttling brazenly along the wall by the door. The firebox was cold and filled with debris that had fallen down the chimney—parts of a bird's nest, the bones of a squirrel.

Pellia did not like the empty room. She could not understand why it was so dirty. Had the family left to visit relatives? If so, when would they come back and clean it up and light a cheerful fire?

"Momma?" she called, and flinched when the rats suddenly stopped moving and looked at her.

Had they *heard* her?

Pellia took a few careful steps toward them as she called again for her mother.

The rats cheeped in alarm and fled into the walls through a hole in the wainscoting.

"Wait," she cried suddenly. "Don't go!"

The last rat paused in the mouth of the hole and looked at her with its small black eyes, whiskers twitching.

"I won't hurt you," she said. "You can hear me, can't you?"

The rat watched her, and she did not approach it any closer for fear of chasing it away. She wished she had a crumb of cheese to give it.

"Do you know where my momma is?"

The rat lingered a moment longer, its cheeps no longer filled with panic.

Then it was gone.

Pellia stood there. She felt very alone, which was worse than feeling lonely. The house around her did not seem right. It felt empty. And when she turned to look at her own painting, she saw others on the walls that had not been there before her nap.

There were two of men—one about twenty and the other much older—who looked strangely like her brothers. But that was silly. Why would they paint death portraits that made her brothers look all grown up?

There was a painting of Momma, though again the artist had made her look too old. But it *was* her. The same eyes, the same freckles. Faded, though. And her mouth was sad and she looked very tired.

"Momma?" she said.

Then Pellia left the sitting room and went running up and down the stairs, along each hall, in and out of every room.

Momma was not there. Daddy was not there, nor were her brothers, her aunt, or . . .

Anyone.

She was alone in that great house. Alone in the cold shadows and dust. Alone with the rats.

Pellia screamed for a long time.

She wept for a longer time.

She went into the attic and down into the cellars, but they were empty, too.

It took all her courage to open the big front door and go out into the garden. It was a tangle of creeper vines, weeds, and strange old trees. Nothing was familiar anymore. Where were the flower beds? Where the fruit trees and herb garden by the kitchen door?

She wandered, lost in places where just yesterday she had known every plant and bush and bird. Even the carriage road was a tangle of weeds and trees, some of which looked ancient.

The family crypt had been built like a barrow into the side of a hill, and the iron door was rusted now and leaned out on a single twisted hinge. Dried leaves littered the floor inside and crunched under her slippers. That surprised her, made her gasp, because never once since she died had Pellia made a single sound. Not even to her own ghostly ears. But the leaves crunched, and when she paused to think about it, she realized that each of her footfalls had made sound. They were such ordinary sounds that it had not occurred to her until now.

She bent and picked up a leaf and was both frightened and delighted that she *could* pick it up. Pellia held the leaf to her chest and wept.

Actual tears.

They ran down her cheeks and fell onto the leaf she clutched. They fell onto her hands.

"Momma," she said through her tears.

Momma had not been in the house. She was there in the crypt, though.

Pellia had been good with letters and reading, which had always pleased the governess. She was the pride of her parents, the talk of the family.

Now, though, she wished she had never learned to read. Not now. Not with what was chiseled into stone on the sarcophagus in the corner. She read the name.

Momma's name.

And beside her, Daddy's.

She found both her brothers in their stone coffins. And her aunt. And dozens of others, including Mellis, who was just her aunt's newborn. The years cut into the stone said that Mellis had lived sixty-one years.

But that was impossible.

All Pellia had done was to take a little nap in her painting. Just a nap. Only a few hours.

The stone of those sarcophagi was old. Stained and covered with moss and mold.

Pellia sank down to her knees, calling the names of everyone she loved. Of everyone who had ever loved her. Tears burned on her face. Her heart hammered in her chest as if she were still alive . . . but she knew she was not.

No one she loved was alive. While she slept, they had grown old and died.

How long ago?

She begged for them to rise as ghosts from their dreamless sleep. She pleaded with them to find her.

To find her.

To find her . . .

Outside, the day became night and became day and night again. Over and over again. Pellia sat there in the crypt, begging her beloved dead not to leave her alone.

Not again.

Not forever . . .

<hr>

CHAPTER SIXTY-NINE

SEVEN DAYS EARLIER

"And this happened *when?*" demanded Lord Nespar. The standard with the bloodstained yellow cloth lay on the map table in what had become the strategy room in the palace.

Jakob gave him the details, word for word, as related to him by the courier.

The chamberlain's face went pale and then flushed with anger. He touched the cloth.

"This is cut from a Raven's cloak," he said, his voice hushed but charged with shock.

"I thought so, too," agreed Jakob. "But the symbol . . . Gods of the Pit, Nespar . . ."

The painting was crude and sloppily applied, but it was the symbol itself that mattered. The precise design was new, but not its component pieces.

"The silver disk represents the Silver Empire," said Nespar.

"Anyone can see that. There are silver disks like this painted on walls from Sunderland to Nelfydia."

"Yes, useless protests intended as threats," said Jakob. He touched the circle of roses. "This troubles me greatly."

Nespar licked his lips and nodded. "Very greatly. That is the sigil of the Poison Rose."

"Without a doubt," said Jakob. "But what does it *mean*?"

The chamberlain stood staring down at it for several moments before he spoke. "There was one person whose family line has always used a similar sigil—that of climbing roses wrapped around the hilt of a dagger."

"The Vales?" suggested Jakob.

"Yes," said Nespar. "Though the symbol was first used as a crest on the shield of Lady Bellapher, the general who conquered Hakkia during the rebellion. Bellapher, the hard right hand of that era's Silver Empress. Have you read those histories?"

"I have," said Jakob bleakly. "Bellapher was a brutal conqueror who slaughtered the priests of Hakkia's faith and burned all their churches."

"She was a monster. In Hakkia, parents use her as a threat to get their children to do their chores and say their prayers. Grown men blanch when her name is spoken aloud, Jakob. It's true . . . and not just peasants. I've seen seasoned soldiers—officers— make the warding sign at the mention of her name."

"Are you saying this was done in Bellapher's name?"

"No, no . . . If that were the case, I would not be as frightened as I am now."

Jakob laid a hand on his friend's shoulder. "Tell me, then. What do *you* see when you look at this sigil?"

"I see the ghost of Bellapher's descendant. Lady Marissa Trewellyn-Vale."

"The Poison Rose," echoed Jakob faintly.

"Some version of this was passed down generationally through

Bellapher's family until it became the personal sigil of Lady Marissa. The question is, whose symbol is it now?"

"Surely Kagen Vale," said Jakob, but Nespar shook his head.

"All of our spies agree that he has fled the country, and possibly the empire itself. If our raider caught up with the Therian ship on which Kagen and his allies took passage and was, as our lord believes, sunk, then it's highly possible that Kagen has fled to one of the islands. Likely an unaffiliated one. Do you know how many islands are in the Western Reach?"

"Two thousand eight hundred and sixteen," said Jakob. "I read that in a report."

Nespar nodded. "So someone *else* is using the sigil and has enough of his or her own allies to ambush and slaughter a patrol of Ravens."

"Gods below," breathed Jakob. He swallowed and said, "The Poison Rose had a lot of children. Nine, I believe."

"Yes. Seven sons and two daughters," replied Nespar. "And Hastur alone knows how many cousins. The family is spread throughout the empire."

"Three are dead," said Jakob. "Hugh, a palace guard, was killed defending the Seedlings and the empress on the Night of the Ravens, and Lord Degas, the eldest, was crucified and burned a few days later. And the cleric, what was his name?"

"Herepath," supplied Nespar.

"Yes. According to the documents I've read, he went missing on an expedition to the Winterwilds and is presumed dead. That leaves five brothers, including Kagen, and the two sisters. If Kagen was not behind the massacre, then who was?"

"I don't know," said Nespar.

"If you had to guess," prompted Jakob.

"The ones they call the Twins. Jheklan and Faulker. I have a stack of reports a yard high about them causing trouble long before we invaded."

"*This* kind of trouble?"

"No. They are ostensibly soldiers of the empire. Or were. But mostly they were a pair of rakes. Gamblers, duelists, adventurers."

"Would a pair of louts like that be able to do something like this?"

"Alone? No. They are reputed to be superb fighters—as are all of the children of the Poison Rose—but not what you might call 'joiners,' or even leaders."

"Then we are down to three Vale children. Hendross, Belissa, and Zora. Which of them might be behind this atrocity?"

"We're not certain it is one of the Vales," said Nespar.

"It has to be," said Jakob. "The rose and dagger? I would think anyone *not* of the same bloodline would use the sigils of the Silver Empress rather than the Vale house sigil."

"There is another possibility," said Nespar, "and it frightens me very much indeed."

"Tell me."

"What if this is a trick?"

Jakob stiffened. "A trick?"

"Yes. What if this is a subtle ploy played on us by the Therians, or possibly the Samudians?"

"Why? They have no allegiance to the Vale family."

"I don't think it's about allegiance, Jakob. If they sent agents into Argon to *pretend* that their atrocious act was local insurrection . . ."

"Then we would look in the wrong direction," finished Jakob. "You're right; that is frightening. Very much so." He paused. "Either way, I don't think we've seen the last of this madness. War—civil or international—is not merely coming, Nespar . . . it's here. That massacre was the first blow. And even if this is a Therian plot, I think the Vales are involved. I feel it in my bones."

Nespar went over and poured himself a cup of wine. His hands were shaking so bad he sloshed some of it down the front of his robes.

"I . . . I have to tell the king about this right now." His eyes were wide and nearly wild with fear.

Lord Jakob Ravensmere watched the chamberlain hurry away like a frightened stork. When he was alone, the historian poured himself a cup of wine. His hands did not shake at all, and his smile was for himself alone.

CHAPTER SEVENTY

It was a bird who brought Kagen back to himself.

One of the nightbirds. A ragged crow, which looked as weathered and ancient as the twisted pine in which it perched. It gave a long, low caw. Strange and plaintive, but with an almost human quality.

Kagen heard it as he lay there, panting, weary from grief, sick at heart and sick of his own weakness. Sick of being a failure to everyone who mattered, on earth and in the heavens.

The crow spoke again. Sharper, with perhaps a note of reproof.

Kagen got to his knees and sat back on his heels and glared at the animal.

"What the hell do you want?"

The bird cocked its head to one side and stared at him with black-within-black eyes. Kagen heard rustling and turned to see that the pine tree was filled with other nightbirds. Scores of them, huddled together for warmth. Watching like patrons at a circus. Or jurors at a trial.

In a fit of childish pique, Kagen snatched up a fist-sized stone and nearly hurled it at the closest bunch. Jinx and the string of stolen horses stood grazing on withered grass. Kagen looked down at the rock he held and then slowly opened his fingers, letting it fall with a clatter. He took a very deep breath and exhaled raggedly.

"Who are you?" he demanded. "*What* are you?"

The bird cawed once more. And this time Kagen was positive

there was a scolding note to it. Which made Kagen look at himself in that moment as if observing from an objective distance. A grown man kneeling in the dirt, weeping, moaning, begging.

Whining.

All of which was true. All of which flooded him with shame and anger in equal parts.

"Gods-damned piece of shit," he told himself.

The crow cawed again.

"Okay, okay, I'm getting the hell up," growled Kagen as he lumbered to his feet. "You happy now? I'm up. I'm not pissing my pants. I'm not . . ."

He stopped, aware that the birds had all fallen silent and still. They were watching him with cold, intense, unblinking eyes.

Kagen muttered something under his breath, bent, and slapped mud from his knees and chest. He went through the routine of touching the hilts of his daggers and patting his clothes to check that his various other knives—short-range fighting, throwing, utility, and the rest—were all secure. That, too, was childish, at least in the moment, but it nevertheless steadied him. It was a routine and orderly thing to do, and routine had always been his shelter. But there was a bitter sweetness to it, because that habit had been instilled in all of the sons and daughters of the Poison Rose.

"Know where your weapons are," she often said. "That way you will know that you are always ready."

Ready? Sure. But for what?

Kagen felt that sour conversation happen in his head.

He drew the two matched daggers. The blades were forged on Tull Heklon by the priestesses of the Sacred Trust. Finer than the best Bulconian steel. Rare and nearly unbreakable, and each was honed to such a razor sharpness that they could cut through leather and bone and even most armor as easily as through soft cheese.

He considered the knives. On the blades, high up near the crossguard, were identical etched symbols: vines of climbing roses in a precise circle. Two of his brothers, Jheklan and Faulker, had the full sigil—climbing roses swirling around representations of these very daggers—tattooed on their chests, over their hearts.

Seeing those roses on the steel weapons seemed to anchor him to the ground. To help him stand. The blades were not currently smeared with *eitr*, the deadly god-killer poison, but the blades were deadly enough as they were.

The nightbirds rustled now, filling the trees with a sound like waves on a sandy beach. And once more the old crow cawed. Kagen raised the knives until they were high over his head, the steel catching the sunlight and blazing as brightly as if they were torches.

"I live," Kagen told the sky. "Damned or not, I live."

The nightbirds grew agitated.

"Herepath," he said, his voice thick with a tangle of too many emotions to catalog, "I will find you. I will kill you. I will *end* everything that you've become."

Somewhere far, far away, thunder rumbled. Only once, but the echo came rolling across the tops of the trees, shivering every pine in the forest.

"I will end you," said Kagen, and now he did not despise the tears in his eyes. They were cold and bitter tears. A killer's tears.

He slid the daggers back into their sheaths and took a step toward Jinx. Then he paused, turned, and without knowing exactly why, bowed deeply to the tree full of nightbirds.

The old crow watched him with those bottomless black eyes.

Then Kagen mounted and rode away.

CHAPTER SEVENTY-ONE

The Witch-king listened to Lord Nespar's report. The standard with the Poison Rose sigil lay across his lap.

When the chamberlain was done, the hall fell into silence. The pack of hounds, their bellies filled with unspeakable horrors, lounged all around the dais. The pack leader alone was awake, and she sat beside the throne, her eyes fixed on Nespar, her broad chest filling and emptying slowly, her crooked tail occasionally twitching.

Finally, the King in Yellow spoke.

"Who is our man in that part of Argon?" he asked.

"Captain Amurel, subcommander of the One Hundred Seventh Light Infantry," replied Nespar, who had made a point of checking before coming to make his report.

"Have him visit the fort where the murdered Ravens were garrisoned. Tell him I want a complete report immediately. Tell him to use gallopers to get it to me. And also tell him to send patrols out to interrogate the locals."

"What . . . ah . . . *level* of interrogation should they use, Majesty?" asked Nespar.

"For now, no needless violence. Offer any reward that you feel will loosen tongues. And promise Amurel a promotion if he brings me an answer within a week."

"As Your Majesty commands," said Nespar, bowing out of the presence.

The Witch-king lingered on his throne. He used the pad of one finger to trace the circle of rose vines. Over and over and over.

CHAPTER SEVENTY-TWO

Snow fell steadily outside the Bear's Mark and the temperature had dropped all day. Inside was a big and comforting fire that filled the room with warmth and a friendly light.

There were few travelers at this time of year. The trade caravans would not start for many weeks yet, and less than half of the tables were occupied. Each group tended to stake out its own isolated spot, and conversation was low and shared only among friends. A lute player plucked indifferently on his instrument and sang a song about a winter hunt that he did not know all the words to, so he faked it, humming his way. No one cared. It was background noise, and pleasant enough for what it was.

Closest to the fire were two comfortable old chairs in which Tuke and Filia sprawled. They had a pitcher of wine on the table between them, and the remains of a meal on metal plates.

"It's a storm down here," said Tuke, "but it'll be worse up in the hills."

Filia nodded. "Aye, and I know this area. There are big winter storms and blizzards that can come out of nowhere and last for hours. I once had three feet of snow dumped on me when I was out past where Kagen was heading."

Concern flickered on Tuke's features. "You think he'll try to make it back today?"

Filia ran fingers through her short red hair. She usually wore a leather vest over bare skin but today had opted for a heavy woolen shirt and a scarf wound many times around her throat. Her boots were off, though, and set aside, because they were damp from a long walk she and Tuke had taken before they ate.

"If he's smart, Tuke, then he'll stay at that garden," she said, wiggling her bare toes in front of the dancing flames. "It'll be cold, but a damn sight better than trying to make it all this way in a storm."

"Kagen's a city boy, Filia," said Tuke. "I know he's been out in the country before, but I doubt he's ever been in a blizzard this far north. Frankly, I don't know how much he knows about what to do."

"He's smart and practical," said Filia.

"Smart is fine," said Tuke, "but it's no replacement for experience."

Filia grinned. "Don't tell me you're worried about him, you old woman."

"Of course I'm worried," said Tuke, taking no offense. "But by the speckled balls of the jaguar god I'd never tell *him* that."

"Of course not."

A gust of wind buffeted the shutters over the north-facing windows.

"He'll be fine," said Filia. "Even a city boy like him knows enough to get in out of a storm."

"Yeah, but it's not just that," said Tuke. "I'm worried about *him*, you know? It's been weeks since he fought the Witch-king, and he hasn't really talked about it."

"What, you want him to share his feelings so you can both have a good cry about it?"

"Don't be a condescending bitch," scolded Tuke. "And don't pretend you're not worried about him, too. The poor bastard saw his parents killed, he saw the empress and her kids butchered, and *believes* that his gods turned their backs on him. Then, after spending three months mooning around, either drunk out of his skull or amusing himself by killing Hakkians, he goes into the Tower of Sarsis and all that weirdness happens. And to top it off, not only does he *fail* to kill the Witch-king, he finds out that the man who caused all that bloodshed is his own fucking brother."

"It's a lot," conceded Filia.

"A lot? A *lot*? Pits of fire, woman, it's too much. And how much has he talked about it since?"

"He's done nothing *but* talk about it."

But Tuke shook his head. "No, he's talked about the Night of the Ravens, about the death of his parents, about the dead Seedlings, and about his plans to raise an army to fight back . . . but he has barely mentioned Herepath since. A few times, sure, but he hasn't had a real conversation with us about him. Or about the enormity of what Herepath's betrayal means. How it came about."

"Okay, that's true." She sipped her wine.

"And," continued Tuke, "he's barely said a single word about the fact that two of the Seedlings are not dead but have somehow been adopted by the Witch-king and have turned into weird, corrupt little shits. You've known him longer than I have; don't you think he's acting strange?"

Filia shrugged. "Maybe." She moistened her finger and ran it around the rim of her cup, trying to make it sing, but it was too cheap. She sighed. "Okay, sure . . . it's strange. He's a mess, no doubt about that. But between you and me, Tuke, he was a bit strange before. You could never really place a bet on where his mood would land. If he didn't have a cock, I'd wonder if it was his time of the month."

"You really are nasty sometimes," he said, but she only shrugged.

"My guess is that his whole reason for visiting that garden is to think it through and sort things out," mused Filia. "As for sharing with us . . . we should allow him to get around to things at his own pace."

Tuke mumbled something unintelligible, and they drifted into a contemplative silence.

Half an hour later, Filia said, "There's something else *we* haven't talked about."

"Hey, I only glanced at that barmaid. I didn't—"

"Not that, dumbass," laughed Filia. Her face grew serious and she leaned close. "Look, Tuke, we know who the Witch-king is, but neither of us has written to Mother Frey to tell her."

"That's up to Kagen," said Tuke.

"Is it? Why? Just because they're brothers? Herepath is everyone's enemy and everyone's problem. Frey has that cabal of hers. They *need* to know this."

"Sure," said the big Therian, "and we'll tell them, once we talk about it with Kagen."

"I don't think that's good enough. Days are passing."

"Okay," said Tuke, "tell me why *you* haven't written to Frey."

"I have." Then she gave a sheepish grin. "But, okay, not about Kagen's brother. All I told her was that we were with Kagen at the palace and that we're going north to escape the Ravens looking for us."

"Did you tell her that we're going to try to get Kagen accepted into the Unbladed?"

"Yes," she said.

"But not about Herepath?"

Filia let out a long sigh. "It's so fucking complicated, isn't it? We spy on Kagen and send coded reports to Frey, but we withhold the most important detail because we don't want to hurt Kagen's feelings? What is that all about?"

Tuke fished for his pipe and began to light it. Then he blew a stream of smoke up to the ceiling. "We're a couple of real treats, lass, aren't we? Spies and liars."

Filia shrugged. "I won't apologize for it. We each did what we thought was right, but neither of us betrayed that one confidence. I didn't tell Mother Frey the Witch-king's name and neither did you. Unless you did and you're a better liar than I think you are."

"Ha," he said, shaking his head. "I did not so much *lie* as omit information. Not the same thing."

"Then we're both cut from the same cloth."

They drank.

"Tell you one thing, Tuke," Filia said a few minutes later.

"What's that? Another secret?"

"No," she said, "just a truth."

"Then tell me."

"Let me say it this way . . . I've known Kagen for a long time.

We have history, as you say. He's good in the sack, which, sadly, few men are." She grinned. "Present company excepted."

He toasted her with his cup.

"And Kagen is a hell of a fighter," continued Filia. "Better, I think, than even he knows. Maybe as good as his mother. And if not better yet, he'll get there."

Tuke nodded. "The boy's got some talent, I grant."

"However," said Filia, "before all this I never had a lot of respect for him as a person. Do you understand? I mean, he's decent enough, but he has a soft side, a kindness that, while admirable, can be a weakness. More than that, because he was born to wealth and status, he's never really had a chance to prove his worth, and to be frank, I never thought he had much depth to him. He seemed . . . shallow and rather foppish."

"He should hire you as his personal minstrel, because you sing his praises with such zeal."

"Hush, I'm trying to make a point," said Filia. "What I mean is that I think I was wrong about him. The things he's done since the Night of the Ravens. Oh, and I don't mean him mooning around feeling sorry for himself and turning into a violent drunk. That's grief. No, what I mean is what he's done since he found his footing again. He's had fights with groups of Hakkians. Fights that the person I *thought* he was should have lost. Hell, those were fights either of us might have lost. Then he went into the Tower of Sarsis, a place where great kings, princes, knights, and champions went and all died . . . and he came out with information, magical weapons, and the love of an immortal witch . . . or whatever she is. We've both made fun of him, saying that he enchanted her with his magic cock, but that's because we like jerking him around."

"True."

"I think Maralina saw something in Kagen that no one else did. Or could."

"What is it you think she saw?" asked Tuke, interested.

"If you laugh, I'll cut your balls off."

"I won't laugh," he promised.

"I think she saw a hero."

A big grin formed on his mouth. "A . . . hero?"

"I told you not to laugh."

"I'm not laughing," said Tuke. "I think maybe I'm agreeing with you."

"That fight on *Dagon's Swan*? He turned the tide of that battle. Him and those creepy birds."

"Nightbirds," corrected Tuke

"Whatever. I mean, think about *that*. A flock of magical birds is following him around and joining his fights. They fought the ravens on the night of the coronation, and they helped aboard the ship. Not for either of us, but because of *him*. Because of Kagen."

Tuke sat back and sipped his wine as he stared into the flickering fire.

"Hero . . ." he murmured, tasting the word, savoring the nuances.

"Or something," said Filia. "Maybe it's a word we don't know. Hell's bells, I don't know what else to call it."

"Did you tell Mother Frey any of this?" asked Tuke.

"I told her *all* of it," she said, "except, as I said, about Kagen's brother."

A small smile played on Tuke's lips. "So did I."

She shot him a piercing look. "You called him a hero too?"

"Not as such," he drawled. "But my guess is that the old bat would read it the same way you did. The same way I do."

Filia nodded. "We're not going to tell Kagen that, though."

"Oh, hell no," he agreed. "Worse thing in the world is to tell a hero that that's what he is. We don't want the damn-fool city boy to think he's invulnerable, do we?"

"No," she said. "No, we do not."

The storm rattled the shutters and swirled down the chimney to kick sparks from the burning logs.

"All that said," Tuke murmured, "it would be a damn shame if he froze to death out there."

"He'll be fine," she said.

They both looked long and hard at the tavern door as if expecting Kagen to come in out of the storm. He did not. The wind howled outside, and the hours seemed like years.

CHAPTER SEVENTY-THREE

FIVE DAYS EARLIER

Captain Amurel, subcommander of the 107th Hakkian Light Infantry, stalked across the parade ground of Fort Sunrise, hands clasped into angry knots behind his back, jaw thrust forward and set, eyes snapping left and right in anger. The remaining soldiers—the ones that had not accompanied the unfortunate Lieutenant Vorlon—stood in precise rows. Behind the captain were the troops he'd brought with him to help him investigate the massacre. A dozen hard-faced Ravens. Sunlight struck fire from the glittering tips of their spears.

Everything in the fort was neat to the point of obsessiveness; the troops were dressed and their kit was completely correct, down to the number of pleats in their cloaks. Even the horses were properly groomed, with manes braided and hooves oiled so they sparkled in the sunlight. But it all annoyed Captain Amurel so much that he had to bite down on the comments that rose to his mouth.

Hepto, the junior lieutenant in charge of the garrison while the senior officer was on patrol, was a nervous grasshopper of a man with sandy hair and weak eyes. Amurel disliked him at once, and more so because with Lieutenant Vorlon dead. The fort was left in the care of a weakling. Even the rawest recruits looked more reliable than Hepto. Amurel mused that his own favorite whore was likely a better soldier than the man.

When the obligatory inspection was completed—not a long task, as the fort was a small one in an unimportant part of Argon—the captain turned and glared icily at Hepto.

"How in the nine hells did you manage to let your superior officer and an entire platoon get butchered, Lieutenant?"

Hepto snapped to attention so rigidly that his helmet nearly fell off. His yellow cloak billowed and clung to his sword handle and the various metal fittings on his highly polished cuirass.

"I . . . I . . ." was all Hepto could manage.

The captain stepped very close. He was taller and broader than the junior officer, and his face was still marked by scars from the Night of the Ravens. Although not in that elite group himself, Amurel believed that he would one day get the call to become a Raven . . . or he *had* believed so, until Vorlon's patrol was torn to pieces.

"Find your tongue or lose it forever," he said sharply.

Hepto swallowed, tried to stand even straighter, and forced words out past the stricture in his throat. "I was ordered to remain here with the day watch and the reserves, sir," he said. "Lieutenant Vorlon said he wanted to do the patrol."

"And you let some untrained partisans *kill* him?"

"Sir . . . I was following his orders to remain here."

"That is a shit-poor excuse, Lieutenant," snarled Amurel. He was aware that he was being totally unfair and unreasonable. This was entirely on his shoulders. But if he could find some way to make Hepto take the blame, then he might skate clear of the cracking ice.

"Sir, I—" began Hepto, and then he abruptly lurched forward, slamming into Amurel with such force that the captain staggered backwards to the edge of the catwalk on which they stood. The captain pinwheeled his arms, fighting for balance, but Hepto kept leaning toward him.

They were midway to the ground, thirty feet below, when the captain saw the barbed head of an arrow standing redly from the center of the lieutenant's throat. He began to scream, but then the ground seemed to reach up and punch him. The shock of impact and the devilish pull of gravity made the lieutenant land atop him with such force that the arrow point punched into the captain's right eye.

Amurel screamed and screamed, but his cries were lost amid the shouts and yells and shrieks of dying soldiers as arrows arched over the walls and rained down on them in a storm of death.

CHAPTER SEVENTY-FOUR

The day turned dark, and Kagen, slumped in a semidoze in the saddle, jerked awake as he became aware of the change of light and a marked drop in temperature. He straightened and looked around to see a false twilight. The blue was gone and now storm clouds the color of old lead were stretched across the horizon. Even as he watched they darkened further still until all definition was gone, leaving that featureless and threatening gray. He pulled Jinx to a halt and raised his head to sniff the air. There were many miles to go to get back to the Bear's Mark in Traveler's Rest. The storm promised a bad day and a worse night if he got stuck out here.

"Snow," he said. "Ahh . . . *shit*."

Kagen had a rough sense of this land, having studied maps before riding out to the garden early that morning, but finding his way back depended on either a view of the sun's position or landmarks, and if it snowed that evening, he'd have neither.

He thought about the ruin he'd passed when coming out and judged that it was—at most—an hour's ride from where he currently sat. If he could get there, then he and his new troop of horses could wait out the storm and then make for town at first light.

As if in encouragement, or perhaps a threat, the wind whipped sharp-edged flakes of snow against his cheek. Leaves tore themselves from the shivering arms of the trees, and pine needles assailed him like flights of arrows from some pygmy army. A few of the horses nickered nervously.

"Come on, Jinx," said Kagen, tapping the animal with his heels, "let's move."

The snow began falling in earnest within a quarter hour, and by the time Kagen felt that the ruin should have been in sight the world had turned to an eerie fantasy of black shadows and gray-white daggers of snow. The temperature plummeted, too, and Kagen feared for the horses. And himself.

How the hell do people live out here? he wondered. *And why, by all the gods?*

He quickened the pace, though normal caution would have made him creep along. His nascent woodcraft did not extend to survival out in the open in weather like this, and he knew that he had to find shelter or a grave. No other options seemed likely.

Jinx, tired and frightened as he was, pushed ahead into the teeth of the wind, and the string of horses followed.

In the maelstrom, though, Kagen thought he heard a sound. At first it sounded like a child lost in the snow. Kagen paused his horse and stood up in the stirrups, trying to steal the truth from the whistling wind. Was it the nightbirds? he wondered. Were they dying out there in this blizzard, too?

The sound came again, high-pitched, plaintive, filled with terror.

He strained to hear, to pin down the direction, but the wind was a trickster. When the cry came a third time, Kagen kicked Jinx and they surged forward, certain now that the lost child was up ahead in the direction he was going.

Immediately he thought the young one must belong to some travelers who took refuge in the same place he was heading, and that the boy or girl had strayed. Maybe drawn to the swirling snow. Children and adults tend to see a heavy snowfall in vastly different ways.

The child's parents were probably frantic and searching desperately for him. That made it none of *his* business.

And yet . . .

He had been the captain of the cadre of palace guards whose sole job was to protect and defend the Seedlings. His failure there was comprehensive. And though this lost child was likely not a noble and certainly not of the specific group of children he had sworn his own soul to protect, he felt the obligation. No, more than that, he felt pity. No one had been able to save Empress Gessalyn's children. How terrified and abandoned they must have felt. All of the promises made by parents and palace staff and stalwart soldiers had come to nothing. Those children had died in terror.

"Mother Sah," he bellowed as he pushed his horse into the teeth of the storm, "Father Ar . . . you may hate me, but *you* did nothing to protect the Seedlings either. Get off your celestial asses and help me save this child. I, Kagen whom you've damned, beg you. I *beg* you to help me."

The cry tore through the air. Closer now.

"*Child!*" cried Kagen. "Can you hear me? Where *are* you?"

Another cry, but this time with a sharper note. Had the child heard? Kagen repeated his call, over and over.

And then he saw something move across the path not a dozen paces ahead. Small. Quick. Pale, too; barely seen in the darkness.

Kagen abruptly slid from the saddle to examine the snow where he thought he'd seen something. A child? Or had it been some animal? There were marks in the newly fallen powder, but in the storm's darkness it was impossible to tell what they were. He knelt with his back to the wind and brushed at the loose, dry snow, which was several inches deep now. He pawed it carefully back and then, with nearly numb fingers, took flint and steel from a pouch on his belt. There was nothing to burn, but the sparks he struck gave him flash images of the ground. The soil was hard, nearly frozen, but there was yet enough moisture to take a faint print.

Kagen frowned at it, though, because it was not a child's footmark. Nor an adult's, or anyone's. Instead, the mark he saw was cloven, like a goat's print. Kagen was no skilled tracker, and like most city-bred nobles, was only an indifferent hunter. He raised his head once more to see if he could hear the cry again. When only the howl of the wind spoke to him, he listened to his own memories of the cries he'd heard. *Had* it been a goat and nothing more? There had been no words that he made out, only the wail of the lost.

The sounds did not come again. And now he was certain it was no child. Something out there was taunting him.

"You bloody fool," he told himself as he got heavily to his feet. He gripped his daggers as he listened for another half minute, then shook his head.

"Idiot."

As he reached for the saddle horn to pull himself up, a thought occurred to him, and he glanced nervously at the sky.

"Okay, so I was wrong," he told the gods. "Didn't mean to offend you."

There was no answer from above.

Of course there was not. Only heavier snow and a sharp increase in the wind.

He climbed into the saddle and looked ahead. The snow was even heavier now, and even his own footprints were filling up. Those of the animal were already gone.

"Gods-damned goat," he said aloud, though even he, with his city-bred common sense and pragmatism, did not really believe it was a goat. Telling himself that, though, was a shield, however flimsy, against other kinds of speculation.

Magic has returned to the world.

Those six words floated through his mind as if a chorus of voices spoke it. Maralina, the Witch-king, Selvath, his own dead mother. He growled at Jinx and cursed the wind and tried to drown that thought out.

Twenty minutes later he found the ruin.

CHAPTER SEVENTY-FIVE

FOUR DAYS EARLIER

The galloper thundered into the courtyard and leapt from his horse. As guards approached him, he held up a yellow badge edged in black and green on which a raven in full flight had been embroidered. That marked him as a special courier riding on king's business.

The sentries waved him through, and a sergeant ran with him to clear the way. Within moments the rider was ushered into the strategy room. Lord Nespar, the scar-faced General Grenleth, and Jakob Ravensmere looked up as one as the man entered.

"My lords," gasped the galloper, "I've just come from Fort Sunrise."

"What is the news?" asked Jakob.

The courier reached into the pouch slung across his chest and produced a carefully rolled piece of yellow cloth that was the same hue as his cloak. He handed it to the historian and waited as the thing was unrolled and laid flat on the table. There was the same image of rose vines encircling crossed daggers set against a disk of silver.

"Tell us what happened," cried Nespar.

The courier described the massacre at the fort.

"They killed nearly everyone," he gasped. "But they singled out those of us with this badge." He touched the official emblem that hung on a leather cord around his neck. "There were three of us.

The bastards killed two—my mates Johub and Brielle—but they let me live. They said that I had to deliver this to the Witch-king's very hand, my lords."

He shivered with exhaustion and terror. Sweat ran down his weathered face and he kept cutting looks toward the door as if expecting the King in Yellow himself to appear and punish him for having survived.

"By Hastur's staff, who *did* this?" growled General Grenleth.

The courier shook his head. "They all wore hoods, sir," he said. "But the one who handed that cloth to me said to say that the Sons of the Poison Rose were coming for the Witch-king and that they would . . ." He paused, unable to continue.

"They would *what?*" asked Jakob coldly.

Grenleth handed the man a cup of wine, which he drank down greedily.

"They said they would skin him alive and piss on him," said the man in a nervous whisper. "And then they would line the palace walls with the heads of every Hakkian invader. Those were his actual words, my lords."

"What else can you tell us?" urged Grenleth.

The galloper seemed to look for answers in his empty cup. "That was all they said. Then they knocked me about a bit. Not much. Just having some kind of cruel sport with me. Thirty of them and one of me. After that, the one who gave me that cloth told them to leave me alone. They let me mount and take two additional horses with me. I left as fast as I could and rode through the night. I changed horses three times at our outposts."

His knees abruptly buckled and he sagged down. None of the royal advisors tried to catch him.

"My lords . . . the things they did to the other soldiers," moaned the galloper from the floor. "They . . . tore them apart. Skinned some and butchered the others. I could still hear the screaming of the ones they flayed. The sound chased me for miles."

He burst into tears and covered his face, his body racked by sobs. Nespar called for guards to take the wretch out and see to his needs.

When they were alone, he turned to the others. "And so we have it," he said bluntly. "Sons of the Poison Rose. It must be the remaining Vales who did this. Jheklan, Faulker, and Hendross. This is revenge and insurrection."

"We need to tell the king at once," said Grenleth forcefully, pounding a fist into his palm.

Jakob went over to the table and stood looking down at the map of what had been the Silver Empire. "And what do you think our master will do?"

Nespar thought about it, then said, "I read your reports about the weapon brought to us by the Hollow Monks. Was it really as terrible as it sounds?"

Grenleth shivered. "Worse. I have never seen anything like it, and I've been on battlefields all my life. The person under the curse—if curse is the right word—attacked with such savagery that it chilled the blood in my veins. With a single bite he was able to pass along the curse, and soon each victim—or those he attacked—was transformed into a similar monster. They swept through the village and killed everyone. 'Killed,' I say, but they did not die any normal death, Nespar. Gods below, no. They became monsters. They were neither alive nor dead but in some other state of being that I do not and cannot quite understand. A kind of living death. I have had nightmares ever since." He narrowed his eyes. "Why do you ask this now?"

Nespar said nothing.

"Gods of . . ." began Jakob, his voice trailing off. Then he took a breath and in a fierce whisper asked, "You don't think our master would use . . . *that* in retaliation, do you?"

"Yes," said the chamberlain as he went over and poured himself more of the strong local wine. "I think he will."

"He's right," said the general.

"But that weapon is so dangerous," protested Jakob. "How could we possibly hope to control it? When we tried it in that village, we had the place surrounded and we disposed of all the cursed." He turned to the chamberlain. "You understand, Nespar, that each victim of that curse had to be killed by arrow shots to the head? Nothing else seemed to stop them."

"What choice do we have, Jakob?" mused the general. "This is different than Samud or Vahlycor putting an army into the field against us. This is guerilla warfare, and everyone knows you can't win that kind of fight in straight-up combat.

"But . . . if this is released in a way that allows it to spread beyond our control . . ."

Nespar gulped down the rest of his wine. He tried to set the cup down on the table but missed and it fell. The three men looked down at it . . . the Hakkian crest was stamped into the side of the pewter goblet, and now it lay dented and spilling wine as red as blood onto the floor.

"May Hastur protect our souls," whispered Lord Nespar.

CHAPTER SEVENTY-SIX

By the time he saw the building, the wind was a shrieking thing.

Young pines bent painfully under the relentless assault; older and less flexible trees cracked and died. Snow began piling up, inch by treacherous inch. The blankets covering the horses were nowhere near enough for warmth or protection, and the animals screamed as the gale gnawed at them with teeth of ice.

Then the storm seemed to spread its wings, and suddenly a building seemed to materialize out of the gray and wild nothingness.

"Thank the . . ." Kagen began, but stopped short of actually citing the gods. Not his gods, anyway. Instead, he clamped his jaws shut and pressed on. There was still a quarter mile to go, and every yard forward was a torment for him and the horses.

As he drew closer, the building took more definite form. He had glimpsed it on the way to the garden but had not given it much study because it was clearly old and deserted and of no interest then. But now he strained to pick out every detail.

The place had clearly once been a mansion of considerable size, built in the old style, with a huge central building rising to two lofty stories and wings that stretched out and curled around to enclose a central courtyard. Whole sections of it had long since collapsed, and trees—some of them at least a century old—rose from the wagon turnaround and from the ruined places glimpsed through shattered sections of walls on both wings.

The main part of the structure seemed intact, though, and Kagen made straight for that. All he needed was a hall or stable or anything enclosed by four walls and a roof.

There was a grand entrance framed by marble pillars and rows of statues, the faces of which had long since eroded to vagueness. Kagen stopped in front of a pair of doors that towered a dozen feet above his head. Massive things, of some dark wood he did not recognize, banded by steel set with heavy, pointed rivets. Both wood and metal were covered with the unmistakable pockmarks of arrows, the wounds of sword and axe, but also other marks, some of which looked like claw marks. But from what kind of animal—bear, hunting cat, or wolf—he could not tell. The marks were old and already caked with snow and ice.

Kagen slid painfully from the saddle; his legs ached from the bitter cold and his ankles felt brittle. He tied Jinx's reins to the arthritic arm of a crippled pine and lumbered to the door. Up close he was even more certain that this place was deserted, but his city-bred manners made him bang on the door anyway. Even through the howling wind he could hear the doleful echoes reverberating emptily inside.

He tried the huge iron door handles, but that was a waste of effort. They remained steadfastly shut, though whether locked or frozen closed it was impossible to determine.

Kagen stepped back and studied the door, looking up at its towering height.

He had no illusions about the doors being his way in, though. They were closed and did not even seem to rattle as the winds punched them with fists of ice. But there was a smaller door set discreetly in the wall near the main entrance. A servants' door of some kind. Kagen pushed on it and felt it yield a tiny bit.

Encouraged, Kagen put his shoulder against it and threw all of his strength and need against the portal. He was only medium height but very strong, and his desperation amplified his strength.

"Come on, damn you," Kagen cried as he rammed himself against the door over and over again. Behind him, Kagen heard the horses whinnying in distress. He looked over his shoulder and saw them—a cluster of figures turned ghostly in the blinding snow—stamping restlessly, pawing the snowy ground, tossing their heads and pulling against the rope leads that attached them all in a single string. He knew he had to hurry or they'd panic and break loose.

And then the door moved.

It did not want to, but in the end it yielded to Kagen's relentless assault. The cries of rusted metal hinges were higher and sharper even than the eerie sounds the pale goat had made. Then, after moving a few stubborn inches, it suddenly burst inward as if pulled open by a strong hand inside the mansion. Kagen pitched forward and fell in a bone-jarring sprawl. But he sprang to his feet, his right hand whipping a dagger out as he crouched and turned in a quick circle, looking for whoever had opened that door.

The room was draped in shadows.

"Who's there?" he bellowed.

Only silence answered him.

Kagen felt his way to the wall and then around it and found nothing. The screams of terrified horses tore through the air.

"Shit," he growled, feeling time flying faster than the snow. He groped his way until he found another door, then opened it, dagger ready. This door groaned as well but did not resist him more than ordinary rust and disuse would explain. Kagen entered a bigger room—something he could tell from the echoes his steps made—and followed basic logic around to where the main doors had to be. He found them, felt a heavy timber laid into brackets, grinned as he sheathed his knife, and then braced himself to lift the crossbar up. As soon as he did, the wind pushed the doors in at him and faint blue-white light from without painted everything. He saw the frightened horses and rushed out to them, taking Jinx's reins, and with a combination of commands, soothing noises, and curses, guided the whole string into the building. Then he shoved the door closed once more, heaved the crossbar into place, and sagged against the door, panting and nearly spent.

He had never before been caught in a blizzard in the wild, and the experience was both terrifying and humbling. Argon was his home and it lay in a temperate zone with all four seasons, but none ever in extremes. How in the many hells could—or indeed *would*—anyone choose to live in such a climate as Nelfydia?

"This morning I was in a warm gods-damned bed," he muttered. "What the hell is wrong with me?"

Inside his chest his heart hammered, and despite being in out of the storm, he did not feel at all safe.

Not even a little bit.

CHAPTER SEVENTY-SEVEN

After a long moment he pushed himself away from the door and half-staggered over to Jinx—barely seen in the lightless room—and removed from the saddle a small bundle of logs he carried for camping purposes. They were lightweight, dry pine that would burn easily. A smaller bundle of kindling fell out as he removed the wood, and Kagen dropped to one knee, fished out his flint and steel, and in seconds had a small blaze going.

The fire shoved the shadows back far enough for Kagen to see that he was in a large entrance hall. Old paintings of brooding people in antique clothes stared down from the walls with stern disapproval. None of the faces were rendered with smiles, and Kagen could see their point. Moth-eaten tapestries hung in dusty threads, and a coat of arms carved in dark hardwood was wreathed in withered spiderwebs.

The horses were shivering, restless with cold, hunger, and fear. Even with stout walls between that chamber and the storm, the air was viciously cold. Kagen himself felt a strange lassitude, as if the cold were that of the grave and it was whispering an end to pain if he were to but yield to it.

"Gods of the burning Pit," Kagen snarled, though his teeth chattered so much that it weakened the curse to something closer to a whine.

He immediately set about tearing down the paintings, kicking them to pieces and using the heavy wooden frames to build several fires in different parts of the foyer. He was tempted to burn the paintings, too, but hesitated in the act of commission as some vague superstitious dread stayed his hand. He let the paintings fall and kicked them into the shadows and took the dense, carved wood. The extra fuel built the fire big and bright. Soon the light and the heat banished the rest of the shadows to the farthest corners, and they filled the hall with warmth. Spiders that somehow flourished in the cold rose from their hiding places in the cracked floor and scuttled away from the heat. A centipede as long as a child's forearm crawled up a wall. Kagen drew his knife and swiped at it, but the thing vanished into a deep crack.

"Gods of the Pit," he swore.

Kagen stood for a moment between two of the fires, soaking in the warmth, feeling his muscles thaw even if his nerves were still frozen with apprehension. He did not like this place. No, not one bit.

Jinx blew sharply, calling him back to his duties. Kagen shook his head like a confused hound, then put feed bags on each of the mounts, knowing that warmth, light, and food would go a long way to soothing the nerves of skittish horses. He removed their saddles and baggage, shook the melting snow off their blankets, stroking and patting the animals as he did so.

Then Kagen used strips of tapestries and a bit of cooking oil from his pack to make torches. The dry cloth burned quickly, so he kept his explorations short. What he found was that the entry hall opened up into several rooms, including a grand hall big enough to hold a tournament. There was furniture in almost every room, which gratified him, because they were made of old hardwood that would burn slowly, but also concerned him, because the stuff was expensive and yet looters had left it.

Very odd, and in no way a comfort.

He returned to the entrance and made sure to close all of the connecting doors.

As he finished that, he realized that something was gnawing at his awareness, and it took him a moment to sort it out. Then, alarmed, he turned toward the horses, all of which were busily munching feed from their bags. Kagen quickly counted them.

"What in the burning hells?" he said softly. Including Jinx, there were thirteen horses. Not fourteen as there should have been. He picked up the end of the rope that trailed behind the last horse. It was cut.

But no, not precisely that.

Kagen turned to allow more light to fall on the rope. The end was not cleanly severed, so it was not some opportunistic thief who'd stolen one while he either struggled through the snow or searched for a way into the mansion. The end was frayed. More than that, it looked like it had been *chewed* apart.

Kagen dropped the ends of the rope and his hands strayed toward his dagger hilts.

Chewed?

"Tears of the Harvest Gods," he said, forgetting in the moment that the Gods of the Garden had abandoned him. "That was no damned goat."

But the words echoed and came back to him as if the banished shadows were a mocking chorus. Kagen checked the door again to make sure it was firmly secured. It was, but somehow it did not offer any real sense of safety. The blizzard outside howled, the heavy winds buffeting the mansion's ancient walls.

Kagen stood there, one palm flat against the door and the other gripping the handle of a sheathed dagger. His heart pounded, and despite the cold, he was sweating.

He checked each horse more closely and his concern deepened. Some of them—the ones who had been crying out the most—had scratches on their hind quarters, legs, and withers. A few of these wounds were deep, and caked with blood that was hardly dry.

Something had been out there in the storm with him. It had mocked him with false cries, and now he was certain that it *had* been a child's cry he'd heard. One being hunted by whatever had taken the horse. Or, could it have been the false cry of a child made by . . .

By *what*?

Kagen had no idea, and what had been weird and strange before, now became terrifying. His hands clutched the handles of his daggers.

This part of the world was completely unknown to him, being at the very top of the Silver Empire. Even the borders seen on maps were what he had heard called "soft" borders, meaning that they were drawn by mapmakers but were in no way official. As a child he had never thought to ask why those borders had been drawn at all. Why had Nelfydia not claimed a greater territory? Why had no other county claimed possession? Vahlycor, Zaare, and Bulconia all shared their northern borders with the wastelands. Why draw their borders where they had and not take another inch of land?

He'd always assumed that it was because there was nothing worth owning this far north—merely snowy wastes, fragments of the glaciers that had covered the whole continent in ages past, and nothing else. But having come here, Kagen saw that there were animals here to hunt for fur and meat. There were endless forests to provide timber for building homes and ships and wagons. The dichotomy confounded him. Was that the truth? What kept men clustered in the south? What made them hesitant or afraid to push north?

This ruin made those questions even more frustrating. If there was nothing north of here, why would someone have built so fine and large a mansion on the very edge of it? The very size and presence of this place spoke to some opportunities, some reasons for being here.

It also made him wonder why this place was deserted. And why all of the valuables had been left behind and never looted.

Kagen was city-born and -bred and did not like mysteries of this kind, not at the best of times, and certainly when he had no other choice. If not for the howling storm of snow and ice outside, Kagen would have left right then and camped in the forest. But it was death out there for sure.

What, then, was in this place?

On impulse he drew both daggers and yelled aloud, "Come for me, you bastards, and I'll gut you and watch you bleed."

Once more the echoes turned his bold challenge into the frail and defensive cry of a child afraid of the dark. He knew that Tuke and Filia would have mocked him for his fear. But they were not here, and they could both go fuck themselves, he decided.

No creature—human, animal, or monster—materialized to take his challenge. There was only the darkness, the flickering firelight, the cold, the sounds of nervous horses, his own frightened breathing, and the unknown.

After a long time, Kagen reluctantly sheathed his daggers. He finished quickly with the horses and then took pieces of the thinner picture frames and used a hatchet to cut them into thick triangles, then kicked these under the edges of every door that opened into the hall. None of the doors opened outward into the other rooms.

Doing that made him feel marginally more comfortable, though some of the horses still cast anxious eyes at the shadows that capered at the edges of the fire glow.

Then something occurred to him, and Kagen took a torch, drew one dagger again, kicked one doorstop loose, and went stealthily back to the little servants' entrance through which he had first entered. The torch showed more of the room, and he saw things he hadn't observed before. There were five bedrolls on the ground, and each of them was torn and slashed, the ragged fabric stiff with old blood. And near the door itself he found a doorstop like the ones he had created. Kagen squatted down to examine it. The thing was a wedge with a long slant, the slope cut by the edge of the door under which it had been positioned.

Apart from that dent, the stop was whole.

Kagen's frown deepened.

The door was heavy and stout, the gap beneath it thin but with enough space for the doorstop to have been deeply and securely positioned. It should have required half a dozen men with a battering ram to open it. So how had he done it with only his shoulder? *And* without doing any damage to the door—or to the doorstop, for that matter? It was almost as if the door—or the house—had yielded to allow him inside.

Had this been one of the stories his father read to him as a child it would have been a happy circumstance. But Kagen did not for a moment believe the house was extending benevolence and mercy to him. The grim demeanors of the faces in those portraits hinted that kindness had never dwelt therein.

Kagen pivoted on the balls of his feet and studied every inch of that small room. The hairs on the back of his neck stood up and he felt goose bumps rise that had nothing to do with the chill air.

He rose. Kagen was a brave man, but in that moment he felt as weak and vulnerable as a child caught in a nightmare. His mother had long ago told him that the dark itself was not to be feared but that those things that knew how to hide and move through it were.

In the storm he'd seen a small, pale shape. It had tried to fool him with a cry like a lost child. Had it actually lured him here? Was it that thing that had bitten through the rope on the last horse in the string?

The horse had not cried out, though, and if the thing in the dark had been a wolf then all of the horses would have screamed. There would have been snarls and growls as the wolves dragged down a horse. Horses were timid at times but could fight like devils if attacked. Besides, wolves were not mimics, and the pale thing was, of that Kagen was certain.

Outside, the winds screeched like a horde of banshees. Inside, the cold shadows seemed to lurk, to wait, to watch.

Kagen began to speak a prayer to the Harvest Gods, but it died on his tongue. They would not listen to his prayers. Now or ever. He retreated to the entry hall, secured the door, and checked the horses, counting them once more. No more were missing, but did that mean they were safe? He truly did not know.

Kagen left the hall one more time, dragging two heavy chairs back. Once dismantled they would give him more than enough fuel to keep the hall bright and warm. And safe? Again, Kagen did not know.

He stood in the middle of the room for a long time, just listening. Trying to *feel* the house. If there were secrets in that place, the old stone and timbers did not whisper them to him. Not in any way his ears could hear. The horses, however, stood together in a tight group right in the middle of the room, not merely to share heat but also because that was where it was brightest.

"Gods protect me," whispered Kagen.

CHAPTER SEVENTY-EIGHT

TWO DAYS EARLIER

"Show me," said the Witch-king.

The three advisors had agreed that General Grenleth was the right one to make the presentation. He brought the swatch of cloth to the foot of the dais and—mindful of the bitch hound's baleful glare—handed it to the king, who in turn laid it on his left thigh. The first of the yellow cloths lay across his right. They were not identical, as if each had been painted by a different hand.

The general bowed and retreated to stand with Nespar and Jakob.

"The entire garrison is dead?" asked the Witch-king.

"All of them, Majesty," said the general. "Including the extra troops Captain Amurel brought with him. Only the courier was spared, because they wanted this sent. They wanted us to know who did this."

The Hakkian monarch touched the circle of thorns and roses with his fingertips, tracing them thoughtfully.

"Sons of the Poison Rose," he said softly.

"It is a new version of the sigil of the Poison Rose," said Nespar.

"That much is clear. Something particular to this group, though I don't think we can rule out a cult dedicated to her. We've seen that kind of thing before."

"Yes," agreed the Witch-king. "We've seen hints of this and I've been expected more."

In truth there had been a small group of young Argonian soldiers who had called themselves the Thorns of the Poison Rose. They ambushed two junior Hakkian officers on a night-darkened side street right there in Argentium. However, they were drunk and clumsy and were arrested within hours. All five of them were tortured until it was clear that their group had been cooked up that very day over too many drinks. No one believed, then or now, that they were part of any larger or better-organized rebellion. Those soldiers were put into a cell and told to fight, and that the survivor would be spared. After nearly an hour of savage combat, the bloody winner was told that he was, indeed, to be spared, but it meant that he would be left in the cell with his dead comrades. The only food offered to him was the flesh of his friends; the only drink was their cooling blood. That man lasted three days before beating his own brains out by running head-first into the bars over and over again. The hounds had the leavings.

"Lord Nespar," said the Witch-king, "you don't believe that Kagen Vale is behind this?"

"I do not, Majesty," and he gave the same explanation that he and Jakob had discussed a few days earlier.

"I agree," said the king.

"Majesty," said Grenleth, "it is even possible—perhaps likely—that it is not directly a Vale thing at all. It could have been created by any supporter of Lady Marissa Trewellyn-Vale. She is being promoted as a martyr, and I'm sure that in any hidden cell of Garden believers she has been canonized. As much or more so than the empress herself."

"Agreed," said the Witch-king again.

"Most of the empress's closest allies have fled Argentium to their rural estates," said Nespar. "Who knows what foolish plans they are drawing in secret meetings. With the Green Faith in tatters, people cleave to anything that gives them hope and comfort. Martyrs fill that need quite easily."

"They do," said the King in Yellow.

Lord Nespar turned to his master. "I can have Ravens begin searches of rural estates and—"

"Pardon me, my lord chamberlain," Jakob said to Nespar, cutting him off. He turned to the monarch. "May I speak, Majesty?"

"You may."

"If we begin raiding those estates, we risk creating more problems," said the royal historian. "If anyone resists and is hurt, we generate more drama and more martyrs. If great homes are ransacked, we will be viewed as a group of thugs rather than liberators from the harsh restrictions of the Silver Empire. So far we have done good work in sharing our propaganda that the Night of the Ravens was a thing to celebrate, and that toppling the Faith of the Harvest was a blow struck for religious freedom. Things have settled down since then, and the way we managed the narrative following the attempted assassination has kept the fires of insurrection banked very low."

"Tell that to the Ravens who were slaughtered by whoever carried this standard," growled Grenleth.

Jakob gave him a placating bow. "Oh, I totally agree, General," he said. "But these are two incidents committed by what is very likely one group of partisans. I think it's at worst a random act of violence by a group of disgruntled thugs. Perhaps unemployed soldiers, since the size of the Argonian army has been reduced by two thirds. More likely, though, it was an experiment—a statement of a kind to see how easily we can be provoked and how we will react."

"Are you saying that we should *not* react?" asked Grenleth, appalled.

"I am saying that we should not *over*react," said Jakob.

"We must respond," cried Nespar. "If we do nothing, then we will appear weak."

"And if we react too strongly, then we will look like barbarians," said Jakob, "and we will appear frightened. Frightened people lash out. And, make no mistake, we are being watched very closely by spies of the submonarchs. Although they were willing to participate in the coronation, it does not mean they are truly loyal. They have been unusually quiet, which makes me wonder what that silence is hiding. Any of them could be behind these atrocities. They might be curating this in order to study our reactions. There are many kinds of apparent weaknesses—over and under reactions are equally telling. I think we need to be restrained in our response."

The Witch-king nodded. "Lord Ravensmere," he said slowly, "I appreciate the calm sobriety of your comments. You do not want more violence. That is, it seems to me, a scholar's viewpoint. War is destructive and scholars are hoarders and gatherers."

Jakob gave a small bow but made no comment.

"This," said the King in Yellow as he placed his hands on the two swatches, "is not a small act of little consequence. This is a declaration of war."

"Surely not, Majesty," protested Jakob.

But the Witch-king shook his head. "There is subtlety here. There is guile. I do not for one moment believe that this is the work of a band of rabble-rousers."

He picked up the pieces of cloth, folded them, and placed them on a side table as he rose. Without haste he stepped down from the dais and walked, hands clasped behind his back, to a wall upon which a tapestry was hung. The embroidered pattern showed a misty vale choked with blue-gray mist. Barely seen in that mist were figures—people, though their postures were odd, almost animalistic. General Grenleth studied it as well, and for him it called to mind the awkward and unnatural postures of the cursed in the small town he had seen torn to pieces.

"We have been discussing war since the night Kagen Vale tried to kill me," said the Witch-king without turning. "We knew it was coming, but we did not know what form it would take." He turned. "Now we do. Our enemies are sly, gentlemen. They think we will buy this story of rebel groups making small attacks in remote places. The nations of the Silver Empire have always underestimated Hakkia," continued the Witch-king. "Always. For a thousand years they have regarded us weak, ineffectual, impotent."

He walked over to stand in front of his three advisors.

"The kings and queens saw our palace invaded and my life threatened without punishment or response. No doubt it made them sure that their assessment of Hakkia was correct. Despite all we did on the Night of the Ravens, Kagen Vale *proved* to them that we are not invincible. Because we have not used great magicks since then, that has likely convinced them that our one best arrow has been fired and we have nothing of consequence left in our quiver." He sighed. "Such arrogance. Such lack of vision."

"What will we do, then, Majesty?" asked Grenleth.

The Witch-king looked at him for a long moment. "You have *seen* what we will do, General. As have you, Lord Ravensmere. And you, Nespar, have read every report."

"My . . . my liege," gasped Jakob. "Surely you would not use that . . . that . . . weapon in open warfare!"

"We are greatly outnumbered, and on any field of battle we do not have the military might to win a war against an empire," said the Witch-king. "Our enemies disparaged us all these years, but the empresses and their assassin, Lady Bellapher . . . they knew. They understood. They tried to crush us because they realized how dangerous we might be. It is time, my friends, to show them—and all the world—that they were right to fear Hakkian retribution."

He turned away.

"Nespar, summon the Hollow Monks. We have much work to do."

CHAPTER SEVENTY-NINE

Kagen made some food and ate it while watching first one door and then another.

Once his cooking gear was stowed away again, he thought about how he might fight something that was beyond his experience. He knew that magic was returning to the world, and his knowledge on that subject was as thin as that of most of the citizens of the Silver Empire. He wished he knew as much about it as Tuke and Filia seemed to. But for someone like him, magic was for history books, drunken tavern tales, and to scare children into eating their greens. Except that now it was here, and he knew nothing about how to fight it.

Nor, for that matter, did he know about how to fight the *natural* creatures that lived this far north. He had heard tales of white bears that stood fifteen feet tall and could disembowel a horse with a single swipe of their claws. He had seen drawings of white snow apes, pale leopards that hunted the more remote reaches, and other dangerous beasts.

All of those memories bonded with his fears of the unknown, making him feel deeply uneasy. It was the kind of reductive feeling that brushed aside vain imaginings of how older and more worldly friends like Tuke would mock him for his fears. Tuke, damn his eyes, was not here, and Kagen believed that even his towering giant of a friend would not sit easily in this place. Together they might laugh at the shadows and make bold declarations to one another, using braggadocio and company as shields to protect their doubts and insecurities. Kagen was afraid of no man—not in combat of any kind—but he feared this place and its unseen secrets.

He recalled one of the lessons he'd learned as a lad.

"Order and habit and all mundane tasks keep the hands busy and the mind focused."

One of his mother's many aphorisms, and he seized it, taking from it a new and more useful meaning than he had before.

"Get about it," he told himself, trying to make his voice sound normal. It was a good enough effort to shake him loose from fearful immobility. He fished for his cooking gear and a skin of water and set about preparing a hot meal. He boiled water and took some beef slices that had frozen solid, along with a handful of herbs and his last potato, and with that made a stew. His cooking was as indifferent as his woodcraft, but it was edible and hot. With each steaming bite he could feel warmth return, however reluctantly, first in his belly and then in his limbs. He leaned into the steam to let it soothe his chapped face. The herbs called to mind happier days in the palace kitchen.

When he'd eaten his fill, he put the pot on the edge of the fire to simmer. He thought about the skin of wine but passed on that and instead took a bundle of leaves and made some strong tea. The horses seemed to calm down as well, perhaps because they, too, had full bellies, or maybe because, empathetic creatures that they were, they took comfort from his returning confidence. Kagen checked on them, patting each and pausing for a moment to lean his forehead against Jinx's.

Then he returned to his spot, opened the leather pouch in which he kept a few precious items, withdrew a small crystal vial, and held it up to the light. It looked delicate but had so far survived battles and hardships and remained intact. Nor had the cold frozen the contents. It was nearly full of a liquid that was the pale golden color of autumn cider. A casual observer might have mistaken it for a vial of perfume, or perhaps something to add savor to a king's soup. But Kagen knew its nature and secret.

It had been a gift to him from Maralina, the strange woman who lived in the Tower of Sarsis in Vahlycor. A woman he'd tried to rob of a legendary treasure—the Chest of Algion—before he'd fallen under her spell. Even now, Kagen was not sure exactly *what* she was. There were fragments of memories from dreams shared while he and Maralina made love, and in the throes of their passion they seemed to drift through centuries of time. Maralina, daughter of the queen of faeries. She was the lover and victim of an ancient vampire. What she had become in the untold ages since was a kind of tortured creature who was part of both worlds but accepted in neither. Ancient, ageless, powerful, and profoundly sad. Maralina lived now in his heart and dreams, but he had no idea if he would ever see her again.

If not for the gifts she had bestowed on him when he left her tower, Kagen knew he might have easily let himself believe she was nothing but a dream. A fantasy conjured by his broken heart, his longing, and his despair.

The vial was real, though. It was proof of her reality.

When she gave it to him, Maralina had said, *"It is something very old. It has no name in Argonian or the common tongue, but ages ago it was called* eitr. *In ages past,* eitr *was both the source of life and a certain means of ending it. Once, before the world was made, gods battled each other for the right to rule this planet. When fragments of ice from a great kingdom of frost encountered the fires of a burning realm, that sacred ice melted and the runoff was this. Some believe that* eitr *was the water of life that gave birth to all living things, but as it gives life, so it can take it. Be very careful with this. Allow a drop to run along the length of your mother's daggers. Let it dry completely before you dare touch it."*

He had asked what it did, and Maralina had given him a wicked smile.

"This poison was said to be deadly enough to kill gods, though I do not

know if that is true. It is at its most potent, however, when it touches enchanted flesh. If you fight the Witch-king and can cut him with this, much will be revealed. If he is mortal, he will bleed and become sick. Perhaps he will die. But even if he does not, his mortal weakness will be revealed to anyone who sees him so afflicted. If he is a god or a demon, then his true form will be fully revealed. It may not kill him, but it may show him for the monster he is, and that may help your dreams of rebellion."

With that poison, Kagen had come close to killing his brother, Herepath. The *eitr* on his blades had allowed him to slaughter many of the Witch-king's soldiers, but the lord of Hakkia had escaped. Only just. When, during their fight in the great hall of Argentium, the Witch-king's lace veil had been torn away and Kagen had glimpsed that familiar—that impossible—face beneath, he had faltered. That hesitation had allowed Herepath to flee—uncrowned, yes, but unpoisoned and undefeated. That failure burned so hot in Kagen he wondered that it did not turn the blizzard into a spring mist.

"Maralina," he murmured, conjuring her lovely face in his mind. "How disappointed you must be in me."

The building shuddered as the winds increased. Kagen cut wary glances at the doors, but the wedges held them closed.

He used a few precious drops of that poison to season the steel of his daggers, and he dribbled more into the sheaths. He sat down with his back to a solid wall between two fires. If whatever was in this place drew breath or pumped blood, then the poison would likely kill it. If it could kill gods—if that part of Maralina's story was true—then maybe it would save him from monsters or ghosts.

A year ago, Kagen would have laughed at himself for even believing such things existed. Back then, the Silver Empire ruled the west and magic had been banished a millennia ago. Ghosts and demons belonged to campfire stories and threats to make children eat their vegetables. They were not real.

Until the Witch-king conquered the Silver Empire with magic.

Until the Hakkians resurrected the cult of Nyarlathotep, conjured a razor-knight and awakened other supernatural threats. Until Kagen had met a woman who was half faerie and half vampire and doomed to immortality.

Until . . .

Everything since last year had torn away any possibility of a disbelief in a much larger world than the one taught in the gardens. It forced upon him, instead, a certain knowledge that there were unclean things in the shadows.

Magic had returned to the earth.

Kagen sat there, clutching his poisoned daggers, feeling his fear conjure ice in his blood despite the burning wood. He sat there long into the night, intending to stay away until dawn.

He was exhausted but relied on training, discipline, and fear to keep him awake.

The night, the storm, the darkness, and the atmosphere of the mansion conspired otherwise, and he fell asleep, hands still closed around his knives. Kagen slept, and dreamed . . .

CHAPTER EIGHTY

They were not soldiers. They were a farrier and a woodsman.

The farrier had no hammer, no comforting length of iron. All he could find was a wooden bucket with a sturdy leather handle. The woodsman's axe was long gone—buried in the skull of that man's second cousin—and he had no weapon worth a damn except a small kitchen knife with a three-inch blade that was good for cutting onions and sausages but damn little else.

They crouched behind a burning warehouse, squeezing themselves into a downspill of shadows cast by a broken door that hung from one twisted hinge. The door was burning, too, and soon its light would burn off the shadows. Or the flames devouring the warehouse would also feast on them.

They huddled together, shivering and clutching each other like children, as they watched their town burn. Screams tore through the air and tore into each of them. It was hard to tell the difference between the shrieks of men or women when they were in that much pain. The cries and wails of children had faded out already. Maybe they were all dead; perhaps some were hiding. Most likely, they thought, the children—or what had *been* children—were now . . . *them.*

There was no name for what those things were. Not men and women. Not anymore. Not the living or the dead. These were surely monsters, demons like those in old stories. Foul things that inhabited the flesh that each man knew so well—neighbors and friends, cousins and in-laws.

And the others.

Monstrous, ravenous, howling abominations who wore the faces of their wives and parents and children like carnival masks. Terrible nightmare figures that snarled and bit and ate and hungered.

The farrier and the woodsman looked around, hoping and praying to see someone left alive. Left un—They did not even know the word. Possessed? Was that it? Cursed? Driven mad with some kind of sickness?

They looked and saw only those creatures—running, shambling, staggering, crawling, or bent over torn lumps of things that were so thoroughly ruined that they could not carry the burden of the curse alone. Things that had once been people and were now only creatures. Shapeless, inhuman.

The farrier tried to make a warding sign in the air, but his hand was shaking too badly. The woodsman looked down at the blade in his bloody hand and wondered if it would save his soul if he plunged it into his own heart.

Above and behind them, the warehouse burned.

The flag of their small town, Kuppinshal, and the national flag of Ghenrey, hung from the mayor's office across the street. As they watched, the flagpole caught fire. They watched the flames crawl upward until they stroked the limp sheets of color cloth, and then the flags were burning too.

"We have to—" began the woodsman, but that was as far as he got, because the warehouse roof, weakened by the fury of the flames, collapsed inward and the force punched all of the walls out. The two of them were buried under three tons of flaming debris.

Theirs were the only deaths in that little Ghenreyan town that could in any way be described as natural. If anything inside the walls of that town could use that word on such a night.

A half mile outside the walls, a knot of figures on horseback watched Kuppinshal burn.

Four of the six riders held bows. One of the remaining men held a small torch, ready to light more arrows. But after another half an hour of watching, he dropped the torch. The archers put their arrows back into their quivers and unstrung their bows.

"A good night's work, lads," said the sixth man. "Let's go."

The six of them turned and melted into the night.

CHAPTER EIGHTY-ONE

No one alive knew his real name.

Even he did not know it, was never sure he ever had one. Orphans left outside a guardhouse seldom had names. They had no families, no lineage, no history. All that he knew of his own origin was that he was estimated to be a week old. He was half-starved, frail, and discarded.

Like many such children, the boy was sent to one of the many orphanages funded by the Faith of the Harvest. It was in a poor corner of the Argonian farmlands, tucked into the border shared by eastern Nehemite and western Bulconia. He was given a name, Radhu, but that was in honor of the soldier who brought him to the garden. The soldier, a young man of nineteen, was unmarried and did not want to raise a child, but he left a small bag of coins he'd collected from the other guards on his watch. Enough to pay for the child's care for a few months.

Radhu was not a popular child, and not a very good-looking one. Nor particularly ugly. He was completely average in height, weight, build, hair, and eye coloring. He could as easily been Argonian, Nehemitian, or Bulconian . . . but also Zehrian, Hakkian, or Ghenreyan. Medium brown hair, brown eyes, mildly olive skin.

The only thing about the orphan that set him apart from his peers was his intelligence. He excelled in classes, reading far above his level and displaying a talent for languages. By the time he was ten years old he could speak the common tongue, Argonian, and also Nehemitian, with smatterings of others. And he demonstrated a knack for accents. He could speak with a refined Argentium upper-crust accent one moment, shift without effort to the broader midlands farmer's drawl, and then rattle away in the rapid patter of a southern caravan merchant.

When Radhu was sixteen, having never been adopted—prospective parents always found something disagreeable about the look in his eyes, the angle of his knowing smile, or his ability to detach from emotions—he left the Garden and enlisted in the military. Not out of patriotism, for Radhu owed allegiance to none. He felt that he belonged to no nation, no community. He had no theology and no politics, though he understood both very well.

In the army he was valued because of his language skills, though promotions came rarely because he never played politics the right way, never went out of his way to flatter his superiors, never went to lengths to demonstrate his loyalty. He left the service at twenty-two and found employment as an interpreter for various merchants. One of these was a Hakkian seed merchant named Colrik Nespar. Colrik's older brother was ostensibly a courtier and an official but was actually a spymaster. It was this older Nespar, soon to become the lord chamberlain of Hakkia, who was the first to see the true value of someone who in no way drew attention to himself because he looked absolutely ordinary. Radhu's talent with languages was key, but it was his skill at speaking with all the varied dialects, and doing so with great fidelity and subtlety, that most appealed to Nespar. He groomed Radhu, paid him well, treated him with respect, and even showed true kindness. As Lord Nespar rose in political power, Radhu rose with him, though never publicly, never in the light. He loved the shadows and thrived there, and soon he was the spymaster for the new chamberlain.

No one else in the entire Hakkian court knew that Radhu existed. Different officials and nobles met Gibly, the Zehrian caravan scout, and Jolner, the Argonian spice merchant. They met Sergeant Wollix of Zaare and the minor Samudian noble, ul-Zhek, and had brief encounters with Zurr, a corn farmer from Vahlycor or Captain Quamian, owner of a Behlian shrimper. The name Radhu was never used, and each of those identities was utterly forgettable.

Which made Radhu the most powerful weapon in Lord Nespar's arsenal, and—if anyone was able to review the details—the most effective and dangerous spy in the west.

When Nespar tasked him with uncovering spies working for the submonarchs of the former empire, his chief agent melted into the ebb and flow of humanity and appeared to vanish entirely.

The only trace of him was in the small scrolls, written in a special code, that appeared every now and then under the pillow on Nespar's bed. Even the lord chamberlain had no idea how they got there. He had excellent guards and sophisticated locks. None of that mattered to Radhu.

CHAPTER EIGHTY-TWO

Kagen often remembered one dream per night in great detail, but he was aware on some level that he had many dreams. Some he recalled as fleeting images—an old face, an event from that day, a fantasy of something improbable, a snatch of conversation his waking mind knew he'd never had.

Sometimes he was aware of the weight of a dream pressing down on the edges of his consciousness, but even sitting on the side of a bed, or cross-legged atop a bedroll out in the wild, he was unable to pull details out of the darkness.

And then there were dreams that came to him with such exquisite detail that he knew he would never—*could* never—forget them.

As he slept in that empty hall in the dead mansion, he had one such dream.

He was not in Nelfydia but far away, in a small town in western Vahlycor, in a tall tower that overlooked the ocean.

And she was there.

She.

Maralina.

The tower was the same, the chamber was the same, but there was something different that he did not yet understand as the dream began to unfold.

The chamber was much as he remembered it, with a thousand candles burning and dripping wax. Sticks of incense were thrust into some or stood in clusters in little bowls of sand set before altars of such exotic design Kagen had no idea what gods or saints they represented. Massive tapestries hung on the walls, and Kagen eyed them suspiciously, for he knew firsthand that each of these was not mere cloth but a doorway into another place, another time, perhaps even other worlds.

Against one wall was a huge and ornate spinning wheel and a loom of incredible beauty and antiquity. Both were inlaid with gold and silver, amethyst and pearl. Hung on the wall between and above these was a round mirror as big as a battle shield. Its surface was so heavily polished that it reflected the rest of the room as surely as a looking glass. And yet as Kagen studied the mirror he saw that the reflection of that chamber was merely a veneer, and beneath it was a different thing entirely. The mirror reflected an ancient road with massive paving stones so heavily overgrown that it was barely a road at all. Beyond, at the very range of sight, were stoneworks of some vast and improbable city with architecture that seemed entirely unreal and unsuited for human habitation. The buildings did not seem to be constructed according to any logic or engineering Kagen could grasp. There were gigantic structures like cones, some smooth and others terraced, and each topped by unusual tubes, the function of which seemed to be to allow passage, but the scale was off. Nothing ever made by man would require so grand a corridor as those.

Scattered throughout the visible section of the city were pyramids, like the crumbling relics scholars studied on the island of Skyria, but much larger. Three, four, and even ten times bigger, and made from blocks of stone that had to weigh hundreds of tons. How such blocks could be cut and dressed, let alone transported and arranged, boggled his mind. Other structures looked like five-, six-, or eight-pointed stars, some leaning backwards or forward at such angles that surely magic of some unknown kind kept them from toppling. The rest of the city was lost to gloom, distance, and the rampant lushness of the jungle.

Kagen had never been to that place, though he had been to something similar, a fragment of a city where the greater percentage was buried beneath uncountable tons of volcanic slag. He and three of his brothers visited that forgotten place once, many years ago, when Kagen was still a lad. It was deep in the heart of Vespia, a strange land on the eastern side of the Cathedral Mountains. History books said that Vespia was once as high and sophisticated a land as Skyria, and much older, and that the people there were great builders and mathematicians and astronomers. However, some strange and unknown doom came to Vespia, collapsing the civilization and casting the survivors of that calamity into barbarism, cannibalism, and madness. The nations that patrolled its borders did so to make sure none of the mad flesh-eaters tried to invade civilized lands. Yet, in all the centuries since its fall, there was not one story of the Vespian dog soldiers, as they were called, ever crossing their own borders. The Vale brothers had barely escaped with their lives, and all of them swore never to return.

The city in that mirror was either the one he'd been to, either in the past or somehow excavated from the obsidian that covered nearly all of it, or it was another, greater place. Kagen's instinct told him it was the latter.

He looked around at the rest of the room. At the uncountable books on shelves and in stacks, at the bins of scrolls, and easels on which clay tablets were placed for contemplation.

There were couches upholstered in soft velvet of purple and black and indigo and divans whose embroidered pillows spilled onto the floor. Astronomical and astrological charts were spread out on tables. And everywhere he saw chests and boxes of jewelry of unparalleled craftsmanship and beauty but covered in dust, as if their intrinsic worth did not matter at all.

Then he turned again, and she was there.

Even though Kagen dreamed about her nearly every night, and though he had lived with her for a month and spent every moment, awake or asleep, with her, the sight of Maralina nevertheless stole his breath away.

She was very tall—inches taller than Kagen—and had lustrous black hair that hung down to her waist. When he first met her, that hair was streaked with red and silver, but now it was black within black within black. That intensity highlighted her skin, which was pale as moonlight on a clear winter's night.

Maralina wore a gown of rich electric blue, and it was fitted to her form like a second skin. Seeing her awakened his memory of her when they made love. Clothes leaned her, disguising lushness of breast and hip, hiding the elegant curve of her back from good shoulders down to a narrow waist.

Even with all of that, it was her face that most enchanted him. She had high cheekbones and a broad, clear brow. She had a patrician nose and full lips that could be sensual or cruel or amused with equal artfulness.

And her eyes. Never in his life—nor in any painting he'd ever seen—had he seen eyes like Maralina's. The color seemed impermanent and changeable with her moods. They could brood darkly or flash with green fire; they could soften the moment with blue serenity or stir the conversation with swirls of hazel and green and yellow. In every mood, the one constant was her intelligence. She possessed an obvious wisdom that was far, far older than her apparent years.

"Kagen," said Maralina as she approached him. "I've called you so many nights and you have not come to me."

"I . . . I did not hear your call," he said.

Her reply was a small, sad smile.

"I'm here now," Kagen said quickly, rising from the couch on which he sat and reaching for her.

"No," she said, "you are not."

Kagen took her in his arms and kissed her. It was a long kiss. Deep and sweet, and their tongues danced a slow waltz that set Kagen's heart ablaze. But then Maralina pushed him gently back to arm's length.

"This is but a dream, my love," she murmured.

"Then it's a dream," he replied. "Who cares? We found each other again."

But Maralina shook her head. "I did not come to make love with you, Kagen Vale," she said. "I—"

"No," he said sharply, cutting her off. "Please . . . I don't want to hear more of prophecies and Witch-kings and warfare. I found you after all my dreams and wandering and I want to just be."

Maralina looked at him with such profound sadness that Kagen felt his own eyes tingle with unshed tears.

"Oh, my wandering knight," she said, forcing the smallest of smiles. "We have so little time, and night has come for the world."

"Then let us have the time we have," he said.

She reached out and caressed his cheek with fingers that were as cold a winter's morning. Then she took one of his hands and placed it on her chest, between her breasts and over her heart. Somehow, with that action, they were gone from the chamber with the loom and mirror. Now he stood beside her bed in another part of the tower. They were naked, and firelight painted her pale skin in the softest of golden tones.

She reached down and clasped his erect cock, stroking it gently.

"Kagen," she said, as she had once before, "I'm so cold. Keep me warm."

He raised a hand and traced a slow line down the side of her throat and down over her collarbone, following the soft swell of one full breast all the way to the soft pink nub of her nipple. He took it between thumb and forefinger, coaxing it to hardness. Maralina's moan was low and husky as Kagen bent to bite the nipple with infinite tenderness. It tightened and he sucked it gently.

Maralina placed her hands on his shoulders and pushed him down with gentle insistence, and he sank to his knees. His hands brushed the length of her, from breasts to ankles and back up, rediscovering the beautiful landscape of her. He kissed her stomach and then each full hip, pressing his nose and mouth into the softness sheltered by the hip bone, and nipping the flesh with his teeth.

He turned and guided her down onto the bed, and as she lay back, Kagen moved to the foot of the bed and lay on his chest between her alabaster thighs. He bent forward and once more pressed his mouth against her, but this time into the tangle of silky dark hair. And there he lingered for a long time, using tongue and teeth, lips and breath to draw gasps and finally a piercing shriek from her.

After, she pulled him up and rolled him onto his back, then swung a leg across with such grace and delicacy and sureness of action that as she sat down he was inside her.

Kagen did not know how long they made love. A few minutes or forever. He became as lost in his love and passion as he had been when he first came to that tower and fell through a tapestry into a series of other worlds. But this was all sweetness and beauty, and unutterable sadness.

When the lovers were spent and lay in a tangle of sheets, breathing gradually slowing, Maralina placed her hand over his heart and he responded with the same gesture. In that moment it became a symbol between them, though its exact meaning was something he could not yet define.

"Are you in your tower still, my lady?" he asked.

"I will always be there," she said.

"Even now that magic has returned to the world? Surely there is some spell that can set you free."

"Only my mother can free me, Kagen, for it was she who cast that spell. But she is gone far away, through the veils and into a world so distant that even with my mirror I can no longer find her. She might even be dead, if the queen of the Baobhan sith can die. I know we can, but she is different. Older and stronger, and even by our standards, infinitely stranger."

"There must be something . . ."

She patted his chest. "I have dwelt in my tower for more years than you know, my love. I have accepted that it is my fate. Besides . . ." She began to say more, then paused.

"Besides . . . what?"

"You know my story, Kagen. You know what I did and what was done to me. You know what I became."

He did know, too. She told him the horrific and tragic tale of how she, as a young faerie princess, had fallen for what she thought was a human nobleman, Duke Sárkány. He seduced her, and then after he had taken her in every possible way, he revealed his true nature to her. He was no man at all—not anymore—but was an ancient and powerful vampire. He fed on her and then forced her to feed on him. Then he cast her out—literally threw her from his window and left her dying on the lawn below.

Her mother came to find her, and when Maralina's new hybrid nature asserted itself and she rose from what should have been her death, the queen of the faerie folk cursed her and drove her away. Later, the queen, out of grief and shame, imprisoned Maralina in the Tower of Sarsis, and there she was doomed to remain.

"How can I help you?" begged Kagen.

"You cannot save me," said Maralina. "If I were somehow free of this place, free of my mother's magicks, then I would become more like Duke Sárkány. You have seen the graveyard outside of this tower. You know that I have those same red hungers. How many kings and princes and champions are buried *there? How many ghosts haunt this palace and cry in voiceless voices in vain hope of driving away any other mortals, lest they fall prey to me?"*

She said this in a calm voice, nearly a whisper, but it punched Kagen like fists.

He rubbed tears of love and frustration from his eyes and said, "I can't do nothing, Gods damn it."

"Perhaps my hour will come, Kagen Vale," she said. "But now is the hour of the Witch-king, and he is drawing his allies to him. The Hollow Monks have raised a terrible weapon that should have died with the ancients. And the Prince of Games is alive again. He wields no sword, but his whispers can topple nations. Beware of the Hollow Monks, Kagen, but fear the prince all the more."

"Who are they?" he demanded.

But he was alone and Maralina was gone from his dreams.

He was in the mansion in the woods of Nelfydia. The blizzard howled like forty demons and yet Kagen did not wake. Instead, he turned over and plunged into dreams once more.

CHAPTER EIGHTY-THREE

At the top of the tower stairs, Gavran and Foscor stopped, crouching by the heavy door that was shut and locked from outside. There was a slot on the bottom of the door, through which trays of food could be passed.

The children flattened out on the floor and peered in through the slot. The opening was not very big, only high enough for a tray with a wine bottle laid on its side. One such tray sat inside, the food untouched and crawling with roaches. Two other trays were nearby, clearly pushed farther into the room as each new one was shoved inside. The smell of rotting meat was strong, though there were more powerful and pungent scents hanging in the dank air.

Voices spoke within the room, though the children could not see anyone. They turned and pressed their ears to the opening, straining to hear. It took a while to still their own breathing so that the sounds they made did not interfere with the muffled conversation.

". . . your name," said a voice. It sounded like their former governess, Lady Kestral, but not entirely. This voice sounded too old, too thin, too sickly.

"Wh-where am I?" begged a male voice. It was as thin as hers and sounded frightened and confused.

"You are in the palace in Argentium," replied the woman. "Tell me your name."

"I . . . Gods of the Pit . . . what's wrong with me?" There was a pause, and the same voice spoke again, the voice climbing to a higher register as fear turned to panic. "Am I dead? Please . . . tell me that I'm not dead. I beg you . . ."

"Tell me your name," repeated the woman, trying to put enough steel into the words to make them a command.

"Save my soul," cried the man.

"Tell me your name and I can help you," said Kestral.

There was a pause, and then something mumbled that the children could not understand.

"Say it again," ordered the witch.

"I . . . I am . . ."

"*Tell me.*"

"Trochnar," blurted the man. "I am Trochnar, sergeant of the Fifth Spears."

Another pause. Then Kestral spoke again, and now they could hear in her voice a sadness bordering on grief, perhaps despair.

"You are Hakkian," she said, not making it a question.

"I . . . I serve the Witch-king," said the man, and now he wept. "I pledged my life to—"

And then the voice was cut off.

The twins stared at each other, trying to make sense of what they had heard. It was Foscor who mouthed a word.

Ghost?

Before Gavran could answer, the sound of sobbing filled the room beyond the door.

"I cannot do this," wept the woman. "By the grace of the Shepherd God . . . I *cannot* do this anymore."

The smell of blood and fresh urine filled the air as the sobs rose to a maniacal pitch.

The children frowned at each other. Lady Kestral was their favorite of anyone in the palace. Although mercy played very little part of their emotional awareness, it was not absent. They lay there and prayed that she was not as far gone as she sounded.

The sobs turned to shrieks, and the wild madness of that chased them all the way down the stairs.

CHAPTER EIGHTY-FOUR

"I'm telling you, lads," said the beadle of the town of Chestnut Grove in central Argon, "there's trouble brewing."

He spoke in a low, confidential voice, and his two friends—Mullet the gamekeeper from the big estate on the edge of town, and the city scribe, Pollor—leaned in to listen. They were in a cell in the beadle's office. The cell door stood open because there hadn't been a prisoner there since the last Harvest Day celebration, when the beadle locked up three local lads for drinking too much and singing love songs very loudly to the virgin daughter of Chestnut Grove's mayor. A board was set on a barrel and a game of Castles and Kings was paused midway through a defensive move. They were all indifferent players, and conversation—along with strong, hard pear cider—was more to their liking.

"You're talking about what happened at the fort?" asked Pollor.

"Aye, and elsewhere," said the beadle. "I've heard there's been six different attacks on the Hakkian outposts."

"Six?" grunted Mullet. "I only heard about four."

"Six," insisted the beadle. "There was a patrol ambushed and cut to pieces up by Lake Lyra two weeks ago. Twenty Hakkian regulars and an officer."

"Damn," breathed Mullet.

"And the other?" asked Pollor.

"There was a border garrison by that little town right over the border in Nehemite. You know the one, where they have the horse sales every spring."

"Xanthel?" suggested Mullet.

"That's it," said the beadle. "Two dozen Hakkians, including a visiting patrol of six Ravens."

Pollor sipped his cider and belched. "As a man of faith I'd like to say that I'm sorry for the poor souls sent on to their reward, but . . . I don't like to lie."

They all laughed at that. However, the laughter was thin and faded out quickly.

"Truth is, lads," said the beadle, "with these Sons of the Poison Rose making such a fuss, I'm afraid of what the Hakkians will do."

"Do to who?" asked Pollor. "Ain't none of us riding under that standard. And no one I know, either."

"Well, someone's killing those Hakkians," said the beadle. "And if the Hakkian pricks can't find the ones actually doing it, tell me you don't think they'll start crucifying just any-damn-one so they can make a point."

"Yeah," said Mullet. "Kind of surprised that hasn't happened already."

They drank and thought about it.

"Tell me," said Pollor to the beadle, "you always seem to hear gossip before the rest of us. Have you heard anything? Do you have any idea who's behind this? I mean 'Sons of the Poison Rose' . . . that suggests something to me, at least."

The beadle nodded. "There are a lot of Vale siblings out there," he said.

"You think it's Kagen? The one who had a run at the Witch-king?"

When he said the name of the Hakkian monarch, all three of them turned and spat on the floor.

"Maybe," said the beadle. "He tried once, which means he has the balls for it."

"So, you think it's him?"

The beadle shrugged. "If it was a Vale and I had to guess," he mused, "I'd say it was probably those two they call the Twins. Jheklan and the other one."

"Faulker," supplied Mullet.

"Them. They were always getting into trouble, and if half of what's said about them is true, they're not afraid of cutting the odd throat."

The conversation ran on along those lines.

They spoke quietly. No one outside of the office could have heard a word. But Radhu, spymaster of Hakkia, was not outside. He was wrapped in dark cloth the exact color of the ceiling and strapped to one of the thick beams that crisscrossed above the three men. The light from the small fireplace did not even reach him.

However, every single word did.

―――――――――――――――▶ **CHAPTER EIGHTY-FIVE**

DREAMS OF THE DAMNED

In dreams Kagen was seldom the man he was and instead walked abroad as a lad of fifteen years. His thoughts were a blend of his younger mind and the adult, with an emotional bias toward the former. He had his boyhood sense of wonder and trust, but also the unrefined fears and untested courage.

In his dream he stood in the great hall on the other side of the stone wall against which he slept. But when he reached out casually to touch the wall, the surface burned his fingers with a deep and shocking cold. Kagen stepped closer and brushed at the stone, and saw the dusty granite flake off and fall away, pieces of it drifting down like the last dead leaves of autumn, revealing a far paler stone beneath. At first Kagen thought it was marble, but then the truth became manifest as he bent close to study it.

Not marble at all. The wall behind the granite facade was ice. Very old ice. Kagen looked around, and in the moment of doing that, the mansion itself vanished and he stood in a great hall of ice that he recognized from other dreams. He was inside a glacier, somewhere in the vast nothingness of the Winterwilds.

"It's all ice, little brother," said a voice, and Kagen whirled to see a tall man behind him. Dour, nearly gaunt, with dark eyes and a high, clear brow. A man dressed in green robes edged with woodland brown, with faint leaves embroidered along the hems. Despite the clerical robes and lugubrious scholar's face, the man wore a sword at his hip.

"Herepath," said Kagen, and in a strange moment he heard that name inflected in two distinctly different ways. The boy spoke with excitement, with filial love, with joy at seeing his favorite brother. The older Kagen hissed the name, filling the three syllables with bile and hurt.

Herepath smiled at him. That cold smile of his that barely lifted the corners of his mouth. A knowing smile—superior, amused, with a promise of contempt for fools and the unenlightened. Jheklan and Faulker always mocked that tone, imitating it at family dinners. Herepath had always ignored the mockery, though, as if descending to their level even to be offended was far beneath him.

"You're not here," said Kagen, forcing his current mind to speak through the young mouth.

Herepath's eyebrows rose, haughty and amused. "Neither are you, Kagen."

Kagen drew both daggers, quick as a flash, and slashed at Herepath, crossing the blades under his chin in a killing move that should have cut his throat all the way to the spine. However, the blades met no resistance of skin or muscle. They passed through Herepath as if he were a ghost.

Herepath sighed. "You used to be the brightest of our brothers, Kagen, but I suspect you've grown into a fool."

Kagen tried stabbing, but he might as well have been attacking smoke, for all the good it did.

Herepath stepped closer and reached out to touch one blade. Kagen felt the knife move slightly in his hand. He chopped at the fingers, but again there was no contact. The fact that Kagen could make no contact seemed to amuse Herepath.

"The world is full of wonders," he said. "You have glimpsed the merest bit of them, Kagen. You have no idea what is coming."

Kagen straightened, though as a boy he was much shorter than his tall older brother. Even so, he spoke with a man's voice. "You have no idea what is coming, either. I will find you and kill you for what you've done."

"Will you?" mocked Herepath mildly.

"You slaughtered Mother and Father, damn your soul to the blackest hell. You killed Hugh and the empress and the Seedlings . . ."

"Oh, I've done much more than that, Kagen," laughed Herepath. "Much, much more."

"But why, damn it?" demanded Kagen. "You were a Gardener!"

Herepath waved it away. "A means to an end."

"You killed our parents!"

Herepath's eyes darkened. "This is a hungry world, little brother. It needs to be fed. It demands sacrifices."

"But Mother? Father?"

"Even them," said Herepath. "Them and everything else I have ever loved."

Was there a whisper of sadness in his brother's voice?

"To what end?" demanded Kagen. "You're not even Hakkian. You're not in the Witch-king's bloodline."

Herepath's smile seemed to flicker, to become somewhat forlorn, and in that was all the more mysterious. "You do not understand how this world works, Kagen. Maybe you'll live long enough to grasp its subtleties, but I doubt it. I will have your blood, and with it . . . your dreams."

"I will kill you first," snarled Kagen.

"Kill me?" said Herepath. "And why do you think that would matter?

After all you have seen so far, do you truly believe that death is an end?" He waved his arms toward the ice walls and, following the gestures, Kagen saw something he'd seen in other dreams—shapes inside the ice, human and . . . not. Some were static, truly frozen into immobility except for their eyes. Others seemed to writhe and move within the solid ice itself—amorphous things made of darkness that kept changing shape as if hoping to find one capable of breaking free. Kagen felt an ancient chill. The boy aspect of him was confused by the shapeless masses; but the older Kagen remembered a time when he, Jheklan, Faulker, and Herepath had visited one of these glaciers and, by accident, released a shapeless, shambling thing. Only luck had allowed them to survive that encounter.

In that frozen place, the echoes of the monster's weird cry filled the frigid air.

"Tekeli-li! Tekeli-li!"

With that sound came the name Herepath had given it.

Shoggoth.

Meaningless in any language.

Were the things in these walls like that other thing? Herepath had named it as if he knew it, as if he understood what it was.

Herepath walked past him and touched the ice by one of those writhing shapes.

"Magic has returned to the world," he said without turning. "I have done this thing."

"You're a monster," said Kagen.

Still not looking at him, Herepath nodded. "Yes," he said. Then he half-turned. "The ice is melting, Kagen. Did you know that? When it does, the secrets of the past will no longer be trapped. I will have them. You will see wonders, boy. Maybe they will change you; maybe you will understand why I have done the things I've done. Or . . . maybe you are too weak, and these things will blast your mind. Time will tell, but that time is coming. Oh yes, Kagen the Damned, that time is coming soon."

Kagen turned away, not wanting to hear more.

Silence filled the hall of ice. When he turned back, Herepath was gone.

The shadowy shapes with the ice continued to watch him, though. And some of those horrific shoggoths continued to scratch their way toward freedom.

Kagen reeled backwards, turned and fled.

Within three steps he was in the great hall of the deserted mansion once more. He had two visions, each appearing for the space of a step or two, each vanishing except for the images burned into his memory.

In one, that hall was bright with banners and torches, and the air was alive with laughter and song. A great lord sat upon a throne at one end, a brimming wine cup in one hand, his bearded face alight with happiness and pride, with a joy shared by the hundreds who talked and drank and danced. He was dressed in yellow—nearly but not exactly the same shade as the garb worn by Herepath, the Witch-king. The banners hanging from the wall were all of the same sunlight gold, and they fluttered with a breeze created by the dancing nobles. The guards standing sentry had their armor festooned with garlands of many-colored flowers. The room was warm and filled with the scents of energetic sweat, expensive perfume, rare incense, and cooking meat. When one song ended and another began, the lord stood and lifted his voice in song, and it was sweet and beautiful, rich and wonderful.

Kagen wanted to linger there, to dive into that celebration and become a smiling reveler.

But then, one step later, the room changed and everything was different. It was still the same room, but the color and gaiety and light were gone. Figures still moved, but these were not the revelers in their finery. These things seemed garbed in colors of sadness and sickness, and they reeked of sorrows so deep and perverse that it polluted the very air. On the throne, the lord in yellow now wore a crown of jagged spikes, and his face was covered by a veil of yellow lace that was stained with drops of blood. Monstrous forms created by firelit shadows cavorted ponderously on every wall.

"Gods of the Pit," cried Kagen, stumbling backwards. The dancing throng moved with a frantic energy that was miles beyond mere madness. It was an orgy of thrashing limbs, of screaming faces, of terror embraced as erotic joy.

Some of the dancers turned toward him even in the midst of their frenzy. They beckoned obscenely and yelled promises of delights that sickened him. He kept backing away.

"Come dance with us," they yelled, their voices twisted out of humanity into dreadful shrieks. A few broke from the melee and stalked toward him, tearing at their clothes to expose pendulous breasts covered in running sores, to show penises engorged to impossible lengths and girths, to tempt him with wounds whose lips were foul imitations of vaginas.

The young and older Kagen screamed and turned to run.

Hands grabbed at him, snagging wrists and ankles, his clothing and his hair, preventing him from fleeing, tearing at him, pulling him back toward—

Kagen was torn from the dream by something that coiled around his thighs and waist and throat and tried to crush the life from him.

He heard the horses screaming and tried to scream as well, but the creature that held him only squeezed more tightly.

CHAPTER EIGHTY-SIX

The thing wrapped around him as forcefully as a boa constrictor, squeezing the air from his lungs, pinning his arms, trying to crush the very life from him.

The coil around his throat forced his chin up so all he saw was the ceiling and some of the wall. On both surfaces, though, were bizarre shadows cast by the firelight. He saw himself writhing in the grip of something that looked like tentacles. But they were not, he was sure of it. He felt a rough, dry texture against his skin as he fought it. It was as if some vast serpent or water beast was wrapped in old cloth. That was impossible, but it was happening.

He fought for air, but the stricture around his throat was too fierce, too powerful. Black and red poppies seemed to burst in air before his eyes.

Kagen scrabbled for his knives, but the tentacles fought him as if they understood that sharp steel was the real threat. The thing plucked him off the ground and slammed him against the cold stone wall.

Over and over and over again.

Pain exploded in Kagen's back and shoulders. He tried to diffuse the impact with the flats of his feet, but then the thing whipped him high into the air and smashed him down on the floor. Air boiled to poison in his chest as the choking force increased the murderous pressure. He could hear Jinx and the other horses screaming in abject terror. Their hooves clattered as they sought in vain to flee, but flight was impossible. All of the doors were closed and secured with wedges and bars.

Kagen's fingers clawed their way along his torso, down toward his waist, battling for every inch of distance. If he could get a single blade out . . . even one of the smaller utility knives . . .

A sound filled the air, lower in tone than the horses, but robust, and so strange. It was like the bellow of some great animal—a hippopotamus or water buffalo—but muted as if the screaming head was somehow smothered. The sound was weirdly dry and dusty, for all its volume, and the roar was ugly and hungry. The strangest aspect of all was that the roar came from all around Kagen, from the things that ensnared him, and he could not tell if it was one howling monster or a dozen.

His fingernails scraped something hard and cold.

Steel.

It was the crosspiece of one of his daggers. He braced his feet on the floor and heaved his weight in that direction, trying to turn his hip more sharply toward his fingers. The thing that held him tightened further still, trying to thwart him. The lights in his mind were burning out and the oxygen trapped in his lungs threatened to burst his chest.

But Kagen's fingers curled around the handle, and with a final burst of strength fueled by his hatred, his terror, his need to kill Herepath and rescue the imperial twins, and the towering, aching, burning desire to avenge his mother's death, he tore the blade from its sheath.

The thing attacking him roared again, but there was a sharper note to it, as if it suddenly realized its own peril.

Kagen slashed at the coil that was cinched around his throat. His eyes were blind with air deprivation, but he could feel blade meet resistance. The blade bit deep, but it did not feel like flesh and muscle. The steel passed through it but there was no spill of hot blood onto his fist. He stabbed again and again, then slashed and chopped and sliced as his mind began to tumble into darkness that would hold no dreams . . . only the eternal peace of death.

Or the fires of damnation.

That flickering thought gave him a last spoonful of power.

And then the stricture was gone. It snapped backwards from his stabbing blade, nearly tearing the dagger from his weakening grip. Another of those weird, dry howls filled the room, but now it was ten times louder and filled with pain and outrage.

Kagen toppled sideways, gagging, fighting to draw breath, coughing and gasping.

Air—sweet and delicious—flooded his lungs, dragging him back from the edge of death and into the living world of madness. For in that moment, he *saw* what it was he fought.

Not a serpent, or even a nest of them. Not the tentacles of some subterranean horror. Nothing as understandable as that. The thing that coiled around him, that was trying to crush the life out of the horses . . .

Was *cloth*.

He stared for a moment, too dumbstruck to move. The wall hangings and banners, the tapestries and flags, had all come to life and were attacking as if they were hell's own legion of serpents.

"Gods of—" he began, but it disintegrated into coughing because the air was filled with centuries of dust shaken free by the wild movements of those impossible coils.

Kagen staggered to his feet, drawing the second dagger. He blinked his eyes clear and tried to grasp the situation.

Several sections of coiled cloth lay by the wall where he had been sleeping. The rest still writhed like titanic snakes. The daggers were an anchor to reality in his fists, but it took his oxygen-deprived mind to grasp a critical truth.

The cloth he'd stabbed had sagged down and lay without moving. Dead? Or was that part of this thing now deprived of its driving force? He glanced at his daggers and the truth was there. Before sleep he had seasoned the blades with *eitr*, with the god-killer poison.

"*Yesss,*" Kagen hissed, getting it now. Magic poison for magical creatures. Understanding brought power back to his trembling muscles. "Now," he bellowed, "if you want me, take me."

But it was *he* who attacked the creature. Kagen rushed forward, slashing and stabbing with the Poison Rose's daggers. With every touch of the blades, the strangling cloth recoiled, shuddered, collapsed.

The thing did not want to yield this field without a fight, though. It slapped at him, trying to knock the blades from his hands. Kagen ducked and rolled, slashing each time, killing more of the supernatural force that animated the old tapestries. Kagen fought his way to Jinx and shredded the coils that were trying to kill his horse. They fell, and Jinx reared up and kicked at other coils that still rose like cobras. One coil shoved one of the other horses at Kagen, but he dropped flat under it, scrambling backwards by kicking with his heels so that he passed between the animal's hooves. One hoof caught him in the thigh, but Kagen bit down on that pain, used it to chase the last of the black midnight from his mind. He sliced the coil of cloth open; it spilled dust and the desiccated carcasses of old spiders before it shuddered like a dying thing and collapsed. Another tentacle, made up of coiled flags, reached for him from behind, but Jinx reared again and drove it away before it could take hold. Kagen pivoted on the balls of his feet and stabbed the coil.

He waded into the cluster of horses, his blades moving with terrible speed and ferocity. He did not know how long the *eitr* would last and he wasted not a second, not a moment, in saving his animals.

And then . . .

Then it was over.

The remaining coils sagged down and either whatever force had possessed them vanished or, perhaps, the effect of the god-killer poison did its full work. Hundreds of pounds of cloth dropped heavily to the floor and lay there, twisted and dusty and dead.

Kagen crouched over it, legs wide, fists locked around the knife handles, chest heaving. Despite the cold, hot sweat poured down his skin.

Around him the fires had all burned low and morning light peered in through high windows. The horses stood in their huddle, watching him with fear in their animal eyes, as if they also had glimpsed his dream. Drool hung from their mouths and fear sweat lathered their flanks. They panted with a terror only barely contained.

When he was sure there was no lingering deception, Kagen sheathed his knives and quickly checked the horses. A few had serious friction burns from struggling against the rough fabric of the tapestries. He soothed and patted them while at the same time peering into every corner, every nook.

Apart from him and his horses, the room was still.

Kagen staggered over to his saddlebag, tore it open, pulled out the vial of *eitr*, and immediately smeared some on his knives again. He was surprised at how much was left. Surely he was near the end of the poison. But when he held the vial up and studied it against the firelight, he saw that it was filled to the brim.

"Maralina . . ." he breathed. "My love."

For a moment a scent wafted through the room. It was the same geranium and rose incense he remembered from his sweet dream of making love with her.

"My love," he said again.

He took several long breaths, feeling inside his body for damage and finding only the hyperawareness of fear. All the hairs on the back of his neck and along his forearms stood straight up. He kept glancing at the tapestries and banners, expecting them to twitch, to reanimate. His mouth went dry and he had to suck spit from inside his cheeks to swallow.

"To the blackest hells with this place," he gasped, his voice hoarse and unfamiliar.

Then he realized something that he hadn't had time to pay attention to before.

It was quiet.

The wind no longer howled, nor did the walls of that ancient place shudder from the blizzard's assault. He went to the door and listened. Nothing. And beneath the door was a line of soft white light.

It was dawn, and that long night was over.

He wondered how much of his salvation was because of his poisoned blades and how much was because daylight had come. He had no way to know, because all of this was beyond his experience.

He thought about that and corrected the thought. It was *part* of his experience; he simply did not understand how such magic worked. Was this a spell of some kind conjured by his brother? Was the Witch-king hunting him with more than squads of

Ravens? Was this the action of some local god because he had killed those red monks? Or was it simply that haunted houses existed—not merely in bedtime tales or campfire yarns but in real point of fact—and he had made the damn-fool mistake of sleeping in one?

Too many questions and no answers he could grab.

Nor did Kagen Vale want to linger and investigate. In another time he would have sent a message to the Office of Miracles, perhaps to that old hag Mother Frey, and let her do the research. All he wanted, more even than answers, was to be quit of this place.

Within ten minutes he and his horses were out of there.

Tired as the horses were, they seemed happy to gallop hard enough to leave that place far, far behind.

CHAPTER EIGHTY-SEVEN

"Read this," said Nespar, holding out a piece of vellum on which was a decoded message from his spymaster, Radhu.

"What is it?" asked Jakob Ravensmere, reaching across the table to take it from him.

"A report," said Nespar.

Jakob read it. "Oh my. More mischief from the Sons of the Poison Rose."

"'Mischief'? Conspiracies everywhere. More of our soldiers butchered."

"My apologies, brother," said Jakob. "I tend to hide behind sarcasm and understatement when I'm distressed. This is appalling and frightening."

Nespar pinned the note to the tabletop with a stiff forefinger. "I should share this with His Majesty . . ."

Jakob studied him. "You seem uncertain about that. Tell me, what is your concern?"

"What do you think? Overreaction."

"Our people are being killed," said Jakob. "Do you even know how many Hakkian heads have been taken in these attacks? Have you heard the grumbling from the generals? Everyone who matters is looking to the Witch-king for a response. Surely you can't withhold key intelligence."

Nespar got up and walked over to the fire, leaned a bony hand on the mantle, and stood in silence for a while, looking deep into the writhing flames. After a few moments Jakob came over and stood with him and spoke in a gentle voice.

"Are you all right, my friend? I've never known you to hesitate like this before."

Nespar closed his eyes and sighed deeply. Then he opened his eyes and looked hard at Jakob.

"I *can* trust you, can't I?" There was almost a note of pleading in his voice. "What we say stays between us, no matter what?"

Jakob placed his hand flat on his own chest. "I have no honor to swear by," he said, "but I will swear on my life. Yes. What we say stays between us. Now and always. You and I *need* to share trust, to stand back to back in these troubled times. You and Kestral brought me into more than the Hakkian government; you accepted *me*. You were my advocate when I stood before the Witch-king for the first time. You spoke up for me, Nespar." Jakob took Nespar's hands and squeezed them. "I can never forget that. I *will* never forget it. I owe you far more than my silence."

The chamberlain was at a loss for words for a long moment, then he nodded and returned the grip.

"So," said Jakob, "tell me what troubles you."

Nespar took a long, steadying breath and exhaled slowly, nodding as he did so. "If I bring this note to the king, I am afraid that he, in his righteous anger, will strike back with such force that it may do more harm than good. The political situation is so fragile.

Right now, we balance on the edge, with the other nations poised to strike but hesitant to do so. Remember that with Empress Gessalyn dead and no living heirs, the empire technically exists but is in a crisis. Any of the monarchs can put forward a claim to the throne because they are all 'cousins' of the empress, at least in legal terms. That's in the charter their own ancestors signed when the empire was established. Every one of them has a firmer legal right to forward such a claim because they can prosecute a case of their own loyalty to the empire, while the Witch-king is still a usurper. If we overreact to what these so-called Sons of the Poison Rose are doing—if we hold the Argonian nobility accountable and begin nailing them to their front gates—then we invite them to ally against us. The king has already said that he cannot reproduce the magicks used to conquer the empire, and you know as well as I do that we don't have a tenth as many troops as are needed to defend this palace, let alone win a war against an entire empire."

"What then?" asked Jakob as he went over to the table and returned with their wine cups.

Nespar sipped. "I may be alone in this, but I believe that the Sons of the Poison Rose are a small, radical group. I don't think they are working with the support of the other monarchs. Nor, Jakob, do I believe they are funded by the great houses of Argon. The level of savagery does not speak 'nobility' to me. And the choice of targets is timid. Remote outposts, patrols on distant roads. No . . . there is no sophistication behind this."

"You don't?" asked Jakob surprised. "Who is behind them, then?"

Nespar shook his head. "I don't know. My spies are looking."

"Well," said Jakob, "I hope they find the right answers."

"Yes."

"How long do you think you can keep that report from the king?"

Nespar chewed his lip. "I don't know. A few days, perhaps. If he asks, I can say that I was waiting on confirmation. I just pray that there are no more attacks in the meantime."

Jakob tapped his glass against Nespar's. "I'll add my prayers to yours, brother."

CHAPTER EIGHTY-EIGHT

"Now what?"

When the gate watchman of Xifial spoke, his friend Budley looked up from the wooden doll's head he was carving for his youngest daughter. The face was that of the Poison Rose, though he planned to change the hair and eye color so as not to raise suspicions. He was happy that he had Lady Marissa's cheeks and brow right, though.

"What's that, Moze?" he asked.

"Look at this," said Moze, indicating something on the other side of the wall. Budley set the doll aside and stood, squinting into the eastern sun. It was not yet noon and the sun glare was harsh in the cool air.

"What am I looking at?" he began. Then he said, "Oh."

Coming along the road, pulled by a pair of burly donkeys, was a small wagon of a kind not often scene in northern Hakkia. It had tall hoops on which was stretched a canvas painted in the bright primary colors of red and yellow and blue, plus green.

"Odd," said Budley. "Looks like a Samudian festival wagon."

"Can't be," said Moze, keeping his voice down. "Wrong time of year for it, and . . . besides . . . now that things have changed, His Majesty the Witch-king won't ever allow a Sower's jubilee. Not since the Ravens tore down all the gardens and did all that ugliness to the nuns and such."

Budley nodded. Neither of them were soldiers, nor had they

any strong political views. The new king was a new king . . . it did not much change the day-to-day affairs of farmers this far from the cities. Each of them had gone to the town garden for weddings and funerals, holidays and town meetings, and if they were not deeply devout men, they harbored no animosity toward the nuns and monks. When the Ravens destroyed the gardens in other countries, Budley and Moze—like all of the tavern regulars—chewed it over as they drank. Sure, they knew about Lady Bellapher and how her armies had marched into Hakkia and burned *their* churches, but after three centuries, payback seemed pointless. They understood the anger and resentment behind the attacks on the gardens, but the rape and murder was too much. It was unholy by anyone's beliefs. As time went on, though, and the rage against the Harvest faith expanded, they fell silent, afraid to speak aloud what they all thought.

Seeing a wagon festooned for celebrations of a Garden holiday was queer. It made no sense in such times.

Budley nodded uneasily. "Okay, I hear what you're saying, Moze, but that's definitely what that is down there. I saw them a few times when I went to Samud to visit my wife's family. Why *here*, though? And why now?"

They watched the wagon roll along the road toward the town gates.

"Maybe the Ravens confiscated it to use for the tax collectors," suggested Moze.

"Nah," said Budley. "From what I heard they're going to cut taxes."

"Believe that and I have a gold mine I'd like to sell you."

"Ha ha," said his friend. "Then *you* explain it."

Before Budley could come up with an alternate suggestion, the wagon rolled to a stop below where they stood. The driver was a dusty little man dressed like a Samudian serf.

"Looks the part," murmured Moze.

Budley picked up the small black flag used to indicate an official parlay.

"Who approaches?" he demanded, trying to make it sound formal.

The Samudian raised a hand in greeting. "Peace to you and prosperity to your fields," he said, using a greeting that had, until the Night of the Ravens, been a common phrase exchanged by strangers.

The guards exchanged a brief look.

"Peace and good Harvest to you and yours," replied Moze, though after everything that had happened these last few months, the words felt strange, even risky to say aloud. But the driver smiled and doffed his cloth cap. He had dark hair and a heavy beard trimmed in the spiky Samudian fashion.

"State your business, friend," called Budley.

"Trade," said the man. "Stuff to sell, things to buy."

"And yet you roll up in a carnival wagon?"

The Samudian laughed. "Bought it cheap, back home," he said. "They're selling everything that wasn't burned. I'll get around to repainting it once I sell off what I brought."

"What's your cargo?" asked Moze.

The driver jerked a thumb over his shoulder. "I have twenty bushels of apples and four of pears. Looking to sell them in town and buy some rice and beans. Maybe some good Hakkian lemons, if you have any."

"We'll have to inspect the goods before we can let you in," said Moze. "Wait right there."

He tapped Budley on the shoulder and the two of them climbed down the ladder and together lifted the heavy timber pole used to secure the gates. Like a lot of border towns, there was a tall fence left over from less civil times. The original gate had been built more than a thousand years before, when Samudian raiders regularly crossed the border into Hakkia, and even after the peace of the Silver Empire it was rebuilt a dozen times, and kept in good order. There was peace and there was common sense, and walled towns like theirs were common from Behlia to Zaare. Many of those towns kept the walls in good repair but left the gates open—or at least they had, prior to the Night of the Ravens. Now everyone was on high alert, especially there in Hakkia, and strangers were seldom welcome.

A simple apple seller from Samud, though, was very welcome, because an early frost had ruined almost a third of the local fruit crop.

Each man took one gate and leaned against it, walking it outward until there was a space more than wide enough for the wagon. Even so, they waved the driver down and began strolling toward the back to see what kind of bounty was there.

"We might need to sample the wares," suggested Moze, and the driver gave a small, knowing smile and touched the side of his nose.

"Here," said the Samudian as they moved behind the wagon, "let me loose the flaps."

He quickly untied the leather straps holding the canvas in place and whipped the cloth out of the way. The interior was dark, and the guards had to lean in to see.

Hands shot out and dragged Moze and Budley inside the wagon, where there was no smell of apples or even of pears. Instead, the interior of the wagon was filled with a stench like rotting meat. They fought against the hands, but knives moved inside that darkness and both men died right there, with neither having time to cry out.

Without apparent haste, the driver sauntered to the front again and climbed up onto the bench seat. He clicked his tongue for the donkeys, who began moving at once. The wagon passed inside the town walls. The driver slid down, looked around, and saw an empty quarter acre of hard-packed dirt just inside. There were no other guards, though racks of spears and barrels of arrows stood ready under the catwalk.

"Let's go, lads," he said. "No time to waste."

Four men piled out of the wagon, each of them dressed like Argonian serfs. They ran to where he pointed and began dragging the spears and arrows outside. Then they returned and two of them climbed inside.

A moment later two figures—a man and a woman—came toppling out of the wagon and thudded into the dirt. They were filthy, their clothes in rags, hair matted, and skin crusted with mud and dried blood. They thrashed and snarled like beasts, but with their ankles and wrists bound they could do nothing else.

The two Hakkians who had climbed into the wagon began handing out sections of lumber that were cut to specific lengths and sizes. Then they jumped out, one carrying a bucket of long spikes and the other with an armful of heavy hammers.

They jogged outside while two others closed the gates nearly all the way, leaving only a slit wide enough for a man to slip through.

The driver drew a knife and slit the thongs binding the feet of the thrashing figures. Then, moving with professional speed and efficiency, he slashed the bindings on their wrists, turned, and ran like hell for the door. Both figures scrambled instantly to their feet, snarling and snapping at the air with their cracked teeth. They chased him, but the driver dove through the opening as the other four slammed the doors shut with such speed that the lunatics slammed into it and rebounded.

Immediately, the five men thrust the precut boards into place, centered their spikes, and with all the speed and desperation they could summon, nailed shut the gates of the town.

The sound of the hammering and the howls of the two crazed people drew curious people from homes and shops nearly to the gates, and the driver lingered long enough to hear the noise of people coming to investigate.

"Let's go," he said in a fierce whisper. He climbed onto the wagon seat while the others got into the back.

Even before the driver had the wagon turned, the air was filled with screams and yells and hungry snarls from the other side of the gate.

CHAPTER EIGHTY-NINE

Eyes watched Kagen ride through the snowy pine forest.

The deer and foxes and bears and wolves watched him. Thousands of nightbirds in the trees watched him. Other eyes watched him, too. Eyes that burned with fire. Eyes that were slitted like serpent eyes but looked out of human faces. Eyes of creatures that had crawled out of holes in the ground in which they slept through the centuries. Eyes that belonged to things that had never before lived on earth but that had come through the broken pathways.

They all watched Kagen and his string of horses ride past.

Some watched with indifference, others with a biting curiosity. Some feared what they saw, while others hungered for the meat and blood of man and beast.

And one set of eyes watched from far away. Eyes whose lids were closed and whose body was crushed beneath hard-packed dirt and chiseled stone, whose grave had been sealed so long ago that not even the most ancient legend hinted at it. A race of sorcerer-warriors had each shed their own blood to bury the monster, and their magicks had kept the world safe for uncountable years.

For all those years the thing beneath the earth slept. And dreamed.

Now, though, it was awake. Buried. Hungry. And very much awake.

Beneath all that weight of dirt and stone, and separated by many hundreds of miles, it stretched out with senses vast and strange, and it beheld Kagen of Argon riding through the snow.

In its dark grave, the ancient thing smiled.

PART THREE
THE UNBLADED

The name "Unbladed" has always been a source of confusion and misunderstanding. They are not allowed to carry swords because of a foolish and ill-considered rule established by people who think that an understanding of politics inevitably includes insights into what it means to be a warrior. They think that to limit one's weapon means that the warrior is somehow unarmed and incapable of fighting. They are too familiar with ordinary soldiers and not those men and women who have made a true study of warfare and the philosophy of combat. The truth is that a true warrior can pick up a stick and with it defeat an enemy with the greatest sword ever forged. The truth is that it has never been about the weapon but the person who wields it.

—GENERAL HEGUSTUS AUGLIAN OF NEHEMITE, FROM MEMOIRS
WRITTEN IN THE SIXTH CENTURY OF THE SILVER EMPIRE

Night was falling softly over the snowy landscape when Kagen rode into town. Because the little village of Traveler's Rest was at a lower altitude than the garden, the snow was not as deep and most of it was melting slush. Jinx, seeing the town lights and recognizing the road to the stable, whinnied as eloquently as any traveler returning from a rough journey.

Kagen rubbed his mount's neck. "You earned some extra oats, boy." The horse bobbed his head. Kagen smiled. "And by the gods I need to drink about a gallon of strong red wine."

The brightest lights blazed inside the tavern on the edge of town, and it created such a warm and inviting sight that Kagen felt depressed rather than elated. He remembered too many visits to his grandparents' villa in the north of Argon, where the Vale family would go to celebrate the winter holiday of Sunrest. On the shortest day of the year there would be feasts and songs, old stories told by the roaring fireplace, snowball fights with his brothers and sisters, and rides through the forest on a sledge pulled by four big, retired warhorses. There would be ice fishing with the family's unofficial twins—Jheklan and Faulker, who were a year apart but looked identical—and the big feast of roast boar with the last of the autumn vegetables. Such good times.

Gone now.

His grandparents had died six months apart, four years back. His parents and brother Hugh were dead. Degas, too, if the rumors were true. And . . . Herepath was a monster. Lost and dead in a different way. As for the others? Scattered and currently beyond his reach, if they were even still alive.

"Herepath," murmured Kagen as he rode toward Traveler's Rest. "What happened to you?"

It was a question that bit at him constantly ever since that night. How could a scholar and an ordained *Gardener* of the Green Faith fall to so low a point? How could so strong a person as Herepath become seduced and corrupted? That dream he had the previous night kept trying to whisper answers, but real understanding hovered beyond his reach.

On some level he even wondered—or *hoped*—that Herepath was under some kind of spell, or that he was possessed. That would make sense. That would, at least, offer a slice of cold comfort. If not, then Kagen had to reevaluate everything he remembered of his brother to try to determine when Herepath had strayed. How and why he had become the monster he now was.

"Gods of the fiery Pit," he grumbled as he rode on toward the inn.

Ahead he saw the tavern, and standing in uneven ranks along the pitched roof were the nightbirds. Silent, watchful.

A piece of shadow under the eaves of the tavern detached itself and resolved into a tall man who stepped into the middle of the road in Kagen's path. A heavy cloak of dark bear fur was draped around his broad shoulders, and his face was covered in gray-green tentacle tattoos that coiled from inside his tunic, wrapped around his throat, and curled across his countenance. He wore several gold rings in each ear, and these caught sparks from the torches burning outside the inn. He waited patiently as Kagen approached, taking big bites from a turkey leg and chewing thoughtfully.

"We'd given you up for dead," said Tuke Brakson. "Filia said you were waiting out the storm. I said you were either frozen stiff or someone was taking your head back to Argentium on a pike. I've lost five silver dimes."

Kagen, unamused, gave him a flat stare. "You bet on whether I was dead or not?"

The tattooed giant shrugged. "Let's face it, brother, that's not an unreasonable assumption."

"Fuck you."

The big man laughed. Then his eyes ticked past Kagen to the string of horses.

"By the lightly frosted balls of the ice giants," said Tuke, waving his drumstick toward the horses, "there has to be a story behind all that."

"You have no idea," said Kagen wearily, slowing to a stop and sliding from the saddle. "But trust me when I say it needs a hell of a lot of strong drink to tell it."

"They hang horse thieves in Nelfydia, you know."

"I didn't steal them, Tuke."

The Therian walked along the string of horses, lifting saddlebags and rugs, checking the flanks of each.

"Now that is very interesting," he remarked. "No brands."

"Not a one," agreed Kagen.

"They're not colts or fillies either, so you didn't steal them before they were branded."

"I already told you . . . I didn't steal them."

"Uh-huh. These are all full-grown but without owner's mark of any kind, Kagen. Which means no one can dispute your ownership," said Tuke. "But will anyone come looking for them?"

Kagen snorted. "The owners are sorting things out with the odd little god they pray to. And by 'sorting things out' I mean meeting their god face-to-face."

"*Twelve* of them?"

"Thirteen, actually," said Kagen. "I lost one horse in the woods."

"Thirteen," marveled Tuke. "By the absent balls of the god of geldings."

"It was a strange couple of days," admitted Kagen, fighting the urge to shiver at the memories of that mansion. He was proud of the fact that his voice sounded calm, though beneath his furs and leather he was trembling badly, and not from the cold.

"I definitely need to hear this story," said Tuke, grinning.

Kagen nodded, patting the pouch of coins he'd taken from the dead monks. "I'll buy the wine."

"Oh, I think you should," agreed the big Therian. "Anyone who goes out for a day for sober reflection in a deserted garden and comes back with a dozen good horses can always buy me some wine."

CHAPTER NINETY-ONE

Lord Nespar came into the entrance foyer, his staff thumping with impatience on the marble floor. A guard trotted along beside him, looking nervous and frightened.

"He said that he was sent for," insisted the guard.

"Sent for by *whom*," snapped the chamberlain. "I have sent for no one. Did Lord Ravensmere summon this person?"

"No, my lord chamberlain," said the guard quickly. "He said that it was an imperial request."

Nespar cut him a look, then turned away with a grunt of disgust. The guard was an imbecile. There was no damned empire and—he feared—such a thing might never exist.

"If this is a joke, my lad, I'll have your guts for garters," Nespar promised.

The guard could not summon anything by way of reply but increased his pace so that he reached the door first and pulled it open.

The foyer was lined with benches for the comfort of guests, with side chambers for more prestigious persons to sit in some comfort. The walls were hung with tapestries showing important moments of Hakkian history. A man stood looking at one of them—the Battle of Kelplass Fields, which had been fought 1,300 years before. He was not a tall man, though his posture, narrow waist, broad shoulders, and slender neck gave him the illusion of greater height. Despite the cold, he wore a sleeveless gown of gray and green, had thin arms knotted with wiry muscles, and a head crowned with masses of curly dark hair that was almost brown and almost black but seemed exactly neither. His long-fingered hands were clasped behind his back.

"My Lord Nespar," said the stranger without turning, "do you know the full story of this battle?"

"Who are you, sir, and what is it you want?"

The man ignored that and said, "The history books say that Kelplass was the seat of power for an upstart princeling who challenged his own uncle for the throne. But that was never true. Or, not precisely true. That prince had sold the blood of his first-born child—his own *heir*—to a demon who promised him that he would sit on the Hakkian throne. But . . . demons should never be trusted. Any fool knows that. The prince led his troops onto the field, and when he was confronted with five times his number, spoke the prayer that the demon swore would raise a legion of ogres. Instead, every man in the prince's army began shitting and pissing himself. They vomited worms and beetles and tried to flee. The army of the king slaughtered them all. Except for the prince, of course. He was brought before his uncle, and there, standing beside the king, was the demon. Grinning and laughing because he had served *his* king so well. This, of course, was not how history recorded it, but it is what happened."

"Who *are* you?" demanded Nespar, more than a little unsettled.

The man turned very slowly, as if he had all the time in the

world and even the chamberlain of the Witch-king was not sufficient to hurry him along.

"I have come to see your master," said the man. He was pale
and handsome in an unpleasant way, with a beaked nose and full
lips and eyes whose color was impossible to determine. They
seemed to swirl with unpleasant greens and yellows and browns,
as if the irises were stirred by night winds.

"I . . ." began the chamberlain, but he faltered and had to clear
his throat before trying again. "I asked you your name, sir."

The stranger smiled. He seemed to have a lot of very white
teeth, and in an ancient Hakkian dialect he said, *"Keth-um jiskro
tellif aulir."*

It took Nespar a moment to translate the words.

I am the Prince of Games.

Nespar's mouth went dry. It was a name he had heard his master use with some weight, some reverence.

He straightened. "Are there, ah . . . credentials you would like
me to present?"

The prince continued to smile. "Your master does not require a
calling card, Lord Chamberlain. Go and tell him I am here."

"This is irregular and—"

"And the world is irregular," said the prince, amused. "But your
master and I will do our very best to set it to rights. Now . . . off
you go."

Then he turned and continued studying the tapestry.

Nespar lingered. Anger and outrage warred with fear and a
sense of duty. When those wretched and terrible Hollow Monks
had arrived, the king had seemed excited at the thought that it
was the Prince of Games who came calling, and had been visibly
disappointed that it was not he. What was it the Witch-king said
at the time?

"He is never one to come when called but appears in his own good time."

"Very well," said Nespar with cold formality. "Wait here until you are summoned."

He heard the man chuckle softly at that. Nespar turned and hurried off to tell his master that a long-awaited guest had arrived.

CHAPTER NINETY-TWO

Tuke steered Kagen toward a blazing fire in a private corner of the tavern that fronted the inn. Their companion, Filia alden-Bok, was already there, and judging by the roses blooming in her cheeks and the lights in her eyes, it was clear she had already made inroads with the wine.

Her dog, Horse, sat beside her chair, ugly head resting on her thigh, eyes alert to any chance of a dropped piece of food.

"Gasp!" Filia cried in mock horror. "What shambling horror darkens my threshold?"

Kagen gave her a sour grunt and went to stand with his buttocks to the flames, rubbing his hands together, happier now that he was indoors. The horses had been turned over to a bemused stable girl, and a platter of hot food was promised by the landlord.

"I'm half frozen is what I am," said Kagen.

"I was right," she said. "You did wait out the storm somewhere."

"Kagen had some adventures," said Tuke.

Filia cocked an eyebrow. "Oh . . . what *kind* of adventures?"

"My quiet day of reflection turned out to be something else," said Kagen.

"Meaning . . ."

"Things got a little weird."

"Weird?" said Filia, amused. "In an empty garden?"

Tuke said, "He came back with a dozen unbranded horses, a pouch of coins, and the promise of story to go along with them."

Filia brightened. "Nothing better than a good story on a cold night," she said. "If you're done broiling your ass, why don't you sit down and tell us."

Kagen slumped into a chair, accepted a wine cup from Tuke, knocked it back, held the cup out for a refill, sipped that, and then told it to them in chunks, pausing at the point where he reached the mansion but not yet telling the rest. Tuke and Filia listened with great interest, occasionally asking him to repeat certain details.

"Describe those idols again," said Filia, when he'd finished the part about the attack in the garden. After Kagen did so, she looked at Tuke for a long moment. "What do you reckon? Blood priests of Tsathoggua?"

"Has to be," said the Therian.

"What in the realms of the underworld are blood priests of Tsathoggua?" asked Kagen.

"Technically they're monks," said Filia, "with an actual priest as the leader of their coven."

"Coven? You mean they're witches?"

"No," said Tuke. "I'm using *coven* because I don't know a better word for it. *Cult*, maybe. They're part of a secret religious society. Small bunch. Secretive, transitory, and not from around here."

"So . . . where is Tsathoggua? Is it a city or—"

"No," said Filia. "Tsathoggua is their god. Those idols are probably of him, though I never saw one of their temples or shrines. Never saw a statue of that god. Did you bring one back?"

"Hell no," said Kagen. "I've pissed off enough gods lately. I left the statues undamaged back at the garden."

Filia leaned over and kissed his cheek. "Clever boy."

"I might have seen something like what you described," said Tuke after some thought. "When I was on a ship working those little islands between Theria and Tull Belain. There's scores and scores of them, so don't ask me which one. But what you described sounds like Tsathoggua to me. Never met any of the actual blood priests, though. I'm not surprised you haven't heard of them."

"I've never been this far north before," said Kagen, nodding. "And I haven't been to any of those islands. Why would these priests of Tsathoggua be after me? I don't recall offending any *other* gods recently."

"Give it time," murmured Tuke.

"First," said Kagen, "go fuck yourself."

"Oh, if I only could."

"Eww," said Filia with a wince.

"Second," continued Kagen, "are these red priests and their god aligned with Hastur?"

"Not that I've heard," said Filia. "But who knows? These days, I'd believe just about anything."

"Good thing you didn't run into any of Tsathoggua's *other* servants," said Filia. "I heard that he has some creatures at his command that he'll send to his worshippers if they use the right prayers."

"Oh, that's just terrific," said Kagen glumly. "What kind of monsters? Are they white? Like strange goats, perhaps?"

Filia frowned as she scratched Horse's head. "Not at all. The ones I heard about are supposed to be these black, shapeless things. Or maybe that's the wrong word. *Amorphous* is closer, I suspect. Blobs of black goo that can take any shape they want. And hard as hell to kill."

Kagen leaned back and studied the fire for a moment.

"Uh-oh," said Tuke, "it looks like he's thinking. Nothing good can come of that."

Kagen ignored the jibe. "Not thinking . . . remembering." He sipped his wine. "A long time ago, back when I was a lad, I went on an adventure with three of my brothers. Jheklan and Faulker, who everyone calls the Twins because they look so much alike except for hair color, but they're really a year apart. And . . . well . . . Herepath . . ."

"Shit," said Filia. Tuke did not make a joke.

"We went to one of the glaciers and found an entrance into a small cavern. Bones and old weapons everywhere. Clearly, other people had gotten there before us and came to a bad end. We couldn't figure out how or why until we accidentally cracked open one of the walls and this *thing* came out. It was what you described, Filia. Black and shapeless, but it kept taking on different forms. Animals and people and such. We nearly died and added our own bones to the pile. It was more luck than anything else that allowed us to cause the cavern to collapse, and we got the hell out of there. We thought those things were trapped, but now I wonder."

The others looked at him for a long time.

"For someone who keeps saying that he has no experience with magic," said Filia slowly, "you've had a hell of a lot of *direct* experience. More than anyone I've ever met."

Kagen grunted and muttered under his breath something they could not hear.

"Hold on. Go back a bit. You went with *Herepath*?" asked Tuke, leaning on the name.

"Yes. Back when he was a young scholar working for the Garden."

They sat with that for a bit.

"I have to wonder," said Tuke slowly, "if that adventure, as you call it, is a clue to how your brother became what he is now."

"Yes," said Kagen. "I thought about that too."

"Might also explain why those priests were after you."

Kagen shrugged. "Maybe."

"It could be that," said Filia, "or it could be something else. I mean, let's face it, these are weird times. With magic returning to the world, who knows what else will be crawling out from under the floorboards. A lot of religions and cults that the Silver Empire supposedly destroyed actually went underground. I think we can expect to see more of them come out to play."

Kagen grunted again. He hadn't yet told them about what happened inside the mansion.

Tuke pursed his lips in thought. "There's a little fragment of something like that floating in my mind, but I can't grab it. Tsathoggua is, I think, a god who rules over a city of priests and monsters."

"A city?" asked Kagen. "Where? On one of those islands?"

"Not sure," said Tuke. "I seem to remember hearing that it exists in another dimension. Or . . . maybe on another planet. I can't recall the details. Let's face it, I was young and likely drunk at the time."

"That's not very helpful," said Kagen.

Tuke gave him a withering look. "Well, if I'd known at the time that your brother was going to take the identity of the Witchking of Hakkia, invoke the Shepherd God Hastur, and conquer the fucking world, I'd have taken notes."

"Yeah, yeah, I was just saying . . ." Kagen glanced at Filia. "How do you know about them?"

Filia refilled everyone's cups, settled back in her chair, and leaned down to scratch Horse's back. "While I was running with the Unbladed I heard all sorts of stories. Those lads tend to work on the fringes of society anyway, and that's where the freaks and cults and maniacs tend to congregate. I first heard of the red priests after they raided a Bulconian settlement four or five years ago. They're big fans of flaying whole families. Something to do with how that releases a special kind of blood magic that their god feeds on."

"Charming," said Kagen. "Makes me feel less guilty about what I did yesterday."

"The Unbladed group I was with were paid to protect a village near the settlement," Filia said. "There were eight of us, and those bastards came at us just before dawn. Thirty of them, on fast horses. They rode through the center of the village, flinging torches onto rooftops and through windows. It wasn't their normal method of attack, so we figured they'd been tipped to our presence and wanted to force us out into the street for what they thought would be an easy kill."

"How did that work out for them?"

"We lost six," said Filia with a shrug. "And we put thirty heads on pikes that we placed all around the village."

"Did they leave the village alone?" Asked Kagen.

Filia's eyes darkened a bit. "For the rest of that year and well into the next. Then, long after we were gone, they came back and killed everyone. Skinned every man, woman, and child and left them crucified in the town square. They even skinned the family dogs."

"Shit," said Kagen.

"By the sea god's dripping balls," growled Tuke.

"Yeah," said Filia with a sigh. "Nothing we could do. We were hired to protect the town for a season. But I suppose any cult whose members have kept mostly secret for a thousand years is used to being patient."

"Why would they go after Kagen, though?" asked Tuke. "I mean, beyond it being a public service because he's such a pain in the ass."

"Fuck you," said Kagen.

"As I recall, the red priests are pretty solidly dedicated to Tsathoggua," continued Tuke. "I can't see them bending the knee to Hastur, let alone the Witch-king of Hakkia."

"The gods only know," said Filia.

"Maybe they're just greedy," said Kagen. "The reward on my head is pretty hefty these days."

"It is," said Filia. "I've lain awake many a night wondering if I should cut your throat and drag your dead ass back to Argentium so I can get rich and retire."

"Except they'd arrest you and torture you for a couple of very long months," said Kagen.

"Well, sure, there's that." She grinned. "Spoilsport."

"Nice thought, though," said Tuke.

He and Filia clinked glasses.

"It's nice to know I'm among friends," said Kagen. "Not *my* friends, but someone's friends."

"A thin-skinned city boy," said Filia, then poked Kagen in the stomach. She did it hard and grinned when he winced.

Tuke shook his head, then cut a look at Filia. "Hey, my dear, if there were eight of you and thirty of them, that makes—what?— three or four each? And my boy Kagen here slaughtered a baker's dozen."

"Now I'm your boy?" said Kagen.

"Don't let it bug you," said Filia. "It's how Tuke was brought up and trained. Kick a mule and then give it some sweet apples. The Therian way."

"I've noticed," said Kagen sourly.

She grinned. "Tell you what, though, lads . . . Tuke's right. You did well today. Almost like a hero. We should celebrate."

"*Almost?*" Kagen muttered. "I should at least get a song out of this."

"Ah, if there were only witnesses," said Tuke sadly.

"Friends," said Kagen again, giving it the same emphasis he would have used for remarks on horseshit. "My wine cup's empty. How'd that happen?"

He shook the bottle, but it was spent. So Kagen reached across the table, snatched Tuke's cup, and drained the last of it in three long gulps.

"By the sweat dripping from the balls of the god of the forge," cried Tuke in mock outrage.

"That one's a bit complicated," said Kagen as he wiped his mouth with the back of his hand.

"How about 'fuck you' then?" demanded the Therian.

"Concise, but less poetic," observed Filia.

"I'd also like to know," said Kagen, "how they knew to find me at that garden."

Filia looked uneasy. "The walls have ears . . . ?" she suggested. It was a poor joke and landed flat. They sat in uncomfortable silence for a bit. When they resumed their conversation it was in lower tones.

Filia frowned as she studied Kagen's face. "There's something else, isn't there? Something else that happened out there?"

Kagen looked up at the ceiling beams, watching the way the firelight made shadows dance.

"There's more to my story," said Kagen. "And we're going to need a hell of lot more wine for the rest of it."

Filia raised her hand and snapped her fingers for the barmaid.

CHAPTER NINETY-THREE

The King in Yellow sat upon his throne in the great hall. Now that all possible blood samples had been collected for Lady Kestral, the room had been thoroughly cleaned, the great windows—damaged by lightning strikes—were repaired, and the throne of the Silver Empresses was reupholstered in Hakkian yellow, trimmed with black. The new throne, intended for use after the coronation, had been taken and stored in a basement because the Witch-king did not wish to see it.

He was surrounded by his pack, one hand resting on the handle of his sword. The great black blade was still sheathed, but the king had loosened it.

The man who walked toward him was a stranger, but only as defined by the flesh and substance of the waking world. In dreams, he had spoken with this so-called Prince of Games. During long nights of slumber, as the Witch-king floated on clouds of poppy smoke, he wandered through veils and worlds and places whose nature had no actual name and had spoken to shadows who, in turn, whispered secrets to him. One such was a being—a ghost, perhaps, or demon, or maybe a trickster, even he was not certain—who called himself by that name and promised that when a Witch-king sat upon the throne of the Silver Empresses, he would come to offer his counsel.

And now, here he was. Or, at least, someone claiming that name.

The Witch-king had not known what to expect. A towering figure of great physical power, perhaps. Or a wizened sorcerer upon whom centuries hung. Yet this man seemed so . . . *ordinary*.

That was the first impression, and the Witch-king was too worldly to rely on such things. He waited, along with the rows of guards positioned between each flickering torch and the hounds who had all risen to their feet. If this man was false, then no power on earth would save him.

The Prince of Games walked to within a yard of the foot of the dais, which was closer than guests were permitted. Nespar began to say something, then he stopped. Not because his master signaled him to do so but because he seemed incapable of it in that moment.

The prince bowed. It was a very grand bow, with a flourish of arms and a head bent nearly to the floor. There was nothing about the act that held true reverence. Nor was there an insult. If anything, it was as if the prince was making a comment about all such formalities and doing so with the confidence that his audience would grasp his meaning.

The Witch-king merely nodded.

As the prince straightened, he offered a wide smile that showed a lot of very white teeth.

"My lord, Gethon Heklan, first of your name, Witch-king of Hakkia," said the visitor, "I have come to offer my services to you in your holy quest to create the Yellow Empire, and in doing so, to honor the God in Yellow, our lord Hastur."

"I know your title," said the Witch-king, unimpressed, "if title it truly be. What is your name?"

"Oh, my king, I have had a hundred names. A thousand. Ten thousand. Elegga, Juha, Nicodemus, Anansi, Coyote, Renart the Fox, Flagg, Kappa, Mbeku, Merlin, Yaw, Păcală, Cin-an-ev, Baron Samedi, Talihsin, Nanabozho . . . and more than even I can remember. Take your pick, lord. What is a name, after all?"

"What do you call yourself?"

"I do not call myself anything," said the prince, "for I know who I am. Perhaps I am only the jester to a court of fools."

Amused, the Witch-king nodded. "Prince of Games will do, then."

The visitor gave another elaborate bow. "As Your Majesty pleases." As he straightened, the prince flicked a finger toward Nespar and merely raised an eyebrow.

"You may leave us, Nespar," said the king.

"Sire, I—"

"Now."

Nespar bowed as graciously as a ramrod-stiff back would allow. He turned, tried to wither the prince with a lethally cold glare, failed utterly to do so, and then fled.

"And your guards?" asked the prince, taking a half-step forward.

"They remain."

"As you please, lord."

"Tell me, prince," said the Witch-king, "I know that you have traveled far to come here. Tell me why you have made that journey and what value your presence is to me at this time."

"The west is arming for war," said the prince. "You sit on the throne of the Silver Empire and yet it is not your throne. Not truly and not yet. You are stuck here. If you return to Hakkia and try to rule from there, it will look like a retreat and a concession to failed plans. So you remain here, occupying the house and the throne of the former empress, and that cannot feel good. It is not an *imperial* throne, after all. For all your grandeur and celestial patronage, you are an occupying usurper. And that is beneath your station. It is unworthy of what you can and should become."

The Witch-king said nothing.

"I have come to share wisdom and insight," continued the prince. "To offer counsel."

"What do you know of war?"

"Oh . . . I know everything about the ways in which men enjoy slaughtering each other for pieces of ground upon which to stand and gloat. I have seen skies darkened with ten thousand arrows, and I have seen whole cities destroyed in glowing clouds of fire and smoke."

"I already have a historian," said the king.

"Yes. Jakob Ravensmere," replied the prince, making a small face of disapproval. "You own his life and he has promised his soul, but he is a devious little shit. Use him—oh yes!—but never turn your back on him."

The King in Yellow dismissed that with a wave of his hand. "I am aware of Lord Ravensmere's capricious loyalty."

The prince took another step forward and now stood at the very base of the dais. The hair on the back of every hound stood straight as brush bristles. The huge bitch bared her teeth at the visitor, but he only smiled. "Perhaps one day it would be entertaining and even enlightening for us to have a conversation with him when there is no one around to hear."

"My guards are not afraid of screams," said the king.

"Of course not. But I don't speak of his screams, Majesty," said the prince. "I suggest that he may have things to say that you would not want anyone else to hear. No, not even your lord chamberlain. But . . . that is a conversation for another time."

"You presume much."

"I always have," said the prince. "Yet I offer much for all my presumption."

"Prove it, Prince of *Games*," said the king. "You are highly skilled at making cryptic comments, but I have yet to see why I should not have you thrown out. Or crucified."

"Oooh . . . threats. I enjoy threats," said the prince, his eyes twinkling with merriment. "I always have." He paused, letting all of the implications of that sink in. Then his smile faded just a bit and he said, "There are secrets in the ice. There are many things waiting to be told. So far you have heard only whispers."

"And what do you know of ice or the secrets it holds?" asked the Witch-king, leaning back in his throne. "Speak truth, but be warned yourself, trickster, I have the god Hastur as my patron."

"Your patron was defeated by a dozing squid, sire," said the Prince of Games. "He was chased off by a sleepy godling. Do not put your faith in such beings."

"You . . . *dare*?"

"Oh yes," said the prince, and now there was no smile at all. His eyes swirled with ugly colors and the hall itself seemed to grow colder. As the prince spoke, his breath plumed with steam. "You *think* your god is in league with your desires, but he is not. None of those so-called gods are. They have never been in league with mortal man. Mankind is, at best, a mistake of evolution to them, though more likely they regard you all as a cosmic joke. You are nothing but a convenience, and most often, an annoyance. You believe them all-powerful, but the truth is that they fled from the stars, from things vastly more powerful than them. They came to earth and met their defeat at the hands of *primitive* men. They sleep through the ages in hopes that your kind wipe each other out and leave an untroubled world for them. If you wake them from their slumber, they will not thank you for it. In their dreams they *rule* this world. Would you wake them to the truth that they are defeated beings who lack the strength to conquer puny creatures such as yourself? No. Would you wake them to the truth that they are *trapped* here? That they have slept through uncounted ages of self-deception in which they dream of conquest and of godhood? Why do you think even the mighty Cthulhu returned to his slumber after defeating his half brother, Hastur? Awake, he is fully aware of his limitations, but in dreams he rules all. He has left the waking awareness that he was defeated by talking apes and has returned to his dreams beneath the green waves."

"This is madness," growled the Witch-king. "It's lies."

"Lies? Are you so certain? Send your guards away and I will speak absolute truth to you," said the prince in a fierce but hushed tone. "Or shall I speak your name here and now?"

The Witch-king almost flinched. His hounds growled and the sentries close enough to hear the dogs turned their heads toward the confrontation. But the king did not call for them to attack.

"Guards," he said. "Leave us. Close the doors and let no one in until I give the word."

They snapped to attention and bowed themselves toward the door. The last one, the captain of the retinue, lingered for a moment in the doorway as if waiting for his master to change his mind. Then he bowed once more and pulled the doors shut.

The pack of hounds remained standing, their teeth bared, eyes blazing, muscles rippling with barely contained energy. They wanted to lunge forward and tear this man to pieces, and the merest word would set them to their red feast. The threat was as real in the air as if it had been shouted. As was the prince's total indifference to the threat.

"Now, Herepath, son of the Poison Rose, brother to the damned, traitor to your own blood, beloved of ravens . . . your usurpation is stalled because your put your faith in the false promises of a failed being, a creature who pretends godhood but is no less mortal than yourself. No, I do not lie. You believe him to be immortal because he has existed for millions of years. But to a mayfly you are no less an immortal being because you live for decades and it lives for hours. The difference is the same. If you declared yourself the emperor of the ants, that would be no different. To them you *would* be a god, or no different than what they, with their limited intellect, imagine a god to be. They fear you, they are in awe of you, and you wield power beyond their understanding, but does that make you an actual god?" He paused and laughed. "You do not answer because you understand the truth now. What value, then, is the worship or esteem of the powerless and ignorant?"

"What, then? Do you ask me to bow to you?"

"Ha! Bow to *me*? By all the gods that have ever lived, no. What an absurd thought. Bow to me? Not now or ever have I asked or desired to be worshipped. I do not crave adulation. It is meaningless to me. No, my dear king, I want to *join* you in this conquest. I want to be part of a *true* conquest. I want to bathe in tears and blood. Give me that and I will give you an empire that will last for ten thousand years."

"You promise this and ask this and yet you do not fear the gods?"

"I fear no god," said the prince.

"Who do you fear? Mother Frey? Kagen the hero, Kagen the Damned?"

"The only person I have ever feared is dust and bone these fifty millennia," said the Prince of Games. "And no, I will not speak his name. No, nor any of his names. But for all his power, he was mortal, in his way. And he is dead. I live and cannot die. I am sewn into the fabric of this world and it must forever endure my footfall. It must forever listen to my song."

"You claim immortality?" asked the Witch-king, leaning forward with interest now.

"The world we know is only a thin coat of paint on a canvas upon which infinite images have been wrought. Mankind has risen and fallen times uncountable. There have been floods and asteroids, wars and plagues, poisoned skies and ice. Oh yes . . . the ice. That was the last catastrophe. The world burned and then froze, and glaciers miles high covered nearly all the land. Life was pushed to the edge of extinction. Mankind fell from a great height, Herepath, a very great height. Fell and rose, fell again and rose. And now there is this world. Your world. The ice tore the old continents apart, drowning some, raising others, creating new lands. All of the old continents have been reshaped by cycles of ice ages and ages of volcanic fury."

"Continents? You mean there is more than this one?"

"Oh, yes. Many, though vast oceans separate them. There are tales of ships finding lost lands, and not all of these are born from the mind of drunken bards. Nor have all the ships lost at sea been consumed by the waves; some of them found those other lands and were content to stay. Or unable to leave. Beware if you go looking, Herepath or Gethon—whichever face you wear—because the seas are filled with horrors."

The king looked at the prince, at the strange man who came uncalled and unarmed to the court of the conqueror of half the known world.

"Have you come to talk about the world that was or the world that will be?"

"Both," said the prince, "for life is a wheel."

"What can you tell me that is of *use* to me?" demanded the monarch. "What can you say that will allow the Yellow Empire to be born?"

"Ah," said the prince, "those are the correct questions to ask, and I will say these things first. I know that your necromancer, Kestral of Ulghareth, daughter of Zheseth and granddaughter of Murestra the White-Haired, is even now working to raise a razor-knight to serve you. Had I been here sooner, I would have cautioned you against wasting so precious a resource as Kestral to create another of Nyarlathotep's battle demons."

"Do you prophesize that she will fail?"

"Not at all. I have every hope she will succeed."

"Then why mention it, unless to show off your intelligence gathering?"

"Oh, I just hope she solves your problem before her life force is all spent. In my dreams I have glimpsed important work that she has still to do."

The Witch-king said nothing.

"You mentioned Mother Frey. Ah . . . she has a bloodline that goes back further than men can count. Even she is unaware who her forbears were, and best for all if she never finds out. You would be well served to have her found and killed on the spot. Do not tarry with interrogation or torture, for while her heart beats, your empire teeters on the edge of a knife."

The Witch-king said nothing.

"And I have heard the darkness speak a name," said the prince. "Not a true name, but the one by which she is called. I do not yet know more, but I do know this . . . the Widow walks abroad. Her heart is broken and her mind is a furnace. She does not yet know her power, nor even its palest edge, but woe to you if she ever allies herself with Frey and Kagen."

"Who is this 'Widow'?"

"I do not yet know her name or where she is," said the prince. "Not yet. But my dreams are never wrong. And I am aware of how much importance *you* place on prophetic dreams. Oh, yes. As for the Widow, I cannot urge you strongly enough to have your spies listen for mention of her, for if she comes for you, she will not come alone, and the beat of great wings will shatter the walls of this palace."

Outside, there was a crack of thunder. Distant, but its echoes rattled the windows in their frames. The Prince of Games smiled and nodded.

"Even the skies whisper their warning, my king."

"Tell me more," said the Witch-king. "Speak truth to me and couch it not in riddles."

The prince stepped back from the dais, and for a moment he looked weary.

"I cannot say more right now." He ran a hand over his face and his shoulders sagged. "The years are heavy on me and I have slept long. So, so long . . ."

Then he raised his head and that devilish smile returned. If it was not as bright, it nonetheless held power and humor.

"Give me a room and a meal," he said. "And before midnight's bell has struck send two virgins to me. It matters not if they are male or female or one of each."

"This is not a brothel," said the king.

The prince's eyes suddenly swirled with furious colors. "Oh, I only intend to enjoy the flesh of one of them, my lord. As for the other . . . well . . . there is so much one can learn when innocent flesh is opened in the right way, with the right tools, and in the right hour. Kestral is not the only haruspex in your palace. Surely, Majesty, you understand this."

The Witch-king studied him for a very long time. There was a second rumble of thunder, but it was very far away now, like a lion that, having uttered his challenge, was slinking away.

"Very well, Prince of Games," said the king, "you shall be my guest and what you require will be provided. For I have dreamed *your* name and foresaw your coming."

"And yet I am such a surprise, am I not?" asked the prince with a mocking laugh.

He bowed again and stood smiling as Lord Nespar was summoned to see to his every need.

CHAPTER NINETY-FOUR

"Am I drunk, or crazy?" said Peder Gross.

He knelt on the grass and looked down at the flowers that bloomed so aggressively at the foot of the cross. The body that had been nailed there was only bones now, and soon those would fall as birds and insects ate away the last of the cartilage that held the sagging skeleton together.

His friend Garrick was standing in the middle of the road, looking at the long lines of crosses stretching off to the crest of the hill. There were more beyond that. Behind them were seven empty crosses, scattered over a mile of the way they'd come. Garrick consulted a list of names and locations. The seven sets of bones were in canvas bags in the back of the wagon, and they had nine more to collect for the families that had obtained permission to bury their dead. He and Peder were making good money doing this, but it was ugly work. Grave digging was bad enough as a profession, but taking down the crucified was worse. They had known some of these people. Luckily, none were close friends or—thank the gods—family. It was tough enough to do this for families who paid them. Overpaid them, really, because even most family members lacked the stomach for work like this.

Garrick realized that Peder had said something a moment ago. "What was that?" He asked distractedly.

"Look at these," said Peder.

"At what?"

"Come and look, damn it."

Garrick sighed and walked over to where his friend knelt. He looked over Peder's shoulder and then frowned.

"I . . ." he began, but had nowhere to go with it.

At the foot of the cross was a bunch of wildflowers. The shape was unusual—some species of tulip, he reckoned—but that was as close as he could come to identifying them. The shape was hard to see, to understand. Not because the flowers were deformed but because of the color.

"What color are they?" demanded Peder.

"I . . ." said Garrick again. "I mean . . ."

They looked at each other for a moment and then down at the flowers.

They were no color at all.

It was not that they were colorless but that the color they were made no sense. They were not any shade of red or blue, yellow or green. They were not purple or white or . . . anything.

The color was something impossible to understand because it was not part of the world as they knew it. They were not a shade or even a blend of any other colors.

"Gods of the Harvest," murmured Garrick, and he made a warding sign in the air. A circle bisected by a rising vertical line. "I can hardly look at it."

"I know," agreed Peder. He licked his lips and began to reach for one, to pluck it so he could take a better look.

"Don't!" cried Garrick. "Don't touch it."

Peder almost laughed. He almost made a mocking comment. Almost.

Instead, he withdrew his hand and stood up slowly.

"I don't like that," said Garrick.

Peder licked his lips again. They were dry, and his throat was dust.

They looked up and down the road. Then up at the bones.

"Who was he?" asked Peder.

Garrick consulted his list. The Hakkian official who had signed permission for this job had given numbers that corresponded with those cut into the post of each cross. But families had supplied the names and, in most cases, the professions. Garrick knew that it was in hopes that familiarity with the dead, and respect for their professions, would translate into greater care and reverence when collecting the remains.

"Cross one hundred seventeen," he said. "Celesta del Haas. Nun of the Antoline Garden."

"A nun?" echoed Peder, and this time he made the warding sign. "Gods above."

They looked up at the bones of what had been a devout daughter of the church, a handmaiden of Mother Sah. A holy woman, even if a minor one in a rural garden. Then they looked down at the indescribable flowers.

"I don't like this at all," repeated Garrick.

They stood there for several silent minutes.

"What should we do?" asked Peder nervously.

Garrick touched the tattoo of a leaf he kept hidden beneath his tunic. It was a crime to show any sign or symbol of the Green Faith, now that the Hakkians were here. His tattoo was old, and he wore a cotton undershirt beneath the tunic. It seemed to throb as he looked from the bones to the flower and back again.

"We have to take her down," he said.

"Shit."

"We have to."

Peder glanced at him, and there were tears in the corners of his eyes. "This is wrong," he said. "I want to get the hell out of here."

Garrick nodded.

They stood there.

It took nearly half an hour for them to summon the courage to fetch the ladder and a fresh canvas bag from the wagon. Once they began working, though, they moved fast. Perhaps too fast, because one arm fell from the skeleton and dropped among the flowers.

They used a branch cut from a tree to coax the bones free. They cut a piece of cloth to use when they picked it up. Neither was willing to touch anything that had touched those flowers. Once the bag was in the back of the wagon, the two men climbed onto the seat and fair whipped their donkey bloody getting out of there.

CHAPTER NINETY-FIVE

Jakob Ravensmere loved codes. He was good at them, and the talent was useful for someone who spent a great deal of time translating works written in many languages, including ancient texts in dead tongues. Language always had some internal logic, and cryptographs of all kinds set the wheels of his mind in useful ruts.

Translating his own writing into coded messages was so easy he did not need a key, though he used one on the off chance that a simple mistake might lead to an error in understanding on the part of the recipient.

Alone in his room, the door double-locked and a single candle burning on his desk, he encrypted the note. Even if it was intercepted and decrypted—the former always a risk, but the latter no risk at all—the code was unbreakable. There were different keys for each of his many agents, and different master keys for each day of the month. Even if one of his agents was captured and forced under torture to reveal his code for any given note, it would only decipher that one message. Moreover, Jakob was deliberately obtuse in his phrasing. The note he composed after his meeting with Lord Nespar ran this way:

> Be on the lookout for any mention of the Sons of the Poison Rose.
> There are reports of them west of Andulin River.
> If spotted, notify Captain Hwrellin at once.

The phrasing could only be interpreted as a warning to a local spy to be aware of the radical group operating in a certain area, and the Hakkian officer to whom all pertinent information should be reported. Nothing about it was dangerous if decoded.

He finished the note, blotted it with sand, blew off the particles, enclosed it in a leather envelope, and used yellow wax and his signet ring to seal it.

Less than a full day later, the note was handed to a girl who served as a runner. She wrapped it in corn leaves and tossed it over a certain wall on a quiet street as the watchman struck the evening bell in the town's tower.

The man who picked it up slipped it immediately inside his clothes before entering the back door of the deserted house that wall embowered. He went down into the basement, pulled on a stack of barrels that moved with some reluctance on hidden gimbals, then passed through into the basement of the adjoining house, where two others waited. He closed the secret entrance behind him.

"Was there word?" asked one of the two.

"Aye," said the first man. He went to a table on which was an oil lamp. He broke the seal and removed the note from the envelope, spread it out, and spent five minutes translating the code into the traveler's tongue. When he was done, he turned to the others and gave them a dark grin. "We're on, lads."

"Where and when?"

"No specific time, which is good," said the first man. "Gives us time to gather the others."

"And the target?"

"The Hakkian garrison west of the Andulin."

The third man produced a map of that part of northeastern Argon. They opened it and bent to study the details. The first man touched a thin blue line.

"That's the river, and here," he said, moving his finger a little, "is the fort. Thirty soldiers under Captain Hwrellin. Either of you know him?"

"Aye," said the second man. "From the capital. He was with the first wave into Argentium that night."

"A Raven?"

"Nah, just a field man. Been in some scrapes, though. Pretty tough."

"Too tough for the Sons of the Poison Rose?" asked the first man, grinning.

The other man grinned like a hungry wolf. "Not a chance."

CHAPTER NINETY-SIX

Kagen told his friends the rest of his story about the goat, or goatlike creature, he'd glimpsed in the storm, the missing horse and the wounds on the others, and everything that had happened in the mansion.

Filia stared at him, her eyes wide. Tuke made no jokes but sat like a statue, gripping the edge of the table as if he was in danger of falling. When Kagen's narrative was complete, they sat in silence for several long minutes. Tuke touched the small pouch in which he kept his icon of Dagon, and Filia made a warding sign.

"Those . . . snakes," began Filia. "Or carpets, or whatever . . . Are you sure you weren't dreaming?"

Kagen just gave her a flat stare.

Filia swallowed and made another warding sign. Tuke began refilling his wine cup without realizing it was already full. Kagen touched his hand and the Therian looked down at the spreading pool of red.

"By the . . . balls of . . ." he began, but that was all he could manage.

Filia looked shaken. "I've ridden that path before, lads. Two or three years back. I remember seeing ruins. And maybe I'm mis-remembering, but I thought the whole place was little more than a mound of timber and stone with only a single standing wall."

"Can't be the same place," said Kagen.

She shook her head, dipped her finger into the wine, and on the tabletop drew a rough map of the region. "This," she said, tapping a winding line, "is the only road from this town to the garden. The only ruins out there are what I saw."

Kagen leaned back and drank half a cup of wine. "I don't know what to tell you," he said. "It was a huge old house. The main hall was bigger than this whole tavern. I slept in the entrance foyer with all of my horses. It's how we survived the blizzard. And, no, I wasn't dreaming it. Those . . . *things* woke me from a dream about Herepath. Believe me when I say I was very much awake."

"When I was looking for brands on the horses," said Tuke, "I saw some scrapes and raw spots . . ."

"The tapestries attacked them, too," said Kagen.

Filia repeated the warding sign and touched wood to reinforce it.

After another quiet moment, Tuke asked, "We know the world has gotten stranger of late. Is it possible that a destroyed *house* can have its own ghost? Could that be where you spent the night?"

Kagen had no answer. Filia stared down at the map and then up at the ceiling. None of them spoke for many minutes.

CHAPTER NINETY-SEVEN

"Shhh," cautioned Foscor. "He's coming."

She pulled Gavran down behind a stuffed rhinoceros that dominated the second landing of the south stairwell. Footsteps could be heard ascending from the rear door of the great hall. They flattened out and, invisible in inky shadows, peered out from between the animal's leathery legs.

Lord Nespar's bald and vulturine head appeared first, and then the plumed helmets of a pair of guards. As they reached the landing and turned to continue climbing, another pair of royal guards appeared, but in front of them was a small man with curly hair and a sleeveless robe.

As the procession passed, the curly-haired man turned his face toward the stuffed animal, and then lowered his eyes to look directly at the children. He winked one eye and then the other, and when he smiled his lips seemed to writhe and crawl, and the color of his eyes changed into a poisonous swirl of swampy tones that completely obscured the whites of his eyes. The twins nearly cried out, and in their horror, they clutched each other. Hand to hand.

And in doing so, they were Alleyn and Desalyn.

The stranger's smile grew larger and he laughed aloud. A single sharp bark of delight.

Nespar paused and turned. "Something, my lord?" he asked.

"Oh," said the stranger, "it's nothing at all. I just thought of something amusing."

The chamberlain looked from him to the rhinoceros, saw nothing of note, nodded, and kept climbing the stairs.

When the party was gone, Desalyn looked down at her brother's hand.

"He *saw* us," she said. "He *knows*."

Alleyn had tears in his eyes. All he could manage was a breathless nod.

CHAPTER NINETY-EIGHT

Tuke broke the dark mood by staggering to his feet, and with great dignity he proclaimed, "I need to piss."

"By all means do so, anywhere but here," said Filia.

Tuke gave a low, wobbling bow. "Of course, my fair lady."

He tottered out. Kagen caught the look in Filia's eyes as she watched the big Therian go. He felt a small pang, because he had slept with her a couple of months before the assassination attempt. It was not the first time, and afterward he had realized that he had genuine feelings for her. However, he saw that there was more than affection in Filia's eyes. There was love. He reached out and gave her forearm a squeeze.

"He's a good man," said Kagen. "I'm glad for you both."

Her eyes darted to his and there was a moment of challenge as she looked for the joke or snub. Finding none, she relaxed and nodded. "Totally not my type," she said.

"Why, because he's a lout, a slob, and—worse yet—a Therian?"

"Oh, hell no. Those are some of his best qualities."

"Then what?"

She took a moment with that. "I'm not the type who falls in love. I'm notoriously unsentimental. You know that firsthand. I'm selfish and mean and hard as hell to get along with. I prefer not to have strong connections because I want the freedom to just up and go."

"Tuke is a lot like that, too, Filia," said Kagen gently, then repeated his earlier comment. "He's a good man."

Filia's smile was in part agreement and part personal. "He is that."

Kagen said, "I owe him a great deal. When he found me, I was swimming at the bottom of a bottle. Grief and frustration were killing me, and I was aiding and abetting. He helped me back to my feet and gave me a kick in the ass."

Filia sipped her wine. "There's a lot to him. Behind the bluster and bombast, I mean."

"And his obsession with balls."

"And that, yes," she laughed. She gave him a curious glance. "What about you and that witch person? Your half-vampire faerie princess. And Gods of the Pit, that feels weird to say out loud."

Kagen grunted. "Imagine what's it like to hear you—the most practical and least fanciful person I know—saying it. But . . . what about us?"

"Are you going back to see her?" asked Filia. "Now, or when this is all over?"

Kagen traced the filigree on his knife handle with a thumbnail. "I don't know."

"Why? I thought you were falling in love with her."

"Oh, I'm already there," admitted Kagen. "Despite all common sense, I love her . . . but what of it? For one thing, she's immortal. And probably batshit crazy . . . and given all the bodies in her front yard, likely *actually* evil, at least by the moral standards of the Garden and the Silver Empire."

"Neither of which exist anymore," Filia pointed out.

He glanced at her. "Mm. There's that. But even so, she'd outlive me in what to her would be a blink of time's eye. And let's face it, I'm young and strong now, but when that all fades, I'd be nothing more than a figure of pity. Or maybe the next set of bones in her garden."

Filia sighed. "I remember when you used to be lighthearted, optimistic, and fun."

"I remember when my parents were alive, I had a job I was good at, my gods hadn't kicked me out of paradise, and my brother wasn't a black-hearted sorcerous madman."

Despite everything, they laughed and clinked glasses. When Tuke returned he looked less drunk and wore a frown.

"What's wrong?" asked Kagen. "Couldn't find your cock? You do know that cold shrinks things, right? And when it's already that small to begin with . . ."

Tuke didn't rise to the bait. He sat and took a small sip of his wine, then leaned back in his chair and rolled the cup between his big palms. "Thinking about tomorrow, actually," he said.

"Ghuraka?" suggested Filia.

"Yes. She's a tough old bird, and no fan of anyone noble born."

"What's Ghuraka's story?" asked Kagen. "Why is everyone so afraid of her?"

"I'm not," said Tuke. "I rather admire her."

"Ha," snorted Filia. "You only like her because of her collection."

"Collection?" asked Kagen.

"Ghuraka has forty-some tobacco pouches on her wall," said Filia.

"My brother Jheklan collects old maps," said Kagen. "So what?"

"They're made from the scrotums of men she's killed," Tuke explained.

"Ah," said Kagen with a wince. "Ouch."

"She's like an angel to me," said Tuke dreamily.

"That's some hobby," said Kagen.

"More like a trophy wall," said Filia. "And they're hung in the room where she meets guests. It makes a statement."

"Yes, it damn well does," agreed Tuke.

Kagen laughed, but he also reflexively crossed his legs. He said, "What do you think will happen? What's the plan once we reach her camp? And, moreover, do you think she'll really be even willing or able to help us?"

"Help us infiltrate Argentium again?" mused Tuke. "To try to kill the Witch-king again? To risk death with very little chance of reward? Gosh, let me think."

"This was *your* damn suggestion, Tuke," growled Kagen.

"Was I sober when I made that suggestion?"

"Yes, you were."

"There you go, then. I make all of my best decisions when I'm drunk."

Kagen peered at him. "Tell me again why I haven't slit your throat before now?"

Tuke merely laughed.

Filia said, "The Hakkians aren't happy with the Unbladed at the moment. Even though the ones who helped us at the coronation were only pretending to be Unbladed, it's soured the whole lot of us for the Ravens. There have been arrests."

"Quite a few arrests," agreed Tuke. "Some executions, too."

"How do you know that?" asked Kagen, then shook his head. "No, let me guess. Secret messages from Mother Frey?"

"Smart for a city boy," said Filia.

"Again I ask, though," said Kagen, "why are we going to see the one person least likely to thank us for that state of affairs?"

"Because if we can win her to our side, we have the army you said we needed," said Filia. "An army that is virtually invisible. An army that is well situated in every city and town in every country from the mountains to the ocean. And an army with more individual combat experience than any bunch of half-trained plowboys marching under a national flag."

Tuke pointed to her. "What she said."

➤ **CHAPTER NINETY-NINE**

"Your Majesty," said Lord Nespar, bowing so low he had to grip his staff for balance. "Now that we have seen to the comfort of your, ah . . . *guest*, is this a good time to discuss matters of state?"

The face behind the yellow lace veil moved subtly, and there was a pause before he answered. Nespar, who had built a career on being able to read people, tried to infer something from the movement, the pause, and even the king's body language. But as so frequently happened, what he saw did not easily lend itself to insight.

"State?" murmured the Witch-king. "Ah. Yes. I suppose we must make sure the taxes are collected, the streets swept, and the widows and orphans seen to."

Nespar was sure that was sarcasm but was unsure if it was an actual joke, so he merely smiled. A friend once told him that his smiles looked like the grimaces of someone with a troubled stomach and piles, but it was what he had to work with.

"Where would you like to begin?" asked the Witch-king.

"The Samudian king has officially closed his embassy here in the capital," said Nespar. "And my agents tell me that Vahlycor is considering a similar action."

The Witch-king nodded. "And Theria?"

"Notably quiet, Majesty."

"Which means they are contemplating a military move. They always were a closed and secretive bunch." The king shifted in his great throne. "Reach out to our network of spies. I want something more than vague suspicions, Nespar. We need troop numbers. And not a rough head count. I want reliable numbers of foot, light, and heavy cavalry, archers, siege engines, and warships."

"I have already sent those instructions, Majesty," said the chamberlain.

"Do so for all of the nations in the west. Have good ears in each court. After what happened here, there will be discussions ongoing about alliances. Theria, Vahlycor, and Samud were allies once, supplying ships and men to a fleet of coastal pirates."

"That was over a thousand years ago, Majesty . . . and they were allied against the first Silver Empress."

"True enough," said the king. "But less than fifty years after the Silver Empire was established, they *served* the second empress in a war against the same pirate armada. Be adult about this. Alliances come and go and are built on necessity. *We* are the enemy. If they can summon the courage to do so, they will march on us."

"They fear your magicks, Majesty. Surely there would not be open rebellion after what happened on the Night of the Ravens."

"Don't fool yourself. They won't see it as rebellion. The more romantic among them will view it as patriotism and revenge. As for the more pragmatic in that bunch . . . well, with the Silver Empire gone they are all technically free states now. They can rally together against a common enemy without breaking any oaths to the empire. They did it once before. Do not forget, my friend, that Bellapher, the Silver Thorn, slew the last Witch-king of Hakkia on his throne. And he was a powerful sorcerer, too."

"True, Majesty, but he was not on *your* level. You are the most—"

"Stop. When I need my ass kissed I'll send for a whore," said the Witch-king irritably. "You are a great administrator, Nespar, but sometimes you lack empathy, and empathy without sentimentality is how one gets inside the head of the enemy and sees the world from their perspective. The monarchs of every imperial nation saw me thwarted in my attempt to become their legal emperor. They saw a handful of fighters, led by Kagen Vale, throw all of our careful plans into total disarray. They saw another god battle our god, and though Hastur was not defeated any more than *I* was defeated, the people gathered here that night saw that we have limitations. That even if we cannot be easily defeated, we can be stopped. Do you not think that is fueling the fires of their rage right now? Instead of emperor I am only usurper. I am an interloper and criminal, as they see things."

"You are still a powerful sorcerer," insisted Nespar. "I don't say that to flatter, Majesty, but to make the point that they might grumble and hold secret meetings and talk of rebellion, but how can they ever dare to take real action? The Witch-king who was murdered by the Silver Thorn did not have the power to transport troops to every capital city at once. He could not transport his entire fleet into Haddon Bay as you did. They *fear* you, and rightly so."

The Witch-king reached for a wine cup on a small, ornately carved table beside the throne. He lifted the hem of his veil and took a sip. Nespar had only a brief glimpse of the monarch's strong chin and mouth, and then the veil dropped again.

Was there a small curl of the yellow king's lip? Was he aware that Nespar was trying to see more of that hidden face? Was the lifted veil a tease? Nespar thought so, on all counts.

"I want the size of your intelligence network expanded," said the Witch-king. "Doubled and even trebled. We will need it for what is to come. War is inevitable, Nespar. War will break apart the bones of the old Silver Empire and suck out the marrow. My coronation would have prevented it, smothered such a thing in its crib. Alas, there is no legal empire, and we are surrounded by enemies."

"But . . ."

"But nothing. War is coming," said the Witch-king. "And that will present a new set of challenges for us. And a new path to glory."

"How so, Majesty?"

"Because we will conquer the lot. Every nation that belonged to the Silver Empire. Every independent island in the Western Sea, from Tull Orgas to the Dragon Islands. We will see our Ravens march into Bulconia—and, in time, across the Cathedral Mountains."

"Majesty . . ." gasped the chamberlain.

"The Hollow Monks and their *gift* are not my only weapon, as I seem to have to remind you and my generals. And now the Prince of Games has declared himself a friend to Hakkia."

"As Your Majesty pleases," said Nespar, "though I do not yet understand what role that person will play."

He intended that to encourage a reply; however, the Witch-king said no more. The chamberlain bowed and left.

CHAPTER ONE HUNDRED

The seven horsemen wore cloaks that were as gray as the leaden Hakkian sky.

A large patch of that cloud cover flickered with other colors— fierce red, hungry orange, and lifeless black—reflecting the inferno that used to be a town. There were still a few lingering screams, but even as the riders paused on a knoll to listen, those cries changed from the shrieks of the dying to the howls of the cursed. Soon even these died out and the night was dominated by the slow, steady, inexorable roar of fire.

"We've a long ride ahead of us, lads," said the leader of the group. Like the others, he wore a spiky black beard. The few arrows remaining in his quiver had the gold and red fletching of the elite Samud archers.

They kicked their horses into a canter, following the pale clay of the road that wound up from the valley to a bigger route that zigzagged through a forest. Once there, they rode along the verge to avoid the wheel tracks cut into the surface by centuries of caravans.

The leader rode out in front with another soldier, a longtime friend and confidant.

"What if they get out?" murmured the other rider, pitching it too low for the rest to hear.

"Then, laddie," said the leader, "we are well and truly fucked."

His friend cast a nervous glance over his shoulder. "You mean because they'll blame us?"

"No, brother, because if those damned souls get out, then who or what could stop them?" He made a warding sign. "Lord Hastur save our souls, because if that happens, they'll eat the whole world."

They turned and headed south toward Ghenrey, and then home to Hakkia.

CHAPTER ONE HUNDRED ONE

The ship was not the same one that brought Ryssa to Tull Yammoth. That one, the *Dreaming God*, was in dry dock to have its hull scraped of barnacles and seaweed. Instead, the Widow stood on the forward bow of a much larger warship whose name, *Turn'ghftor gn'th*, meant *Green Sea*.

It had a crew of 203, tall masts crammed with sails that were so white it hurt the eyes to look at them in full sunlight. Small catapults squatted in rows, their carriages lashed tightly to ringbolts set into the oak decking. Lines of various thickness and purpose seemed to weave around the Widow like the work of titanic spiders. She neither knew nor cared what each did, nor cared she for the science of sail handling, navigation, or any other aspect of the sailor's trade. When the officers attempted to engage her interest, she only smiled faintly and turned away.

All through the day, with only short breaks, she stood as far forward as was possible, looking out past the figurehead of a great fish riding a curling wave. She looked forward. Always forward, never back.

Once in a very rare while, when some unusual splash pulled her from her thoughts, the Widow would look down into the water. Most often it was a dolphin or killer whale or some other mundane thing. Once or twice she caught brief glimpses of something else—huge and sleek and mottled with turquoise and blue—as it swept past, faster than the ship, faster than the waves.

Each of those times she murmured a single word, *Miri*, in the hope that somehow those more mysterious creatures could carry her voice down to wherever her lover's body lay in the unlighted depths.

The ship sailed on and on, and the Widow watched the horizon. True to what the Prince of Games had said, her mind was a furnace, and it burned her thoughts. Not to black ash but to a penetrating hardness, the way a blaze will turn a sharpened stick into a spear. The way a forge will turn iron ore into glittering steel.

CHAPTER ONE HUNDRED TWO

The food was long gone, the last bottles of wine standing empty, the fire guttering.

"I'm for bed," said Filia, getting to her feet. She yawned and stretched, filling the air with small popping sounds from joints and backbone. She poked Tuke in the chest. "Are you coming?"

He was bleary with drink but managed a smile, placed both hands on the table, and heaved himself up as if lifting a laden cart horse. His body sang its own chorus of too many years of hard use.

"I've got to piss again," he mumbled, not directing it to anyone, then shambled off toward the door. He paused and turned red-rimmed eyes to Filia. "See you upstairs."

"It's cold out there," she cautioned. "Try not to let your cock freeze off."

"I'll do my best."

Kagen watched her watch Tuke, and he felt a flush of emotion. Not jealousy—there was nothing malicious or grasping about it— but definitely a kind of piercing envy. He did not make her the villain, though. Nor Tuke. The world was broken and he was twice as fractured. Damaged goods were hardly appealing.

Filia turned and must have caught something in his eyes.

"Are you all right, Kagen?"

No "city boy" or "boy" this time.

He forced a smile into place. "It's been a rough couple of days," he said.

"Why don't you get some sleep, too?"

"I will, in a bit," said Kagen. "I need to go through everything that happened at the garden and that mansion. And go over what you and Tuke had to say. Red priests and all that. I'll be fine. I'll sit here and watch the fire burn out."

"That's gloomy," she said. "Maybe put it all aside and get a good night's rest. Things may make more sense tomorrow."

Tuke returned, shivering and stamping. "Be well, brother," he said, and wrapped his brawny arm around Filia's slender waist.

Kagen toasted the lovers with his nearly empty cup and watched them walk over to the steps and vanish upstairs. He let his gaze linger on the empty staircase for a moment, thinking about the two of them.

Filia was as tough as anyone he'd ever met, but she was alone. No family that she ever spoke about, a body covered with scars from hard use, and a cynicism she wore as armor over a true heart. Her loneliness was palpable, though. Even now. Even in love.

As for Tuke, the big Therian loved to bluster, but his bombast was as much armor as Filia's jaded exterior. He felt a great and deep affection for them both. And that, strangely, gave him a buffer against his own sadness. He knew that even after nearly four months since the Night of the Ravens, he had not properly grieved. Any hopes that the visit to the garden would allow him the contemplative quiet to allow that process to unfold had been ruined.

Tomorrow they were heading farther north to see Ghuraka. There would be hardships along the way, there would be fighting once they got there—and probably some bullshit politics—and then the road would open up again to find Mother Frey. To build an army. To slaughter their way back to the throne room of . . .

Herepath.

"Damn," said Kagen to the dying fire. "Damn, damn, damn, damn."

CHAPTER ONE HUNDRED THREE

The Prince of Games and the Witch-king sat at one corner of a vast dining table. There was enough food for ten men, but they were the only diners.

"I hope your accommodations are satisfactory," said the king.

"Are we doing small talk?" mused the prince. "Then, sure. Lovely suite of rooms. Nice view of a grove of fruit trees about which I care just a little less than nothing. But as my arrival was unannounced, I shouldn't complain."

"No," said the Witch-king, "you should not."

The prince smiled, speared a slice of veal with a fork, shoved it in his mouth, and chewed noisily. Grease ran over his lips and hung in fat oily drops from his chin.

"Is being offensive a habit or something deliberate to try to keep people off balance?" asked the king.

"Oh, a bit of both. And it's fun."

"Ah."

The prince swallowed, washed it down with wine, and then wiped his chin with a great show of delicacy. "Better?"

"I did not say I was offended," said the Witch-king. "I'm merely curious. I've read a great deal about you, though much of it is in dense and archaic verse that reads as if it was written to be deliberately cryptic."

"Very likely. I may even have written some of that myself."

"I daresay," murmured the Witch-king. "I also gather that your behavior is intended to convey a message that, despite being my guest, you are not my subject or my inferior."

"And how does that make you feel?"

"It's a minor irritation."

"To your pride?"

"No, to my desire to see things moving forward in their proper course and at a useful speed."

"And yet *you* began the conversation with polite chitchat."

The Witch-king nodded. "A fair point."

The Prince of Games winked at him. Then he set his cutlery down and pushed the plate away, even though he had taken but a few bites. "Then let us get to it, shall we?" he asked.

"By all means."

"I know you have your own spy network. Networks, I should say. Each branch of your military has its agents, your intelligence service has more, and then there are the spymasters and their people. You have yours, as do your chamberlain—am I the only one who thinks he looks like an affronted ostrich?—and your court historian."

"Your point being?"

"I have my sources as well, and I daresay they are rather better than most."

"Is that a boast or is there substance to it?" asked the king.

Strange little lights ignited in the prince's eyes. "How about this? Did you know that the blood priests of Tsathoggua found

Kagen Vale? They were enticed by the reward, but more so, I believe, by the thought that capturing him for you would result in you inviting them into the—how should I put this?—family of cults and fringe groups that have emerged from the shadows now that the oppression of the Silver Empire is ended."

"The blood priests found him?" said the Witch-king sharply, then he settled back against his chair. "Found is not the same as captured, I take it."

"Sadly, no," said the prince offhandedly. "They tracked him from where the Therian ship landed him in Vahlycor—after it sank your Hakkian raider with all hands. Pity, that. They followed him north into Nelfydia, far up to the border, but did not want to make their move until he was alone. Kagen was traveling with the same two fighters who brought him to the palace and pissed all over your coronation. Tuke Brakson of Theria and Filia alden-Bok of Vahlycor. Both fighters of considerable skill, as you saw firsthand. Filia is particularly dangerous, though the Therian is no oaf, for all his size. Anyway, when Kagen rode off alone to visit a garden, they followed discreetly, and when they were sure he wasn't going to meet a group of armed allies, they set upon him."

"A-a-and?" asked the Witch-king, drawing the word out.

"Oh, Kagen butchered the lot."

The king glanced away out the window for a moment. "And escaped unharmed, I take it."

"The red priests are a vicious lot of bloodthirsty madmen," said the prince, "but they are hardly great fighters. They came for Kagen in broad daylight, and in a place where he had room to maneuver, believing that numbers were all the advantage they required."

"No survivors?"

"There was one," said the prince. "A witness, not a participant. A junior monk who traveled with them as a servant. He was tending the horses but fled to a place of safety when the priests failed to emerge from the garden and instead a blood-spattered Kagen did. The monk watched young Vale take all of the horses and ride off just as a blizzard was about to strike. He tried to follow but was on foot and got lost in the storm."

"When was this?"

"Yesterday," said the prince.

"But . . . how could you know of it already?"

The Prince of Games smiled that ugly, unnatural smile of his. "You have your ways, my king, and I have mine."

"And you're sure of this?"

"I am."

The Witch-king sat in silence for a while. "Where in Nelfydia?" The prince told him, naming the closest town as well. "Do you have any way of locating him now? Can you track him?" asked the king.

"That, alas, is not how things work. But trust me that Kagen Vale was there at that garden yesterday afternoon." The prince leaned forward, resting his elbows on the table. "There is a danger, and you can't see it."

"I see much," snapped the king. "I have spies in every court and country."

"Yes, and your spies will tell you what you need to know about troop movements and rebellion from within the corpse of the Silver Empire," said the prince, "but it is not of that I speak, O king."

"Then tell me my peril."

"Kagen Vale is your true enemy on earth," said the Prince of Games. "He and that witch, Frey. I have met their kind before. Many times before. They are human, and by all the stars and shadows you should be able to snap your fingers and erase them from existence. And oh how that would simplify the mathematics of conquest. But alas, my king, Kagen has become something more than the brother of your flesh."

"And what is that?"

"He has become a hero."

"What are heroes but the first to fall or the last to recognize the futility of their cause?" laughed the Witch-king. "The bones of heroes fill the potter's field east of this palace."

"Oh, no, my liege," said the prince, his eyebrows lifting from wide eyes. "We are not talking about some pigheaded thug with a storied sword, or the decorated champion of a grand hall. No. That would be easy; that would be no threat at all. I speak of hero in the grander sense. A cosmic sense, if you will. You think of him as a rogue knight bent on revenge, but he is wiser than you guess. Because you have memories of him as a boy, you think you understand the man. It is the one vulnerability you possess, my king. You are wise, and your eye sees far and sees much, but Kagen is a blind spot in your perception. You authorize a king's ransom for his head and heart, but that seems more of a reaction out of pique than of strategic sophistication."

"I can deal with a hero."

"Maybe," said the prince, "though I can tell you firsthand that many great kings and queens, and other kinds of powerful leaders, have thought the same of heroes in the past. And sometimes they are right, which pleases the composers of tragic ballads and dramatic plays. But don't let hubris cloud your vision, my king. When a real hero rises, a *true* hero—whether his own gods or people recognize him as such at the outset—he draws to himself allies. Powerful people, powerful *forces*. You have torn the veil between worlds, and many beings in the larger world love you for it. I do, as a matter of fact, because my own return is as much your doing as mine. But we are on one side of this war and there are forces of equal power on the other. Your Ravens, your Hollow Monks and razor-knights and necromancers and all of them, are pieces on one side of the board, and at this moment it appears you have the strongest position, but the game of Kings and Castles is a tricky one. A single wrong move on your part, and a decisive countermove on the other can change everything. Everything.

"I have come to help you deal with those other forces. You have *learned* magic, great king, but I *am* magic. Unlike you, I was never a mortal man born of woman and raised from a mewling infant. I was created with the world itself and I have always been. Heroes like this Kagen have even killed my body, and in their naïveté, they thought that would kill me. Such childish myopia. I *wear* this body, but I am not defined by it."

The Witch-king sat unmoving while the Prince of Games spoke. He was not afraid, but he was surprised and did not care to show it or allow it to flavor his voice. The things he had learned about the Prince of Games—in this or other aspects—added up to more mysteries than answers, and this diatribe only made that stranger. A thousand questions occurred to him, but asking them, especially now, might show weakness. So he allowed the affectation of a calm posture, the obscurity of his yellow veil, and his silence to control the moment.

The prince reached across the table and took some fat purple grapes from a bowl. He tossed one into the air and caught it in his mouth the way a child—or a lout—might. The Witch-king caught those strange eyes watching him, looking for a telling reaction, but he gave none.

That made the prince smile, and he gave a small nod of approval. He ate another grape and tossed the others onto the table, where they rolled this way and that. "I have eyes watching for Kagen Vale," said the prince.

"Yes," said the king.

"I *will* find him."

"Yes."

"And . . . I think I may have some idea where he might go."

"If he is in northern Nelfydia," said the king dryly, "then he is likely to seek out the Unbladed. Lady Ghuraka has a training camp up there."

"Oh, no doubt he'll go there," said the prince. "And no doubt things will not go his way."

"You know something?"

The prince merely shrugged.

"And if Kagen survives?" mused the king. "What then? What strategic insights does your wisdom offer?"

Again, the prince nodded approval. "I have given that a great deal of thought, my king," he said, his voicing losing the comedic tone. When he spoke again, it was—as the Witch-king viewed it—an ordinary voice. Peer to peer, and that was good. It was as if some test had been presented and the results satisfactory. "Kagen is gathering his allies, and that includes those he has not yet met."

"Mother Frey?"

"And her cabal, yes. I know they exist, but so far my eye is blocked in seeing where they are." The prince shrugged. "That will change in time. I am newly reborn into this world. My fingers reach far, but not as far as they will."

The Witch-king nodded. "Go on."

"Kagen, Frey, and that lot had three really good options to dethrone you," said the prince. "The first was to cut your throat, and they made a closer run at that than anyone could have guessed. It was not something they could have done without help. I suspect either Xeran Cohall, Earl Veus, or Lady Maralina. No one else could have gotten him to the very foot of your dais."

The Witch-king nodded. "Of those three, who would you guess?"

"Tricky question, because I can make a good case for each."

"Let me add a detail that will help," said the Witch-king. "Kagen Vale was known to be in western Vahlycor shortly before coronation night."

The prince blinked in surprise. "Is that a fact? How very interesting. Then Lady Maralina it is." He smiled. "I hope you have not done something rash like sending assassins to try to cut her throat."

"No."

"Good. Even though her mother exiled her, the queen of the faerie would take it amiss if her daughter were murdered. Believe me when I say that you do not want the Baobhan sith to enter on the wrong side of this coming war."

The Witch-king nodded and took a sip of wine. He was not particularly careful as he raised his veil to do so, allowing the prince to glimpse part of his face.

"The rumors are true, then," said the prince, "that Kagen Vale cut you with one of his mother's daggers. Clearly not poisoned, though I take it they were when that fight started. He killed too many of your soldiers in a crowded room for it to be anything else. You have the luck of the devil."

The Witch-king smiled faintly. "The assassination was one of Kagen's options. You said there were two others?"

"Yes. Neither is quick or easy, which means you will have time to arrange something to prevent these plans from coming to fruition."

"Tell me."

The Prince of Games smiled. "He will either go to the Winterwilds, to the glaciers where the last dragon is imprisoned. Poor Fabeldyr. She is so old now, isn't she?"

"You *know* of the last dragon?"

"Oh, my king, I know *much* of what is hidden up in the ice," said the prince. "Much more than you do, I dare say."

"Perhaps. An expedition to the Winterwilds would take months and require extensive outfitting."

"Yes," agreed the prince, "so the third option is most likely. A well-armed and moderately provisioned party could reach it in less than a month."

"Reach . . . *what?*"

"Vespia," said the prince. "And you know what he would go there to find. You know what that hag, Frey, would *want* him to find. Not one great book, but a collection of them, bound in the skin of saints."

The Witch-king shook his head. "I spent months there, and the Seven Cryptical Books of Hsan are not in Vespia."

"Then you did not look hard enough," said the prince. "The books *are* there. They are where they have always been, in the city of Ulthar, in the sacred temple of Ig-ulthan, which can only be entered through a hidden door."

"Ulthar," said the Witch-king. "I know that name, but in the Mitithian Grimoire the scholar claimed that it was utterly destroyed even before Vespia fell."

"Ah," said an amused prince. "That's because the copy of the Mitithian Grimoire you have is the translation and not the original."

"How could you know that?"

The prince laughed. "Trust that I know. Did it have sixty-nine chapters or seventy-two?"

"Sixty-nine."

"Translation," said the prince with a dismissive sniff, "and not a good one. My guess is that it's the copy that was taken to Skyria by their priests. They scoured the ruins of the ancient world looking for books of great magic. They found many, as you and other more modern scholars know. But works like the Mitithian Grimoire were translated by generations of mystics long before the Skyrians built their first pyramids. That is one of the dangers, my king: some translations are faulty because the language in which they are written is so long dead that no attempt at translation can ever hope to be completely faithful. Nuance and subtlty are lost, and translations are often filtered through the culture of the translator. That renders much of the contents of questionable integrity and accuracy. You have some experience in that on a personal level, I believe."

The Witch-king said nothing.

"Yes," murmured the prince, answering his own observation. "No matter. The point, dear king, is that much of the most powerful truths, the most sacred knowledge, has either been lost entirely or survives as watered-down versions. The copy you have is a translation by scholars from the fourteenth century of the pre–Silver Empire world based on a Skyrian translation of an older translation by Sendrellan scholars who were the first to visit the ruins of Vespia four thousand years ago. The Sendrellan language is largely lost to time, and what few relics have been unearthed since have been wrongly attributed to an offshoot of the Ghestilan cave peoples. There is no way that a proper translation could possibly exist. And while I applaud the scholarship displayed at various historical points, even the most earnest of them was working with faulty tools."

"You are a charming houseguest," said the Witch-king with a touch of frost. "But getting back to the Hsan books. I wonder if Maralina could read them. She's old enough."

"Oh, without a doubt," said the prince. "Which means that we can never let Kagen or Mother Frey get hold of them. If they engage Maralina to translate them, then we may be lost."

The Witch-king nodded. "We will have to prepare for that eventuality. Since we cannot safely move against Maralina, we will have to make sure that none of Frey's agents can ever get those books to her, should Kagen somehow obtain them."

"Perhaps quadrupling the size of the Garrison in the town of Arras?" suggested the prince. "Maybe even building an actual fort around the Tower of Sarsis. That might . . ."

He paused, distracted by a rat that scuttled across the floor beneath a tapestry showing dueling wyverns. One of the king's hounds raised its head and snarled, muscles bunching as it prepared to attack, but the prince snapped his fingers and the dog yelped as if struck and turned away.

"Forgive my bad manners," said the prince. "Chastising your dog. But I rather like rats. Nearly as much as I like cats."

The Witch-king said that it was of no importance, but he was troubled that his faithful hound had obeyed this strange man. Obeyed and feared.

"Even if what you've said is true," said the king, and despite his best efforts, there was uncertainty in his voice, "if I could not find the original text, which, as you suggested, is still hidden in the city of Ulthar in Vespia, then what chance does Kagen have?"

"Oh, he has every chance. And why? For two very good reasons, my king: because Kagen was there once. He and three of his brothers. You may have some memory of that, yes?" The prince chuckled. "But the city was a nameless one to the Vale brothers. They searched and searched but they found nothing because they had no understanding of Ulthar's secrets. The truth was *so* close. Kagen Vale actually stood near to the entrance but had no idea."

He clapped his hands and laughed. It was an uncouth donkey bray, and the Witch-king endured it, his fists balled on the tabletop. The laughter died away and the Prince of Games dabbed at his eyes and then sat in a considering silence for a moment before continuing his comments.

"And the other chance Kagen has of finding it," he said, "is because Mother Frey knows exactly where those books are. If we are ever so unfortunate as to allow Kagen Vale to *meet* and *talk* with that witch, then everything you have worked toward your entire life may come to dust."

The Witch-king rose from the table and walked across to the window. He stood looking out at the thrashing blue waves of Haddon Bay.

"I will stop him," he said.

"You must," said the Prince of Games. "But you are not try-ing hard enough. You are using the gift of the Hollow Monks to frighten the nobility of this fallen empire. Playing a devious little game of trying to blame each other for the delicious atrocities your field teams have inflicted with that curse. But you have been circumspect . . . allowing it to be used in walled towns, where the curse cannot spread."

"I want to conquer the empire," said the king with asperity, "not destroy it. That weapon is far too dangerous to be allowed free rein."

The Prince of Games came over to stand with him, staring until the king turned to meet his eyes.

"Oh, forgive me for being blunt, but it's just us here," said the prince airily. Then his eyes, his mouth, and his tone all hardened to bitter ice. "That is a timid response and a weak parry. You are many things, my dear king, and you have so many qualities . . . surely when it comes to the decisions that shape history and re-shape the world, you are not timid. Are you . . . ?"

The room grew very quiet. The hounds raised their heads and looked at the two men.

"No," said the prince. "I suspect that you are not timid at all."

CHAPTER ONE HUNDRED FOUR

They met in secret, in a room that only a handful of people in Samud knew about, even within the palace household. The door-way was built into the wall of a stairwell that led to a T junction that split left to the royal apartments and right to King al-Huk's private library. The door itself was built into the granite wall so seamlessly that it was impossible to find without knowing it was there. It required a special touch of a certain duration on a part of a bronze bust of Hrollan al-Huk, a cousin of the king's great-grandfather.

When Major General Culanna yl-Sik, deputy field marshal of Samud, slipped in through that secret door, she closed it firmly and ran her fingers along the edges to make sure there was no air passing through. Closed properly, it allowed nothing—not a breath, and certainly not a sound.

Confident that it was secure, she turned and passed through a curtain and into the chamber. There was a bright fire of hickory logs, and two chairs pulled close. King al-Huk sat staring into the flames, but he waved her to the empty chair.

"How bad is the news?" asked the king.

"Bad, Majesty."

Al-Huk closed his eyes for a moment. Then he took a breath. "Tell me."

"They are calling it the return of the Red Curse," said the general, and she waited for him to react. When he did not, she added, "Though many refer to it as the Samudian Plague."

"Is it?" asked the king.

"I . . . don't know. The Red Curse swept Samud nearly fifteen hundred years ago. It was a plague of madness and cannibalism. No one knows how it began, or even where it came from, but the first cases of it were here in Samud, hence the nickname. This time it struck first in Argon, then Nehemite, and then Hakkia. It manifests the same way, from what we have been able to establish. The madness, or disease or curse or whatever it really is, strikes one person and drives him or her completely mad. They lose all ability to speak or communicate. It's as if their minds are totally gone. That alone is bad enough, because that much would be heartbreaking."

"Like senility," said al-Huk quietly. "Like what happened to my father."

"In a way," said the general, "but unlike senility, these people go quite mad in the most terrible of extremes. They attack any other person around them. Animals, too. They fall on them like ravenous beasts, killing and feeding on them."

"Gods of the Harvest," breathed the king.

"What makes it so much worse is that anyone bitten, even if they are bitten to death, will rise as hungry monsters and attack someone else. It spreads like that. It is fast, it is terrible, and no one is immune." Culanna leaned forward, forearms on her thighs. "I was able to get an agent into Xorat, the Hakkian city tucked into an unimportant corner bordering Nehemite and Ghenrey. A small town built on the bones of an old fort. My agent saw firsthand what happened when Hakkian militia tried to take control of the city and arrest the . . . cannibals." She shook her head. "It was a slaughter. Even swords through the body did not stop them. They killed a few by cutting off heads, but the whole town was overcome with the curse. The Hakkian militia were slaughtered. Two escaped. One was unharmed but the other had a bite on his arm. He fell ill and was isolated in a tent, but within hours he broke free from the restraints and attacked the other local soldiers. By the time a platoon of Hakkian regulars arrived the curse had claimed everyone in the camp. The regulars used their bows, and it took a dozen arrows each to bring down the cursed."

"Gods . . ."

"It was after that massacre, when officials could examine the bodies of the dead, that the first talk of the Samudian Plague began."

"How was that connection made?"

The general licked her lips nervously and hesitated so long the king turned to her.

"Tell me," he ordered.

"In two ways," said the general. "Each as damning as the other." She reached into a pouch tied to her belt and removed the feathered ends of six arrows. The fletching on each was stained with soot and blood but they were otherwise identical. She held one up so the king could see the red and gold feathers used in the fletching. "One from each site, sire. There were hundreds of arrows stuck in walls, animals, and people. They are all like this."

King al-Huk took the arrows from her and held them in his palm. He selected one and studied it with an archer's practiced eye. He ran his thumbnail along the teeth of the nock.

"If those are fakes, my lord," said Culanna, "then they used feathers from Samudian geese and are familiar with our process of dyeing and construction."

Al-Huk tossed them onto the small table that stood between the chairs. "Arrows can be copied. What else do you have?"

"Sire," said the general, her face tight and pained, "when the officials examined the whole town, they found two bodies hidden in a barn. They wore Hakkian clothes but did not look the part, and so my officers examined them, stripping the bodies to look for regional tattoos or something along those lines. Tattoos were found. Each was identical, and tattooed on their lower backs, where they would not be easily noticed. My king, they were tattoos of gold falcons."

The king's eyes went wide. "No . . ."

The falcon was the official bird of Samud, and only the most elite of the Samudian royal guard had golden tattoos inked onto their skin as a mark of trust and honor.

"Is this *true*?" croaked al-Huk.

"My operative was able to see those corpses. He saw the tattoos and is certain he recognized one of the dead men as yl-For of Igtha. He was—"

"I know yl-For, damn your eyes. It *can't* be him. He retired with high honors not two years ago. He is fiercely loyal, a true son of Samud."

"His reputation as a patriot is very well known, my king," said the general.

"I don't believe that man in Hakkia is my former guard. I *won't* believe it. Send word to his family. Half the people of Igtha are cousins of him. Find someone who knows where he is so we can put this nonsense to rest."

The general looked deeply pained. "Sire, I did that before I came here. A week after the Night of the Ravens, he and some other veterans led an attack on a Hakkian barracks. They killed eleven Ravens. I sent you a report on that."

The king looked stricken and only managed a nod.

"Yl-For and his friends went missing after that. No trace of them has been found . . . until now."

"No . . ."

"There's more, sire . . ."

The king gripped the arms of his chair as if expecting to be knocked out of it. "Tell me all of it, damn it."

"Three miles outside of Igtha is the last place where the Red Curse was ever reported. A village was overrun, and the authorities at that time slaughtered the cursed and buried them in a mass grave. That mound is still there. Overgrown, but still avoided. Red Hill it's called. Sire . . . if that curse is something else, a disease perhaps, like the gray pox or the blood cough, then it is possible the disease survived in that mass grave. Red Hill is an easy walk from where yl-For lived. If he and his friends wanted a weapon powerful enough to strike back at the Hakkians . . ."

She left the rest unspoken, because there was no need to say a single word more.

CHAPTER ONE HUNDRED FIVE

There were corpses everywhere.

Twenty-three men and seven women in the armor of Hakkian regulars. Fourteen general staff. Forty-six horses. Eight goats, two milk cows. Three dogs and a cat.

All dead. Killed by a group of men wearing silver sashes across their chests.

The leader of the group sat on an overturned bucket, slowly

wiping gore from his sword as his men went through the process of cutting off heads and stacking them into a pyramid.

"Hey," he yelled, "let's not be sloppy. Use the smaller ones on top. There . . . that's better. Nicely done."

The fighters in his group were a mixed lot, and most were not even from that side of the Cathedral Mountains. There was a black-haired Inaki and an Ikarian with dark skin and cat-green eyes. There was a pair of red-haired giants from Kierrod Sund and three heavily tattooed pirates from the small islands near Tull Mithrain. A few were Berclessians and the others a scattering of cutthroats and brigands from the remnants of the Silver Empire.

No Hakkians.

No Argonians.

No Vales.

The leader, who was raised on a coastal raider and had no real idea of lineage or nationality, was a muscular brute with a sword scar that ran from his right temple to the point of his left jaw, with a path of terrible scarring that turned an ugly face into that of a monster. Although he had hated receiving that cut—the parting gift of a Therian, just before the leader gutted him—he loved the effect. People were afraid of him even before he drew his cleaver of a sword. Even his own people found it hard to look him in the eye because it was impossible not to stare at the pulpy red scars.

"Hurry it up, lads," he growled. "It's time we were gone."

The last of the heads was placed atop the pyramid. The leader's number two, a barrel-chested Korthan, handed him a pole on which was a standard. The leader stood, sheathed his sword, and took the standard. It was fashioned with a short crossbar near the top, and on that was pinned a piece of sheepskin.

He walked over, raised the pole, and carefully fitted it into the pyramid. Because of awkward angles of cheeks and foreheads and chins, he could not make it stand straight, but when he stepped back and looked at the crooked, blood-spattered standard, he nodded.

"Has a bit of style to it," he said to his number two.

"Oh, aye," said the Korthan. "A rakish angle."

"That's it exactly."

"Artistic, that is," said the Korthan.

They grinned at each other. Then the leader put two grimy fingers into his mouth and blew a sharp call. The soldiers came running, many of them with shirts that bulged with whatever they'd stolen. They mounted their horses and rode out.

The standard, with its declaration from the Sons of the Poison Rose, leaned away from the pyramid. A single trail of blood rolled very slowly down its length.

CHAPTER ONE HUNDRED SIX

Tuke fell back, gasping, drenched in sweat, heart pounding.

"Gods of the watery deeps," he wheezed. "You're going to kill me."

Filia lay beside him, her skin glowing with sweat, eyes filled with post-orgasmic lights, mouth smiling like a wolf.

"It's the only way you'll die happy, you grouchy bastard," she laughed.

They lay together on the ruins of the bed. The furs and pillows had long since been kicked into tangled heaps on the floor. The air in the room smelled of sweat, burning pine logs, and sex. Filia's pale skin had a few red welts on buttocks, thighs, and breasts. Tuke was as comprehensively scratched as if he had spent the night wrestling with bobcats. Gentle lovers they were not.

She peeled herself off the bed, padded naked to the window, and threw up the sash. Cold air swirled in, bringing with it flakes of pure white snow. She leaned out to take several long, deep breaths and let the icy wind dry her sweat and raise gooseflesh from collarbones to ankles. Then she sighed and pushed herself away from the sill, leaving the window open.

Filia was not a tall woman, and she had few curves. Instead, her body was lean and hard, crisscrossed with scars from a life spent in conflict. Adventurer, caravan guard, ruthless fighter, and a member of the Brotherhood of Steel—the Unbladed. It was a choice rather than a necessity; she had the papers that allowed her to carry a sword, because of her work with the silk and spice merchants. Membership in the Unbladed, however, allowed her to make good money doing nasty little jobs here and there.

As she walked slowly back to the bed, Tuke propped himself up against the headboard. His body was broad and heavily muscled, but because of his height, those muscles were long and made him appear leaner than he was. Like her, he had a collection of scars that told stories about his adventures. The tentacle tattoos that covered part of his face coiled around his neck and down his torso, never actually attaching to a squid or octopus body but instead merely circling and swirling. Here and there were smaller tattoos of brightly colored fish that stood in elegant contrast to his dark brown skin. His chest was still heaving from their last bout of lovemaking. His mass required more effort to move, and keeping up with Filia in bed demanded much of him.

He patted the mattress beside him, but instead of lying down, she climbed up and sat cross-legged, her elbows on her thighs, chin on her palms.

"Tuke?" she asked quietly.

"Mmm?"

"I saw a messenger arrive this evening, just before Kagen showed up."

Tuke winced. "Did you now?"

"I saw him slip you a note and saw you stuff it into your shirt."

"Ah."

"It was from Mother Frey, wasn't it?"

Tuke sighed. "It was."

"When were you going to tell me?"

"In the morning," he said. "First there was Kagen and his stories about those monks and that creepy damn mansion. Then we all drank too much, and after that we came up and shagged each other silly. When have I had the time?"

"Have you read it?"

He paused. "Yes."

"Will you tell me what it said?"

"It was short. She said that she was at the palace on coronation night."

"What?"

Tuke nodded. "She saw us with Kagen. She was with two members of the cabal. Hannibus Greel, a countryman of mine, and someone named Helleda Frost, whom I don't know."

"I do. She's a rich noblewoman who is as cold as her name. But her politics are worthwhile. What else did Frey say?"

"Not much. She got your message about taking Kagen to Ghuraka. She named three different inns in Vahlycor, and the approximate dates when she might be there. She said that she'd look for our sigils on the door frames."

Filia nodded. It was a custom of the Unbladed to cut small and unique marks outside of any tavern, inn, or roadhouse where they were staying. The marks indicated that the Unbladed whose sigils they represented were available for hire. Frey knew the sigils each of them used.

"She wants to meet with Kagen and try to enlist him into the cabal."

"Does she have an actual plan?" asked Filia.

"That old witch always has a plan. Hell, ten plans."

"Aye," agreed Filia. "True enough."

They sat and thought about it for a while, listening to the wind.

"I wasn't planning on telling Kagen this," said Tuke. "Not until and unless he passes the test to be an Unbladed."

Filia nodded. "Good."

Then she reached out and took hold of his cock.

"I have another plan, too."

He gaped at her. "Already? Gods of the Pit, I'm spent, half dead, worthless . . ."

She proved he was none of those things.

CHAPTER ONE HUNDRED SEVEN

"You sent for me, Majesty?" said Lord Nespar. As he bowed low, he cut a sly look in the direction of the figure standing beside and slightly behind the throne. The Prince of Games. And that creature was looking directly at him. Smiling like a reptile—a blend of merriment and hunger, without any trace of warmth or humanity.

"It is time to separate the wheat from the chaff," said the Witch-king.

"Majesty?"

The Witch-king gestured toward a bundle of scrolls tied with a yellow ribbon that lay upon a table on the other side of his throne.

"Have these delivered immediately."

"Of course, Majesty, but . . . may I know what they are so I can be sure to handle them properly?"

The Prince of Games turned away to hide a different kind of smile, and Nespar did not like the look of it at all. He felt his skin crawl.

"Invitations," said the King in Yellow. "One for each of the sub-monarchs, inviting them to either visit my court or send an official of sufficient rank and authority to discuss matters of grave political importance."

"Of course, Majesty. Er . . . *which* matter is in question?"

"The Samudian Plague," answered the king. "We must determine who will stand with us if we are to go to war with Samud."

"But I . . ." began Nespar, and then stopped. "I beg your pardon, sire. I will attend to this directly."

"Do so," said the king, then turned away from him to whisper something to the Prince of Games, who laughed.

Nespar took the scrolls and hurried out.

CHAPTER ONE HUNDRED EIGHT

DREAMS OF THE DAMNED

Kagen lay awake on his bed for what seemed like days, though he doubted it was more than an hour. Time seemed to be as broken as everything else in the world.

He tried not to hear Filia and Tuke romping away. Failing that, he tried not to care, and failed there, too. His mind tortured him by conjuring vivid images of Filia naked, astride him as she had been a few months ago. His body joined the conspiracy against him and produced a large, painfully hard erection that he was as unsuccessful ignoring as the rest.

He forced his mind away from the lovers and by main effort of will brought a different face and form into the front of his thoughts. She stood there, naked and exquisite, with a headdress of horns and spikes and decorative skulls. Her body was ripe, and suddenly it was she who filled his memory with precise recollections of planes and curves, of tastes and scents, of pressures and releases.

"Maralina," he breathed. And in the next moment he toppled off the cliff of wakefulness and dropped deep into the chasm of dreams.

It was there, across the chamber, and he had not seen it because it seemed to fade into the gloom. But Kagen snatched up the torch and walked halfway toward it. He stopped, afraid to get any closer as the firelight picked out the details.

The creature hung from the wall, draped in chains that were ancient and crusted with red rust. The chains were fixed to massive rings driven deep into the rock. Its head drooped low, its wings were spread wide as if in a cruel mockery of flight, but dozens of heavy iron spikes had been driven through them. The thing's body was crisscrossed with a thousand cuts. Ten thousand. Flesh and scales had been excised from its body, leaving old scars and new bleeding wounds. The thing was massive, filling that whole side of the chamber.

As the fire's glow flickered and danced on the floor and on its massive body, the thing raised its grotesque head and opened huge eyes that were cat green but shot through with lines of sickly red. The huge chest moved so slowly, as if each single breath was a painful labor that taxed it to the limits of what strength and life remained.

"Gods of the . . ." began Kagen, but his words trailed away, leaving his mouth as dry as dust. He felt tears burning in the corners of his eyes, but as they broke and fell, they froze to ice on his cheeks.

The thing looked at him, and in its eyes he saw wisdom as old as the world. And pain. So much pain. An agony so profound that it went miles deeper than the torture inflicted upon it. It was a pain filled with self-awareness. An existential torment so profound that Kagen felt himself crumpling down to his knees.

"I'm sorry," he said. Knowing that he meant it, though not knowing why he said it. Or why he meant it. "I'm so sorry."

The version of him that slept in the drying mud, the damned version of him, spoke the same words. Damned now as he was then. And for the same reason.

On the wall, cruelly pinned, the dragon wept tears of fire.

Another snatch of conversation seemed to fill the air, but it was only sound, as if he listened at a closed door.

"Fabeldyr is the last of her kind because your kind decided that they were evil, and over many thousands of years they hunted those magnificent beings to the point of extinction," said Maralina, her voice filled with passion and heartbreak. "She is all that's left. There are no male dragons left on this world, on this side of the veil. Fabeldyr is all there is and will ever be of her race here on earth, and the whole world should weep at that."

"Why?" demanded Kagen. "I don't understand. Dragons were monsters."

"Dragons are truth," snapped Maralina. "Dragons are magic. Without them the world would have been overrun with darkness of every kind. They should have been protected rather than exterminated."

After that the voices faded out and Kagen sank lower into a dreamless sleep that was a mercy. But it did not last, and soon clawed fingers reached for him—for his dreaming self—and tore at him.

CHAPTER ONE HUNDRED NINE

"Is there news from the west?" asked Vulpion the Gray, king of Zehria.

The gaunt, stooped figure of Mantis, his spymaster, closed the secret door and scuttled over to the chair across from her master. Her face was creased with worry.

"There is, sire," said Mantis, "and I fear it is not good."

Vulpion sighed. "Tell me anyway."

Mantis sat, leaning forward, fingers woven together in her lap. "Samud has attacked Hakkia."

"Attacked?" cried the king. "Gods of the Harvest, how? When and where? With what force of arms?"

"It is not an open attack, sire," said the spy, and she explained about the small towns in Hakkia that had been utterly destroyed. "They are calling it the Red Curse," she said. "Though some have named it the Samudian Plague."

"Samudian arrows?"

"Everywhere. And there were no survivors that I know of. A complete slaughter."

"Have the Hakkians responded?" asked Vulpion.

"Not as yet, sire," said the spy. "Given the delicacy of current affairs, and the failed coronation, it is possible, even likely, the Witch-king is waiting for more information. His spies are everywhere, so clearly he is aware of this, but it's not at all clear if this is an official act of war, the actions of a rogue group of soldiers—always a danger now—or something else. And I daresay he is watching what the other nations do. Word of this will undoubtedly get out, and this kind of news will spread like wildfire, and that may force other rulers to either make a move, declare neutrality, or form other alliances."

"Oh, by Father Ar's golden plow, yes," growled Vulpion. He chewed on that for a moment, then he asked, "Damn, Mantis, do you think this is tied in some way to the massacre of Hakkian soldiers by that rebel group?"

"The Sons of the Poison Rose?" asked Mantis. She considered it. "Possibly. But I tend to doubt it. That group is hitting military targets. The Samudians are attacking civilians."

"Who do you think these Sons are? The Poison Rose's actual sons? Is this Kagen and his brothers?"

"If it's Kagen, sire, then he is pulling strings from afar. I have reliable intelligence that he fled north after the failed assassination. He was spotted in Vahlycor with that Therian giant and the red-haired woman. I have people trying to find them, and the most recent theory is that they've gone into hiding in Nelfydia."

"Why there?"

Mantis shrugged. "A couple of possibilities. It's already winter up there and anyone with wits can find a place to hole up and let distances and bad weather provide some breathing room. Time to regroup and plan."

"That's smart. What's the other possibility?"

"Lady Ghuraka," said Mantis. "She has a camp up there, and if he can enlist her aid in this fight, he'll have an army."

"One *hell* of an army," agreed Vulpion, but then he shook his head. "I've never met her. Have you?"

"Oh, yes," said Mantis. "She is brutal, domineering, narcissistic, violent, and fickle. But she's also smarter than she looks—something she plays on—and apolitical. Self-interest matters far more to her than crowns. It's always been hard to place a winning bet on which way she'll go in any situation."

"She's Silver Empire, though," protested the king. "Surely she'll offer aid and comfort at the very least. Or, if she's afraid of the political repercussions, she'd turn them away and not report them."

"I'm not at all certain that her loyalty was ever to the empire, sire. Ghuraka is loyal to herself first and her people second. Beyond that . . ." She spread her hands. "But, sire, to return to your question. At this moment I don't know who is behind the Sons of the Poison Rose. Because of the nature of the attacks, I think the strongest possibility is a group of knights belonging to houses the Hakkians hit hardest, using the Poison Rose as their rallying cry. She was, after all, the second-most famous person in the Silver Empire. Empress Gessalyn was naturally more well known, but she stood for peace. The Poison Rose was a fighter and leader, and that makes for a different kind of martyr. Imagine if the Hakkians had managed to murder Lady Bellapher? The sack of Hakkia would have been fifty times worse."

"Hm. Dig into that, Mantis. Find out."

"Of course, Majesty."

"Getting back to al-Huk's game," said Vulpion. "I'm troubled by those attacks."

The spymaster nodded. "Beyond the obvious, sire, what troubles you most?"

"Why was this done so openly? Even without leaving witnesses, clearly any bloody fool knows what a Samudian arrow looks like." He shook his head. "Al-Huk is subtle bastard and this is clumsy."

"To be fair, sire, a lot of people are considerably off their game right now," Mantis said.

They were old enough friends for the conversational doors to stand open on topics other court officials would not dare to walk through. "When you returned from the capital, you were visibly shaken by what happened. By what you saw."

"Gods fighting in the air," said Vulpion softly, then he shivered.

"And not *our* gods," said Mantis. "Hastur and Cthulhu fought, but Father Ar and Mother Sah did not appear. That has been somewhat marginalized in public conversation, because of the assassination attempt and the death of the king of Theria. But as days pass, the fact of that absence is going to seep into everyone's mind like a spiritual poison."

"I feel it myself," admitted the king. "I would never say it publicly, but it's shaken me to my core. All of the scriptures, the prophecies, the teachings, and the gods of the Garden did not, as promised, appear in our hour of greatest need. It calls faith itself into question."

"And there, sire, is where we might have an insight into why al-Huk would strike back with such ferocity. He has always been devout. Openly, but—as my spies tell me—privately as well. And he could have taken action and put an arrow in the heart of the Witch-king. He *should* have done this."

"We should all have done something," said the king.

"May I be frank, sire?"

"In here? Between us? Always, Mantis."

"Then . . . yes. Had the submonarchs allied and killed the Witch-king, much would be different. Whether a new Silver Empire rose, or something like it, or even a return to neighboring states with no overall central government—any of those options would be better than uncertainty and the potential for tyranny."

The king rose and began pacing, hands gripped tightly behind his back.

"There is no direct word from King al-Huk, sire," said Mantis, who stood also but remained by her chair. "I've sent messages to my agents in his palace and expect to hear something. But so far all he is openly doing is building up his military in the same way we all are."

The king stopped and stood looking at a map of the world hung on the wall. It was very old, hand-painted, and illuminated by a famous monk of the garden there in Zehria.

"This has given me much to think on, Mantis," he said. "I used to believe that I was astute and objective enough to guess at the probable future even years out. Now I have no idea what will happen tomorrow, let alone next year. The world feels broken. It feels like we are all in different rooms of a burning house and all the doors are nailed shut."

He turned.

"We have no choice but to redouble our efforts to arm for war. The Bulconians are massing at our northern border and Hakkia is to the south. We are caught between the hammer and the anvil."

"What will you do?" asked the spymaster.

But the king turned and stood staring at the map and did not answer.

CHAPTER ONE HUNDRED TEN

Kagen rose early, fleeing a troubling dream in which strange creatures hunted him in the recent blizzard. As the dream unfolded, those monsters slaughtered each of the horses in turn until only Kagen, astride a bleeding and terrified Jinx, raced through the blinding snow. Howls filled the air, and within those cries Kagen thought he heard a guttural voice, as if the things that pursued him were speaking to one another, calling out to set a trap. He rode on, though, not knowing in which direction the trap was. As he and Jinx veered off the main road to follow a game path that promised some measure of safety, something huge and white leapt from a high pine limb. Kagen had a brief image of a gaping mouth filled with yellow fangs and long claws that took Jinx across the neck. Blood exploded in a hot spray and Kagen pitched forward and down—

And woke on the floor beside his bed, his body soaked with sweat, his heart beating like a kettle drum. The drab and familiar walls of the Bear's Mark stood around him. Kagen lay there for several minutes, still half asleep, unsure whether what had happened was in a dream or a memory. Or was it a premonition?

Shaken to his core, he rose and dressed without bothering to sponge away the fear sweat. He needed sunlight and the sound of people.

Magic has returned to the world.

That phrase echoed in his head. Everyone seemed to have said that in one way or another, and the weight of it was becoming oppressive. Kagen did not want to live in a world where monsters and demons, ghosts and sorcerers roamed free. It tore at the fastenings of the world as he had always known it. He felt cheated by this sudden, drastic, awful, and potentially permanent alteration in the fabric of reality. This was not *his* world, and although he would never say as much to Filia or Tuke, he was terrified. His friends were more worldly and already mocked him for being city-bred. Kagen wondered what made them nimble enough of mind to pivot toward acceptance?

He wondered how his mother would have reacted? But as far he knew, her first encounter with sorcery was the razor-knight that killed her.

He suddenly went very still. Was he right about that? Everything had happened so fast that terrible night, and now, in the silence of his room, Kagen fought to remember *exactly* how things had unfolded. He closed his eyes and drifted back to the Night of the Ravens.

He'd awakened drunk and naked in a whore's bed. The city of Argentium was already swarming with Ravens, Hakkian regulars, and mercenaries. They used cannisters of banefire—an ancient alchemical mixture that exploded with enough ferocity to destroy stone walls. Kagen killed several Hakkians, at first to acquire clothing and weapons, and then he stole into the palace through secret ways that he and his brothers long ago discovered. When he reached the empress's suite of rooms, he found his brother Hugh and his father, both dead, and his mother in a fierce battle with the invaders. She was winning that fight, though the war itself was already lost from one end of the empire to the other.

Then a monster appeared. Even Kagen, who had been frightened by ghost stories spun by his older brothers, knew what a razor-knight looked like. There were paintings of Lady Bellapher fighting one during the suppression of the Hakkian Witch-kings three centuries before. He pieced together every moment of what happened.

"*Kagen—ware!*" his mother had cried, seeing the threat before he did.

But the monster hit Kagen from behind. The blow hurled him across the chamber, and as he lay there, dazed and hurt, he saw the razor-knight in the flesh. It was big, gigantic—far taller and more powerfully built than even the towering Hugh. It loomed over him, dressed all in black, with a helmet that hid the face beneath, so that only a pair of red eyes glared out. Around its shoulders and covering both arms was a kind of cloak made from long blades of painted steel, and each of those blades was sewn into a canvas of the same stygian hue. When the thing raised its arms, it looked like the wings of some titanic bird. And all around the creature—Kagen could not think of it as a man—was a strange swirl of shimmering air, as if the thing had just stepped from the heart of hell's furnace.

The creature moved with incredible speed and the confidence

of a killer who knows that nothing and no one can stop it. For all of the steel in its black wings, the thing moved in utter silence, as if the darkness of midnight had itself been given form.

There were no stories about anyone besting a razor-knight in combat, and Kagen realized that the stories of Lady Bellapher did not actually explain how she vanquished the one she fought. If she even had. Legends tended to grow in the telling.

When his mother stared up at the creature, Kagen saw the light of despair ignite in her pale eyes. She was exhausted, badly wounded, heartsick, and too old for a sustained battle. The poison on her blades was surely spent now, wiped off in increments on each Raven she'd killed. He saw in her eyes the certainty that she could not survive this fight.

"Kagen," cried the Poison Rose, *"Gods of the Garden . . . run! You cannot defeat this thing. No one can. Run, for the love of all. Find the Seedlings. Save them, I beg you."*

Then the massive wings of black steel seemed to enfold the Poison Rose and he heard her scream as it butchered her.

Kagen had snatched up a cannister of banefire and hurled it at the monster. The resulting explosion tore the razor-knight apart—along with Kagen's mother and the other Hakkians . . .

Kagen thought about his mother's words. She had not only known what the creature was but she knew for sure that it could not be defeated by ordinary force of arms. What would have happened, he wondered, if her daggers had still been oiled with poison? Would she have stood a chance?

He glanced over to the chair where his belt was slung, the daggers resting in their leather sheaths. The poison he had was *eitr*, the god-killer. Would that stop a razor-knight? Could he even get past that cloak of knives to land a telling blow?

Outside the window, the morning birds began their songs. He rose and dressed, and as he did so, Kagen went through the habitual routine of checking the other knives sewn into pockets here and there. His hands paused, though, when he touched the throwing spikes secreted in hidden pockets of his leather jerkin. He was as good with one of those as with his daggers. On impulse, he spun, drew, and threw a spike. It shot across the room and *thunk*ed into the exact center of the windowsill and thrummed softly.

He felt a coldness creep through him. Not of fear, but of a certain kind of calmness.

There was a flicker of regret, too. Had he seasoned those spikes, the fight with Herepath might have ended much differently.

"Next time, brother," he said. "Send all your monsters and I will send their hearts and balls back to you, pickled in oil."

He spat upon the floor and stamped on it to seal the threat.

Kagen nodded to himself, finished dressing, packed his gear, and went downstairs.

CHAPTER ONE HUNDRED ELEVEN

A reluctant dawn was breaking behind sheets of gray clouds, visible even through the grimy windows, as Kagen went down to the tavern. A handful of people were hunched over plates of eggs and sausage. Kagen leaned heavily on the bar and demanded wine.

The bemused publican smiled. "Starting early are we, sir?"

"Fuck you," growled Kagen.

"Ah, well put, sir," said the owner, and went away to fetch a bottle. He set it and a cup on the counter and moved off to polish already clean wine cups, avoiding Kagen's eyes.

But the wine tasted sour in his mouth. Kagen pushed the cup away and tossed coins on the bar top, overpaying because he was embarrassed. He slunk outside and went to check on his horses. Jinx, happy to see him, blew down his long nose and bobbed his head. Kagen leaned his forehead against the animal's. If the stable girl thought this was at all strange, she was wise enough not to say so.

A loud voice from outside roused Kagen from his silent communion with Jinx, and he went to the stable door to see what was happening. A fat man in the green and white livery of a town crier stood on the steps of the small building that served as the official office for the little hamlet. He held up a sheet of parchment and read from it in a loud, nasal, and officious voice.

The content of that message chilled Kagen to the bone.

The document was from the court of the Witch-king, monarch of Hakkia and de facto ruler of the Silver Empire, and it described Kagen, Tuke, and Filia, though it gave only Kagen's actual name. The descriptions were very good, too. Alarmingly so. And it included the amounts payable for the capture and delivery of each to Hakkian authorities. The reward offered was huge. Absurdly so. A cartful of gold, an estate, a title, and more.

"Gods of the Pit," breathed Kagen.

The crier read the announcement twice and then hammered it to the front door of the office with silver nails. Several people hurried over to study the notice, and Kagen thought at least one of them glanced over his shoulder at the tavern.

Kagen shrank back into the shadows of the stable. He licked his lips and hastily sorted through his options. That did not take long, because there was really only one viable course of action.

He whirled. "Girl . . . saddle the horses."

"Which ones, master?"

"All of them, and be quick. There's two silver dimes if it's done in ten minutes. Say nothing about this and there's two more on top of that."

The girl's eyes snapped wide. Four silver dimes was more than she could earn in two full years. Kagen just hoped the girl had not heard the announcement, or if she had, that she was not smart enough to make the connection between the fugitives and paying customers.

But the girl paused, one hand on Jinx's flanks.

"I won't tell," she said. "If that's what you're worried about."

Kagen turned to look at her but said nothing.

"I know who you are," she said.

It was the first time he'd really looked into the girl's eyes, and he realized straightaway that this was no muddle-headed child. There was wisdom and clarity there that was beyond both her years and her station.

When Kagen remained silent, the girl said, "Most of the people who stay here are travelers. Rough trade, because better people can afford a nicer inn in a better town. My pa dresses me as a boy because he knows what strangers would try to do to me. I know, too, because even when I was a wee thing and didn't yet have breasts to see, travelers would try things. I had some close calls." And the ghosts in her eyes told Kagen that they were more than close calls. "Now I bind my breasts and dirty my face and act like a boy."

"Why are you telling me this now?"

"I already told you I was a girl," she said.

"Yes, and that was a dangerous and stupid risk."

"No," she replied, "I *know* people. My ma was like that, too. And my grandma. That's how my ma knew my pa was a good man. She looked at him and she knew."

Kagen said nothing, but the image of the witch Selvath came into his mind. She had the same kind of gift. More magic, but not the wicked kind.

"You could have done whatever you wanted with me," she said. "You could have raped me and what could my pa do? You and your friends are hard cases. Warriors. Unbladed, I think. What could someone who runs a shitty little inn like this do to you? Even if he called the beadle, he's an old fool who couldn't find his ass with both hands and a set of directions." She shook her head. "No, you could do anything you wanted."

"I'm not a good man, girl," he said. "I'm a failure, an outcast, and my own gods have abandoned me. I would have nothing to lose if I—"

She shook her head and that stopped the flow of his words. "I think I knew who you were before that fat fool read the descriptions. Even with the beard and the longer hair, I knew."

"How?"

"I told you. I *know* things about people."

"Gods below, girl, but you take a lot of risks."

She laughed. "I'm a girl in *this* world, master Kagen. I don't mean offense, but what does a *man* really know about risks?"

He sighed and nodded.

She pointed to the door. "Right now, everyone's reading that notice. That disguise you have—and it's not really that good, is it?—isn't going to hold up. An Argonian man with daggers, a really tall Therian, and a short, red-haired woman riding together. You could wear hoods and dress as puppeteers and everyone would know who you are." She stroked Jinx once more. "If you and your friends ride out in broad daylight, someone would follow and send word to the Hakkians. That reward? Gods of the Harvest, it would make everyone in this town rich. There are people here in town that would kill their own brothers for a tenth as much."

"But not you?"

"No," she said. "Not me."

"Why? Because I didn't try to rape you?"

She looked at him as if he was dim-witted. "Your mother was Lady Marissa," she said. "You are the son of the Poison Rose. There's no one in the entire empire who doesn't know her. She should be a saint. Every girl wanted to be her. And you carry her knives. You're trying to stop the Hakkians."

"I—" he began, but she cut him off.

"Please, let me finish. We have a garden half a day's ride from here. Do you know what they did to the nuns? They brought them

420 ✦ JONATHAN MABERRY

into town, right into the square. They tied them over a barrel and raped them. Every Hakkian soldier. They even raped them after the nuns were dead." Tears fell from her eyes and carved paths through the grime on her cheeks. "They made all of us watch."

"Gods below," breathed Kagen.

"And you ask me why I wouldn't turn you in for a reward? Son of the Poison Rose? I offer help in *her* name. And because you are her son."

She was a child, but her words were not childish. Her understanding was not. Kagen, strong and dangerous, felt weak in her presence.

"I . . . I'm so sorry, girl."

The girl shook her head. "It's how it always is. Fathers tell their sons about fishing and fighting and becoming men. Do you know what mothers tell their daughters? They tell us how not to get raped. They tell us how to avoid being seen as women, to hide our sex, to not provoke men. Even in an empire ruled by a woman, and I expect it's the same everywhere."

The girl walked over to the door and peered out. He came and stood next to her, both of them in the shadows beyond the spill of daylight.

"You have to get out of here," she said. "Right now. Go get your friends. I'll saddle as many horses as I can, but whatever I have done by the time you get back will have to be enough. Then I need you to beat me up and tie me to a post."

"The fuck I will," he cried.

"Would you rather they tortured me to find out where you went? And when you left?"

Before Kagen could construct a proper response, she turned away and began saddling Jinx.

Kagen ran out the back door and raced up the exterior steps to the second floor. Nightbirds squawked and scattered, scolding him with creaky voices.

"Oh, bugger off," he snarled.

Once inside he checked that the hall was empty and then hurried to the suite at the end of the hall. He tapped on the door, then entered without waiting for a reply.

Filia and Tuke lay naked among the furs on the narrow bed. They peered groggily at him.

"By the rocky balls of—" began Tuke, but Kagen cut him off.

"Get dressed. We're leaving right now."

"Why?" demanded Filia, springing out of bed, more alert than her lover, though her eyes were red-rimmed and her coloring sickly from too much drink the night before. "What's wrong?"

He told them.

They had a thousand questions but asked none of them. Instead, they dressed with the kind of haste acquired by soldiers, mercenaries, and fugitives. Kagen told them about the town crier, the notice, the attention it attracted, and about the girl in the stable. Filia paused in her packing to study Kagen's face. Something passed between them—a conversation on some level beyond words. She nodded and he replied in kind. Tuke noticed none of it.

Like thieves they crept down the exterior steps and went into the stable to find that the stable girl had indeed gotten the horses ready.

"If you go out the back," said the girl, "you can lead the horses behind the buildings and go into the southern woods. There's a line of spruces and a trail at the end of it. Go that way and mount once you're inside. Go about a mile and you'll come to a crossroads with a stone well. Roads lead off in all directions. Don't tell me which way you'll take."

Tuke grunted. "You're a smart one, aren't you?"

Kagen produced a small bag of coins. "Hide this," he said. "If things get bad here, use this to get away."

"My family is here."

Filia, who was clearly hungover, nevertheless pushed past Kagen and gave the girl a second pouch. "Take your family. And listen to me and *hear* me. If you need to run, try to get down to Vahlycor. There's a town about forty miles over the border. Rosehill. In that town is a pewtersmith's shop. It has a sign of a tankard with eagle wings above the door. Go inside and when you're alone with the smith, tell him that Filia sent you. Tell him I said that you're there to buy fittings for a coffin. He'll take care of you."

The girl began to ask about that, but then nodded.

"Thank you," she said.

"No," said Kagen, "thank you. There's blood on the ground between us."

The girl surprised them by giving him a nasty grin. "You tried to kill the Witch-king. You and your friends. Do us all a favor and try harder next time."

Tuke laughed. "Oh, I like this one. What's your name?"

The girl hesitated, then said, "Jeal."

"May the gods keep and protect you, Jeal," he said. Filia hugged her. Kagen, feeling oafish and awkward, gave her a nod and a grunt.

The girl hid the bags of coins under a loose floorboard and then dragged a bale of hay over it.

"Now," she said, "you better hit me and tie me up."

Kagen balked, though. Tuke raised his hands, turned away, and pretended he was somewhere else. Filia gave them both a withering glare, took the girl by the shoulders, tilted the child's head to a certain angle, and then punched her fast and hard. The girl's head rocked back and her eyes rolled up. Filia darted forward and caught her as she fell.

Cursing under his breath, Kagen helped tie, blindfold, and gag the girl. They left her sprawled on her side in the middle of the floor, where anyone entering the stable would spot her.

"The world is mad," said Kagen.

"You're just now learning that, city boy?" said Filia. Then she stopped, swayed for a moment, and suddenly ran to a corner and vomited. A lot. Her sickly color now looked like week-old milk left in a hot sun. "Gods of the Harvest, just take me now," she mumbled, then hunched over as another wave of nausea hit her. Tuke tried to comfort her, but Filia whirled on him with her knife half drawn. He backed away quickly.

"Weren't you the one who made fun of me when I was seasick?" asked Kagen unkindly.

"Gods of the fucking Harvest," she croaked, "I hate you."

Kagen, feeling vindicated, turned to do a last-minute check on the horses, while Filia forced herself to stand up straight. She washed her face with handfuls of water from a trough, rinsed her mouth out, spat, and gave a weak nod.

"Let's go," she said.

Kagen glanced at the unconscious girl and silently offered a prayer for her to Mother Sah. The gods may hate him, but that girl was both an innocent and a courageous soul. He wished her well.

Then the companions led the horses quickly but quietly out the back and into the woods. Once there, Tuke drew one of his machetes and cut a couple of lush pine branches. He backtracked and used the boughs to wipe out their tracks in the morning's light snowfall. Then he tied the boughs to the tails of three of the horses and positioned them at the back of the string. Kagen watched, impressed.

"It won't fool a good hunter," said Tuke as he climbed back into the saddle, "but it might slow things down."

"Enough," said Filia. "Let's ride."

And ride they did.

Ghuraka's Unbladed camp was over two full days' journey into the snowy northern wastes. The horses Kagen took from the dead blood priests of Tsathoggua were in a string behind them. Gifts for the unofficial queen of mercenaries, they decided.

Filia's dog, Horse, trotted beside Dog, the horse.

The riders were bundled into furs against a day that started cold and grew colder still as morning became afternoon. A wind came out of the northeast and bit them with sharp teeth. No matter how many scarves and blankets they wrapped around themselves, the cold found them.

Tuke studied the sky. "I don't much like the look of those clouds. It's going to snow again."

"In the frozen north?" said Kagen, fighting an unending series of shivers. "You shock me. Who ever heard of such a thing?"

"You can kiss my horse's balls, city boy," said the Therian.

"You're riding a gelding, dumbass."

"You're missing my point."

"I will knife you both if you don't *shut up*," said Filia. Her hangover had gotten worse, thanks to the cold wind and the jogging of the horse. The two men lapsed into silence, guilty as a pair of schoolboys caught in a prank.

It was a very long day.

When they camped for the evening, the spot they picked was a clearing sheltered by huge broken rocks that blocked the wind well enough that the ground was dry and clear of snow. There were some hardy old trees and many shrubs, and that allowed them to secure plenty of wood for a big fire. The rocks hid much of the glow from their blaze.

Tuke did the cooking because, of the three, he was by far the best at it. Kagen was a cook with no imagination, and he'd already used his store of spices, and everything Filia cooked taste like roasted lizard skin.

They ate in thoughtful silence, watching as dark clouds gradually devoured the whole of the sky, blotting out the last sunlight and gobbling the stars. Kagen stacked firewood near each of them so that whoever woke at any point could keep the blaze and its heat constant. Then they wrapped themselves in furs and drifted off.

While he slept, Kagen dreamed. He groaned in his sleep, but nobody heard him.

CHAPTER ONE HUNDRED FOURTEEN

DREAMS OF THE DAMNED

Once more Kagen walked through corridors of ice.

"Why here?" he asked aloud, and with that same internal awareness that marked these kinds of dreams, he felt the mouth of his sleeping self move to form those words. In the dream he heard them echo through the endless corridors. "What is it about this place that keeps pulling me back? Why these dreams?"

Silence was the only reply.

He had no idea where he was or where he was going. Not specifically. Instead, he felt drawn by some impulse or force, and he did not try to fight it, even though with every step fear grew in his heart. Not merely of this strange place, but of the why of the place. He knew, from instinct and conversations with Herepath, that there were uncountable secrets trapped within these mountains of ice. Herepath had come here with his team to try to understand them, study them, unlock them.

The adult Kagen who was a passenger in the body of his teenage self knew full well that Herepath had succeeded. Somewhere in this bitter and lonely place his brother had discovered dark knowledge which had— somehow—changed his very nature. Where Herepath had always been aloof and secretive in the way scholars often are, he had changed into a man capable of committing unspeakable atrocities. He had conquered the Silver Empire, perhaps destroying any chance of it ever returning. He had ordered his troops to slaughter the Silver Empress and her children. Herepath had let his men butcher his own parents and one of his brothers. He sent his Ravens to every garden in the empire, encouraging them to rape the nuns and monks and to crucify the Gardeners. There seemed to be no end to his bloodlust and villainy.

Kagen was sure that Herepath's nature had been different when he was younger, when they were still brothers, their hands unstained by innocent blood. So what was it that changed his brother? Was it something always latent within him that was cultivated here? Was it some infection of the soul to which he was exposed in the heart of the glacier? Was he under some evil spell?

Kagen did not know. However, he felt certain the answer was here. Somewhere. Every corridor down which he ran seemed the same as the last, and it gave him the dizzying feeling that it was the same corridor, and that he was doomed to run through it throughout eternity.

"Kagen . . ."

A voice called out and he skidded to a stop, turning to look behind. That way was dim and full of shadows. He strained for echoes to provide a clue, but the ice went silent.

Kagen stood panting, listening. Waiting.

"Please," he breathed.

There was only silence.

However, that silence was not empty. He was sure of it.

It felt like the pause when someone is watching. His brothers Jheklan and Faulker played games like that sometimes when they ventured deep into the bowels of the palace. Ghost voices in a game of hide-and-seek.

But that had been playful. This did not feel at all that way.

"Kagen," murmured the voice again. So softly it could barely be heard.

Was it sneaky or spiteful? Or was it merely weak?

Kagen's hand sought the handles of his poisoned daggers, but their reality did nothing to dispel his unease.

"Who are you?" cried Kagen. "Where are you?"

The ice fell silent for a long time.

So long that he convinced himself that he had imagined it. He took a breath and exhaled a plume of steam into the cold air. Eventually his hands fell away from the knife handles and he began walking again.

"Kagen!"

This time the voice was sharper, clearer.

And . . . female?

He heard the echoes clearly now. The voice was undoubtedly that of a woman, and it was eerily familiar.

Not his mother's, nor any of his sisters. Not Filia's voice, either.

This voice was rich and deep, a contralto with rough edges. There was a sense of age about it, though not of infirmity.

"Where are you?" he called again. "Tell me."

"Please find me, Kagen Vale," said the voice, and it seemed to be coming from everywhere, the echoes moving toward and away from him, floating like unseen spirits along each corridor.

"Tell me how to find you," yelled Kagen.

"I am lost, Kagen," said the voice, and now he could hear a mix of emotions in that voice. Fear and pain; despair and a profound loneliness. "I am so lost."

"Who are you?" But as soon as he asked that question, a thought occurred to him. "Are you Maralina?"

"I am lost in the cold darkness, Kagen," replied the voice, without answering his question. "You must find me, or all will be lost."

He began moving again, following the strongest echo in hopes that was the true source of the voice. His boots clicked loudly on the ice and he kept stopping so as not to drown out her voice.

"Maralina? Is that you, my love?"

He was in his younger self's body but that question—even the timbre—was a grown man's.

"Kagen, you must hurry," said the voice, and he knew for sure that this was not his immortal lover. It was a stranger's voice. Strange . . . and yet familiar in some way he could not adequately define. "If he is left unchecked, this world will fall. Do you understand, Kagen?"

"I do," he said, though he did not. "I'll kill Herepath. I'll stop him."

He ran down halls of blue-white ice, running through patches of light from torches set into the walls, and through shadows into which no shadow dared intrude. Kagen tore his daggers free and ran with them in his hands. Ready to fight, to kill.

"The world is breaking, Kagen. Can you hear its bones crack?"

Kagen reached the end of one very long tunnel and jerked to a stop at the entrance. It was completely dark inside and the air was weirdly warm and humid. Not at all like the dry and frigid air everywhere else. And it reeked of foulness. A rancid stink of living flesh that was nonetheless rotting. The stench of a sickness so profound that it was completely beyond his understanding.

There was no part of Kagen that wanted to step through that entrance. Fear coated him like a diseased second skin and slivers of ice stabbed down through his stomach and groin.

"Gods of the . . ." he began, but then let the rest die on his tongue.

"Kagen," called the voice again, and now it was irrefutably coming from within that darkened chamber. "Save me. Kagen, save the world . . ."

And Kagen Vale woke up.

CHAPTER ONE HUNDRED FIFTEEN

It began snowing around noon of that new day, but it was only a moderate storm. The snow was dry and powdery, and the breeze pushed it around, building drifts but not blocking the road very much. The temperature was a bit more bearable, though, and they made good time.

Filia was in a better frame of mind, her hangover miles behind. She even broke into a song, lifting her voice to fill the air with an old ballad about a young princeling and his doomed love for a princess who was under a curse. The melody was pretty and she sang it well enough. Kagen knew the tune, but in Argon the lyrics told a different tale—that of a sailor in love with a mermaid. He remarked on that, which sparked a conversation about the chameleon nature of folk songs and folk tales.

"That was a Therian song first," said Tuke, but they ignored him. He typically claimed cultural ownership of anything good or worthy and tended to claim that bad songs, bad wine, bad horses, bad stories, and bad decisions all originated in countries other than his own.

"Kagen," began Filia, "does that song remind you of Maralina?"

He sighed and nodded. "It does."

"It's not about her, I don't think," she said. "But there are a lot of songs about the doomed faerie lady who lives in that tower. Your Maralina, though under half a dozen different names."

"Are there?" he asked, interested.

"Oh, yes. In most she is a cruel seductress, a hideous monster who uses magic to make herself appear young and beautiful. She lures kings and heroes, princes and champions to her tower—or in some versions to a grotto deep in elf land—and there she drains the life from those men. They don't die, though. Not completely, anyway. They linger as pale ghosts who try in vain to warn other potential victims away."

"You're just saying all that because I told you what happened in there," complained Kagen.

"Not entirely," said Filia. "And that's not why I sang that song. But . . . the connection, the similarities . . . you have to admit that it's too close to be coincidence. I'm just glad you escaped with your whole skin."

"This is all very charming," remarked Tuke. "But do you know any happy songs? Something with wine, swordplay, and women with big tits?"

Filia ignored him and instead looked thoughtfully at Kagen. "Perhaps it isn't the blood of those champions that sustains her. Yes, she is part vampire, if what she told you is the truth—hard as that is to even imagine! But in the song, it suggests she feeds on something. Maybe it's life force or maybe it's their souls."

Kagen sighed and nodded. "And I am damned. My soul—if I even have one anymore—is tarnished. Unpalatable."

"Damned, my ass," said Tuke under his breath. "That's a lot of horseshit and you know it."

But Kagen shook his head. "I saw Father Ar and Mother Sah that night. They filled the sky no differently than Hastur and that squid god—"

"Cthulhu," supplied Filia.

"Whatever. The gods appeared to me, and they turned their backs on me."

"Or," suggested Tuke, "maybe they turned in the direction of your destiny and expected you to get up and follow them. Ever think of that?"

"That is a profoundly stupid idea," said Kagen. "And I'm not in the mood for jokes."

"Who's joking, brother," said Tuke. "I'm as serious as a kick in the balls."

"Much as it pains me to agree with him," said Filia, "he makes a good point."

Kagen just shook his head, and that was the end of conversation for the new few hours.

"Once we're done with this business," said Tuke later, as they were setting up camp once more, "perhaps it might be worth the effort to find some of your siblings, Kagen."

"Yes," said Kagen, but left it there.

While dressing a rabbit for the spit, Tuke made another attempt at conversation. "Filia and I are out here away from town a lot more than you ever were, and—"

"And I'm a city boy," snapped Kagen. "I know."

"That wasn't where I was going," said Tuke patiently. "My point is that we've had glimpses of magic even before the Witch-king made it all worse. In the city, you probably never have. What's your feeling on it?"

The question was a reasonable one and Kagen gave it real thought.

"I had a lot of time to chew on that," he admitted, stirring dried beans into boiling water. "The world is getting stranger, and I have to admit that, even with everything I've seen, it's taken me a long time to accept that magic is real and that it's awake in this world. That's not easy for me because growing up in Argentium, working in the palace, I was force-fed all of the antimagic dogma. On reflection, I can see the conflict within that. I mean, on one hand we're told that magic doesn't exist in the world, and on the other we know that the Silver Empire squashed it out. But that doesn't really hold up to scrutiny, though a thousand years of Gardeners have done their jobs by confusing it. Now I wonder how the hell anyone bought that obfuscatory cant."

"*Obfuscatory*," echoed Tuke, nodding his appreciation.

"Let's face it, even if the Silver Empire squashed magic out of existence, they did so only within the borders of the empire. There's a whole world beyond that. The islands in the Western Ocean; unfederated states like Bulconia—"

"Bah," growled Tuke. "Bulconians are so gods-damned pragmatic. No imagination at all. They wouldn't know a goblin or a vampire if one buggered their granny in front of them."

"Always so charming," said Filia under her breath.

"And all of the nations east of the Cathedral Mountains," continued Kagen. "Surely magic exists everywhere. So . . . yes, I am being a lot more open-minded about things. I think the last of my skepticism burned off after I was attacked by the gods-damned *drapes* at that mansion. Mind you, I am probably more messed up about things than even I know. My head is full of bees. But I'm trying to stop mooning around in shock. I know I haven't been quite right since the Night of the Ravens. There's more than a chance I've been out of my mind. Now, though, I want to get my feet under me and go after Herepath in some way that might actually work."

Filia studied him as she turned the spitted rabbit. "That's pretty encouraging to hear."

"Is it? I suppose so," said Kagen. Then he added, "Your friend, Mother Frey, used to be the chief investigator for the Office of Miracles. If anyone knows the truth about magic—and its implications in the world as it is now—then it's her. So, no matter what happens tomorrow at Ghuraka's camp, I want to go see her."

"You're sure?" asked Tuke.

"I am."

Kagen kept stirring the beans. They ate in silence and afterwards they took pipes from their saddlebags. Filia's was a long-handled cherrywood, while Tuke and Kagen had cheaper clay ones they'd bought in Traveler's Rest. They smoked for a while.

After a long and companionable silence, Tuke touched Kagen's arm.

"Tell me, brother," he said gently, "how will your brothers react when you tell them who the Witch-king really is?"

Kagen sighed and stared into the fire.

"It will kill them," he said.

CHAPTER ONE HUNDRED SIXTEEN

"Have you received any replies?" asked the Witch-king.

He stood in front of one of the tapestries. It showed a dragon hung from a pale blue-white wall, its great wings nailed in place, chains on its limbs, countless scars cut into the scaly hide. Although fashioned from woven threads with additional embroidery on top of it, the image nonetheless was as vivid and clear as the finest painting. Nespar had not seen this tapestry before and he was struck by the look of bottomless misery on the beast's face.

It was so striking an image that he realized he'd paused too long before responding. He cleared his throat and bobbed his head.

"We have, lord," he said. "Ghenrey, Zehria, Narek, the Waste, Behlia, and Nehemite have all responded. Each of them will be sending a highly placed official."

"I take it none of the monarchs themselves will come?"

"Alas, no, sire."

The Witch-king raised a hand, and without actually touching the surface of the tapestry, traced the outline of the dragon's face.

"Have we received any refusals?"

"No, Majesty. Though some have yet to reply."

"Nothing from Samud?"

"No, Majesty."

"Very well. You may leave me."

Nespar bowed and left.

When the chamberlain was gone, a figure stepped out of the shadowy niche, a celery stick in one hand. He bit a piece and chewed noisily as he came to stand beside the king. They looked at the dragon for a long time.

"Poor Fabeldyr," said the Prince of Games. He swallowed and took another bite.

"Poor Fabeldyr," agreed the Witch-king.

"You do know al-Huk will never set foot on Argonian soil as long as you reign. Not unless he has been brought to heel."

"Yes."

"It is notable, Majesty, that Theria, Vahlycor, Zaare, and Nelfydia have each abstained from replying. They are watching and waiting to see if you will retaliate against Samud. Actually, all of them are, even the ones sending officials. It's a waiting game for them all."

"And if I declare war on Samud?"

"Some may step out as allies," said the prince, his white teeth crunching on the celery. "Especially if they think that what Samud is doing threatens them. Ghenrey, for sure."

"Yes," said the Witch-king, drawing out that word. "Perhaps it will be best if there is no doubt that the Red Curse threatens them all."

He and the Prince of Games smiled at one another.

CHAPTER ONE HUNDRED SEVENTEEN

They were up at first light and covered the last miles under a faultless blue sky.

"We'll be at Ghuraka's camp soon," said Filia. "Things can get pretty wild there, so best to put on your fancy clothes."

By that, Filia meant armor, and they each dug into their saddle bags. Tuke pulled on a knee-length coat of thick goat hide set with many small plates of steel that would give him protection and yet allow a lot of flexibility. He strapped on buckler and greaves on which the Therian tentacles writhed, and on his head he placed a steel cap lined and ringed with seal fur.

Filia's outfit was all of leather, though there were wafers of iron sewn between the layers. She fitted on a harness that covererd her chest, and her shoulders were cupped in skull-faces made of brass, above which were two bands of ancient copper coins and between them smaller skulls, each the size of a robin's egg.

Kagen's armor was a hodgepodge of things he had scavenged from soldiers he killed. Mostly Hakkian leather over a lightweight coat of Bulconian ring mail. As he fitted it on he found that his mood was slipping from uneasy optimism to sour. He was tired of the cold, being in the saddle all day, and sleeping on the frozen and rock-hard ground.

They worked in silence, mounted, and headed off.

"Where are your feathery friends?" asked Tuke. "I haven't seen them since we left the inn."

"How the hell should I know?" growled Kagen.

That quieted conversation down for the next several miles.

They paused at the crest of a hill and looked down at a cluster of huts, tents, and yurts near a stream fed by runoff from a range of mountains rising in the north. The peaks were vast, though not as imposing as the Cathedral Mountains in the west, which divided the entire continent.

"What do we do?" asked Kagen. "Do we just ride up or send up a smoke signal?"

"Just wait," said Filia. "They know we're here."

"How? I don't—"

An arrow whipped through the air less than a yard from Kagen's nose. It struck a tree to their left. Suddenly, figures clad in white fur and cloaks seemed to materialize out of the snow. A dozen stout fighters with drawn bows or deadly spears surrounded them.

"Don't move," said Tuke under his breath. "If there are a dozen here then there are that many still in hiding."

"I'm good sitting right here," said Kagen, trying to keep his voice calm.

Filia stood up in her stirrups and touched her face, drawing a bowed line from cheek to cheek, missing her nose. Then she sat back down and placed her left palm over her heart.

Tuke repeated the same gesture.

"Should I . . . ?" asked Kagen.

"No," said Filia. "It's a greeting between Unbladed."

He nodded and said nothing else.

One of the white-clad figures stepped forward and eyed them, then he made the same gesture.

"Name yourself and your company," he said in a rough voice. He spoke the trader's tongue, which was the common tongue shared by everyone in the Silver Empire. His accent, though, was Samudian.

"I am Filia alden-Bok of Vahlycor. I am late of the Gray Company."

"Who was your saint?" demanded the man, and Kagen understood that this was part of an important ritual of greeting. Saints were what the Unbladed called the mentors who guided new members through their training and taught them the secrets of the group.

"Quill van-Gert was my saint, and he is buried in Bethryn Pass near the Bulconian border."

The man's eyes narrowed. "I have not heard that Quill is dead. How did he die?"

"A Bulconian arrow through his eye," said Filia. "We were guarding a caravan of nutmeg, ginger, and cinnamon and were set upon by border guards."

"What happened to the guards?"

"Their ghosts serve Quill in hell," said Filia.

The man nodded and looked at Tuke. "I know you, I think, but name yourself and your saint."

"I am Tuke Brakson of Theria, and yes you do know me, you dog. You were crew when my saint—my uncle Nethis—took those two pirate ships from Tull Aranzal. You are Venlys al-Toor, and *your* saint was Gemelin ur-Beil, known to all of us as Gemelin the Gremlin because he was the ugliest son of a Samudian whore that ever walked this earth. How is that horse-faced bastard?"

Venlys barked out a rough laugh. "The Gremlin lives, but he is retired. He has four wives and nine children and—gods save us— they are even uglier than he is."

"That's hard to imagine."

"You should see his wives," said Venlys, grinning. "The best looking of them would scare the balls off a snow ape. And now that I think of it, she might *be* a snow ape."

His smile faded as he turned to Kagen. "And this one? He did not make the sign."

"He's not yet part of the brotherhood," said Tuke. "Which is why we're here."

"What is his name?"

Filia said, "He is a fugitive from Argon and his name is best not given to the open wind."

Venlys walked over to Kagen and gave him a long and thorough appraisal. "He doesn't look like much."

"I wasn't aware that appearance mattered to a real fighter," said Kagen. "But if you want to tap blades . . ."

The other sentries rankled at this and edged forward, all of their arrows and spear points now directed at Kagen. Tuke closed his eyes and shook his head.

"By the vaporous balls of the god of ghosts," he muttered.

But Venlys only laughed again. "He has spirit, if nothing else."

"I would be happy to show you what else I have," said Kagen, moving his hand an inch toward a dagger hilt.

"Ghuraka will have fun with this one," Venlys said, giving Tuke a knowing look. Then he turned, gestured to the others, and began walking down the hill. The cadre of sentries fanned out to create a ring around the six horses.

As they moved forward in Venlys's wake, Filia spoke in a quiet tone to Kagen. "You do understand that there is no law out here but Ghuraka, yes? Mouthing off to one of her people is a quick way to get your throat slit."

Kagen gave her a thin smile. "Your friends need better manners."

"Save me from gods-damned city boys," she breathed, shaking her head.

They went the rest of the way in silence.

CHAPTER ONE HUNDRED EIGHTEEN

"Gods above, I hate this place."

The shorter of the two soldiers glanced at his companion.

"That's hardly news, Timon," he said. "I hate everything about Argon. I wish our legion had stayed the hell back in Hakkia."

But his friend shook his head. "No. That's not what I mean, Brix. It's this place, this palace . . . it gives me the creeps."

Brix and Timon were in the third hour of a long night's patrol through the maze of corridors, rooms, halls, and cellars of the palace in Argentium. They were ordinary soldiers, not the elite Ravens, and jobs like this were usually tedious and boring. But the former home of the Silver Empress and the heart of the entire Silver Empire seemed incapable of either tedium or boredom. It was incredibly vast, covering more than nine hundred thousand square feet—a staggering twenty-one acres, not counting the exterior grounds. It dominated a massive chunk of land on a great hill overlooking Haddon Bay. The main and upper floors had the usual grand halls and reception rooms, the elegant apartments for the imperial family and assorted nobility, and countless rooms for business, storage, staff bedrooms, kitchens, armories, and more. And below the palace, cut into the limestone hill, were level upon level of basements and dungeons.

When the 18th Hakkian Foot were detailed to come to Argentium following the defeat of the empire, they were given tours, maps, and lectures on how to navigate the palace. Not that it helped much, because even people who had once lived in that palace often got lost. Brix, who had guarded castles and forts several times in his career, had his doubts that the maps were accurate. Most such maps never were. All such buildings had secret rooms, restricted areas that never made it to public knowledge. New chambers—ranging from closets to suites of rooms—were being discovered all the time, there in the palace.

Timon stopped and studied his friend's face. "The creeps? Why? What have you seen?"

Brix glanced up and down the otherwise empty corridor. When he spoke, his voice was quieter. "It's not what I've seen, mate," he said. "It's what I've been hearing."

"Like what? Ghosts rattling chains?" Timon grinned, but Brix did not.

"Heard from some of the other guys," said Brix. He looked down at the floor and then along the hall to where the closest torch painted a patch of bright yellow, and without saying a word he moved to that spot. He stood in the firelight and waited for Timon to join him.

His friend wore an expression that was half amused smile and half confusion.

"What is it they've been telling you?" asked Timon. "You've been getting twitchy for weeks now."

Brix leaned back against the wall and rubbed his eyes. Then he glanced back the way they'd come. The long hall stretched far, and the pools of light seemed insufficient to show it with a comforting clarity.

"People have seen things," he said. "And heard things."

Timon's crooked smile was still in place. "Heard and seen what *kind* of things? Are we talking Argonian spies hidden in secret compartments? Assassins moving through hidden passages? I mean . . . if there's any kind of real threat here, Brix, we should be reporting it to the lieutenant, not gossiping about it here, or in the barracks."

"It's not that kind of thing," said Brix, though it was obvious he was reluctant to say more.

But Timon wasn't having it. "Come on, now. There's no one listening. We're all alone here. It's the middle of the damn night. You won't get in trouble for telling me. Or . . . don't you trust me?"

"I trust you, Timon," said Brix. "You know I do."

"Then what is it?"

"It's not spies or assassins or anything like that." Brix touched a small yellow icon that hung from a chain around his neck. It was the profile of a man in heavy furs holding a shepherd's crook—a representation of Hastur, the Shepherd God, patron of the monarch in yellow. Although Brix had not been in the right part of the palace to glimpse the manifestation of Hastur that dominated the sky on coronation night, he had heard every account of it. He prayed nightly to Hastur for strength and protection.

Timon shook his head. "You are pissing me off, Brix. Just fucking say it. What are the other guys afraid of?"

Brix finally summoned the courage to say the word.

"Ghosts."

Timon stared at him, his smile faltering. "Ghosts," he said. Too surprised to even inflect it as a question.

Brix nodded. "Some of the guys have been seeing things. Feeling things." He paused. "It's hard to explain."

Timon folded his arms across his chest. "Try."

"Well . . . it was Garther who saw it first."

"*It?*"

"The lady in the upper gallery," said Brix, lowering his voice even more.

"What lady?" asked Timon. "Are you talking about Lady Kestral? I admit she's a bit strange, but—"

"No," said Brix quickly. "Not her. And not any living lady. Gods above and below, I wish I hadn't said anything."

Timon held up his hands, palms out. "Okay, sorry, brother. Take a breath and tell me what Garther said. Tell me who he saw."

Brix once more checked the hallway. Then he drew a breath and said, "They see *her*. Or her ghost . . . walking along the corridors, covered in blood, clothes slashed to ribbons. And her eyes . . . Garther said they were empty, and I don't mean without expression. He said that her eyes were gone and the eye sockets were black as midnight."

Timon's smile was gone, though doubt clouded his expression.

"Her? Do you mean the old empress? Is he seeing Empress Gessalyn's ghost?"

"What? No," said Brix. "*Her*. The one who fought the razor-knight. The one whose son tried to kill His Majesty."

It was clear that he could not bring himself to say the name. Timon began to make a joke, but a chilly breeze blew past them, coming out of nowhere and making the torchlight tremble and writhe. Both men shivered and then stood staring at the torch closest to them. It took nearly half a minute for the disturbed fire to settle down.

Timon did not mention the name of the Poison Rose, either.

All along the corridor the pools of torchlight seemed smaller, fainter. Weaker. And the shadows were infinitely dark.

CHAPTER ONE HUNDRED NINETEEN

"Lord Ravensmere," said a voice, and it made the historian jump from his chair and utter a squeak exactly like that of a frightened rat. He whirled to see the Witch-king standing there. The door was still closed and there had been no sound at all.

"M-my lord," he sputtered, bowing awkwardly. "I would have been more than happy to wait upon you, had you sent word."

The king ignored that. He seemed unusually tall and imposing, and it occurred to the historian that he had never stood on even ground with the man. Jakob, though of medium height, felt dwarfed by the King in Yellow. If not in actual stature then in personal power.

"You have been away from the palace quite a lot since coronation night," said the king.

"It is my pleasure and honor to continue the work you have assigned me, Majesty."

"Is that all you have been doing?"

Jakob stiffened. "Sire?"

The Witch-king raised his hand and showed it to the historian.

"The Sons of the Poison Rose," murmured the king. "What a clever idea."

Jakob could not speak.

"All those attacks on the garrisons," continued the king. "All of those deaths. The outcry from our people. The outrage we have all felt."

Jakob said nothing.

"There are so many Vale brothers—and sisters, for that matter—out in the wind. Of course they would attack. Of *course* they would want revenge. Who would ever doubt such a thing?" The Witch-king held the sigil up so that firelight shone through it. "And so many Argonians have stepped out in support, as, I'm sure you know, dissident groups in Samud and elsewhere."

"Sire?" croaked Jakob.

"As it turned out, we are seen to be the victims, both inside our own borders and without. That is excellent political game playing."

The Witch-king stepped close and held the cloth out to Jakob, who, after great hesitation, took it. "In any other circumstance, Lord Ravensmere," he said softly, "I would have your eyes spooned out of your head and make you eat them."

Jakob's knees tried so hard to bend, to fail, to make him fall. He would never thereafter understand how he found the strength to keep upright.

"However, it is a clever plan," said the Witch-king. "In fact, you have been quite an inspiration. Were it not for your deviousness and subtlety, I might not have taken the gift of the Hollow Monks and used it to such effect as I now have."

He began to turn, then paused.

"You earn praise this one time, my friend," said the king. "However, if you do anything behind my back again, I will do more than have you blinded."

With that, the Witch-king swept out of the room. The door

seemed to open for him and close behind him, as if moved by an invisible hand. Jakob noted that, even as his knees finally failed and he collapsed onto the floor, weeping, gasping for breath, pissing himself.

CHAPTER ONE HUNDRED TWENTY

Lady Ghuraka was everything Filia and Tuke described. Short but nearly as wide as her height; muscular, battle-scarred, and ugly by even the most broadminded standard of beauty.

"What have we here?" she barked, as Venlys led the visitors through the camp and up to a clear spot outside of her tent. She wore a kind of tunic that was a patchwork of bear and goat pelts, with crisscrossed leather knife belts, wool leggings, lightweight fencing boots, and a breastplate made from finely hammered brass. She had elaborate shoulder armor fashioned of steel but made to look like skulls, each crowned with coiling vipers. Ghuraka's eyes were sky blue, her hair black but shot through with gray, and silver rings pierced her ears, nostrils, and eyebrows.

The procession stopped and the Unbladed soldiers fanned out in a half circle, their weapons still pointed at Kagen, and marginally less so at Tuke and Filia.

Filia and Tuke both made the Unbladed hand signal. Kagen merely nodded at the leader of all the mercenaries of the north.

"We meet at the crossroads," said Filia aloud. It confused Kagen for a moment, since the camp was in the middle of a field, nowhere near any roads, but then he realized that it was some kind of ritual phrase.

Ghuraka studied her for a long moment. "We touch blades at dawn or dusk."

"And watch each other's backs throughout the day and night," said Filia, completing the formal greeting.

"Filia alden-Bok," said Ghuraka, looking her up and down.

"You look like you've been through one of the hotter rings of hell. You too, Tuke Brakson."

"And yet you look as lovely as dew on spring grass," said Tuke smoothly.

That knocked a laugh from Ghuraka. "Smooth-talking Therian bastard. Don't think that'll get you into my cooze."

"A man can hope," said Tuke.

It took Kagen great effort not to roll his eyes.

Ghuraka walked over and looked up at Kagen. "I don't know you and yet I do," she said. "Kagen Vale, son of the Poison Rose; Kagen the Damned, or as some call you, Kagen the failure. Once captain of the palace guards, oath-bound to protect the Seedlings. How did that work out for you?"

"About as well as your hopes of being named the most beautiful woman in the west," said Kagen.

He heard Filia's sharp intake of breath. Somewhere behind him someone cursed, and there was the sound of blades being drawn. But Ghuraka burst out laughing.

"Gods of the Harvest," she roared, "you have a pair of balls on you, damn if you don't. Maybe I'll hang them on my wall."

Kagen layered both palms on the saddle horn and gave her a benign smile, but said nothing.

Ghuraka turned to Filia, her eyes hard and penetrating. "You come here and bring *this* man to my door. What you three idiots did that night in Argentium has caused nothing but troubles for the Unbladed. Much trouble. The Hakkians have Unbladed on the run all over the place."

"We did what we felt was right," said Filia, not flinching from the woman's harsh words. "If things had gone well, we would have killed that evil bastard and the Hakkians would be on the run from us."

"You should not have had your allies disguised as Unbladed," countered Ghuraka.

"That was not our doing," said Filia. "The Argonian nobles chose their own disguises. As for Tuke and me . . . we have every right to present ourselves as Unbladed—or, for that matter, as Unseen."

The Unseen were sons and daughters of the great houses who, because of some personal disgrace, wore concealing helmets and sought adventure among the mercenary class.

"Some of our people have died," said Ghuraka.

"And that's too fucking bad," snapped Kagen. "My mother and father were butchered before my eyes. Two of my brothers are dead. The empress and nearly all of her children are dead. Gardens from here to Sunderland have been burned and the clerics brutalized and murdered. Maybe if you stopped hiding all the way the hell up here and did something, took some action, showed some loyalty to the empire, your Unbladed would have died for a reason."

The Unbladed who surrounded them gasped. Tuke closed his eyes and winced as if he was in genuine pain. Filia sat rock still.

Kagen hooked a leg over his horse's neck and slid from the saddle. Bowstrings creaked as arrows were drawn back, but he did not care. He stood face-to-face with Ghuraka, looking down into her eyes.

"I have killed better men than you for so much less," she said.

"And I have killed better women than you in battle," said Kagen. "I ride with a woman who is worth ten of you."

"You dare?"

"Yes," said Kagen, "I dare. You have the numbers because you're all hiding up here, afraid to do what's right. If you want me dead, then tell your archers to shoot. I guarantee you that I'll die with your blood on my blade."

"Kagen," warned Tuke, but Kagen ignored his friend.

"You call me Kagen the Damned, and that's fair enough. The Harvest Gods abandoned me. You call me Kagen the failure, and I will accept that as well, for I could not save those children. Two yet live, and if I can, I will save them yet, but in truth I have failed.

Just as I failed to kill the Witch-king. But I got to the foot of his dais, I fought him there and I marked him with my dagger. It's a scar he'll wear the rest of his life, even if he is too much of a coward to show his face. Every day he will remember that *I* marked him." He gestured to his companions. "Filia alden-Bok and Tuke Brakson fought beside me and we heaped a mountain of Hakkian Ravens around us. We filled hell with their souls. Tell me, Ghuraka . . . since the empire was invaded, what have *you* done? It's a serious question. Apart from hiding up here, what have you done that allows you to be so arrogant, so condescending?"

Ghuraka's blue eyes seemed to exude fiery heat, and Kagen wondered if he had overplayed this. If he had, he would live up to his promise. Of all the Vale brothers, he was the fastest at drawing a knife—either to cut or to throw.

But Ghuraka surprised him. She did not laugh and make light of things, like someone nervous about how her followers would see her react. No, she was genuinely tougher and more confident than that. Nor did she hurl threats or try to win the argument.

Instead, Ghuraka merely smiled. "Tough words, Kagen Vale. Let's see if your steel is as sharp as your tongue."

With that, she turned away toward a large tent on the other side of the camp. Filia and Tuke dismounted and flanked Kagen.

"You are absolutely out of your gods-damned mind," whispered Tuke.

"That was stupid," said Filia.

Kagen ignored them and followed Ghuraka.

■■■■■■▶ **CHAPTER ONE HUNDRED TWENTY-ONE**

The girl screamed for as long as she could.

She was young, barely a week past her menarche, completely pure. Innocent, with all the power that comes with that. She would have been beautiful, too, even for a peasant.

Now she lay naked, with eyes that stared upward into the well of infinity. Arms and legs spread and tied to rings set into the floor. Mouth open as if she was screaming still.

The Prince of Games squatted over her. He, too, was naked, though that was not really necessary for a haruspex. He preferred it, though, because he rather liked his courtly clothes and divination of this kind was not kind to fine silks.

He held the purple-red ropes of her intestines, moving them from hand to hand, letting them fall and studying the patterns. Repeating it. Adding her heart and liver to the divinatory mix.

The answer was the same every time.

Finally he stood, blood running down his chest and stomach, over his engorged penis, sluicing down his thighs and puddling around his feet. His toenails were long and black and pointed like talons, and they left scratches on the floor. He turned to the Witch-king, who stood just outside the circle of protection. The prince's eyes flowed and swirled with colors and his lips were slack and rubbery.

"Tell me what you see," said the Witch-king.

The prince spoke—or tried to—but at first the sound that came from his throat was a weird bass roar that was impossibly loud. Not at all a human sound. More like a bull's. He paused, swallowed, and tried again, and this time his voice was human, though jittery with excitement and energy.

"East," he said.

"Whither?"

The prince raised a bloody hand and pointed.

"Vespia," he croaked. "Your victory lies that way."

The Witch-king waited.

"Your victory or your downfall," said the prince. "East. Your enemies will go that way. As I warned you, they will seek the Seven Cryptical Books of Hsan in the dead cities of Vespia."

"Hastur protect us," murmured the Witch-king.

"Mother Frey knows the location of the city of Ulthar, my lord," panted the Prince of Games. "And it may be that she knows where the temple is located. There is time, but not much. A month at most. Unless we are quick—so very quick—they will reach it first. If Mother Frey gets the Hsan books, we may be undone." He gasped and dropped to his knees, vomiting blood onto the floor. "East, my king. Your glory or your doom lies east."

CHAPTER ONE HUNDRED TWENTY-TWO

"So, how's this work?" asked Kagen.

He stood at the edge of a circle marked out on the floor by a ring of small painted stones. The space inside was about twenty feet in diameter and of hard-packed dirt that was frozen to iron hardness. Around the circumference were bales of hay, over-stuffed pillows, disused saddles, and some wooden crates, and the audience sat on these. Torches on long poles bathed the room in yellow light, and there was a single beam of sunlight falling slantwise from the smoke hole at the top of the tent.

Lady Ghuraka sat on a kind of rough throne made of bales and boxes and covered in a heavy wine-colored velvet. Four massive Unbladed flanked the throne, and a half dozen fighters were clustered nearby, heads bent in conversation with their leader. Venlys was there, too, and kept turning to give Kagen dark and ominous smiles. Scores of other Unbladed filled the tent.

Filia and Tuke stood with Kagen on the far side of the ring, speaking to him in low tones.

"Are we fighting with live blades?" asked Kagen.

"Yes," said Tuke.

"I mean sharpened ones . . . or the dulled blades they use in tournaments?"

"This isn't the city," said Filia. "And this isn't a sparring match."

Kagen nodded and fluttered his fingers on his dagger hilts. "I figured. There's no poison on my blades today."

"Good," said Tuke. "They'd take that as cheating . . . even for the son of the Poison Rose."

"Ghuraka will pick a champion," Filia said. "It'll be someone she knows can do you some damage."

"How much damage are we talking?"

"Remember that row of mounds we passed a mile out?" asked Tuke. "Those are graves."

Kagen gave a philosophic shrug. "Do we deliberately fight to the kill?"

"No," said Filia. "You fight until someone is too badly injured to continue or until Ghuraka calls a halt. Normally she'd not let anyone get too seriously damaged, because then one or even both of the players are out of commission, and that's not useful."

"But you did a damn good job of pissing her off, my friend," said Tuke. "So if you're losing, she might let her man keep going until you either yield—"

"Not a chance," said Kagen.

"Or are dead," finished Tuke.

"I'm good with that," Kagen said. "Sounds like fun."

Filia shifted around to look him dead in the eyes. "This is no joke," she said.

He gave her a small, hard smile. "Who's joking?"

Before she could say anything else, a squat little man with long, intricate braids and a walrus mustache stepped out into the center of the ring. He had scars of all kinds and was missing most of his left arm and a chunk of his nose.

"He's charming," murmured Kagen. "Who's he?"

"That's Badger," said Tuke. "Ghuraka's master of ceremonies. Official title is Master of the Ring. Been Unbladed for twenty years. Before that he was captain of a Zehrian axe battalion. Back in his day he was a bit of a legend. Once killed two water buffalo with a hatchet. A *hatchet*, mind you, not even a full axe."

"Hush," said Filia, "it's starting."

"Everyone shut the fuck up and sit the fuck down," bellowed Badger, and this resulted in a lot of laughter that melted down into expectant silence. He grinned with a few jagged teeth and a lot of good humor. Badger turned in a slow circle. "Our good friends Filia of Vahlycor and Tuke of Theria have brought us a candidate. Someone who thinks he has what it takes to be one of us, to be Unbladed."

That provoked a chorus of boos, catcalls, and ill-humored laughter. Kagen let it all slide off.

"Now," said Badger, "you lot already know who our guest is. Kagen Vale, formerly captain of the palace guards and defender of the imperial Seedlings."

More boos, rude laughter, and even some threats.

"This lad even tried to cut the throat of the Witch-king," roared Badher. "Now how about that?"

Mocking laughter this time. Someone threw a half-cooked potato, but it wasn't really intended to hit the target. The point was made, though.

"He comes all the way up here to our garden paradise," continued Badger, "and for all intents and purposes, pisses in Lady Ghuraka's teacup."

This time there were far more threats than anything.

"But her ladyship is fair, and no one knows the rules better than her," said Badger, waving them all to silence. "She's decided to let our guest prove himself with steel."

Applause.

"And to help him make his case, Lady Ghuraka has invited her friend and yours, *the mighty Branks!*"

He shouted the last few words as the crowd parted and into the ring stepped what Kagen at first took to be an arctic bear. The man was easily as tall as Tuke, but even broader across the shoulders and deeper of chest. He wore a cloak of snowy bear fur and a circlet around his head to hold back his long golden hair.

"Branks the Horsekiller," breathed Tuke. "Oh, shit."

"What?" asked Kagen.

Tuke looked at him and then back at Branks. "Oh . . . *shit*," he repeated, this time with much more emphasis.

Filia said nothing, but her face went pale beneath her tanned skin.

"Horsekiller?" echoed Kagen.

"When he was a soldier in Vahlycor," said Tuke, "he was in a battle with Bulconian raiders who came up through the wastelands and attacked from the north. You've seen those big damn horses they ride. The ones with the furry feet? Well, the leader of the raiders broke through the line and was just about to take the head of Branks's captain, but then Branks jumped up, wrapped his arms around the horse's neck, dropped with a twist, and people said the sound of that animal's neck breaking could be heard from one end of the battlefield to the other. The horse went down and killed the raider in the fall. After that, the Vahlycorians rallied and wiped the Bulconians out."

"He killed a horse with his bare hands?" asked Kagen, eyebrows raised.

"Yes, he did."

"Well . . . shit," said Kagen. Then added, "I like horses."

"Are you even fucking *listening*?" growled Tuke.

"To every single word," said Kagen.

Branks strode to the center of the circle as if he owned it and everything around him. He unclasped a heavy steel brooch and let the bearskin drop to the ground, revealing a muscular build that seemed to be constructed of bundled steel cables of the kind used to raise drawbridges in the bigger castles. His hands were massive, his wrists thick, and his forearms absurd. He moved not with the lumbering gait of a brute but with the panther-like grace of a dancer. His heels never seemed to touch the ground but were lifted to allow his weight to balance on the balls of each foot. The handle of a short sword rose above his left hip, and a pair of slender daggers were strapped one to each thigh. Like all the Unbladed, he had old and new scars, but none seemed to have been serious wounds, which meant that he was either lucky or simply that good a fighter. Kagen rather thought it was both.

Branks imitated Badger by turning in a slow circle, but he held his arms out to both sides, fingers splayed, grinning like a ghoul, nodding as the crowd erupted into thunderous and sustained applause.

"He thinks a lot of himself," said Kagen.

"And for good reason," said Filia.

Kagen watched the crowd. The loudest cheers were from the youngest men and women in the tent. Obvious hotheads who loved a good blood sport. However, some of the more experienced-looking faces wore different expressions. He saw doubt, confusion, and even some frowns that looked like disapproval.

"Not everyone seems to adore him," said Kagen.

"He has his followers," said Filia. "And there are some who can't stand him. He's arrogant, and he's entirely Ghuraka's creature."

"How good is he?" asked Kagen. "With weapons, I mean. Not with horses."

Tuke snorted. "Sadly, just about as good as he thinks he is. Strong as an ox and quick as a tiger."

"You in love with him?"

"Kiss my balls," said Tuke. "Listen, city boy, I'm warning you. Don't underestimate him. Branks is smart; he's been in more fights than you've had cooked meals. I've seen him kill men with a single blow. Not with a knife, just his fist. And he sometimes likes to close with his opponent and either systematically carve him to pieces or grab him in a hug and break arms, ribs, and then spine."

"Charming."

Filia punched Kagen's arms. "Listen, gods damn it. Ghuraka doesn't send Branks out to test people. He's a killer and she wants you dead."

Kagen nodded. "I hear you. But tell me . . . isn't that against the Unbladed rules? Outright killing? I thought that if it happens, fine, but it's not the point."

"Maybe that was the case before you insulted her," snapped Filia.

"Answer my question," said Kagen. "Is this intended to be a fight to the death?"

"No," said Filia. "Not by Unbladed law, of course not."

"But that's what she wants?"

"Branks doesn't usually audition people," said Tuke. "He's her enforcer if there's serious trouble." He leaned even closer. "The match hasn't started. There's still time to call this off and ride out of here."

Kagen looked past his friends to where Ghuraka sat enthroned. Her blue eyes bored into him and her face was a smiling mask of ice. He studied her, reading her as best he could. There was something about her attitude, right from first meeting, that raised his hackles.

"No," he said. "I think we're past that now."

With that, he walked away from them and circled around to stand in front of Branks. As he did this, the crowd noise dwindled and died away. Kagen removed his heavy sheepskin coat, without haste, and tossed it to Tuke, who caught it. He stood in a leather vest, wool trousers, and weather-worn boots. Branks had a thick jerkin and thick leather bracers on his forearms, with matching greaves around each shin. His shoes were expensive and looked new, and they had thin, flexible soles and short heels, perfect for quick footwork.

"Nice shoes," said Kagen.

Branks grinned. "You'll enjoy how they feel when I kick them up your ass, shitface."

"Shitface? Is that my name now?"

"It's what your mother called you when she shat you into this world."

Kagen gave him a big, warm, friendly smile. "Don't talk about my mother."

Branks goggled for a moment and then burst out laughing. "Did you hear that? He doesn't like it when I make fun of his mule-fucking whore of a mother. Isn't that precious. Little city boy is going to cry."

Kagen continued to smile. He turned his back on the big man and looked at Ghuraka. When he spoke, though, he pitched it loud enough for everyone to hear.

"They call me Kagen the Damned," he said. "Outcast of Argon, outcast from the Harvest faith. A fugitive with enough of a bounty on my head to make everyone in this tent rich." That sent a small murmur through the crowd. "I came with my friends. They are my sponsors here. My *saints*. They are Unbladed, and everyone here knows who they are."

He noticed that the heads that nodded belonged almost entirely to the older, more sober members of the crowd.

"I'm here to audition for membership in the Brotherhood of Steel," said Kagen. "Although I grew up in the palace in Argentium, I've known several of your brotherhood. Men and women of fierce skill, unquestioned courage, and unbreakable honor. If I did not believe in the honor that is at the core of your brotherhood, I would never have made this journey. And I tell you now that if I pass this test and win your trust, I will try to encourage as many of you as I can to join the fight against the Witch-king of Hakkia and his Ravens."

He gave that a moment. Ghuraka's blue eyes were narrow and calculating.

"Tuke Brakson brought me here because I saved his life and there is blood on the ground between us. No one in the world respects that more than the Unbladed. No matter what happens to me, I know that he will be treated fairly, with dignity, and with brotherhood."

That earned a smattering of applause.

Now Kagen spoke directly to Ghuraka. "When I came here, you insulted me. Maybe that's your way. *Your* way, I say, and not the Unbladed's. I don't care. I gave as good as I got and there is no debt between us. I ask nothing of you, Lady Ghuraka, but the chance to prove that I am worthy of carrying a personal sigil to mark me as one of you."

The ensuing silence was massive, ponderous. Kagen bowed to her. She did not respond, but her eyes flicked to Branks and she gave the tiniest of nods. Kagen turned back to the powerful Branks, and as he began to turn, he caught out of the corner of his eye a huge fist hurtling toward him.

━━━━▶ **CHAPTER ONE HUNDRED TWENTY-THREE**

The punch should have killed him.

The punch *would* have killed him, if it had landed.

But Kagen knew it was coming. It's why he turned his back on Branks in the first place. No honorable fighter would have tried a blind punch like that, and Kagen wanted to give Branks a chance to establish what kind of man he was. He knew he'd read him the right way.

As Kagen made that turn, he crouched and pivoted fast and low so that he went under the monstrous blow. Kagen drove his own fist into the man's crotch. Kagen was barely half the man's size, but he knew how to hit and where to hit. He twisted on the balls of his feet so that every ounce of his body was behind that punch, and the power coiled up from the floor. Ankles and knees, thighs and waist, and all of the hard muscle of Kagen's shoulders and right arm was funneled down into the two big knuckles of his right hand. The blow spiraled as it hit, and the angle was sharply upward.

There was a codpiece beneath Branks's trousers, but Kagen had seen that. He aimed for it, so the force of his blow turned the hard edge of the leather groin protection inward and upward.

The blow folded Branks in half. He let loose with a whistling shriek of pain and staggered backwards. Kagen followed with a leap, twisted hard in midair, and turned the jump into a savage punch across Branks's jaw. The *crack* shocked the crowd to silence. Branks toppled sideways, barely catching himself with one bracing hand while the other seemed unable to decide whether it wanted to cup his balls or try to hold his broken jaw in place.

Kagen walked forward, grabbed Branks's yellow hair, jerked his head up, and then hop-stepped as he brought his left knee around to hit the other side of that shattered jaw. Teeth, blood, and spit spattered the watchers in the front row.

Branks would have fallen, except for Kagen's grip on his hair.

"What did you say about my mother?" he growled, and punched Branks with a hard chopping blow that exploded his nose. "Tell me what you called her?"

He hit him again.

And again.

"My mother died trying to save this empire from the Witch-king." He kicked him in the ribs.

"It took a gods-damned demon-from-hell razor-knight to bring her down, and you—you pathetic, cowardly piece of shit—dare to sully her name in my presence?"

He stamped on Branks's bracing hand, splintering the bones.

"What have *you* done for this empire?"

Another kick.

"What have you done to avenge the deaths of thousands of Gardeners and nuns? Have you seen what they did to the nuns in your own country?"

He kicked Branks's balls again. And again.

The crowd was on its feet, yelling, screaming. Some of the younger ones began to rush the combatants, but Filia and Tuke stepped up and drew steel.

"No one interferes," Filia roared.

Branks was bleeding badly, coughing blood down the front of his jerkin. With a huge grunt of effort, Kagen hauled the man to his feet. He spat in his face, headbutted him, released him and—moving so quickly that gravity had no chance to pull the big man down—pivoted and stamped his heel on Branks's left knee, smashing it inward and backwards until bones tore through flesh and cloth and stood white amid the spraying blood.

Only then did Kagen release his grip and let Branks fall.

He bent over the giant, and with a movement too quick for the eyes of the audience to follow, drew his daggers and slashed back and forth, back and forth, until Branks was crisscrossed with a dozen cuts. None fatal, but all serious.

Then Kagen stepped back and turned very slowly toward Ghuraka. He pointed both bloody daggers at her.

"I came here to audition for the Unbladed," he said in voice that was far colder than the frozen ground on which he stood. "I saw you give the signal to Branks to attack me when my back was turned. Tell me, Ghuraka, is this all the honor of the Unbladed means?"

He did not wait for an answer but instead turned to the audience. They stood in shocked silence, mouths open, some with drawn weapons and others with knives half out of their sheaths.

"*Is this the honor of the Unbladed?*" he roared. "Is the Brotherhood of Steel built on cowardice, treachery, and murder?"

His words were like thunder and the tent was filled to bursting with his rage.

"I am Kagen Vale, son of the Poison Rose, and I have come here in good faith to join you. Where is the honor of the Unbladed? Tell me . . . *Where?*"

There was no answer, and he began to lower his knives, his heart sinking below the level of his rage.

But then a voice spoke out. "No!"

Kagen turned to see Badger—the oldest, the most battered, the least capable of the fighters in the room—draw a slender dagger. He walked over to Kagen and looked up at him.

"This is not the Unbladed way," growled Badger. "I live and die by the honor of the Brotherhood of Steel," he said. Then he tossed his knife onto the dirt at Kagen's feet. "There is blood on the ground between us."

The moment stretched as Kagen and Badger faced each other.

Then, astonishingly, Venlys stalked over, pulling a heavy war axe from over his shoulder. He stared into Kagen's eyes as he dropped it.

"This is not the Unbladed way," he said. "There is blood on the ground between us."

Then the older members of the audience pushed past the hot-heads and came and repeated the words and the actions. A handful at first. Then a dozen. And then scores of them. The younger Unbladed stayed where they were, looking frightened and uncertain.

As if by agreement, they all turned toward Ghuraka, who sat white-faced, hands clutching her own knife handles.

Kagen stood his ground, his chest heaving, eyes full of fire.

It seemed to take forever, but Ghuraka rose slowly from her throne of boxes and velvet and stood there, her body trembling with a mix of emotions at which Kagen could not even guess. She looked past Kagen to the ruin of Branks. Her champion, her ally— and, Kagen thought, her lover too?

She drew her knives.

"Th-there is . . . blood on the ground . . . between us," she said, tripping over it, barely able to speak loud enough to be heard.

And she let both knives fall.

CHAPTER ONE HUNDRED TWENTY-FOUR

In the shadowed halls of the palace in Argentium, a silence fell without warning but with great force.

It was as if some huge bell had been rung or the earth had trembled, though neither thing had occurred. In truth there was nothing anyone could thereafter point to or name to explain the sudden stillness.

And yet every tradesman paused in his work, every groom in the stable stopped midway through brushing their horses' coats. The blacksmiths' hammers poised midstrike; the milkmaids' hands gripped the dripping teats but ceased their rhythmic pulling. Soldiers dropped their hands to sword hilts. Diners looked up from their plates of food or froze with tankards half raised to thirsty mouths.

They all listened for some confirming sound.

There was only stillness.

In the Hall of Hakkian Heroes, Lord Nespar and two generals looked up sharply, searching for echoes of whatever had ground that moment to a halt. In her tower, Lady Kestral, withered and nearly dead, paused in her labors, blood dripping from her skeletal hands as she searched the darkness with rheumy eyes. Even the goblin shadows that cavorted around her paused in their capers.

Nothing.

The Witch-king, who knelt in supplication at his shrine to Hastur the Shepherd God, jerked his head up. His face was bare of mask or veil, and his mouth hung open, the prayer dying on his tongue.

"What . . ." he said aloud, but there was no one to answer.

Deep in the lower dungeon of the palace, the Prince of Games faltered in the process of using a beaker filled with dry salt to draw a ring around himself. The salt poured out like sand to form a pyramid at his feet. He cocked his head and listened to the crushing silence.

"No," he said. Had Nespar or Jakob, Kestral, or even the Witch-king been there to hear that single word of protest and denial, each would have been shocked to hear fear in the strange man's voice.

Deep fear.

In a high tower, Foscor and Gavran were stilled midmotion, their training swords going still in their small hands. They looked around, but even Sir Giles of Hock had seemingly turned into a statue. The children were immediately and profoundly terrified, and without thought they sought each other's free hand. Gavran and Foscor vanished in that moment and in their place were Alleyn and Desalyn. The swordmaster was too deeply entranced by whatever had happened to realize this.

The children were the only ones in that palace who smiled. They each mouthed a single word. The same word. Their lips formed it, but they dared not give it actual voice.

The word they said was *Kagen*.

But even they did not know why.

■━━━━━▶ **CHAPTER ONE HUNDRED TWENTY-FIVE**

"Gods of the watery deep," breathed Tuke in a ghastly whisper.

He and Filia huddled together by an ancient pine tree with roots that looked like arthritic fingers clutching the ground for dear life. It was the only shelter—and even then, really more of a suggestion of shelter than any real defense against the bitter wind.

A hundred yards away stood a solitary figure wrapped in a gray cloak, his face turned into the icy wind, hair riffling, body swaying only slightly with the heavier gusts. If Kagen knew he was being watched, he did not react or even turn.

Tuke turned to Filia, who stood beside him, her body tense and rigid, small muscles at the corners of her jaw bunching and flexing. "What just happened in there?" he asked quietly.

Filia turned her head very slowly and looked up into his eyes. "I think maybe you just met the *real* Kagen Vale."

"But . . . you've known him for years," protested Tuke. "Have you ever seen anything like *that* before?"

She shook her head. "This isn't the Kagen I used to know."

"What do you mean?" asked Tuke.

"If the Witch-king is really Herepath," Filia said softly, "then he must have known *this* was inside Kagen all along. This is why there was such a huge bounty on Kagen even before the coronation night. Tuke . . . I think this is the Kagen Vale that the Witch-king fears."

Tuke licked his dry lips. "Yeah, well he's not the only one."

They fell into silence and stared at the lonely, powerful, dreadful figure standing in the bitter wind.

PART FOUR
ILL MET IN ZAARE

There are times when we can see history transform into leg-end. Two people meet, by chance or design, and it is as if the invisible scribes of the universe pause, pens hovering above the sacred scrolls, and then they toss away the old page and begin again. History and the very course of the future changes in such moments. When Kagen the Damned met Mother Frey, those same celestial scribes gasped and took a breath, then with fresh vigor wrote the foreword to the next age of this world.

—HETHLYAN THE UNSPEAKING, CHIEF SCRIBE
OF THE TEMPLE OF REASON

Kagen felt eyes on him as he prepared to saddle his horse. He tried to ignore them as he brushed inside of the saddle pad, removing bits of road grit and pine needles. He gave it a final shake, placed it across Jinx's back, and pulled it to the withers. At first he thought it was Tuke and Filia, or the Unbladed, who were trying to figure him out.

Let them try, he thought as he examined the saddle, which was atop a wood rail. He made sure the girth strap was attached to the right side of the saddle. Then he flipped the right stirrup and laid the girth strap over the saddle to get them out of the way.

"Come on, boy," he said. "Let's get this on you and we can get the hell out of here."

He picked up the saddle while holding the right side straps up and approached Jinx from the left side. He had a comfortable traveler's saddle, designed for long rides. It was heavy, but Jinx was a big, strong, and young animal. Kagen placed the saddle on his back with the horn right above the withers. He began to string the thick, black tie strap through the ring on the girth strap, but then a dry rustling sound made him turn. There were no people watching him from the camp. Not at that moment. Instead, thousands of small black eyes watched him. Nightbirds lined the corral rails, stood on the tops of tent poles, clustered together in the branches of the pine trees, or merely squatted on the frozen ground.

"And you're still with me," he said.

The birds shifted and flexed their wings and kept watching him.

"It's been bad enough so far," he told them. "Going to get worse."

A few birds—the older and wiser ones—cawed softly.

Kagen looked away to the southeast.

On the way to Ghuraka's camp, Tuke and Filia told Kagen about everything they had shared with Mother Frey—and everything they had, out of respect for Kagen, withheld. As he adjusted the saddle, Kagen reviewed it all. What, before, had been hypothetical and possible irrelevant information now seemed to fit into a pattern from which possibilities now emerged. Rash plans like the one that had failed during the coronation now seemed childish to him. Or, worse, naive.

Tuke had told him that Mother Frey wanted to meet Kagen once he was done in Nelfydia. The old woman's coded messaged named three taverns in different parts of Zaare, each one closer to both the Bulconian border and the western slopes of the Cathedral Mountains. She provided dates, too.

Kagen had been indifferent to what Frey wanted; now he accepted the need to connect with her and the cabal of which she was part. Filia had long argued that Frey's allies had the things Kagen lacked to make a meaningful move against the Witchking—an intelligence network, contacts, and a hell of a lot of money.

Kagen understood her motives—she was part of the religion that the Hakkians had torn down, and no doubt she lost many friends in the purges—but as he did not know actually know her, he was uncertain about many things. The main aspect that was still dark to Kagen was why *him*. There were other soldiers out there. And there were other Vale siblings. Given that he had failed to save the Seedlings—failed on a spectacular level with Alleyn and Desalyn—and had been discarded by Father Ar and Mother Sah, why him and not some other Vale sibling? Even Tuke and Filia had to admit they did not know.

"Do you know what that old witch wants?" he asked the birds.

The old, ragged crow he'd come to regard as the leader of the strange flock opened its mouth and uttered a nearly silent cry. Kagen nodded as if that was a reply, and on some level far below his conscious awareness, maybe it was.

He went back to saddling Jinx.

Filia and Tuke came over, approaching him slowly and with evident caution. They stood and watched him tie the last straps in place.

"Where are we going?" asked Tuke.

Kagen turned to them. His eyes were unreadable.

"To see your old witch," he said.

"And after that?"

Kagen turned and gave him a look that was dark and complex and nearly unreadable.

"After that I plan to start a gods-damned war."

And that was all he would say, then or for the rest of that day.

Ten minutes later the three friends left the camp. They rode a very long way in silence. The weight of everything that had happened seemed to drag behind him. If Kagen noticed the odd looks Tuke and Filia shared, he did not comment on it.

The miles melted away behind them as they pushed on through the frozen landscape.

 CHAPTER ONE HUNDRED TWENTY-SEVEN

The Widow sat in the mouth of the cave and watched the waves tumble over the sands. Seagulls wheeled and cried in the faultless blue sky, and far out near the horizon a pod of whales blew pillars of mist into the air. Tull Yammoth was many miles to the south, and the great desert that was the island nation of Skyria was a smear of tan on the northern horizon. The island on which she sat was on no map. There was nothing of worth there except caves bored into the blighted coastline by a million years of relentless waves.

"You should have told me," the Widow said, even though she was the only living soul on that entire stretch of beach. Except for seabirds, lizards, and tortoises, she was the only thing alive on the whole nameless island.

A small driftwood fire crackled, releasing old-wood perfumes as it burned.

"I could not raise my god alone," said a soft voice. "You cannot defeat the Witch-king alone."

The Widow turned and looked into the eyes of Miri. She sat there, wrapped in white linen draped with seaweed. Her skin was nearly colorless and completely transparent. All of her was like that. The Widow could see the side of the cave wall through her.

"Then we are lost," she said.

But Miri smiled. A soft, small smile. The way she used to smile before the Hakkians came and ruined the world. The way she smiled when they woke in bed together, naked, the sheets knotted from the passions of the previous night. And yet the energy spoke of innocence and purity.

And love.

"We are not lost, my sweetheart," said the ghost.

"You're dead," snapped the Widow. "And your *god* sleeps again in the green depths. The Witch-king sits upon his throne and no one can stand against him. How are we *not* lost?"

"Because we are not alone."

"I am."

"You're not. I'm here."

The Widow snatched up a seashell and threw it at Miri. It passed through her and broke upon the wall.

"You're not even real," she cried.

Miri leaned toward her, the smile faltering but not vanishing. "It is lost if we fight separately. But, my love, we are *one*. If you accept it, allow it, open to it, what we will become is so much greater than what either of us is. But there is a great risk."

"I have already lost my home, my country, and my love," wept the Widow. "My heart is a broken thing in my chest. What else is there to lose?"

"There is everything to gain, sweet Ryssa."

"How? How can we do anything? Do I have to die, too? Did you bring me all the way to Tull Yammoth just to break my heart?"

"I brought you to my home because I love you. I will always love you, Ryssa."

"You're a monster."

"No," said Miri. "A monster sits on the throne of the west. A monster nearly as great stands in the shadow of his throne. We are not like them. We are something else, Ryssa. We are something they have never seen."

Tears broke and rolled down the Widow's face. Sobs tried to punch their way out of her chest.

"Gods of the Harvest, I miss you so much!"

"I am here, my love," said the ghost. "Take me in your arms." She rose and reached for the living girl who trembled and wept by the lonely fire.

"I cannot! You're dead. You're not real."

Miri's smile changed, becoming somehow both brighter and yet darker. "Come and find out if I am real, sweetheart," she whispered.

The gulls in the sky all cried out as one as the Widow slowly stood.

Far out to sea, halfway between the sand and the horizon, massive green and gray tentacles broke the surface of the water, waving and thrashing as in joyful celebration.

CHAPTER ONE HUNDRED TWENTY-EIGHT

"How do you even know he's still alive?" asked the taller of the two men.

They stood side by side on the edge of a narrow ravine in one of the most rural parts of Zaare, pissing into the stream below, out of sight of the road and of their companion.

"He's alive," said the shorter man, aiming his stream at a rat, which hissed when it was splashed and scurried off into the brush, chittering furiously. The short man grinned, wondering what the rat was telling him. He wished he spoke rat, because they might have some useful insults to add to his collection. His name was Hop Garkain, and he prized a good insult nearly as much as strong wine, willing women, and thick steaks given only a passing acquaintance with a cookfire.

"Yes," said his companion, "but how do you know?"

"I know."

"You see?" complained the other. "Comments like *that* are why people don't like you, Hop. It's not even a proper answer."

"It's the best I can do while pissing," said the short man.

Hop Garkain was a former huntsman from the dense forests of Behlia in the deep south. He'd left his family and their fleet of leaky shrimp boats to become what he liked to call an "adventurer." Some of those adventures were legitimate enterprises, or close enough—guarding caravans, hunting for treasure, fighting pirates on the trade routes through the Dragon Islands, and occasionally searching for gold in the rivers that snaked through the Cathedral Mountains. Some of his other adventures involved *being* a pirate in those same waters, working as a freelance thief, or breaking legs for a moneylender in Nerek.

He was nearly a foot shorter than his friend, though far more heavily built, and seemed to be made up entirely of chest, arms, and shoulders. Hop had a fierce black beard that grew high on his cheeks, a snub of a nose, and very little neck—which he was happy about, because if he was ever sent to the chopping block, the executioner would have the devil of a time getting a good, clean cut. It tickled him to think that in his last second of life he would score that small victory. His legs were short and bowed, giving him a distinctly simian appearance.

He was dressed in leather pants and a jerkin tooled with images of improbably busty mermaids and coiling sea serpents. There was skunk fur trim around his boot tops, the hem and collar of his cloak, and the base of a spiked cap. That cap was an antique Hop had looted from a tomb near the Lonely Sea, and it was covered in delicate words in an unknown language. No one knew what it meant, and Hop tended to lie whenever anyone asked about it, claiming that it was anything from prayers to one of the old gods, to blessings from the vampire witches of the Red Gate, to erotic poetry about maidens getting it on with satyrs. Sometimes he claimed to be one of the legendary dwarf warriors from the mines of Kierrod Sund, but that was a lie. He was a little too tall, and in truth there were no mines filled with dwarves, but the story enchanted many drunken women out of their knickers, and so he kept to it.

An axe hung down his back, the handle angled for a quick grab, and at his waist was a heavy-bladed, curved desert knife of a kind called a "camel killer."

His companion was Bracenghan al-Fahr, known as Brace to his few friends and as "that gods-damned bastard" by his family. He was a former Samudian knight whose run of bad luck, gambling debts, and duels with the wrong sons of the wrong nobles had been the ruin of him before his twenty-fifth birthday. His black hair was dyed blond, and like many northern Samudians, he had very blue eyes. He was handsome in an inbred noble way, with a long, curved nose that looked like it had been punched at least once from every possible direction, high cheekbones, a clear brow, but not enough chin. Brace had a pinched little mouth that was ill-suited for smiling, and he was almost, but not quite, as handsome as he thought he was.

Brace began whistling to coax his bladder to release. It did, and his stream chased the same rat that had been assaulted by Hop.

They finished their business, shook off, wiped their hands on leaves that still dripped from a rain shower an hour before, and adjusted their clothes. Brace wore a surcoat of gray over a shirt of light chain mail and leather britches, and on his chest was a discolored place where the embroidered family crest had been removed. Forcibly removed. The al-Fahrs of Samud were a very old and very proper family, and the youngest son had been exiled, cast out of the clan because of his troubles and misadventures. His share of the family fortune had been divided among his siblings and a stone had been buried in the cemetery to mark his date of "death" to his blood kin. Samudian nobility were a very fussy lot, and the brash last-born had never managed to "sow his last oats and settle down" as his mother had predicted. So his father had four retainers beat the young man bloody and then cast him adrift on the road with a skin of wine, a crust of bread, a single silver dime, and a dire threat of worse to come should he ever return. His fortunes had not improved much since.

Both of them had joined the Unbladed, though there was something about their looks that scared off the better-paying clients.

Brace indicated the top of the hill with an uptick of his chin. "You think herself is done?"

Their companion was an old woman. They had left her to use a leafy rhododendron as a privacy screen.

"No idea," said Hop, then he cupped his hands around his mouth. *"Hey! Are you done shitting?"*

Brace punched him on the arm. Hard. *"Gods of the Garden,* Hop, but you are a sorry excuse for a human being."

"Oh, why is that? Because I don't phrase things with flowery delicacy?" He snorted and spat. "As if mothers of the Garden don't take shits."

"That's hardly the point."

"Then what *is* the point? Or should I have used some kind of euphemism like 'Has the lady finished her rest' or 'Are you ready to ride on'?"

"Yes. Exactly," said Brace, keeping his voice low and jerking on Hop's sleeve to encourage the same. "Either of those would be better. Literally *anything* would have been better. And how does a barbarian like you know a word like *euphemism*?"

"How does an overbred fop like you *not* know that women take shits?" replied Hop.

"You," said Brace, "are a cretin."

"You," said Hop, "have a stick up your ass."

There was a rustle and an old woman came out of the foliage on the top of the hill. Mother Frey wore the black robes of a mourning widow, which—along with her age—rendered her virtually invisible to most people. She was not pretty, did not look rich, and kept her eyes averted until *she* wanted to observe.

"I believe we may continue our journey," said Mother Frey. If she was embarrassed by Hop's graceless question, it did not show. She wore, as always, a faint, bland whisper of a smile.

Both of the men gave her courteous bows—Brace's being more elaborate and flowery—then they hustled up the hill to help her into the saddle of her placid bay. Neither of them knew exactly how old she was, though anyone could see that Mother Frey had seen a lot of years, and many of them hard ones. Nor did they know where she was from. That she had been pretty once, possibly even beautiful, was writ clearly to see in her cheekbones, brow, and bearing, but the nuns of the Garden were celibate and lived very hard lives. There were scars on her hands and face, and the two men had privately agreed that some of them were of the kind earned in battle, not in solitary prayer. One night Brace had tried to draw a story out of her about those scars, but Mother Frey merely smiled and offered no explanation.

Once the old woman was mounted, Brace and Hop climbed onto their horses and the three of them continued their journey.

It was a humid early winter morning and the air was filled with ten thousand chittering birds. The forest was an old one and the road that wound through it was very well maintained but little more than a dirt path.

Mother Frey had met the two young Unbladed on the recommendation of Hannibus Greel of Theria, for whom they had done good work. They had no idea what was in Greel's sealed note of recommendation, but Mother Frey had taken them on and placed a great deal of trust in them. Before doing so, though, she made them swear blood oaths, which both did without jokes or questions.

Over the last few weeks, they had accompanied her to several out-of-the-way places across Vahlycor and only once had to draw steel in her defense. That was when a small group of teenagers tried to rob them. The two mercenaries had given them a sound thrashing, stripped them naked, and chased them all the way into town.

Now they were heading to a roadside tavern in one of the most remote stretches of back road in Zaare, where Mother Frey hoped to catch up with a certain young Argonian nobleman. A man whose name neither Hop nor Brace liked saying out loud because throats were being slit from the mountains to the ocean just on *rumors* of him. Worse, there were rumors drifting throughout the Unbladed community that the Argonian had fought Branks and left him on the point of death. Neither Hop nor Brace believed that, though, because they had seen Branks in action and nothing short of an angry rhinoceros could take him down.

A few miles into the new leg of their journey, Brace—trying to sound completely casual—asked. "So, Mother, how do you really know for sure this, um, *chap* is even alive?"

Mother Frey did not answer. It looked like she was dozing in the saddle.

Hop made a big show of looking completely exasperated. "Of *course* he's alive, jackass."

"You say that, but what makes *you* believe it?" demanded Brace.

"Because I know a man who knows a man who knows someone who saw him at Ghuraka's camp," said Hop.

"Oh, well, that's fine then. That's very comforting," said Brace. "You've totally allayed my fears."

"You know what your problem is?" asked Hop.

"I'm sure you'll tell me," sniffed Brace, "and I'm equally sure it will be bullshit."

"Your problem," said Hop, "is that you don't believe in anything. I mean, you swear by the gods, but you don't believe in them."

"I'll believe gods when I see them *do* something for someone," said Brace.

"You don't believe in governments."

"Neither do you."

Hop smiled. "Not governments per se, no, but some of the actual people, sure. I like the red ladies of Zaare. I like the dance hall maidens I met in Narek. I like the—"

"You like your dick," said Brace. "And anyone you can pay to touch it."

"I don't have to pay all of them . . ."

"You are such an uncouth lout."

"My point," said Hop, unperturbed, "is that *you* don't have even a piss-drop of faith in what other people say."

Brace gave him a withering look. "People have been great disappointments to me."

"You really need to—" began Hop, but a voice cut him off.

"He's alive," said Mother Frey.

The men turned sharply to look at her. The old woman's eyes were shut and her chin still down on her chest, but she spoke slowly and clearly.

"No matter what the rumors say," she murmured, "no matter what you hear in taverns, Kagen Vale is very much alive."

Brace began to say something, thought better of it, and closed his mouth.

Hop leaned out of the saddle, tore a handful of sweetgrass from the side of the road, selected the longest and fattest strand, put it between his teeth, and chewed it, all the time grinning at Brace.

CHAPTER ONE HUNDRED TWENTY-NINE

"Nearly two hundred people lived here," said the royal historian. He paused and repeated that one dreadful word. "Lived."

Jakob put no additional emphasis on the word. It needed none, and any hint of drama would cheapen the moment from tragedy to something maudlin. Instead, he turned away from the entrance to the town of Xola and let his eyes move without lingering across the small sea of faces. None of those eyes met his. They were all focused on what had been revealed moments ago, when a pair of Hakkian soldiers had opened the doors at Jakob's command.

Beyond was horror.

Beyond was death and madness.

The interior space was set aside for wagons to off-load goods from other towns and to take on locally grown late-season corn, pumpkins, and garlic. Those crops were heaped high, but now they crawled with a dozen species of flies or their maggots. Several wagons were nothing but heaps of charred wood and heat-twisted metal fittings. The savaged corpses of horses lay where they had died, their throats and bellies torn open, the lips of each wound ragged but clearly showing teeth marks. None of the marks had been made by animals.

The loading area covered a half acre and then washed up against the first rows of homes. Small houses, wattle huts, tiny stores, a single official-looking building, and a church. Or rather, the bones of these. Nothing in Xola had escaped the hungers of fires that had spread unchecked.

Bodies lay everywhere. Spread-eagled and nearly stripped to the bone. Curled around small children in a mockery of protective embraces, though none of those little ones were whole and many of those adults had died with young flesh between their teeth. Others lay where a hard blow to the head, a dagger to the heart, or arrows through their eye sockets or temples had dropped them. Like the wagons and the buildings, they also were burned.

The group of investigators, minor nobles, and royal representatives of a dozen nations moved forward with the smallest steps, none of them wanting to be there. Or see this. Or accept it.

They edged their way into the town in a kind of ghastly silence, as if none dared to breathe. Jakob stepped to one side, no longer needing to be their guide. He did not speak, waiting for them to write the history of this moment in their own words.

It was a major from the army of Zehria who spoke first.

"Everyone?"

Jakob nodded.

As if that single word by the major gave permission to the others, or perhaps broke the spell of shock, everyone began speaking. A jumble of questions and answers tumbled one over the other.

"The gates were closed?" asked a duke's man from Ghenrey.

"Looks like archers defended the gate," said a Therian sea lord.

"I've never seen this many arrows except on a battlefield,"

growled a deputy minister of war from Nehemite. "There must be a thousand arrows."

"Twice that many," countered the major.

"Flaming arrows, too," said a Vahlycorian captain of scouts.

"Look at the fletching," said a Zaarean count, tearing an arrow from the dirt at his feet. He held it up to show the red and gold feathers. A political strategist from the Waste took the arrow from him and held it out to show the others.

"Samudian, without a doubt," he proclaimed. The others stared at the arrow and then looked around at the duplicates of the one the strategist held up. Red and gold. Everywhere.

And there it was. Spoken by someone of official rank who was not in any way connected to Hakkia. It took a great deal of effort for Jakob Ravensmere to keep a smile from his face.

CHAPTER ONE HUNDRED THIRTY

Hop and Brace rode ahead of Mother Frey, who once more appeared to doze in her saddle. They kept their voices low as the miles drifted past.

"Look, Hop," insisted Brace, "there's just no way I'm going to believe that this Kagen fellow beat Branks in a fair fight."

"From what I heard," said Hop, "it wasn't fair at all."

"Then there you go—"

"No, I mean Branks tried to pull a fast one on the lad and got his ass handed to him. And the friend of a friend of a friend who told me said the big man was acting on Ghuraka's orders."

"You're saying Branks and her ladyship *cheated* someone during an audition?" Brace snorted and then spat. "That's what I think of such nonsense."

"It's what I heard," said Hop stubbornly. "And all the Unbladed who were there were so outraged by what Ghuraka and Branks did that they threw their blades at Kagen's feet and swore a blood oath."

"Such twaddle."

"It's what I heard," said Hop.

"Then you're an idiot for believing it," said Brace.

They rode on.

Behind them, slouched in her saddle with her eyes closed, Mother Frey nonetheless smiled.

CHAPTER ONE HUNDRED THIRTY-ONE

The small man was ushered into the throne room of King al-Huk. The procession from the huge doors to the foot of the royal dais was done in a stately fashion, with the Samudian chamberlain, Orsin ol-Tek, leading the way and six archers accompanying. Courtiers of various kinds, most from Samud but more than a dozen from other nations, parted like curtains, their robes and gowns rustling and hissing in an otherwise silent room.

The small man wore a brocade jacket of yellow silk embroidered with black thread. Its high collar fanned outward with night-black raven feathers. His gloves were dove gray, as were his slippers. He was clean-shaven and his hair was cropped so close to the skull that it gave the impression of a skullcap. From the time the doors were open and all the way to the royal presence, he smiled.

No one else in that room wore a smile. There were looks of grave concern, doubt, curiosity, surprise, naked dislike, and even scowls of outright disdain. On either side of the throne was a pair of tigers. It was a mated pair in the full flush of their youth and power, and the slender gold chains that drooped from their collars to rings set into the sides of the throne fooled no one. If those tigers lunged, they would snap the soft metal of their chains. However, they had been hand-raised by King al-Huk and were as loyal and attentive as the best hounds.

The procession reached the point on the ornately tiled floor where the wings of a hunting falcon stretched wide, the upper edges of each creating a subjective barrier.

Chamberlain ol-Tek stopped and bowed. Everyone else in the room except the guards did the same. Al-Huk replied with a small nod and the barest lift of his hand. He was dressed in light chain mail of strong steel links covered in gold and scarlet enamel. His surcoat was of the same color.

"Who comes without invitation to my hall," said al-Huk. Like the others, there was no trace of a smile on his face.

"Your Royal Majesty," said the chamberlain, "an envoy has arrived from the court of Gethon Heklan, Witch-king of Hakkia, usurper of the Silver Empire, and seeks an audience."

"Who speaks for the Witch-king?" demanded al-Huk.

The envoy did not wait for ol-Tek to make the introduction but instead took a half-step forward so that he was very nearly at the foot of the dais. The tigers rose from where they sat and shifted closer to the king. They did not snarl or growl, but these were massive animals, ten feet from fangs to tails, and each weighed more than six hundred pounds.

"Exalted king," said the envoy, "my name is of no importance whatever. I come to you as but a humble servant of His Royal Majesty Emperor Gethon Heklan, first of his name. What I wish to say is only what I have been asked to say, and therefore I am but the mouth of my king."

It was unusual phrasing, and the chamberlain seemed to be searching his thoughts to find an insult buried somewhere therein. King al-Huk was unperturbed.

"Speak your piece, envoy," he said.

The envoy bowed again and produced a slender scroll from the inner pocket of one voluminous sleeve. It had a seal of yellow wax and he held it out to the king and then the chamberlain.

"The seal is intact," said the chamberlain. This was a bit of normal court theater, but ol-Tek scowled regardless, as if expecting a trick.

The envoy broke the seal and unrolled the document. He did not look at the scroll but began speaking as if reading from it, though he gave the briefest preamble.

"What I say now are the words of my king," he pronounced, looking around at the gathered courtiers. He rattled off the usual formal and flowery greetings of king to brother king and then paused. When he restarted, his voice was noticeably different, and those among the gathered nobles who had been in the presence of the Witch-king gasped, because it was that voice which came from the envoy's mouth.

And it came out as a roar of fury, of indignation, of outrage.

"Why has Samud attacked my people?"

The force of that voice was such that everyone in the room staggered backwards. Even King al-Huk slammed backwards against the padded splat of his throne. The tigers cried out in fear and cowered down. Every torch in the hall flared and then guttered, nearly burning out.

"Village after village," continued the Witch-king's voice. *"Town after town. Not forts, not military installations, but the innocent people! Why have you attacked them with your dreadful Samudian Plague? Why have you resurrected that ancient curse and turned it against farmers and millers and shepherds? When Hakkia overthrew the Silver Empire, it was to end a thousand years of oppression and religious intolerance. Our attacks on the gardens, however brutal, were repayment for generations of our priests who were murdered, for the scholars of our faith hunted like animals and butchered. We repaid that in kind, and the scales are balanced."*

The envoy paused as the echoes bounced off every wall and then faded out, leaving the king and his courtiers gasping.

"*There is war, and that is bloody enough,*" said that terrible voice. "*But we did not attack your towns without cause. We did not take incurable and dreadful diseases and use them as weapons of war. Even we, whom you name as monsters and villains, did not do this. But you, King al-Huk, have created a storm of blood that has killed thousands of innocent Hakkians. How can you ever justify these crimes? How can you dare to use such weapons and then claim the moral high ground? Who are you to prey upon the unarmed, the innocent, the good people who bear no ill will to you or any of their neighbors in the western lands?*"

Then the envoy turned to face the courtiers on the left side of the room.

"*I see among you nobles from Nehemite and Theria, from Ghenrey and Sunderland.*"

He turned to the right.

"*Among you are important courtiers and diplomats from Zehria and Vahlycor, from Behlia and the Waste.*"

He turned back to the throne.

"*So many important people, representing the crowns of the monarchs of lands that once bent the knee to the Silver Empress. All of the kings and queens, princes and princesses had joined together to welcome me, to see me crowned as lord of a new empire—one built on tolerance, religious freedom, a celebration of every nation's unique culture, a sharing of arts and sciences that would have ushered in a new golden age. Yet you stand here now with a king who would rather embrace hatred and genocide.*"

He paused.

"*Or do you? Do you stand with him or merely near him? Have you come to his court to bow to him or to raise your own voices in protest over these atrocities?*"

King al-Huk slowly got to his feet.

"How. . . . *dare* you come here and make these spurious claims?" he snarled. "How dare you accuse me of these crimes?"

The envoy untied the belt of his robe and reached inside. When he withdrew his hand, he held a fistful of arrows. Some were caked with dried blood, many were scorched from fires. All of them had the gold and red fletching that marked them as Samudian. The envoy flung them onto the floor before the dais.

"Each of these arrows represents a town—an entire town— destroyed by the Samudian Plague. Count them. Or do you not even know the scope of the horrors you have wrought?"

The arrows lay where they had fallen, and the gathered nobles— particularly those who were visiting from other lands—gaped at them.

Then, one by one, they raised their eyes and looked at King al-Huk.

The envoy spoke once more in the voice of the Witch-king.

"I have sent this man to be my voice, for I know that my own life is forfeit should I step on Samudian soil. I do not trust that Samud will honor the treaties and protocols which govern—and should guarantee— the safety of diplomats and monarchs. You have no honor, King al-Huk. You have done these things to provoke war. When I used my magicks to end the tyranny of the Silver Empresses, I extended my hand in peace to every brother and sister monarch, and this is your reply. You want war. Let us see who stands with you in support of your crimes and who will stand apart in defense of peace. One of the towns that was destroyed by the Red Curse of Samud was across the border in Ghenrey, a nation that has caused no offense to anyone. A land of peaceful agriculture. And yet everyone from that town is dead—either torn by the teeth of the infected or pierced with Samudian arrows. Was that a mistake, O king? Or was it what it appears: a warning to the other nations that if they stand with justice or stand apart, they too will drown in a tidal surge of innocent blood?"

Many eyes turned toward the ambassador from Ghenrey, whose face had gone chalk white.

But the Hakkian envoy was not quite done.

"*The world is watching,*" he proclaimed. "*The people of the west are watching. My fellow monarchs are watching. I have spoken.*"

With that, the envoy bent forward as if exhausted. He dropped to one knee, gasping, sweat running down his face.

King al-Huk walked slowly down the steps of the dais and stood in front of the man. His face was livid, and he too was sweating. His fists were balled to bony knots at his sides and he panted as if after a long race. To everyone watching, it seemed as if he was going to strike the envoy. But then he turned away and looked across the sea of faces.

"I have not done this thing," he said.

It was a weak riposte. They all knew it. He knew it, too.

The silence that followed was terrible.

CHAPTER ONE HUNDRED THIRTY-TWO

"Here we are," said Hop. "Told you it was on this road."

"Well, at least you're right about *something*," said Brace waspishly.

The three of them slowed their horses to a stop and looked at the only building they'd seen in three days. The old roadside inn, tucked between a pair of ancient and moody old elms, looked like it had grown up with those trees. As if it had always been there. The walls were a haphazard mix of oak and pine, the pitched roof was covered with dried mud and wreathed with ivy. Fragrant smoke—rich with the smells of roasting meat, bitter ale, and steamed vegetables—curled from the chimney like a sleepy snake. Muted conversation in a dozen travelers' tongues rolled outward when the door was open, and now and then a burst of laughter escaped even when the door was closed. A handful of horses were tethered to a bar outside, and in the seedy stable on the far side of the narrow lane, twice that many—and a few mules—dozed in their stalls.

A rusty old pair of iron lanterns on posts were positioned on either side of the road, one to light the way to the inn door and the other to indicate the presence of a stable where overnight guests could leave their horses. A lad lay dead asleep in a rickety wooden chair by the stable, his feet splayed wide and chin sunk down on his chest. Though he was no more than twelve, there was a wine bottle standing beside his chair and a cup clasped in his hand. His mouth was open and he snored loudly.

"Relative of yours?" mused Hop, but Brace ignored him.

A grimy and weatherworn sign hung on chains above the inn door read "The Cavorting Bear."

Brace grunted at the sign. "Do they have a pet bear or something?"

"I wish," said Hop.

"No, seriously . . . why 'cavorting'? Do they have a bear that does tricks? Dances or juggles?"

"Truth is that no one in the vicinity seems to know why it's called that," said Hop. "My guess is that the original owner was a soldier with that nickname who, upon completion of some cavorting worth remembering, retired and bought this place."

"Not *all* taverns are owned by ex-soldiers," said Brace.

"No? Name two that aren't."

Brace ignored the question. "Did this hypothetical former soldier actually *cavort*?"

Hop shook his head. "Gods of the Harvest, Brace, you have no poetry in your soul."

"It's a fair question, given the name," insisted the Samudian.

"Tell you what," said Hop, "we can ask the landlord once we get in out of this cold."

The two men dismounted. Brace pressed his fists against his lower spine and bent backwards so far that there was a rattle of creaks and pops.

"I'm getting old," complained the young exile.

"I have codpieces older than you," said Hop.

"Yes," drawled Brace, "and strangely none of them are yours."

Hop began to reply but admired the barb too much to want to spoil it. It was a good one that he might use at some future time.

They helped the old woman down from her horse, and both were gentle about it. The ride had been a long one that day.

"And you're sure this is the place?" asked Brace, looking around. There was a corral in which a couple of dozen horses were watching them with mild interest. A small lantern on a hook hung beside the weathered front door.

"How many roadside inns in this part of Zaare do you think are named the Cavorting Bear?" asked Hop.

"Okay, fair enough. But what if this Kagen fellow isn't even here?"

Mother Frey spoke up, her voice pitched low and confidential. "Hop, tilt the lantern so I can see the jamb. The left side, not the right."

Hop did so and they studied the many scratches, graffiti, and marks left by generations of travels.

"There," said the nun, pointing with a crooked finger. "See it? Right there."

On the jamb, just above where the eye would naturally fall when reaching for the door handle, was a small symbol that had clearly been carved recently into the wood. It was crude—a cross whose upright shaft was encircled by a coiled line that ended in a rough approximation of a rose. The kind of mark someone could cut in a few moments with a sharp utility knife.

Brace traced the mark. "Son of the Poison Rose," he said softly, then glanced at the old woman. "That's what they call him, yes?"

"Yes," sad Mother Frey. "And without a doubt that's his Unbladed sigil."

"I'm always right," Hop said with a happy grin. "Except when I'm wrong."

"I don't get this fellow, Mother," said Brace. "He's the most wanted man in the west and yet he leaves his sigil where anyone can find it?"

"Tell me, son," said Frey, "if you did not know that was Kagen's sigil would you guess it?"

"Well . . . not . . . as such . . ."

She nodded. "Besides, he's been an Unbladed for less than a month. This is only the second time he's made that mark. The first was near Erthus, and I missed him by mere days."

"What's this, then?" asked Hop. "One in a series of potential meeting spots?"

"Exactly that."

"Smart. Done that myself a few times."

Brace looked up and down the road, then gave a dubious shake of his head. "I don't like it," he said.

"You don't have to like it," said Hop. He led the horses to the corral, opened the gate, and led them inside. It was balmy for a winter night and moisture glistened on grass that was still more green than brown. The horses, weary as they were, set to munching. He lingered for a moment, looking at the other animals. Six of the horses were roped off in a corner with the lushest grass. The saddles were well-worn but of good quality.

"Is Kagen traveling alone?" he asked as he rejoined the others.

"Why do you ask?"

He told her about the saddles and horses. "The horses in the corral are top quality. Not farmer's hacks. Nor the sad-faced nags traders use. They look almost military."

"Kagen is traveling with two people I know. A red-haired woman from Vahlycor and—"

"A giant of a Therian?" finished Hop. "Gods of the green corn, that's the other two who were supposed to be with your boy when he did for Branks."

Brace, whose face had gone a few shades paler, said, "That

description also matches the two maniacs who helped your, um, *friend* when he tried to cut the Witch-king's throat. That's who we're here to meet? The three most wanted people in all the west?"

"Well," said Brace, "unless they each have several excellent packhorses, there may be other rough trade in there."

They looked at the horses for a moment longer and then Frey turned toward her companions. Her eyes glittered like polished obsidian. "Listen to me, boys . . . there is no Kagen Vale in there. Do you understand? We are not here to meet anyone named Kagen Vale. We know no such person, nor ever have. We are here to hire an Unbladed—or maybe three of them—and that is all. Give me your word on this."

Hop smiled and placed his hand over his heart. "You already have my word, Mother. Once given, you can trust me forever."

Brace, not to be outdone, said as much and added his mostly courtly bow.

They went inside.

━━━━━▶ **CHAPTER ONE HUNDRED THIRTY-THREE**

King Vulpion the Gray met his spymaster, Mantis, in the secret room in the palace in Zehria. A piece of parchment lay slumped across his thighs. His hand trembled as he reached for his wine cup.

"This is a faithful transcript?" he asked.

"It is, sire," said Mantis. "Several people in attendance in Samud wrote an account of what was said. They did not, I fear, entirely trust al-Huk's court scribe in this matter. Several key diplomats met afterward and compared their recollections. What is notable is that they each remembered the words with a remarkable fidelity. Down to the smallest article and noun."

"Well, given the way it was delivered, how could they not?"

The king paused. "What about the ambassador from Ghenrey? What was his reaction?"

Mantis shook her head. "The ambassador left immediately. He made only the most perfunctory remarks but did not engage in any meaningful conversation, even with his friends among the attending courtiers. He and his entourage headed directly back to Ghenrey."

"What do you infer from that?" asked the king. "That he did not know of the massacre of that village? Or that he wanted to determine if it is was true and kept silent for fear of saying the wrong thing?"

"Both, would be my guess."

The king picked the transcript up and read it for the fourth time, then tossed it toward the fire. The parchment twisted in the air and missed the firebox, striking the plinth and landing instead on the stone hearth. They both watched the golden light and smoky shadows dance on the words of the Witch-king's envoy.

"But did al-Huk *do* this?" demanded the king. "Is he behind this Red Curse?"

"Who else?" asked Mantis.

"You don't think this is some mad plan by the Witch-king to start a war?"

The spymaster shook her head. "I can't see how. Or why. His forces are under siege from the Sons of the Poison Rose—whoever they are. Several garrisons have been wiped out. That, at least, makes some sense. But this Red Curse . . . Our most conservative estimates put the loss of civilian life at close to nine thousand. All Hakkian civilians."

"So many?" gasped Vulpion.

"Likely half again as many, sire. What good could come of such a sacrifice? How would it benefit the Witch-king's goal of uniting the nations under his banner?"

Vulpion chewed on that for a moment. "If he was a complete

madman," he said slowly, "he might do something extreme to make himself the victim in the eyes of the other monarchs."

"Nine *thousand* of his own people?" said Mantis, raising her eyebrows. "Whole towns? Besides, lord, he has been devious without doubt, but nothing he has so far done suggests that he is literally insane. If anything, there are arguments to be made in favor of his restraint. He could have killed everyone who served the Garden. And, yes, his troops committed atrocities there, but mostly it was one in ten killed, or one in twenty. He has hung many of his own Ravens and ordinary soldiers for rapes, theft, and other crimes. Not counting, of course, what happened on the Night of the Ravens. Since then, he has not persecuted the people, he has allowed trade to flow. No, he is many things, but I don't think he's a madman."

Vulpion threw back the last of his wine, dragged a hand across his mouth, and then launched himself from his chair to pace the room. He made a half dozen paces back and forth and then stopped, bent, and snatched up the document and stood reading it again.

"The Hakkian usurper used magic to deliver his message," said the spymaster after a moment. "That was not idly done. By speaking through his envoy's mouth, he reminded everyone in that room that he is not called the *Witch*-king for nothing. That level of magical ability is a terrifying reminder of what could happen if Samud goes to war. Moreover, it sends a very clear message to anyone that might align with al-Huk in some kind of campaign of genocide, which this Red Curse could easily become."

The king cut a look at Mantis. "I've asked this before," he said. "Did al-Huk *do* this?"

"Sire, I can't see how it can be anyone else."

"And *my* options?"

The spymaster winced. "They are few and they are terrible," said Mantis. "Do nothing and you will be seen to be complicit by lack of punitive action. Ally yourself with Samud and face the magic and fury of the Witch-king."

"Damn, damn, damn," breathed the king. "Zehria is too small to stand on its own if the west goes to war. If nothing else, Bulconia will snatch us up. They've only held back this long because of the strength of the empire. And they fear the Witch-king as much as anyone. One way or another, we have to pick a side."

"One way or another, sire, everyone has to make that same choice. And time is burning away."

CHAPTER ONE HUNDRED THIRTY-FOUR

The *Ravenheart* was one of the fastest ships ever to sail from the vast shipyards of Hakkia. It was the new model of trireme, with 170 men pulling on the three banks of oars, a massive mainmast and small foremast, each with square sails. Burly steersmen wrestled the two stern-mounted steering oars. It cut like a finely honed sword blade through the blue waters.

The captain of the ship had spent his life plying the waters of the Golden Sea and knew every island, islet, atoll, and reef from the capes of Samud to the Dragon Islands. He knew this island, too, even if only as a place to refill water casks. There were no people living on the nameless island, and only a few scattered blocks remaining from some unknown structure that had been consumed by sea wind, salt, and time. The place had no known history, and unlike many deserted islands, it did not even have a ghost story or pirate legend associated with it.

And yet the Witch-king's advisor, the Prince of Games, had ordered the *Ravenheart* there at speeds that nearly killed some of the rowers. Now those men lay slumped over their oars, gasping, running with sweat. The captain and a platoon of seasoned Ravens trudged along the beach toward a cluster of small caves set high in a cliff wall.

"Sir," said a sergeant, who had to run to keep up with his commanding officer, "how will we know what this Widow person even looks like?"

The captain ran a few steps before answering. "The prince said we'd know."

They moved on in silence.

At the foot of the cliff was a rocky path that would barely welcome a goat's sure feet, but it was the only way up, and so they climbed. Carefully, clinging to the side of the cliff face, moving as slow as snails, they climbed.

The sergeant was the first to reach the level of the one cave from which a faint curl of pearl gray smoke coiled upward. At the edge of the opening he paused, drew his sword, took a deep breath, and then stepped inside.

He was the first to die.

He was not the last.

CHAPTER ONE HUNDRED THIRTY-FIVE

Inside the Cavorting Bear, the air roiled with the mingled smells of sweaty leather, good ale, cheap wine, fragrant wood smoke, and hot food. The conversation dimmed for a moment as the three travelers entered and patrons looked up from tankards or dice, giving the trio a quick up and down. They saw a short and shabby man, a tall and fussy man, and an old woman. None was particularly well dressed, and they looked road-worn and weary. The patrons lost interest because these strangers were not wearing any kind of official uniform—notably yellow Hakkian cloaks. Conversation resumed and the strangers were ignored.

Hop scanned the crowd and felt a wave of unease. He leaned close to his companions and murmured, "Pretty rough trade for a place like this."

"Oh, I don't know," said Brace cheerfully. "Seems friendly enough."

"Then you're blind," said Hop. "Either way, watch what you say, Brace, and don't refer to her ladyship's former profession. The Zaareans have no love for Hakkia, but you can't tell who's a local in for a pint and who's a spy for the Bitch-king."

Mother Frey touched his arm. "Given that," she said dryly, "perhaps it would be best not to mock the Witch-king at all while we're here."

Hop grinned sheepishly. "Yeah, yeah, okay. I'll *think* it, though."

Frey gave him a small curl of lip. "As will we all."

He heard her say "Bitch-king" under her breath.

The publican came ambling over, walking crookedly on a peg leg as he wiped his hands on a dirty cloth. "Welcome, welcome, my friends. What can I do for ye?"

"You're new," said Hop. "I thought Jane the Cat had this place."

The landlord shook his head. "Ah . . . Jane up and married her an ivory dealer. Moved down south and lives in a fancy estate on Lake Lyra. I bought the Bear last spring. Making it my retirement, as you might say. Me and my daughter, Nell."

"Tell me," asked Hop with elaborate casualness, "were you by any chance ever a soldier?"

"What's that?" The landlord laughed and snapped his fingers. "Oh, the leg. Yes, yes, I was a pikeman in the Fifty-Third Light out of Riker's Pass. Lost the leg to a Bulconian bastard when they tried to annex the northeastern provinces. I did for him, but that was the end of my soldiering days. Bought this place and have been enjoying the peaceful life. Or at least things *were* peaceful, before the empire changed management, as you might say."

"Always an honor to meet another ex-soldier," said Hop. "I had the pleasure of serving with the Rangharn Rangers back home in Samud."

"Really? I heard some wild tales about you lads," laughed the landlord. He gave them a more professional appraisal. "Running with the brotherhood now, I take it?"

"Doing the odd job or two, yes."

"Well, best to you." He beamed and shifted his attention to Mother Frey. "My name is Holnaar. How can I be of service?"

Frey pulled off her hood, revealing white hair clipped quite short. She stood very erect and exuded an elegance that suggested wealth. It was a useful thing, which Hop had seen her use before. He enjoyed seeing the landlord's attitude change from friendly to overtly deferential, and he even gave the impression of standing to attention.

"A table in a quiet corner, Goodman Holnaar," Frey said. "Some ale for my companions and wine for me, if you please. Food, too, if your kitchen is still open. And we have horses in the corral."

"Of course, of course. Whatever you need, your ladyship," said Holnaar, and he quickly led them on a winding path through the tavern and to a curtained alcove. The publican pushed back the curtain, revealing a table.

Hop and Brace both offered supporting arms to the old woman, but she declined with a smile and slid into the bench, settling snugly into the back of the alcove. The men removed their cloaks and hung them on pegs, then sat on either side of her. Brace had to adjust his sword as he sat, but Hop had an axe slung down his back, which he removed and merely stood on end, the handle leaning against his thigh.

"Not seeing anyone who looks like the, um, man in question," murmured Brace.

Holnaar hurried over with a plate of cold cheese and hot bread, and the promise of soup, steamed vegetables, and the best cuts of beef the region had to offer. He set a clean glass and a dusty bottle of wine down in front of the old woman, and then poured two tankards full of dark brown ale for the men.

"Will you be wanting rooms for the night, milady?" asked Holnaar.

"If convenient," said the woman. "A single and a double. Clean linen, too."

"Of course, your ladyship," said the publican, bobbing his head. "Only the finest for a noblewoman and her servants."

"Thank you," said Frey.

When the man was out of earshot, Brace bristled. "*Servants?* If I wasn't here on business, I'd thrash him within an inch of his life."

"Oh, do shut up, you effete snob," said Hop.

"Why? He should have some respect."

"For what? A traveler with no sign of rank or station? He's an innkeeper not a seer. You're a gods-damned bully, Brace, and no mistake."

"And you're a peasant who doesn't understand how the world is run, Hop Garkain. And what's with the Rangharn Rangers nonsense? You were never in the military."

"You think you know everything," said Hop, laying a finger alongside his nose. "Besides, it's good to relate to people. Even if the truth needs a little paint now and then."

"A little—You don't even have a passing acquaintance with the truth, let alone honor and—"

"Enough," said the old nun, and though her voice was soft and her tone quiet, they shut up as surely as if she'd shouted. Brace looked into his mug for a moment, then drank about half of it down. He sighed and dabbed at the corners of his mouth with a surprisingly delicacy.

Across from him, Hop drank, too, but he kept his tankard tilted high until the entire pint was gone. Then he wiped his mouth with the back of his hand, belched softly and aromatically, and waved to a tavern wench with his empty mug. The girl came over with a pitcher, refilled both tankards, and was convinced to leave the pitcher when Hop pressed a coin into her hand. He held that hand for a moment longer than was absolutely necessary before releasing it and offering a wide smile. He had a gap between his front teeth that made him look a bit comical, and despite his fierce black beard and terrifying axe, his eyes were merry. The girl gave him a look that lingered as long as his grip had, then she was gone, taking with her the ghost of a smile.

"Mother Frey," said Hop when they were alone, "are you sure you don't want to take your meal in your room? Maybe rest and refresh before we look for your friend?"

The old woman patted his forearm. "You're always so considerate," she said, "but I'll be fine here."

The food arrived and they set to like hungry wolves. Even the old lady worked her way through a steaming heap of greens, half a loaf of dark bread rich with molasses and raisins, and nearly half of her steak. When the jug of beer was empty, Hop signaled for the waitress to bring more. She did, and made sure to refill Hop's first, pouring slowly while she looked into his eyes and matched his smile with one of her own.

"Tell me, sweetheart," said Hop, "what time do you get off?"

"Why . . . I'm nearly done now," she said, contriving to lean a hip against him while she reached across the table to splash half a pint into Brace's cup. Most of the rest of the beer landed on the table and on the young knight's lap.

"Hey!" cried Brace. "Watch it, you clumsy slut—*Oww!*"

His words ended with an abrupt cry as the flat of Mother Frey's steak knife whapped the back of his wrist.

"Manners," she said sharply.

Brace rubbed his hand and scowled, but he kept his tongue. Hop looked like he was in real physical pain from trying to contain his laughter.

The old nun looked at the young woman. "Girl, there is a man here, possibly staying at this inn? One of the brotherhood. Medium height, well made. Curly black hair, gray eyes, fine to look at. He may be wearing a pair of matched daggers with pearl handles."

The girl's eyes flicked away to the only other curtained alcove across the room. She said nothing but instead gave Frey a small smile before turning away.

"We have found him," said the nun.

CHAPTER ONE HUNDRED THIRTY-SIX

Lords Nespar and Ravensmere sat on one side of the table, with the Prince of Games across from them and the Witch-king at the head. They were alone in the hall, and even the pack of hounds had been banished to the kennels.

Maps lay scattered across the oak tabletop, and upon these were a litter of letters in flowery script and notes in arcane codes. Wine cups and bowls of fruit anchored the documents. Outside, a hard gray rain chipped away at the palace walls.

"Ghenrey has withdrawn its ambassadors from Samud," said Nespar. "That is a win for us."

"It is," agreed the prince, and for once he did not try to make an ordinary comment into some kind of snark or spin it into mystery. "They have no real choice, though, do they? What are they but a strip of farmland between Samud and Hakkia?"

"The question is whether they *believe* that al-Huk is behind the Red Curse or not," said Jakob.

"We haven't given them much room for doubt," said Nespar. "The city we picked is right on our border. That part of Ghenrey is remote and there are no clear borders to mark where Ghenrey ends and Hakkia begins. Even a fool could build a case that Samudian soldiers *thought* they were in our country and merely attacked the wrong town. From there, you could literally throw a stone into Hakkia."

The Witch-king nodded. "Which is precisely what we want them to think. That Samud is so determined to attack us that they do not even care to be precise."

"Or," suggested the historian, "that al-Huk doesn't care if there is collateral damage."

"That, too," said the king, nodding.

"What is next, then?" asked Jakob. "Do we allow the Hollow Monks to continue their work? Or pull back and wait to see what happens with the various royals?"

"If I may, Your Majesty," said the prince, smiling an oily and unpleasant smile. Nespar and Jakob sat back in their chairs, avoiding eye contact with each other lest the prince could somehow eavesdrop on an unspoken conversation.

The Witch-king gave the smallest of shrugs. "By all means."

"There is another town," began the prince. "A rather more important one. A trade hub that is very popular with caravans because of the dining, the quality of taverns and inns, and—most critically—the Museum of Trade, which is of more importance than the actual number of goods that pass through there. Everyone respects that museum, and its curator is the famous Joshah Ogreal, former minister of agriculture for the Silver Empire. That museum is something of a shrine to them."

"You're talking about Meadowvale," cried Nespar.

"That's in Nehemite," said Jakob.

"Why there?" asked the king.

"When your Ravens took down the capital cities of each member nation of the empire," said the prince smoothly, "they did not attack those towns and cities that are trade hubs. That was not only wise of you in your planning, sire, but it meant that despite the change of government the movement of goods was not significantly interfered with. Rich families in every nation—be they nobles or entrepreneurial commoners—were not affected. I understand the subtlety and wisdom of this, and I applaud you for it.

All of our spies have reported that this assurance of mercantile consistency is a major contributing factor in the subordinate nations not rising up in unified rebellion. It, in fact, contributed greatly to your intentions to make that change of government legal."

"And you want to now disrupt that trade?" asked Nespar.

"No," said Jakob quickly. "No, no, I see where the prince is going with this. Now that Samud has its back to the wall because a lot of people on all social levels are buying into the story that the Red Curse is, in fact, of Samudian origin, if that plague should strike a major hub like Meadowvale, with the resulting impact on trade . . ."

"Then Samud will be doubly a villain," said Nespar, catching up now. "Unlike us, *they* will be picking everyone's pockets by stopping caravans from moving."

"Exactly."

"But Meadowvale is an unwalled city," said Jakob. "If the Red Curse is released there, nothing can prevent it from spreading. And there are too many people for our agents to take down using Samudian arrows."

"It is on our northern border as well," cried Nespar, his face going tight. "Surely you are not suggesting we allow the plague to run rampant in Hakkia?"

The Prince of Games smiled thinly. "You forget your own geography, my lords. Meadowvale is, despite its name, not in a meadow. It is bordered on the east and west side by strong rivers, and they join in the south to form the great River Pilo. We know that those infected with the Red Curse cannot swim. They lack the intelligence for that. They would be swept away and eventually thrown into the sea. And as for the north . . . that's where the actual meadowlands are, and in open country like that they can be hunted down without too much difficulty."

They all bent over the map and studied the region.

"As you can see," said the prince, "there are no other towns within two days' ride."

"It's a terrible risk," said Nespar. Sweat glistened in beads across his forehead.

"When has war been without risk?" asked the prince.

"That is hardly the point," snapped the chamberlain. "What you are talking about is tantamount to setting fire to a house to chase out the mice."

"Only if we bungle things badly," countered the prince. "And at several key points."

Nespar began to reply but the Witch-king silenced him with a curt gesture.

"Lord Ravensmere," said the king, "you look less distressed. What are your thoughts on this?"

Jakob chewed his lip for a moment. "I agree with both Lord Nespar and the prince," he said. "There are risks but there are also strong strategic advantages. My personal view is to continue to explore the prince's idea but to not rush into anything, so we have time to weigh the risks and rewards. And, sire, to see if we can put into place whatever forces are necessary to guarantee our control over the spread of the curse."

"I can live with that," said the prince, smiling his oily smile. After a moment, Nespar gave a nod so grudging that it looked physically painful.

"Shifting focus for a moment, if I may," said Jakob. "We have a few Samudian courtiers in our pocket. If one of them were to 'overhear' that his king was considering releasing the Samudian Plague on our northern border, that person could be properly shocked at what his own king is planning. That same person, desiring to prevent his king from making a mistake fatal to all parties, might risk everything to bring a warning to the court of Queen Lliaorna of Nehemite . . ."

He let the rest hang. Nespar looked dubious, but the Prince of

Games beamed a great smile. "I can see why you hired this lad, Majesty. *He* has vision."

If he leaned a bit on the word *he* while looking sidelong at Nespar, no one made a comment.

The Witch-king brooded on Jakob's suggestion for a full five minutes before giving a slow nod. "I want you and Lord Nespar to share every bit of intelligence you have on whomever you pick to deliver that message. If there is even the slightest hint that he—or she—may be compromised, then move on to pick someone else. We cannot afford a leak, no matter how small."

The two advisors bowed.

"Now," continued the king, "as to the prince's scheme, that will take more thought and planning. We need to make sure we have enough of our own troops on the border before this is attempted. And subtlety is paramount. Our preparations cannot be visible. We will need earthworks, covered trenches, and tunnels to hide our numbers."

"I will see that done," said the prince. "And, of course, I play well with others, so I will enjoy working with our lord chamberlain and our esteemed historian to make sure that all fears are allayed and that we are in agreement with each step."

Nespar and Jakob both nodded, though there was obvious caution in both men's eyes.

"Now," said the king, "as regards the *other* matter . . ."

"Majesty," said the prince quickly, "there are aspects of that other matter I feel would be best discussed in private. Perhaps while Lords Nespar and Ravensmere begin their preparations for dealing with the Samudian spy, we can . . . ?" He let it trail off.

It was clear that Nespar—perhaps more strongly than Jakob—wanted to object, but the king gave no opening.

"Leave us," he said, and his tone was such that no invitation for dispute was offered. The two advisors bowed and withdrew.

Jakob looked thoughtful as he departed; Nespar avoided the prince's eyes for fear of letting the man see the fury in his own.

When the door was shut, the prince took two clean wineglasses from a sideboard and filled them with a naturally sparkling dry white wine from southern Bulconia. He handed a glass to the king.

"Let us talk of Kagen Vale and the lost cities of Vespia," said the Prince of Games.

CHAPTER ONE HUNDRED THIRTY-SEVEN

Kagen watched through a narrow parting of the alcove curtains as a short man walked across the tavern toward him. The fellow had too much beard and too little nose, Behlian features, with lots of earrings of the kind favored by sailors and pirates, and a double-bladed war axe slung over his shoulder. Kagen had seen him come in a few minutes before in the company of an old woman and a foppish young man.

The Behlian did not come directly over but took his time, moving here and there, ostensibly looking at the names seared onto the lids of beer barrels stacked against the wall, or at paintings of woodland hunting scenes hung between the windows. He was trying to look casual and was making a middling job of it. Nothing that would fool a keen observer, but nothing that would draw attention. Kagen found it amusing.

It was possible, even likely, that the old woman was Mother Frey, but Kagen had no idea who the men were. More Unbladed, perhaps? He did not get his hopes up about that, though, because they could just as easily be Hakkian agents and this could be a trap.

Kagen shifted his body a little so that one foot was braced against the alcove floor in a way that would allow him to spring out of the booth if this was an attack. He quickly scanned the other patrons to gauge whether any of them were likely confederates of the short Behlian. None seemed to be, though. Even so, Kagen did not relax. Instead, he let one hand drift down to fall on the pommel of one of his poisoned knives.

The short man eventually reached the booth and leaned a brawny shoulder against the outside wall. Without directly looking at Kagen, he said, "Saw your sigil."

Kagen said nothing.

"We meet at the crossroads," said the man quietly.

Kagen studied him for a moment, then gave the Unbladed's ritual response. "We touch blades at dawn or dusk."

"And watch each other's backs throughout the day and night," said the stranger.

Kagen kept his hand on the knife. "Speak your piece," he said.

"Name's Hop Garkain," said the bearded Behlian. "I won't ask yours."

"And?"

"There's a lady here who'd like a word."

"Sure," said Kagen. "Send her over."

"She'd like you to join her over yonder," said Hop without pointing. "She's old, so be a gent."

Kagen looked him in the eye and held the contact. "Trust is earned," he said.

Like the Unbladed ritual greeting, this, too, was a code. The little man's thick beard parted to show a lot of white teeth.

"Let me make sure I got this right," Hop said, then leaned a few inches closer. "Trust is a leaf on winter's wind."

Kagen relaxed, but only a little. It was the response agreed upon through Frey's correspondence with Tuke. There were four alternate answers, each one indicating some level of threat. The one Hop recited was the only one that told him things were safe.

He slid out of the booth and stood. Although Kagen was not a particularly tall man, he towered over Hop Garkain.

"Take me to her."

Hop grinned up at him and, without a further word, led the way across the room to the other alcove. The curtain was mostly closed and Hop pulled it back, stepping aside to let Kagen enter. Inside was the second man—a young Samudian dandy with a drooping mustache—and a woman who looked to be about three years older than the world itself.

Kagen stood at the end of the table, his thumbs hooked into his belt, which placed the edges of each hand close to the pearl handles of his daggers. He did not even try to make it look casual anymore. It was an implied threat, and he wanted the implication to be clear from the outset.

"Okay," he said, "so you're Mother Frey."

"What is left of her," said the old woman.

"Who's the mustache?" asked Kagen, indicating Brace with an uptilt of his chin.

Frey introduced Brace and explained that he and Hop were Unbladed she had engaged as bodyguards.

"You two any good as lookouts?" asked Kagen.

"Sure," said Brace. "Why?"

"Then go over to the bar and keep watch."

"Hey!" cried Brace, but Mother Frey patted his arm.

"It's fine," she said. "You lads go have a drink, but stay sober."

Brace began to protest but Hop pulled him out of the booth. Before they left, though, the Behlian leaned on the table and gave Kagen a long, hard, challenging look.

"You don't make a very good first impression," he said. "So far I can't say I like you much. I'm only trusting you because she does. But if you try anything . . ."

Kagen started to say something offensive, but instead merely nodded. He fished a silver dime from his pouch and tossed it to him. "On me. Enjoy your drinks."

Hop snatched it deftly from the air. "Remember what I said."

Kagen turned away. "Close the curtain."

Once they were alone, Kagen shifted a little closer to the old woman.

"Before we get into this," he said, "I want something a little more than Tuke's code. You've been in their conversations since the Night of the Ravens. They seem to think the sun shines out of your ass, but I don't know you at all. So why not tell me why I should listen to anything you have to say. Tell me why I should trust you."

Mother Frey nodded. "I would expect nothing less than healthy skepticism and great caution."

She reached into a pocket concealed inside her voluminous sleeves and from it removed two objects: a slender silver vial and a small scroll tied with green string. These she placed on the table, her eyes never leaving Kagen's.

"So?" he asked.

"This scroll is a map," she said.

"Let me guess . . . a treasure map?"

"Of a kind."

"Not interested," said Kagen flatly. "What's in the vial?"

"Blood," said Mother Frey. "And placental fluid."

"Okay, that's creepy," said Kagen. "And kind of disgusting. Your time is almost up."

"Don't you want to know *whose* blood and fluid it is?"

"Not even a little." Kagen ticked his head toward his own alcove. "I have wine over there that needs drinking."

Mother Frey picked up the vial and considered it for a moment.

"Before I began working for the Office of Miracles," she said slowly, "I was a midwife in a birthing house in Argon. The big house in Argentium, right on Haddon Bay."

"Again I ask . . . So?"

"I kept a vial with drops of blood and placental fluid for every child I ever delivered." She held vial toward him. "Read the name on this one."

"Why?"

She didn't answer, nor did her ancient hand quaver as she held it out for him.

Finally, Kagen sighed and took it, hoping to get this nonsense over with and get back to his wine. He took it a bit roughly and held it up, angling it toward the light.

The moment froze.

The whole room seemed to vanish, taking all of the sound with it. Kagen felt like he was standing in a vast empty room, but the floor of that room was slowly tilting. There, etched with great care into the small vial was, indeed, a name. His lips moved as he read it.

Marissa Trewellyn.

Kagen's mouth went dry.

It was his mother's name.

CHAPTER ONE HUNDRED THIRTY-EIGHT

Kagen forced himself to remain outwardly calm, but everything in his heart and head was a storm.

"You're saying this is my *mother's* blood?"

"Yes," said Mother Frey.

Kagen closed his fist around the silver vial, trying so hard not to let the last image he had of his mother fill his thoughts. That image came, nonetheless. Lady Marissa, falling beneath the whirling blades of the razor-knight. A woman who had never once lost a fight against man or beast, torn to pieces by something supernatural.

"My friends tell me you were with the Office of Miracles," he said evenly. "Now that I think on it, I believe I heard of a Frey who was a troublemaker and a busybody."

"That's as fair a description as any," Frey said, looking faintly amused.

"My mother told a story once about you and an apprentice— Miri, I think her name was—getting involved in something. I don't remember all of the details," said Kagen. "Something about a sorcerer in the town of Anaria in Zehria. There was a man claiming that he had the power of the gods and could strike down his enemies at a distance. Story has it that an entire mountain blew up, but it wasn't a volcano. It put paid to the sorcerer. Don't suppose that was you?"

Mother Frey leaned back and her smiled broadened. "Ah, Miri. Clever girl. She's a full investigator herself now. Or was, before the Hakkians. Worked out of the Garden of Argentium. But, like so many of my sisters, she vanished when the empire fell, and I fear the worst."

"So it's true?" asked Kagen. "You blew up a mountain?"

Mother Frey shook her head. "Of course not. How could an old woman do such a thing? And with what?"

Kagen watched her eyes and she knew she was lying. He found that very interesting.

Mother Frey took a piece of radish from her plate and nibbled on it. "Your mother was a sweet girl. She grew into a wise and powerful woman. A hero and champion, and that's not hyperbole. I considered her a friend. Even with the Hakkians everywhere, people still tell stories about her. She is revered—more so even than her forebears, and that is saying much. History may value her as much as Lady Bellapher, the Silver Thorn. I grieved when I heard that she had fallen during that awful first night. The details are vague, though, and like the tale of Miri and me in Zehria, it has perhaps become distorted in the telling. May I ask how she died?"

Kagen felt the pain flicker across his face and tried to hide it by drinking. When he lowered the cup, he saw that Mother Frey's green eyes were locked on his. She was no fool, he mused, and warned himself to be cautious.

"She was slaughtered by a razor-knight," he said.

There was no surprise on Frey's face. "Then the rumors are true," she murmured sadly. "And some say that you killed that creature."

Kagen shrugged.

"How did you manage that?" asked Frey, though Kagen thought she already knew.

"Banefire."

"Tell me," she said, and Kagen did.

After a moment's thought, Frey said, "I would like to engage your services. Or is becoming one of the Brotherhood of Steel merely a means to an end?"

"No doubt Tuke and Filia gave you all the details," said Kagen. "And this is beginning to feel more like a dance than a conversation. Let's cut right to it, shall we? Tuke and Filia have gone to great lengths to sell you as someone I needed to meet. They say that you have connections and resources. That's what we need to talk about, not family history."

Frey nodded. "Very well. We have a shared enemy. We have both suffered terrible losses, but we both have more resources than the Hakkians know. The fact that you managed to get into the palace and force the Witch-king to come to blows suggests more than physical courage and ordinary cunning. There was magic in that. Tuke has told me some of it. He hired you to help him secure the Chest of Algion—"

"Which, as it turns out, is bullshit. The chest is the bait in a very old trap."

"As we now know," said Frey. "The legend is so old and so thoroughly accepted that we thought it was worth the risk. But . . .

you found some other weapon in the Tower of Sarsis. You found the witch who lives there."

"She's not a witch," said Kagen. "Surely Tuke or Filia told you."

But Frey shook her head. "Your friends are loyal to you, Kagen. More so than to me. They've kept me apprised of your movements but have omitted much because they felt it was your story to tell."

"Are you lying to me?" asked Kagen.

"I am not," she said without rancor. "Give me that vial back and I will swear on it."

Kagen shook his head. "If I tell you what happened in the tower, and in the palace, what will you tell me? This has to be a fair exchange or I'm out."

"What do you want to know?"

"They said you are part of a cabal. Who else is in it? What are your plans? How many troops do you have? I want all that and more."

Before Frey could reply, there was a discreet tap on the wall beside the curtain and the tavern maid poked her head in, accompanied by the tantalizing smell of freshly grilled beef.

"Sir," she said nervously, "your steak is done, but I didn't know if you wanted it here or in the other alcove."

Kagen glanced at Mother Frey, studying her. "Here will do."

The food was placed and the curtain drawn. Kagen inhaled the aroma of a rare country steak beautifully prepared. "Tell you what," he said, cutting a piece from which steaming blood ran freely. "I'm going to eat. You have until I finish my steak to convince me I'm not wasting my time here."

Mother Frey sipped her wine and once more lowered her voice. "I will give you the bones of it," she said, "but some things are best left until we are far from strangers."

Kagen shook his head. "Here or nowhere."

Frey sighed. "Very well. The cabal is a group of nobles from virtually every corner of the empire," began Frey, "with perhaps a bias for Argonian, Vahlycorian, and Therian persons. That is happenstance, though, because they were closest to hand when the Ravens invaded. We have since expanded our network to include key people in every nation of the former empire. Each of us has sustained great harm from the Hakkians." She paused, and for a moment her cold eyes went colder still. Cold as winter steel. "The Witch-king has much to answer for."

"Yes," said Kagen. "More than you know."

She studied his eyes for a moment and nodded. "I daresay you have your own tale to tell. But for my part, because of my position in the Garden, which required me to travel far and wide, I have many useful contacts on all levels of society. Tuke and Filia are examples, but there are many others. Some may surprise you."

Kagen cut another piece and put it in his mouth.

"We are acutely aware that the Silver Empire was not without its faults," she continued. "Some might view them as crimes. The heel of the Silver Empresses was ever on the Hakkian neck. That began because the empire feared the Hakkian devotion to magic in all of its less savory forms. But since it is difficult to separate black from white magic, it was long ago decided that *all* magic be suppressed. That could—and in retrospect *should*—have been handled with a less heavy hand, and even, I daresay, with mercy and tolerance. That is water under the bridge, and we cannot undo the actions of our ancestors."

Kagen sipped wine and ate another piece of the excellent steak.

"There are few experts on the subject of magic among the citizens of the Silver Empire, excluding the Hakkian priest caste. Understand, we have sorcerers in the Garden, but they are really only scholars who study the old ways of healing and agricultural magic, even to the point of performing rituals, but they possess no actual powers. Perhaps you've heard of Alibaxter? No? He is a Belianan who is—or was—second senior assistant to the group of scholars who were studying the ancient ruins of Skyria. When he was a lad, he apprenticed to your brother, Herepath, though he did not accompany Herepath on the journey to the Winterwilds." She paused, studying him. "What's wrong? Your face . . . you went dead pale. Are you unwell?"

Kagen swallowed the chunk of steak and nearly choked on it. He washed it down with the rest of his wine and poured himself another cup, coughing still. When he could speak, he said, "It's . . . nothing. Just swallowed wrong. Keep talking."

He could see that Frey was suspicious, but she continued nonetheless. "The only real sorcerers left that we know of are the Hakkians," she said. "Some years back I filed a report with my suspicions that the priest caste had not, as we thought, been exterminated by Lady Bellapher, but I was not believed, and no action was taken."

"Whoever ignored that report ought to be horsewhipped," muttered Kagen.

"That was High Gardener Woeth," she said coldly. "He was forced to watch every member of his staff—all eighty-three of them, male and female—be flayed alive and then drawn and quartered. Then he was crucified on the door of his garden, with the rotting bodies heaped around him. He has more than paid for his lack of vision."

"Sorry for his people," said Kagen. "Not so much for him."

"To one of your other points," she said, changing direction. "We do not yet have a standing army, but I daresay we could hire one of some considerable size."

"You *could*," said Kagen, "but have not. Let me guess why. Magic."

"Of course. We do not want to waste time and resources on a move that could not only fail but even take what heart is left among the people of the empire."

Kagen nodded. He cut another piece of his dwindling steak.

Frey took a sip and did not comment further on that. Instead she said, "In the meantime, we are compiling as much information as we can about the Witch-king."

Kagen sat back, chewing slowly. "And what have you learned?" he asked, his tone neutral.

"Gethon Heklan was a priest of Hastur and a scholar of middling fame within Hakkian circles," Frey said. "He is a fifth cousin of the last Witch-king, making him the only person with a potentially legal claim on the throne and title. He worked briefly with several Gardeners on research projects involved with ancient mysteries. During that time he wrote two notable papers. Very learned but a bit radical. The papers were rejected by Lord Hroth, Chief Gardener of the Office of Official History. The rejection of his papers resulted in Gethon being dismissed from all official field research. One highly regarded Gardener stood in support of Gethon, but his letter of appeal was sealed by Lord Hroth. Even I have not been able to secure a copy of it."

Kagen's eyes were fixed on her as she spoke.

"The refutation of his work by the Office of Official History was a crushing blow to Gethon," continued the old nun. "He became addicted to the Flower of Dreams and as a result became erratic, prone to hallucinations, and also physically ill. He was diagnosed with a wasting disease, and seven years ago he was predicted to die within a year."

Kagen cut one last piece of steak.

"Gethon sold what little property he had," said Frey, "and decided to go on one last expedition in hopes of finding a cure among some rare texts and ancients codices that were rumored to be in a secret vault in one of the forgotten cities of Vespia. That part of his story ends in that strange land, though there are rumors that he found only more clues there and proceeded on to the Winterwilds, but no one has been able to corroborate this. Until he rose to power this year, it was believed he was either killed by Vespian cannibals or died during the arduous journey to the glaciers. Then he appeared as the Witch-king, clearly restored to health and possessing enormous and terrible powers."

Kagen leaned back in his chair. "You may be wrong about that, old mother."

"You think so?"

"I do, but we'll get to that," said Kagen. "Keep going. I still have a little steak left."

"One of the most trusted members of the cabal—Hannibus Greel of Theria—has been visiting key members of the royal houses. Rulers as well as influential court advisors in Samud, Theria, and elsewhere. Our hope is to secure a promise of military action if things align the right way."

"Good luck with that," said Kagen. "Or maybe you haven't heard about the Red Curse. What some are calling the Samudian Plague. If any governments are going to take action, it will be either in support of Samud or—more likely—as unhappy allies of the Ravens in a war to crush King al-Huk."

"The Red Curse is something we will discuss later," said Frey. "I admit that it has caught us all off guard. My agents cannot even agree if al-Huk *is* responsible or not."

"From the talk I've heard over the last few weeks," said Kagen, "most people seem to think it's a Samudian countermove against Hakkia that is going awry."

"If that is true, then it is both out of character for someone as wise and restrained as al-Huk and also a potentially suicidal move."

"Which leaves us where?" asked Kagen.

"There are still some options open to us," said Frey. "They are few and they are very risky, but each offers a chance of making this fight a more even one."

"How? With your pet wizard? What was his name? Alibaxter?"

"The answer to that is why I wanted to meet you. Even if we can build an army with ten times the numbers the Hakkians can put into the field, there is still the certain knowledge that the Witch-king's magic will tip the scales his way. We do not yet have magic on our side, nor even any quantities of banefire. The Witch-king is rending the veils between this world and the infinite realms that compose what can best be called the 'larger world.' Already there are reliable reports of vampires, a clan of werewolves, ghosts of many different kinds, night-gaunts, and others."

"I hope you don't think *I'm* some kind of magician."

"No, though your mother said you had a gift," said Frey. "Dreams that were possibly prophetic. But, like a dutiful daughter of the Harvest faith, she did not encourage that talent in you. Such gifts often manifest during puberty. She said that you stopped having them by the time you reached your sixteenth year."

Kagen shook his head. "No. I just stopped telling my mother about them."

"That's very interesting," said Frey. "Also to be discussed later."

"We'll see," said Kagen.

"In any case," continued the old woman, "you visited the Tower of Sarsis. You met the creature who dwells therein and lived to tell the tale. No one else has done so."

Kagen pushed his plate away. "You wanted Tuke to find that stupid chest. He would have tried, had he not been injured in a fight. Considering the legends surrounding that tower, you were clearly willing to let him risk his life in that venture."

"Of course I was," she said with some edge to her voice. "This is war."

"And you're what? A general?"

"In my own way," she said coldly, "yes. Tuke is a strong, smart, and very resourceful man. I sent him rather than one of my other agents because I believed he had the best chance of success. When he told me he was injured but had met you, that seemed like a stroke of unusually good luck. And . . . you succeeded."

"What was the goal, though? Why send him there at all, considering you didn't even know what might be in the Chest of Algion?"

"I believe that we need to fight magic *with* magic."

"I figured that much," said Kagen. "And before you ask, the lady in the tower is not going to join your cabal. She can't leave the tower. Some kind of curse."

"Ah," said Frey. "I'll admit I'm disappointed, but not surprised. There had been some old writings suggesting that. But we had to try."

"Was that your only plan? Because if so, we are in deeper shit that I thought."

"No," Frey said. "There are two other possibilities. Both very risky, but each with the potential to give us an actual weapon. The only reason we did not try them first was because each involves a journey of some distance and some danger. Considerable danger."

"We're surrounded by conquering armies lorded over by a sorcerer," said Kagen. "Things are already considerably dangerous. Don't tell me that you are thinking of sending assassins into the heart of Hakkia itself."

"That's being considered," she said. "However, I am talking about two places that *you* have been. Places outside of the Silver Empire. Places I daresay you would not willingly return to."

Kagen set down his knife, the last piece of meat untouched. "Say the names."

"Vespia and the Winterwilds."

Kagen laughed. "You are out of your gods-damned mind."

"I am not," said Frey.

"What could there possibly be in Vespia that could help? The people are savage cannibals, the whole place is a wild jungle where everything seems to want to kill you. And the cities are just empty ruins so creepy that even the Vespian dog soldiers are too afraid to go there."

"They may be a fallen race," said Frey, "but somewhere, locked in their shared memory they know that there is a great darkness in those cities. Ghosts of the ancient things that built the cities, for it was not their own ancestors. Those cities were built by god-like beings from other worlds. Their ghosts or something worse still dwell there."

"Okay, that speaks to my point," Kagen said, tapping the tabletop with a stiff forefinger. "If ghosts of creatures that powerful dwell there, why would you want to send anyone? What's to be gained?"

"Books of dark magic," said Frey flatly. "Notably, the Seven Cryptical Books of Hsan, which I believe are hidden in the Vespian temple of Ig-ulthan, in the city of Ulthar."

Kagen snorted. "Oh, that's just bloody brilliant. Books of magic from a culture that died out thousands of years before *our* culture rose. Hidden in a lost city in the most dangerous place on earth. Gods below. Who do you think will be able to even *understand* those books?"

"To be frank, Kagen, I don't yet know. Alibaxter, perhaps. Or someone else I have in mind, who is the foremost scholar on such matters. But we need those books, even if only to keep them out of the hands of the Witch-king."

"For fuck's sake . . . that's not even a plan. It's a pipe dream."

"Would you rather we do nothing?" she asked, but she did not wait for him to reply. "That said, the alternative—the Winterwilds— offers the best chance of making the Vespian venture successful. The person who may be our best choice to decipher the Vespian books is there, and I believe it will require a bit of the Vale luck and daring to find him."

"What makes you think I'd go all the way to the Winterwilds— half the world away—when the fight is here?"

"No, Kagen, I don't want you to go there."

"Good, because—"

"I've already sent a team there."

Kagen sighed and shook his head. "Then I hope you told then

to pack their own burial shrouds. There are *things* up there that never went to sleep when the Silver Thorn crushed out the magic here. Gods of the Pit, you have no idea. Only a bunch of suicidal madmen would venture there."

"Don't you want to know who I sent?" she asked, her eyes glittering.

"Sure, though I don't know anyone insane enough to undertake such a mission."

"I sent your brothers," said Mother Frey. "I sent Jheklan and Faulker."

Kagen's mouth dropped open.

"You did what?"

"It is my dearest hope that they succeed," she said, reaching across and taking his hands in hers. Her fingers were cold but surprisingly strong. "You see, Kagen, in all the gardens of the Silver Empire there is only one person whose understanding of magic is so deep, so vast, so insightful that he might be able to *use* the Vespian books to fight the Witch-king on his own terms."

"Who?" demanded Kagen.

She looked surprised. "Why . . . your brother Herepath, of course."

CHAPTER ONE HUNDRED THIRTY-NINE

War is loud and bloody, and it shakes the land with thunder and fills the sky with shouts and screams.

Strange that the road to war is often so quiet.

In Samud, King al-Huk spent weeks watching his troops drill. Spearmen raced in lines toward targets. They practiced boxing in cavalry amid a forest of spear points; they practiced deceptive retreats that were really traps. Old and new strategies, trained to a level of precision that was terrifying or encouraging—depending on who was watching. The Samudian archers darkened the skies with their massed flights of arrows or ran in loose skirmish lines to turn and fire, turn and fire. Captured ravens were released in their thousands and the archers tore them from the sky with their shafts.

In tiny Behlia, squads of light cavalry mounted on armored zebras ran complex hit-and-run patterns, with variations for open fields, mountain slopes, and city streets. Their curved swords seemed to flow like mercury through the humid southern air.

Vahlycorian heavy cavalry charged in unbreakable lines across the plains, sometimes trampling unharvested fields, going wherever their generals sent them. Doing it faster and better every single time.

In the Waste, the generals from the various unaffiliated city-states met to discuss tactics and then worked with their own diplomats and strategists to blend the smaller forces into something approximating a standing army. At first they were a rowdy and uncooperative lot, but with each new report about cities torn to pieces by those infected with the Red Curse, they got better. And better still.

All across the bones of the Silver Empire the armies marched and trained and prepared. No declaration of war had been issued, but even those soldiers of the meanest intelligence could read the direction of the wind.

However, except for the soldiers of Samud, the vast majority of those men and women being trained, from Ghenrey to Narek and from Nelfydia to Sunderland, had no idea on whose side they would fight.

CHAPTER ONE HUNDRED FORTY

Kagen stared long and hard at Mother Frey. He felt a smile try to form on his lips. It was small and cold and felt ugly. He didn't like the feel of it, but he could not stop it.

"You sent Jheklan and Faulker to the Winterwilds to try to find our brother Herepath?" he murmured.

"I did," said Frey."Tell me what troubles you about that."

"Oh," said Kagen, "everything."

"Why? Your brothers are tough and resourceful," said Frey. "They told me that they've been to the Winterwilds. With you and Herepath, in fact. It's not like I sent them to some uncertain doom."

"You may have," said Kagen bitterly. "Or you may have wasted two excellent resources in a completely futile gesture."

"Futile? If there is even the slightest chance that we can locate Herepath and enlist his aid, then—"

"Listen to me and hear me, old woman," growled Kagen, leaning toward her, his face flushed, eyes filled with dangerous lights. "There is not that slightest chance they will find Herepath there. Not one gods-damned chance in the coldest corner of hell."

"How can you be so sure?" she asked, leaning forward. "Do you know something about Herepath that I don't? Gods of the Harvest, please don't tell me that the Hakkians got to him first. Is he a prisoner? Is he dead?"

Kagen leaned back and rubbed his eyes. "Dead?" he murmured. "Oh no, he's not dead. Though I wish with every fiber of my being that he were so. I wish that I was bathed head to toe in his blood."

Mother Frey gaped at him. "Why would you say such a horrible thing about your own brother?"

"Why?" asked Kagen, his voice now eerily calm. He even wore a small, twisted smile. "Why? Because my brother Herepath is the Witch-king."

CHAPTER ONE HUNDRED FORTY-ONE

"*Nooo!*"

The old woman's scream rang out and was immediately cut short.

Hop and Brace whirled away from the bar toward the sound, and they saw the curtain of the alcove tremble. The entire room went dead silent.

Then the two men were running, drawing their weapons.

"We should never have left her alone with that madman," snarled Brace, fear pushing his voice to a higher register.

"I'll kill that Argonian son of a bitch," roared Hop. "I'll—"

He jerked to a stop midstep as a figure rose from a table and laid the blade of a machete across his throat.

"Hey!" yelped Brace, but then the heavy, curved blade of a Vahlycorian fighting knife swung out of nowhere and the razor edge pressed against his crotch.

"Stop right there, lads," said a woman's cold voice.

As if from nowhere, a slim redhead stood at a quarter angle to Brace, her blade making very hard contact. The machete was in the hand of a massive Therian with facial tattoos, and its twin hovered inches from Hop's face. A very large and very ugly dog crouched between Mother Frey's bodyguards, lips peeled back from rows of sharp white teeth.

Brace looked petrified, but Hop's hands tightened on his axe-handle. He glared at Tuke with no trace of fear on his face. Then his eyes went wide as the patrons at every tables suddenly got to their feet, throwing back cloaks to reveal jerkins or light chain mail. The air was filled with the slithery sound of steel weapons being drawn. Hop and Brace looked around at a sea of knives of every description, axes, hatchets, a bow with a drawn arrow. One even had a marlin spike.

Without taking her eyes from Brace, the woman yelled over her shoulder. "What's going on in there, Kagen?"

Kagen shoved back the curtain and stepped out of the booth. "The old witch fainted," he said. "Someone get me some water."

Hop and Brace stared in uncomprehending astonishment as one of the patrons hurried over to the bar and quickly returned with a bowl filled to the brim with water. He passed it to Kagen.

"What?" asked Brace.

"What?" asked Hop.

Everyone ignored them.

"Don't tell me she had a damned heart attack," the woman fired back. "I told you to break it to her easy."

"Yeah, well . . ." said Kagen. He leaned into the alcove, then called back, "She's breathing."

"A stroke would be pretty damned inconvenient, too," said the big Therian. "By the twitching balls of the jackrabbit god, you are a clumsy oaf."

"Shut up and give me a hand with her."

The redhead glanced at the other patrons. "Keep an eye on these two."

She lowered her knife and stepped away as a pair of fighters with scarred faces stepped up and disarmed Hop and Brace with professional speed and competence. One put a dagger point against Brace's kidney, and the other put the edge of a heavy woodsman's hatchet to the side of Hop's thick neck.

"What the hell is happening here?" demanded Hop.

The big man tapped the side of Hop's face with the flat of a machete. "Be quiet. It might be that you're among friends. If not, well . . ." He let that hang and punctuated it with a charming smile. Then he followed the woman over to the alcove.

The room stood still for several moments and Hop looked around as best he could. A realization dawned on him very slowly. He looked at the two men now guarding him and took a chance.

"We meet at the crossroads," he said.

The closest guard gave him a look of chilly appraisal, then shrugged. "We touch blades at dawn or dusk."

"Wait," said Brace, a half step slower, "you're *Unbladed*?"

"They all are," said Hop levely.

"Clever lad," said the guard with the hatchet. "Now shut the fuck up."

Across the room, the big Therian took hold of the table and pulled it out of the alcove, setting it against the tavern wall. Then

Kagen stepped inside and lifted Mother Frey in his arms. He stepped out, with Filia holding the old woman's hand and whispering in Frey's ear. The nun seemed to be awake but dazed, and her face was streaked with tears.

"Holnaar," he called, and the publican hurried over. "Where's her room?"

"This way, this way."

Hop and Brace watched Kagen carry the old woman away, and a moment later footfalls sounded on the stairs. The redhead went with Kagen while the Therian walked over to the two men under guard. He sheathed his machetes.

"If he hurts her . . ." began Hop, but the big man gave them a surprisingly warm smile.

"Mother Frey is safe with us," he said. He nodded to the guards, who lowered their weapons and stepped back. "So are the two of you . . . if you behave yourselves."

CHAPTER ONE HUNDRED FORTY-TWO

Mother Frey was terrified.

She was a not a woman prone to extremes of emotion. Though not a physically powerful person, her most effective armor had been always been intellect and insight, empathy and understanding, knowledge and pragmatism. She had never once fainted in her entire life.

Until she met Kagen Vale and heard his terrible pronouncement. Then the world turned to fire and then to utter blackness. She was conscious of becoming unconscious—a strange and terrifying new experience. She felt herself fall away from Kagen's words and into a dark well that had no bottom. She fell and fell . . .

Even when her body went limp, she had some residual awareness. She felt a strong hand lift her and carry her. She could feel the jolt as she was carried upward, step by step. She felt herself being lowered onto the mattress. It was careful. Gentle. And that frightened her because it was so disconnected to the shock that had sent her tumbling. Kagen's words had been a fist, a knife to her heart, a cudgel to her mind.

Frey was not aware of when the darkness took her completely. No. But when she began to float like a bloated corpse to the surface of awareness she felt that. It was awful, and she wanted to flee, to return to utter darkness.

The world, however, was not kind to her.

She was awake for nearly a full minute before she opened her eyes. Before she dared step back into the fires of reality. She spoke two words.

"Herepath."

And then, a moment later, in a crushed voice that even to her ears sounded either very young and helpless or very much older. And helpless.

It was another voice that answered. "Yes," it said.

CHAPTER ONE HUNDRED FORTY-THREE

Nearly a thousand miles away, in the great palace of the Silver Empresses in Argentium, on a promontory that looked out on the glittering waters of Haddon Bay, those two words—*Herepath* and *Yes*—echoed with complete reality through the minds of four sleeping people.

The Prince of Games, weary from plots and intrigues, sodden with drink, glutted from excess, slept and dreamed his dark dreams. When those words reached his deepest mind, he groaned and turned over, clawing a pillow to him, heedless that his fingernails—grown long in the dark—raked the cooling flesh of the woman he'd taken and used and killed. The words made him smile as he slept, though had he known that, even he could not have said why.

In another part of the palace, the twins Foscor and Gavran slept in their separate beds, with Madam Lucibel between them, rocking away the hours in her chair. Her wand of kindness lay across her lap and her hands clutched it every now and then while she slept. In the minds of the Witch-king's stolen children, the words *Herepath* and *Yes* echoed over and over again, each time taking on new and subtle meanings. Important meanings, though both aspects of each child were not yet—but almost—able to grasp their importance. And so the children groaned in their sleep and turned onto their sides. Gavran reached his hand toward the left side of the bed; Foscor reached her hand toward the right. Had they shared a bed, their fingers might have touched.

Behind stout walls and long stairwells guarded by the most seasoned and brutal of the Ravens, the Witch-king lay naked upon his thick mattress, the firelight making the sheer yellow bed curtains glow. His lean and muscular body was painted in dozens of subtle shades of yellow and gold, saffron and ochre. He heard those words, and in the tangle of dreams they seemed to both call him and warn him off.

He dreamed that he heard those words. *Herepath* and *Yes*.

His fists closed into white-knuckled balls as his body twisted and turned. In his mind a worm of fear wriggled and turned; but in his heart there was a dark flower—a black rose of unspeakable beauty—grew and his dreaming mouth smiled.

CHAPTER ONE HUNDRED FORTY-FOUR

"She's coming around," said Filia.

The Vahlycorian sat beside the bed, applying cool compresses soaked in peppermint oil to Mother Frey's brow. The old woman's eyes fluttered and then opened very slowly, as if she was reluctant to step back into the waking world. She looked up at Filia and tried to smile, but no smile would fit.

"Did I fall?" she asked faintly.

"You fainted, Mother."

"Fainted?" Frey tried to sit up and Filia helped her. "Don't be absurd. Of course I didn't faint."

She looked past Filia to the two men who filled most of the rest of the small room.

"Tuke," she said, reaching out a hand, and the big Therian took it and kissed her knuckles.

"You gave us quite a scare, Mother," he said gently.

Frey looked past him at the other man. "Kagen Vale."

"Yes," said Kagen. "Sorry for shocking you the way I did."

Under his breath Tuke said, "Clumsy idiot." Filia did not gainsay him. Nor did Kagen.

For a moment Mother Frey's eyes seemed to cloud, and then they cleared and hardened to diamond clarity.

"Herepath," she said, making it a statement and a question.

"Yes," said Kagen. "Herepath."

Mother Frey sat up straighter, no longer requiring help. "And you are certain?"

"I saw his face at the palace that night," said Kagen. "I *spoke* to him."

She turned away and looked at the closed and shuttered window for a long moment. "Did he offer any explanation?" she asked.

"No," said Kagen. "Beyond some vague justification that the empire oppressed the religious freedom of Hakkia."

"Which it did," said Frey. "I'll be the first to admit it."

"Which it did," agreed Kagen.

"Do you *understand* it?" she asked, turning back to him, her eyes pleading. "Does it make any sense at all? Were there signs? Warnings?"

Kagen came around and sat on the side of the bed opposite to Filia. "Mother Frey," he said, "I just don't know. Ever since the Night of the Ravens I have been having more of those dreams I told you about. Many of them—nearly all, in fact—are either re-membered conversations I had with Herepath long ago, or new ones. I think that he may be aware of my dreams, too. Hell, he might actually be talking to me in dreams."

Frey looked very frail, almost deathly, but Kagen saw her begin to pull at the threads of her dignity. She straightened and there was a slow transformation as she worked to calm herself. It was impressive, like watching a seasoned warrior put on armor before a fight. Kagen admired the strength he saw, the control. It spoke to an inner toughness totally belied by her age. It was a small thing that many might have missed, but he saw it, felt it, knew it. He understood some of why Filia and Tuke respected her and trusted her. He was starting to feel the same.

"Those dream conversations," said Frey, her voice closer to normal, "I wonder if they were only happening when both of you were actually asleep. I have read about such things in ancient texts."

"Does that mean he can read my mind?" asked Kagen, alarmed.

She shook her head. "I don't know, though I don't think so. If he could, then his soldiers would have found you already."

"Cold comfort," said Tuke, "but beggars can't be choosey."

"The problem is that the dreams don't seem to fit any kind of sequence," said Kagen. "Some are even older dreams, but rewrit-ten somehow, with snatches of conversation from other dreams or borrowed from actual talks I had with Herepath in the wak-ing world. Some are so strange and cryptic that even though I'm engaged in the conversations I have scant idea of what the real meaning is." He shook his head. "Maybe there were warnings in those dreams, but if so, I never discerned it. After all, even at his best and most gracious, Herepath was a closed one. He prized se-crets in all their forms. His loathing for politics was well known, even though his understanding of it was unquestioned. But . . .

did I know? Did I even suspect that Herepath had this level of darkness and corruption in his soul? No. I wish I could say otherwise, but . . . no."

They sat in silence with that, each of the four digesting the implications and chewing on the mysteries.

"Were they dreams or actual prophecies?" asked Tuke.

"How the hell should I know?" snapped Kagen, but before Tuke could reply he held up a hand. "No. I take that back. Peace, brother. It was a fair question." He thought on it for a moment. "I think they were both, and that's what confounds me the most. How can I tell which elements are reliable and which are merely the constructs of a dreaming mind?"

"Some of it has been verified, though," said Filia. "You dreamed of a dragon and Maralina told you that it exists, and even gave you her name."

"Fabeldyr," said Kagen. "Yes."

That brought Mother Frey to even sharper attention. She grabbed Kagen's sleeve. "Fabeldyr *lives*?" she cried. Then a moment later, she gasped out a name. "Maralina? Gods of the Harvest, Kagen Vale . . . there is much you need to tell me."

Kagen smiled wanly. "And if I tell you my whole tale, will I then need to go outside and dig you a grave? By the Pits, old woman, I'm not trying to burst your heart."

Frey colored, but then her face grew stern. "I fainted once in all these years. I do not expect to do so again, so mind your manners."

Her tone was so commanding that Kagen straightened so sharply that he gave the impression of standing to attention and saluting. Filia turned away to hide a smile. Tuke laughed out loud.

"And you can wipe that grin off your face," snapped Frey. "Both of you, for that matter. You could have found a way to get this information to me long ere now."

"It wasn't ours to share," protested Filia. "Out of respect for Kagen, we—"

"Hush!" scolded Frey. "If we are to be allies, then there can no longer be secrets between us. Kagen, I need you to tell me all of it. Now."

"That's a lot of telling," said Kagen.

Mother Frey reached behind her head and plumped her pillow. "We've all eaten, and I'm perfectly comfortable," she said. "Shall we get to it?"

CHAPTER ONE HUNDRED FORTY-FIVE

The riders moved through the countryside like phantoms.

One hundred of them, traveling in groups of two or four or eight. Never more than that. Each with a purpose. Each riding fast, pushing their horses to the limit to make remount stations. Miles burned away to dust as they passed.

They wore travelers' clothes in case they were seen. Some looked like Unbladed hurrying to catch a caravan; others wore the garb of regional couriers—though they changed clothes when they crossed national lines. None wore Hakkian colors of any kind, nor had anything yellow at all about their persons or mounts. Each was chosen for their fighting skills as well as the ability to speak any of the many languages of the old Silver Empire, or to speak the merchants' tongue—the common language—with regional accents that marked them as being from Vahlycor or Zaare or anywhere that was not Hakkia.

They left Argentium from a dozen different ways and then headed into Nehemite before striking east through Zehria. They entered the Cathedral Mountains in Nerek or Ghul, and then turned north.

Riding to Vespia.

Each of those one hundred riders carried with him vials of liquid prepared by the Hollow Monks and given to them by Lord Nespar.

Somewhere, they knew, Kagen Vale was almost certainly heading to Vespia, too. Although each rider was loyal to the death to the Witch-king and would never have asked for a copper penny more than their regular pay, the lord chamberlain had told them that whoever brought back Kagen's head and heart would be granted a baronetcy and a fortune beyond counting.

The riders bent over their horses, teeth gritted, minds churning on the importance of their mission and the glories of success.

Riding hard through the days and nights.

CHAPTER ONE HUNDRED FORTY-SIX

When he was done, the tavern below had grown quiet.

Mother Frey's first questions were about her two bodyguards. "What happened to Hop and Brace? Where are they? Are they unhurt?"

"They're downstairs with my friends," said Kagen.

Frey glanced at Tuke and Filia and frowned. "Friends?"

"Everyone down in the bar are Unbladed," explained Filia. "Once we left Ghuraka's camp we picked up some willing souls along the way."

"My guess," said Tuke, "is that our lads have your boys—Hop and Brace, is it?—drunk and overstuffed by now."

"They are also Unbladed," said Frey.

"So they said, and the others assured them that you are among friends and in good hands."

Frey pursed her lips for a moment. "What about the innkeeper?"

"He's in the brotherhood, too," Tuke assured her. "That leg he lost? It wasn't from his time in the military. He was working guard for smugglers bringing Bulconian wine into Zaare.

He can be trusted. As for the others . . . yes. We have a score of them downstairs, and deputized scouts out looking for more. All trusted. Unbladed. We handpicked them. People we knew, or know through friends whose words are solid. It's a slow process, though, because we have to select those fighters whose hatred of the Hakkians is as strong as our own. People who won't be tempted to shuck their honor in favor of the reward on Kagen's head."

Filia nodded. "As I mentioned in one of my reports, Ghuraka nearly sold Kagen out. She was always greedy, so I don't know why I'm surprised. Although we don't think she was actually in league with the Hakkians, she was willing to kill an applicant and sell his head and heart to the Ravens."

"Maybe it's me," said Tuke, "but somehow that's worse than a political betrayal. The brotherhood is only as good as its word."

Frey nodded. "Her people saw all this, yes? Well . . . they are unlikely to ever forget. And so many swore blood oaths to you."

"Even Ghuraka," said Tuke, "but I wouldn't gamble a gelding's balls that her word is any good."

"Nor would I," said Frey.

"Personally," said Filia, "it wouldn't surprise me if someone either challenged her for the right to lead the Unbladed . . . or cut her throat while she slept."

"I'm fine with either," grumbled Tuke.

Frey's color was better now and she sipped hot wine that had been mixed with cinnamon, licorice, and apple peel.

"What does this do to the two plans you were telling me about?" Kagen asked. "My brothers are already on their way to the Winterwilds. They won't find Herepath there, so is there anything they *might* find that will help us?"

"There is no way to answer that question," said Frey. "They are smart lads."

"That they are," said Kagen. "Tough as nails, too. But the question is whether Herepath left a contingent of Ravens up there as either a trap for anyone sniffing around or to continue whatever work he was really doing there."

"What about the dragon?" asked Filia. "What are they likely to do if they find a great beast chained to the wall?"

They all looked at Kagen, who shook his head. "I have no idea."

"Will they kill it, do you think?" asked Tuke, directing the question to anyone.

Frey shook her head but made no reply.

Kagen said, "Those lads will happily chop the head off someone who cheated at cards, but a helpless, tortured creature?" He shook his head. "Not saying they would risk setting it free, but I cannot see them killing it. Either way, though, we need to get word to them. They need to know how things are. They need to know about Herepath." To Frey, he said, "Mother, does your network of agents stretch that far?"

"No," she said. "Perhaps before the fall of the empire I could have arranged something, but many of the most reliable people were Gardeners. Only one in fifty survived the Witch-king's purges. My most reliable agents are scattered, or they're involved with espionage in the various kingdoms, because anyone can tell that war is brewing. By the time I can reallocate those resources, your brothers will have reached the Winterwilds. They are likely on the far side of the Cathedral Mountains by now and making their way northeast through the Shadowlands."

Filia made a warding sign. The Shadowlands was a vast area of permafrost, dense pine forest, steppes, and ruins. Like Skyria and Vespia, the cultures that once dwelt there were long gone, swallowed by the dust of history. The current occupants of the Shadowlands were tribes of nomads known by outsiders as Shadow Riders, who were hostile to visitors and tended to attack, murder, and rob rather than ask questions. Only the Vespian cannibal dog soldiers were more feared. None of the eastern nations, like Alya-Ta, Ashgulan, Gefhelm, or Jakata, seemed interested in annexing the Shadowlands, which made economic sense because those lands were mostly barren, with few resources to make the effort profitable. Fear of the Shadow Riders, however, likely influenced those decisions.

"How many fighters did you send with my brothers?" asked Kagen.

"None," said Frey. "They said they knew where to pick up some likely lads and lasses—and here I'm quoting Faulker—so I gave them gold to help that process."

"Likely lads and lasses," echoed Tuke, then cut a look at Kagen. "What do you say to that?"

Kagen shrugged. "Jheklan and Faulker know people everywhere. They make friends easily and people tend to be oddly loyal to them."

"Because," said Filia, "despite all their boyish bullshit, silly banter, and frequent bouts of drunkenness, they are true."

"True?" asked Tuke.

"Their word is unquestioned," said Filia. To Kagen, she added, "Don't look so surprised. You may have introduced me to them, but I've been involved with them on certain outings. I was there when they auditioned for the Unbladed."

"You're out of your mind," said Kagen. "The Twins aren't Unbladed."

"Yes, they are," said Frey and Filia at the same time.

"What?"

"You are sometimes unbearably clueless about certain things, boy," said Filia. "The Twins became Unbladed so they could get caravan work. Why do you think they've been away for long stretches so often? Unless you bought their fiction of being 'adventurers.' That's just a word some people use when they don't want to admit they're Unbladed."

"They carry swords . . ." began Kagen.

"Because they are noble born and official knights of the empire," said Filia. "You know, there are many Unbladed who still carry swords. I do myself every now and then. Not all Unbladed are outcasts or intinerant muscle."

"I actually did not know that," said Kagen.

"Ha!" laughed Tuke. "If you hadn't pissed off your gods, you could have a sword, too."

Kagen pointed at him. "You can start looking for fire ants in your bedroll henceforth."

Filia, ignoring the two, spoke to Frey, prompting her back to the topic. "Vespia and the Winterwilds . . . ?"

The old nun nodded. "My desire to send a team to Vespia still stands."

"Even knowing that my brother is the gods-damned Witch-king?" asked Kagen.

"Oh, even more so. I wanted to obtain the Seven Cryptical Books of Hsan and get them to Herepath because he is the person most likely to be able to interpret them and use their power. Now we must hurry to *prevent* those books from falling into his hands. With that ancient knowledge, the Witch-king can do more than create his new Yellow Empire. Oh, no . . . that would only be the beginning. If we allow Herepath to unlock the secrets of the darkest of all magicks, then he will become immortal. He will become as a god. His powers will grow exponentially, and he will rule this world forever."

She took a breath and looked around at the stunned expressions.

"But you're forgetting Maralina," said Kagen into the silence. "Surely she might be able to read those books?"

"Possibly," said Frey, but there was no enthusiasm in her voice. Her eyes were filled with thoughts of terrible things. "An hour ago . . . my greatest fear was that we were on the brink of a great and terrible war. At the coronation I saw that the Witch-king was not all-powerful and I dared to hope that we could stop him and restore the empire. Now my fear has grown to a terror deeper than any I have ever imagined. And now I know what our task is. We four here, and those allied with us, are all that stand between the world of humankind and the beginning of a dark age of terror and madness."

Tears rolled over the cracks and seams of her old face, but the look in her eyes was a blazing inferno.

Filia once more made a warding sign in the air, drawing it with a trembling hand. Tuke's dark skin paled to a sickly yellow-brown. Kagen Vale stood with his fists locked tight around the handles of his poisoned daggers.

He said, "When do we leave for Vespia?"

CHAPTER ONE HUNDRED FORTY-SEVEN

The following morning they all met in the tavern. There were no guests at the inn except the Unbladed that Kage, Tuke, and Filia had hired on the long ride from Nelfydia to Zaare. Holnaar, the former Unbladed who owned the place, personally vouched for the barmaid, the cook, the drunk stable lad, and the maids, as they were all his children.

Mother Frey sat at the head of a long table created by pushing all of the smaller tables together. A burly brute of a Nehemitian named Dilhoolie volunteered to watch the door and the road outside. He sat on a stool with a huge double-bladed axe laid across his thighs.

"That's weird," he said as he took up that post.

"What is?" asked Tuke.

"The birds," said Dilhoolie. "They're everywhere. More than I've ever seen at one time. What the bloody hell?"

"Can you see any ravens out there?" asked Filia.

"Ravens? The birds? Nah. Bunch of crows and a mixed lot of the rest. Blackbirds, mostly. Why?"

"They're mine," said Kagen, and everyone looked at him. When he offered no explanation, there was some quiet muttering, but no one challenged him on the remark.

Hop and Brace wrestled, kicked, and cursed their way to Frey's side and flanked her at the table. Kagen sat across from her, with Filia and Tuke on either side. The rest of the Unbladed—thirteen men and seven women—sat or stood, waiting, as the room settled down to an expectant silence.

Tuke opened the conversation and filled them all in on the backstory of his adventures with Filia and Kagen. He told much of Kagen's own story, omitting the part where he was abandoned by the Harvest Gods and glossing over all the days Kagen had spent drunk and murderous throughout the Vahlycorian countryside a few months back. It was clear to all that most of them knew large pieces of this story, but the Unbladed went still and pale when Tuke gave them a full and complete account of the failed assassination on the night of the coronation. He said the name Herepath only once, and even hushed his voice as he did so, but the name hung burning in the air.

Kagen did not speak yet but sat and listened, taking small sips of beer and watching the faces of the gathered fighters. When it was time to tell Mother Frey's story, the old woman spoke. She did not rise, nor did she raise her voice very loud, but the room went totally silent and everyone bent close to hear.

Frey explained about the cabal, though she did not name any members, for safety's sake. She related the tale of how she and two friends attended the failed coronation, and told about what had happened there. Everyone knew some version of the story, though such tales always tend to grow in the telling. Her version did not have armies of angels and demons warring above the palace, nor was there a mass slaughter of a thousand Hakkian soldiers. Even so, the parts about the two warring godlings, Hastur and Cthulhu, battling in the sky as lightning flashed was true.

She also explained about the imperial twins, Alleyn and Desalyn, and how they had fallen under the Witch-king's spell.

"He has stolen the heirs of the empire," said Frey, "and has sickened their souls. He calls them Foscor and Gavran now. If we can rescue them and somehow break the spell that binds them to the Witch-king, then we can use that as a rallying cry to bring all the nations under the same banner. As long as those children live, the Silver Empire endures."

That was a sobering moment and she let them work it through in their minds. A thin Nerekian woman with ice-blue eyes was the first to raise her cup.

"To the heirs of the empire," she declared. The whole company echoed her words with fierce shouts.

Frey nodded her approval, then she went on to explain her reasoning for sending Jheklan and Faulker Vale to the Winterwilds, and how that plan was in danger. She said that word would be sent out to every one of her agents in the hopes that someone would be able to follow the Twins and warn them in time. Kagen noticed that she omitted all mention of Fabeldyr, even as Filia had withheld the same information. He accepted that, because it might be one step too far for practical fighters raised in an empire that did not officially believe in magic—or that at least pretended that magic was gone from the world.

Kagen personally disagreed, because he trusted these fighters. They were adults; they were practical. He believed they could handle that truth. But he did not contradict Filia and Frey.

The last part of the long tale was the other mission: Vespia. She explained about the Seven Cryptical Books of Hsan, which were believed to be hidden in a temple in the city of Ulthar. The room was utterly silent except for her creaky old voice.

"Our immediate mission then," Frey concluded, "is to find those books so we can attempt to learn from them and add some measure of magic to our own arsenal, and make sure at all costs to keep them out of the hands of the Witch-king."

She sat back, exhausted from the long narrative. Hop took one of her hands and Brace the other.

"Vespia?" asked Redharn, one of the Unbladed. He was a big man with a face scarred by the talons of combat-trained hawks. "Apart from the cannibals, the whole place is an overgrown jungle. Those cities are buried under vines and leaves. How can we hope to find any of them, let alone this Ulthar?"

"I've been there," said Kagen. "A long time ago, with Jheklan and Faulker. And, yes, we went there with Herepath."

Several of the Unbladed gasped and made warding signs.

"Don't do that," snapped Kagen with sudden anger. "Herepath may be the Witch-king and he may be a damned wizard, but he is mortal. He will not appear if you say his name aloud." He laughed. "If he would, then I'd have yelled his name a hundred times ere now and butchered him when he appeared."

No one spoke until Frey broke the silence. "The Witch-king has enough power already. Let's not give him any more. Say his name. All of you. Say it."

Tuke and Filia said it first, though neither liked the feel of it on their tongues and winced as they spoke. Not to be outdone, Brace and Hop said it. Then Redharn. Then everyone.

When the last of them had spoken the true name of the Witch-king, the room grew quiet again.

Gi-Elless, a Samudian archer with olive skin and sharp features, spoke next. "Okay, so Captain Kagen has been there. But what do we really know about Vespia? Other than it being dangerous and haunted."

"Fair question," said Mother Frey. "Vespia was a great nation once. One of the most advanced nations on earth, with cities of such magnificence that it seemed impossible that men could have built them. Vast temples made of huge blocks of stone—marble of a kind that is so rare no one knows where it was quarried, and of such size that nothing we now know about building can explain the construction. There are more wild tales than accurate histories. Some say that Vespia was first settled by a race of gods from beyond the known stars; others say that giants from the moon built those temples."

"I heard it was lizard people from the hollow center of the world," said Brace, and Hop nodded.

Frey ignored that and produced a small scroll—the same one she'd been prepared to show Kagen the night before—and unrolled it. Everyone bent close to see that it was a section of a map.

"This was cut from a very old map of northeastern Vespia," she said. "If placed on any standard traders' map of the eastern side of the Cathedral Mountains, it should blend right in. Does any of you have one?"

"I have one in my saddlebag," said Hoth, a moody Ghenreyan with dueling scars on his face. He fetched it and spread it out on the table. Kagen took the fragment from Mother Frey and placed it over the spot she indicated. Indeed, it was a perfect match, but unlike the rest of the map, the swatch had more detail and a clear indication of the location of Ulthar.

Frey touched the map. "See there? That's where Ulthar is. It is unlikely the Witch-king has something like this fragment. If his soldiers go to Vespia, they will not know where to look, and that should buy us the time we need."

"It'll take a while to get there," said Hoth. "And as long to get back. Things may be much worse by then. War is brewing."

"Aye," said Redharn, one of the senior Unbladed, "and the king of Samud seems to have lost his damn mind. He struck back at Hakkia with the old Red Curse that nearly destroyed his own country."

"It is not certain that King al-Huk is actually responsible," said Frey.

"You know otherwise?" asked Redharn.

"Know?" she asked, then shook her head. "But I know al-Huk well enough to have some faith in his reason. Given the terrifying way that plague spreads, I find it hard to believe that he would release it even if the legions of Hakkia were marching down Archers Way to invade his palace and take his head."

Brace and Gi-Elless, both Samudians, growled their agreement, and Kagen saw that many of the older and wiser Unbladed among them nodded, too.

"Then what is it?" asked Tuke. "More of the Witch-king's sorcery?"

"Sorcery, treachery, or innate malevolence," said Frey. "Take your pick. But I would bet much that the Red Curse is the Witch-king's weapon."

"Which leaves us where?" asked Hop.

"In need of haste," said Frey.

"I'm still of two minds," admitted Kagen. "The sane and civilized part of me wants to stay here, raise an army, and do whatever I can to put Herepath's head on a spike."

"What about the rest of you?" asked Hoth.

"Ah, well . . . there you have me," said Kagen. "I am a Vale after all, and if my brothers are crazy enough to go all the way to the gods-damned Winterwilds, then I might be crazy enough to go looking for magic books in Vespia."

The room grew quiet again and Kagen looked around.

"All of you know about what happened at Ghuraka's camp," continued Kagen. "You know how I earned my membership in the Brotherhood of Steel. You know that every Unbladed there swore an oath that there was blood on the ground between us. They cast their blades at my feet and swore to answer when I called. Well . . . except for Tuke and Filia, who are my blood family now, none of you lot were there. I hired you to accompany me here and fight against the Witch-king. But this mission—this insane and likely suicidal mission—is not what you signed up for. I release you from your work bond. You owe me nothing and there is no debt between us. None of you are honor bound to go to Vespia with me."

The Unbladed glanced at one another. Tension filled the air of the tavern. Mother Frey gripped Hop and Brace's hands, and her mouth was a hard, determined, frightened, rigid line.

Finally, Redharn stood and looked down at Kagen.

"You give the least encouraging recruiting speech I've ever heard, and I've worked for the Bulconians. You're right, Kagen, there's no blood on the ground between us, which means I'm making bad choices completely on my own." He folded his massive arms. "I'm in."

And so were they all. Every man and woman.

Mother Frey looked as if she was able to take her first real breath since meeting Kagen last night. Filia gave Kagen a sly wink, and Tuke beamed a great and happy smile.

CHAPTER ONE HUNDRED FORTY-EIGHT

They snuck into the great hall in the dead of night. Two figures, moving with incredible stealth, quick but silent, careful to check every corner. The chamber was empty and all of the torches were cold and dark in their sconces.

They crept along the wall, careful not to touch the tapestries. They had been warned about those embroidered hangings and knew that guards, and even two courtiers, had been flayed alive for touching them. There were rules to break for fun, rules to bend for new knowledge, but some rules were not worth the risk.

Gavran and Foscor were young, but they were crafty beyond their years.

When they reached the dais they paused, looking around once more to make sure there was no one there. They tried to sense whether anyone was peeking in, but all of the doors were shut.

Like careful cats, they climbed the stairs and stood on either side of the throne.

"You go first," said Gavran, nudging his sister. She looked at him, biting her lip in mingled fear and anticipation.

"You're sure?"

"Yes," he hissed.

"What if we're caught?"

"Then we get a beating," he said. "So what? This is ours anyway. Father said so. This throne and one he's having built that's just like it."

Foscor touched the arm of the throne. "But is this one mine or yours?"

Gavran shrugged. "What's it matter? Come on, don't be a sissy. *Try* it."

Foscor took a long, steadying breath and then a huge grin spread over her face, chasing the worries away. She climbed onto the throne. It was far too big for her, and when she sat back it nearly swallowed her. In imitation of their father, she settled back and laid her hands on the arms of the huge chair.

Gavran stepped back and gave her a wildly overdone courtly bow. "Your Imperial Majesty," he said gravely.

When he straightened he saw the lights in her eyes. They were dark but they glittered.

"Imperial Majesty," she murmured, liking the taste of it on her tongue.

Gavran grinned. "Now it's my turn . . ."

They spent a large part of that morning making plans, but the process was not as difficult as Kagen had feared.

"You're saying you prepared for this?" he asked Mother Frey.

"Oh yes," she said. "As soon as your brothers set out for the Winterwilds, two of my dearest and most trusted allies, Hannibus Greel and Lady Helleda Frost, took on the task of gathering supplies and horses for the Vespia mission. They are in a warehouse near the entrance to the Sligor Pass."

Kagen bent over the map and located the pass. Vespia was south and a bit east from the Cavorting Bear. The Sligor Pass paralleled a branch of Thunder River, which was a main waterway that cut through northern Bulconia. The river itself was heavily patrolled and exceptionally dangerous. One or two people might slip through in a canoe, but a force of any size would be detected. The Bulconians did not suffer unwelcome travelers gladly and were known to kill and rob them without bothering to ask for travel documents. Especially that far north, away from the bigger cities in the west and south of that big nation.

"This isn't the same one we took when Herepath, the Twins, and I went to Vespia," said Kagen. "We came up through Argon to Zaare and cut east, entering the mountains along the old silk trade route established by the merchants of Alya-Ta."

"That's safer," said Filia, studying the map closely, "but it would add days. Frey's right. Sligor Pass is the fastest way to Vespia."

"You know the region?" asked Kagen.

"I know that section of the Cathedral Mountains," said Filia, "and some parts of Bulconia. As for Vespia, I used to say you couldn't get me to cross that border even under torture." She shrugged and smiled. "Times change."

"And the world gets stranger," mused Tuke.

Kagen tapped the network of rivers that crossed the whole of northern Vespia. "We'll need boats for some of that. I recall reading that the rivers are both wide and deep."

"They are," Filia assured him.

"There are boats in the warehouse," said Frey. "Collapsible ones, I believe, but sturdy enough when assembled to carry horses and supplies if you make several trips."

Kagen turned to look at the Unbladed they'd hired. Hop and Brace were with them, sharpening their weapons and making friends.

"Have you told them yet that they're not going?" he asked the old nun.

"I did," said Frey. "Didn't you hear the shouting?"

"I was outside, seeing to the horses," said Kagen.

"It was loud," said Tuke. "And by the lucky balls of the god of chance, that little bearded fellow can curse like a hero. I wonder if we're related."

"They don't like staying behind," said Frey, "but I played the frail old lady card and said that I needed their strength, courage, and protection." She shrugged. "It worked, but they aren't well pleased."

"They kept calling us all a bunch of bloody bastards," said Filia.

Kagen grinned. "Bloody bastards, eh? I rather like that."

Frey studied Kagen. "Twenty years ago I would have gone with you."

Kagen saw in her rheumy eyes the absolute awareness of the limitations of her age, the knowledge that her reach was no longer as sure as her vision. He knew, from stories Tuke and Filia had told him, that Frey was once a very formidable person. Not a warrior in the same way as the Unbladed, but cunning, ruthless, focused, wise, and dangerous. It hurt his heart to see her acceptance of the realities of old age's inevitable victory.

"My guess," said Kagen, "is that twenty years ago you would

have picked up a sword during the coronation and cut my brother's head clean off."

Mother Frey did not answer, but there was a sudden flash of old mischief in her smile.

CHAPTER ONE HUNDRED FIFTY

They left at noon.

Before they departed, Kagen took Frey aside for a last private chat. Only Tuke and Filia joined them.

"Do you think war will break out before we get back?" Kagen asked.

"I fear it might," said Frey.

"And is it your belief that Herepath is using this Red Curse and not al-Huk?"

"I do."

Kagen nodded. "I think you're right. In any war where we would have a chance we need al-Huk. He has the ships and the best standing army at the moment. Other nations are likely reading the writing on the wind and are building up their armies. But the Samudians have always *been* ready." He paused. "It's funny, but for a while Empress Gessalyn was concerned that Samud might try to break from the empire."

"I heard that, too," said Frey, and Filia nodded.

"If you're right about the Hakkians using the Red Curse against their own people," mused Kagen, "then I can see some strategic sense in it. It weakens Samud and could turn their allies against them. It paints al-Huk as someone so filled with fear that he would risk an outbreak of a deadly disease just to punch back at Hakkia. Or it reveals that he is every bit as corrupt as the Hakkians. In either case, it would isolate Samud, and there goes the backbone of any real alliance."

"You speak truth," said Frey.

"Why use such a dangerous weapon?" asked Filia. "Herepath already has great magic. Why risk a plague affecting his own people when he could cast some kind of spell? Just because he hasn't used much since the night of the coronation doesn't mean he's lost his powers."

"I can make a guess," said Frey. "It isn't like in the fairy tales, where a magic user has unlimited power and never tires. Rather, the reverse. There is a cost to the user. Remember that the source of magic is believed to be the blood or tears—or both—of dragons. In the days when magic flourished everywhere, there were many dragons alive in the world. We're talking thousands of years ago. As they died out, or were hunted and killed, magic diminished. It never truly died out, but it was so thoroughly weakened that when the Silver Empire was born, they were able to drive nearly all of it out of the west."

"Fabeldyr is still alive," said Kagen.

"Yes she is," agreed Frey, "but from what you told me of your dreams, she is old, enslaved, and possibly dying. Clearly Herepath has discovered some method of drawing on Fabeldyr's powers to fuel his enchantments. There is no other explanation for the degree of sorcerous power he used on the Night of the Ravens. But he is drawing on the life energies of a dying creature, and each use drains some of his own life force. That takes time to replenish. He has to be conservative in how he uses it."

"Even if there is a war?" asked Filia.

"Very much so, yes. It is in Hakkia's best interests to try to trick submonarchs into fighting one another. That will almost weaken any chance of an empire unified against a usurper. Don't forget that the Red Curse is also known as the Samud Plague. Herepath is smearing al-Huk's name and shifting focus from Hakkia to Samud as the most dire growing threat. If he is successful, the other nations will spend their soldiers' lives in ground wars and naval battles, with one side actually defending Hakkian. The effect is that all of the nations involved in that war become weaker and the Witch-king will not need to use more of his magic to emerge as the most powerful force. All that time, he will be growing stronger again."

"That's not particularly encouraging," said Tuke.

"It's not meant to be," admitted Frey. "That is why my friend Hannibus Greel is meeting with the submonarchs to help them grasp the subtlety of the Witch-king's plans."

"And how long will it take for Herepath to regain his full strength?" asked Kagen.

The old nun shook her head. "I have no idea. Which is why we cannot waste time."

Kagen ran his thumb along the crossbar on one of his knives. "How bad can this plague really get?"

"The only reason we are all alive to have this conversation," said Frey, "is because the outbreaks were in remote corners of Samud. Had it reached the biggest cities, nothing could have stopped it. The Samudians had to sacrifice whole villages, some that were only partly infected, in order to save the nation and the empire."

"You're serious?" gasped Kagen.

"Completely. If allowed to spread unchecked, the Red Curse will be many, many times worse than the whole of Hakkian army and all the sorceries of the Witch-king."

Kagen rose from the table. "Then we need to get moving."

They went outside and found that the stable lad—now sober and awake—had gotten their horses ready, and the Unbladed were waiting.

Mother Frey, despite being a scholar and researcher and not a Gardener, spoke prayers as the company knelt in the dirt beside their waiting horses. She blessed them and promised to pray for their success and their souls.

Only Kagen remained on his feet and stood apart. Nevertheless, Mother Frey looked at him when she called on the Harvest Gods to bestow protection on the enemies of the Witch-king.

Kagen, sourly amused, hoped that the old woman had a better relationship with the gods than he did. He turned and looked up at the nightbirds in the trees and in rows along the eaves of the tavern. He nodded to them, and the ragged old crow gave him a soft caw of response.

When the prayers were done, Kagen growled, "Okay you bloody bastards, mount up."

They did and Kagen gave the old woman a curt nod before he kicked Jinx into a cantor. The company—the Bloody Bastards—rode after him. And soon the flocks of nighbirds threw themselves into the wind and followed.

Mother Frey, flanked by Hop and Brace, stood watching for a long time.

PART FIVE
IN THE CITY OF THE DEAD

———

In dreams I went to Ulthar, there in the burning west, set hard along the River Skai, which is born in the mountain of Lerion, where the fading recollections of Elder Gods are spoken in sighs that all can hear and few can understand. Lerion is vast, the greatest mountain in the world, rising more than seven miles into a troubled sky. Snowmelt starts the river, and it flows into Mynanthra, but it is likewise fed by rainfall lower down, and by fetid streams vomited from goblin caves into which the unwary wander and never return. Skai flows uncountable miles until it passes ancient Ulthar, and in that city the cats watch all, and their eyes of yellow and orange and green miss nothing.

Miles away, but not far enough, are the ruins of Ygiroth wherein dwells the Thing in the Yellow Mask, known as the High Priest Not to Be Described or the Elder Hierophant. On his golden throne in his kingdom of cracked stone, old bones, and gray dust, the Thing in the Yellow Mask looks out across the rivers and the mountains, the valleys and the wastes, watching over the secrets he and the Elder Gods have entrusted to the troubled earth.

Dare you go there? Do you risk your sanity and your soul? If I go there, not in dreams but in flesh, will you go with me?

—PRIEST KING B'KETHLAN SOMTON OF ALYA-TA, LAST AND
UNFINISHED WRITINGS, FROM A FRAGMENT DISCOVERED 1,635
YEARS BEFORE THE FOUNDING OF THE SILVER EMPIRE

CHAPTER ONE HUNDRED FIFTY-ONE

The Bloody Bastards rode as quickly as stealth would allow.

Four of the Unbladed rode at a distance from the group—one far ahead, riding point; one to either side, staying a mile out; and the sharp-eyed Gi-Elless, watching everyone's backs. The Bastards were all highly skilled, and in the weeks that elapsed after leaving Ghuraka's camp in far Nelfydia, Kagen learned about each rider—their pasts, their personalities, and their skills. He, Tuke, and Filia had interviewed more than a hundred Unbladed during that journey, and the score of fighters they'd picked were the best of a very talented lot.

The Bloody Bastards settled into a kind of military structure, with Kagen as captain, Tuke and Filia as lieutenants, and Gi-Elless and Redharn as sergeants. Everyone else was equal, and all of them accepted this structure as right and proper.

During the longer and more dangerous expedition to Vespia, he saw friendships and alliances form within the group. Although conventional wisdom on hazardous missions was to keep an emotional distance from everyone else because of the high risk of death and the dangerous effects of grief in combat, Kagen knew firsthand that soldiers of all kinds tend to fight hardest in defense of their fellows. That loyalty among brothers and sisters in arms was a powerful thing. He considered it a secret weapon that the Witch-king was likely to underestimate and also to not have among his own troops. The Hakkians relied on fear to maintain order. It worked most of the time, but it was hardly a rousing rallying cry. Kagen preferred a familial love, friendship, mutual respect, and shared stakes in the growing crisis.

Also, every member of the Bloody Bastards had lost friends or family to the Hakkians during or since the Night of the Ravens. Revenge, Kagen knew, was also a powerful weapon. He just hoped he was captain enough to use that weapon effectively.

CHAPTER ONE HUNDRED FIFTY-TWO

"There it is," said Kagen, pointing with a gloved finger.

Tuke signaled a halt and stood up in the stirrups to look past the heads of the riders in front of him. They had just emerged from a section of woods high on a mountain slope. Far below they could see that there was a wide, curving line beyond which the land sloped sharply down into green shadows and roiling mist. It was as if they glimpsed part of the lip of some vast bowl.

"That's Vespia," said Kagen as the others gathered around.

"Looks inviting," said Tuke, not meaning it.

"When we came here before," said Kagen, "Herepath told us that the reason Vespia seemed to sit in a kind of basin was that it formed when a falling star slammed into the earth fifty millenia ago. How he knew such things was always vague. He said the impact killed most of the life on earth and toppled all of the existing civilizations. He said ancient and immortal creatures came to earth in that falling star, and it was they who built those cities."

"Do you believe that?" asked Filia.

"I believed everything Herepath told me. So did the Twins. Herepath seemed to know everything."

"What can you tell us about the place?" asked Redharn.

"Everything is different down there. Everywhere around is a

wilderness of pines, but down there it's a rain forest. The weather is completely different. Much hotter, and with different kinds of foliage. Strange trees, ferns, and like that. More like the southern reaches of the Jungle Belt. Never snows there, either, and don't ask me why. Even Herepath didn't seem to know. Even without the threat of the cannibal dog soldiers, it was the least hospitable place I've ever been. Mosquitoes, scorpions, fire ants, centipedes as long as a child's forearm, and even poisonous plants. It was as if the whole region conspired in a desire to kill every intruder."

"Another of your speeches of encouragement," sighed Redharn. "You should have gone into politics."

Kagen grinned. "Would you rather I lie?"

"A bit, yes."

"Okay, it's a paradise of fruit trees and weaterfalls and naked women."

"Hey," said Filia.

"And naked men."

They grinned at each other.

Then Kagen sobered and said, "There's a creek down the slope to the left. Fill your waterskins and drink as much as you can. Water the horses, too."

Hingol, a young, sandy-haired Unbladed who had never been in this part of the continent, said, "If it's a rain forest, captain, won't there be plenty of water everywhere?"

It was Filia who answered. "Do you have basil or neem leaves in your pack?"

"No . . ." said Hingol uncertainly. "Why?"

"Any gooseberries or vetiver?"

"Not as such . . ."

"Then no coriander or cilantro?"

"No, of course not."

"Even though we told everyone to stock up on those items?" asked Filia.

"I'm not much for salads," said Hingol, then he realized that several of the older and more experienced members of the group were chuckling, and at his expense. "Why? What's that have to do with anything?"

"Because, lad," said Redharn patiently, "those herbs and berries and such purify water that's been tainted."

"Tainted?"

"With venom, natural poisons, and suchlike that will, at best, make you shit your colon out, and at worst will kill you."

"It's Vespia," said Tuke blandly. "Everything wants to kill you."

"I . . ." began Hingol and then let it trail off.

"Don't worry, son," said Redharn. "If you die we'll make sure to send a Harvest wreath to your folks."

Hingol looked at the dense green wall of the jungle and then at the other Bastards. "I hate you all."

Everyone had a good laugh—even Hingol, though his was more nervous and not entirely genuine—and the party went down to the stream to get clean water. The creek was much closer to the wall of jungle, and Filia stood looking at it, taking small sips from her waterskin.

"This is as far as I've ever been," she said. "Frey said that there were no roads . . ."

Kagen shook his head. "There are roads, and some of them are as broad as imperial avenues. Wider than the roads the old Skyrians built. But they're covered over with vegetation and dirt."

"That's not particularly useful," mused Tuke, who stood close by.

"Actually, it is," said Kagen. "I know how to find those roads."

In a lower voice, so that the others could not hear, Tuke said, "You were here exactly once, when you were only a lad."

"True enough," said Kagen quietly. "But Herepath was leading that expedition, and he taught Jheklan, Faulker, and me how to survive in Vespia."

Tuke flinched at the name, but asked, "How did *he* know, though?"

Kagen shrugged. "Don't know and really don't care."

They remounted and Kagen addressed his team. "Okay, you Bloody Bastards, time to earn your pay."

As they made their way down the slope, Kagen spoke with his two friends about the Vespians. "They were a great people once," he said. "Even though their civilization has fallen beyond repair, and madness of some kind has warped them, on some level they seem to remember some aspect of their greatness. My mother said that she hoped that one day a generation of Vespians will rise and reclaim their heritage and their culture. Quite frankly, I hope that for them, too."

"Even though any dog soldier in that jungle right now would gleefully kill and eat you?" asked Tuke.

"Even though."

"Fair enough," said Tuke. "But just to be clear, Kagen, the Vespian dog soldiers aren't keen on letting people wander around and survey. As I understand it, they tend to be a bit bitey."

"True enough," said Filia. "And it's not like there are only a few of those dog soldiers. There are a hell of a lot of them, as I've been told. They act like little tribes until someone comes across the border in force, and then suddenly there are a couple hundred thousand screaming maniacs with teeth sharpened to fangs. They will throw their children onto spear points if it will allow them to take advantage of a distraction."

"By the thorny balls of the god of rose bushes," muttered Tuke. Then he grunted and looked around. "Hey, where are your gods-damned birds? They were behind us this morning."

"I . . . don't know," replied Kagen. "I didn't even realize they'd gone."

"So . . . wait," said the Therian. "Are you saying that even your spooky damned magical nightbirds—who were at the fight in the palace, on our ship when it was attacked, and everywhere else where there was bloodshed and danger—are afraid of entering that jungle?"

Kagen had no answer, and Tuke lapsed into a very heavy and uncomfortable silence as they made their way to the jungle wall.

The party of well-armed Bastards reached the bottom of the slope, paused for a long moment, and then, moving in a single line, crossed both the border of the nation of Vespia and entered the dark and endless jungle. When the last of them passed inside, the whole landscape seemed to go still. Apart from hoofprints in the grass, there was no sign of them at all, as if the forest had swallowed the Bloody Bastards whole.

CHAPTER ONE HUNDRED FIFTY-THREE

"You look unhappy," drawled the Prince of Games as the Witch-king stalked into the Hall of Hakkian Heroes. He lounged on a divan, one leg hooked over the scalloped back, the foot moving as if in time to music, though the room was otherwise silent. He held a very old parchment scroll that trailed down to the floor. "What's wrong? Did you catch Nespar licking your dog's ass?"

"I'm in no mood for your jests," snapped the king. He went to a sideboard, snatched up a bottle of extremely old Bulconian brandy, and poured four fingers into a glass.

The prince sat up, letting the scroll fall to the floor like a discarded snakeskin. "Tell me," he said.

"Princess Theka will be coronated tomorrow at noon."

"That's hardly news," said the prince as he wandered over to pour himself some brandy. "We have plenty of spies in Theria keeping an eye on things."

"That is my point," said the Witch-king. "Two of those spies reported in, each from a different arm of our intelligence network and each saying the same thing. There are rumors circulating within certain channels in that government that Theka will use her coronation to announce that she is going to going to openly side with Samud against us."

"That is unfortunate, but not entirely unexpected, Majesty," said the prince.

"Think of the consequences," snarled the King in Yellow. "If Theria takes Samud's side, then we will almost certainly see Vahlycor join them."

"What if they do? None of the other nations will dare join them. They are either too remote or too weak."

"Those three have more than triple our troop strength, and each has a fleet."

"And we have the Red Curse."

"Which we cannot use in open warfare without revealing its true source," countered the king.

The prince waved that away. "Maybe, though it would be a bit late at that point."

The Witch-king turned sharply to him. "You would rather see the empire united against us? Or, worse, the west laid waste by our own plague? I want to rule this empire, not be caretaker of a graveyard." He paused and studied the other man very closely. "You are not a Hakkian. You are not even human. At moments like this I wonder if I have trusted too easily and place too much faith in your loyalty to my cause."

The Prince of Games set down his untouched glass. For a moment his eyes swirled with that strange mix of sickly greens and browns, but that distortion passed and his eyes became human again within moments. The prince nodded slowly to himself.

"A danger of being who and what I am," he said, "is that I don't take great matters of state with an acceptable sense of grandeur. Time means nothing to me, and I have seen more than mere empires rise and fall. I am the seedling blown along by the winds of time, but I seldom tarry and rarely take any kind of root. However,

I tell you now, mighty Witch-king, that I have a great personal investment in seeing you succeed in your plans to establish the Yellow Empire."

"Do you?"

"Yes," said the prince, "I do."

"Why?"

"My reasons are my own, my king," said the prince. "But I swear to you now, that for as long as you wear the mantle of the Witch-king, I am your servant, your ally, your fist, and your friend. This is a pledge I have made few times in my endless life, but I make it now. Look into my eyes and tell me what you believe."

They stood there for a long time. Whole minutes passed as the Witch-king searched the eyes of the Prince of Games, and the prince both endured and allowed it. Their conversation was one of silence but not of inaction. The tapestries in the hall began to flutter. Some scraps of parchment blew off the map table and swirled around them, and then each of those burst into flame. Ashes fell like snow. In the fireplace, the logs split and fell apart, belching sparks onto the marble floor. In an anteroom, the entire pack of hounds threw back their heads and howled, long and plaintive.

The moment stretched and stretched, and then the Witch-king nodded his head. He did it once, very slowly.

"We have much work to do," he said.

"Oh, yes," said the Prince of Games, his smile returning. "We do."

CHAPTER ONE HUNDRED FIFTY-FOUR

"Oh, yes. We do."

Those words filled the empty air of the tower room even though the speaker was in another and distant part of the palace. The entire conversation was as clear as if the king and the prince were standing only inches away.

The listener lay on the cold stone floor. Lady Kestral wore a robe of stained white silk, but it might as well have been a shroud, for her body was wasted and skeletal. Her skin was a jaundiced yellow and there was a milky film over her eyes. What hair she had left—for most had fallen out—was gray and dry and lifeless.

She lay panting from the effort of casting what should have been a simple spell. Blood trickled from her mouth and nose, from her anus and vagina, staining the robe even more and spreading into a small pool beneath her. The stain did not spread far, though, because she had so little lifeblood left. Her chest heaved with the effort of drawing even the smallest breath.

All around her were patches of dried blood. Most, though, was not hers. Those other areas were each surrounded by circles of mingled salt, powdered onyx and carnelian, and the ground-up bones of crows and starlings. Within each circle were burn marks and the smudged remains of footprints, some of which were human. Others were cloven or clawed. In a few circles were shapeless lumps of meat and bone, but they did not look like they truly belonged to any creature, human, or animal. They looked like lumps of discarded modeling clay, though they reeked of rotting tissue.

The conversation between the Witch-king and the Prince of Games faded out, drawing with it the taint of their energies. Kestral lifted one hand, which required a great deal of what little strength she still possessed, and she snuffed out a bloodred candle that stood inside its own protective circle.

For nearly half an hour she lay there, fighting for breath, rebuilding her strength a very little at a time. The room was cold, but she was far beyond the point where that mattered. Her whole body felt like ice and had for many weeks.

When she could manage it, she got to her hands and knees, and then eventually to her feet. She staggered over to where a crooked walking stick leaned against the wall, and she steadied herself with it. Then she tottered across to one more sacred circle. This one was intact, and the mixture of powders and ground minerals was thicker than the others. In it stood a column of smoke that swirled with a thousand shades of gray and white, black and red. The column turned but did not dissipate as even its smoky substance was trapped within the confines of her spell.

The smoke was not completely undefined. At times it seemed to grow legs and a torso, or a head on massive shoulders, and hands that ended in sharp spikes. It had eyes, and they burned with the reddest flame she had ever seen. Redder even than those of a similar monster she had conjured early on the Night of the Ravens.

"Child of Nyarlathotep," she said, her dry tongue nearly tripping as she spoke, "sp-speak to me."

At the sound of her voice the smoky form suddenly coalesced, taking on a far more definite shape. It towered several feet above her and was dressed all in black, with a helmet that completely hid the face beneath so that only those burning eyes glared out. The creature had a vaguely human shape but was in no way human. Around its shoulders and covering both arms was a kind of cloak made from long and slender blades of steel painted a midnight black. It raised its arms as far as the circle would allow, and those blades gave it the eerie appearance of some titanic bird. It also wore a long coat of black silk, leggings, and boots with spikes on the toes. And all around the creature was a strange swirl of shimmering air, as if the thing had just stepped through the door to hell itself.

"Speak to me," she croaked.

The eyes flashed at her and she recoiled from their heat. "Speak of what, witch?"

"Speak to me of Kagen Vale," she said. "Speak to me of Kagen the Damned."

The monster bared its teeth at her, and apart from the eyes, they were the only thing that was not pitch black. Those teeth were long and yellow, tapering to fangs like those of a wolf or bear. Its black tongue writhed like a snake for a moment. Then the razor-knight spoke.

It spoke not in the same stentorian voice with which it had demanded an answer of her a moment ago. Now it spoke in a softer, more cultured voice. A man's voice.

The voice of Kagen.

It spoke to her of the Unbladed and of a group of them who called themselves the Bloody Bastards. It spoke of the journey to Vespia. It spoke of the search for the Seven Cryptical Books of Hsan hidden somewhere in the temple of Ig-ulthan, deep within the city of Ulthar.

Lady Kestral listened to all of it.

And for the first time in longer than she could remember, she smiled.

CHAPTER ONE HUNDRED FIFTY-FIVE

Two figures walked through the dense jungle that was the western reach of Vespia. They moved without apparent haste and yet they had come many hundreds of miles since their journey began. Distance meant little to them. Their brothers had traveled even greater distances and now walked through the green shadows of the southern and eastern jungles. All of them at the same deliberate pace. Six in all, three pairs of two, dressed identically in gray robes with rope belts, strange sigils embroidered in yellow thread on their breasts. As they walked, they kept their arms folded and their hands tucked into voluminous sleeves.

On the shoulder of each man sat a raven. These were young, strong, fine birds, each in the full flush of its vitality. The birds had not come all the way from Argentium on the shoulders of these Hollow Monks. Instead, they flew ahead, following some beacon in their minds, and were waiting for the monks. An un-kindness of ravens, in point of fact.

As the monks approached the jungle wall, the ravens had flown, one to each of them. The monks then paused, for the first time in many days, and tied around the legs of each a small glass vial filled with red liquid that looked like blood mixed with water.

The monks lingered long enough to whisper a series of com-plex prayers in a language that no human tongue could manage. Then the monks lifted the ravens onto their shoulders and entered Vespia.

Now, deep within that country, the Hollow Monks approached three villages. They walked directly past the sentries—sharp-eyed killers who missed nothing, except that they did not see the monks at all. The monks did not wish to *be* seen.

Not until they stood in the center of each village. And then they spoke the words that shed the glamour and revealed their presence.

It was a moment of shock and horror in those nameless villages. It was a moment of sudden anger, fear, and rage. Men and women, even children, whirled around as they became aware of the robed figures, and the drama played out nearly identically in those towns.

The Vespians—from youngest stripling to oldest hag, from cooks to weavers to the most skilled fighters—howled their out-rage as they snatched up any weapon they could and rushed at the monks. There was no call for explanations, no demands, no questions. There was only the desire to kill these things that had snuck onto their sacred land. The weapons rose and fell, rose and fell. The gray robes were hacked to pieces, the bodies within dis-integrating beneath blade and cudgel. The ravens made no move to escape and therefore they were hacked to blood and feathers. In each case, as each monk and bird was smashed to ruin, the small vials were shattered. The bloody red liquid splashed the maddened Vespians.

Splashed.

Touched.

Infected.

Destroyed. And in doing so, the evil within that fluid proved to every Vespian that there was a level of rage that even they had never reached.

Until then . . .

CHAPTER ONE HUNDRED FIFTY-SIX

Getting to the border of Vespia required patience and stealth, but Kagen relied on Filia to find their way. She was the most experienced caravan guard among the Unbladed, and she knew every trick. It was slow going, but her canny strategies for avoiding Hakkian patrols in Zaare, and Bulconian guards, allowed the Bloody Bastards to move like ghosts through the forests and mountain passes. Stealth eats time, though, and Kagen felt the loss of every minute spent hiding or taking a detour. He bit down on his own complaints, and when they were at the Vespian border, he thanked Filia, because they had not lost a single fighter or horse during the arduous journey.

"Now," said Filia, "it's up to you. I've never been to Vespia and hoped never to add that to my life list of places visited. And you— you crazy city boy son of a bitch—have been there and back."

"Aye," said Kagen. "Now let's see if I can get us to where we're going."

"Oh, that's encouraging," said Tuke. "You have all of my confidence."

"Kiss my ass," said Kagen.

"Get us out of Vespia alive, my friend," said the Therian, "and I'll hire a dozen of the prettiest whores in Zaare to kiss your ass."

They laughed and crossed into the land of cannibals and madness.

The jungle was a monster. It clawed at them, bit at them, resisted them every step of the way. Within a few miles, the ground cover thickened to the point of being nearly impenetrable. The horses nickered and whinnied as they tried to muscle through, but hairy vines, deadfalls, monstrous spiderwebs, and gigantic ferns with razor-sharp leaves fought them.

To Kagen, the interior of Vespia seemed as if it had been smashed together by infant children of mad gods. There were swampy marshes in which twenty-foot-long crocodiles lurked, visible only by merciless eyes peering out from between water lilies. Clouds of mosquitoes, gnats, and biting flies spiraled up from the shadows of ravines cut into the land by runoff. Stands of trees seemed to have been corralled by hairy vines as thick as a grown woman's forearm. Then, with sudden drama, cliffs would rise hundreds of feet into the air, cloaked in moss and grasses or laid bare as if hand-scraped, revealing old tree roots and rocks as if they were bones of some ancient race of giants. Ferns whose breadth of leaves stretched as wide as thirty feet; carnivorous plants that perfumed the air with honey-sweet nectar; hordes of monkeys that chattered and screamed but were never actually seen.

Rivers cut through, running with intense vigor or creeping along with despairing slowness. In the former, huge silver fish leapt and splashed as bears clung to fallen trees and tried to claw them out of the air; in the latter, water snakes of impossible size cruised with no fear, because they owned those waterways. There were places where the foliage was crushed and torn and splashed with blood from some recent and savage slaughter. Ticks as large as silver dimes crawled to the end of drooping leaves, waiting for their prey with the patience of all such monsters. Centipedes the color of blood wriggled along the ground, sometimes catching unwary nesting birds and tearing them to pieces. Huge bats slept upside down beneath the shadowy canopy of overlapping trees.

Rains came out of nowhere—since the sky was often hidden by that canopy—drenching the travelers, but then the heat would boil every last drop off in moments. Then the humidity would reassert itself, pulling sweat from every pore as the travelers forged through the green hell.

"This is insane," said Filia, who rarely complained about any kind of hardship.

Tuke, who had sweat pouring down his muscular frame, rode point and swung both his machetes, one to either side, to try to carve a path. But the vegetation seemed to merely close behind him again, offering no clear path for the rest of the Bloody Bastards.

Finally, the frustrated Therian slid from the saddle, tied the reins to the back of his belt, and laid to. Redharn came forward and joined him, and the two big men worked in grunting, sweating, swearing partnership to forge a path. It was brutal work, and soon others had to join them.

Filia, who rode just ahead of Kagen, turned in the saddle. "Are you even sure this is the way?"

"Sure enough," said Kagen, though he was aware that his voice lacked conviction because doubt weighed so heavily on him. He let his horse walk a dozen steps forward and then made a disgusted sound and dismounted. He handed the reins to Filia and moved up the line, calling for Tuke and Redharn to stop. The whole company paused behind them and everyone fished for their waterskins.

Tuke leaned against a tree, dug a rag from a pocket, and mopped his streaming face. He gave Kagen a weary and sardonic smile. "If you're going to tell us to hurry, I can tell you where to shove that."

"No," said Kagen. "You lads are doing fine."

"The hell we are," gasped Redharn, whose face was as red as his name. "I've never seen jungle like this."

"I have," said Kagen, "but it gets better once we find one of the old highways. Even though they're completely overgrown, they tend to be used as game trails. They're wider, firmer, and easier to navigate."

Tuke reversed a machete and offered the handle to Kagen. "If you want to try to find one, then by all means."

But Kagen shook his head. "You lot rest here for a bit."

"That's kind of you—" began Tuke, but Kagen cut him off.

"I need you fit and ready to fight," he said. "You're no use to anyone if you're dead on your feet."

"Or," said Redharn, digging at the thick red hair on his chest, "just dead." He plucked off a tick and crushed it with his thumbnail. "Little bloody bastard."

"Maybe I should have hired him," said Kagen.

Redharn spat on the mess on his fingers and wiped it off on a tree. A cockroach the size of a mouse scrambled away, spitting and hissing.

"Going on record now," said Tuke, "but I hate this fucking place."

"Stay here," said Kagen. "Let me see if I can find that damned road."

He moved past them and walked half a dozen paces. When he paused to look over his shoulder the jungle had closed so completely behind him it was as if it had swallowed his company whole.

"Gods of the Pit," he breathed.

———————▶ **CHAPTER ONE HUNDRED FIFTY-SEVEN**

"How many have arrived?" asked the Witch-king.

He sat on a simple and unadorned chair that was set before a window that offered a wide view of Haddon Bay. Hundreds of ships and smaller craft plied to and fro in the azure waters. Gulls with feathers of incredible whiteness floated on the thermal winds, and brown pelicans swooped to snag fish from the choppy wavelets.

Lord Nespar stood just behind the chair, wringing his thin hands nervously.

"Not many," he said. "A few."

"Who?"

"Emissaries from Ghenrey, Nehemite, Zehria, Sunderland, and Behlia, my king."

"None from the north?"

"Not so far, Majesty."

"No monarchs?"

"Ambassadors only, sire," said Nespar. "But I am assured they are each empowered to speak the will and wishes of their masters. I am reliably informed that they are here to pledge their fealty and support to Hakkia." He paused. "And to you, Majesty."

The Witch-king watched the seabirds. Nespar saw that a golden icon of the Shepherd God, Hastur, lay across the king's thigh.

"I will be down in a quarter hour," said the King in Yellow.

CHAPTER ONE HUNDRED FIFTY-EIGHT

Tuke and Filia sat on a half-rotted tree stump, passing a waterskin back and forth and watching the subtle and constant movements of the jungle. A parrot of startling colors—red, green, yellow, and blue—was on a low branch cracking nuts with its sharp beak.

"He's been gone a long time," said Filia.

"He's fine," said Tuke.

"Nearly an hour."

"He's fine."

"Even though he's been here once before," she said, "he's still a city boy."

"He's fine," Tuke repeated.

"I'm glad you think so," Filia said irritably, "but I'm worried about him."

"He's—" began Tuke, and then Kagen Vale came crashing through the wall of green a yard from where they sat. He was racing like a madman.

"What the hell?" cried Filia as she leapt to her feet.

As if in eloquent reply, a half dozen arrows whipped through the leaves, missing them by inches. The arrows missed Kagen, too, who was dipping and dodging as he ran. One of the shafts struck the parrot, though, and pinned it to the tree. It squawked once and died.

"Run!" roared Kagen as more arrows punched through the walls of leaves.

<hr>

CHAPTER ONE HUNDRED FIFTY-NINE

"Are you dying?" asked the boy.

"She looks like she's dying," said the girl.

Foscor and Gavran squatted on either side of the withered husk of Lady Kestral. They were dressed in their fencing clothes and had swords with bamboo blades tucked into their belts. Gavran had a whip mark on her cheek from Madam Lucibel's wand of kindness. Foscor had red welts across the backs of both hands. Both were smiling.

"I bet we could just kill her," said Gavran. "Right now. No one would know."

"Father would know," said Foscor, and for a moment both of their smiles flickered. They cut a look toward the doorway as if the Witch-king would suddenly appear.

The door remained closed and so they turned back to the woman who lay beside the salt circle. Within the circle, smoke—formless but dense—swirled slowly.

Kestral was so weary that she could not move. All day she had wrought complex and careful spells, and each one, each aspect, had taken more from her than she could reasonably afford.

"She smells," said Foscor.

"She smells like shit," said Gavran.

"And piss," said Foscor.

"And puke," added Gavran.

They giggled.

They were very close to her, and Kestral could feel their heat. It was, she knew, a quality of being so deathly cold, but the living, vibrant heat of the children's healthy bodies was like being between two furnaces. Like a vampire, she drew it in, feeding on it to keep the flickering candle of her life from going out.

Foscor reached out and poked her. Despite having just turned six, her little finger was strong from all the training with swords and daggers, axes and bows. The poke rocked Kestral's body.

"Still alive," said the girl.

"She looks dead to me," said Gavran.

"So poke her," suggested Foscor. "She's still warm."

Gavran reached out to poke Kestral's face. He pressed his fingertip into the sunken hollow beneath the jutting ridge of cheekbone.

"Seems pretty dead to me," he said.

And in a move as fast as a snake—so fast it surprised the children and even Kestral herself—the dying woman caught Gavran's wrist.

"Hey!" he cried, pulling back but finding the icy fingers were as strong as steel. "Foscor, help me."

His sister grabbed Kestral's wrist and pulled, but as soon as she did so, the sorceress grabbed Foscor's arm as well. Now she held both children in her grasp, and everything she was, everything she had ever been, and all that she had left in this world—in that body—went into maintaining that grip. No, to more than that. She pulled the two small arms with savage, desperate strength.

"Let . . . go!" cried the children, throwing their weight against the grabs. But Kestral fought to own this moment. To achieve one thing of importance. To build on what she had already tried to set in motion.

Using all of her strength, she forced the two small, pink, bruised hands toward each other. The children, seeing their peril, screamed.

And screamed.

And then they stopped.

Foscor and Gavran stopped screaming.

Because Alleyn and Desalyn did not want to scream.

CHAPTER ONE HUNDRED SIXTY

The air was alive with death.

Arrows whipped through the leaves, punching holes in them, tearing some off the stem as the barbs sought the flesh of the scattering invaders. A spear arced over a wall of dense shrubs and punched through the rib cage of one of the horses. The animal reared and screamed, and its thrashing hooves caught another horse in the face. Both animals collapsed in a broken tangle.

"*Run!*" roared Kagen. Everyone else took up the same warning cry, even though it was obvious to them all that the Vespian dog soldiers had found them.

Kagen twisted aside to avoid a pair of arrows. One missed, but the other cut a burning line across the outside of his left bicep. He ignored the pain as he grabbed the reins of four horses and jerked them to safety behind a stand of thick rubber trees. He crouched there and took very quick stock of the situation.

Two horses were down and a third was walking in a slow, awk-ward circle, three arrows standing out from its right hip. It looked confused and whinnied piteously. One of the Bastards sat with his back to a kapok tree, fixed there by a spear. Blood bubbled on his lips and he kept trying futilely to draw his short sword. Another man crawled like an iguana toward a dead horse, staying flat to let terrain and that dying animal soak up the arrows. Kagen saw that it was Dilhoolie, a broad-shouldered Nehemitian axman and the group's cook. Redharn broke from cover, grabbed Dilhoolie by the collar, and dragged him to safety on the far side of the path he and Tuke had chopped.

He heard Filia's dog, Horse, snarling, and then there was a piercing, wet, and ugly cry that came from the same spot as the dog's growl.

Kagen could not see Filia, but he did see Tuke as the Therian pulled his bow and a quiver of arrows from his horse. The big man knelt behind a tree and began nocking, drawing, and firing arrows with incredible speed. Somewhere behind the screen of trees one of the Vespians uttered a shrill cry and flopped out onto the path. In the moment before the gap of leaves closed up again, Tuke sent two more arrows and earned two more horrible screams.

That seemed to rally the Bloody Bastards, and in the space of a heartbeat they went from a panicked, fleeing crowd to professional soldiers organizing a brutal counterattack. Men and women grabbed their bows and returned fire, and Hingol, who could not find his quiver, simply pulled Vespian arrows out of trees or the dirt, knocked debris from the barbs, nocked, and fired. He was a better archer even than Tuke, and all of the young man's feckless demeanor melted away there in the heat of battle.

From the number of arrows and spears, Kagen reckoned that there could not be more than two dozen of the attackers. His memories of Vespia told him that dog soldiers mostly traveled in packs about that size. Also, the attack was coming from one side of the path, and that suggested that the dog soldiers had found them by accident. If they'd been hunting the Bastards, they would have set a better trap, encircling the company and turning the path into a killing floor.

Kagen rose and moved laterally, going to the end of the string of terrified horses. Then, after checking to reassure himself that the focus of the attack was the head of the path, he cut across and moved like a ghost into the woods. As he moved, he saw leaves tremble just ahead of him, and then two figures emerged. Filia and Xeptog, a jovial former king's guard from Behlia. They paused when they saw him, but then he moved forward, angling left now to circle behind the dog soldiers. A third Bastard, Yill the Bulconian, seemed to materialize out of thin air, her assassin's daggers clutched in tight fists.

The four of them moved fast and quiet. Filia raised a hand, fist clenched, and they all froze on one side of a thick wall of wild bamboo. She gestured to Xeptog to go left with her, and for Kagen and Yill to go right. She peered between the bamboo stalks and then used her fingers to give a count of how many of the enemy were there. Six to the left and seven to the right.

Then she chopped down with her hand and the four of them split into pairs, raced around the bamboo, and attacked. Kagen, trained by his warrior mother, was not the kind to yell when attacking. Although he understood the logic to yelling—trying to instill fear in the enemy while summoning courage in the attacker—he preferred stealth.

"Move like a scorpion," the Poison Rose had told her sons and daughters. *"Don't worry about frightening them. Go for the kill and make every movement count. Make every cut tear screams from the enemy."*

Kagen moved very fast indeed. Whatever mercy he had or compassion he felt was left behind as he broke cover and ran straight at the closest dog soldier. The Vespians wore loincloths and rope sandals, with thick pieces of tree bark strapped to their bodies as armor. Their hair was a dark golden brown and pasted into wild crests; their skin was caked with some green pigment that allowed them to blend into the vegetation. Each had ritual marks painted on their exposed skin, but the patterns varied wildly from one to the other. Perhaps family markings or something sacred.

Kagen did not know, and in that moment he did not care. His matched daggers were in his hands, the blades coated with *eitr*, the god-killer poison, and he slashed at the flanks of the closest man. The razor tip of the dagger bit deep. Blood welled, bright and intensely red, but Kagen knew that at the same moment that gore ran from the wound, more blood was carrying the poison deep.

Before the dog soldier could even complete his scream of pain, his knees buckled and he went down. But Kagen was already moving, slashing at a second Vespian. This man, alerted by movement and that scream, whirled and brought up his bow, but Kagen slashed downward at an angle, cutting through the flexible yew wood, the nocked arrow, and a muscular wrist. He let the poisoned man stagger backwards and pivoted to press his attack on the dog soldiers.

Filia moved like a dancer, lithe and nimble, graceful in her own way, using a straight sword that would have gotten her arrested in any town in the empire. The longsword glittered in the slanting sunlight and filled the air with blood and screams. Yill used her wavy-bladed knives the way a good infighter does, carrying the fight to the enemy, pressing them with ferocity and damage so that the wounded, the dying, and the frightened collided with each other in an attempt to flee.

Xeptog fought beside Filia, and he used a combination of short dagger and spiked mace. It was an unusual pairing, and the way the man fought suggested a background in the Bulconian gladiatorial rings.

The dog soldiers fought like demons. Kagen had to give them that. If they retreated, it was only to gain better ground or to draw an enemy out of cover. They screamed and howled as they fought, and the wild sounds called to Kagen's mind the first time he'd heard them, all those years ago. Those sounds had utterly terrified him and his brothers—except Herepath, who never showed much emotion—and haunted Kagen's dreams for years. Even now he felt echoes of that fear, though it neither gave him pause nor drained any iron from his muscles. If anything, it was a spur, galvanizing him into ferocious action. His blades moved like silver fire and the dog soldiers fell all around him.

Horse came bounding out of the brush, his muzzle red and his teeth snapping as he launched himself at a Vespian. Dog and dog soldier toppled backwards into a flowering shrub and a scream began but immediately disintegrated into a wet gurgle.

Then, as if the world fell suddenly under a spell, the arrows stopped flying and there were no more screams. Kagen, Filia, and the others turned, looking for more of the enemy, but although there were dog soldiers everywhere, none moved.

"Tuke," yelled Kagen. "Redharn!"

The leaves parted and several of the Unbladed came through, each covered with sweat and blood, the weapons in their hand painted with crimson.

"We did for all the evil pricks," said Redharn. He had a deep cut across his forehead that poured blood down and turned his face into a red mask. Tuke had some minor cuts but was otherwise unharmed.

"How many did we lose?" demanded Kagen.

"Two of the lads are down," said Tuke. "Purley and Dross the Behlian. May Father Dagon take their souls into the quiet deeps."

Kagen cursed. "What about the horses?"

"Lost three," said Redharn, pawing the blood out of his eyes. "Your horse, Jinx, took an arrow, but it isn't bad. Stuck in the hide but doesn't look like it did much harm to the muscle."

Filia and Horse took some of the fighters into the woods and did a full sweep. She returned at a casual pace, her sword sheathed. She shook her head. Horse looked deeply disappointed.

"Let's get out of here," said Kagen. "That was a loud fight and

I don't want to be here when another party of these damn dog soldiers comes looking for their friends."

Tuke, who still held the bow, pointed with it to where the path he and Redharn had chopped ended. "Go where?"

Kagen grinned. "I found the road."

CHAPTER ONE HUNDRED SIXTY-ONE

They were Alleyn and Desalyn, and they clung to each other. They wept and clawed at each other's clothes to pull themselves closer into a fierce embrace. It had been nearly two months since the last time their true selves had emerged. During that time, they were aware of being trapped inside their stolen bodies, suppressed within the minds of Foscor and Gavran as if they were in a real prison forged by the "children" of the Witch-king.

On the floor, Lady Kestral kept her hands locked around the children's, refusing to allow even the possibility of their letting go.

"Please," she whispered. A plea and a prayer both. "Please."

The twins looked at her, at the total ruin of the beautiful lady they had once feared yet admired. The sorceress who served as advisor to the Witch-king and conjured dark magic at his command.

Now, though, she was a broken thing. Emaciated, jaundiced, covered in sores, and clearly at the edge of death's abyss. Seeing her so weak and helpless moved Alleyn and Desalyn. They bowed their heads and wept for her.

That was who they were. That empathy, the compassion for pain and suffering, for weakness and helplessness, defined who they were. Kestral, dying, saw this. She saw all the way into them and knew that what she saw was what the Witch-king feared. It was what the Prince of Games feared.

"Please," she begged, "hold on to each other while I do something that will allow you to *remain* yourselves. Do you understand?"

They nodded, but there was much doubt and confusion in their eyes.

"I need to take blood from each of you," she said. "Just a drop. It won't hurt."

Desalyn managed a small smile. "It's okay. We're used to pain."

Kestral flinched as if those words were physical blows. "I'm sorry for what we have done to you. We have blackened our own souls, my dears. But . . . perhaps I can put some of it right."

"How?" asked Alleyn.

Instead of answering, the sorceress used the tip of a small blade to nick each child on the forearm. As promised, it caused only a few small drops of blood to well out. Kestral—careful not to touch the blood with her own skin—used the blade to scrape it up, and then with great delicacy she painted a small symbol on each. It was a double loop that created one continuous line. She explained that it was the symbol of infinity but also of sacred connection.

Next, Kestral cut strands of their long hair, and then some wispy strands from her own threadbare scalp. She sat hunched over in a chair and, as the children watched, wove the strands of hair into two braids and tied them into circles. Her fingers were still nimble enough for that task. When she was done she placed one braided loop over the head of each of the twins, tucked low behind ruffles and folds of cloth.

When that was done, Kestral closed her eyes and spoke very slowly and haltingly in a language neither child understood. Finally, she opened her eyes and slumped back against the chair.

"It is done," she said wearily. "Let go of each other."

The looks they gave her were full of doubt and suspicion and fear.

"We don't want to go back to being *them*," said Gavran.

"We hate being them," said Foscor. "They're so mean."

"It will be better," said the sorceress. "Trust me."

It took so much time and so much strength, but they finally let go. Each had tears in their eyes and they panted like frightened rabbits. Their clenched hands relaxed and slid apart and the connection was finally broken. Alleyn and Desalyn froze, breath caught, eyes wide with fear.

"I . . ." began Alleyn.

"I'm not . . ." said Desalyn.

"You are both yourselves," said Lady Kestral. "You must never let anyone see those braids, and you must never take them off. Do you understand?"

They nodded, and hope blossomed as slowly as the first flowers of spring.

"Now, children," wheezed Lady Kestral, "we have much work to do."

CHAPTER ONE HUNDRED SIXTY-TWO

"Who are you that you come without invitation to my hall?" demanded the king of Samud.

The Prince of Games stood, framed by armed guards, before the throne of King Hariq al-Huk. He wore a simple robe of yellow edged in black, carried no weapon of any kind, and brought with him no gift or letter of introduction.

"I am the left hand of the Witch-king of Hakkia," he said, pitching his voice to fill the hall. "I am advisor to the King in Yellow and I have been sent by my master to deliver a message. Abuse me, O king, and fire will rain down on you and your line, for I am an emissary who comes here on imperial business."

"Do not dare to threaten me in my own hall," snapped al-Huk.

"Was that a threat or a promise that I made?" asked the prince, smiling.

Al-Huk could feel the weight of stares from the courtiers and advisors, from his officers and the guards.

"Speak your piece," he said. "But do not waste my time."

"Then I will, at your invitation, mighty king, be both brief and blunt," said the prince. "The Red Curse is spreading throughout Hakkia and has struck villages in Ghenrey and Nehemite and Zehria. Innocent people are dying of what everyone calls the Samudian Plague. We know that this curse has its origins in this land, Majesty. Is it so strange, then, that nowhere in Samud has it appeared? No Samudian has been struck down with it. Only Hakkians and the good, free people of our neighboring lands have suffered from it. The whole of the west whispers that King al-Huk has released this to punish anyone who stands with the Witch-king. This goes against all treaties and agreements, all sworn oaths and customs of warfare."

His words echoed in the hall and everyone who heard him held their breaths.

"The Witch-king has a valid and legal claim to the throne," continued the prince. "He has worked to achieve his goal of founding a new, fair, and tolerant empire that is free of religious oppression, genocide, and hatred. And yet you have broken with all civilized custom to use plague—*plague*—as a weapon of war. There is no defense for such an abominable act. There is no justification for treachery of this kind. My king has sent me to tell you that there is blood on the ground between us, mighty king. May the gods have mercy on your soul, for you will find no mercy here on earth. I have spoken the words of my king and have no more to say to you or anyone on Samudian soil. Allow me to take my leave unmolested."

As the prince spoke, al-Huk's face first paled to the color of spoiled milk and then gradually flared with the dark crimson of a fury only barely contained. His hands gripped the arms of his throne as if he was ready to launch himself at the man and throttle him. But everyone was watching, and he fought back the words that first came to his lips.

When he trusted himself to speak, he said, "You have brought me false words from a usurper. You have come these many miles to trade in lies and baseless accusations. If you were not an emissary I would have you stripped and beaten and dragged behind my horses all the way back to Argentium."

The room was utterly silent.

"But because I am *not* the barbarian that your king describes in this message, I will allow you to leave unharmed. I send no message back to your king because I do not recognize him as a peer or as a rightful *anything* except Hakkian trash. Begone now, before I change my mind."

The Prince of Games smiled. His eyes went totally dark, losing pupil and sclera both as green and brown and yellow swirled like a witch's brew. From that angle, only King al-Huk could see this grotesque and dreadful transformation, and he shrank back involuntarily.

"Begone!" he cried, and the sudden fear in his voice was heard by all.

The Prince of Games bowed, and as he turned, his eyes became normal once again. He smiled at the gathered soldiers and nobles and left the hall with his head held high.

CHAPTER ONE HUNDRED SIXTY-THREE

The Bloody Bastards followed Kagen through the woods, down a slope to a gorge, and then down a series of switchbacks to reach the floor of the chasm.

"The road is down there?" complained Tuke, who was having a very hard time leading his horse along the treacherous path, which was little more than an irregular ledge. "By the cloven balls of the god of goats."

Filia, who was behind him and battling with spiraling swarms of gnats, said, "Goat balls aren't cloven, you half-wit."

"I'm clinging to a wall and trying not to die," Tuke fired back. "It's the best I can manage."

"The road is down there," said Kagen, picking his way with great care.

When they reached the bottom, half the company sat down on the mossy floor as if needing to commune with solid ground. One of them even made a warding sign. And there were some muttered comments about Kagen, his personal habits, his hygiene, and his sexual proclivities. Kagen ignored all of that and allowed the group to rest for ten minutes.

After that he led them along the floor of the gorge to a place where the walls were even more sheer and unforgiving, but the path widened. Still leading Jinx, he stamped the ground a few times to show how solid it was. Redharn knelt and pawed at the soil until he uncovered a flat sheet of granite. The others clustered around.

"That's a road sure enough," he said.

"Yeah . . . well," groused Tuke.

Kagen said, "We can follow this road for a good while, but we need to be careful. About nine miles from here is a stream. It's shallow, but beyond it is a small village. Once we find the right landmarks, I think I remember how to skirt that village by going along a side path."

They began moving along the path, and in the relative cool of the gorge's shadowy bottom they made good time, even with a road that was mostly covered with dirt and plant roots. Eventually they were able to mount and the miles fell away behind them. They heard the gurgle of the stream before they reached it, but Horse, who was ranging ahead, suddenly stopped. He crouched low, hair standing straight along his spine, teeth bared.

"What is it?" whispered Kagen as Filia and the others clustered around.

"That's what's wrong," said Filia, pointing up.

Above them and about a mile farther along, the sky was filled with dark shapes that circled slowly.

"Vultures," said Tuke. "Shit."

Kagen dismounted. "We'll leave the horses here with two men. The rest come with me. Stay quiet and stay sharp."

With the bulk of the company at his heels, Kagen moved through the shadows in the direction of the Vespian village.

Redharn touched his arm. "Something's coming this way," he said.

They all crouched behind whatever cover was available, weapons drawn, eyes alert. Within seconds there was a rustling in the bulrushes that grew in the marshy soil. Kagen had both his daggers in hand as he knelt behind a boulder. Horse, who was very well trained, lay flat in the weeds beside his mistress, but his body rippled with tension.

A figure emerged around a bend in the path. It was a woman wearing a sarong, her face painted with Vespian tribal colors. She walked uncertainly, staggering and nearly falling several times, and Kagen wondered if she was drunk. As she moved from gray shadows into a slanting beam of sunlight, he saw that the woman's problems went miles deeper than too much wine.

Most of her throat was gone. There were dreadful wounds on her arms and breasts and one thigh. The injuries looked like bites. Blood ran down her limbs and she left red footprints behind her on the green moss.

"Gods of the Pit," murmured Filia. "Look at her eyes."

Kagen could not help but stare at those eyes. They were pale, milky, and totally vacant. There was no hint of pain or even of shock. The eyes held nothing at all. And, as awful as that was, it was her mouth that sent an icy thrill through Kagen. Her jaws opened and closed with relentless consistency, as if she was chewing, but there was nothing in her mouth. She bit the air itself. Snapping at it, grinding her teeth as if feasting on the most savory meat.

"What's wrong with her?" asked Tuke.

He spoke quietly, but not quietly enough. The woman's head turned sharply in his direction and those empty eyes widened and the snapping mouth snarled. Then she rushed toward Tuke with no preliminary tension, no word of challenge, not even a howl to alert the rest of the village. One moment she was shambling and the next she was racing at horrific speed toward the crouching Therian.

Tuke rose up and tried to avoid her. She was not a fighter, that much was clear, and was both unarmed and badly injured. He did not want to hurt her, but she flew at him with such savage force that he began backing away, using the flats of his machetes to try to deflect her reaching, clawing, grasping hands.

"Dagon's sacred balls!" cried Tuke. "Help me with her."

Redharn and Xeptog rushed to his aid and their presence seemed to momentarily confuse the injured woman. She kept lunging at one and then another as they circled her. Xeptog darted in and caught one arm, but as he tried to jerk her off balance, she sprang at him. She was half his size and weight, but the sudden ferocity of a hundred pounds slamming into him bore the man down. The others lunged for her, but she was fast. Gods of the Pit she was fast. She sank her teeth into the flesh of his cheek and tore at him. Even as Tuke and Redharn yanked at her, pounded her with fists, kicked her, she tore away a flap of skin. Xeptog screamed as blood erupted from the wound. The woman, her mouth filled with flesh, tried to bite again and again, as if no amount of meat could ever satisfy the hunger that burned within her. Her bloody teeth snapped down on Xeptog's windpipe and now a geyser of red shot a dozen feet into the air.

Tuke, horrified, stopped punching her with the fists holding his machetes and instead slashed at her. Once, twice, again and again.

Her body seemed to come apart as the big blades cut through meat and tendon and bone.

She never stopped biting as he cut her to pieces.

Horse pranced around, snarling and snapping, but he clearly feared the woman and would not get close. Only when Redharn grabbed her by the chin and the hair and wrenched her head all the way around—snapping vertebrae with a sharp and sickening crack—did the power and madness come to a complete and instant halt. The woman sagged in his grip and he cast her aside with a grunt of mingled anger and disgust. Tuke dropped his machetes and used his hands to try to stanch the awful spray of blood from Xeptog's ruined throat.

He tried.

But it was too late before he even attempted. The blood slowed and then stopped, and the man's thrashing limbs settled, with only a few residual tremors.

Then everything froze. The company, the horses, the dog, and even the breeze seemed to pause. Kagen and the rest of the Bloody Bastards looked down at the two corpses. The Vespian woman who lay in pieces like a broken doll. And Xeptog, spread-eagled in a lake of his own blood.

"Gods . . ." began Kagen.

But then Xeptog's eyes opened.

"Wait," cried Hingol, pushing his way through the crowd to reach his friend's side. "He's still alive. Someone get me some bandages and—"

And then Xeptog came up off the ground with shocking force and speed. He grabbed Hingol by the hair and jerked the man forward, mouth stretching impossibly wide, teeth snapping shut. The brief stillness was shattered by a new and awful scream. Fresh blood splashed Xeptog's face. Hingol beat at him with panicked fists. Redharn and Kagen grabbed at Xeptog while Filia and Dilhoolie tried to pull Hingol out of danger. Kagen punched

Xeptog in the face. Once, twice, again. Tuke pummeled him with fists and knees and elbows, roaring at him to let go. Xeptog was far beyond understanding, let alone obeying. His friends tried, though.

They tried. They tried so hard. But in the end, they had to kill him to stop those gnashing teeth. Hingol coughed blood as he sagged to hands and knees, and then he seemed to puddle down into a boneless sprawl. Dead.

Dilhoolie looked down at his two dead friends and then around at the other Unbladed. "What?" he demanded. "What . . . ?"

No one had an answer. Above them the vultures circled faster, driven to madness by the smell of so much blood.

CHAPTER ONE HUNDRED SIXTY-FOUR

Silent as shadows, the imperial twins moved through the corridors and passageways of the palace. When one hall was occupied, they used another, and twice opened secret doors in the walls and felt their way through cobwebby darkness.

Stealth requires patience, and despite their pounding hearts and a constant terror of being discovered, they did not falter in either direction or purpose. Rats scuttled out of their way and then turned to watch them with their red eyes, sniffing at the air with twitching noses as if they could smell intent.

It took a very long time for the children to reach the secret stairway that led to the Witch-king's private alchemy laboratory. There were two sets of stairs, one that the Witch-king used and one that had been disused for a long time and was sealed up before the Hakkians invaded Argon. The children knew, though. With their brothers and sisters, they had discovered all of the secret ways within the palace. Two of the sons of the Poison Rose had taken their older siblings on adventures, and those sisters and brothers had passed the knowledge down to their younger kin.

And so Alleyn and Desalyn reached the hidden door, confident that no one had, or even could have, followed them. They bent close to a hole that Jheklan—or was it Faulker?—had cut into the wall. At that time, this room had been used by their older brother Herepath, and they would sneak in and leave obscene drawings in his most sacred texts or put pregnant mice in his cupboards.

Now Herepath was their father. Or, at least he said he was. That made no sense to the children. Their father had died along with Mother and everyone else in the family the night the Hakkians came. That mystery had to wait, though. Lady Kestral had sent them on a very special mission, and she had begged them to hurry as much as they could.

They pressed their ears to the door, but there was no sound at all. Alleyn reached into a hidden niche, his fingers feeling for a slender wire.

"I can't find it," he whispered.

"It's there," insisted Desalyn. "Keep trying."

"Got it," he cried. There was a faint *click* and a narrow section of wall shifted a little. Desalyn pushed it open a few inches and peered into the laboratory.

"It's empty," she said.

They crept inside. The room was big and quiet, with two oil lamps burning. The door to the main stairway was closed, and when Desalyn pulled on the handle it was clear that it had been locked from without. That made her feel a little better.

The chamber was very strange. There were all manner of bottles and vials, heaps of books and scrolls, skeletons hanging from hooks, and parts of creatures suspended in jars. It stank of chemicals and death. They tried not to look up at the stuffed animals hanging from the rafters. Both were familiar with taxidermy because the palace had scores of heads on walls, and they knew the eyes were only glass, but it was impossible not to feel as if these eyes were watching them. Nor did they want to look at the row of huge, thick-walled glass tanks. The things in there seemed far too alive, and none of them were animals either of them had seen, even in storybooks.

One thing that did draw their attention was what looked and felt like a huge block of ice. It stood against a wall and there was some shape within that looked like a man, but the ice was hard to see through. The fact that the ice did not seem to melt was disturbing on a level neither of them could quite articulate, and so they turned away and tried not to see it. Both of them felt as if the figure in the tank watched them. Alleyn even turned back, thinking that the thing had turned its head, but as he stared at it, the form within the tank was absolutely still.

"I hate this place," he said, his eyes huge and round.

"Me, too," said Desalyn, shivering. "Come on, we have to hurry."

They went to a chair set beside a table. On it was a yellow cloak and upon that was a veil—one of many the Witch-king always wore. Desalyn snatched up the veil and turned it over in her hands, scrutinizing it while Alleyn examined the cloak.

"There's nothing," she said, but Alleyn raised a hand in triumph. Caught between his fingers was a single strand of dark hair. Desalyn frowned. "Are you sure it's his?"

"Who else's?"

They shared identical small, nervous, hopeful smiles.

Desalyn produced an empty glass vial from an inside pocket of her indigo robe, removed the stopper, and held it steady while Alleyn slid the strand of hair inside. Then she corked it and hid it in her pocket. "Let's go," she said.

Alleyn looked around the grim and strange room. He made no argument. They hurried away and soon the room was empty and silent once more. The only movements therein were the flickering flames of the lamps and the dark eyes of the thing in the ice. It stared at the place where the secret door had closed. It blinked slowly and waited with infinite patience.

> ### CHAPTER ONE HUNDRED SIXTY-FIVE

They stood in a ragged circle around the bodies of Hingol and Xeptog. No one spoke, and even Dilhoolie stopped asking for answers that were no one's to give. Horse sniffed at the bodies and then retreated a dozen paces, sat down, and whimpered like a frightened pup.

Tuke knelt very slowly beside Xeptog and studied the man. When he could finally manage to speak, he said, "I don't understand this. He went as mad as that woman."

"It's sorcery," said Filia, making the warding sign. Many of the others did the same.

Tuke suddenly straightened. "By Dagon's scaly balls, I think I know what this is. It's the Red Curse."

Gi-Elless gaped at him. "In *Vespia?*"

"It has to be," said the Therian. "What else could it be?"

"Tuke," warned Kagen, "don't touch him. Everyone get back."

"Red Curse or not, I don't understand," said Borz, a dour caravan scout from Ghul. "Xeptog was dead, damn it. Then he wasn't."

"He must not have been dead," said Gi-Elless. "In a coma, mayhap, and then the Red Curse did whatever it does and he woke up with his mind broken. Kagen, you told us about the Vespian dog soldiers being insane. Is this the same thing?"

"No," Kagen replied. "You all saw how ferocious they were this morning, but none of them tried to *bite* anyone. I think Tuke is right; this is the Red Curse. It's how Mother Frey described it to us."

Tuke bent to pick up his machetes and began cleaning them on the leaves of a big fern. "How in the burning hells is it here in Vespia, though?" he muttered.

Which is when Hingol woke up.

Like Xeptog, he came awake all at once and leapt to his feet, eyes wide but blank, hands reaching, mouth snapping at the very air. It happened so damned fast. One moment he was a dead man and the next he rushed at Tuke. Filia and Kagen both grabbed Tuke and dragged him backwards with such desperate force that the Therian staggered a dozen feet and nearly fell. Hingol threw himself at Bor'ak, a blond-bearded Vahlycorian, but the fighter pivoted nimbly, slapped the side of Hingol's head, and sent the young man crashing into a tree near where the horses were clustered. The animals screamed and reared and suddenly half a dozen hooves punched into Hingol's face and arms and chest. Bones splintered audibly, flesh tore, but Hingol—impossibly— did not go down. Instead, like a marionette on tangled strings, he staggered toward another of the company, reaching with shattered arms. Pieces of broken teeth slid from his mouth on a thin wave of dark blood.

Kagen stepped up and slashed with a dagger, not expecting much to happen but needing to know if the god-killer poison had any effect on Hingol. The young Unbladed took another step. Another. And on the third his leg buckled and he fell forward like a scarecrow cut from its crossbar. He made no attempt to break his fall, and after a single rippling shudder, he lay totally still.

Once more they all stood like statues, staring at the dead men who had been their friends and comrades.

"What . . . was that?" gasped Gi-Elless. She was a very tough woman, a leader of fighters, but her voice was as fragile as spun glass. "Both of them were damn well *dead* and both of them got up and attacked us." She looked around. "Am I wrong? We all know death when we see it."

"Aye," said Kagen. "They were dead."

"What are you saying?" growled Borz. "That the Red Curse brought them back? How are we supposed to fight insane Vespians *and* this . . . this . . ." He stopped and shook his head.

Kagen looked at the three corpses. "We know that the god-killer poison works. Not sure if that's magic or alchemy or what. But that woman only died after Redharn broke her neck."

"So . . . they're immune to regular blades?" suggested Dilhoolie.

"No . . ." said Kagen, chewing on it. "No, Xeptog was killed by the horses. His skull was shattered."

"What does that tell you?" asked Redharn.

"I don't know for sure," said Kagen. "But it's suggestive. A broken neck and a shattered skull."

"And your poison," said Borz. "Do, um, you have enough for all of us?"

"Not nearly," said Kagen. "The head and neck, though . . . there's got to be something in that."

"I agree," said Filia, though she looked uncertain.

"Well," said Tuke, laying his hands on his sheathed machetes, "I think I'm going to start lopping off heads. Just to be sure."

"Yeah," said Borz. "Me, too."

Kagen looked around and walked up the path to the turning. He stopped there, stood frozen as the full weight of what was happening struck him. When Tuke and the others saw his expression, they hurried over, each of them with weapons in their hands. Around the bend was the Vespian village. It was tiny, a cluster of a dozen huts.

Everywhere they looked they saw blood. Big pools of it. Sprays of it on the sides of the huts. Streaks of it on the ground.

"Where are the people?" asked Filia.

The village was empty. Bloody footprints wandered off in all directions. Into the woods, up the slopes, and farther along the path they needed to take.

"Where are the people?" she asked again, but they all knew the answer. They understood even before the screams and howls split the forest silence.

"May the gods save our souls," whispered Bor'ak. He made the warding sign and then drew his weapon. There was a fresh wave of screams.

Closer.

Coming their way.

CHAPTER ONE HUNDRED SIXTY-SIX

The first of the infected burst through the jungle wall. It was a dog soldier, painted in his sacred markings but covered from mouth to belly with glistening blood. Part of his face was gone, cheek and nose torn away, leaving ragged flesh and edges of white bone. He carried no weapons, but the disease had made *him* a weapon. With reaching hands and snapping teeth he charged at Dilhoolie, but Kagen pushed him out of the way and met the charge with his poisoned daggers. The silver blades whipped back and forth only once, and immediately all sense and purpose vanished from the running legs. The Vespian fell forward and slid on chest and face along the path.

The forest was alive with screams, though, and Kagen backpedaled. "Bows!" he bellowed, and the Unbladed ran to their horses to fetch the weapons.

Two more victims of the Red Curse broke from the foliage—another dog soldier and a teenage girl. Both wore the marks of the bites that had infected them; both had empty eyes and gnashing teeth. Filia and Tuke raised their bows and fired at the same instant. Tuke's arrow took the dog soldier in the throat and spun him around, dropping the madman to his knees. Filia shot the girl in the right eye socket and the arrow punched through eyeball, brain matter, and out the back of her skull. She toppled forward and rolled in an artless sprawl less than a yard from where Filia stood.

The dog soldier, however, got back to his feet. The arrow transfixed the man's throat, entering below the left side of the jaw and sticking out behind the right ear. It still did not stop the cursed soldier.

"Shit," cried Tuke as he reached for another arrow.

"The eye," yelled Kagen, but Filia had an arrow nocked. She fired and took the dog soldier in the forehead, just above the left eye. At that range the arrow bit deep and the Vespian simply collapsed.

The Unbladed stared at them, and Borz hurried over, raising his huge axe, waiting to see if they rose again. They did not.

Tuke glared at Kagen and pointed to the dog soldier. "Explain that to me, damn it," he snarled. "Redharn broke that woman's neck. I shot this one clean through the throat and neck."

Kagen shook his head.

It was Filia who answered. "Redharn *broke* the neck. The horses smashed Xeptog's skull. My arrows pierced the brains of those two. Without a doubt it's the brain. That's the key to killing them. Brain or spine."

"I don't understand it," said Kagen, "but that's worth trying. Destroy the brain, break the neck, or cut the head off."

Three more of the cursed—an ancient village shaman and two more dog soldiers—smashed through the brush and charged. This time they were met by a flight of arrows. Every Unbladed was a good shot, and the range was nearly point-blank. The infected crumpled down, each with at least one arrow in eye socket, temple, or forehead.

"As a working hypothesis," gasped Tuke, "I approve."

"Hush," said Gi-Elless as she inched toward the forest wall and cocked her head to listen. When she spoke it was in a whisper.

"I can hear more of them. But not close." She turned. "Kagen, if you know where this damned city is, then we need to move our asses."

"Yes, we damn well do," said Kagen. "Everyone mount up. The only path is around the bend and through that village. Can anyone not shoot from the saddle? No? Good. We're going to ride hard and push through whoever or whatever is there. We ride in two columns so everyone has a partner. No pauses, no hesitation. If it moves, kill it."

He swung into Jinx's saddle.

They rode hard. They rode fast. There were a dozen villagers on their feet. They all turned at the sound of the approaching horses. Another seven burst from the forest. The Bloody Bastards filled the air with flying death. The screams tore the morning apart.

And then the company was through and riding hard, leaving only death behind them.

━━━━━▶ **CHAPTER ONE HUNDRED SIXTY-SEVEN**

Far away, in a high room in a slender tower that looked out on a troubled sea, a figure stood with her hands lightly touching the sill. She wore a gown made of climbing roses and moss. Ladybugs and crickets wriggled beneath the green leaves. Behind and around her a hundred cats sat in perfect stillness, their eyes—sun yellow, pumpkin orange, or jade green—stared at their mistress, seeing whatever she saw.

The woman's face was cast in sadness and two vertical lines were cut beneath troubled brows. This window did not face the ocean, but was east-facing. The woman cast her gaze far past the town and the fields and the vastness of lush Vahlycor. She saw nothing of that nation, but instead looked beyond. Past valleys and rivers and the jagged spires of the Cathedral Mountains to a place where cities old beyond counting lay beneath grave-blankets of jungle green.

She saw the drama unfolding in ancient Vespia. She smelled the blood and tasted the tears of the dying and felt the heat of thundering horses. She saw him there.

Him.

In ten times ten thousand years she had never loved a mortal man. Not true love. Not love without the lust of blood and the hunger to consume that sweet and final exhalation as the soul leaves the dying body. Her garden was filled with old bones and weeping ghosts. Those men were not her lovers. They were her crimes.

But Kagen Vale.

She loved that man. Impossibly young, troubled, damned, filled with fear and hate.

Kagen.

Maralina, the Lady of the Tower of Sarsis, saw him. His face, his heart, his past, and the perils that closed in on him from every side. She saw all of that. But try as she might, even with all of her magicks, she could not see his future.

And Gods of the Earth, that was terrific.

Gods of Air and Fire that was magnificent. A man whose very existence swirled in the midst of a storm of chaos.

"Kagen," she whispered.

CHAPTER ONE HUNDRED SIXTY-EIGHT

"Did you get it?" gasped Kestral.

The necromancer sat slumped in her chair. Her face was as gray as dust, her eyes sunken so deeply into shadowy pits that they almost vanished, and she panted like an old, sick dog.

"Yes," cried Desalyn, running to her while Alleyn quietly closed the door. "Here!"

In the little girl's hand was the vial containing the strand of hair.

"Gods of—" began Kestral. Then she cut herself off and instead said, "Give it to me."

Desalyn handed the vial over. Alleyn, lingered by the door, looking down at the infinity symbol on his arm. Fear sweat had caused the mark to run and thin. "I . . . I'm feeling sick," he said. "I can hear Gavran in my head. He's not gone. He's in there and he wants to come back out."

"Me, too," said Desalyn. "Foscor is scratching at the inside of my head. She's under my skin."

"Come here, children," said Kestral quickly. She set the vial down with great care and picked up two necklaces. Each had a pouch that clicked softly as stones within them moved. "I made these for you, and you must wear them constantly. Hide them at all costs."

"What's in them?" asked Alleyn weakly.

"Black tourmaline for grounding yourself into your own energy," said Kestral, "clear quartz for deflecting negative energy, black obsidian to attract positive and healing energy, black jade to deflect the insights of the wicked, and amethyst because it helps to promote calm, serene energy and can guard you against being overwhelmed. You'll need that calm in order to pretend to be Gavran and Foscor. Amethyst, in conjunction with the other stones, offers great spiritual and emotional protection and guards your peace. Now please, put them on and tuck them out of sight."

The children did not hesitate. The change was immediate. Both of them suddenly took deep breaths as if released from unseen constriction. They smiled and hugged each other and then Kestral.

"Mind that you play your roles well," warned Kestral. "Madame Lucibel and Sir Giles are shrewd, and they will be watching. Do nothing that will arouse their suspicions. Much depends on this. Do you understand?"

The smiles faded and the children nodded. The sorceress seemed to take comfort and strength from them.

Kestral let out her own pent-up breath. "Now," she said, "let's see what mischief we can get ourselves up to."

■■■■■■■▶ **CHAPTER ONE HUNDRED SIXTY-NINE**

The Bloody Bastards rode for their lives, pushing the horses to their limit. But the animals seemed acutely aware of the peril and did not complain, even as foam flecked their mouths and sweat streaked their laboring bodies. Horse ran along beside Filia, unwilling to move far from his mistress. Though the hound feared no normal man or beast, the cursed terrified him.

Kagen led the way, following instinct as much as memory. He never strayed from the ancient stone road as he searched for modern versions of landmarks he remembered from boyhood: an ancient and massive kapok tree on which he, Faulker, and Jheklan had carved their names; a pair of broken stone pillars straddling the path; a waterfall that zigzagged down the mountainside. They were all there, and it gladdened his bitter heart.

"Kagen," called Redharn, who was at the rear of the string. "They found us."

Kagen turned in the saddle and saw figures running through the murky shadows. Then he heard a series of yips and cries, and words spoken in a strange language filled with clicks and barks.

"More of the cursed," yelped Borz.

As if in reply, a half dozen arrows slashed through the air. One struck a packhorse and it stumbled and fell, screaming in agony, but the other shafts missed.

"The cursed don't use arrows," growled Filia. "Those are dog soldiers. Ride, damn you!" She kicked her horse and they surged forward with speed born of panic.

They rode for their lives. The dog soldiers, running instead of riding, fell behind, but even without being infected, they were relentless. They fired as they ran and filled the air with arrows. One struck Tuke's horse, but the barbed shaft merely buried itself in his waterskin.

Up ahead, not a hundred yards distant, Kagen saw the thing he was most desperate to find. It was a pile of granite stones of immense size that had fallen across the road, leaving only a narrow gap.

"There it is," he yelled as he urged Jinx on.

An arrow tore through the leaves of a rubber plant and opened a hot line across his thigh. He cursed and begged Jinx for more speed. The horse needed no urging, though, and it bore him like the wind through that green hell. Then Kagen reached the cleft. He laid his body low across the horse's withers, flattening down because the passage was dangerously low. Stone scraped his back, nearly tearing the leather jerkin from him. But then he was through and the way ahead was clear.

Filia was next, and as she burst through the cleft, Kagen jerked Jinx to a halt, flung himself from the saddle, snatched his bow and quiver and ran back. He knelt just inside the opening and fired past the company at the dog soldiers. Unlike the running Vespians, who jostled their own aim as they ran, Kagen steadied himself against the stone and fired one arrow after another. He missed the first man he aimed at, but the arrow caught a man behind him in the groin. The dog soldier screamed and fell, tripping another behind him. A third vaulted his fallen comrades even as he nocked an arrow, but Kagen took him in the chest.

Filia dismounted and joined him, and together they provided covering fire as the rest of the Bloody Bastards poured through the opening.

Once Redharn was through, all of the Unbladed joined Filia and Kagen.

"There's too many of them," cried Gi-Elless.

"Retreat," ordered Kagen. "They won't come into the city."

"City?" said Borz, looking around and seeing only massive hills of mossy rock.

"Trust me. Now fall back, blast you."

They did, pulling their horses with them as they followed Kagen away from the cleft and around a thick stand of rubber trees. Tuke paused there and looked back, and sure enough, the dog soldiers stopped on the other side of the opening. A few fired arrows, but these were done more out of frustration than with any hope of making a kill.

"Damn, city boy," he said. "You're right."

The company stopped running and peered through the rubber trees, watching the dog soldiers as the Vespians stopped and merely stood in the road. They howled and shook their weapons at the invaders, but they did not cross the line.

"By the fortunate balls of the god of luck," said Tuke, his big body trembling with fear and exhaustion.

"Why did they stop?" asked Dilhoolie.

"They fear this place," said Kagen.

"They fear a ruin?" asked Bor'ak, frowning. "Why?"

"Kagen," asked Gi-Elless, "what about the cursed? Will they stay outside, too?"

All Kagen could do was shake his head.

CHAPTER ONE HUNDRED SEVENTY

Lady Kestral huddled in a chair, unable to stand even when the Witch-king entered her room.

"My lady," said the king, "the hour has come. Have you accomplished the task I set for you?"

It took her several tries before there was enough spit in her mouth to answer. "Yes," was all she managed.

The King in Yellow went to a side table and poured water into a cup. He held it for her to drink. She took three sips, then sagged back, gasping from the effort.

"Tell me," said the king, looming over her.

━━━━➤ CHAPTER ONE HUNDRED SEVENTY-ONE

They did not tarry there but took a kind of rest as they walked their horses through the green hills. It soon became apparent to them that all the hills were, in fact, ruins. In an awed silence, the Bloody Bastards passed between pinnacles and cones of what looked like granite, but dressed so finely that the dense stone felt like silky, polished marble to the touch.

As the city became more evident, its size and strangeness stilled every voice. Everything was of a scale that dwarfed anything they had ever seen. Even the palace in Argentium, made from blocks of two or even three tons, was a child's dollhouse in comparison. Many of the structures seemed—impossibly—carved from single blocks of stone so huge as to challenge the sanity of the viewers. Finally, the company stopped at the foot of a long sloping fairway that led up and into the city.

Titanic cones and pyramids soared hundreds of feet into the sky, blotting out the clouds all along the eastern horizon. There were what looked like gigantic cube-shaped blockhouses, a hundred or even two hundred feet per side, but without marking, doorway, or window. And these lay in rows as if placed there, though what force could have ever maneuvered such pieces was beyond comprehension. No human hands could have done this. They were all sure of that much, if unsure of anything else. There were lines of cones, ranging from those that were cut to points and others deliberately truncated. Some of these had terraces or walled ledges, and behind those were darkened openings that seemed too tall and too geometrically odd to be windows or doors. Every now and then these rows were interrupted by massive stone globes connected by arched walkways, though these were far above the ground. A few, though, had collapsed, and their fragments showed a kind of flagstone used for roadways that alternated red, red-gray, and brown in oddly hypnotic patterns. Other interruptions in the lines of cones were structures that looked like stars with five, six, seven, or eight points. The shortest of these stars was about a hundred feet tall, and the largest, which had toppled backwards and shattered long ago, had to have stood a thousand feet high.

Needlelike spires rose here and there, each of them slender and most of them broken or cracked, and wherever they had been built were amphitheaters of various sizes, constructed with ascending curved terraces of seats, though each seat was far too tall and deep to have been meant for humans.

"Who *built* this place?" asked Filia in a hushed voice.

"A race of giants," said Kagen. "Or at least that's what my brother said."

"This is the city of Ulthar?" asked Borz.

"Aye," said Kagen. "Now we need to find the temple of Ig-ulthan."

"And how are we supposed to do that?" asked Gi-Elless. "It will take us months to scour this place."

"When I discussed this with Mother Frey, I described the buildings my brothers and I entered all those years ago. One of them matched a place she'd read about, and she's certain that it's the temple."

"You know where it is?" asked Tuke.

"I do," said Kagen, for now he was feeling much more confident about things. Remembering a forest path was one thing—after having been on so many, it presented challenges to recall a specific one—but this city was unique in his experience. It was impossible to forget. "It's a pyramid with a flat top. It has a big staircase on the front—huge steps, as tall as a man, so we'll need to climb. There's a second stairway in the back, not as grand but the steps are still as tall. The pyramid is on one of the sides of the city facing the jungle. Even though it's been a long time since I was here, I can find it. Come on."

He climbed back into the saddle. The others also remounted, and together they cantered deep into the heart of that ancient and terrible city.

Tuke rode beside him. "You never did say why the dog soldiers are afraid to follow us here."

"I actually don't know," admitted Kagen.

"Did your, ah . . . *brother* know?"

"His name is Herepath, damn it. Stop acting like a sissy and say his name."

"Fine. Did *Herepath* know why the dog soldiers were so afraid?" said Tuke.

"I don't know. Maybe. He made some vague comments about race memory, or maybe it was cultural memory. Something like that."

"Which is . . ."

"Memories of the gods or demigods who built this place, stored in the mind of every person of Vespian blood. He said that they are born afraid of Ulthar and some of the other great cities. Herepath said it was a scar on the minds of every Vespian, the memory of living as slaves to immortal giants. Part of it is a worshipful fear of the gods, but it is also what he called *certain* knowledge. When Faulker pressed him on it, Herepath said that the believers in the Harvest Gods, or you Therians with your devotion to Father Dagon and Mother Hydra, have awe and fear based on what you believe. The Hakkians, too, with their belief in Hastur. But the Vespians did not require faith in the same way because they lived in the same city as their gods."

"Okay," said Tuke, "that explains them clinging to a religion after all these years—certain knowledge passed down. I get that part. But if they lived *with* their gods, why do they now fear to enter those same cities?"

"Herepath was less certain about that. He said that there are references in some old texts to a race of slaves that were less than these Elder Gods but many times more powerful than the human Vespians. Shoggoths, they were called. Creatures either created by the Elder Gods or perhaps brought with them when those gods descended from the stars. He said that the shoggoths were beings of immense power but were still slaves. And one day the shoggoths rose up and overthrew their masters. Depending on the version of the story you read—and Herepath said there were several conflicting accounts—the shoggoths either killed the Elder Gods or drove them back to the stars. Or under the sea. Again, I'm not sure. Once free, the shoggoths demanded that the Vespians worship them. Some did, but for some reason this did not please the new masters. There was a war or rebellion, this time with the Vespians rising up against these shoggoths."

"If the shoggoths were so strong, how could ordinary mortals hope to win?"

Kagen laughed. "I asked that same question. Herepath said it came down to numbers. The shoggoths were few and the Vespians were many. The legends say they fought the shoggoths in what scholars called the Nightmare War. And before you ask, Tuke, it was called 'nightmare' because the shoggoths were true monsters. They were shape-shifters, capable of taking on the form of anyone with whom they made physical contact, usually by consuming them. So the Vespian armies had to face armies of shoggoths who had taken on the appearance of dead friends, family members . . . even their own children. Herepath said this was what drove the Vespians mad."

"And they stayed insane all these years?" asked Tuke.

"Again, Herepath said that the madness is as deep a scar on the Vespian race as their memories of the Elder Gods they once worshipped. And, I suppose, the same as their fear of the shoggoths, who they still believe live in these cities."

Tuke stared at him. "Was there a point in our very long journey where you were planning on telling us all of this?"

Kagen did not answer.

"You are a right bastard, Kagen Vale," growled the Therian.

"So I've been told," said Kagen before falling silent once more.

CHAPTER ONE HUNDRED SEVENTY-TWO

Five cursed Vespians squatted in a loose circle around a grisly meal that had been a trio of dog soldiers minutes before. Seven other infected lay sprawled in the grass with arrows in their eye sockets or heads cut from their shoulders.

Sunlight slanted down, and in its yellow beams flies and gnats swirled. A hundred or more nightbirds watched from the highest branches, their glittering black eyes missing nothing. Then, abruptly, the insects fled, shooting off into the protection of the trees as the air where they had been began to shimmer.

It was a subtle thing at first, a small distortion that looked like heat haze, but with each second the shimmer took on a more definite substance. The feasting cursed did not notice this until the shimmer began to swirl like a dust devil. Then they looked up, but still reflexively.

It wasn't until the shimmering cone lost its transparency and took on color that they stopped to really look at it. The air in that swirl darkened from pale gray to charcoal and finally to pitch black. The one closest to it sniffed the air like a dog and then bared his bloody teeth. He rose slowly and even let drop the forearm on which he had been gnawing. That it had once belonged to his own brother was something the infected Vespian was incapable of understanding.

He took a step toward the black spiral. The others rose, too, though their interest was not yet murderous. An observer might not even understand why the cursed were drawn to the shape. It gave off no smell of living flesh, no maddening aroma of blood. It merely *was*.

And then it was so much more.

The swirling cone of energy pulsed once, twice, and then flashed outward like ripples after a huge stone is dropped into a pond. These waves slammed into the cursed, knocking them backwards onto the ground; they tore bark from the closest trees and stripped leaves from the branches. The nightbirds squawked in alarm and fled the treetops. Small fires ignited and began to burn the weeds, and the water in the marshy puddles boiled and steamed.

The energy flared and then faded.

In place of the shimmering whirlwind was a figure. Massive. Taller than a man. Broader. Intensely black, so that it appeared more like a shadow than a person.

Then it spread its arms wide and leaned back, mouth open to take its very first breath.

"*I live!*" it said in a huge, booming voice that sent echoes rolling through the forest.

The cursed clawed their way off the ground, dazed, bleeding, flash-burned . . . and hungry. They saw the towering thing and smelled flesh within all that darkness. They got slowly to their feet as the monstrosity turned toward them. It wore a helmet that completely hid its face except for a pair of red eyes in which actual flames burned. From its mighty shoulders hung a cloak made of long blades of black metal. When it stretched its arms out to the sides, that cloak fanned out like the wings of some nightmare bird.

The infected Vespians did not care. They were physically stunned but otherwise incapable of being intimidated or afraid. All they were was hungry, and that hunger was so deep, so profound, so bottomless that it could never be assuaged.

With a collective howl of red madness, they charged at the giant.

Laughing, the razor-knight let them come.

The nightbirds settled back on the trees to watch the slaughter.

"It's there," said Kagen.

They were deep inside the city of Ulthar now. Since escaping the dog soldiers, they had walked for hours among the titanic buildings. The place was eerily quiet, with no birdsong or buzzing insect. The only sounds they heard were the sounds they themselves made.

As they rode, though, they all became visibly uneasy. Weapons were unsheathed and the naked blades laid across thighs. Bows were slung and quivers given small shakes to make sure the arrows would be easy to pull. Horse ran ahead of Filia at first, but after sniffing a few patches of unusually dense shadow, the hound retreated to his mistress's side. Everyone had seen that brute in combat, which made Horse's obvious fear even more intimidating.

Once inside Ulthar, it took far less time to find the pyramid than Kagen had feared. It was indeed on the outer edge of the city, and about five miles in. Whether by blind chance, or perhaps a bit of divine guidance—for every single one of the Bloody Bastards had found a renewed devotion to their gods—it was on the first side of the city they tried.

The seven-sided pyramid was built in a natural depression, so that from a distance it looked shorter than it was, but as they followed the paved road it angled down to a plaza below the structure. From there, its immensity was absolutely apparent. They tethered their horses in the shade of a kapok tree and stood for a long moment marveling at what the ancients had wrought.

"God's bones," said Redharn, squinting up. "It has to be five hundred feet or I'm a fishwife."

"Seven hundred ninety-eight feet," said Kagen. "My brothers and I measured it. And twelve hundred feet exactly per side. Faulker worked out how many square feet it was, but I forget. It was a lot, though."

"Those steps have to be decorative," said Filia. "No one could ever use them."

The grand staircase rose from the plaza all the way to the top and looked like an ordinary palatial stairs except in scale. Each riser was six and a half feet tall and eight feet deep. Even the flat banister was six feet wide.

"The legends say that the Elder Gods were giants," said Kagen.

"But priests and staff had to get up there somehow," Filia insisted. "There must be another way in. An entrance for mortals, and some better way to ascend. Didn't you say there was another staircase in back?"

"It's narrower, but the scale is otherwise the same," said Kagen. "And we looked for exactly what you described, a normal-sized way in, but although we spent two whole days looking, we never found it. So we had to scale those stairs the hard way."

Filia cursed.

The company unsaddled their horses, fed and watered them, and left them under the guard of a single Unbladed—Pergun, a good fighter but with a thigh wound from the fight with the dog soldiers. Horse, who would not go within a dozen paces of the pyramid even if he could have climbed the steps, was also left behind. He whined piteously at Filia, more of a warning than a plea for comfort. She grabbed his jowls, kissed his ugly head, and told him to grow some balls. Then she hurried off to join the others in that long climb.

It was a long and exhausting undertaking, and the sun, with no jungle to filter its intensity, blasted them. They each carried long coils of rope, saddlebags, weapons, and themselves, and every incremental step required boosting one another and hauling their own weight. It was brutal and took nearly three full hours to reach the summit. By the time they did reach it, all were weary, dripping sweat, and quivering with tension.

The top of the pyramid was flat, with a surface made from granite paving stones that had long since cracked from the relentless assault of pernicious weeds and wild trees. The bones of some kind of enormous serpent lay curled near the top step, and other bones of less recognizable origin were scattered about. Some looked like human bones, perhaps from the race of giants who once lived there. It troubled Kagen that those bones had not turned to dust after all these thousands of years exposed to wind, rain, and sun.

In the center of the big square was a cluster of buildings of various sizes, each decorated with bas-reliefs of strange gods with the bodies of men but the face and skin of reptiles. Only the eyes of these sculptures still retained any traces of paint, and the yellow irises with black slits for pupils seemed to watch everything these intruders did.

"If I had a hammer and chisel," said Dilhoolie darkly, "I'd do for those eyes and no mistake."

"That might *be* a mistake," warned Kagen. "My brother Jheklan said the same when we were here, and Herepath warned him not to defile any sacred image."

The axman muttered something and turned away, but he—like all of them—found himself glancing nervously from time to time at those watchful serpent eyes.

"These buildings are different," said Tuke, running his hands along the facade of one of the structures. "Stones are rougher. Craftsmanship isn't nearly as fine. Makes me wonder if humans built them."

"That was Herepath's theory," Kagen agreed. "He told us that ancient Vespians were forced to build them by the shoggoths and not the Elder Gods, who had been vanquished by then. Herepath thought this area up here was used for public worship and sacrifices."

"Sacrifices to whom? The shoggoths slew their own gods."

"No idea," said Kagen. "Herepath had a dozen theories, but none that stood out. My personal guess was that some of the shoggoths realized that they *needed* their gods after all. The cities were falling into ruin and there was conflict with the natives. Maybe the sacrifices were an attempt to appease them and bring the Elder Gods back."

"Unpleasant thought," muttered Tuke.

"It is," said Kagen.

There were eleven structures in all, and they looked nearly identical. Kagen, Tuke, and Filia walked among them, trying different doors, studying the bas-reliefs.

"Which one is it?" asked Filia.

Kagen dragged an arm across his face to mop up the sweat. Atop the pyramid it felt like the afternoon sun was within arm's reach. He was boiling inside his leather jerkin but dared not remove it.

"I'm trying to remember," murmured Kagen. He closed his eyes and tried to pull memories from the deep well of his mind. Details floated toward him and then darted away like koi in a pond. The four Vale brothers had been in each of these buildings and had camped right where Kagen and his friends now stood. He remembered Herepath consulting a journal in which were written all manner of clues. Mother Frey provided some suggestions, but her words—spoken in the comfort of the Cavorting Bear—seemed somehow disconnected from the reality of where he stood. It was like trying to assemble something from a box of fragments but with no idea whether any of the pieces belonged, or what shape it would take if it was ever put back together again.

A sound made him turn and look up as a big crow flew overhead and then landed over the lintel of the fifth of the buildings. It settled there, rustling its old feathers and looking directly down at him.

"That one," said Kagen.

Tuke and Filia glanced at him, up at the bird, then at each other. Tuke held his hands up, palm out. "Normally I'd have something witty or amusing to say, but right now I have nothing. We're following the directions of a bird."

"We're following the directions of a bird," agreed Kagen.

He approached the door, which was closed.

"Do you at least have a key?" asked Filia.

"We didn't need keys," said Kagen as he began to run his hands along the frame. There was a very narrow gap between the structure and the stone door, just big enough for his questing fingers. He worked his way around, inch by inch. "There was some kind of trick to it. We spent two days attempting to break in, and just when we were about to give up, Faulker found . . . oh . . . wait . . ."

There was an audible *click*. Kagen glanced at his friends, took a breath, and then pushed. The massive stone door moved as easily as if it were a light wooden panel on well-oiled hinges.

"By the armored balls of the armadillo god," marveled Tuke.

"That was the easy part," said Kagen. "We searched each of these buildings for weeks and did not find any hidden room filled with magic books."

"Your optimism is inspiring," said Filia. Despite everything, Kagen grinned at her.

Before they could enter, the big falconer, Redharn, came running toward them. "Kagen, there are Vespians in the city."

"I thought that was impossible," said Filia.

"Which *kind* of Vespian?" demanded Tuke. "The good kind or the bad kind?"

Redharn blinked. "Is there a good kind?"

"Are they insane or cursed?" asked Kagen.

"You mean are they living or living dead?" mused Filia.

"You tell me," said Redharn as they all hurried to the top of the stairs.

Far below them a swarm of people was racing toward the pyramid. They fell upon the horses, ripping with fingernails and tearing with teeth. Jinx and Dog reared up in panic, lashing out with hooves. Horse barked furiously and then whirled and ran deeper into the city, fleeing a fight he could not win.

Pergun fought like a hero, killing several of the infected, but it was a fight he couldn't win, either. He slashed the tethers of the panicking horses. By then the living dead were swarming over them and Borz's horse went down beneath a wave of the madmen. As it fell, the thrashing animal staggered sideways, sending Pergun careening. The man's bad leg buckled and he fell with a cry. The horse collapsed and was swarmed by the dead, but Pergun slithered away under some shrubbery, vanishing from sight. The Vespian undead turned toward the grand staircase and followed its lines with their eyes until they stared up at the row of Unbladed silhouetted against the sky. The howl the mass of them sent up was truly terrifying.

What was far, far worse was the answering howl from within the jungle. More and more of the bloody, mangled, mindless, endlessly hungry dead poured out of the forest and hurled themselves at the steps. They lacked coordination or intelligence, but the forces that drove them were relentless. They leapt up to grab the edge of the steps and pulled themselves up even as their fellows grabbed them and used other infected as ladders. It was slow, it was clumsy, and many times whole masses of them collapsed under the weight of so many bodies. They fell over and over again, but there was never a pause as they scrambled up and tried again.

When some of them gained the top of the first step, Gi-Elless drew an arrow and fitted it to her bowstring.

"Save it," said Kagen. "You can't guarantee a killing shot to the head from here."

The archer lowered her weapon, easing the tension on the string. "So what, then? We wait until they climb up here?"

Kagen turned away. "Do you have a better suggestion?"

With that he headed back to the cluster of stone buildings.

Far below, the infected Vespians howled their hunger as they climbed.

CHAPTER ONE HUNDRED SEVENTY-FOUR

"Has he found it?" asked the Witch-king. His voice sounded calm, but he sat forward at the table, clutching the edge of it with his hands as if the whole room might tilt downward and send him tumbling into the pit.

The Prince of Games did not answer immediately. He sat cross-legged on the floor between the king and the fireplace. He was naked, his body painted with arcane symbols of protection, power, and insight. The Witch-king knew that those same symbols, placed on an ordinary mortal, would tear the soul out, but he suspected the prince had no soul. He had no such weakness.

"Tell me, damn your eyes."

"He is close," said the prince.

"How close?" demanded the king. "Will the razor-knight reach it first?"

The prince turned his face toward the monarch in yellow. His eyes swirled with colors and his skin had faded to a corpse-like pallor.

"Reality is a maelstrom," he said in a ghostly voice. "The future is hidden from me now. I do not know why. I can see the past and I can see this moment, but there are dozens upon dozens of possible outcomes trying to splinter off. Each breath, each thought, each footfall creates another possibility."

"I need to know," said the Witch-king. "Kagen cannot be allowed to find the temple."

"Kagen has *already* found it," said the prince.

"By Hastur's staff, has he—"

"No," interrupted the prince, "he has not found the books. Not yet." He paused. "The razor-knight draws near. There is still time . . ."

> **CHAPTER ONE HUNDRED SEVENTY-FIVE**

It moved through the jungle of Vespia, following the ancient stone road.

Nightbirds flew ahead, landing now and then to watch its progress. The old crow they all followed studied the razor-knight, making no sound except a flutter of wings as it left one tree to find another so that it was always ahead of the creature's progress.

Buzzards circled high in the steamy sky, though there were fewer of them than before. Many of their comrades were down on the ground, feasting on what was left of the group of infected who had first attacked the monster. The rest, wise and patient, waited for the next meal, knowing that today was a red day. A feast day.

The razor-knight walked with a steady precision, step upon step, striding quickly along that road. Turning neither left nor right but instead following the path taken by Kagen and his company. It did not sniff the air like a dog or search the ground like a hunter, but it never strayed from the right path.

Only once more did it pause, and that was when an arrow whistled out of the trees and struck its chest with lethal force.

Lethal, had the target been a human.

The razor-knight gave a small grunt of amusement as he plucked out the shaft, snapped it between his fingers, and tossed the pieces away, even as a knot of six dog soldiers emerged from the brush. They were all painted for war, but not this war. Not this battle.

With howls like those of animals, the Vespian fighters closed like a fist around the massive intruder. They fired arrows, stabbed with spears, slashed with flint-bladed hatchets. Every single blow landed.

And it did them no good at all.

CHAPTER ONE HUNDRED SEVENTY-SIX

Kagen ran back to the building, whose door he had opened. Borz had used a big chunk of the old skeleton to wedge the door open. None of them had dared to enter, though.

"Filia, see what you can do to prepare a useful greeting for our friends down there," said Kagen, tilting his head in the direction of the grand staircase. "Conserve your arrows. Maybe use the rest of that skeleton."

"In hopes we crush a skull with each vertebra?" she asked.

"You have a better idea?"

She narrowed her eyes thoughtfully and moved off to look at what advantages circumstances provided. Kagen tapped four of the fighters to help him—the dour Borz; Giffer, a former Gardener from Zaare who had strayed from his vows; the popular and likeable Lo-fan of Nerek; and the moody Ghenreyan poet and duelist, Hoth. They pushed the door wide, turning their heads as a cloud of unpleasant-smelling dust belched out. Borz fetched another heavy piece of bone to keep the door wedged wide. Hoth used flint and steel to light oil-soaked torches and then handed them around.

"Come on," said Kagen, letting the burning torch lead the way. "Be careful."

As he stepped across the threshold, he felt a sudden chill that he remembered from long ago. It was not the change in temperature—that sensation was there every time he or his brothers had entered any of the buildings in Ulthar. It was as if those places were unable to hold real warmth and they were as cold and damp as an underground crypt. As the others entered behind him, he heard gasps and soft curses. And prayers.

Everything inside the building was ornately carved. There were statues of monsters—gods or demons, he did not know—in niches all around the walls. Low benches were set in odd patterns, as if the attending worshippers were not all allowed to face the same way, or to serve some other function, the nature of which was lost to the ages. A sacrificial table was set on a low dais, the cold stone still showing bloodstains that seemed infused into the surface. How many lives had been spent there to have stained a stone as impermeable as granite?

On one bench he saw the initials carved there by Jheklan and Faulker. On another was a crude sketch of a woman with improbable breasts. More of Faulker's work, which Kagen recalled had earned him a stinging rebuke from Herepath.

Between the niches were long rows of images—hieroglyphs, Herepath had called them—but they told no clear story to Kagen. There were no clues as to where the sacred books were hidden. If those books were there at all. After all this time, who knew how many looters had braved the dangers of Vespia. Even if he found the hiding place, it might be filled only with shadows and dead spiders.

Several smaller chambers led from the main room, and the others explored those while Kagen searched the big room, which he thought was a chapel of some kind. He moved here and there, driven by faulty old memories and gut instinct.

Despite the torches the Unbladed carried, the shadows seemed unwilling to withdraw entirely. The firelight did not so much vanquish the shadows; rather, the darkness yielded ground briefly. And in some places the darkness seemed especially dense and reluctant to flee. It was not natural, and Kagen knew it, but he did not know how to properly think about it. There was an almost oily viscosity to the shadows.

Tuke stuck his head in through the doorway. "Anything?"

"No. How are things out there?"

The screams and howls of the cursed Vespians were constant and growing louder.

"The good news is they're close enough for us to kill a bunch of the bastards," said Tuke. "The bad news is we're going to run out of arrows long before we run out of people to kill. If we don't get out of here soon, Kagen, then we never will. Have you found those gods-damned books yet?"

"We're trying."

"Try harder," yelled the Therian. Then he vanished.

"Shit," muttered Kagen as he stretched out on the floor beneath the altar and ran his fingers along a double line of ornate carvings.

He prayed for a latch or something. And as he fumbled along, he tried to conjure Maralina in his mind, wishing there was some practical way to speak to her, to ask her for advice. Surely a sorceress of her power would be able to find something as simple as a hidden door. Several times he felt a coldness pass through him and his heart jumped, his need and his love believing that he had in fact touched her across all those miles.

"Maralina," he whispered, "help me . . . *please* . . ."

The screams of the infected grew louder, and he felt dread mounting within him. Those creatures, were they alive? Or were they, as it appeared, actually dead, yet also somehow alive? What did that make them? Not living, not dead. Living dead, perhaps? The very concept offended his rational mind and shook him to his core.

He also felt the terror of failure. When he and his friends had tried to kill the Witch-king that night, the stakes had been lower. It was more about revenge than saving the empire. Or the world. Now those stakes were so much higher, and everyone seemed to be looking to him to save everyone, to be a hero.

"Bloody fools," he growled as he worked. It appalled him that Tuke, Filia, the Unbladed, the Bloody Bastards, and Mother Frey all seemed to regard him as a hero or champion when he knew himself to be a failure . . . and a literally *damned* one at that.

At the precise instant he had that thought, one of the carvings moved beneath his fingers. There was a soft grinding sound, and the entire altar began to move.

"Gods of the fiery Pit . . ." breathed Kagen. "I think I found it . . ."

━━━▶ **CHAPTER ONE HUNDRED SEVENTY-SEVEN**

Tuke knelt on the edge of the pyramid's platform, drawing another arrow back, sighting along the shaft, the yew bow creaking with the tension.

"By Dagon's scaly balls," he said, and loosed. The arrow shot through the air, following the slope of the gigantic staircase, and the barb struck home in the left eye of the foremost infected. The creature's head snapped back and Tuke thought he could hear the snap of a vertebra. The cursed thing toppled backwards, striking the ones below it, and at least half a dozen went crashing down, striking their fellows and the edges of the granite steps.

This was the rhythm he had established and which the other Bastards were now imitating. Wait for one to reach the edge of a step and knock it back. There were so many of the infected climbing up that their own numbers were their enemy. Even when an arrow struck a nonlethal spot, the force and the fall did terrible work. Those that recovered from the fall without crippling injuries would then have to climb up again. That climb was hard enough for sane people capable of thinking. It was much more of a challenge for the mindless living dead.

He replayed those thoughts and that logic, because it was all he had as a shield against the fact that there were now *thousands* of cursed Vespians.

Redharn, ten feet away, was hastily replacing a snapped

bowstring and caught Tuke's eye. "All the way here from Zaare," he said, "I thought that the worst we would face would be cannibal villagers and dog soldiers. I mean, sure, that's bad enough, but Gods of the Harvest, I wish that's who we were facing now. They'd have chased us all the way to this thrice-damned city but would have at least left us alone. Kagen said they wouldn't come in here. But these spooky sons of bitches will chase us to hell itself."

Tuke drew another arrow and used it to point down at the mass of creatures swarming up toward them. "I bet the Vespians wish that you were right, too. If any of them are still left alive."

Redharn sighed and nodded as he bent his bow to take the new string. "Aye. But, how the hell did the Samudian Plague get *here*?"

Tuke shook his head. "Between you and me, Redharn, I'm not even sure that this Red Curse really *is* Samudian. I've read some of the histories and I don't recall ever reading that the dead actually come back to life. And you saw what I saw."

"Then what is this?" asked Redharn.

"Fuck if I know," said Tuke. "Raising the dead is what necromancers do, and which country do *you* know that has necromancers? Sure as hell isn't Samud."

"Shit," said Redharn.

They fired.

And fired. Every arrow killed one of the infected. Every falling body dragged others down. But for each one that fell there seemed to be a dozen scrambling to take its place, and more kept streaming out of the jungle. Flocks of nightbirds swirled overhead, occasionally diving down to slash at the Vespian undead, but the cursed neither flinched nor cried out, even when a talon tore across an eye or slashed a cheek. The infected swiped and grabbed at the birds. Not to ward off their attacks but to crush their hollow bones and bite through feathers for blood and meat. The nightbirds kept attacking, regardless. Then suddenly the whole flock of them veered away and flew high into the sky as the front wall of the jungle shuddered.

"Wait," said Redharn, suddenly lowering his bow and pointing. "What the hell is *that*?"

Tuke leaned over to see that many of the infected had paused in their assault and were looking behind and down at something that emerged from the woods and walked toward the pyramid. It looked vaguely like a man in full armor, but that armor was a uniform and featureless black. And it was big. Too big to be an ordinary man. It was nearly twice the size of the Vespian infected who thronged the plaza below and littered the stairs like bugs.

The living dead seemed to be startled, puzzled by the newcomer. They stared at it, and many moved toward it, but they did not immediately attack it. The black thing seemed to care little about them as it stalked relentlessly toward the first step.

A small knot of infected stood between the pyramid and the intruder. One of them pawed at the black thing, trying to grab at its cloak. There was a dark blur of movement and then the reaching arm flew high into the air, trailing black blood.

Then the armored thing was among the cursed. It did not use a sword but instead swept left and right with the edges of its cloak. Tuke thought at first that it must have some kind of blade hidden beneath that cape, but it was quickly apparent that the cloak itself was the weapon. Any of the living dead who stood in the way were immediately cut to pieces. Heads and arms, legs and torsos flew everywhere.

The cursed attacked it with howls of fury, breaking their fists on its armor. It merely swept its own path clear of obstructions. Then it reached the bottom of the stairs, stretched high with one black-gloved hand, and pulled itself up to the second step. Despite its massive size, it climbed with the agility of one of the great mountain gorillas. Any infected Vespian not in its direct path turned away from it and looked back up at the men and women defending the platform.

Tuke felt his heart turn to ice in his chest as understanding slowly dawned on him. He knew what this thing was. He had read about it as a child, and Kagen had described it in great detail. He turned to Redharn and saw the exact moment when his comrade realized what was coming for them. Redharn's eyes dulled, his nostrils flared, and his mouth fell into sickness.

"Hell's gate has opened," moaned the big falconer.

It was a *razor-knight*. A creature conjured by the darkest of magic. It was the same kind of monster who had single-handedly slaughtered the Poison Rose.

A razor-knight. And, surrounded by an army of the living dead, it was climbing the long staircase. Coming for Kagen.

Coming for them all.

CHAPTER ONE HUNDRED SEVENTY-EIGHT

"*It . . . is . . . there . . .*"

The words were spoken with great effort, each breath costing so much more than Lady Kestral could afford to spend. Tiny droplets of blood flecked her lips.

At her words, the Witch-king turned from the maps on the table.

"Who?" he demanded. "Has Kagen found the books or—"

"The . . . knight," wheezed Kestral. "He has . . . found . . . Kagen . . ."

She slid from the chair on which she had huddled. The Prince of Games was close enough to catch her, but instead he stepped aside to let her fall. He looked down at her with a wormy smile wriggling on his lips.

"Help her, damn your eyes," barked the Witch-king, but although two guards rushed to help, the prince did not.

"She's done her work," he said. "She raised your demon."

"She's dying."

"Oh, without doubt. I can taste it in the air," said the prince. "Such a piquant taste. Just the right tang."

The Witch-king pushed past him and knelt to gently raise the sorceress and restore her to the brocade chair. He called for guards to fetch a blanket and send for tea and medicines.

"That will only prolong the inevitable," said the prince.

"Shut up and get out of the way," said the Witch-king. "She is important to me."

"Is she? So important that you let her spend her life force to kill one man?" The prince shook his head. "So important that you set her a task that you *knew* would kill her?"

"This is war," said the king.

"It is, and spending her life is the cost of waging war. I accept that, but why shed tears over it?"

The blankets and other items arrived, and the Witch-king tucked the blanket gently around Kestral. He lingered, stroking the thin strands of her remaining hair. Then he took her hands in his. Her fingers were thin and cold and already felt like those of a corpse.

"You have done great things for the empire, my lady," he said tenderly, "and I love you for it. No one else has done as much. No one else has been as true."

Tears welled in her eyes and fell slowly down her dry and withered cheeks.

"If I can bring you back from this brink, I will," said the Witch-king.

She raised her eyes to his, seeing only the shadow of his face through the yellow lace veil. "What I do," she said slowly, letting fragments of the sentence ride each careful, shallow exhalation, "I do for my people. For Hakkia. For the empire."

"I know, my lady, and you will be remembered forever for this."

And that made her smile. Though it was a strange smile, and it made the king frown.

"For my people . . ." said Lady Kestral, and then her eyelids fluttered shut.

The prince sniffed. "Is she dead?"

The king shook his head. "No. But I fear she may not wake again."

"What of it?" asked the prince.

The king stared at him with mingled apprehension and dismay. "How can you be so wise in so many ways and not understand the peril of this? Do you not understand how a razor-knight is invoked? How it is constructed?"

"It's a demon in the body of golem," said the prince. "That is magic from the cult of Nyarlathotep. Not my particular skill set, I'll grant, but again . . . what of it? She has made this thing and it is where we need it to be. It cannot be stopped by any ordinary means. Kagen and his pack of idiots lack any sorcerous powers, and we know that arrows and blades will not save them. Let your witch die in peace, content in knowing that her last conjuration will end with Kagen Vale's death."

"You're a fool if you think that," said the Witch-king. "All this time, I thought you were close to omniscient, yet you reveal yourself to be ignorant of some basic truths. By Hastur's staff you are useless."

The prince did not appear to take umbrage. "Then, pray, educate this poor, uncouth fellow."

"This razor-knight was called into existence with Kagen's blood. That's crucial—blood, hair, or something that carries the life force of the individual. The razor-knight in Vespia is tied to him, anchored in this world by Kagen, just as the last one was tied to the blood of the Poison Rose. Our spies had obtained strands of her hair. But the knight is also tethered to this reality by the life force of the necromancer who conjured it. Lady Kestral. If she dies, the razor-knight will lose substance. It will fade. *Now* do you understand?"

It was a rare thing indeed for the Prince of Games to look surprised, but that emotion was clear on his features. When he spoke, there was no more mockery or challenge in his voice. He offered the Witch-king a small conciliatory bow.

"After all these years I suppose an old dog can still learn new tricks."

It was not an apology, but the Witch-king knew it was as close to one as he would get from the creature.

The monarch called for a guard to fetch the royal physician, and within minutes a very fat man in voluminous black robes appeared. He carried with him a heavy carpetbag filled with potions, herbs, and tinctures.

"She is very ill," said the king. "Do whatever you can to keep her alive."

"But Majesty," cried the healer, "she is dying. I am amazed that she is not dead already. I fear there is no hope for her."

"Pray that you are wrong, Doctor," said the king. "For if she dies before the sun sets, then you will join her in the grave."

The doctor blanched, but then nodded and began pulling items out of his bag.

The king turned as the Prince of Games removed an object from a pocket inside his robes. It was a piece of quartz crystal. "What is that and what are you doing?" he demanded.

"Making myself useful," said the prince. He raised it so that he could see the flames in the fireplace through the facets of the quartz.

"What do you see?"

It took the prince a long time to answer, and as moments fell away around him, he seemed somehow less substantial, almost translucent. When he spoke, his voice was lower, harsher, grating. Almost inhuman.

"The razor-knight has reached the temple of Ig-ulthan," he intoned. "He is climbing the main staircase. The undead are with him."

"What about the dog soldiers?"

The prince laughed. "They are irrelevant now. Let's just say that the gift of the Hollow Monks has helped focus their attention."

"And Kagen?" demanded the king. "What of him? Has he found the books?"

That trembling smile returned to the prince's lips. "Oh, I think it's closer to the mark to say that the books have found *him*."

CHAPTER ONE HUNDRED SEVENTY-NINE

Kagen could not hear the yells from outside.

He could not hear anything but his own breath. It rasped in and out very fast, as if earth's breath was trying to catch up with the jackrabbit speed of his hammering heart. When the altar shifted, it revealed a set of stairs that led down into darkness. Borz fetched a torch for him, and the others clustered around, ready to follow.

He went down into a place where no light had burned in thousands upon thousands of years.

It *felt* like that, too.

If the darkness in the upper chamber had seemed oddly solid, with each step he felt as if he was stepping into something that, in every awful and unnatural way, was alive. The bright yellow light of the torch should have washed it all back, but it roiled there in that confined space, pushing back against the glowing intrusion. The shadows even muffled the sound of his boots on the stone steps. It was the strangest sensation . . . like entering a pool, but without wetness. He could feel the shadows lapping against his thighs.

With each step he crunched on the bones of rats and other animals that had somehow found their way into the temple and down to this crypt only to be consumed by . . .

By what?

Every fiber of his being screamed at him to turn around, to go back upstairs, to pit himself against the Vespians—both living and undead—rather than risk whatever waited for him below.

"Coward," he scolded himself, but the darkness took that word and bounced it around, warping the echoes so that it was as if a chorus of ghosts mocked him.

With his free hand he drew a dagger, clutching it less as a weapon than as a talisman. His mind conjured a memory of his mother's face, the way she looked when she returned from a battle: bitter, hard, her mouth a tight line and her eyes still holding the memory of the things she had seen and done. Such a deep sadness, such horror at the realities of the world, and so much self-hatred for the person she sometimes needed to be in order to serve the empire.

Then, another image overlaid that one. His mother in her last moments, her face weary and filled with pain, her eyes glittering with a sharp acceptance of her own defeat. Begging him to run, telling him that he had a duty to perform. Saying that because she had no idea that the children he had sworn to protect were already dead.

Or so he had thought.

Another step down and now he saw the faces of Alleyn and Desalyn. Beautiful children, powerful in their innocence. Or they had been. His last memory of them was on the night of the coronation—bitter, twisted, impish. Self-aware of their own corruption and reveling in it. Owned, body and soul, by Herepath. Claimed as his own children.

And suddenly something flickered past his awareness as he took the next step.

Fragments of memories. Small snatches of conversation that ended abruptly when he walked into a room. Significant looks shared covertly when they thought no one was looking.

Who, though?

Another step. The memories crystallized. Still broken, but those pieces forming a strange mosaic.

Step.

Herepath was there. Younger. The way he was before he left for the Winterwilds a bit over six years ago. He was always there in the palace. Reading in stuffed chairs, wandering the aisles of the library. Talking with . . .

With?

Step.

With her. Talking with her. Walking in the gardens with her. Discussing books with her.

With her.

"No . . ." breathed Kagen, refusing to accept that this was insight rather than delusion. "No, no, no."

Step.

A voice in his mind whispered to him.

There are no lies down here, Kagen Vale, it said. *There are only truths here.*

Step.

"No, gods damn it," insisted Kagen.

Just because the truth draws blood does not make it evil, whispered the darkness.

Kagen stopped, panting, waving the torch around to see if it was an actual person who spoke. But all he could see were the steps, stone walls, and . . .

Darkness. Moving away from the torchlight.

There are no lies here in Hsan, said the voice. *There is only truth. Are you brave enough to listen, Kagen Vale?*

"Shut up," said Kagen tersely as he resumed his descent. "This isn't true."

Do you fear the truth so much? Have you not already seen the worst truth of your life?

And that brought with it the moment in Argentium when Kagen had looked past the torn veil and beheld the Witch-king's true face. Herepath's face. That had nearly broken him, nearly snapped his mind. It had broken his heart. Herepath was the monster who had killed the Poison Rose. And Father, and Hugh. The murderous fiend who had slaughtered all the Seedlings. Except two.

The twins. Alleyn and Desalyn. Herepath had spared them. Why?

Why?

You know why, said the darkness.

Step.

Those shared glances between Herepath and the woman who was infinitely beyond his station. The two of them sharing knowing, secret smiles. Lovers' smiles. And then suddenly the banishment. Herepath sent to the farthest place on earth. To the icy nothingness of the Winterwilds. Not willingly. Kagen now understood that. Exiled. Discarded. Intended to die.

Sent there by . . .

"No!" cried Kagen.

But he remembered standing on the parapet of the palace on a fine summer morning, watching as Herepath rode off, leading a train of horses packed with books and supplies. Heading away.

Away forever.

Leaving home because . . .

Because he could not be allowed to stay, said the shadows. *Because she would not allow it. Could not allow it.*

She.

"Please," begged Kagen, hating the truth that filled him.

The pieces of that mosaic moved in the darkness, the pieces sliding toward one another. Finding matching edges. Becoming whole. Becoming the truth.

Step.

In his memory—his very real memory—he remembered turning to the person standing farther along the wall of that parapet. A woman, watching Herepath leave. A woman dabbing discreetly at tears she could not risk showing.

"He will be missed," said the woman, pretending a smile.

"Yes, Your Majesty," said young Kagen to the empress.

The faces of Alleyn and Desalyn filled his mind, and he *saw* them now as he should always have seen them. As they truly were, not as the versions the members of court needed to see.

Step. The last step.

Alleyn, with Herepath's pale eyes and Gessalyn's strong nose. Desalyn with her mother's full mouth and her father's smile.

"Gods save my soul," whispered Kagen.

CHAPTER ONE HUNDRED EIGHTY

"She's dead," said Desalyn, tears springing into her eyes. But Alleyn took her hand and gave it a fierce squeeze.

"No," he said.

"I can't *feel* her anymore," wept his sister.

Alleyn shook his head. "I can. She's still alive. Close your eyes," he said. "Feel for her. She's still there."

Desalyn looked dubious and frightened, but she wiped her tears away, took a breath, and closed her eyes. It was dark behind those closed lids—much darker than it should have been. It was totally lightless. No diffused light through skin. No flicker of firelight. Not even the strange patterns of moving light she always saw when trying to sleep. All there was to see was a formless, bottomless nothing.

"I can't find her . . ."

"Keep looking," said Alleyn. "I can feel her. Wait, listen . . . hear that?"

"I . . . wait . . . I hear something." She chewed her lip as she struggled to stretch out with her senses. "It's slow . . . like a far away drum. There is it again. What is it?"

"That's her heartbeat," said Alleyn, clutching tight his sister's hand.

"It's slowing down. Gods of the Harvest, it's so slow. She's dying."

"Dying," said Alleyn. "But not dead yet."

They opened their eyes and stared at the swirling black mass in the center of the big circle of protection. The glowing red eyes glared back at them. Its massive fists opened and closed with fell intent. Without warning it punched the inner wall of the shimmering circle. The entire circle pulsed with white-hot sparks from the impact, and yet it held. The razor-knight struck again and again, each time causing the circle of protection to flare.

"He's going to break out," cried Desalyn.

"No," said Alleyn. "He can't. Not while *we* live."

There was no trace of certainty in his voice, though. Not one bit.

CHAPTER ONE HUNDRED EIGHTY-ONE

"Gods of the watery deep," breathed Tuke, "tell me that isn't what it is."

Filia looked over the edge at the massive bulk of the razor-knight. Her sweaty face went dead pale and for a moment she closed her eyes and appeared to deflate. She started to make a warding sign, but then let her hands go slack.

The other Bloody Bastards all stopped to stare. Above them, the terrified nightbirds continued to swirl in agitation. A few dozen landed on the buildings on the plaza, but they shivered and jostled in obvious distress. It was the first time Tuke had seen them like that—afraid. It turned his bowels to ice.

The infected climbed with the creature, but they did not attack it. They seemed indifferent. Instead, they looked up at the Unbladed and shrieked out their hunger and their need.

The knight grabbed each next step and hauled its bulk up and over the edge of the risers, repeating the movements without evident fatigue.

"I heard that Captain Kagen killed one of those things," said Falric, a stocky Nehemitian with stars tattooed all over her face.

"That he did," said Filia.

"Then they can die," grunted Redharn, drawing an arrow.

"He used banefire," said Tuke.

"Even so," said Redharn, "if they can die then they can die."

He drew back on the bowstring, took careful aim, and fired. The razor-knight was still a fair way down the steep staircase, but he was a good shot. The arrow zipped down the slant and struck home, catching the razor-knight in the shoulder, between the heavy trapezius muscles and the collarbone. It hit hard and held fast . . . and the razor-knight did not even flinch. Nor did the thing pause to pluck it out. It kept climbing.

"Shit on me," murmured Redharn.

"What's banefire?" asked Furley, a member of the Crocodile clan from Behlia. "Can we make any?"

Filia glanced thoughtfully at him. "No . . . But maybe we can improvise." She stepped back sharply. "Axmen, on me!"

With that she turned and ran to where some scrub pines and maple had grown like weeds from cracks in the platform. Dilhoolie and Redharn grinned at each other, unslung their axes, and ran to follow.

CHAPTER ONE HUNDRED EIGHTY-TWO

Kagen stood in the crypt as tears burned in his eyes. The mosaic conjured in his mind by the voice of this darkness was still there to be seen. Herepath and Empress Gessalyn. And their children. A monster, a murdered woman, and their bastards. This was why Herepath hated Gessalyn so terribly. She had cast him out and sent him north. Was that the reason Gessalyn had banished him? To cool his illicit ardor with unending cold? Kagen knew this was poetry, but it was also partly true. It had to be. The empress had indeed frozen the heart of her secret lover, and in doing so—by breaking that heart before freezing it—had created the monster who now ruled the west.

How could Herepath's heart not go cold and dark? It had loved and dared so much to be with Gessalyn and then become expendable because of a pregnancy that might have split the empire apart. The Imperial Consort was from Vahlycor, a union that had elevated that entire country. The truth and its implied betrayal would surely have torn the peace with civil war. Thousands would die and the empire itself might collapse under the weight of those unwise actions.

What then was one man's life if it would hide the secret and sell the lie? Was peace not worth more than that?

And what of banished and heartbroken Herepath? Brooding away the endless cold of the Winterwilds. Venting his rage and hurt by digging too far, too deep into the glacier. And finding . . .

What? Were the things anyone would eventually find, or were they revealed in the heat of a heart turned to furnace?

Hatred tried to own Kagen. It wanted to take him and cut out his beating heart and replace it with the coldest of stones. Or with bitter ice from the glaciers of the Winterwilds.

Ice.

But what use was that knowledge now, he wondered? He was here in Vespia, and his friends were fighting and probably dying to buy him time to find lost books, and yet he stood there weeping for those lost children, weeping for an empress who he now knew was flawed and human and also bitter and cruel. And weeping for Herepath. Grieving for his enemy.

Kagen pointed his dagger up at the ceiling as if he could see the faces of the Harvest Gods above him.

"You allowed this!" he roared. "You claim to intervene on the side of goodness, of truth, of justice, but you permitted this to happen *and did nothing*. And yet you damn me? Damn you, and all of you. I hope the Elder Gods return and tear down all your gardens and burn your fields. I hate you for what you've done. I hate you more for what you could have done and did not do. Gods of love . . . I spit upon you."

He did spit, too, and then stamped on it and ground the spittle into the dusty granite floor. He lowered the knife and stared at the poisoned blade, then he glanced upward once more.

"Maralina said that *eitr* is the god-killer poison," said Kagen to the gods. "May it be so, and may I stand before you one day with my mother's blades in my hands so I can cut your hearts out. I would swear this on my soul, but you have stolen that, so I swear it on these knives. I, Kagen Vale, son of the Poison Rose, declare that I am your enemy now and forever. If there is any true justice in the universe, then I will end the tyranny of false gods. Even if in doing so I am truly damned to the burning pits for all eternity. Hear my words and know them for the truth. Hear my vow and know it to be your doom."

He turned away from the ceiling as if dismissing the entire pantheon of Harvest Gods. With rage burning every inch of his body, with frustration and bloodlust boiling beneath his skin, he swung around and thrust the torch into the darkness.

And now it recoiled from him.

There, at the end of the spill of light, was a table made of obsidian and carved with the faces of gods whose names he did not know and did not care to know. On that table were scrolls. A line of them, each neatly rolled and bound with scarlet string. Not bound books, but books nonetheless, for there were seven of them.

He approached them, shocked that they were really here, that they were literally within reach. He had found the key to defeating Herepath.

The scrolls had not crumbled to dust after all these years. He saw, with some curiosity and alarm, that they were not even dusty. Everything else was coated with dust, but they looked as clean and tidy as if they had been placed there only an hour ago. He found a bracket on the wall, placed his torch in it, and walked in a slow circle around the table. The light from the torch spread a circle of gently flickering light, but there seemed to be another light source that Kagen could not quite understand, and it illuminated the scrolls.

But no, it was not some hidden light, nor even a crack in the wall through which stray sunlight fell. As he bent to study the scrolls it became immediately clear, without a fleck of doubt, that the scrolls themselves provided their own light. Very pale, visible only because of the dense shadows, but it was there. Something within the cylinder of each scroll glowed with a pale rose-red luminescence. Or maybe it was the actual material of the scrolls. He did not know and was leery of touching them.

And what did it mean? Was it proof that these were, indeed, books of magic? Was it some kind of trap or test? Kagen had no idea, and he wasn't at all sure he wanted to touch them with his bare hands. He had not brought a saddlebag or satchel down there with him. He touched the fabric of his traveling cloak and wondered if it would provide protection—if that was needed.

No matter what, though, he had to get the scrolls out of here, out of Vespia, and into the hands of someone who understood these sorcerous matters. Frey, perhaps, though Kagen felt that

Maralina would be best. She was a powerful sorceress, though the Tower of Sarsis was thousands of miles away on the coast of Vahlycor.

As he stood there, trapped within his indecision and uncertainty, he could almost see Herepath's thin, ascetic face smiling at him with that old condescension, that same haughty superiority. That memory was overlaid with the brief glimpse Kagen had gotten on the coronation night, when the yellow veil failed to hide the truth.

"Herepath," Kagen said, despising the taste of each syllable in his mouth. In his chest, in the dark soil of his soul, dangerous flowers bloomed, their crimson petals unfurling to release his hate.

The darkness seemed to close in on him, encircling.

"I am coming for you, Herepath," he said, making another vow he knew was sacred. A voice tied to everything that he was. "I am coming for you, my broken brother. I love you, but I will kill you. I will save your children. That is the only mercy I offer to you."

Which is when that coiling darkness lashed out with tentacles made of shadow, which wrapped around Kagen's torso and thighs and throat and began to crush the life from him.

CHAPTER ONE HUNDRED EIGHTY-THREE

Redharn and Dilhoolie were big men who had fought on scores of battlefields with a variety of weapons, but an axman was at heart always an axman. They stood on opposite sides of a medium tree, nodded to each other, and began to swing their heavy blades. Those steel half-moons that had cleaved armor, cut heads, killed warhorses, and shattered shields chunked deep into the living wood. Chips and splinters flew, and the men fell into a rhythm, working together as if they had spent their lives as loggers.

Nearby, Filia was directing several other Unbladed to gather branches and bundles of weeds. Gi-Elless and Bor'ak, each of whom always had a bottle of liquor in their packs, gladly yielded them to Filia. The rest of the Unbladed worked the edge of the stairs, firing carefully to make best use of the arrows they all had left.

"Whatever you're doing over there," gritted Tuke, "make it fast."

Below them, the razor-knight climbed and climbed, and the army of the living dead followed.

CHAPTER ONE HUNDRED EIGHTY-FOUR

There is no way to prepare for the unexpected.

That was a lesson Kagen learned long ago from the Poison Rose.

"You can prepare the body for combat, refine the mind for strategy, and cultivate pragmatism, but the unexpected will always have the advantage."

"What then can I do, Mother?"

"I will tell you instead what you may never do. Never panic."

"Even if I'm terrified?"

"Especially if you are terrified, Kagen. You cannot ever prepare for the unexpected. All you can do is react. All you can do is fight to survive. Fight to live."

Coils of darkness encircled him with unbelievable force. They seemed to come not from one great being but from every corner and cleft where shadows could hide. Kagen knew what this was, though. He had spoken of these monsters to Tuke, and his sleep had been haunted by them since he was a lad.

Years ago, when he was a teenager, he had gone with Herepath, Jheklan, and Faulker to one of the closer, smaller glaciers in the Winterwilds. It was the only time Kagen had ventured so far, and he swore thereafter that he would never return. Because of a monster like this.

Because of a shoggoth.

It had been trapped in the ancient ice—caught within the

glacier's walls but not frozen. Not entirely. Merely weakened. But even through that thick ice, the Vale brothers had seen it moving. Not quite liquid, not entirely solid. Some parts were bulbous where the mass was thicker, but there were wispy tendrils that stretched outward as if through veins in the ice. And as it moved, there seemed to be a strange luminescence from within—a sickly green that was unpleasant to look at. It had eyes, too. Many eyes, appearing and disappearing all over its amorphous bulk. Kagen now understood why he and the other Unbladed had felt like they were being watched ever since entering Ulthar, and more so here in this temple.

Because they *were* being watched.

The shoggoths—whatever they were—had dwelt here through the long millennia, patient as the stars. Waiting for the unwary. There now was no doubt why the dog soldiers feared entering this city. They feared the thing that was not merely *in* the dark but *was* the dark.

Now it had him. Coil upon inky coil slithered around him.

He fought with all of his strength, pushing one tentacle away from his mouth and then gagging as two others slapped themselves around his face. A questing tip of one tried to push its way into his mouth. He heard, or thought he heard, a voice speaking. No . . . *voices* . . . as if there were many of these things in that small chamber with him. Or perhaps they all shared a single mind.

"*Fahf bthnkor c' ah,*" they whispered, and somehow—impossibly—Kagen found that he could understand the alien tongue.

This meat is ours.

That understanding nearly tore the heart from him. He began thrashing and kicking. The torch fell and rolled toward the table on which the sacred books lay, the flame nearly extinguished.

"*Ymg' goka l' c', orr'enah shuggoth,*" whispered the darkness. "*C' gokln'gha.*"

Yield to us, mortal man. Feed us.

He saw faint circles of strange light appear and realized with horror and disgust that these were the shoggoth's eyes. They leered at him from the shadows, forming on the thickest parts of the tentacles, then fading to appear elsewhere. First one or two, then ten, then a thousand, then only one. Opening and closing, *seeing* him. Knowing him.

Kagen clawed at the tentacles, but they would not yield. They held him off the ground, waving him sickeningly back and forth. He gasped for air as flowers of fire seemed to ignite before his eyes.

The creature began to pull Kagen toward the lightless space behind the table, where the shadows were tainted by a hellish green radiance. He could hear that low voice muttering.

"C' gokln'gha l' set c' na'ah'ehye."

Feed us to set us free.

A terrible smell, like rotting fish and decaying vegetable matter, suddenly permeated the chamber. Somehow Kagen knew that it was this monster, and others like it, that had slain the giant serpent outside and the vermin here in the temple. Small lives to keep it alive through the long ages of the world. With that knowledge came the deeper insight that these shoggoths needed more than meat and blood; they hungered for human souls. The Vespians knew this and even in their madness would not dare cross into Ulthar.

Would the living dead feed these things? Even as the monster throttled him, Kagen knew this answer to be no.

They fed on life force, on consciousness, on thought and immortal souls.

And he had brought them his own soul and his flesh to satisfy their hunger.

As his oxygen-deprived mind began to die, faces seemed to float before his eyes. Not the hated Herepath or the flawed Empress Gessalyn. Nor even Filia and Tuke or any of his friends.

No, the faces that watched him from the flickering shadows of his mind were those of two beautiful children.

Alleyn and Desalyn. Their true faces, not the masks of corruption and possession they'd worn that night in the palace. It was as if Kagen could look across the gulf of miles between him and them. Bright eyes filled with hope and with fear. Eyes in which some sliver of trust still burned.

Trust in him. Trust in the man who had knelt and sworn a blood oath to protect them.

But these faces were fading as his mind began its tumble into that bottomless darkness. Even then, even dying, Kagen's reflexes were still alive, still trying to do what the Poison Rose had taught him.

"You cannot ever prepare for the unexpected. All you can do is react. All you can do is fight to survive. Fight to live."

The fingers of his left hand closed around the hilt of one of the two matched daggers. He could feel the pearl and sculpted silver of the weapon. He scratched at it with trembling fingernails. Clawing at it. Using the last of his fading strength to curl his fingers around the handle.

His mouth formed the names of Alleyn and Desalyn.

Of Maralina, too.

And the knife hand moved.

A little. A half an inch.

An inch. More. The tendril wrapped around his waist shifted to try to stop what he was doing, but it closed around the guard and the blade as well. In its eagerness to stop what he was doing, it tightened against four inches of exposed steel.

Sharpened steel. *Poisoned* steel.

The shoggoth screamed. It flung Kagen away from itself. He flew across the crypt and struck the wall with such force that the last air in his tortured lungs was punched from his chest. He fell hard to the floor, sprawling, gasping, gagging, vomiting, as all around him the night-black tentacles writhed and thrashed.

"*H' fm'latgh!*" shrieked the voice. "*H' fm'latgh!*"

Those words and their true meaning pulled Kagen back from the brink of his own death.

It burns! It burns!

Kagen rolled over onto his hands and knees, the dagger now clutched in one fist. He scrabbled for the other and drew it, even as he clawed more air into his lungs.

"*Llll hastur,*" screamed the shoggoth, "*h' fm'latgh.*"

By Hastur, it burns.

Kagen staggered to his feet and stood there, chest heaving, clothes torn and stained with black ichor, the matched daggers of the Poison Rose burning like cold fire in his fists.

He took a staggering step forward and slashed at the tendrils that snapped and thrashed around him. The blade bit deeper this time, and the pleas of the shoggoth turned to screams. No potion, no elixir, no magic spell could have done more to put iron back in Kagen's limbs—and courage back in his heart—than those screams. Kagen felt himself come back to life—no, roar back to life.

He stepped into the mass, slashing wildly. The pearl-handled daggers sliced through black flesh and pale eyes with savage force.

"*All you can do is fight to survive. Fight to live.*"

And so he fought.

Once upon a time, Herepath had told him that such creatures could not be hurt, but Kagen knew that on this his brother was wrong. That Herepath had been younger, less learned, more naive about the magicks he would later bring back into this world.

And Kagen was now older, more learned, and less naive about his own ability to fight back. To fight to live. As he slashed with his blades, he did more than harm this ageless monster. He was killing it.

It recoiled from him, the tentacles now shuddering with horror at its own mortality.

"*Tekeli-li! Tekeli-li!*" it screeched. He'd heard a shoggoth scream that all those years ago and knew that there was no translation in either human tongue or human thought. The fear within it was so very eloquent, and every fiber of his being told him that this monster—*these monsters*—were driven past the walls of their own arrogance and were beseeching the Elder Gods they themselves had killed. Or driven away. Begging them for mercy and salvation.

There was no mercy left in Kagen's soul. He had no salvation to offer.

He waded into the tangle of whipping tendrils, slashing and stabbing, chopping and cutting. The *eitr* on his blades burned the shoggoth from the inside out. The eyes were filled with fear now. They bulged and burst, spraying him with dark goo. They pleaded, and he responded with more slashes and stabs.

The beast sought escape, but Kagen chased each part of it into every corner of the crypt, under every ledge, into every crack.

The last living piece of it huddled beneath the table on which lay the Seven Cryptical Books of Hsan. Kagen ignored them as he dropped to his knees and flung himself at the shoggoth, snarling like a wolf, stabbing with mad ferocity. The shoggoth screamed in its ancient language. Kagen could hear it beg its dead gods for salvation. He could hear it beg *him*.

For mercy.

He bared his teeth and let it see with whom it was pleading.

Kagen the Damned.

━━━▶ **CHAPTER ONE HUNDRED EIGHTY-FIVE**

In Argentium, in the palace of the Silver Empresses, the Witch-king staggered as if struck. He reeled away from the Prince of Games, his hip striking the map table and nearly overturning it, sending glasses and bottles crashing to the stone floor. The table righted itself but the Witch-king's knees buckled and he fell.

The doctor gave a single sharp cry and fell backwards to lie twitching on the carpet by his chair. Outside the palace, thunder exploded with such shocking force that the entire building shuddered.

The Prince of Games stood stock-still, shocked by the thunder and the sudden distress of his patron. He tried to catch the Witch-king but missed because his legs would not move.

The Witch-king lay as one dead upon the floor. The Prince of Games stood as if turned to stone. The doctor gave a single twitch, and then from between his parted lips came the slow, distinctive clicks of a death rattle. As his last breath exited, his whole body settled down and lay utterly still.

Lady Kestral opened her eyes and saw all of this. With the insight granted to the very old or to those who feel death's soft kiss upon their lips, she alone understood what was happening.

"Be damned to you all," she whispered, in a voice too small and faint for anyone to have heard.

CHAPTER ONE HUNDRED EIGHTY-SIX

"Filia, hurry damn it!" cried Tuke. "I'm almost out of arrows."

"Take mine," called Jonal, a hatchet fighter from Sunderland. He tossed his quiver to Tuke, though there were only five shafts left. He tossed his bow away, drew both heavy-bladed choppers from his belt, and took up his station on the edge of the plaza.

All of the others had already emptied their quivers. Only three of them had spears; the rest had drawn their steel and crouched on the edge of the platform, staring with horrified eyes as the undead crawled upward. Tuke fired at the razor-knight, hoping for a hit to either eye, but the creature seemed to sense this, and each time the Therian shot, it moved very slightly left or right, turning its head to take the arrow on the framework of its helmet. That reinforced Tuke's belief that its eyes were as vulnerable as the eyes of the infected.

"We're going to die here," muttered the Behlian, Bitler.

Jonal laughed. "Better here than old and sick in bed."

"I'll take old and sick," said Urri, giving him a broad smile.

The joke wasn't that funny, but they all laughed at it. Laughter was sometimes a better piece of armor than a steel-banded hardwood shield. Even Bitler managed a lopsided grin.

Filia looked up from what she was doing and saw the Bloody Bastards—among the toughest fighters she'd ever known—standing there ready to die. That was how she saw it. They were always ready to fight, but now there was a resignation in the line of their shoulders, an acceptance in the set of their jaws. They all believed that this was the end of every road they had traveled, that they would all die here in this lonely, forgotten place. It was a dreary death for fighters who had earned their reputations, who had always stood between the helpless and the angel of death. Worse, it would be a pointless death because there seemed to be no chance at all that even if Kagen found those damnable books that any of the fighters would survive to get them to Mother Frey. The mission had been a risky and unlikely one from the outset, and now these heroes would fall and be consumed. Maybe they would all rise as slavering, flesh-eating monsters. Or maybe they would be stripped to the bone and only their ghosts would haunt this godless place. Either way, it was a tragedy. No one would ever tell the tale—not even their enemies. Every one of these men and women were going to die, and no one would survive to sing their songs or tell their tales. Which made their courage and fatalistic humor all the more admirable. In that moment, she loved every one of them.

Even as these thoughts stabbed her, Filia kept working.

The Witch-king got slowly to his feet. Sudden pain lanced through him and he cried out and clutched the edge of the map table to keep from falling back down. He leaned there for a long minute, his legs trembled and heart raced. He gulped in careful lungfuls of breath and hissed them out while the room spun sickeningly around.

His mind cleared by slow degrees. He saw the doctor sprawled on the rug, eyes wide and sightless. On her chair, Lady Kestral looked dead as well.

"What . . . what *was* that?" he gasped. When his chief advisor did not answer, he turned to see the Prince of Games sitting with his back to the wall near the fireplace, his face in his hands. "Speak, damn you. What happened?"

The prince's eyes swirled with color and his mouth was open, lips slack and rubbery.

"Do you live?" demanded the king. "Damn your soul to everlasting hell if you've died. Speak!"

"I . . . live," wheezed the prince. He shook his head like a dazed hound, but his eyes slowly regained focus and humanity. Then those eyes showed sudden alarm. "Check the witch. Did she die?"

The King in Yellow shambled over to her chair, pausing along the way to look down into the open and glassy eyes of the dead doctor. Then he knelt by Kestral and pressed his fingers against her throat while he held his own breath. Then the Witch-king exhaled slowly, nodding with relief.

"She yet lives," he said. He staggered to the sideboard and poured himself a glass of wine, and after a moment, he poured one for the prince. They drank the glasses dry. "Again I ask, what *was* that?"

The prince got to his feet. The Witch-king saw the strange man's hands shaking and wasn't sure if that degree of human vulnerability was comforting or distressing. He decided that it was equal parts both.

"For the second time today," said the prince, affecting a voice of calm that was totally at odds with his disheveled clothes and stricken face, "I find myself at a loss, and when I tell you that this is an exceedingly rare thing for me, I pray you take me at my word."

"I do," said the king. He looked around and saw much of the glassware had shattered; wine dripped like blood from the table. The maps were stained with it. There were thin cracks in the walls and one that ran crookedly across the stone floor. Guards pounded on the door, but the Witch-king snarled them away.

He refilled and drained the cup a second time. "We must understand this," he gasped.

The prince took the bottle and drank it dry. They both leaned against the table, not trusting their own strength. Lady Kestral groaned very softly but did not open her eyes.

"Tell me, my lord," said the prince, his eyes narrowed and fixed on the necromancer, "how much do you trust the lady?"

"Kestral?" said the Witch-king. "With my life. Why?"

"Mm," murmured the prince. "I find myself wondering how greatly the lady values that trust."

"What do you mean? Look at how completely she has spent her life and strength to do my will."

"That," said the prince, "is what I mean."

The Witch-king studied him for a long and silent moment. "No," he said. "You are wrong."

"Perhaps, Majesty," said the Prince of Games, "but in the meantime, it might be wise to gather all of the magicians of your court. Every diviner, all the scholars of the ancient ways, and to do that without a moment's further pause."

And this the Witch-king did.

CHAPTER ONE HUNDRED EIGHTY-EIGHT

Kagen rose to his feet and leaned on the table. His daggers were coated with black blood and the rotting fish stench was overpowering. Spread out before him were the books Mother Frey said could save the world. In that moment Kagen wanted to burn them and go on to destroy everything and anything that was tainted with magic. He hated it all.

But he looked down at his knives. *Eitr* may, itself, possess magic qualities. It was gifted to him by an immortal sorceress. The conflict that offered was impossible to ignore.

Upstairs he could hear the shouts and furor of battle. A battle that was being fought to buy him the time needed to gather up these books and get them out of Vespia. Upstairs his friends were fighting and very likely dying. And yet he did not move. Not yet. He lingered there, still clutching the handles of those knives. He felt his lips move before he realized that, despite everything, he was praying. Not to the fickle Harvest Gods. Not to Hastur or Cthulhu, nor even Dagon.

He prayed to whatever gods there might be whose love was red combat, the gods of war and vengeance. And the gods of hate.

Then he took a sweat rag from a pocket and used it to wipe the black blood of the shoggoth from the steel. When it was thoroughly clean, he fished in his pouch for the vial of *eitr*. There was very little left. Maybe not enough.

He took the cleanest corner of the rag, let the pale liquid soak into it, and began seasoning those daggers with the god-killer poison.

CHAPTER ONE HUNDRED EIGHTY-NINE

The two Bloody Bastards with spears—Wilfreth the Gray of Narek and Moonie of Tull Belain—positioned themselves on either side of Tuke as the Therian fired his next-to-last arrow.

"See you on the other side, brother," said Wilfreth as he raised his spear.

Moonie grinned. "First drink in hell is on me."

They both laughed. Even Tuke smiled as he drew his last arrow.

"Make a hole!" cried a voice, and they turned to see Redharn rushing toward them with a huge log held over his head. Bundles of sticks were lashed to it, and these blazed with bright flames.

Tuke leaned sideways, pushing Wilfreth out of the way. Moonie stepped aside, his grin even brighter now. With a roar of anger, Redharn ran to the very edge and hurled the flaming log down at the razor-knight.

"*Go back to hell!*" he bellowed.

The monster was only twenty feet from the platform, and with the infected crowded around, there was no chance or space to evade. The log struck the knight full in the chest.

Or should have.

At the last moment—and with appalling speed—the razor-knight bashed it aside with a mighty fist. The burning log spun sideways, struck two of the cursed, crushing one skull and snapping the other's neck, and then fell among the undead. The blistering sun had dried their hair and clothes, and as the log struck over and over again, it set little blazes here and there. The cursed screamed in rage but not in pain, even as they burned. The falling bodies and the flames slowed the mass of Vespians, throwing them into confusion, knocking dozens of them backwards and down.

And yet the razor-knight kept climbing.

Redharn, Dilhoolie, Filia, and the others lit one after another of the logs and hurled them down. Scores of the infected fell, some crippled and broken, others burning. Each burning body created a kind of fiery infection of its own. The blaze swept through the Vespians, and as the logs landed at the bottom of the pyramid they sent arms of fire reaching up to ignite more of the living dead. Soon hundreds were burning. A wall of flame swept upward, setting ablaze everything it touched and pushing before it a great wind of burning air.

Wilfreth was leaning out to stab down when the blazing wind reached him. He saw his doom a moment too late, and then he was wreathed in yellow fingers. His cloak and tunic and beard caught fire before Moonie could save him, and the Narekian toppled forward, using his last conscious thought to fall toward his enemies, and so became a counterpunch of fiery destruction.

It was he who slammed into the razor-knight.

And they fell together.

But as Wilfreth continued to roll and bump downward to ultimate destruction, the razor-knight shot out a huge hand and caught the step below where it had been. Its fingers gouged the granite, such was the monster's power, and it pulled its massive bulk up to that step, and the one above, and the one above that.

Moonie began stabbing at it with his spear, thrusting with all the force of his heavy muscles and towering terror. His spear point struck the armored shoulder of the knight, but then the creature once more darted a hand out, this time catching the shaft behind the leaf-bladed steel head. With a savage jerk it pulled Moonie off the ledge and hurled him backwards and down into the reaching hands and snapping teeth of the undead dog soldiers.

Then the razor-knight gripped the lip of the platform and pulled itself over the edge.

"Gods save our souls," cried Dilhoolie, his face going dead pale.

"Fuck the gods," bellowed Redharn. "Come on, brother, let's kill this ugly bastard."

Redharn and Dilhoolie rushed at the knight, swinging their axes with every ounce of power and fear they possessed. The heavy blades struck the creature in the thigh and the chest, staggering the thing so that it nearly fell backwards down the stairs, but as they raised their weapons to strike again, the monster crouched to regain its balance. Its red eyes glowed with malice, and the mocking laughter boomed from its mouth. The nightbirds on the buildings and in the air screamed at the sound of it.

Then the razor-knight attacked.

One side of its cloak whipped upward, the ink-black set of blades tearing through the air. Redharn flung himself to the left, hitting the platform floor and rolling. Dilhoolie tried to check his swing and block the attack. He brought the axe handle up, but the knight's stygian blades sheared through it.

And through the big Nehemitian.

For a fragment of a second Dilhoolie stared down at himself, eyes and mouth wide in surprise. Then everything above the waist slid sideways and fell. His legs remained standing for a moment longer, and then they, too, fell as blood shot into the air.

"No!" cried Redharn in horror. He swung his axe again, this time catching the razor-knight's shoulder. It spun the thing and Redharn hit it again and again. But the razor-knight did not fall. Instead it braced its feet to take the blows and abruptly pivoted with its left wing toward the falconer. In a splintered piece of a second Filia flung herself at Redharn, catching him around the waist and barreling him over and down. They landed on the top step amid a handful of the infected. Cold, dead fingers plucked at both of them, pulling them toward red mouths.

Above, the razor-knight began marching toward the temple, pulled by the call of its creator to find the Books of Hsan.

The remaining Unbladed were caught in that terrible moment of indecision—fight the infected or fight the razor-knight. Death leered at them from either choice.

Tuke shattered that hesitation with a howl of murderous glee. He knew he was going to die and he was damn well going to fill hell with as many of his enemies as possible. He leapt onto the top step, a machete in each hand, and laid into the infected who were trying to kill his lover and his friend. Arms, legs, and heads went flying through the air. He kicked crippled Vespians down the stairs, further confusing their ascent.

Filia pulled Redharn to his feet and they scrambled up to the platform, then both turned and offered hands to Tuke, but instead he tossed his blades up to them, caught the rim, and hauled himself up, landing in a crouch. He took his weapons back, still grinning.

"There are no poets here, alas," he laughed, "but by the burning balls of the god of the forge we will write our own song in the blood of these monsters."

He, Filia, and Redharn turned and stood in a line as the living dead poured over the rim and swarmed forward. Gi-Elless, Giffer, Yill, and Bor'ak ran to defend the door to the chapel.

"Kagen is still inside looking for the books," said Giffer. "We need to give him all the time he needs. We can't let that monster get in."

"Hold the line," said Gi-Elless. "No matter what, we hold this line."

The razor-knight saw them, and from its chest rolled that deep, booming laugh.

"Pray to your useless gods," it bellowed. "You will see them soon enough."

It raised the bladed ends of its cloak like the wings of a monstrous bird and rushed their line.

CHAPTER ONE HUNDRED NINETY

"Where's Kagen?" cried Alleyn, staring into the swirling vortex that surrounded the trapped demon spirit Kestral had conjured. They saw other people—men and women they did not know but who stood between the knight and the open door of a stone chapel.

"I can't see him," said Desalyn, "but we have to do the next part or it'll kill him."

"Lady Kestral said she would help us, though."

His sister gave him a hard look. "She told us what to do. I think she knew she might not be able to do it herself."

Alleyn gasped. "But . . . what if we get it wrong?"

"Then we're stupid and we'll die," said Desalyn.

The boy closed his eyes, fighting tears.

"Alleyn," said Desalyn, "we have to try." She pulled the necklace from her tunic and showed it to him. "Or do you want to go back to being Gavran?"

The sheer terror in her brother's eyes was his most eloquent answer.

"Get the vial," said Desalyn. "Hurry!"

CHAPTER ONE HUNDRED NINETY-ONE

Kagen knew he was out of time. He removed his cloak and laid it over the line of scrolls, then stepped back in case something happened. When the cloth did not burst into flames, he drew closer again and very carefully touched one finger to the cloak at the point where it lay curved over a scroll. Nothing.

Greatly relieved and more than a little surprised, he wrapped the cloth around the Hsan books.

"Borz," yelled Kagen as he slung the bundle slantwise across his back and tied it securely around his chest, "what's happening?"

The Ghulian appeared in the doorway, his face streaked with dirt and sweat. "Everything's going to shit."

Kagen slid his daggers into their sheaths, careful not to scrape the *eitr* from the steel. "What's wrong? Have the cursed reached the summit?"

"Worse than that," said Borz.

Kagen turned to him. "What the fuck is worse than an army of undead cannibals?"

Borz licked his lips. "A razor-knight."

Those words hit Kagen like punches, like arrows. He staggered back a pace and had to grab the edge of the table.

"No . . ." he breathed.

But then the deep, booming, bass thunder of the razor-knight's voice—a roar of bloodlust and triumph, punctuated by the screams of the fighters outside—reached him.

"A razor-knight?" he said hollowly. "Here? *How?*"

"I don't know, Captain, but we are losing this fight. By the Harvest Gods, I don't know how we're getting out of this."

Kagen glanced at the shadows in the room, remembering how they had come alive as the shoggoth emerged. Remembering how they died. He pushed off the table and clapped Borz on the shoulder.

"Maybe I do," he said, and without explaining, he rushed from the crypt and raced up the stairs.

CHAPTER ONE HUNDRED NINETY-TWO

The map room was filling up with men and women in yellow robes. Each set of robes was embroidered with alchemical and astrological symbols, some with fragments of spells and words of power from the oldest dialects of the Hakkian language. Every one of them wore ornate jewelry of silver or platinum, and each was either carved into the likeness of a patron god or servant demon or was set with crystals or gemstones cut into key elements of sacred geometry. A few had familiars—a leopard on a golden chain, a raven with albino wings, a cobra with three eyes. Every magician in the court of the Witch-king was there, crowding the space, jostling cheek by jowl with one another but making every effort not to touch the King in Yellow or his princely advisor. None would even dare step on the shadow of either man.

There were alchemists and animists, mages and archmages, druids and elementalists, old-style enchanters and modern mentalists, shamans and herbalists, wizards and sorcerers, enchantresses and warlocks.

A platoon of heavily armed and armored soldiers took up station outside of the room, with orders to kill anyone who attempted to enter—or leave—without the Witch-king's permission. Lord Nespar and Jakob Ravensmere sent word in that they were outside and available to help, but the king did not bother to reply.

The Witch-king told his gathered magic users of the battle being fought in distant Vespia. Some of the attending magicians already knew, for they had worked with the Hollow Monks and the Red Curse. Others knew that Lady Kestral had been laboring to conjure a razor-knight. All of them pledged their skills and their lives to their master.

"We need to stop Kagen Vale and the Unbladed scum accompanying him," said the Witch-king. "They have gone to Vespia to find great and ancient books of magic. The truest drafts of the Seven Cryptical Books of Hsan."

That tore gasps of shock and wonder from the crowd.

"If he is allowed to bring those books out of Vespia," warned the king, "then Hakkia is in peril. War is already coming for us. We still hold the power, but there are forces aligned against us and they are helping Kagen. This must end today."

One of the most senior of the magicians, Ekluster the Seer, stepped forward. "Majesty," he said, his hands placed over his heart, "tell us what we, the Family of the Unknowable, may do to help."

The Witch-king touched Ekluster's shoulder. "Ever you have served us with wisdom and piety. You and all who have come in answer to my call are beloved of Hastur and I count you as *my* family." They all bowed. Some even wept at these words. "Now, listen to me, all of you. There is wild and awful work to be done. It will require much of each of us, for this is the darkest and most dangerous of magicks."

And he told them.

The Prince of Games stood apart and looked out the window instead of at the gathering. His eyes swirled and shifted, and he cast his thoughts onto the wind and let it carry his mind far, far away.

CHAPTER ONE HUNDRED NINETY-THREE

Tuke and half the Bloody Bastards held the top step of the platform. Gi-Elless and the rest held the line at the door. Tried to hold.

Tried.

The dead kept coming. In their hundreds, in their thousands. The forest trembled with the numbers of them that rushed to the sound of battle and the smell of flesh. Driven by the scent of fresh blood, they climbed, scrambling over one another, kicking and clawing and even snapping at their fellows to be first to the feast. Scores of them lay crushed and broken at the foot of the grand staircase, but they served as no warning, provided no caution to the others. As new infected arrived they merely trod upon the crippled and the dead, which made it easier to gain the first step. They grabbed belts and sashes, tunics and hair as they scaled their own kind to reach the next step, and the next.

The razor-knight was fighting its way to the door of the chapel, but the Unbladed there were making the thing earn every inch. They circled it, slashing high and low, working with the coordinated ferocity of fighters who had only ever survived as many battlefields as they had by knowing how to work together. A handful of skilled soldiers working in harmony were worth ten times their number of less-experienced warriors. Each time the razor-knight moved toward the door, they would attack from all sides, slashing at its legs and hands. Gi-Elless tore off her cloak and hurled it over the knight's head, momentarily blinding it, and

Giffer, former scholar and ascetic, snatched up the skull of the skeletal serpent and brought it down with crushing force on the monster's back.

The impact drove the razor-knight to one knee, and both Yill and Bor'ak rushed in to stab the creature in the throat.

The knight jerked its arms up, bracing fists against its helmet and letting the encircling wings of its cloak take the thrusts. Yill's blade snapped; Bor'ak's knife caught in a cleft between two of the long, flexible blades. As the knight surged back to its feet, Bor'ak's knife was torn from his hand. The knight pivoted, letting the hem of his cloak swirl around like a deadly whirlpool. The blades inside the cloak slashed Bor'ak's chest and throat to rags and caught Yill as she tried to dance out of the way. The tip of one blade raked her across the waist and she stumbled back, pawing at her middle with her hands, trying to keep her entrails within, and failing utterly. She dropped to her knees and the razor-knight turned away, not even interested enough to watch her die.

Gi-Elless and Giffer jumped out of the way; she hit the chapel wall and Giffer tripped over more of the skeleton. They both went down, badly dazed. The door stood unguarded now, and the razor-knight's thunderous laughter once more filled the air, louder even than the howls of the living dead.

Tuke heard the roar and risked a backwards glance just in time to see the armored monstrosity squeeze its bulk into the chapel. "Dagon's blood," he cried. "We're lost!"

CHAPTER ONE HUNDRED NINETY-FOUR

Desalyn got up and ran to a small table set by the chair where Lady Kestral had been before the Witch-king's men came to fetch her. The children had been hiding and were helpless to prevent it, but the lady had told them it would happen. Just as she had prepared for what was to come.

"Don't spill it," warned Alleyn as he removed several items from a pouch Kestral had given him.

Desalyn walked as carefully as if she were picking a safe path through a field of broken glass. The bowl was cupped in her small hands and she tried not to wince at the acrid smell. She stopped a few yards from where the soul of the razor-knight was still fighting to break free of the circle of protection. Within that swirling cone of shimmering energy, Desalyn could see flash images of what the knight saw. Alleyn looked up, too, and watched as the razor-knight approached a stone building. Soldiers the children did not recognize stood ready to sell their lives dearly to protect that doorway.

"Who are they?" asked Alleyn.

"I don't know," his sister answered as she lowered herself carefully to her knees and set the bowl down.

One of the defenders rushed at the knight with a pair of wavy-bladed daggers, but the razor-knight cut her to pieces. It was all very quick and messy and horrible. The woman with the knives seemed to fly apart as if she were made of paper, her bright blood splashing the faces of the other defenders.

CHAPTER ONE HUNDRED NINETY-FIVE

Kagen and Borz ran up the stairs to the chapel just in time to see Lo-Fan, staggering backwards, clutching his chest. The Nerekian turned to them and tried to speak, but all that came from his mouth was a torrent of red blood. He dropped to his knees, fingers clawing at his sternum, and to his horror, Kagen saw that the whole front of Lo-Fan's chest was dented inward as if from some terrible blow. Lo-Fan gurgled once and fell sideways, eyes fixed on a spot high on the wall as if it were a window to infinity.

A shadow filled the chapel doorway, and *it* was there.

The razor-knight was even bigger than the one that had killed the Poison Rose. Easily eight feet tall, with a barrel chest, massive shoulders, and those raven wings in which dozens of blades were hidden. Its eyes glowed with the red fires of hell, and the thing turned toward Borz and Kagen.

Gi-Elless, weak and smeared with blood from a scalp wound, appeared in the doorway behind the knight, and Giffer—looking even worse—was behind her.

"Get back," yelled Kagen.

"Do you have the books?" begged Gi-Elless.

"Yes, now get the hell back. Both of you. Gods of the Pit . . . run! You cannot defeat this thing."

Even as he spoke, he could hear his mother making a similar plea to him.

"*Kagen . . . Gods of the Garden . . .* run*! You cannot defeat this thing. No one can. Run, for the love of all.*"

His mother had died then. But would she have if she'd fought the thing with her knives coated with poison? No, he thought, she would not have. Her daggers had been coated with some other toxin. It was not *eitr*.

Kagen drew those same weapons now.

"You want the Books of Hsan?" he asked calmly.

"I will take them from what is left of your body, Kagen Vale."

Kagen raised his daggers and showed the blades to the monster. "Come and try, if you dare."

The razor-knight laughed. So, too, did Kagen.

And then, with mutual roars of bloody hatred, they flew at each other.

CHAPTER ONE HUNDRED NINETY-SIX

In the palace map room, the sorcerers gathered around the table. The maps had been pushed to the floor and a big bowl was placed on the hardwood top. In it were dozens of pieces of parchment on which each of the magicians had written their own name, the name of their patron demon, the sacred name of Hastur, and key lines from the most powerful of spells. A few of the magic users hesitated, uncertain of the purpose and consequences of that kind of magic.

"This is a very old spell," said the Witch-king, who had sent for items from his alchemy laboratory. As he ground various minerals and spices together, he explained. "It is known by many names—the Heart of Fire, the Blood of the Gods, the Blood of Chaos—but I learned it as the Tears of Hastur. It is dangerous, so be warned, but we are all in peril. The navies of Samud, Vahlycor, and Theria are preparing to sail. The Red Curse may soon sweep the land. Rebellion is in the air, and soon we will all be engaged in a bloody civil war. Even our wisest augurs cannot predict the future. Everything is in flux, now that magic is awakening. Most critically, we are engaged in a fierce battle more than a thousand miles from where we stand. Kagen Vale is even now in the sacred city of Ulthar in Vespia, and he has found the Seven Cryptical Books of Hsan. He and his Unbladed allies want to give those books to our enemies."

"By Hastur's staff," said the Hakkian high priest, who was one of the most powerful sorcerers alive, "with that he can undo all that we have worked for."

"Yes," said the Witch-king fiercely. "That is his plan, and if he succeeds then not only will we be in danger of losing the war, but the old Silver Empire will rise again. This time they will not be content with repression of our culture and suppression of our religion. No, they will exterminate our race. We will be wiped from the face of the earth. It will become a crime to even remember that we ever lived. We are now in a fight for our very survival. I warn you all, though, that there is no small danger here. Though you do not fight for Hakkia with swords and spears, what I ask of you comes with risk. Terrible risk."

"Whatever you require from us," said the high priest, "we will do. For you, our Witch-king, and for the glory of Hastur the Shepherd God."

The Witch-king reached out a hand and the Prince of Games placed a small silver knife in it. The handle was very plain wood, the blade sharp and gleaming. He took the knife in his left hand, balled his right into a fist, and held it out over the bowl. Then, without hesitation, he drew the edge across his forearm. Blood welled from the wound and he squeezed his hand to encourage the flow until several ounces had dripped into the bowl. Then he turned to the high priest and offered the weapon.

The high priest bowed and repeated the action, his face tightening with the pain. Then they all did this, until the items in the bowl were completely saturated with dark red. When the last of them had completed the blood sacrifice, the blade was passed to the prince, who set it in the coals of the fire. The fingers of flame that touched his hand left no marks at all, for he was the Prince of Games and fire—that quixotic and chaotic thing—was his friend.

The sorcerers all watched as the Witch-king bent over the bowl and spoke in a language long forbidden in the Silver Empire. The language of the Elder Gods.

"Ph'nglui hastur's vulgtmoth yaah Y' goka fahf vulgtmor ot gn'th'bthnk ng r'luh," he intoned.

As he spoke, the air in the room seemed to change, to become thicker, warmer, more humid. In the fireplace, the blaze leapt up, growing bigger and brighter, belching sparks onto the floor. Outside, they could hear ravens squawking in alarm.

"Y' l' uln orr'ee ot vulgtmoth fm'latghor l' c' hafh!"
I call upon the spirits of the holy fire to aid us!

The floor beneath their feet rumbled and fresh cracks appeared. Dust plumed from fissures in the walls. Thunder boomed in the clear sky outside the window. Inside the bowl, the soup of herbs, crystal powder, parchment, ink, and blood pulsed with an inner light. However, that light was not red but instead flared with yellow intensity. The color of the Witch-king's robes. The color of every painting of Hastur the Shepherd God. With each pulse the amount of liquid in the bowl seemed to grow, to swell, rising toward the rim. The sorcerers backed away in fright, but the Witch-king held his ground, hands extended, palms down, as he repeated his entreaty over and over. The timbre of his voice swelled, too, until it was unbearably, impossibly loud.

Then all at once the bowl and its contents exploded. A fireball of golden light hung for a moment above the table, rotating and swirling and throbbing.

The Witch-king screamed the prayer one last time and the fireball shot toward the window, shattering the glass and tearing huge chunks of masonry away. It hurtled into the sky, growing larger and flashing faster. Then it shot—faster than any eye could follow—to the northeast.

Toward Vespia.

CHAPTER ONE HUNDRED NINETY-SEVEN

Kagen drove forward and then immediately ducked as one wing of the razor-knight's deadly cloak tore through the air at head level. As he evaded that killing blow, he slashed with both daggers. One blade was checked by the metal faulds that made up the monster's armored skirt. His other knife cut along the bottom of the breastplate and Kagen felt his edge move through something that yielded.

The razor-knight suddenly roared in shock and pain. He back-handed Kagen with a vicious blow that sent him flying. Kagen crashed into Borz and knocked the former caravan guard flat.

Despite the pain, Kagen rolled off and scrambled back to his feet as the razor-knight charged again. His hopes of killing it with but a touch of the *eitr* were crushed, because the thing kept moving. Kagen dove behind an altar to avoid those black and bladed wings. He rolled on one shoulder, came up fast, spun and attacked the knight again, once more slashing with both blades. This time he aimed for the night-dark skin visible beneath the line of the helmet. But his blades only scraped on steel as the razor-knight turned and hunched to protect itself.

Kagen danced backwards toward Borz. He kicked the man in the hip, jolting the Nerekian from his dazed state. "Get out, gods damn your eyes," snarled Kagen. "Get out of my way. Go help the others. *Go!*"

Borz cut a terrified look at the knight and then ran without a word. Gi-Elless and Giffer, still lingering at the door, retreated with him, their conflict about leaving Kagen alone with the monster burning in their eyes.

This gave Kagen more room to maneuver as the razor-knight charged him. Kagen, smaller, faster, and more agile, ducked and dodged, slipped and twisted away from each sweep of the cloak of knives. He kept hoping the god-killer poison was at work in the knight's bloodstream—if the thing even had blood. It did not seem to be slowing, though, and that worried Kagen. The bundle of scrolls on his back, though inconsequential in actual mass, nevertheless weighed him down with their importance. He regretted not giving them to Borz.

"You cannot hope to win," mocked the razor-knight as it charged again.

Kagen put a foot on the edge of the altar, kicked himself into the air, twisted over the slashing wing, and stabbed backwards as he landed. The impact sent a painful shock up his arm and the razor-knight roared in pain.

In pain.

Kagen pivoted as he landed and pressed his attack at the knight, which now retreated from him.

"Die, you miserable bastard," screamed Kagen, but once again the knight did not fall. Kagen could not even be sure if it was the *eitr* that tore the painful cry from the thing or simply the steel of the knife.

"You cannot kill me," growled the knight, even as it backed away, blocking with lightning-fast movements of the armored cloak. Still Kagen pressed his attack, trying to sneak the edge or point in, under, or around the armor.

The razor-knight blocked and parried, deflected and evaded as they dueled back and forth. All of the gods and demons carved onto the altar and the walls seemed to watch, and Kagen could swear their eyes followed him as he moved. For some reason he could never understand, it amused him.

Then he realized that the knight was moving to a pattern, edging Kagen step by step toward one corner of the chapel. Trying to cut him off so that it could dominate the human with its bulk and winglike cloak.

Kagen made himself look very frightened—something that required very little playacting—and appeared to hesitate. The knight laughed, checked its own zigzag movement, and rushed forward for the kill. But Kagen was ready for that, hoping for it.

As the razor-knight barreled in, cloak raised high and wide to envelope Kagen in the same lethal way the other knight had killed the Poison Rose, Kagen made his play. He hurled himself toward the monster, leaping high into the air, fists raised above his head, and then stabbed forward with every ounce of strength and need that he possessed. The dagger points glittered with silver fire as he punched downward into the eyes of the razor-knight. Those blades bit deep, piercing the fiery eyes and driving all the way into the creature's brain with such force that the points of each dagger rang sharply on the inside of the helmet.

The razor-knight screamed with an agony so massive, so towering, that the very sound of it was like a fist that punched into

Kagen and sent him flying, the handles torn from his hands. He struck the corner of the altar, rolled, and tumbled into the open stairs that led down to the crypt. He fell badly, and each stone step struck a blow on thigh and hip, ribs and shoulder. He hit his head on the floor and then all the lights in the world went out.

CHAPTER ONE HUNDRED NINETY-EIGHT

The flower petal bowl lay on the floor where Lady Kestral had placed it. Alleyn and Desalyn knelt on either side of it, watched by the glowing red eyes of the demon spirit within the nearby conjuring circle. It had gone still and no longer fought to break out, and those burning eyes seemed to dim sharply. It watched, though. They could *feel* the probing and intrusive fingers of its mind touching theirs.

The mixture in the bottom was dark and smelled awful. There were flakes of Kagen Vale's dried blood, salt water from the ocean, the heart of a dove, moth cocoons, ground bone, mugwort, hellebore, and salt from the deserts of Skyria. There was a slip of paper floating on the top; Kagen's name was written upon it in silver ink.

"Give me the vial," said Desalyn, and Alleyn did so, placing it very carefully in her palm. With infinite care she tugged the cork stopper free, placing her finger over the opening to prevent the contents from spilling out. Then, with Alleyn cupping his hands around hers, she tipped the vial over and shook the single strand of hair out. It wafted to and fro as it fell, and they held their breath, begging the Harvest Gods to prevent it from drifting away.

The hair fell into the bowl and stuck fast.

"Say the words," urged Alleyn. "Say the prayer to Nyarlathotep."

"I . . . I forget how it goes," said Desalyn.

Alleyn screwed up his face as he racked his own brain to dredge up the words he had heard Kestral say when she first invoked the demon. The exact words were so important; the lady had told them that over and over.

"What if I get it wrong?" he pleaded.

Desalyn had no chance to reply, because the demon laughed. It was mocking, pitiless, and cruel, and that told them everything they needed to know.

"There's no time," whispered Desalyn, her eyes huge. "Say it!"

◤ CHAPTER ONE HUNDRED NINETY-NINE

Kagen opened his eyes very slowly.

It took a few moments to understand where he was. Longer to work out why he was there. The walls of the crypt were close and dark, poorly lit by the torch he'd hung in a sconce mere minutes ago, though it felt like an age.

He lay there, eyes open, staring at the ceiling. Every part of him hurt. Every place the shoggoth had squeezed him with black tentacles. The deep bruises from being hurled against the walls and down the steps to the crypt, and from fighting the razor-knight. Pain was more real to him than his own skin. When he tried to move, he heard something crinkle between his back and the floor, and that immediately brought everything back to him. He sat up quickly and then twisted to one side and vomited as an intense wave of nausea punched its way through him.

"Gods of the Harvest," he moaned, not really cognizant of to whom he prayed. He reached around to assure himself that the Hsan books were still there, still his.

It took some time to organize the basics of how to stand, how to breathe. There was a terrible pain in his head, and when he touched his right temple his fingers came away wet with blood. The lines of everything in the room were blurred, and for a moment he saw two torches and two tables.

Concussed and sick, he shambled out of the crypt and climbed like an old dog up the steps. When he saw the razor-knight sprawled on the ground, it startled him. His mind told him that the monster had somehow exploded, but as he fought for understanding he realized that he was layering what happened on the Night of the Ravens with that fight there in the chapel.

Either way, the razor-knight lay still. Dead, if that word could be properly applied to a thing like that.

"Fuck you," he said to it, but he did not dare touch the knight except to retrieve his knives. Instead, he let the sounds of battle draw him toward the chapel door. "I'm coming, Tuke," he said. "I'm coming, Filia."

He stumbled with every step.

CHAPTER TWO HUNDRED

When Kagen met Mother Frey in the Cavorting Bear, there had been twenty Unbladed apart from himself, Tuke, and Filia.

Now there were eleven.

Ten, without the injured Pergun, who had been tending the horses and fled with them when the first wave of the infected Vespians attacked. Redharn, the scar-faced falconer; Urri, the stocky Nehemitian with stars tattooed on her face; Bitler of the Behlian Crocodile clan; Borz, the battered caravan scout from Ghul; Gi-Elless, the sharp-featured Samudian archer; Jonal, the hatchet fighter from Sunderland; Giffer, once a Gardener in Zaare and now a seasoned fighter; and Hoth, the poet and duelist from Ghenrey. Tuke and Filia rounded out the number.

Ten against ten thousand.

"Here they come," said Tuke, shifting into a fighting stance, his machetes already smeared with blood. He glanced at Filia, who stood ready beside him.

"I love you," he said, pitching it for her ears only.

She laughed. "Don't be such a girl," she said.

"Kiss my balls, then," growled Tuke.

She gave him a wicked grin. "Let's see how the day plays out."

They smiled at each other, knowing this was the last moment. The last time, the last conversation. The last of them.

The Vespians boiled over the wall like cockroaches. With screams of inhuman hunger, they attacked.

"Hold the line!" roared Tuke. Filia took up the shout and then all of them yelled it as the surging tide of the living dead slammed into them.

Tuke chopped down at an angle, taking the head and one arm from the first Vespian to reach him, and Filia kicked that falling corpse into the path of the next two. They went down and her longsword conjured silver magic as it cut through the backs of their necks.

Giffer bashed with a small steel buckler, the edge honed to razor sharpness, and then smashed with a mace. Faces and skulls disintegrated with each blow.

Gi-Elless, even without her bow, cut and slashed, kicked and stabbed, moving with an oiled grace that belied the exhaustion she—like all of them—felt after such a long and dreadful day. Her blood was on fire as she moved.

Redharn had taken a pair of spiked steel gauntlets from the corpse of Moonie and fought like a boxer, delivering blows at angles that snapped chins around so fast it broke necks or clouting Vespians on the crowns of their heads to drive splintered bone into brain tissue. His face was flushed red and his eyes were filled with madness.

Because the Bloody Bastards held the edge of the plaza, the teeming mass of Vespians could only climb up a dozen at a time, and the Unbladed met each fresh wave. Over and over again, killing each of the monsters. But the waves never stopped, because the sheer weight of undead behind them pushed the front ranks up and over the ledge. Many of the cursed were charred, and some still burned. The whole front wall of the jungle near the foot of the staircase was burning. The conflagration was driven by hot winds, and the rising heat was as much of a threat to the Bloody Bastards as it was to the Vespian monsters.

Kagen, who had made it as far as the door to the outside, leaned drunkenly against the frame and took all of this in. His heart, already heavy, sank like a stone.

CHAPTER TWO HUNDRED ONE

The ball of yellow light shot through the air above the lands of the former Silver Empire so fast that it was gone before it registered on any eye. Farmers heard their cows bleat and their chickens squawk, but when they stared up to see what had alarmed the animals, there was nothing above but sky.

The fireball reached the peaks of the Cathedral Mountains and passed between them, angling down now, driving toward a specific place deep in the jungles of Vespia. It did not slow as it arched toward the earth. Instead, it struck the edge of the jungle where ten thousand of the living dead were shoving and clawing to climb the steps. The ball of light struck the center of the mass and detonated, hurling hundreds of pieces of bodies into the air, scattering them everywhere. It set ablaze those trees that had not been touched by the earlier fires, and reignited others that were burning out. Within seconds the entire jungle—five times as large an area as before—was burning. The shock wave knocked hundreds more Vespians from the stairs, killing many. It set many more of them ablaze, and that drove the defenders back from the edge.

Throughout the whole of the jungles of Vespia the birds fled the trees. The parrots and hummingbirds, macaws and toucans rose up and flew in every direction except southwest. Not one flew in the direction from which the fireball had come. Not one. They did not fly toward Hakkia on that day.

The other birds, the black ones and dark brown ones, the

starlings and cormorants and blackbirds and crows—always the crows—flew toward the pyramid to join their brothers there.

Kagen staggered out of the chapel just in time to be hit by the blast of energy. The force knocked him inside again and he fell, inches from the razor-knight.

Outside, Filia hauled Tuke to his feet and they stood on trembling legs, gaping at the devastation. There was a crater forty feet wide in the ground, and everywhere was fire and writhing bodies. The impact had destroyed the bottom three steps.

"Gods of the Pit," gasped Tuke. "What . . . what . . . ?"

They saw thousands of corpses sprawled everywhere. But thousands more of the infected climbed back to their feet. Even with terrible wounds and horrible burns, they staggered forward, reaching for shattered pieces of the steps, pulling themselves up, climbing like a swarm of termites over one another. And the Vespians who had been dazed there on the top of the pyramid rose, too. They looked at the Unbladed with their dead eyes. Except those eyes were no longer blank and lifeless. The infected Vespians no longer *had* eyes. Instead, their eye sockets were charred, and where the eyeballs should be burned yellow flames.

Hakkian yellow. Hastur yellow.

The legions of the living dead opened their mouths and in one voice shouted, *"Kagen Vale, thy doom is upon you!"*

That voice was one that Filia knew. She had heard it in Argentium on the night of the failed coronation. It was the commanding voice of Herepath, the Witch-king of Hakkia.

"Gods above save my soul," breathed Filia.

CHAPTER TWO HUNDRED TWO

They said the prayer together.

Alleyn and Desalyn. Twin six-year-old children. Frightened, certain that they would get it wrong, sure they were going to die.

And yet angry.

So angry.

They hated the man who called himself their father.

The man who had murdered their siblings and their parents. The man who had conquered the Silver Empire and slaughtered the Poison Rose. They hated the Witch-king with more pure intensity than did even Mother Frey or Kagen Vale. The Hakkian sorcerer had put spells on them, to make them *his*, to erase their love for their murdered family.

That hatred burned in their flesh and in their minds as they spoke the ritual words Lady Kestral had taught them. They did not know what any of the words meant, and speaking the language hurt their mouths. Their tongues burned and gums bled. They choked and spat, and yet they struggled on as the demon watched. The red of its eyes was nearly gone, but its power was there, its evil hungers were there.

The last words of the prayer to Nyarlathotep split the lips of both children and caused blood to erupt from their nostrils. They collapsed—*almost* falling across the circular line that kept the demon in check.

Almost.

The room fell silent.

For one full second.

And then the bowl exploded. Shards of pottery flew like arrows through the air, stabbing into walls and books and slashing the tapestries. Had the children not been unconscious on the floor, they would have been shredded. Some of the fragments struck the shimmering cylinder in which the demon stood, and the creature recoiled, flinging an arm over its eyes. But the fragments split into thousands of pieces of burning dust and did not penetrate.

The flash of light that accompanied the bowl's explosion was not fire yellow, nor was it hellish red. Instead, it was a deep azure blue, bright beyond bearing, and the force of it was not confined or stopped by walls of stone and plaster. A sphere of energy expanded outward, moving through walls, floors, and ceiling. The expansion was so fast that a blink could miss it, and within seconds its radiance swept across the whole of the west and even through the iron ore heart of the Cathedral Mountains.

All the way to Skyria in the west and to the icy wastes of the Winterwilds in the north. It flashed south to the Dragon Islands. In its passage it burned across a sandy beach where a young woman in mourning clothes stood in the mouth of a cave facing the sea.

And that azure light reached even as far as distant Vespia.

CHAPTER TWO HUNDRED THREE

The gathered wizards and witches, oracles and sages stood looking out of the ruined window frame at the empty sky. The ball of golden light they had conjured was gone now, but in its wake the very air seemed to flicker.

"Did it work?" asked the high priest, one hand clutching the likeness of Hastur that he wore on a silver chain.

"Yes," said the Witch-king. "It did. I can *feel* it."

The Prince of Games smiled. "So can—"

And then the wave of azure energy burst through the walls and smashed into them all.

CHAPTER TWO HUNDRED FOUR

"Gods below," wheezed Kagen. "Stop fucking around and just kill me now."

His words echoed weirdly in the chapel. The gods of the netherworlds did not, however, grant his request. Once more Kagen had to find strength he was sure he lacked to climb to his feet. His concussed head throbbed abominably, and the double vision was back. There were new bruises and scrapes vying for his attention. Ignoring them was its own particular challenge. How he managed it was beyond his understanding. His feet moved, however reluctantly, and with poor coordination, and he managed to reach the door once more and step out into the bright sunlight.

It was not the sun, though, that painted everything in bright yellow, nor was it the sun's heat that struck him in the face. The world was on fire.

"Kagen," cried a voice, and he squinted into the glare to see Filia running toward him. "Kagen, you're alive."

"Am I?" he mumbled.

She looked into his eyes. "You're hurt."

"I'm fine," he lied, forcing his mind to focus. Then he saw the infected. He saw their eyes. "No," he said, "I'm not fine at all."

"They're coming," yelled Tuke from across the plaza. "Hold the line, you bastards."

"Kagen," said Filia, "something happened." She told him about the yellow fireball and how it had changed the dead Vespians. She told him what the horde had said.

Kagen stared at her for a moment, mouth working soundlessly. Finally he blinked and shook his head to snap himself back into the moment. "The Witch-king knows we're here," he said. "He knows I'm here."

Filia pointed to the living dead. "I think he can see us through them. He must know why we're here."

"Fuck what he knows," said Kagen, grabbing her arm. "Filia, I have the books." He released her and pulled the rolled cloak over his head and thrust it into her hands.

"What are you doing?"

"Listen to me, Filia. Take them," ordered Kagen. "Go down the back stairs. Find the horses and get the hell out of here. Get these scrolls to Mother Frey."

"Me? Are you out of your mind? We all need to go."

Kagen pointed to where the Bloody Bastards were bracing as the wave of Vespians struck their line.

"We're not all getting off this pyramid and you damn well know it," growled Kagen. "One or two can slip away, but the rest of us have to keep the dead here. We need to draw their attention while you get away, otherwise they'll just follow and all will be lost."

"To hell with that," snapped Filia. "If anyone should go it's you."

He shook his head. "I'm half done. I can barely stand and I'm seeing two of everything. I wouldn't get a hundred yards from here, even if I made it down those gods-damned steps. But I can fight, I think. I can do that better than I can run."

Filia wanted to argue, to refuse, to tell him he was insane for even suggesting such a plan, but she was too pragmatic for that. She looked over her shoulder to where her lover and her friends were fighting the renewed attack of the living dead.

"Shit," she said, and her voice broke a little on that one word. She took the cloak and tied it across her body. Then she grabbed Kagen and kissed him hard on the mouth. "Tell Tuke I love him too."

And then she was gone. Filia ran to the staircase on the far side of the pyramid, where it waited, hidden by the cluster of buildings, free of anyone living or dead.

Kagen watched her climb down out of sight. For the first time in a long time, he felt a flicker of hope in his chest.

"May your gods protect you and guide you and keep you safe," he said.

Then he drew his daggers and went to join Tuke in the last stand of the Bloody Bastards.

CHAPTER TWO HUNDRED FIVE

In the tower room of Lady Kestral, the imperial twins, Alleyn and Desalyn, slumped back and stared at the ruins of the bowl. The whole room was in shambles.

Inside the shimmering pillar the demon stared at them.

Its eyes were no longer red. They burned now with azure fire.

CHAPTER TWO HUNDRED SIX

Kagen fell in beside Tuke, slashing at two of the Vespians as they climbed over the edge and tried to stand. The *eitr* on his blade did to them what it had not done to the demonic spirit in the razor-knight—the undead creatures dropped immediately.

"Poison?" growled Tuke.

"Poison."

"Got any left?"

"Not a drop."

Tuke lopped off a head and kicked the corpse down the stairs; it dragged half a dozen with it. "Pity. Would be pretty fucking useful right about now."

They fought.

A very human scream made them turn, and they saw Hoth falling backwards with two of the Vespians atop of his, their teeth buried in thigh and throat. Gi-Elless twisted around and killed the two infected, but dead hands reached over the edge and dragged Hoth out of sight. Even as the poet vanished, dying from bites and the Red Curse, Hoth stabbed at the mob that devoured him.

That left eight Unbladed, and Kagen.

Tuke suddenly looked very alarmed. "Gods! Where's Filia?"

Kagen kicked an attacker in the knee, shattering the joint and causing it to fall backwards.

"She's safe," said Kagen. "I gave her the Hsan books and sent her down the back stairs. We need to buy her time."

Tuke looked stricken for a moment, then his big grin blossomed brighter than the sun or the flames. "When we get to hell, city boy, the drinks are on me."

"That's good, you big son of a bitch, because I'm going to be mighty damned thirsty."

They laughed and fought. Kagen's head still ached, but his muscles were responding to his will. Old reflexes, trained over many years, worked their sorcery. Tuke was moving more slowly, and the fatigue was etched into hard lines on the big man's face.

"Tuke," called Kagen, after they had both knocked a trio of attackers down, momentarily clearing the edge of the platform. "Filia wanted me to tell you something."

"What?" asked the big Therian.

"She said to say that she loves you too."

Tuke actually froze for a moment, mouth agape. "She said that?"

"It was the last thing she said before she left, brother."

He saw tears well in Tuke's eyes. But he also saw his friend swell as if those words had infused him with new vigor.

"Thank you, brother," he said. "Thank you."

"They're coming up again," warned Jonal, and there was no more time for conversation.

As the next wave of infected climbed up onto the platform, the two friends fought side-by-side. Their blades spun silver magic. Their eyes blazed with purpose. Grins of madness born of love and hope even though they knew this was their end. Seconds became minutes and still they fought. Minutes seemed to become eternity, and still they fought.

The legions of the dead, unmindful of pain or injury, were as relentless as the tide, and as the Bloody Bastards grew weary they yielded ground.

Step by step.

Yard by yard.

And with each surrender of a bit of ground, more of the living dead were able to gain the top of the pyramid. The Unbladed retreated toward the buildings. Kagen needed to keep the monsters engaged there on the top of that ancient building in order for Filia to find a horse and get far away. He had no idea if she was still looking for a mount or was already on her way. He had no idea if more of the infected might happen upon her, or if the uninfected but equally lethal dog soldiers would be between her and the border.

All he knew was the fight. The killing. The dying. His daggers, light as they were, seemed to weigh a hundred pounds each.

And yet he fought. As they all fought.

Until . . .

"They're falling back!" cried Redharn. "Kagen, look . . . they're falling back."

Kagen, whose back was nearly to the wall of the chapel building, his eyes nearly blind with sweat, realized that Redharn was telling the truth. The dead were falling back—or at least slowing, stopping. Staring. Their hungry growls died out. The sound of blades on flesh slowed and stopped as the monsters stopped their attack. Only the constant roar of the burning jungle and the blazing corpses filled the air.

"What's happening?" asked Urri.

Kagen did not understand it. The dead stopped completely and just stood there, glaring with their fiery eyes. At him.

No. Not at him. They were all looking at the building against which the defenders had been driven. At the open doorway to the chapel.

Kagen turned, and then he, too, stared. His knees wanted to buckle, because what he saw tore every last shred of hope from him.

There, in the doorway, filling that space, stood the razor-knight.

The Witch-king turned toward the Prince of Games and grabbed him by the tunic, jerking him forward, shaking him. The sorcerers in the room recoiled, gasping and confused.

"Why did they stop? Kagen is within reach . . . why did they stop?"

The prince caught the king's wrists, and with strength impossible to justify in a body as slim and slight as his, pulled those hands free. "You forget yourself, Majesty," he said in an icy voice. "Besides . . . this is your spell. I have nothing to do with this."

"I can see through the eyes of the infected," said the king. "I can *see* Kagen Vale. He is right there. But the Vespians have stopped. They're backing away. They . . ."

His voice trailed off.

"Tell me what you see, Majesty," said the prince. "If they are your eyes, what is it they fear?"

The Witch-king told him.

CHAPTER TWO HUNDRED EIGHT

The razor-knight stepped out into the furnace heat. Fire gleamed on his black armor, glimmered on every blade in his winged cloak. The monster loomed over everything there, and everything froze in awe and terror. Even the dead.

On some level of insight, Kagen was aware of that, and the thought was seared into his mind. *Even the dead fear this thing.*

But as he thought that, he struggled to understand the difference between what was happening now and what had happened when the razor-knight first emerged from the jungle. The dead had attacked it. They had not been afraid at all. Now they seemed terrified—if that could be read in the hesitation and the crouching postures, for it could not be read in eyes of flame.

Kagen looked up at the knight, into *its* flaming eyes. They were not red. They were not burning yellow. The razor-knight regarded him with eyes that blazed with a bright azure light.

It opened its mouth and spoke in that earsplitting, booming, thunderous voice. "Witch-king of Hakkia . . . I am coming for you. Send your armies against me and I will yet find you. Open the gates of all the hells and send forth its legions and I will have your blood on my hands. I know you can see me through the burning eyes of these many dead. See me and know me, Witch-king, for I am your doom."

And then it spread its wings and pushed Kagen and Tuke as if they were nothing to it. It strode past Redharn and Urri; past Bitler and Borz, Gi-Elless and Giffer and Jonal. It walked by *all* the Bloody Bastards without pause, without attacking them. Without even seeming to notice or care about them. The razor-knight walked toward the Vespians, spreading its cloak of knives as it did.

And then the slaughter began.

CHAPTER TWO HUNDRED NINE

"Did it hear us?" asked Desalyn.

She lay on the floor beside her brother. Their hands were inches apart. Blood caked her nose and mouth and ears. Asking that one question, those four words, took much of the energy and life that she had left.

Alleyn's hand moved toward hers, limping like a dying spider. His fingers found his sister's, intertwined, held fast. He could only manage a single word. Just the one.

"Yes," he said.

-1-

The ocean exhaled its breath of waves upon the sand. Then the weight of water slid back from the beach with a long sigh.

The Widow sat on the sand and listened to that slow breath. The Hakkian raiders were scattered all around her. The flesh had been blasted from their skeletons. Bloody debris was strewn everywhere. Every bone was cracked and splintered, every spine twisted and pulled apart. A chorus of fractured skulls watched her as she watched the ocean, their empty eye sockets aware of what had happened and what it meant, but their silent mouths were unable to share those truths.

Seagulls drifting along the coastline veered away from that stretch of beach. As well they should. When the sky darkened and a light rain began to fall, the droplets struck the upturned face of the Widow and hissed themselves into steam.

She smiled. The Widow. Ryssa. She smiled.

And smiled . . .

-2-

The Golden Sea was known on many older maps as the Sea of Storms, and in poems as the Sea of Lost Souls.

Skyria—that ancient land of pyramids and buried tombs, of

ghosts and bones—lay to the west, and the eastern coastline was shared by Samud, Ghenrey, Hakkia, the Waste, and Behlia. That stretch of blue water seemed somehow to attract hurricanes, and the seaports boasted some of the sturdiest construction in the Silver Empire. Because of the vagaries and violence of those storms, attacking fleets often chose to sail the thousands of extra sea miles around Skyria instead of running that thrashing gauntlet. The seafloor plunged thousands of feet, and down there in the impenetrable darkness were countless ships. The whole of Khuprol the Red's pirate fleet was there, as were three hundred triremes that comprised ninety percent of an Ikarian invasion force sunk by a gale five hundred years ago. The safest route was to creep along the shoreline, going north around Samud and into the calmer waters of the Western Reach, or south to the Dragon Islands. That was the conventional wisdom, particularly in the early days of winter, when temperature changes drove the waves to madness and turned the winds into howling monsters.

King Hariq al-Huk stood on a platform of his royal palace, looking down at the ships anchored off the coast of Samud. Eleven hundred troop transports, eighty-three warships, and countless tenders. On the docks and running in long lines back to fields used for staging were his troops. One hundred thousand soldiers. Eight thousand warhorses. Fifty-seven tons of arrows.

He stood with his hands clasped behind his back, an ermine cloak around his shoulders. Major General Culanna yl-Sik, deputy field marshal of Samud, stood beside him. They were alone on that balcony.

"Once we weigh anchor, my king," said Culanna, "there is no going back."

"No going back," said al-Huk softly.

"The Therian fleet has not yet set sail," said the general. "We know Queen Theka has prepared her ships and massed her troops, but so far she seems content to wait."

Al-Huk nodded.

"And the Vahlycorians are dragging their feet as well."

"Which is why this will force their hand," said al-Huk. "When war begins, every nation will have to take a side."

"Majesty, as I have said many times, they may opt to wait and watch. Some, we know, will side with Hakkia because they are driven by fear and self-interest. Some have already said that they *may* support us if things go a certain way, but that is hardly the same thing as a firm commitment. At this moment, we are alone."

As if to mock them both, thunder boomed far out to sea. A line of clouds clung to the horizon. They had been white and puffy and harmless an hour ago, but now the white was only around the edges as a storm built within them. The admiral of the fleet had sworn that there would be no storm, no rains. The thunder growled again, mocking that prediction.

"We should wait until the weather clears," said Culanna.

Al-Huk made an ugly sound deep in his throat. "We *cannot*. Before we raise the first anchor, word of this fleet will be on its way to Hakkia and Argentium. They will know, and any delay would give that yellow-cloaked bastard time to get his own fleet out of port. No, General, we are committed. There is no turning back now."

They watched the lines of soldiers march toward the docks.

The booming thunder rolled across the waves and the first flickers of lightning pulsed threateningly within the banks of clouds.

"Gods of the Harvest, save our souls," prayed the general.

The king stood with his jaws clamped shut and said no more.

-3-

In Argentium, the Witch-king and the Prince of Games stood looking out the shattered window. The prince's face was drawn and haggard, his strange eyes less certain. Beside him, the

Witch-king leaned against the stone frame, his yellow robes torn and stained. His veil hung in tatters, torn by the energies they had conjured.

They did not speak at all. From that window, in that curved tower room, they could see the landscape from the ocean to the forests of the northeast.

In the west they saw that a storm was brewing. A great storm, one whose passing would leave nothing unchanged. It was inevitable now. The storm—and the war—could not be stopped. They could only be endured, experienced, and embraced.

From the east, the razor-knight was coming. It walked through the nightmare jungles of Vespia. It was a thousand miles away, with rivers and mountains to cross. Yet it came on, and they both knew that it, too, was inevitable.

But in the sky above the imperial palace of Argentium, something moved behind the clouds. Something vast—so vast that the mind resisted accepting its reality. The Witch-king did not know how many others could see it. When he glanced at the Prince of Games, that man was looking elsewhere. Did he not see it? *Could he not?*

Or, mused the Witch-king, was it a conjuration of the madness and heartbreak and anger that burned inside his own heart and mind? Was it a phantasm conjured by hope? Or was it a demon come to mock him as the world fell to pieces? Or was it his god coming to aid Hakkia in its darkest house?

The Witch-king did not know, but he believed. There were shades of yellow painted on the clouds above, and he prayed that was a sign. An assurance. He prayed silently as the shape took slow form there amid the darkening clouds.

On every mast in Haddon Bay and every flagpole in the city, gusts lifted sails and banners and whipped them until the flapping cloth was a drumbeat proclaiming conflict.

The wind speaks of war, he thought.

Thunder boomed loud enough to shake the palace. The Witch-king thought he heard something inside the thunder. A voice. The voice of his god.

Hastur turned away from him, and for a terrible moment the Witch-king thought that his god had turned his back on him. But then he realized that this was not a rebuke.

Hastur, reluctant as all gods are when beseeched to intervene in human matters, had made his choice. His back was not turned on the Witch-king. His face—and all his anger and power—was turned instead toward his enemies. Ten thousand feet tall, he stood between the King in Yellow and the world.

If war is coming, the great god seemed to say, *then let it come.*

-4-

The razor-knight walked through the jungles of Vespia.

Animals fled before it. Packs of dog soldiers—those that had not yet met and been overwhelmed by the living dead—harried it, attacking from ambush over and over again. Each time, the razor-knight kept moving. It walked into every trap and left behind screaming horses, dying men, and a river of blood.

When swarms of the infected hounded it, driven by the madness that glowed with sickly yellow light in their eyes, it let them come. Let them try. Let them bite. And it left behind only ruin and final death for the undead.

Constantly moving. Tireless. Relentless. Walking through sunlight and shadow toward Argentium.

-5-

The Hollow Monks stood in a cluster on the slope of a grassy hill. Below them was the meandering creek that formed the border between Hakkia and Nehemite. Hundreds of Hakkian troops were positioned in the dense forests to the south, and there were large patrols moving along the line between those two nations.

Every stretch of land that offered a tactical disadvantage for the release of the Red Curse was watched. Deadfalls and other traps had been put in place and cleverly disguised.

Nehemite had no such defenses. The plague, once released, would sweep north through that country, and as it followed the natural boundaries of deeper rivers, a few lakes, and ridges of mountains, the spread would burn like wildfire toward Samud.

The Hollow Monks waited with their infinite patience for the word to come from the Witch-king to release the Red Curse.

Waiting for the real war to begin.

-6-

Kagen Vale sat on Jinx.

The surviving Bloody Bastards flanked him. Up ahead was the entrance to Sligor Pass, and below was a tributary of Thunder River.

Filia and Tuke were to his left. Filia still wore the Seven Cryptical Books of Hsan slung across her lean body. Catching up to her in the jungle had taken days, even though she had left her sigil cut into the trunks of trees. Filia had ridden as if hell itself were biting at her heels.

Once the Bastards had escaped the pyramid, they scoured the jungle until they found Pergun. His tale of survival during the invasion of the undead was, according to Tuke, worth a song. Pergun had a dozen horses with him, and Horse, the dog. All bloody, but all alive. Together the survivors fled the city of Ulthar and followed Filia's trail. The nightbirds had helped them find her. They had not participated in that battle, but Kagen could not blame them. What use are talons and beaks against reanimated corpses?

He saw the old crow on a branch above the trail ahead and he nodded to it. The bird gave its silent caw in reply.

"The fastest route is ahead," said Filia once they crossed the border and left Vespia behind. Kagen nodded.

"Likely to be some Bulconian patrols," said Tuke.

"Do you care?" asked Kagen.

Tuke laughed. "Not much at all, brother," he said. "Do you?"

"Hell no," said Kagen. "Mother Frey is waiting for us in Zaare. My lady Maralina—the only person who can read those bloody books—is in Vahlycor. My brothers are in the Winterwilds. Alleyn and Desalyn are in Argentium. There is much we still need to do. War is coming; you can smell it. And I'm not about to let anything stop me. Not until Herepath is dead at my feet."

He glanced at his companions.

"Come on, you Bloody Bastards," said Kagen. "Let's ride."

Together they thundered into the west.

THE VALE FAMILY

Lord Khendrick Vale, Kagen's father; nobleman, statesman, and advisor to the empress. Murdered during the Night of the Ravens.

Lady Marissa Trewellyn-Vale, Kagen's mother; the Poison Rose, Blade Mistress of the Silver Empire. Slain by a demonic razor-knight while defending the empress.

Lady Bellapher, the Silver Thorn. Ancestor of Lady Marissa and general of the Imperial Army during the war against Hakkia centuries ago.

Lord Degas Vale, firstborn son of Lord Khendrick and Lady Marissa.

Belissa Vale, second-born child and eldest daughter of Lord Khendrick and Lady Marissa. A widowed alchemist not seen since before the invasion.

Herepath Vale, second-born son of Lord Khendrick and Lady Marissa. Gardener, scholar, and mystic.

Zora Vale, fourth-born child and youngest daughter of Lord Khendrick and Lady Marissa. Married to a poet and living in Tull Mithrain.

Jheklan Vale, one of the Vale "twins," though a year older than the other twin. Captain of the North Riders; adventurer, prankster, and rake.

Faulker Vale, the other Vale "twin." Lieutenant of the East Riders; unrepentant scoundrel, inseparable from Jheklan.

Hugh Vale, famously powerful fighter who died defending the empress.

Kagen Vale, disgraced former captain of the imperial guard, Warden of the Sacred Garden, bond-sworn and oath-bound protector of the Seedlings.

Hendross Vale, red-haired giant, affable and a bit wild, missing and presumed dead.

THE IMPERIAL FAMILY OF THE SILVER EMPIRE
Empress Gessalyn, 53rd and last empress of the Silver Empire.

The Seedlings, imperial children of Gessalyn; all but two murdered on the Night of the Ravens.

Desalyn/Foscor, one of the imperial twins, now under the spell of the Witch-king.

Allyen/Gavran, Desalyn's twin, also under the Witch-king's spell.

THE HAKKIANS
Gethon Heklan, the Witch-king, chief priest of Hastur and king of Hakkia.

Lord Nespar, chamberlain and advisor to the Witch-king.

Lady Kestral, court necromancer and advisor to the Witch-king.

Lord Jakob Ravensmere, royal historian to the Witch-king.

Madame Lucibel, governess of the imperial twins in Hakkia.

THE UNBLADED

Tuke Brakson, a Therian adventurer and one of Kagen's closest friends.

Filia alden-Bok, adventurer, Kagen's trusted friend and former lover.

THE LOVERS

Ryssa, orphan girl from Argentium in Argon; lover of Ryssa, initiate into the Faith of the Dreaming God, Cthulhu.

Miri, former investigator of the Office of Miracles; priestess of Cthulhu, lover of Ryssa.

THE CABAL

Mother Frey, former chief investigator for the Office of Miracles.

Lady Helleda Frost, Argonian noblewoman and financial backer of the rebellion.

Hannibus Greel, Therian merchant, serving as diplomat for the Cabal.

THE LARGER WORLD

Maralina, daughter of the queen of the Baobhan sith, the faerie folk; Kagen's lover, trapped forever in the Tower of Sarsis.

Fabeldyr, the last of the dragons who brought magic to earth; chained and imprisoned in a glacier in the Winterwilds.

The Hollow Monks, a cult of demonic sorcerers.

The Prince of Games, an immortal trickster.

Duke Sárkány, immortal vampire; former lover of Maralina.

THE ROYAL HOUSES OF THE SILVER EMPIRE

Argon, no living monarch after the murder of Empress Gessalyn.

Behlia, Queen Weska.

Ghenrey, Crown Prince Ifduril.

Hakkia, the Witch-king.

Nehemite, Queen Lliaorna.

Nelfydia, King Horogillin.

Samud, King Hariq al-Huk.

Sunderland, King Thespo, formerly known as the Pirate Prince.

Theria, Princess Theka.

Vahlycor, Queen Egnes.

The Waste, aka Tarania, various princes, princesses, and governor-general.

Zaare, Prince Regent Mondas Huvan.

Zehria, Vulpion the Gray.

GODS AND THEIR PANTHEONS

The Harvest Gods, patrons of the Silver Empire; also called the Green Faith.

- *Father Ar,* god of sowing and agriculture.

- *Mother Sah,* goddess of reaping and the cycle of life.

- *Geth,* the Prince of Pestilence and Famine.

- *Lady Siya,* goddess of learning, scholarship, and skepticism.

Gods of ancient and modern Hakkia.

- *Hastur the Unspeakable,* the Shepherd God, the Yellow God, one of the Great Old Ones; half-brother of Cthulhu; patron of Hakkia during the reign of the Witch-kings.

- *H'aaztre the Unspeakable One,* the Yellow King, the Feaster from Afar; former chief deity of Hakkia before the rise of the Witch-king.

The Sea Gods/the Deep Ones, patron gods of Theria and the northern Islands.

- *Father Dagon,* chief of the Deep Ones.

- *Mother Hydra,* queen of the Deep Ones.

- *Cthulhu,* the Dreaming God, patron of the people of Tull Yammoth; one of the Great Old Ones; half brother and enemy of Hastur.

ACKNOWLEDGMENTS

Many thanks to those people who have contributed information and advice along the way. Thanks to my literary agent, Sara Crowe of Pippin Properties; my stalwart editor at St. Martin's Griffin, Michael Homler; Robert Allen and the crew at Macmillan Audio; my film agent, Dana Spector of Creative Artists Agency; my audiobook reader Ray Porter; Cat Scully, my friend and mapmaker; my colleagues at *Weird Tales* magazine; and many thanks to my talented and infinitely patient assistant, Dana Fredsti.

ABOUT THE AUTHOR

© Sara Jo West

JONATHAN MABERRY is a *New York Times* bestselling, Inkpot Award–winning, and five-time Bram Stoker Award–winning author of *Relentless, Ink, Patient Zero, Rot & Ruin, Dead of Night,* the Pine Deep Trilogy, *The Wolfman, Zombie CSU,* and *They Bite,* among others. His V-Wars series has been adapted by Netflix, and his work for Marvel Comics includes *The Punisher, Wolverine, Doomwar, Marvel Zombie Return,* and *Black Panther.* He is the editor of *Weird Tales* magazine and also edits numerous anthologies.

    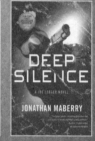
   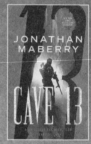